THE VIVERO LETTER

Desmond Bagley was born in 1923 in Kendal, Westmorland, and brought up in Blackpool. He began his working life, aged 14, in the printing industry and then did a variety of jobs until going into an aircraft factory at the start of the Second World War.

When the war ended, he decided to travel to southern Africa, going overland through Europe and the Sahara. He worked en route, reaching South Africa in 1951.

Bagley became a freelance journalist in Johannesburg and wrote his first published novel, *The Golden Keel*, in 1962. In 1964 he returned to England and lived in Totnes, Devon, for twelve years. He and his wife Joan then moved to Guernsey in the Channel Islands. Here he found the ideal place for combining his writing and his other interests, which included computers, mathematics, military history, and entertaining friends from all over the world.

Desmond Bagley died in April 1983, having become one of the world's top-selling authors, with his 16 books – two of them published after his death – translated into more than 30 languages.

'I've read all Bagley's books and he's marvellous, the best.'

ALISTAIR MACLEAN

By the same author

DESMOND BAGLEY

The Golden Keel

AND

The Vivero Letter

HARPER

HARPER
an imprint of HarperCollins*Publishers*
77-85 Fulham Palace Road
Hammersmith, London W6 8JB
www.harpercollins.co.uk

This omnibus edition 2009
1

The Golden Keel first published in Great Britain by Collins 1963
The Vivero Letter first published in Great Britain by Collins 1968
Postscript first published in Great Britain by Collins 1979

Desmond Bagley asserts the moral right to
be identified as the author of these works

Printed and bound in Great Britain by
Clays Ltd, St Ives plc

Mixed Sources
Product group from well-managed
forests and other controlled sources
www.fsc.org Cert no. SW-COC-1806
© 1996 Forest Stewardship Council

FSC is a non-profit international organisation established
to promote the responsible management of the world's forests.
Products carrying the FSC label are independently certified
to assure consumers that they come from forests that are managed
to meet the social, economic and ecological needs
of present and future generations.

Find out more about HarperCollins and the environment at
www.harpercollins.co.uk/green

CONTENTS

THE GOLDEN KEEL

For Joan – who else?

BOOK ONE

The Men

ONE: WALKER

My name is Peter Halloran, but everyone calls me 'Hal' excepting my wife, Jean, who always called me Peter. Women seem to dislike nicknames for their menfolk. Like a lot of others I emigrated to the 'colonies' after the war, and I travelled from England to South Africa by road, across the Sahara and through the Congo. It was a pretty rough trip, but that's another story; it's enough to say that I arrived in Cape Town in 1948 with no job and precious little money.

During my first week in Cape Town I answered several of the Sit. Vac. advertisements which appeared in the *Cape Times* and while waiting for answers I explored my environment. On this particular morning I had visited the docks and finally found myself near the yacht basin.

I was leaning over the rail looking at the boats when a voice behind me said, 'If you had your choice, which would it be?'

I turned and encountered the twinkling eyes of an elderly man, tall, with stooped shoulders and grey hair. He had a brown, weather-beaten face and gnarled hands, and I estimated his age at about sixty.

I pointed to one of the boats. 'I think I'd pick that one,' I said. 'She's big enough to be of use, but not too big for single-handed sailing.'

He seemed pleased. 'That's *Gracia*,' he said. 'I built her.'

'She looks a good boat,' I said. 'She's got nice lines.'

We talked for a while about boats. He said that he had a boatyard a little way outside Cape Town towards Milnerton, and that he specialized in building the fishing boats used by the Malay fishermen. I'd noticed these already; sturdy unlovely craft with high bows and a wheelhouse stuck on top like a chicken-coop, but they looked very seaworthy. *Gracia* was only the second yacht he had built.

'There'll be a boom now the war's over,' he predicted. 'People will have money in their pockets, and they'll go in for yachting. I'd like to expand my activities in that direction.'

Presently he looked at his watch and nodded towards the yacht club. 'Let's go in and have a coffee,' he suggested.

I hesitated. 'I'm not a member.'

'I am,' he said. 'Be my guest.'

So we went into the club house and sat in the lounge overlooking the yacht basin and he ordered coffee. 'By the way, my name's Tom Sanford.'

'I'm Peter Halloran.'

'You're English,' he said. 'Been out here long?'

I smiled. 'Three days.'

'I've been out just a bit longer – since 1910.' He sipped his coffee and regarded me thoughtfully. 'You seem to know a bit about boats.'

'I've been around them all my life,' I said. 'My father had a boatyard on the east coast, quite close to Hull. We built fishing boats, too, until the war.'

'And then?'

'Then the yard went on to contract work for the Admiralty,' I said. 'We built harbour defence launches and things like that – we weren't geared to handle anything bigger.' I shrugged. 'Then there was an air-raid.'

'That's bad,' said Tom. 'Was everything destroyed?'

'Everything,' I said flatly. 'My people had a house next to the yard – that went, too. My parents and my elder brother were killed.'

'Christ!' said Tom gently. 'That's very bad. How old were you?'

'Seventeen,' I said. 'I went to live with an aunt in Hatfield; that's when I started to work for de Havilland – building Mosquitos. It's a wooden aeroplane and they wanted people who could work in wood. All I was doing, as far as I was concerned, was filling in time until I could join the Army.'

His interest sharpened. 'You know, that's the coming thing – the new methods developed by de Havilland. That hot-moulding process of theirs – d'you think it could be used in boat-building?'

I thought about it. 'I don't see why not – it's very strong. We did repair work at Hatfield, as well as new construction, and I saw what happens to that type of fabric when it's been hit very hard. It would be more expensive than the traditional methods, though, unless you were mass-producing.'

'I was thinking about yachts,' said Tom slowly. 'You must tell me more about it sometime.' He smiled. 'What else do you know about boats?'

I grinned. 'I once thought I'd like to be a designer,' I said. 'When I was a kid – about fifteen – I designed and built my own racing dinghy.'

'Win any races?'

'My brother and I had 'em all licked,' I said. 'She was a fast boat. After the war, when I was cooling my heels waiting for my discharge, I had another go at it – designing, I mean. I designed half a dozen boats – it helped to pass the time.'

'Got the drawings with you?'

'They're somewhere at the bottom of my trunk,' I said. 'I haven't looked at them for a long time.'

'I'd like to see them,' said Tom. 'Look, laddie; how would you like to work for me? I told you I'm thinking of expanding into the yacht business, and I could use a smart young fellow.'

And that's how I started working for Tom Sanford. The following day I went to the boatyard with my drawings and showed them to Tom. On the whole he liked them, but pointed out several ways in which economies could be made in the building. 'You're a fair designer,' he said. 'But you've a lot to learn about the practical side. Never mind, we'll see about that. When can you start?'

Going to work for old Tom was one of the best things I ever did in my life.

II

A lot of things happened in the next ten years – whether I deserved them or not is another matter. The skills I had learned from my father had not deserted me, and although I was a bit rusty to begin with, soon I was as good as any man in the yard, and maybe a bit better. Tom encouraged me to design, ruthlessly correcting my errors.

'You've got a good eye for line,' he said. 'Your boats would be sweet sailers, but they'd be damned expensive. You've got to spend more time on detail; you must cut down costs to make an economical boat.'

Four years after I joined the firm Tom made me yard foreman, and just after that, I had my first bit of luck in designing. I submitted a design to a local yachting magazine, winning second prize and fifty pounds. But better still, a local yachtsman liked the design and wanted a boat built. So Tom built it for him and I got the designer's fee which went to swell my growing bank balance.

Tom was pleased about that and asked if I could design a class boat as a standard line for the yard, so I designed a six-tonner which turned out very well. We called it the Penguin Class and Tom built and sold a dozen in the first year at £2000 each. I liked the boat so much that I asked Tom if he would build one for me, which he did, charging a rock-bottom price and letting me pay it off over a couple of years.

Having a design office gave the business a fillip. The news got around and people started to come to me instead of using British and American designs. That way they could argue with their designer. Tom was pleased because most of the boats to my design were built in the yard.

In 1954 he made me yard manager, and in 1955 offered me a partnership.

'I've got no one to leave it to,' he said bluntly. 'My wife's dead and I've got no sons. And I'm getting old.'

I said, 'You'll be building boats when you're a hundred, Tom.'

He shook his head. 'No, I'm beginning to feel it now.' He wrinkled his brow. 'I've been going over the books and I find that you're bringing more business into the firm than I am, so I'll go easy on the money for the partnership. It'll cost you five thousand pounds.'

Five thousand was ridiculously cheap for a half-share in such a flourishing business, but I hadn't got anywhere near that amount. He saw my expression and his eyes crinkled. 'I know you haven't got it – but you've been doing pretty well on the design side lately. My guess is that you've got about two thousand salted away.'

Tom, shrewd as always, was right. I had a couple of hundred over the two thousand. 'That's about it,' I said.

'All right. Throw in the two thousand and borrow another three from the bank. They'll lend it to you when they see the books. You'll be able to pay it back out of profits in under three years, especially if you carry out your plans for that racing dinghy. What about it?'

'O.K., Tom,' I said. 'It's a deal.'

The racing dinghy Tom had mentioned was an idea I had got by watching the do-it-yourself developments in England. There are plenty of little lakes on the South African highveld and I thought I could sell small boats away from the sea if I could produce them cheaply enough – and I would sell either the finished boat or a do-it-yourself kit for the impoverished enthusiast.

We set up another woodworking shop and I designed the boat which was the first of the Falcon Class. A young fellow, Harry Marshall, was promoted to run the project and he did very well. This wasn't Tom's cup of tea and he stayed clear of the whole affair, referring to it as 'that confounded factory of yours'. But it made us a lot of money.

It was about this time that I met Jean and we got married. My marriage to Jean is not really a part of this story and I wouldn't mention it except for what happened later. We were very happy and very much in love. The business was doing well – I had a wife and a home – what more could a man wish for?

Towards the end of 1956 Tom died quite suddenly of a heart attack. I think he must have known that his heart wasn't in good shape although he didn't mention it to anyone. He left his share of the business to his wife's sister. She knew nothing about business and less about boat-building, so we got the lawyers on to it and she agreed to sell me her share. I paid a damn sight more than the five thousand I had paid Tom, but it was a fair sale although it gave me financier's fright and left me heavily in debt to the bank.

I was sorry that Tom had gone. He had given me a chance that fell to few young fellows and I felt grateful. The yard seemed emptier without him pottering about the slips.

The yard prospered and it seemed that my reputation as a designer was firm, because I got lots of commissions. Jean took over the management of the office, and as I was tied to the drawing board for a large proportion of my time I promoted Harry Marshall to yard manager and he handled it very capably.

Jean, being a woman, gave the office a thorough spring cleaning as soon as she was in command, and one day she unearthed an old tin box which had stayed forgotten on a remote shelf for years. She delved into it, then said suddenly, 'Why have you kept this clipping?'

'What clipping?' I asked abstractedly. I was reading a letter which could lead to an interesting commission.

'This thing about Mussolini,' she said. 'I'll read it.' She sat on the edge of the desk, the yellowed fragment of newsprint between her fingers. '"Sixteen Italian Communists were sentenced in Milan yesterday for complicity in the disappearance of Mussolini's treasure. The treasure, which mysteriously vanished at the end of the war, consisted of a consignment of gold from the Italian State Bank and many of Mussolini's personal possessions, including the Ethiopian crown. It is believed that a large number of important State documents were with the treasure. The sixteen men all declared their innocence."'

She looked up. 'What was all that about?'

I was startled. It was a long time since I'd thought of Walker and Coertze and the drama that had been played out in Italy. I smiled and said, 'I might have made a fortune but for that news story.'

'Tell me about it?'

'It's a long story,' I protested. 'I'll tell you some other time.'

'No,' she insisted. 'Tell me now; I'm always interested in treasure.'

So I pushed the unopened mail aside and told her about Walker and his mad scheme. It came back to me hazily in bits and pieces. Was it Donato or Alberto who had fallen – or been pushed – from the cliff? The story took a long time in the telling and the office work got badly behind that day.

III

I met Walker when I had arrived in South Africa from England after the war. I had been lucky to get a good job with Tom but, being a stranger, I was a bit lonely, so I joined a Cape Town Sporting Club which would provide company and exercise.

Walker was a drinking member, one of those crafty people who joined the club to have somewhere to drink when the pubs were closed on Sunday. He was never in the club house during the week, but turned up every Sunday, played his one game of tennis for the sake of appearances, then spent the rest of the day in the bar.

It was in the bar that I met him, late one Sunday afternoon. The room was loud with voices raised in argument and I soon realized I had walked into the middle of a discussion on the Tobruk surrender. The very mention of Tobruk can start an argument anywhere in South Africa because the surrender is regarded as a national disgrace. It is always agreed that the South Africans were let down but from then on it gets heated and rather vague. Sometimes the British generals are blamed and sometimes the South African garrison commander, General Klopper; and it's always good for one of those long, futile bar-room brawls in which tempers are lost but nothing is ever decided.

It wasn't of much interest to me – my army service was in Europe – so I sat quietly nursing my beer and keeping out of it. Next to me was a thin-faced young man with dissipated good looks who had a great deal to say about it, with many a thump on the counter with his clenched fist. I had seen him before but didn't know who he was. All I knew of him was by observation; he seemed to drink a lot, and even now was drinking two brandies to my one beer.

At length the argument died a natural death as the bar emptied and soon my companion and I were the last ones left. I drained my glass and was turning to leave when he said contemptuously, 'Fat lot they know about it.'

'Were you there?' I asked.

'I was,' he said grimly. 'I was in the bag with all the others. Didn't stay there long, though; I got out of the camp in

Italy in '43.' He looked at my empty glass. 'Have one for the road.'

I had nothing to do just then, so I said, 'Thanks; I'll have a beer.'

He ordered a beer for me and another brandy for himself and said, 'My name's Walker. Yes, I got out when the Italian Government collapsed. I joined the partisans.'

'That must have been interesting,' I said.

He laughed shortly. 'I suppose you could call it that. Interesting and scary. Yes, I reckon you could say that me and Sergeant Coertze had a really interesting time – he was a bloke I was with most of the time.'

'An Afrikaner?' I hazarded. I was new in South Africa and didn't know much about the set-up then, but the name sounded as though it might be Afrikaans.

'That's right,' said Walker. 'A real tough boy, he was. We stuck together after getting out of the camp.'

'Was it easy – escaping from the prison camp?'

'A piece of cake,' said Walker. 'The guards co-operated with us. A couple of them even came with us as guides – Alberto Corso and Donato Rinaldi. I liked Donato – I reckon he saved my life.'

He saw my interest and plunged into the story with gusto. When the Government fell in 1943 Italy was in a mess. The Italians were uneasy; they didn't know what was going to happen next and they were suspicious of the intentions of the Germans. It was a perfect opportunity to break camp, especially when a couple of the guards threw in with them.

Leaving the camp was easy enough, but trouble started soon after when the Germans laid on an operation to round up all the Allied prisoners who were loose in Central Italy.

'That's when I copped it,' said Walker. 'We were crossing a river at the time.'

The sudden attack had taken them by surprise. Everything had been silent except for the chuckling of the water and the muffled curses as someone slipped – then suddenly there was the sound of ripped calico as the Spandau opened up and the night was made hideous by the eerie whine of bullets as they ricocheted from exposed rocks in the river.

The two Italians turned and let go with their sub-machine-guns. Coertze, bellowing like a bull, scrabbled frantically at the pouch pocket of his battle-dress trousers and then his arm came up in an overarm throw. There was a sharp crack as the hand grenade exploded in the water near the bank. Again Coertze threw and this time the grenade burst on the bank.

Walker felt something slam his leg and he turned in a twisting fall and found himself gasping in the water. His free arm thrashed out and caught on a rock and he hung on desperately.

Coertze threw another grenade and the machine-gun stopped. The Italians had emptied their magazines and were busy reloading. Everything was quiet again.

'I reckon they thought we were Germans, too,' said Walker. 'They wouldn't expect to be fired on by escaping prisoners. It was lucky that the Italians had brought some guns along. Anyway, that bloody machine-gun stopped.'

They had stayed for a few minutes in midstream with the quick cold waters pulling at their legs, not daring to move in case there was a sudden burst from the shore. After five minutes Alberto said in a low voice, 'Signor Walker, are you all right?'

Walker pulled himself upright and to his astonishment found himself still grasping his unfired rifle. His left leg felt numb and cold. 'I'm all right,' he said.

There was a long sigh from Coertze, then he said, 'Well, come on. Let's get to the other side – but quietly.'

They reached the other side of the river and, without resting, pressed on up the mountainside. After a short time Walker's leg began to hurt and he lagged behind. Alberto was perturbed. 'You must hurry; we have to cross this mountain before dawn.'

Walker stifled a groan as he put down his left foot. 'I was hit,' he said. 'I think I was hit.'

Coertze came back down the mountain and said irritably, '*Magtig*, get a move on, will you?'

Alberto said, 'Is it bad, Signor Walker?'

'What's the matter?' asked Coertze, not understanding the Italian.

'I have a bullet in my leg,' said Walker bitterly.

'That's all we need,' said Coertze. In the darkness he bulked as a darker patch and Walker could see that he was shaking his head impatiently. 'We've got to get to that partisan camp before daylight.'

Walker conferred with Alberto, then said in English, 'Alberto says there's a place along there to the right where we can hide. He says that someone should stay with me while he goes for help.'

Coertze grunted in his throat. 'I'll go with him,' he said. 'The other Eytie can stay with you. Let's get to it.'

They moved along the mountainside and presently the ground dipped and suddenly there was a small ravine, a cleft in the mountain. There were stunted trees to give a little cover and underfoot was a dry watercourse.

Alberto stopped and said, 'You will stay here until we come for you. Keep under the trees so that no one will see you, and make as little movement as possible.'

'Thanks, Alberto,' said Walker. There were a few brief words of farewell, then Alberto and Coertze disappeared into the night. Donato made Walker comfortable and they settled down to wait out the night.

It was a bad time for Walker. His leg was hurting and it was very cold. They stayed in the ravine all the next day and as night fell Walker became delirious and Donato had trouble in keeping him quiet.

When the rescuers finally came Walker had passed out. He woke up much later and found himself in a bed in a room with whitewashed walls. The sun was rising and a little girl was sitting by the bedside.

Walker stopped speaking suddenly and looked at his empty glass on the bar counter. 'Have another drink,' I said quickly.

He needed no encouraging so I ordered another couple of drinks. 'So that's how you got away,' I said.

He nodded. 'That's how it was. God, it was cold those two nights on that bloody mountain. If it hadn't been for Donato I'd have cashed in my chips.'

I said, 'So you were safe – but where were you?'

'In a partisan camp up in the hills. The *partigiani* were just getting organized then; they only really got going when the Germans began to consolidate their hold on Italy. The Jerries ran true to form – they're arrogant bastards, you know – and the Italians didn't like it. So everything was set for the partisans; they got the support of the people and they could begin to operate on a really large scale.

'They weren't all alike, of course; there was every shade of political opinion from pale blue to bright red. The Communists hated the Monarchists' guts and vice versa and so on. The crowd I dropped in on were Monarchist. That's where I met the Count.'

Count Ugo Montepescali di Todi was over fifty years old at that time, but young-looking and energetic. He was a swarthy man with an aquiline nose and a short greying beard which was split at the end and forked aggressively. He came of a line which was old during the Renaissance and he was an aristocrat to his fingertips.

Because of this he hated Fascism – hated the pretensions of the parvenu rulers of Italy with all their corrupt ways and their money-sticky fingers. To him Mussolini always remained a mediocre journalist who had succeeded in demagoguery and had practically imprisoned his King.

Walker met the Count the first day he arrived at the hill camp. He had just woken up and seen the solemn face of the little girl. She smiled at him and silently left the room, and a few minutes later a short stocky man with a bristling beard stepped through the doorway and said in English, 'Ah, you are awake. You are quite safe now.'

Walker was conscious of saying something inane. 'But where am I?'

'Does that really matter?' the Count asked quizzically. 'You are still in Italy – but safe from the *Tedesci*. You must stay in bed until you recover your strength. You need some blood putting back – you lost a lot – so you must rest and eat and rest again.'

Walker was too weak to do more than accept this, so he lay back on the pillow. Five minutes later Coertze came in; with him was a young man with a thin face.

'I've brought the quack,' said Coertze. 'Or at least that's what he says he is – if I've got it straight. My guess is that he's only a medical student.'

The doctor – or student – examined Walker and professed satisfaction at his condition. 'You will walk within the week,' he said, and packed his little kit and left the room.

Coertze rubbed the back of his head. 'I'll have to learn this slippery *taal*,' he said. 'It looks as though we'll be here for a long time.'

'No chance of getting through to the south?' asked Walker.

'No chance at all,' said Coertze flatly. 'The Count – that's the little man with the *bokbaardjie* – says that the Germans down south are thicker on the ground than stalks in a mealie field. He reckons they're going to make a defence line south of Rome.'

Walker sighed. 'Then we're stuck here.'

Coertze grinned. 'It is not too bad. At least we'll get better food than we had in camp. The Count wants us to join his little lot – it seems he has some kind of *skietkommando* which holds quite a bit of territory and he's collected men and weapons while he can. We might as well fight here as with the army – I've always fancied fighting a war my way.'

A plump woman brought in a steaming bowl of broth for Walker, and Coertze said, 'Get outside of that and you'll feel better. I'm going to scout around a bit.'

Walker ate the broth and slept, then woke and ate again. After a while a small figure came in bearing a basin and rolled bandages. It was the little girl he had seen when he had first opened his eyes. He thought she was about twelve years old.

'My father said I had to change your bandages,' she said in a clear young voice. She spoke in English.

Walker propped himself up on his elbows and watched her as she came closer. She was neatly dressed and wore a white, starched apron. 'Thank you,' he said.

She bent to cut the splint loose from his leg and then she carefully loosened the bandage round the wound. He looked down at her and said, 'What is your name?'

'Francesca.'

'Is your father the doctor?' Her hands were cool and soft on his leg.

She shook her head. 'No,' she said briefly.

She bathed the wound in warm water containing some pungent antiseptic and then shook powder on to it. With great skill she began to rebandage the leg.

'You are a good nurse,' said Walker.

It was only then that she looked at him and he saw that she had cool, grey eyes. 'I've had a lot of practice,' she said, and Walker was abashed at her gaze and cursed a war which made skilled nurses out of twelve-year-olds.

She finished the bandaging and said, 'There – you must get better soon.'

'I will,' promised Walker. 'As quickly as I can. I'll do that for you.'

She looked at him with surprise. 'Not for me,' she said. 'For the war. You must get better so that you can go into the hills and kill a lot of Germans.'

She gravely collected the soiled bandages and left the room, with Walker looking after her in astonishment. Thus it was that he met Francesca, the daughter of Count Ugo Montepescali.

In a little over a week he was able to walk with the aid of a stick and to move outside the hospital hut, and Coertze showed him round the camp. Most of the men were Italians, army deserters who didn't like the Germans. But there were many Allied escapees of different nationalities.

The Count had formed the escapees into a single unit and had put Coertze in command. They called themselves the 'Foreign Legion'. During the next couple of years many of them were to be killed fighting against the Germans with the partisans. At Coertze's request, Alberto and Donato were attached to the unit to act as interpreters and guides.

Coertze had a high opinion of the Count. 'That *kêrel* knows what he's doing,' he said. 'He's recruiting from the Italian army as fast as he can – and each man must bring his own gun.'

When the Germans decided to stand and fortified the *Winterstellung* based on the Sangro and Monte Cassino, the war in Italy was deadlocked and it was then that the partisans got busy attacking the German communications. The Foreign Legion took part in this campaign, specializing in demolition work. Coertze had been a gold miner on the Witwatersrand before the war and knew how to handle dynamite. He and Harrison, a Canadian geologist, instructed the others in the use of explosives.

They blew up road and rail bridges, dynamited mountain passes, derailed trains and occasionally shot up the odd road convoy, always retreating as soon as heavy fire was returned. 'We must not fight pitched battles,' said the Count. 'We must not let the Germans pin us down. We are mosquitoes irritating the German hides – let us hope we give them malaria.'

Walker found this a time of long stretches of relaxation punctuated by moments of fright. Discipline was easy and there was no army spit-and-polish. He became lean and hard and would think nothing of making a day's march of thirty miles over the mountains burdened with his weapons and a pack of dynamite and detonators.

By the end of 1944 the Foreign Legion had thinned down considerably. Some of the men had been killed and more elected to make a break for the south after the Allies had taken Rome. Coertze said he would stay, so Walker stayed with him. Harrison also stayed, together with an Englishman called Parker. The Foreign Legion was now very small indeed.

'The Count used us as bloody pack horses,' said Walker. He had ordered another round of drinks and the brandy was getting at him. His eyes were red-veined and he stumbled over the odd word.

'Pack horses?' I queried.

'The unit was too small to really fight,' he explained. 'So he used us to transport guns and food around his territory. That's how we got the convoy.'

'Which convoy?'

Walker was beginning to slur his words. 'It was like this. One of the Italian units had gone to carve up a German post and the job was being done in co-operation with another partisan brigade. But the Count was worried because this other mob were Communists – real treacherous bastards they were. He was scared they might renege on us; they were always doing that because he was a Monarchist and they hated him worse than they did the Germans. They were looking ahead to after the war and they didn't do much fighting while they were about it. Italian politics, you see.'

I nodded.

'So he wanted Umberto – the chap in charge of our Italians – to have another couple of machine-guns, just in case, and Coertze said he'd take them.'

He fell silent, looking into his glass.

I said, 'What about this convoy?'

'Oh, what the hell,' he said. There's not a hope of getting it out. It'll stay there for ever, unless Coertze does something. I'll tell you. We were on our way to Umberto when we bumped into this German convoy driving along where no convoy should have been. So we clobbered it.'

They had got to the top of a hill and Coertze called a halt. 'We stay here for ten minutes, then we move on,' he said.

Alberto drank some water and then strolled down to where he could get a good view of the valley. He looked first at the valley floor where a rough, unmetalled road ran dustily, then raised his eyes to look south.

Suddenly he called Coertze. 'Look,' he said.

Coertze ran down and looked to where Alberto was pointing. In the distance, where the faraway thread of brown road shimmered in the heat, was a puff of dust. He unslung his glasses and focused rapidly.

'What the hell are they doing here?' he demanded.

'What is it?'

'German army trucks,' said Coertze. 'About six of them.' He pulled down the glasses. 'Looks as though they're trying to slip by on the side roads. We *have* made the main roads a bit unhealthy.'

Walker and Donato had come down. Coertze looked back at the machine-guns, then at Walker. 'What about it?'

Walker said, 'What about Umberto?'

'Oh, he's all right. It's just the Count getting a bit fretful now the war's nearly over. I think we should take this little lot – it should be easy with two machine-guns.'

Walker shrugged. 'O.K. with me,' he said.

Coertze said, 'Come on,' and ran back to where Parker was sitting. 'On your feet, *kêrel*,' he said. 'The war's still on. Where the hell is Harrison?'

'Coming,' called Harrison.

'Let's get this stuff down to the road on the double,' said Coertze. He looked down the hill. 'That bend ought to be a *lekker* place.'

'A what?' asked Parker plaintively. He always pulled Coertze's leg about his South Africanisms.

'Never mind that,' snapped Coertze. 'Get this stuff down to the road quick. We've got a job on.'

They loaded up the machine-guns and plunged down the hillside. Once on the road Coertze did a quick survey. 'They'll come round that bend slowly,' he said. 'Alberto, you take Donato and put your machine-gun there, where you can open up on the last two trucks. The last two, you understand. Knock 'em out fast so the others can't back out.'

He turned to Harrison and Parker. 'Put your gun over here on the other side and knock out the first truck. Then we'll have the others boxed in.'

'What do I do?' asked Walker.

'You come with me,' Coertze started to run up the road, followed by Walker. He ran almost to the bend, then left the road and climbed a small hillock from where he could get a good sight of the German convoy. When Walker flopped beside him he already had the glasses focused.

'It's four trucks not six,' he said. 'There's a staff car in front and a motor-cycle combination in front of that. Looks like one of those BMW jobs with a machine-gun in the side-car.'

He handed the glasses to Walker. 'How far from the tail of the column to that staff car?'

Walker looked at the oncoming vehicles. 'About sixty-five yards,' he estimated.

Coertze took the glasses. 'O.K. You go back along the road sixty-five yards so that when the last truck is round the bend the staff car is alongside you. Never mind the motor-cycle – I'll take care of that. Go back and tell the boys not to open up until they hear loud bangs; I'll start those off. And tell them to concentrate on the trucks.'

He turned over and looked back. The machine-guns were invisible and the road was deserted. 'As nice an ambush as anyone could set,' he said. 'My *oupa* never did better against the English.' He tapped Walker on the shoulder. 'Off you go. I'll help you with the staff car as soon as I've clobbered the motor-cycle.'

Walker slipped from the hillock and ran back along the road, stopping at the machine-guns to issue Coertze's instructions. Then he found himself a convenient rock about sixty yards from the bend, behind which he crouched and checked his sub-machine-gun.

It was not long before he heard Coertze running along the road shouting, 'Four minutes. They'll be here in four minutes. Hold your fire.'

Coertze ran past him and disappeared into the verge of the road about ten yards farther on.

Walker said that four minutes in those conditions could seem like four hours. He crouched there, looking back along the silent road, hearing nothing except his own heart beating. After what seemed a long time he heard the growl of engines and the clash of gears and then the revving of the motor-cycle.

He flattened himself closer to the rock and waited. A muscle twitched in his leg and his mouth was suddenly dry. The noise of the motor-cycle now blanked out all other sounds and he snapped off the safety catch.

He saw the motor-cycle pass, the goggled driver looking like a gargoyle and the trooper in the sidecar turning his head to scan the road, hands clutching the grips of the machine-gun mounted in front of him.

As in a dream he saw Coertze's hand come into view, apparently in slow motion, and toss a grenade casually into the sidecar. It lodged between the gunner's back and the coaming of the sidecar and the gunner turned in surprise. With his sudden movement the grenade disappeared into the interior of the sidecar.

Then it exploded.

The sidecar disintegrated and the gunner must have had his legs blown off. The cycle wheeled drunkenly across the road and Walker saw Coertze step out of cover, his sub-machine-gun pumping bullets into the driver. Then he had stepped out himself and his own gun was blazing at the staff car.

He had orientated himself very carefully so that he had a very good idea of where the driver would be placed. When he started firing, he did so without aiming and the wind-screen shattered in the driver's face.

In the background he was conscious of the tac-a-tac of the machine-guns firing in long bursts at the trucks, but he had no time or desire to cast a glance that way. He was occupied in jumping out of the way of the staff car as it slewed towards him, a dead man's hand on the wheel.

The officer in the passenger seat was standing up, his hand clawing at the flap of his pistol holster. Coertze fired a burst at him and he suddenly collapsed and folded grotesquely over the metal rim of the broken windscreen as though he had suddenly turned into a rag doll. The pistol dropped from his hand and clattered on the ground.

With a rending jar the staff car bumped into a rock on the side of the road and came to a sudden stop, jolting the sol-dier in the rear who was shooting at Walker. Walker heard the bullets going over his head and pulled the trigger. A dozen bullets hit the German and slammed him back in his seat. Walker said that the range was about nine feet and he swore he heard the bullets hit, sounding like a rod hitting a soft carpet several times.

Then Coertze was shouting at him, waving him on to the trucks. He ran up the road following Coertze and saw that the first truck was stopped. He fired a burst into the cab just to be on the safe side, then took shelter, leaning against the hot radiator to reload.

By the time he had reloaded the battle was over. All the vehicles were stopped and Alberto and Donato were escorting a couple of dazed prisoners forward.

Coertze barked, 'Parker, go up and see if anyone else is coming,' then turned to look at the chaos he had planned.

The two men with the motor-cycle had been killed outright, as had the three in the staff car. Each truck had carried two men in the cab and one in the back. All the men in the cabs had been killed within twenty seconds of the machine-guns opening fire. As Harrison said, 'At twenty yards we couldn't miss – we just squirted at the first truck, then hosed down the second. It was like using a howitzer at a coconut-shy – too easy.'

Of the seventeen men in the German party there were two survivors, one of whom had a flesh wound in his arm.

Coertze said, 'Notice anything?'

Walker shook his head. He was trembling in the aftermath of danger and was in no condition to be observant.

Coertze went up to one of the prisoners and fingered the emblem on his collar. The man cringed.

'These are S.S. men. All of them.'

He turned and went back to the staff car. The officer was lying on his back, half in and half out of the front door, his empty eyes looking up at the sky, terrible in death. Coertze looked at him, then leaned over and pulled a leather brief-case from the front seat. It was locked.

'There's something funny here,' he said. 'Why would they come by this road?'

Harrison said, 'They might have got through, you know. If we hadn't been here they would have got through – and we were only here by chance.'

'I know,' said Coertze. 'They had a good idea and they nearly got away with it – that's what I'm worrying about. The Jerries aren't an imaginative lot, usually; they follow a routine. So why would they do something different? Unless this wasn't a routine unit.'

He looked at the trucks. 'It might be a good idea to see what's in those trucks.'

He sent Donato up the road to the north to keep watch and the rest went to investigate the trucks, excepting Alberto who was guarding the prisoners.

Harrison looked over the tailboard of the first truck. 'Not much in here,' he said.

Walker looked in and saw that the bottom of the truck was filled with boxes – small wooden boxes about eighteen inches long, a foot wide and six inches deep. He said, 'That's a hell of a small load.'

Coertze frowned and said, 'Boxes like that ring a bell with me, but I just can't place it. Let's have one of them out.'

Walker and Harrison climbed into the truck and moved aside the body of a dead German which was in the way. Harrison grasped the corner of the nearest box and lifted. 'My God!' he said. 'The damn' thing's nailed to the floor.'

Walker helped him and the box shifted. 'No, it isn't, but it must be full of lead.'

Coertze let down the tailboard. 'I think we'd better have it out and opened,' he said. His voice was suddenly croaking with excitement.

Walker and Harrison manhandled a box to the edge and tipped it over. It fell with a loud thump to the dusty road. Coertze said, 'Give me that bayonet.'

Walker took the bayonet from the scabbard of the dead German and handed it to Coertze, who began to prise the box open. Nails squealed as the top of the box came up. Coertze ripped it off and said, 'I thought so.'

'What is it?' asked Harrison, mopping his brow.

'Gold,' said Coertze softly.

Everyone stood still.

Walker was very drunk when he got to this point of his story. He was unsteady on his feet and caught the edge of the bar counter to support himself as he repeated solemnly, 'Gold.'

'For the love of Mike, what did you do with it?' I said. 'And how much of it was there?'

Walker hiccoughed genthy. 'What about another drink?' he said.

I beckoned to the bar steward, then said, 'Come on; you can't leave me in suspense.'

He looked at me sideways. 'I really shouldn't tell,' he said. 'But what the hell! There's no harm in it now. It was like this . . .'

They had stood looking at each other for a long moment, then Coertze said, 'I knew I recognized those boxes. They use boxes like that on the Reef for packing the ingots for shipment.'

As soon as they had checked that all the boxes in that truck were just as heavy, there was a mad rush to the other trucks. These were disappointing at first – the second truck was full of packing cases containing documents and files.

Coertze delved into a case, tossing papers out, and said, 'What the hell's all this bumph?' He sounded disappointed.

Walker picked up a sheaf and scanned through it. 'Seems to be Italian Government documents of some sort. Maybe this is all top-secret stuff.'

The muffled voice of Harrison came from the bowels of the truck. 'Hey, you guys, look what I've found.'

He emerged with both hands full of bundles of lire notes – fine, newly printed lire notes. 'There's at least one case full of this stuff,' he said. 'Maybe more.'

The third truck had more boxes of gold, though not as much as the first, and there were several stoutly built wooden cases which were locked. They soon succumbed to a determined assault with a bayonet.

'Christ!' said Walker as he opened the first. In awe he pulled out a shimmering sparkle of jewels, a necklace of diamonds and emeralds.

'What's that worth?' Coertze asked Harrison.

Harrison shook his head dumbly. 'Gee, I wouldn't know.' He smiled faintly. 'Not my kind of stone.'

They were ransacking the boxes when Coertze pulled out a gold cigarette case. 'This one's got an inscription,' he said and read it aloud. '"*Caro Benito da parte di Adolfe – Brennero – 1940.*"'

Harrison said slowly, 'Hitler had a meeting with Mussolini at the Brenner Pass in 1940. That's when Musso decided to kick in on the German side.'

'So now we know who this belongs to,' said Walker, waving his hand.

'Or used to belong to,' repeated Coertze slowly. 'But who does it belong to now?'

They looked at each other.

Coertze broke the silence. 'Come on, let's see what's in the last truck.'

The fourth truck was full of packing cases containing more papers. But there was one box holding a crown.

Harrison struggled to lift it. 'Who's the giant who wears this around the palace?' he asked nobody in particular. The crown was thickly encrusted with jewels – rubies and emeralds, but no diamonds. It was ornate and very heavy. 'No wonder they say "uneasy lies the head that wears a crown,"' cracked Harrison.

He lowered the crown into the box. 'Well, what do we do now?'

Coertze scratched his head. 'It's quite a problem,' he admitted.

'I say we keep it,' said Harrison bluntly. 'It's ours by right of conquest.'

Now it was in the open – the secret thought that no one would admit except the extrovert Harrison. It cleared the air and made things much easier.

Coertze said, 'I suppose we must bring in the rest of the boys and vote on it.'

'That'll be no good unless it's a unanimous vote,' said Harrison almost casually.

They saw his point. If one of them held out in favour of telling the Count, then the majority vote would be useless. At last Walker said, 'It may not arise. Let's vote on it and see.'

All was quiet on the road so Donato and Parker were brought in from their sentry duty. The prisoners were herded into a truck so that Alberto could join in the discussion, and they settled down as a committee of ways and means.

Harrison needn't have worried – it *was* a unanimous vote. There was too much temptation for it to be otherwise.

'One thing's for sure,' said Harrison. 'When this stuff disappears there's going to be the biggest investigation ever, no matter who wins the war. The Italian Government will never rest until it's found, especially those papers. I'll bet they're dynamite.'

Coertze was thoughtful. 'That means we must hide the treasure *and* the trucks. *Nothing* must be found. It must be as though the whole lot has vanished into thin air.'

'What are we going to do with it?' asked Parker. He looked at the stony ground and the thin soil. 'We might just bury the treasure if we took a week doing it, but we can't even begin to bury one truck, let alone four.'

Harrison snapped his fingers. 'The old lead mines,' he said. 'They're not far from here.'

Coertze's face lightened. '*Ja*,' he said. 'There's one winze that would take the lot.'

Parker said, 'What lead mines – and what's a winze, for God's sake?'

'It's a horizontal shaft driven into a mountain,' said Harrison. 'These mines have been abandoned since the turn of the century. No one goes near them any more.'

Alberto said, 'We drive all the trucks inside . . .'

'. . . and blow in the entrance,' finished Coertze with gusto.

'Why not keep some of the jewels?' suggested Walker.

'No,' said Coertze sharply. 'It's too dangerous – Harrison is right. There'll be all hell breaking loose when this stuff vanishes for good. Everything must be buried until it's safe to recover it.'

'Know any good jewel fences?' asked Harrison sardonically. 'Because if you don't how would you get rid of the jewels?'

They decided to bury everything – the trucks, the bodies, the gold, the papers, the jewels – everything. They restowed the trucks, putting all the valuables into two trucks and all the non-valuables such as the documents into the other two. It was intended to drive the staff car into the tunnel first with the motor-cycle carried in the back, then the trucks carrying papers and bodies, and lastly the trucks with the gold and jewels.

'That way we can get out the stuff we want quite easily,' said Coertze.

The disposal of the trucks was easy enough. There was an unused track leading to the mines which diverged off the dusty road they were on. They drove up to the mine and reversed the trucks into the biggest tunnel in the right order. Coertze and Harrison prepared a charge to blow down the entrance, a simple job taking only a few minutes, then Coertze lit the fuse and ran back.

When the dust died down they saw that the tunnel mouth was entirely blocked – making a rich mausoleum for seventeen men.

'What do we tell the Count?' asked Parker.

'We tell him we ran into a little trouble on the way,' said Coertze. 'Well, we did, didn't we?' He grinned and told them to move on.

When they got back they heard that Umberto had run into trouble and had lost a lot of men. The Communists hadn't turned up and he hadn't had enough machine-guns.

I said, 'You mean the gold's still there.'

'That's right,' said Walker, and hammered his fist on the counter. 'Let's have another drink.'

I didn't get much out of him after that. His brain was pickled in brandy and he kept wandering into irrelevancies, but he did answer one question coherently.

I asked, 'What happened to the two German prisoners?'

'Oh, them,' he said carelessly. 'They were shot while escaping. Coertze did it.'

IV

Walker was too far gone to walk home that night, so I got his address from a club steward, poured him into a taxi and forgot about him. I didn't think much of his story – it was just the maunderings of a drunk. Maybe he had found something in Italy, but I doubted if it was anything big – my imagination boggled at the idea of four truck loads of gold and jewels.

I wasn't allowed to forget him for long because I saw him the following Sunday in the club bar gazing moodily into a brandy glass. He looked up, caught my eye and looked away hastily as though shamed. I didn't go over and speak to him; he wasn't altogether my type – I don't go for drunks much.

Later that afternoon I had just come out of the swimming pool and was enjoying a cigarette when I became aware that Walker was standing beside me. As I looked up, he said awkwardly, 'I think I owe you some money – for the taxi fare the other night.'

'Forget it,' I said shortly.

He dropped on one knee. 'I'm sorry about that. Did I cause any trouble?'

I smiled. 'Can't you remember?'

'Not a damn' thing,' he confessed. 'I didn't get into a fight or anything, did I?'

'No, we just talked.'

His eyes flickered. 'What about?'

'Your experiences in Italy. You told me rather an odd story.'

'I told you about the gold?'

I nodded. 'That's right.'

'I was drunk,' he said. 'As shickered as a coot. I shouldn't have told you about that. You haven't mentioned it to anyone, have you?'

'No, I haven't,' I said. 'You don't mean it's true?' He certainly wasn't drunk now.

'True enough,' he said heavily. 'The stuffs still up there – in a hole in the ground in Italy. I'd not like you to talk about it.'

'I won't,' I promised.

'Come and have a drink,' he suggested.

'No, thanks,' I said. 'I'm going home now.'

He seemed depressed. 'All right,' he said, and I watched him walk lethargically up to the club house.

After that, he couldn't seem to keep away from me. It was as though he had delivered a part of himself into my keeping and he had to watch me to see that I kept it safe. He acted as though we were partners in a conspiracy, with

many a nod and wink and a sudden change of subject if he
thought we were being overheard.

He wasn't so bad when you got to know him, if you dis-
counted the incipient alcoholism. He had a certain charm
when he wanted to use it and he most surely set out to
charm me. I don't suppose it was difficult; I was a stranger
in a strange land and he was company of sorts.

He ought to have been an actor for he had the gift of
mimicry. When he told me the story of the gold his mobile
face altered plastically and his voice changed until I could
see the bull-headed Coertze, gentle Donato and the
tougher-fibred Alberto. Although Walker had normally a
slight trace of a South African accent, he could drop it at will
to take on the heavy gutturals of the Afrikaner or the speed
and sibilance of the Italian. His Italian was rapid and fluent
and he was probably one of those people who can learn a
language in a matter of weeks.

I had lost most of my doubts about the truth of his story. It
was too damned circumstantial. The bit about the inscription
on the cigarette case impressed me a lot; I couldn't see Walker
making up a thing like that. Besides, it wasn't the brandy talking all the time; he still stuck to the same story, which didn't
change a fraction under many repetitions – drunk and sober.

Once I said, 'The only thing I can't figure is that big crown.'

'Alberto thought it was the royal crown of Ethiopia,' said
Walker. 'It wouldn't be worn about the palace – they'd only
use it for coronations.'

That sounded logical. I said, 'How do you know that the
others haven't dug up the lot? There's still Harrison and
Parker – and it would be dead easy for the two Italians;
they're on the spot.'

Walker shook his head. 'No, there's only Coertze and me.
The others were killed.' His lips twisted. 'It seemed to be
unhealthy to stick close to Coertze. I got scared in the end
and beat it.'

I looked hard at him. 'Do you mean to say that Coertze murdered them?'

'Don't put words in my mouth,' said Walker sharply. 'I didn't say that. All I know is that four men were killed when they were close to Coertze.' He ticked them off on his fingers. 'Harrison was the first – that happened only three days after we buried the loot.'

He tapped a second finger. 'Next came Alberto – I saw that happen. It was as near an accident as anyone could arrange. Then Parker. He was killed in action just like Harrison, and, just like Harrison, the only person who was anywhere near him was Coertze.'

He held up three fingers and slowly straightened the fourth. 'Last was Donato. He was found near the camp with his head bashed in. They said he'd been rock-climbing, so the verdict was accidental death – but not in my book. That was enough for me, so I quit and went south.'

I thought about this for a while, then said, 'What did you mean when you said you saw Alberto killed?'

'We'd been on a raid,' said Walker. 'It went O.K. but the Germans moved fast and got us boxed in. We had to get out by the back door, and the back door was a cliff. Coertze was good on a mountain and he and Alberto went first, Coertze leading. He said he wanted to find the easiest way down, which was all right – he usually did that.

'He went along a ledge and out of sight, then he came back and gave Alberto the O.K. sign. Then he came back to tell us it was all right to start down, so Parker and I went next. We followed Alberto and when we got round the corner we saw that he was stuck.

'There were no hand holds ahead of him and he'd got himself into a position where he couldn't get back, either. Just as we got there he lost his nerve – we could see him quivering and shaking. There he was, like a fly on the side of that cliff with a hell of a long drop under him and a pack of Germans ready to drop on top of him, and he was shaking like a jelly.

'Parker shouted to Coertze and he came down. There was just room enough for him to pass us, so he said he'd go to help Alberto. He got as far as Alberto and Alberto fell off. I swear that Coertze pushed him.'

'Did you see Coertze push him?' I asked.

'No,' Walker admitted. 'I couldn't see Alberto at all once Coertze had passed us. Coertze's a big bloke and he isn't made of glass. But why did he give Alberto the O.K. sign to go along that ledge?'

'It could have been an honest mistake.'

Walker nodded. 'That's what I thought at the time. Coertze said afterwards that he didn't mean that Alberto should go as far as that. There *was* an easier way down just short of where Alberto got stuck. Coertze took us down there.'

He lit a cigarette. 'But when Parker was shot up the following week I started to think again.'

'How did it happen?'

Walker shrugged. 'The usual thing – you know how it is in a fight. When it was all over we found Parker had a hole in his head. Nobody saw it happen, but Coertze was nearest.' He paused. 'The hole was in the *back* of the head.'

'A German bullet?'

Walker snorted. 'Brother, we didn't have time for an autopsy; but it wouldn't have made any difference. We were using German weapons and ammo – captured stuff; and Coertze *always* used German guns; he said they were better than the British.' He brooded. 'That started me thinking seriously. It was all too pat – all these blokes being knocked off so suddenly. When Donato got his, I quit. The Foreign Legion was just about busted anyway. I waited until the Count had sent Coertze off somewhere, then I collected my gear, said goodbye and headed south to the Allied lines. I was lucky – I got through.'

'What about Coertze?'

'He stayed with the Count until the Yanks came up. I saw him in Jo'burg a couple of years ago. I was crossing the road to go into a pub when I saw Coertze going through the door. I changed my mind; I had a drink, but not in *that* pub.'

He shivered suddenly. 'I want to stay as far from Coertze as I can. There's a thousand miles between Cape Town and Johannesburg – that ought to be enough.' He stood up suddenly. 'Let's go and have a drink, for God's sake.'

So we went and had a drink – several drinks.

V

During the next few weeks I could see that Walker was on the verge of making me a proposition. He said he had some money due to him and that he would need a good friend. At last he came out with it.

'Look,' he said. 'My old man died last year and I've got two thousand pounds coming when I can get it out of the lawyer's hands. I could go to Italy on two thousand pounds.'

'So you could,' I said.

He bit his lip. 'Hal, I want you to come with me.'

'For the gold?'

'That's right; for the gold. Share and share alike.'

'What about Coertze?'

'To hell with Coertze,' said Walker violently. 'I don't want to have anything to do with him.'

I thought about it. I was young and full of vinegar in those days, and this sounded just the ticket – if Walker was telling the truth. And if he wasn't telling the truth, why would he finance me to a trip to Italy? It seemed a pleasantly adventurous thing to do, but I hesitated. 'Why me?' I asked.

'I can't do it myself,' he said. 'I wouldn't trust Coertze, and you're the only other chap who knows anything about it. And I trust you, Hal, I really do.'

I made up my mind. 'All right, it's a deal. But there are conditions.'

'Trot them out.'

'This drinking of yours has to stop,' I said. 'You're all right when you're sober, but when you've got a load on you're bloody awful. Besides, you know you spill things when you're cut.'

He rearranged his eager face into a firm expression. 'I'll do it, Hal; I won't touch a drop,' he promised.

'All right,' I said. 'When do we start?'

I can see now that we were a couple of naïve young fools. We expected to be able to lift several tons of gold from a hole in the ground without too much trouble. We had no conception of the brains and organization that would be needed – and were needed in the end.

Walker said, 'The lawyer tells me that the estate will be settled finally in about six weeks. We can leave any time after that.'

We discussed the trip often. Walker was not too much concerned with the practical difficulties of getting the gold, nor with what we were going to do with it once we had it. He was mesmerized by the millions involved.

He said once, 'Coertze estimated that there were four tons of gold. At the present price that's well over a million pounds. Then there's the lire – packing cases full of the stuff. You can get a hell of a lot of lire into a big packing case.'

'You can forget the paper money,' I said. 'Just pass one of those notes and you'll have the Italian police jumping all over you.'

'We can pass them outside Italy,' he said sulkily.

'Then you'll have to cope with Interpol.'

'All right,' he said impatiently. 'We'll forget the lire. But there's still the jewellery – rings and necklaces, diamonds and emeralds.' His eyes glowed. 'I'll bet the jewels are worth more than the gold.'

'But not as easily disposed of,' I said.

I was getting more and more worried about the sheer physical factors involved. To make it worse, Walker wouldn't tell me the position of the lead mine, so I couldn't do any active planning at all.

He was behaving like a child at the approach of Christmas, eager to open his Christmas stocking. I couldn't get him to face facts and I seriously contemplated pulling out of this mad scheme. I could see nothing ahead but a botched job with a probably lengthy spell in an Italian jail.

The night before he was to go to the lawyer's office to sign the final papers and receive his inheritance I went to see him at his hotel. He was half-drunk, lying on his bed with a bottle conveniently near.

'You promised you wouldn't drink,' I said coldly.

'Aw, Hal, this isn't drinking; not what I'm doing. It's just a little taste to celebrate.'

I said, 'You'd better cut your celebration until you've read the paper.'

'What paper?'

'This one,' I said, and took it from my pocket. 'That little bit at the bottom of the page.'

He took the paper and looked at it stupidly. 'What must I read?'

'That paragraph headed: "Italians Sentenced".'

It was only a small item, a filler for the bottom of the page.

Walker was suddenly sober. 'But they *were* innocent,' he whispered.

'That didn't prevent them from getting it in the neck,' I said brutally.

'God!' he said. 'They're still looking for it.'

'Of course they are,' I said impatiently. 'They'll keep looking until they find it.' I wondered if the Italians were more concerned about the gold or the documents.

I could see that Walker had been shocked out of his euphoric dreams of sudden wealth. He now had to face the fact that pulling gold out of an Italian hole had its dangers. 'This makes a difference,' he said slowly. 'We can't go now. We'll have to wait until this dies down.'

'Will it die down – ever?' I asked.

He looked up at me. 'I'm not going now,' he said with the firmness of fear. 'The thing's off – it's off for a long time.'

In a way I was relieved. There was a weakness in Walker that was disturbing and which had been troubling me. I had been uneasy for a long time and had been very uncertain of the wisdom of going to Italy with him. Now it was decided.

I left him abruptly in the middle of a typical action – pouring another drink.

As I walked home one thought occurred to me. The newspaper report confirmed Walker's story pretty thoroughly. That was something.

VI

It was long past lunch-time when. I finished the story. My throat was dry with talking and Jean's eyes had grown big and round.

'It's like something from the Spanish Main,' she said. 'Or a Hammond Innes thriller. Is the gold still there?'

I shrugged. 'I don't know. I haven't read anything about it in the papers. For all I know it's still there – if Walker or Coertze haven't recovered it.'

'What happened to Walker?'

'He got his two thousand quid,' I said. 'Then embarked on a career of trying to drink the distilleries dry. It wasn't long before he lost his job and then he dropped from sight. Someone told me he'd gone to Durban. Anyway, I haven't seen him since.'

Jean was fascinated by the story and after that we made a game of it, figuring ways and means of removing four tons of gold from Italy as unobtrusively as possible. Just as an academic exercise, of course. Jean had a fertile imagination and some of her ideas were very good.

In 1959 we got clear of our indebtedness to the bank by dint of strict economy. The yard was ours now with no strings attached and we celebrated by laying the keel of a 15-tonner I had designed for Jean and myself. My old faithful *King Penguin*, one of the first of her class, was all right for coastal pottering, but we had the idea that one day we would do some ocean voyaging, and we wanted a bigger boat.

A 15-tonner is just the right size for two people to handle and big enough to live in indefinitely. This boat was to be forty feet overall, thirty feet on the waterline with eleven feet beam. She would be moderately canvased for ocean voyaging and would have a big auxiliary diesel engine. We were going to call her *Sanford* in memory of old Tom.

When she was built we would take a year's leave, sail north to spend some time in the Mediterranean, and come back by the east coast, thus making a complete circumnavigation of Africa. Jean had a mischievous glint in her eye. 'Perhaps we'll bring that gold back with us,' she said.

But two months later the blow fell.

I had designed a boat for Bill Meadows and had sent him the drawings for approval. By mishap the accommodation plans had been left out of the packet, so Jean volunteered to take them to Fish Hoek where Bill lives.

It's a nice drive to Fish Hoek along the Chapman's Peak road with views of sea and mountain, far better than anything I have since seen on the Riviera. Jean delivered the drawings and on the way back in the twilight a drunken oaf in a high-powered American car forced her off the road and she fell three hundred feet into the sea.

The bottom dropped out of my life.

It meant nothing to me that the driver of the other car got five years for manslaughter – that wouldn't bring Jean back. I let things slide at the yard and if it hadn't been for Harry Marshall the business would have gone to pot.

It was then that I tallied up my life and made a sort of mental balance sheet. I was thirty-six years old; I had a good business which I had liked but which now I didn't seem to like so much; I had my health and strength – boat-building and sailing tend to keep one physically fit – and I had no debts. I even had money in the bank with more rolling in all the time.

On the other side of the balance sheet was the dreadful absence of Jean, which more than counter-balanced all the advantages.

I felt I couldn't stay at the yard or even in Cape Town, where memories of Jean would haunt me at every corner. I wanted to get away. I was waiting for something to happen.

I was ripe for mischief.

VII

A couple of weeks later I was in a bar on Adderley Street having a drink or three. It wasn't that I'd taken to drink, but I was certainly drinking more than I had been accustomed to. I had just started on my third brandy when I felt a touch at my elbow and a voice said, 'Hallo, I haven't seen you for a long time.'

I turned and found Walker standing next to me.

The years hadn't dealt kindly with Walker. He was thinner, his dark, good looks had gone to be replaced by a sharpness of feature, and his hairline had receded. His clothes were unpressed and frayed at the edges, and there was an air of seediness about him which was depressing.

'Hallo,' I said. 'Where did you spring from?' He was looking at my full glass of brandy, so I said, 'Have a drink.'

'Thanks,' he said quickly. 'I'll have a double.'

That gave me a pretty firm clue as to what had happened to Walker, but I didn't mind being battened upon for a couple of drinks, so I paid for the double brandy.

He raised the glass to his lips with a hand that trembled slightly, took a long lingering gulp, then put the glass down, having knocked back three-quarters of the contents. 'You're looking prosperous,' he said.

'I'm not doing too badly.'

He said, 'I was sorry to hear of what happened to your wife.' He hurried on as he saw my look of inquiry. 'I read about it in the paper. I thought it must have been your wife – the name was the same and all that.'

I thought he had spent some time hunting me up. Old friends and acquaintances are precious to an alcoholic; they can be touched for the odd drink and the odd fiver.

'That's finished and best forgotten,' I said shortly. Unwittingly, perhaps, he had touched me on the raw – he had brought Jean back. 'What are you doing now?'

He shrugged. 'This and that.'

'You haven't picked up any gold lately?' I said cruelly. I wanted to pay him back for putting Jean in my mind.

'Do I look as though I have?' he asked bitterly. Unexpectedly, he said, 'I saw Coertze last week.'

'Here – in Cape Town?'

'Yes. He'd just come back from Italy. He's back in Jo'burg now, I expect.'

I smiled. 'Did *he* have any gold with him?'

Walker shook his head. 'He said that nothing's changed.' He suddenly gripped me by the arm. 'The gold's still there – nobody's found it. It's still there – four tons of gold in that tunnel – and all the jewels.' He had a frantic urgency about him.

'Well, why doesn't he do something about it?' I said. 'Why doesn't he go and get it out? Why don't you both go?'

'He doesn't like me,' said Walker sulkily. 'He'll hardly speak to me.' He took one of my cigarettes from the packet on the counter, and I lit it for him, amusedly. 'It isn't easy to get it out of the country,' he said. 'Even Sergeant High-and-Mighty Coertze hasn't found a way.'

He grinned tightly. 'Imagine that,' he said, almost gaily. 'Even the brainy Coertze can't do it. He put the gold in a hole in the ground and he's too scared to get it out.' He began to laugh hysterically.

I took his arm. 'Take it easy.'

His laughter choked off suddenly. 'All right,' he said. 'Buy me another drink; I left my wallet at home.'

I crooked my finger at the bartender and Walker ordered another double. I was beginning to understand the reason for his degradation. For fourteen years the knowledge that a fortune in gold was lying in Italy waiting to be picked up had been eating at him like a cancer. Even when I knew him ten years earlier I was aware of the fatal weakness in him, and now one could see that the bitterness of defeat had been too much. I wondered how Coertze was standing up to the strain. At least he seemed to be doing something about it, even if only keeping an eye on the situation.

I said carefully, 'If Coertze was willing to take you, would you be prepared to go to Italy to get the stuff out?'

He was suddenly very still. 'What d'you mean?' he demanded. 'Have you been talking to Coertze?'

'I've never laid eyes on the man.'

Walker's glance shifted nervously about the bar, then he straightened. 'Well, if he . . . wanted me; if he . . . needed me – I'd be prepared to go along.' He said this with bravado but the malice showed through when he said, 'He needed me once, you know; he needed me when we buried the stuff.'

'You wouldn't be afraid of him?'

'What do you mean – afraid of him? Why should I be afraid of him? I'm afraid of nobody.'

'You were pretty certain he'd committed at least four murders.'

He seemed put out. 'Oh that! That was a long time ago. And I never said he'd murdered anybody. I never said it.'

'No, you never actually said it.'

He shifted nervously on the bar stool. 'Oh, what's the use? He won't ask me to go with him. He said as much last week.'

'Oh, yes, he will,' I said softly.

Walker looked up quickly. 'Why should he?'

I said quietly, 'Because I know of a way of getting that gold out of Italy and of taking it anywhere in the world, quite simply and relatively safely.'

His eyes widened. 'What is it? How can you do it?'

'I'm not going to tell you,' I said equably. 'After all, you wouldn't tell me where the gold's hidden.'

'Well, let's do it,' he said. 'I'll tell you where it is, you get it out, and Bob's your uncle. Why bring Coertze into it?'

'It's a job for more than two men,' I said. 'Besides, he deserves a share – he's been keeping an eye on the gold for fourteen years, which is a damn' sight more than you've been doing.' I failed to mention that I considered Walker the weakest of reeds. 'Now, how will you get on with Coertze if this thing goes through?'

He turned sulky. 'All right, I suppose, if he lays off me. But I won't stand for any of his sarcasm.' He looked at me in wonder as though what we were talking about had just sunk in. 'You mean there's a chance we can get the stuff out – a real chance?'

I nodded and got off the bar stool. 'Now, if you'll excuse me.'

'Where are you going?' he asked quickly.

'To phone the airline office,' I said. 'I want a seat on tomorrow's Jo'burg plane. I'm going to see Coertze.'

The sign I had been waiting for had arrived.

TWO: COERTZE

Air travel is wonderful. At noon the next day I was booking into a hotel in Johannesburg, a thousand miles from Cape Town.

On the plane I had thought a lot about Coertze. I had made up my mind that if he didn't bite then the whole thing was off – I couldn't see myself relying on Walker. And I had to decide how to handle him – from Walker's account he was a pretty tough character. I didn't mind that; I could be tough myself when the occasion arose, but I didn't want to antagonize him. He would probably be as suspicious as hell, and I'd need kid gloves.

Then there was another thing – the financing of the expedition. I wanted to hang on to the boatyard as insurance in case this whole affair flopped, but I thought if I cut Harry Marshall in for a partnership in the yard, sold my house and my car and one or two other things, I might be able to raise about £25,000 – not too much for what I had in mind.

But it all depended on Coertze. I smiled when I considered where he was working. He had a job in Central Smelting Plant which refined gold from all the mines on the Reef. More gold had probably passed through his hands in the last few years than all the Axis war-lords put together had buried throughout the world.

It must have been tantalizing for him.

I phoned the smelting plant in the afternoon. There was a pause before he came on the line. 'Coertze,' he said briefly.

I came to the point. 'My name's Halloran,' I said. 'A mutual friend – Mr Walker of Cape Town – tells me you have been experiencing difficulty in arranging for the delivery of goods from Italy. I'm in the import-export business; I thought I might be able to help you.'

A deep silence bored into my ear.

I said, 'My firm is fully equipped to do this sort of work. We never have much trouble with the Customs in cases like these.'

It was like dropping a stone into a very deep well and listening for the splash.

'Why don't you come to see me,' I said. 'I don't want to take up your time now; I'm sure you're a busy man. Come at seven this evening and we'll discuss your difficulties over dinner. I'm staying at the Regency – it's in Berea, in . . .'

'I know where it is,' said Coertze. His voice was deep and harsh with a guttural Afrikaans accent.

'Good; I'll be expecting you,' I said, and put down the phone.

I was pleased with this first contact. Coertze was suspicious and properly so – he'd have been a fool not to be. But if he came to the hotel he'd be hooked, and all I had to do would be to jerk on the line and set the hook in firmly.

I was pretty certain he'd come; human curiosity would see to that. If he didn't come, then he wouldn't be human – or he'd be superhuman.

He came, but not at seven o'clock and I was beginning to doubt my judgement of the frailty of human nature. It was after eight when he knocked on the door, identified me, and said, 'We'll forget the dinner; I've eaten.'

'All right,' I said. 'But what about a drink?' I crossed the room and put my hand on the brandy bottle. I was pretty certain it would be brandy – most South Africans drink it.

'I'll have a Scotch,' he said unexpectedly. 'Thanks,' he added as an afterthought.

As I poured the drinks I glanced at him. He was a bulky man, broad of chest and heavy in the body. His hair was black and rather coarse and he had a shaggy look about him. I'd bet that when stripped he'd look like a grizzly bear. His eyebrows were black and straight over eyes of a snapping electric blue. He had looked after himself better than Walker; his belly was flat and there was a sheen of health about him.

I handed him a drink and we sat down facing each other. He was tense and wary, although he tried to disguise it by over-relaxing in his chair. We were like a couple of duellists who have just engaged blades.

'I'll come to the point,' I said. 'A long time ago Walker told me a very interesting story about some gold. That was ten years ago and we were going to do something about it, but it didn't pan out. That might have been lucky because we'd have certainly made a botch of the job.'

I pointed my finger at him. 'You've been keeping an eye on it. You've probably popped across to Italy from time to time just to keep your eye on things in general. You've been racking your brains trying to think of a way of getting that gold out of Italy, but you haven't been able to do it. You're stymied.'

His face had not changed expression; he would have made a good poker player. He said, 'When did you see Walker?'

'Yesterday – in Cape Town.'

The craggy face broke into a derisive grin. 'And you flew up to Jo'burg to see me just because a *dronkie* like Walker told you a cock-and-bull story like that? Walker's a no-good hobo; I see a dozen like him in the Library Gardens every day,' he said contemptuously.

'It's not a cock-and-bull story, and I can prove it.'

Coertze just sat and looked at me like a stone gargoyle, the whisky glass almost lost in his huge fist.

I said, 'What are you doing here – in this room? If there was no story, all you had to do was to ask me what the hell I was talking about when I spoke to you on the phone. The fact that you're here proves there's something in it.'

He made a fast decision. 'All right,' he said. 'What's your proposition?'

I said, 'You still haven't figured a way of moving four tons of gold out of Italy. Is that right?'

He smiled slowly. 'Let's assume so,' he said ironically.

'I've got a foolproof way.'

He put down his glass and produced a packet of cigarettes. 'What is it?'

'I'm not going to tell you – yet.'

He grinned. 'Walker hasn't told you where the gold is, has he?'

'No, he hasn't,' I admitted. 'But he would if I put pressure on him. Walker can't stand pressure; you know that.'

'He drinks too much,' said Coertze. 'And when he drinks he talks; I'll bet that's how he came to spill his guts to you.' He lit his cigarette. 'What do you want out of it?'

'Equal shares,' I said firmly. 'A three-way split after all expenses have been paid.'

'And Walker comes with us on the job. Is that right?'

'Yes,' I said.

Coertze moved in his chair. 'Man, it's like this,' he said. 'I don't know if you've got a foolproof way of getting the gold out or if you haven't. I thought *I* had it licked a couple of times. But let's assume your way is going to work. Why should we take Walker?'

He held up his hand. 'I'm not suggesting we do him down or anything like that – although he'd think nothing of cheating us. Give him his share after it's all over, but for God's sake keep him out of Italy. He'll make a balls-up for sure.'

I thought of Harrison and Parker and the two Italians. 'You don't seem to like him.'

Coertze absently fingered a scar on his forehead. 'He's unreliable,' he said. 'He almost got me killed a couple of times during the war.'

I said, 'No, we take Walker. I don't know for certain if three of us can pull it off, and with two it would be impossible. Unless you want to let someone else in?'

He smiled humourlessly. 'That's not on – not with you coming in. But Walker had better keep his big mouth shut from now on.'

'Perhaps it would be better if he stopped drinking,' I suggested.

'That's right,' Coertze agreed. 'Keep him off the pots. A few beers are all right, but keep him off the hard-tack. That'll be your job; I don't want to have anything to do with the rat.'

He blew smoke into the air, and said, 'Now let's hear your proposition. If it's good, I'll come in with you. If I don't think it'll work, I won't touch it. In that case, you and Walker can do what you damn' well like, but if you go for that gold you'll have me to reckon with. I'm a bad bastard when I'm crossed.'

'So am I,' I said.

We grinned at each other. I liked this man, in a way. I wouldn't trust him any more than I'd trust Walker, but I had the feeling that while Walker would stick a knife in your back, Coertze would at least shoot you down from the front.

'All right,' he said. 'Let's have it.'

'I'm not going to tell you – not here in this room,' I saw his expression and hurried on. 'It isn't that I don't trust you, it's simply that you wouldn't believe it. You have to see it – and you have to see it in Cape Town.'

He looked at me for a long moment, then said, 'All right, if that's the way you want it, I'll play along.' He paused to think. 'I've got a good job here, and I'm not going to give it up on your say-so. There's a long week-end coming up – that gives me three days off. I'll fly down to Cape Town to see what you have to show me. If it's good, the job can go hang; if it isn't, then I've still got the job.'

'I'll pay for your fare,' I said.

'I can afford it,' he grunted.

'If it doesn't pan out, I'll pay for your fare,' I insisted. 'I wouldn't want you to be out of pocket.'

He looked up and grinned. 'We'll get along,' he said. 'Where's that bottle?'

As I was pouring another couple of drinks, he said, 'You said you were going to Italy with Walker. What stopped you?'

I took the clipping from my pocket and passed it to him. He read it and laughed. 'That must have scared Walker. I was there at the time,' he said unexpectedly.

'In Italy?'

He sipped the Scotch and nodded. 'Yes; I saved my army back-pay and my gratuity and went back in '48. As soon as I got there all hell started popping about this trial. I read about it in the papers and you never heard such a lot of bull in your life. Still, I thought I'd better lie low, so I had a *lekker* holiday with the Count.'

'With the Count?' I said in surprise.

'Sure,' he said. 'I stay with the Count every time I go to Italy. I've been there four times now.'

I said, 'How did you reckon to dispose of the gold once you got it out of Italy?'

'I've got all that planned,' he said confidently. 'They're always wanting gold in India and you get a good price.

You'd be surprised at the amount of gold smuggled out of this country in small packets that ends up in India.'

He was right – India is the gold sink of the world – but I said casually, 'My idea is to go the other way – to Tangier. It's an open port with an open gold market. You should be able to sell four tons of gold there quite easily – and it's legal, too. No trouble with the police.'

He looked at me with respect. 'I hadn't thought of that. I don't know much about this international finance.'

'There's a snag,' I said. 'Tangier is closing up shop next year; it's being taken over by Morocco. Then it won't be a free port any more and the gold market will close.'

'When next year?'

'April 19,' I said. 'Nine months from now. I think we'll just about have enough time.'

He smiled. 'I never thought about selling the gold legally; I didn't think you could. I thought the governments had got all that tied up. Maybe I should have met you sooner.'

'It wouldn't have done you any good,' I said. 'I hadn't the brains then that I have now.'

He laughed and we proceeded to kill the bottle.

II

Coertze came down to Cape Town two weeks later. I met him at the airport and drove him directly to the yard, where Walker was waiting.

Walker seemed to shrink into himself when I told him that Coertze was visiting us. In spite of his braggart boasts, I could see he didn't relish close contact. If half of what he had said about Coertze was true, then he had every reason to be afraid.

Come to think of it – so had I!

It must have been the first time that Coertze had been in a boatyard and he looked about him with keen interest and asked a lot of questions, nearly all of them sensible. At last, he said, 'Well, what about it?'

I took them down to the middle slip where Jimmy Murphy's *Estralita* was waiting to be drawn up for an overhaul. 'That's a sailing yacht,' I said. 'A 15-tonner. What would you say her draft it – I mean, how deep is she in the water?'

Coertze looked her over and then looked up at the tall mast. 'She'll need to be deep to counterbalance that lot,' he said. 'But I don't know how much. I don't know anything about boats.'

Considering he didn't know anything about boats, it was a very sensible answer.

'Her draft is six feet in normal trim,' I said. 'She's drawing less now because a lot of gear has been taken out of her.'

His eyes narrowed. 'I'd have thought it would be more than that,' he said. 'What happens when the wind blows hard on the sails? Won't she tip over?'

This was going well and Coertze was on the ball. I said, 'I have a boat like this just being built, another 15-tonner. Come and have a look at her.'

I led the way up to the shed where *Sanford* was being built and Coertze followed, apparently content that I was leading up to a point. Walker tagged on behind.

I had pressed to get *Sanford* completed and she was ready for launching as soon as the glass-fibre sheathing was applied and the interior finished.

Coertze looked up at her. 'They look bloody big out of the water,' he commented.

I smiled. That was the usual lay reaction. 'Come aboard,' I said.

He was impressed by the spaciousness he found below and commented favourably on the way things were arranged. 'Did you design all this?' he asked.

I nodded.

'You could live in here, all right,' he said, inspecting the galley.

'You could – and you will,' I said. 'This is the boat in which we're going to take four tons of gold out of Italy.'

He looked surprised and then he frowned. 'Where are you going to put it?'

I said, 'Sit down and I'll tell you something about sailing boats you don't know.' Coertze sat uncomfortably on the edge of the starboard settee which had no mattress as yet, and waited for me to explain myself.

'This boat displaces – weighs, that is – ten tons, and . . .'

Walker broke in. 'I thought you said she was a 15-tonner.'

'That's Thames measure – yacht measure. Her displacement is different.'

Coertze looked at Walker. 'Shut up and let the man speak.' He turned to me. 'If the boat weighs ten tons and you add another four tons, she'll be pretty near sinking, won't she? And where are you going to put it? It can't be out in the open where the cops can see it.'

I said patiently, 'I said I'd tell you something about sailing boats that you didn't know. Now, listen – about forty per cent of the weight of any sailing boat is ballast to keep her the right way up when the wind starts to press on those sails.'

I tapped the cabin sole with my foot. 'Hanging on the bottom of this boat is a bloody great piece of lead weighing precisely four tons.'

Coertze looked at me incredulously, a dawning surmise in his eyes. I said, 'Come on, I'll show you.'

We went outside and I showed them the lead ballast keel. I said, 'All this will be covered up next week because the boat will be sheathed to keep out the marine borers.'

Coertze was squatting on his heels looking at the keel. 'This is it,' he said slowly. 'This is it. The gold will be hidden under water – built in as part of the boat.' He began to laugh, and after a while Walker joined in. I began to laugh, too, and the walls of the shed resounded.

Coertze sobered suddenly. 'What's the melting point of lead?' he asked abruptly.

I knew what was coming. 'Four-fifty degrees centigrade,' I said. 'We've got a little foundry at the top of the yard where we pour the keels.'

'*Ja*,' he said heavily. 'You can melt lead on a kitchen stove. But gold melts at over a thousand centigrade and we'll need more than a kitchen stove for that. I *know*; melting gold is my job. Up at the smelting plant we've got bloody big furnaces.'

I said quickly, 'I've thought of that one, too. Come up to the workshop – I'll show you something else you've never seen before.'

In the workshop I opened a cupboard and said, 'This gadget is brand new – just been invented.' I hauled out the contraption and put it on the bench. Coertze looked at it uncomprehendingly.

There wasn't much to see; just a metal box, eighteen inches by fifteen inches by nine inches, on the top of which was an asbestos mat and a Heath Robinson arrangement of clamps.

I said, 'You've heard of instant coffee – this is instant heat.' I began to get the machine ready for operation. 'It needs cooling water at at least five pounds an inch pressure – that we get from an ordinary tap. It works on ordinary electric current, too, so you can set it up any-where.'

I took the heart of the machine from a drawer. Again, it wasn't much to look at; just a piece of black cloth, three inches by four. I said, 'Some joker in the States discovered

how to spin and weave threads of pure graphite, and someone else discovered this application.'

I lifted the handle on top of the machine, inserted the
graphite mat, and clamped it tight. Then I took a bit of metal
and gave it to Coertze.

He turned it in his fingers and said, 'What is it?'

'Just a piece of ordinary mild steel. But if this gadget can
melt steel, it can melt gold. Right?'

He nodded and looked at the machine dubiously – it
wasn't very impressive.

I took the steel from his fingers and dropped it on to the
graphite mat, then I gave Walker and Coertze a pair of
welders' goggles each. 'Better put these on: it gets a
bit bright.'

We donned the goggles and I switched on the machine.
It was a spectacular display. The graphite mat flashed
instantly to a white heat and the piece of steel glowed red,
then yellow and finally white. It seemed to slump like a
bit of melting wax and in less than fifteen seconds it had
melted into a little pool. All this to the accompaniment of
a violent shower of sparks as the metal reacted with
the air.

I switched off the machine and removed my goggles.
'We won't have all these fireworks when we melt gold; it
doesn't oxidize as easily as iron.'

Coertze was staring at the machine. 'How does it do
that?'

'Something like a carbon arc,' I said. 'You can get tem-
peratures up to five thousand degrees centigrade. It's only
intended to be a laboratory instrument, but I reckon we can
melt two pounds of gold at a time. With three of these gadgets and a hell of a lot of spare mats we should be able to
work pretty fast.'

He said doubtfully, 'If we can only pour a couple of
pounds at a time, the keel is going to be so full of cracks

and flaws that I'm not sure it won't break under its own weight.'

'I've thought of that one, too,' I said calmly. 'Have you ever watched anyone pour reinforced concrete?'

He frowned and then caught on, snapping his fingers.

'We make the mould and put a mesh of wires inside,' I said. 'That'll hold it together.'

I showed him a model I had made, using fuse wire and candle wax, which he examined carefully. 'You've done a hell of a lot of thinking about this,' he said at last.

'Somebody has to,' I said. 'Or that gold will stay where it is for another fourteen years.'

He didn't like that because it made him appear stupid; but there wasn't anything he could do about it. He started to say something and bit it short, his face flushing red. Then he took a deep breath and said, 'All right, you've convinced me. I'm in.'

Then *I* took a deep breath – of relief.

III

That night we had a conference.

I said, 'This is the drill. *Sanford* – my yacht – will be ready for trials next week. As soon as the trials are over you two are going to learn how to sail under my instruction. In under four months from now we sail for Tangier.'

'Christ!' said Walker. 'I don't know that I like the sound of that.'

'There's nothing to it,' I said. 'Hundreds of people are buzzing about the Atlantic these days. Hell, people have gone round the world in boats a quarter the size.'

I looked at Coertze. 'This is going to take a bit of financing. Got any money?'

'About a thousand,' he admitted.

'That gets tossed into the kitty,' I said. 'Along with my twenty-five thousand.'

'*Magtig*,' he said. 'That's a hell of a lot of money.'

'We'll need every penny of it,' I said. 'We might have to buy a small boatyard in Italy if that's the only way we can cast the keel in secrecy. Besides, I'm lending it to the firm of Walker, Coertze and Halloran at one hundred per cent interest. I want fifty thousand back before the three-way split begins. You can do the same with your thousand.'

'That sounds fair enough,' agreed Coertze.

I said, 'Walker hasn't any money and once you've thrown your thousand in the kitty, neither have you. So I'm putting you both on my payroll. You've got to have your smokes and three squares a day while all this is going on.'

This bit of information perked Walker up considerably. Coertze merely nodded in confirmation. I looked hard at Walker. 'And you stay off the booze or we drop you over the side. Don't forget that.'

He nodded sullenly.

Coertze said, 'Why are we going to Tangier first?'

'We've got to make arrangements to remelt the gold into standard bars,' I said. 'I can't imagine any banker calmly taking a golden keel into stock. Anyway, that's for the future; right now I have to turn you into passable seamen – we've got to get to the Mediterranean first.'

I took *Sanford* on trials and Walker and Coertze came along for the ride and to see what they were letting themselves in for. She turned out to be everything I've ever wanted in a boat. She was fast for a deep-sea cruiser and not too tender. With a little sail adjustment she had just the right amount of helm and I could see she was going to be all right without any drastic changes.

As we went into a long reach she picked up speed and went along happily with the water burbling along the lee rail and splashing on deck. Walker, his face a little green, said, 'I thought you said a keel would hold this thing upright.' He was hanging tightly on to the side of the cockpit.

I laughed. I was happier than I had been for a long time. 'Don't worry about that. That's not much angle of heel. She won't capsize.'

Coertze didn't say anything – he was busy being sick.

The next three months were rough and tough. People forget that the Cape was the Cape of Storms before some early public relations officer changed the name to the Cape of Good Hope. When the Berg Wind blows it can be as uncomfortable at sea as anywhere in the world.

I drove Walker and Coertze unmercifully. In three months I had to turn them into capable seamen, because *Sanford* was a bit too big to sail single-handed. I hoped that the two of them would equal one able-bodied seaman. It wasn't as bad as it sounds because in those three months they put in as much sea time as the average week-end yachtsman gets in three years, and they had the dubious advantage of having a pitiless instructor.

Shore time was spent in learning the theory of sail and the elements of marline-spike seamanship – how to knot and splice, mend a sail and make baggywrinkle. They grumbled a little at the theory, but I silenced that by asking them what they'd do if I was washed overboard in the middle of the Atlantic.

Then we went out to practise what I had taught – at first in the bay and then in the open sea, cruising coastwise around the peninsula at first, and then for longer distances well out of sight of land.

I had thought that Coertze would prove to be as tough at sea as apparently he was on land. But he was no sailor and never would be. He had a queasy stomach and couldn't stand the motion, so he turned out to be pretty useless at boat handling. But he was hero enough to be our cook on the longer voyages, a thankless job for a sea-sick man.

I would hear him swearing below when the weather was rough and a pot of hot coffee was tossed in his lap. He once told me that he now knew what poker dice felt like when they were shaken in the cup. He wouldn't have stood it for any lesser reason, but the lust for gold was strong in him.

Walker was the real surprise. Coertze and I had weaned him from his liquor over many protests, and he was now eating more and the air and exercise agreed with him. He put on weight, his thin cheeks filled out and his chest broadened. Nothing could replace the hair he had lost, but he seemed a lot more like the handsome young man I had known ten years earlier.

More surprisingly, he turned out to be a natural sailor. He liked *Sanford* and she seemed to like him. He was a good helmsman and could lay her closer to the wind than I could when we were beating to windward. At first I was hesitant to give him a free hand with *Sanford*, but as he proved himself I lost my reluctance.

At last we were ready and there was nothing more to wait for. We provisioned *Sanford* and set sail for the north on November 12, to spend Christmas at sea. Ahead of us was a waste of water with the beckoning lure of four tons of gold at the other side.

I suppose one *could* have called it a pleasure cruise!

BOOK TWO

The Gold

THREE: TANGIER

Two months later we sailed into Tangier harbour, the 'Q' flag hoisted, and waited for the doctor to give us pratique and for the Customs to give us the once-over. To port of *Sanford* was the modern city with its sleek, contemporary buildings sharply outlined against the sky. To starboard was the old city – the Arab city – squat and low-roofed and hugging a hill, the skyline only broken by the up-flung spear of a minaret.

To port – Europe; to starboard – Africa.

This was nothing new to Walker and Coertze. They had sown a few wild oats in their army days, roistering in Cairo and Alexandria. On the voyage from Cape Town they had talked much about their army days – and all in Italian, too. We made it a rule to speak as much Italian as possible, and while the others were on a refresher course, I didn't lag far behind even though I had to start from scratch.

We had settled on a good cover story to veil our activities in the Mediterranean. I was a South African boat builder on a cruise combining business with pleasure. I was thinking of expanding into the lucrative Mediterranean market and might buy a boatyard if the price and conditions were right. This story had the advantage of not departing too far from the truth and would serve if we really had to buy a yard to cast the golden keel.

Coertze was a mining man with medical trouble. His doctor had advised him to take a leisurely holiday and so he was crewing *Sanford* for me. His cover story would account for any interest he might take in derelict lead mines.

Walker, who proved to be something of an actor, was a moderately wealthy playboy. He had money but disliked work and was willing to go a long way to avoid it. He had come on this Mediterranean trip because he was bored with South Africa and wanted a change. It was to be his job to set things up in Tangier; to acquire a secluded house where we could complete the last stages of the operation.

All in all, I was quite satisfied, even though I had got a bit tired of Coertze on the way north. He didn't like the way I seemed to be taking charge of things and I had to ram home very forcibly the fact that a ship can only have one skipper. He had seen the point when we ran into heavy weather off the Azores, and it galled him that the despised Walker was the better seaman.

Now we were in Tangier, he had recovered his form and was a bit more inclined to throw his weight around. I could see that I'd have to step on him again before long.

Walker looked about the yacht basin. 'Not many sailing boats here,' he commented.

That was true. There were a few ungainly-looking fishing boats and a smart ketch, probably bound for the Caribbean. But there were at least twenty big power craft, fast-looking boats, low on the water. I knew what they were.

This was the smuggling fleet. Cigarettes to Spain, cigarette lighters to France, antibiotics to where they could make a profit (although that trade had fallen off), narcotics to everywhere. I wondered if there was much arms smuggling to Algeria.

At last the officials came and went, leaving gouges in my planking from their hob-nailed boots. I escorted them to their launch, and as soon as they had left, Walker touched my arm.

'We've got another visitor,' he said.

I turned and saw a boat being sculled across the harbour. Walker said, 'He was looking at us through glasses from that boat across there.' He pointed to one of the motor craft. 'Then he started to come here.'

I watched the approaching dinghy. A European was rowing and I couldn't see his face, but as he dexterously backed water and swung round to the side of *Sanford* he looked up and I saw that it was Metcalfe.

Metcalfe is one of that international band of scallywags of whom there are about a hundred in the world. They are soldiers of fortune and they flock to the trouble spots, ignoring the danger and going for the money. I was not really surprised to see Metcalfe in Tangier; it had been a pirates' stronghold from time immemorial and would be one of Metcalfe's natural hang-outs.

I had known him briefly in South Africa but I didn't know what he was at the time. All that I knew was that he was a damned good sailor who won a lot of dinghy races at Cape Town and who came close to winning the South African dinghy championship. He bought one of my Falcons and had spent a lot of time at the yard tuning it.

I had liked him and had crewed for him a couple of times. We had had many a drink together in the yacht club bar and he had spent a week-end at Kirstenbosche with Jean and myself. It was in the way of being a firmly ripening friendship between us when he had left South Africa a hop, skip and a jump ahead of the police, who wanted to nail him on a charge of I.D.B. Since then I had not seen him, but I had heard passing mentions and had occasionally seen his name in the papers, usually quoted as being in trouble in some exotic hot-spot.

Now he was climbing on to the deck of *Sanford*.

'I thought it was you,' he said. 'So I got the glasses to make sure. What are you doing here?'

'Just idly cruising,' I said. 'Combining business with pleasure. I thought I might see what the prospects in the Med. are like.'

He grinned. 'Brother, they're good. But that's not in your line, is it?'

I shook my head, and said, 'Last I heard of you, you were in Cuba.'

'I was in Havana for a bit,' he said. 'But that was no place for me. It was an *honest* revolution, or at least it was until the Commies moved in. I couldn't compete with them, so I quit.'

'What are you doing now?'

He smiled and looked at Walker. 'I'll tell you later.'

I said, 'This is Walker and this is Coertze.' There was handshaking all round and Metcalfe said, 'It's good to hear a South African accent again. You'd have a good country there if the police weren't so efficient.'

He turned to me. 'Where's Jean?'

'She's dead,' I said. 'She was killed in a motor smash.'

'How did it happen?'

So I told him of Chapman's Peak and the drunken driver and the three-hundred-foot fall to the sea. As I spoke his face hardened, and when I had finished, he said, 'So the bastard only got five years, and if he's a good boy he'll be out in three and a half.'

He rubbed his finger against the side of his nose. 'I liked Jean,' he said. 'What's the bludger's name? I've got friends in South Africa who can see to him when he comes out.'

'Forget it,' I said. 'That won't bring Jean back.'

He nodded, then slapped his hands together. 'Now you're all staying with me at my place; I've got room enough for an army.'

I said hesitantly, 'What about the boat?'

He smiled. 'I see you've heard stories about the Tangier dock thieves. Well, let me tell you they're all true. But that doesn't matter; I'll put one of my men on board. Nobody steals from my men – or me.'

He rowed back across the harbour and presently returned with a scar-faced Moroccan, to whom he spoke in quick and guttural Arabic. Then he said, 'That's all fixed. I'll have the word passed round the docks that you're friends of mine. Your boat's safe enough, as safe as though it lay in your own yard.'

I believed him. I could believe he had a lot of pull in a place like Tangier.

'Let's go ashore,' he said. 'I'm hungry.'

'So am I,' said Coertze.

'It'll be a relief not to do any more cooking for a while, won't it?' I said.

'Man,' said Coertze, 'I wouldn't mind if I never saw a frypan again.'

'That's a pity,' said Metcalfe. 'I was looking forward to you making me some *koeksusters;* I always liked South African grub.' He roared with laughter and slapped Coertze on the back.

Metcalfe had a big apartment on the Avenida de España, and he gave me a room to myself while Coertze and Walker shared a room. He stayed and chatted while I unpacked my bag.

'South Africa too quiet for you?' he asked.

I went into my carefully prepared standard talk on the reasons I had left. I had no reason to trust Metcalfe more than anyone else – probably less – judging by the kind of man he was. I don't know whether he believed me or not, but he agreed that there was scope in the Mediterranean for a good boatyard.

'You may not get as many commissions to build,' he said. 'But there certainly is room for a good servicing and maintenance yard. I'd go east, towards Greece, if I were you. The yards in the islands cater mostly for the local fishermen; there's room for someone who understands yachts and yachtsmen.'

'What have you got a boat for?' I asked banteringly. 'Hiring it out for charter cruises?'

He grinned. 'Aw, you know me. I carry all sorts of cargoes; anything except narcotics.' He pulled a face. 'I'm a bad bastard, I know, but I draw the line at drugs. Anything else I'm game for.'

'Including guns to Algeria,' I hazarded.

He laughed. 'The French in Algiers hate my guts – they tried to do me down a couple of months ago. I'd unloaded a cargo into some fishing boats and then I ran into Algiers to refuel. I was clean, see! they couldn't touch me – my papers were in order and everything.'

'I let the crew go ashore for a drink and I turned in and had a zizz. Then something woke me up – I heard a thump and then a queer noise that seemed to come from *underneath* the boat. So I got up and had a look around. When I got on deck I saw a boat pulling away and there seemed to be a man in the water, swimming alongside it.'

He grinned. 'Well, I'm a careful and cautious man, so I got my snorkel and my swim-fins and went over the side to have a look-see. What do you think those French Security bastards had done to me?'

I shook my head. 'I wouldn't know.'

'They'd put a limpet mine on my stern gear. They must have reckoned that if they couldn't nail me down legally they'd do it illegally. If that thing went off it would blow the bottom out of my stern. Well, I got it off the boat and did a bit of heavy thinking. I knew they wouldn't have timed it to blow up in harbour – it wouldn't have looked nice – so I reckoned it was set to blow after I left.

'I slung it round my neck by the cord and swam across the harbour to where the police patrol boat was lying and stuck it under their stern. Let them have the trouble of buying a new boat.

'Next day we left early as planned and, as we moved out, I heard the police boat revving up. They followed us a long way while I was taking it nice and easy, cruising at about ten knots so they wouldn't lose me. They hung on to my tail for about thirty miles, waiting for the bang and laughing to themselves fit to bust, I suppose. But they didn't laugh when the bang came and blew the arse off their own boat.

'I turned and picked them up. It was all good clean fun – no one was hurt. When I'd got them out of the water I took them back to Algiers – the noble rescuer. You ought to have seen the faces of the Security boys when I pitched up. Of course, they had to go through the motions of thanking me for rescuing those lousy, shipwrecked mariners. I kept a straight face and said I thought it must have been one of the antisubmarine depth charges in the stern that had gone off. They said it couldn't have been that because police boats don't carry depth charges. And that was that.'

He chuckled. 'No, they don't like me in Algiers.'

I laughed with him. It was a good story and he had told it well.

I was in two minds about Metcalfe; he had his advantages and his disadvantages. On the one hand, he could give us a lot of help in Tangier; he knew the ropes and had the contacts. On the other hand, we had to be careful he didn't get wind of what we were doing. He was a hell of a good chap and all that, but if he knew we were going to show up with four tons of gold he would hijack us without a second thought. We were his kind of meat.

Yes, we had to be very careful in our dealings with Mr Metcalfe. I made a mental note to tell the others not to let anything drop in his presence.

I said, 'What kind of boat have you got?'

'A Fairmile,' he said. 'I've re-engined it, of course.'

I knew of the Fairmiles, but I had never seen one close up. They had been built in the hundreds during the war for harbour defence. The story was that they were built by the mile and cut off as needed. They were 112 feet overall with powerful engines and could work up over twenty knots easily, but they had the reputation of being bad rollers in a cross sea. They were not armoured or anything like that, being built of wood, and when a few of them went into St Nazaire with the *Campbelltown* they got shot up very badly.

After the war you could buy a surplus Fairmile for about five thousand quid and they had become a favourite with the smugglers of Tangier. If Metcalfe had re-engined his Fairmile, he had probably gone for power to outrun the revenue cutters and his boat would be capable of at least twenty-six knots in an emergency. *Sanford* would have no chance of outrunning a boat like that if it came to the push.

'I'd like to see her sometime,' I said. There was no harm in looking over a potential enemy.

'Sure,' said Metcalfe expansively. 'But not just yet. I'm going out tomorrow night.'

That was good news – with Metcalfe out of the way we might be able to go about our business undisturbed. 'When are you coming back?' I asked.

'Some time next week,' he said. 'Depending on the wind and the rain and suchlike things.'

'Such as those French Security bastards?'

'That's right,' he said carelessly. 'Let's eat.'

II

Metcalfe made us free of his flat and said we could live there in his absence – the servants would look after us. That afternoon he took me round town and introduced me to several people. Some were obviously good contacts to have, such as a ship's chandler and a boat builder. Others were not so obviously good; there was a villainous-looking café proprietor, a Greek with no discernible occupation and a Hungarian who explained volubly that he was a 'Freedom Fighter' who had escaped from Hungary after the abortive revolution of 1956. I was particularly cynical about him.

I think that Metcalfe was unobtrusively passing the word that we were friends of his, and so immune to any of the usual tricks played on passing yachtsmen. Metcalfe was not a bad man to have around if he was your friend and you were a yachtsman. But I was not a yachtsman and that made Metcalfe a potential bomb.

Before we left the flat I had the chance to talk to Coertze and Walker privately. I said, 'Here's where we keep our mouths shut and stick to our cover story. We don't do a damn' thing until Metcalfe has pushed off – and we try to finish before he gets back.'

Walker said, 'Why, is he dangerous?'

'Don't you know about Metcalfe?' I explained who he was. They had both heard of him; he had made quite a splash in the South African Press – the reporters loved to write about such a colourful character.

'Oh, *that* Metcalfe,' said Walker, impressed.

Coertze said, 'He doesn't look much to me. He won't be any trouble.'

'It's not Metcalfe alone,' I said. 'He's got an organization and he's on his own territory. Let's face it; he's a professional and we're amateurs. Steer clear of Metcalfe.'

I felt like adding 'and that's an order,' but I didn't. Coertze might have taken me up on it and I didn't want to force a showdown with him yet. It would come of its own accord soon enough.

So for a day and a half we were tourists in Tangier, rubbernecking our way about the town. If we hadn't had so much on our minds it might have been interesting, but as it was, it was a waste of time.

Luckily, Metcalfe was preoccupied by his own mysterious business and we saw little of him. However, I did instruct Walker to ask one crucial question before Metcalfe left.

Over breakfast, he said, 'You know – I *like* Tangier. It might be nice to stay here for a few months. Is the climate always like this?'

'Most of the time,' answered Metcalfe. 'It's a good, equable climate. There's lots of people retire here, you know.'

Walker smiled. 'Oh, I'm not thinking of retiring. I've nothing to retire from.' He was proving to be a better actor than I had expected – that touch was perfect. He said, 'No, what I thought was that I might like to buy a house here. Somewhere I could live a part of the year.'

'I should have thought the Med. would be your best bet,' said Metcalfe. 'The Riviera, or somewhere like that.'

'I don't know,' said Walker. 'This seems to be as good a place as any, and the Riviera is *so* crowded these days.' He paused as though struck by a sudden thought. 'I'd want a boat, of course. Could you design one for me? I'd have it built in England.'

'Sure I could,' I said. 'All you have to do is pay me enough.'

'Yes,' said Walker. 'You can't do without the old boat, can you?'

He was laying it on a bit too thick and I could see that Metcalfe was regarding him with amused contempt, so I said quickly, 'He's a damned good sailor. He nearly ran off with the Cape Dinghy Championship last year.'

That drew Metcalfe as I knew it would. 'Oh,' he said with more respect, and for a few minutes he and Walker talked boats. At last Walker came out with it. 'You know, what would be really perfect would be a house on the coast somewhere with its own anchorage and boat-shed. Everything self-contained, as it were.'

'Thinking of joining us?' asked Metcalfe with a grin.

'Oh, no,' said Walker, horrified. 'I wouldn't have the nerve. I've got enough money, and besides, I don't like your smelly Fairmiles with their stinking diesel oil. No, I was thinking about a *real* boat, a sailing boat.'

He turned to me. 'You know, the more I think about it the better I like it. You could design a 10-tonner for me, something I could handle myself, and this place is a perfect jumping-off place for the Caribbean. A transatlantic crossing might be fun.'

He confided in Metcalfe. 'You know, these ocean-crossing johnnies are all very well, but most of them are broke and they have to live on their boats. Why should I do that? Think how much better it would be if I had a house here with a boat-shed at the bottom of the garden, as it were, where I could tune the boat for the trip instead of lying in that stinking harbour.'

It *was* a damned good idea if you were a wealthy playboy with a yen to do a single-handed Atlantic crossing. I gave Walker full credit for his inventive powers.

Metcalfe didn't find it unreasonable, either. He said, 'Not a bad idea if you can afford it. I tell you what; go and see Aristide, a friend of mine. He'll try to rent you a flat, he's got dozens empty, but tell him that I sent you and he'll be more reasonable.' He scribbled an address on a piece of paper and handed it to Walker.

'Oh, thanks awfully,' said Walker. 'It's really very kind of you.'

Metcalfe finished his coffee. 'I've got to go now; see you tonight before I leave.'

When he had gone Coertze, who had sat through all this with no expression at all on his face, said, 'I've been think-ing about the go . . .'

I kicked his ankle and jerked my head at the Moroccan servant who had just come into the room. *'Tula,'* I said. *'Moenie hier praat nie.'* Then in English, 'Let's go out and have a look round.'

We left the flat and sat at a table of a nearby café. I said to Coertze, 'We don't know if Metcalfe's servants speak English or not, but I'm taking no chances. Now, what did you want to say?'

He said, 'I've been thinking about bringing the gold in here. How are we going to do it? You said yesterday that bullion has to be declared at Customs. We can't come in and say, 'Listen, man; I've got a golden keel on this boat and I think it weighs about four tons.'

'I've been thinking of that myself,' I said. 'It looks as though we'll have to smuggle it in, recast it into standard bars, smuggle it out again a few bars at a time, then bring the bars in openly and declare them at Customs.'

'That's going to take time,' objected Coertze. 'We haven't got the time.'

I sighed. 'All right; let's take a good look at this time factor. Today is 12th January and Tangier shuts up shop as far as gold is concerned on 19th April – that's – let me see, er – ninety-seven days – say fourteen weeks.'

I began to calculate and to allocate this time. It would be a week before we left Tangier and another fortnight to get to Italy. That meant another fortnight coming back, too, and I would like a week spare in case of bad weather. That disposed of six weeks. Two weeks for making preparations and for getting the gold out, and three weeks for casting the keel – eleven weeks altogether, leaving a margin of three weeks. We were cutting it fine.

I said, 'We'll have to see what the score is when we get back here with the gold. Surely to God someone will buy it, even if it is in one lump. But we don't say anything until we've got it.'

I began to have some visions of sailing back to Egypt or even India like some sort of modern Flying Dutchman condemned to sail the seas in a million pound yacht.

Walker did not go much for these planning sessions. He was content to leave that to Coertze and me. He had been sitting listening with half an ear, studying the address which Metcalfe had given him.

Suddenly he said, 'I thought old Aristide would have been an estate agent, but he's not.' He read the address from the slip of paper. '"Aristide Theotopopoulis, Tangier Mercantile Bank, Boulevard Pasteur." Maybe we could ask him something about it.'

'Not a chance,' I said derisively. 'He's a friend of Metcalfe.' I looked at Walker. 'And another thing,' I said. 'You did very well with Metcalfe this morning, but for God's sake, don't put on that phoney Oxford accent, and less of that "thanks awfully" stuff. Metcalfe's a hard man to fool; besides, he's been to South Africa and knows the score. You'd have done better to put on a Malmesbury accent, but it's too late to change now. But tone it down a bit, will you?'

Walker grinned and said, 'O.K, old chappie.'

I said, 'Now we'll go and see Aristide Theoto-whatever-it-is. It wouldn't be a bad idea if we hired a car, too. It'll help us get around and it adds to the cover. We *are* supposed to be rich tourists, you know.'

III

Aristide Theotopopoulis was a round man. His girth was roughly equal to his height, and as he sat down he creased in the middle like a half-inflated football bladder. Rolls of fat flowed over his collar from his jowls and the back of his neck. Even his hands were round – pudgy balls of fat with the glint of gold shining from deeply embedded rings.

'Ah, yes, Mr Walker; you want a house,' he said. 'I received a phone call from Mr Metcalfe this morning. I believe I have the very thing.' His English was fluent and colloquial.

'You mean you have such a house?' inquired Walker.

'Of course! Why do you suppose Mr Metcalfe sent you to me? He knows the Casa Saeta.' He paused. 'You don't mind if it's an old house?' he asked anxiously.

'Not at all,' replied Walker easily. 'I can afford any alterations provided the house suits me.' He caught my eye, then said, hastily, 'But I would like to suggest that I rent it for six months with an option to buy.'

Aristide's face lengthened from a circle to an ellipse. 'Very well, if that is what you wish,' he said dubiously.

He took us up the north coast in a Cadillac with Coertze following in our hired car. The house looked like something from a Charles Addams' cartoon and I expected to see Boris Karloff peering from a window. There was no Moorish influence at all; it was the most hideous Victorian Gothic in the worst possible taste. But that didn't matter if it could give us what we wanted.

We went into the house and looked cursorily over the worm-eaten panelling and viewed the lack of sanitation. The kitchen was primitive and there was a shaggy garden at the back of the house. Beyond was the sea and we looked over a low cliff to the beach.

It was perfect. There was a boat-house big enough to take *Sanford* once we unstepped the mast, and there was a crude slip badly in need of repair. There was even a lean-to shed where we could set up our foundry.

I looked at everything, estimating how long it would take to put in order, then I took Coertze on one side while Aristide extolled the beauties of the house to Walker.

'What do you think?' I asked.

'Man, I think we should take it. There can't be another place like this in the whole of North Africa.'

'That's just what I was thinking,' I said. 'I hope we can find something like this in Italy. We can get local people to fix up the slip, and with a bit of push we should be finished in a week. We'll have to do some token work on the house, but the bulk of the money must go on essentials – there'll be time to make the house livable when we come back. I'll tip Walker off about that; he's good at thinking up wacky reasons for doing the damnedest things.'

We drifted back to Walker and Aristide who were still going at it hammer and tongs, and I gave Walker an imperceptible nod. He smiles dazzlingly at Aristide, and said, 'It's no use, Mr Theotopopoulis, you can't talk me out of taking this house. I'm determined to have it at once – on a six months' rental, of course.'

Aristide, who hadn't any intention of talking anyone out of anything, was taken aback, but making a game recovery, said, 'You understand, Mr Walker, I can give no guarantees . . . ' His voice tailed off, giving the impression that he was doing Walker a favour.

'That's all right, old man,' said Walker gaily. 'But I must have a six months' option on the house, too. Remember that.'

'I think that can be arranged,' said Aristide with spurious dubiety.

'Won't it be fun, living in this beautiful house?' said Walker to me. I glared at him. That was the trouble with Walker; he got wrapped up in his part too much. My glare went unnoticed because he had turned to Aristide. 'The house isn't haunted, or anything like that?' he demanded, as though he equated ghosts with dead rats in the wainscotting.

'Oh, no,' said Aristide hurriedly. 'No ghosts.'

'A pity,' said Walker negligently. 'I've always wanted to live in a haunted house.'

I saw Aristide changing his mind about the ghosts, so I spoke hastily to break up this buffoonery. I had no objection to Aristide thinking he was dealing with a fool, but no one could be as big a damn' fool as Walker was acting and I was afraid that Aristide might smell a rat.

I said, 'Well, I suggest we go back to Mr Theotopopoulis's office and settle the details. It's getting late and I have to do some work on the boat.'

To Coertze, I said, 'There's no need for you to come. We'll meet you for lunch at the restaurant we went to last night.'

I had watched his blood pressure rising at Walker's fooleries and I wanted him out of the way in case he exploded. It's damned difficult working with people, especially antagonistic types like Walker and Coertze.

We went back to Aristide's office and it all went off very well. He stung us for the house, but I had no objection to that. No one who splashed money around like Walker could be anything but an honest man.

Then Walker said something that made my blood run cold, although afterwards, on mature consideration, I conceded that he had built up his character so that he could get away with it. He said to Aristide, 'Tangier is a funny place. I hear you've got bars of gold scattered about all over the place.'

Aristide smiled genially. He had cut his pound of flesh and was willing to waste a few minutes in small talk; besides, this idiot Walker was going to live in Tangier – he could be milked a lot more. 'Not scattered, exactly,' he said. 'We keep our gold in very big safes.'

'Um,' said Walker. 'You know, it's a funny thing, but I've lived all my life in South Africa where they mine scads of gold, and I've never seen any. You can't buy gold in South Africa, you know.'

Aristide raised his eyebrows as though this was unheard of.

'I've heard you can buy gold here by the pound like buying butter over the counter. It might be fun to buy some gold. Imagine me with all my money and I've never seen a gold bar,' he said pathetically. 'I've got a lot of money, you know. Most people say I've got too much.'

Aristide frowned. This was heresy; in his book no one could have too much money. He became very earnest. 'Mr Walker, the best thing anyone can do in these troubled times is to buy gold. It's the only safe investment. The value of gold does not fluctuate like these unstable paper currencies.' With a flick of his fingers he stripped the pretentions from the U.S. dollar and the pound sterling. 'Gold does not rust or waste away; it is always there, always safe and valuable. If you want to invest, I am always willing to sell gold.'

'Really?' said Walker. 'You sell it, just like that?'

Aristide smiled. 'Just like that.' His smile turned to a frown. 'But if you want to buy, you must buy now, because the open market in Tangier is closing very soon.' He shrugged. 'You say that you have never seen a bar of gold. I'll show you bars of gold – many of them.' He turned to me. 'You too, Mr Halloran, if you wish,' he said off-handedly. 'Please come this way.'

He led us down into the bowels of the building, through grilled doors and to the front of an immense vault. On the way down, two broad-shouldered bodyguards joined us. Aristide opened the vault door, which was over two feet thick, and led us inside.

There was a lot of gold in that vault. Not four tons of it, but still a lot of gold. It was stacked up neatly in piles of bars of various sizes; it was boxed in the form of coins; it was a hell of a lot of gold.

Aristide indicated a bar. 'This is a Tangier standard bar. It weighs 400 ounces troy – about twenty-seven and a half pounds avoirdupois. It is worth over five thousand pounds sterling.' He picked up a smaller bar. 'This is a more convenient size. It weighs a kilo – just over thirty-two ounces – and is worth about four hundred pounds.'

He opened a box and let coins run lovingly through his pudgy fingers. 'Here are British sovereigns – and here are American double eagles. These are French napoleons and these are Austrian ducats.' He looked at Walker with a gleam in his eye and said, 'You see what I mean when I say that gold never loses its value?'

He opened another box. 'Not all gold coins are old. These are made privately by a bank in Tangier – not mine. This is the Tangier Hercules. It contains exactly one ounce of fine gold.'

He held the coin out on the palm of his hand and let Walker take it. Walker turned it in his fingers and then passed it to me reluctantly.

It was then that this whole crazy, mad expedition ceased to be just an adventure to me. The heavy, fatty feel of that gold coin turned something in my guts and I understood what people meant when they referred to gold lust. I understood why prospectors would slave in arid, barren lands looking for gold. It is not just the value of the gold that they seek – it is gold itself. This massive, yellow metal can do something to a man; it is as much a drug as any hell-born narcotic.

My hand was trembling slightly when I handed the coin back to Aristide.

He said, tossing it, 'This costs more than bullion of course, because the cost of coining must be added. But it is in a much more convenient form.' He smiled sardonically. 'We sell a lot to political refugees and South American dictators.'

When we were back in his office, Walker said, 'You have a lot of gold down there. Where do you get it from?'

Aristide shrugged. 'I buy gold and I sell gold. I make my profit on both transactions. I buy it where I can; I sell it when I can. It is not illegal in Tangier.'

'But it must come from somewhere,' persisted Walker. 'I mean, suppose one of the pirate chaps, I mean one of the smuggling fellows, came to you with half a ton of gold. Would you buy it?'

'If the price was right,' said Aristide promptly.

'Without knowing where it came from?'

A faint smile came to Aristide's eyes. 'There is nothing more anonymous than gold,' he said. 'Gold has no master; it belongs only temporarily to the man who touches it. Yes I would buy the gold.'

'Even when the gold market closes?'

Aristide merely shrugged and smiled.

'Well, now, think of that,' said Walker fatuously. 'You must get a lot of gold coming into Tangier.'

'I will sell you gold when you want it, Mr Walker,' said Aristide, seating himself behind his desk. 'Now, I assume that, since you are coming to live in Tangier, you will want to open a bank account.' He was suddenly all businessman.

Walker glanced at me, then said, 'Well, I don't know. I'm on this cruise with Hal here, and I'm taking care of my needs with a letter of credit that was issued in South Africa. I've already cashed in a lot of boodle at one of the other banks here – I didn't realize I would have the good fortune to meet a friendly banker.' He grinned engagingly.

'We're not going to stay here long,' he said. 'We'll be pushing off in a couple of weeks, but I'll be back; yes, I'll be back. When will we be back, Hal?'

I said, 'We're going to Spain and Italy, and then to Greece. I don't think we'll push on as far as Turkey or the Lebanon, although we might. I should say we'll be back here in three or four months.'

'You see,' said Walker. 'That's when I'll move into the house properly. Casa Saeta,' he said dreamily. 'That sounds fine.'

We took our leave of Aristide, and when we got outside, I said furiously, 'What made you do a stupid thing like that?'

'Like what?' asked Walker innocently.

'You know very well what I mean. We agreed not to mention gold.'

'We've got to say something about it sometime,' he said. 'We can't sell gold to anyone with saying anything about it. I just thought it was a good time to find out something about it, to test Aristide's attitude towards gold of unknown origin. I thought I worked up to it rather well.'

I had to give him credit for that. I said, 'And another thing: let's have less of the silly ass routine. You nearly gave me a fit when you started to pull Aristide's leg about the ghosts. There are more important things at stake than fooling about.'

'I know,' he said soberly. 'I realized that when we were in the vault. I had forgotten what gold felt like.'

So it had hit him too. I calmed down and said, 'O.K. But don't forget it. And for God's sake don't act the fool in front of Coertze. I have enough trouble keeping the peace as it is.'

IV

When we met Coertze for lunch, I said, 'We saw a hell of a lot of gold this morning.'

He straightened. 'Where?'

Walker said, 'In a bloody big safe at Aristide's bank.'

'I thought. . .' Coertze began.

'No harm done,' I said. 'It went very smoothly. We saw a lot of ingots. There are two standard sizes readily acceptable here in Tangier. One is 400 ounces, the other is one kilogram.' Coertze frowned, and I said, 'That's nearly two and a quarter pounds.'

He grunted and drank his Scotch. I said, 'Walker and I have been discussing this and we think that Aristide will buy the gold under the counter, even after the gold market closes – but we'll probably have to approach him before that so he can make his arrangements.'

'I think we should do it now,' said Walker.

I shook my head. 'No! Aristide is a friend of Metcalfe; that's too much like asking a tiger to come to dinner. We mustn't tell him until we come back and then we'll have to take the chance.'

Walker was silent so I went on. 'The point is that it's unlikely that Aristide will relish taking a four-ton lump of gold into stock, so we'll probably have to melt the keel down into ingots, anyway. In all probability Aristide will fiddle his stock sheets somehow so that he can account for the four extra tons, but it means that he must be told before the gold market closes – which means that we must be back before April 19.'

Coertze said, 'Not much time.'

I said, 'I've worked out all the probable times for each stage of the operation and we have a month in hand. But there'll be snags and we'll need all of that. But that isn't what's worrying me now – I've got other things on my mind.'

'Such as?'

'Look. When – and if – we get the gold here and we start to melt it down, we're going to have a hell of a lot of ignots lying around. I don't want to dribble them to Aristide as they're cast – that's bad policy, too much chance of an outsider catching on. I want to let him have the lot all at once, get paid with a cast-iron draft on a Swiss bank and then clear out. But it does mean that we'll have a hell of a lot of ignots lying around loose in the Casa Saeta and that's bad.'

I sighed. 'Where do we keep the damn' things? Stacked up in the living room? And how many of these goddammed ignots will there be?' I added irritably.

Walker looked at Coertze. 'You said there was about four tons, didn't you?'

'*Ja,*' said Coertze. 'But that was only an estimate.'

I said, 'You've worked with bullion since. How close is that estimate?'

He thought about it, sending his mind back fifteen years and comparing what he saw then with what he had learned since. The human mind is a marvellous machine. At last he said slowly, 'I think it is a close estimate, very close.'

'All right,' I said. 'So it's four tons. That's 9000 pounds as near as dammit. There's sixteen ounces to the pound and . . .'

'No,' said Coertze suddenly. 'Gold is measured in troy ounces. There's 14.58333 recurring ounces troy to the English pound.'

He had the figures so pat that I was certain he knew what he was talking about. After all, it was his job. I said, 'Let's not go into complications; let's call it fourteen and a half ounces to the pound. That's good enough.'

I started to calculate, making many mistakes although it should have been a simple calculation. The mathematics of yacht design don't have the same emotional impact.

At last I had it. 'As near as I can make out, in round figures we'll have about 330 bars of 400 ounces each.'

'What's that at five thousand quid a bar?' asked Walker.

I scribbled on the paper again and looked at the answer unbelievingly. It was the first time I had worked this out in terms of money. Up to this time I had been too busy to think about it, and four tons of gold seemed to be a good round figure to hold in one's mind.

I said hesitantly, 'I work it out as £1,650,000!'

Coertze nodded in satisfaction. 'That is the figure I got. And there's the jewels on top of that.'

I had my own ideas about the jewels. Aristide had been right when he said that gold is anonymous – but jewels aren't. Jewels have a personality of their own and can be traced too easily. If I had my way the jewels would stay in the tunnel. But that I had to lead up to easily.

Walker said, 'That's over half a million each.'

I said, 'Call it half a million each, net. The odd £150,000 can go to expenses. By the time this is through we'll have spent more than we've put in the kitty.'

I returned to the point at issue. 'All right, we have 330 bars of gold. What do we do with them?'

Walker said meditatively, 'There's a cellar in the house.'

'That's a start, anyway.'

He said, 'You know the fantastic thought I had in that vault? I thought it looked just like a builder's yard with a lot of bricks lying all over the place. Why couldn't we build a wall in the cellar?'

I looked at Coertze and he looked at me, and we both burst out laughing.

'What's funny about that?' asked Walker plaintively.

'Nothing,' I said, still spluttering. 'It's perfect, that's all.'

Coertze said, grinning, 'I'm a fine bricklayer when the rates of pay are good.'

A voice started to bleat in my ear and I turned round. It was an itinerant lottery-ticket seller poking a sheaf of tickets at me. I waved him away, but Coertze, in a good mood for once, said tolerantly, 'No, man, let's have one. No harm in taking out insurance.'

The ticket was a hundred pesetas, so we scraped it together from the change lying on the table, and then we went back to the flat.

V

The next day we started work in earnest. I stayed with *Sanford*, getting her ready for sea by dint of much bullying of the chandler and the sailmaker. By the end of the week I was satisfied that she was ready and was able to leave for anywhere in the world.

Coertze and Walker worked up at the house, rehabilitating the boat-shed and the slip and supervising the local labour they had found through Metcalfe's kind offices. Coertze said, 'You have no trouble if you treat these wogs just the same as the Kaffirs back home.' I wasn't so sure of that, but everything seemed to go all right.

By the time Metcalfe came back from whatever nefarious enterprise he had been on, we were pretty well finished and ready to leave. I said nothing to Metcalfe about this, feeling that the less he knew, the better.

When I'd got *Sanford* shipshape I went over to Metcalfe's Fairmile to pay my promised visit. A fair-haired man who was flushing the decks with a hose said, 'I guess you must be Halloran. I'm Krupke, Metcalfe's side-kick.'

'Is he around?'

Krupke shook his head. 'He went off with that friend of yours – Walker. He said I was to show you around if you came aboard.'

I said, 'You're an American, aren't you?'

He grinned. 'Yep, I'm from Milwaukee. Didn't fancy going back to the States after the war, so I stayed on here. Hell, I was only a kid then, not more'n twenty, so I thought that since Uncle Sam paid my fare out here, I might as well take advantage of it.'

I thought he was probably a deserter and couldn't go back to the States, although there might have been an amnesty for deserters. I didn't know how the civil statute limitations worked in military law. I didn't say anything about that, though – renegades are touchy and sometimes unaccountably patriotic.

The wheelhouse – which Krupke called the 'deckhouse' – was well fitted. There were two echo sounders, one with a recording pen. Engine control was directly under the helmsman's hand and the windows in front were fitted with Kent screens for bad weather. There was a big marine radio transceiver – and there was radar.

I put my hand on the radar display and said, 'What range does this have?'

'It's got several ranges,' he said. 'You pick the one that's best at the time. I'll show you.'

He snapped a switch and turned a knob. After a few seconds the screen lit up and I could see a tiny plan of the harbour as the scanner revolved. Even *Sanford* was visible as one splotch among many.

'That's for close work,' said Krupke, and turned a knob with a click. 'This is maximum range – fifteen miles, but you won't see much while we're in harbour.'

The landward side of the screen was now too cluttered to be of any use, but to seaward, I saw a tiny speck. 'What's that?'

He looked at his watch. 'That must be the ferry from Gibraltar. It's ten miles away – you can see the mileage marked on the grid.'

I said, 'This gadget must be handy for making a landfall at night.'

'Sure,' he said. 'All you have to do is to match the screen profile with the chart. Doesn't matter if there's no moon or if there's a fog.'

I wished I could have a set like that on *Sanford* but it's difficult installing radar on a sailing vessel – there are too many lines to catch in the antenna. Anyway, we wouldn't have the power to run it.

I looked around the wheelhouse. 'With all this gear you can't need much of a crew, even though she is a biggish boat,' I said. 'What crew do you have?'

'Me and Metcalfe can run it ourselves,' said Krupke. 'Our trips aren't too long. But usually we have another man with us – that Moroccan you've got on *Sanford*.'

I stayed aboard the Fairmile for a long time, but Metcalfe and Walker didn't show up, so after a while I went back to Metcalfe's flat. Coertze was already there, but there was no sign of the others, so we went to have dinner as a twosome.

Over dinner I said, 'We ought to be getting away soon. Everything is fixed at this end and we'd be wasting time if we stayed any longer.'

'Ja,' Coertze agreed. 'This isn't a pleasure trip.'

We went back to the flat and found it empty, apart from the servants. Coertze went to his room and I read desultorily from a magazine. About ten o'clock I heard someone coming in and I looked up.

I was immediately boiling with fury.

Walker was drunk – blind, paralytic drunk. He was clutching on to Metcalfe and sagging at the knees, his face slack and his bleared eyes wavering unseeingly about him. Metcalfe was a little under the weather himself, but not too drunk. He gave Walker a hitch to prevent him from falling, and said cheerily, 'We went to have a night on the town, but friend Walker couldn't take it. You'd better help me dump him on his bed.'

I helped Metcalfe support Walker to his room and we laid him on his bed. Coertze, dozing in the other bed, woke up and said, 'What's happening?'

Metcalfe said, 'Your pal's got no head for liquor. He passed out on me.'

Coertze looked at Walker, then at me, his black eyebrows drawing angrily over his eyes. I made a sign for him to keep quiet.

Metcalfe stretched and said, 'Well, I think I'll turn in myself.' He looked at Walker and there was an edge of contempt to his voice. 'He'll be all right in the morning, barring a hell of a hangover. I'll tell Ismail to make him a prairie oyster for breakfast.' He turned to Coertze. 'What do you call it in Afrikaans?'

''*n Regmaker*,' Coertze growled.

Metcalfe laughed. 'That's right. A *Regmaker*. That was the first word I ever learned in Afrikaans.' He went to the door. 'See you in the morning,' he said, and was gone.

I closed the door. 'The damn fool,' I said feelingly.

Coertze got out of bed and grabbed hold of Walker, shaking him. 'Walker,' he shouted. 'Did you tell him anything?'

Walker's head flapped sideways and he began to snore. I took Coertze's shoulder. 'Be quiet; you'll tell the whole household,' I said. 'It's no use, anyway; you won't get any sense out of him tonight – he's unconscious. Leave it till morning.'

Coertze shook off my hand and turned. He had a black anger in him. 'I told you,' he said in a suppressed voice. 'I told you he was no good. Who knows what the *dronkie* said?'

I took off Walker's shoes and covered him with a blanket. 'We'll find out tomorrow,' I said. 'And I mean *we*. Don't you go off pop at him, you'll scare the liver out of him and he'll close up tight.'

'I'll *donner* him up,' said Coertze grimly. 'That's God's truth.'

'You'll leave him alone,' I said sharply. 'We may be in enough trouble without fighting among ourselves. We need Walker.'

Coertze snorted.

I said, 'Walker has done a job here that neither of us could have done. He has a talent for acting the damn' fool in a believable manner.' I looked down at him, then said bitterly, 'It's a pity he can be a damn' fool without the acting. Anyway, we may need him again, so you leave him alone. We'll both talk to him tomorrow, together.'

Coertze grudgingly gave his assent and I went to my room.

VI

I was up early next morning, but not as early as Metcalfe, who had already gone out. I went in to see Walker and found that Coertze was up and half dressed. Walker lay on his bed, snoring. I took a glass of water and poured it over his head. I was in no mood to consider Walker's feelings.

He stirred and moaned and opened his eyes just as Coertze seized the carafe and emptied it over him. He sat up spluttering, then sagged back. 'My head,' he said, and put his hands to his temples.

Coertze seized him by the front of the shirt. '*Jou gogga-mannetjie,* what did you say to Metcalfe?' He shook Walker violently. 'What did you tell him?'

This treatment was doing Walker's aching head no good, so I said, 'Take it easy; I'll talk to him.'

Coertze let go and I stood over Walker, waiting until he had recovered his wits. Then I said, 'You got drunk last night, you stupid fool, and of all people to get drunk with you had to pick Metcalfe.'

Walker looked up, the pain of his monumental hangover filming his eyes. I sat on the bed. 'Now, did you tell him anything about the gold?'

'No,' cried Walker. 'No, I didn't.'

I said evenly, 'Don't tell us any lies, because if we catch you out in a lie you know what we'll do to you.'

He shot a frightened glance at Coertze who was glowering in the background and closed his eyes. 'I can't remember,' he said. 'It's blank; I can't remember.'

That was better; he was probably telling the truth now. The total blackout is a symptom of alcoholism. I thought about it for a while and came to the conclusion that even if Walker hadn't told Metcalfe about the gold he had probably blown his cover sky high. Under the influence, the character he had built up would have been irrevocably smashed and he would have reverted to his alcoholic and unpleasant self.

Metcalfe was sharp – he wouldn't have survived in his nefarious career otherwise. The change in character of Walker would be the tip-off that there was something odd about old pal Halloran and his crew. That would be enough for Metcalfe to check further. We would have to work on the assumption that Metcalfe would consider us worthy of further study.

I said, 'What's done is done,' and looked at Walker. His eyes were downcast and his fingers were nervously scrabbling at the edge of the blanket.

'Look at me,' I said, and his eyes rose slowly to meet mine. 'I think you're telling the truth,' I said coldly. 'But if I catch you in a lie it will be the worse for you. And if you take another drink on this trip I'll break your back. You think you're scared of Coertze here; but you'll have more reason to be scared of me if you take just one more drink. Understand?'

He nodded.

'I don't care how much you drink once this thing is finished. You'll probably drink yourself to death in six months, but that's got nothing to do with me. But just one more drink on this trip and you're a dead man.'

He flinched and I turned to Coertze. 'Now, leave him alone; he'll behave.'

Coertze said, 'Just let me get at him. Just once,' he pleaded.

'It's finished,' I said impatiently. 'We have to decide what to do next. Get your things packed – we're moving out.'

'What about Metcalfe?'

'I'll tell him we want to see some festival in Spain.'

'What festival?'

'How do I know which festival? There's always some goddam festival going on in Spain; I'll pick the most convenient. We sail this afternoon as soon as I can get harbour clearance.'

'I still think I could do something about Metcalfe,' said Coertze meditatively.

'Leave Metcalfe alone,' I said. 'He *may* not suspect anything at all, but if you try to beat him up then he'll *know* there's something fishy. We don't want to tangle with Metcalfe if we can avoid it. He's bigger than we are.'

We packed our bags and went to the boat, Walker very quiet and trailing in the rear. Moulay Idriss was squatting on the foredeck smoking a *kif* cigarette. We went below and started to stow our gear.

I had just pulled out the chart which covered the Straits of Gibraltar in preparation for planning our course when Coertze came aft and said in a low voice, 'I think someone's been searching the boat.'

'What the hell!' I said. Metcalfe *had* left very early that morning – he would have had plenty of time to give *Sanford* a good going over. 'The furnaces?' I said.

We had disguised the three furnaces as well as we could. The carbon clamps had been taken off and scattered in tool boxes in the forecastle where they would look just like any other junk that accumulates over a period. The main boxes with the heavy transformers were distributed about *Sanford*, one cemented under the cabin sole, another disguised as a receiving set complete with the appropriate knobs and dials, and the third built into a marine battery in the engine space.

It is doubtful if Metcalfe would know what they were if he saw them, but the fact that they were masquerading in innocence would make him wonder a lot. It would be a certain clue that we were up to no good.

A check over the boat showed that everything was in order. Apart from the furnaces, and the spare graphite mats which lined the interior of the double coach roof, there was nothing on board to distinguish us from any other cruising yacht in these waters.

I said, 'Perhaps the Moroccan has been doing some exploring on his own account.'

Coertze swore. 'If he's been poking his nose in where it isn't wanted I'll throw him overboard.'

I went on deck. The Moroccan was still squatting on the foredeck. I said interrogatively, 'Mr Metcalfe?'

He stretched an arm and pointed across the harbour to the Fairmile. I put the dinghy over the side and rowed across. Metcalfe hailed me as I got close. 'How's Walker?'

'Feeling sorry for himself,' I said, as Metcalfe took the painter. 'A pity it happened; he'll probably be as sick as a dog when we get under way.'

'You leaving?' said Metcalfe in surprise.

I said, 'I didn't get the chance to tell you last night. We're heading for Spain.' I gave him my prepared story, then said, 'I don't know if we'll be coming back this way. Walker will, of course, but Coertze and I might go back to South Africa by way of the east coast.' I thought that there was nothing like confusing the issue.

'I'm sorry about that,' said Metcalfe. 'I was going to ask you to design a dinghy for me while you were here.'

'Tell you what,' I said. 'I'll write to Cape Town and get the yard to send you a Falcon kit. It's on me; all you've got to do is pay for the shipping.'

'Well, thanks,' said Metcalfe. 'That's decent of you.' He seemed pleased.

'It's as much as I can do after all the hospitality we've had here,' I said.

He stuck out his hand and I took it. 'Best of luck, Hal, in all your travels. I hope your project is successful.'

I was incautious. 'What project?' I asked sharply.

'Why, the boatyard you're planning. You don't have anything else in mind, do you?'

I cursed myself and smiled weakly. 'No, of course not.'
I turned to get into the dinghy, and Metcalfe said quietly,
'You're not cut out for my kind of life, Hal. Don't try it
if you're thinking of it. It's tough and there's too much
competition.'

As I rowed back to *Sanford* I wondered if that was a veiled
warning that he was on to our scheme. Metcalfe was an
honest man by his rather dim lights and wouldn't willingly
cut down a friend. But he would if the friend didn't get out
of his way.

At three that afternoon we cleared Tangier harbour and
I set course for Gibraltar. We were on our way, but we had
left too many mistakes behind us.

FOUR: FRANCESCA

When we were beating through the Straits Coertze suggested that we should head straight for Italy. I said, 'Look, we've told Metcalfe we were going to Spain, so that's where we are going.'

He thumped the cockpit coaming. 'But we haven't time.'

'We've got to make time,' I said doggedly. 'I told you there would be snags which would use up our month's grace; this is one of the snags. We're going to take a month getting to Italy instead of a fortnight, which cuts us down to two weeks in hand – but we've got to do it. Maybe we can make it up in Italy.'

He grumbled at that, saying I was unreasonably frightened of Metcalfe. I said, 'You've waited fifteen years for this opportunity – you can afford to wait another fortnight. We're going to Gibraltar, to Malaga and Barcelona; we're going to the Riviera, to Nice and to Monte Carlo; after that, Italy. We're going to watch bullfights and gamble in casinos and do everything that every other tourist does. We're going to be the most innocent people that Metcalfe ever laid eyes on.'

'But Metcalfe's back in Tangier.'

I smiled thinly. 'He's probably in Spain right now. He could have passed us any time in that Fairmile of his. He could even have flown or taken the ferry to Gibraltar, dammit. I think he'll keep an eye on us if he reckons we're up to something.'

'Damn Walker,' burst out Coertze.

'Agreed,' I said. 'But that's water under the bridge.'

I was adding up the mistakes we had made. Number one was Walker's incautious statement to Aristide that he had drawn money on a letter of credit. That was a lie – a need-less one, too – I had the letter of credit and Walker could have said so. Keeping control of the finances of the expedition was the only way I had of making sure that Coertze didn't get the jump on me. I still didn't know the location of the gold.

Now, Aristide would naturally make inquiries among his fellow bankers about the financial status of this rich Mr Walker. He would get the information quite easily – all bankers hang together and the hell with ethics – and he would find that Mr Walker had *not* drawn any money from any bank in Tangier. He might not be too perturbed about that, but he might ask Metcalfe about it, and Metcalfe would find it another item to add to his list of suspicions. He would pump Aristide to find that Walker and Halloran had taken an undue interest in the flow of gold in and out of Tangier.

He would go out to the Casa Saeta and sniff around. He would find nothing there to conflict with Walker's cover story, but it would be precisely the cover story that he suspected most – Walker having blown hell out of it when he was drunk. The mention of gold would set his ears a-prick – a man like Metcalfe would react very quick-ly to the smell of gold – and if I were Metcalfe I would take great interest in the movements of the cruising yacht, *Sanford.*

All this was predicated on the fact that Walker had *not* told about the gold when he was drunk. If he *had*, then the balloon had really gone up.

We put into Gibraltar and spent a day rubber-necking at the Barbary apes and looking at the man-made caves. Then we sailed for Malaga and heard a damn' sight more flamenco music than we could stomach.

It was on the second day in Malaga, when Walker and I went out to the gipsy caves like good tourists, that I realized we were being watched. We were bumping into a sallow young man with a moustache everywhere we went. He sat far removed when we ate in a sidewalk café, he appeared in the yacht basin, he applauded the flamenco dancers when we went to see the gipsies.

I said nothing to the others, but it only went to confirm my estimate of Metcalfe's abilities. He would have friends in every Mediterranean port, and it wouldn't be difficult to pass the word around. A yacht's movements are not easy to disguise, and he was probably sitting in Tangier like a spider in the centre of a web, receiving phone calls from wherever we went. He would know all our movements and our expenditure to the last peseta.

The only thing to do was to act the innocent and hope that we could wear him out, string him on long enough so that he would conclude that his suspicions were unfounded, after all.

In Barcelona we went to a bullfight – the three of us. That was after I had had a little fun in trying to spot Metcalfe's man. He wasn't difficult to find if you were looking for him and turned out to be a tall, lantern-jawed cut-throat who carried out the same routine as the man in Malaga.

I was reasonably sure that if anyone was going to burgle *Sanford* it would be one of Metcalfe's friends. The word would have been passed round that we were his meat and so the lesser fry would leave us alone. I hired a watchman who looked as though he would sell his grandmother for ten pesetas and we all went to the bullfight.

Before I left I was careful to set the stage. I had made a lot of phoney notes concerning the costs of setting up a boatyard in Spain, together with a lot of technical stuff I had picked up. I also left a rough itinerary of our future movements as far as Greece and a list of addresses of people to be visited. I then measured to a millimetre the position in which each paper was lying.

When we got back the watchman said that all had been quiet, so I paid him off and he went away. But the papers had been moved, so the locked cabin had been successfully burgled in spite of – or probably because of – the watchman. I wondered how much he had been paid – and I wondered if my plant had satisfied Metcalfe that we were wandering innocents.

From Barcelona we struck out across the Gulf of Lions to Nice, giving Majorca a miss because time was getting short. Again I went about my business of visiting boatyards and again I spotted the watcher, but this time I made a mistake. I told Coertze.

He boiled over. 'Why didn't you tell me before?' he demanded.

'What was the point?' I said. 'We can't do anything about it.'

'Can't we?' he said darkly, and fell into silence.

Nothing much happened in Nice. It's a pleasant place if you haven't urgent business elsewhere, but we stayed just long enough to make our cover real and then we sailed the few miles to Monte Carlo, which again is a nice town for the visiting tourist.

In Monte Carlo I stayed aboard *Sanford* in the evening while Coertze and Walker went ashore. There was not much to do in the way of maintenance beyond the usual housekeeping jobs, so I relaxed in the cockpit enjoying the quietness of the night. The others stayed out late and when they came back Walker was unusually silent.

Coertze had gone below when I said to Walker, 'What's the matter? The cat got your tongue? How did you like Monte?'

He jerked his head at the companionway. 'He clobbered someone.'

I went cold. 'Who?'

'A chap was following us all afternoon. Coertze spotted him and said that he'd deal with it. We let this bloke follow us until it got dark and then Coertze led him into an alley and beat him up.'

I got up and went below. Coertze was in the galley bathing swollen knuckles. I said, 'So you've done it at last. You must use your goddamn fists and not your brains. You're worse than Walker; at least you can say he's a sick man.'

Coertze looked at me in surprise. 'What's the matter?'

'I hear you hit someone.'

Coertze looked at his fist and grinned at me. 'He'll never bother us again – he'll be in hospital for a month.' He said this with pride, for God's sake.

'You've blown it,' I said tightly. 'I'd just about got Metcalfe to the point where he must have been convinced that we were O.K. Now you've beaten up one of his men, so he knows we are on to him, and he knows we must be hiding something. You might just as well have phoned him up and said, "We've got some gold coming up; come and take it from us." You're a damn' fool.'

His face darkened. 'No one can talk to me like that.' He raised his fist.

'I *am* talking to you like that,' I said. 'And if you lay one finger on me you can kiss the gold goodbye. You can't sail this or any other boat worth a damn, and Walker won't help you – he hates your guts. You hit me and you're out for good. I know you could probably break me in two and you're welcome to try, but it'll cost you a cool half-million for the pleasure.'

This showdown had been coming for a long time.

He hesitated uncertainly. 'You damned Englishman,' he said.

'Go ahead – hit me,' I said, and got ready to take his rush.

He relaxed and pointed his finger at me threateningly. 'You wait until this is over,' he said. 'Just you wait – we'll sort it out then.'

'All right, we'll sort it out then,' I said. 'But until then I'm the boss. Understand?'

His face darkened again. 'No one bosses me,' he blustered.

'Right,' I said. 'Then we start going back the way we came – Nice, Barcelona, Malaga, Gibraltar. Walker will help me sail the boat, but we won't do a damn' thing for you.' I turned away.

'Wait a minute,' said Coertze and I turned back. 'All right,' he said hoarsely. 'But wait till this is over; by God, you'll have to watch yourself then.'

'But until then I'm the boss?'

'Yes,' he said sullenly.

'And you take my orders?'

His fists tightened but he held himself in. 'Yes.'

'Then here's your first one. You don't do a damn' thing without consulting me first.' I turned to go up the companionway, got half-way up, then had a sudden thought and went below again.

I said, 'And there's another thing I want to tell you. Don't get any ideas about double-crossing me or Walker, because if you do, you'll not only have me to contend with but Metcalfe as well. I'd be glad to give Metcalfe a share if you did that. And there wouldn't be a place in the world you could hide if Metcalfe got after you.'

He stared at me sullenly and turned away. I went on deck.

Walker was sitting in the cockpit. 'Did you hear that?'
I said.

He nodded. 'I'm glad you included me on your side.'

I was exasperated and shaking with strain. It was no fun
tangling with a bear like Coertze – he was all reflex and no
brain and he could have broken me as anyone else would
break a matchstick. He was a man who had to be governed
like a fractious horse.

I said, 'Dammit, I don't know why I came on this crazy
trip with a *dronkie* like you and a maniac like Coertze. First
you put Metcalfe on our tracks and then he clinches it.'

Walker said softly, 'I didn't mean to do it. I don't think
I told Metcalfe anything.'

'I don't think so either, but you gave the game away
somehow.' I stretched, easing my muscles. 'It doesn't matter; we either get the gold or we don't. That's all there is to
it.'

Walker said, 'You can rely on me to help you against
Coertze, if it comes to that.'

I smiled. Relying on Walker was like relying on a frac-
tured mast in a hurricane – the hurricane being Coertze. He
affected people like that; he had a blind, elemental force
about him. An overpowering man, altogether.

I patted Walker on the knee. 'O.K. You're my man from
now on.' I let the hardness come into my voice because
Walker had to be kept to heel, too. 'But keep off the booze.
I meant what I said in Tangier.'

II

The next stop was Rapallo, which was first choice as our
Italian base, provided we could get fixed up with a suitable
place to do our work. We motored into the yacht basin and
damned if I didn't see a Falcon drawn up on the hard.

I knew the firm had sold a few kits in Europe but I didn't expect to see any of them.

As we had come from a foreign port there were the usual Customs and medical queries – a mere formality. Yachtsmen are very well treated in the Mediterranean. I chatted with the Customs men, discussing yachts and yachting and said that I was a boat designer and builder myself. I gave the standard talk and said that I was thinking of opening a yard in the Mediterranean, pointing to the Falcon as a sample of my work.

They were impressed at that. Anyone whose product was used six thousand miles from where it was made must obviously be someone to be reckoned with. They didn't know much about local conditions but they gave me some useful addresses.

I was well satisfied. If I had to impress people with my integrity I might as well start with the Customs. That stray Falcon came in very handy.

I went ashore, leaving Walker and Coertze aboard by instruction. There was no real need for such an order but I wanted to test my new-found ascendancy over them. Coertze had returned to his old self, more or less. His mood was equable and he cracked as few jokes as usual – the point being that he cracked jokes at all. But I had no illusions that he had forgotten anything. The Afrikaner is notorious for his long memory for wrongs.

I went up to the Yacht Club and presented my credentials. One of the most pleasant things about yachting is that you are sure of a welcome in any part of the world. There is a camaraderie among yachtsmen which is very heartening in a world which is on the point of blowing itself to hell. This international brotherhood, together with the fact that the law of the sea doesn't demand a licence to operate a small boat, makes deep-sea cruising one of the most enjoyable experiences in the world.

I chatted with the secretary of the club, who spoke very good English, and talked largely of my plans. He took me into the bar and bought me a drink and introduced me to several of the members and visiting yachtsmen. After we had chatted at some length about the voyage from South Africa I got down to finding out about the local boatyards.

On the way round the Mediterranean I had come to the conclusion that my cover story need not be a cover at all – it could be the real thing. I had become phlegmatic about the gold, especially after the antics of Walker and Coertze, and my interest in the commercial possibilities of the Mediterranean was deepening. I was nervous and uncertain as to whether the three of us could carry the main job through – the three-way pull of character was causing tensions which threatened to tear the entire fabric of the plan apart. So I was hedging my bet and looking into the business possibilities seriously.

The lust for gold, which I had felt briefly in Aristide's vault, was still there but lying dormant. Still, it was enough to drive me on, enough to make me out-face Coertze and Walker and to try to circumvent Metcalfe.

But if I had known then that other interests were about to enter the field of battle I might have given up there and then, in the bar of the Rapallo Yacht Club.

During the afternoon I visited several boatyards. This was not all business prospecting – *Sanford* had come a long way and her bottom was foul. She needed taking out of the water and scraping, which would give her another half-knot. We had agreed that this would be the ostensible reason for pulling her out of the water, and a casual word dropped in the Yacht Club that I had found something wrong with her keel bolts would be enough excuse for making the exchange of keels. Therefore I was looking for a quiet place where we could cast our golden keel.

I was perturbed when I suddenly discovered that I could not spot Metcalfe's man. If he had pulled off his watchdogs because he thought we were innocent, then that was all right. But it seemed highly unlikely now that Coertze had given the game away. What seemed very likely was that something was being cooked up – and whatever was going to happen would certainly involve *Sanford*. I dropped my explorations and hurried back to the yacht basin.

'I wasn't followed,' I said to Coertze.

'I told you my way was best,' he said. 'They've been frightened off.'

'If you think that Metcalfe would be frightened off because a hired wharf rat was beaten up, you'd better think again,' I said. I looked hard at him. 'If you go ashore to stretch your legs can I trust you not to hammer anyone you might think is looking at you cross-eyed?'

He tried to hold my eye and then his gaze wavered. 'O.K.,' he said sullenly. 'I'll be careful. But you'll find out that my way is best in the end.'

'All right; you and Walker can go ashore to get a bite to eat.' I turned to Walker. 'No booze, remember. Not even wine.'

Coertze said, 'I'll see to that. We'll stick close together, won't we?' He clapped Walker on the back.

They climbed on to the dockside and I watched them go, Coertze striding out and Walker hurrying to keep pace. I wondered what Metcalfe was up to, but finding that prof-itless, I went below to review our needs for the next few days. I stretched on the port settee and must have been very tired, because when I woke it was dark except for the lights of the town glimmering through the ports.

And it was a movement on deck that had wakened me!

I lay there for a moment until I heard another sound, then I rose cautiously, went to the companionway very quietly and raised my head to deck level. 'Coertze?' I called softly.

A voice said, 'Is that Signor Halloran?' The voice was very feminine.

I came up to the cockpit fast. 'Who is that?'

A dark shape moved towards me. 'Mr Halloran, I want to talk to you.' She spoke good English with but a trace of Italian accent and her voice was pleasantly low and even.

I said, 'Who are you?'

'Surely introductions would be more in order if we could see each other.' There was a hint of command in her voice as though she was accustomed to getting her own way.

'O.K.,' I said. 'Let's go below.'

She slipped past me and went down the companionway and I followed, switching on the main cabin lights. She turned so that I could see her, and she was something worth looking at. Her hair was raven black and swept up into smooth wings on each side of her head as though to match the winged eyebrows which were dark over cool, hazel eyes. Her cheekbones were high, giving a trace of hollow in the cheeks, but she didn't look like one of the fashionably emaciated models one sees in *Vogue*.

She was dressed in a simple woollen sheath which showed off a good figure to perfection. It might have been bought at a local department store or it might have come from a Parisian fashion house; I judged the latter – you can't be married to a woman for long without becoming aware of the price of feminine fripperies.

She carried her shoes in her hand and stood in her stockinged feet, that was a point in her favour. A hundred-pound girl in a spike heel comes down with a force of two tons, and that's hell on deck planking. She either knew something about yachts or . . .

I pointed to the shoes and said, 'You're a pretty inexperienced burglar. You ought to have those slung round your
neck to leave your hands free.'

She laughed. 'I'm not a burglar, Mr Halloran, I just don't
like shoes very much; and I have been on yachts before.'

I moved towards her. She was tall, almost as tall as
myself. I judged her to be in her late twenties or possibly,
but improbably, her early thirties. Her lips were pale and she
wore very little make-up. She was a very beautiful woman.

'You have the advantage of me,' I said.

'I am the Contessa di Estrenoli.'

I gestured at the settee. 'Well, sit down, Contessa.'

'Not Contessa – Madame,' she said, and sat down, pulling
the dress over her knees with one hand and placing the
shoes at her side. 'In our association together you will call
me Madame.'

I sat down slowly on the opposite settee. Metcalfe certainly came up with some surprises. I said carefully,
'So we are going to be associated together? I couldn't
think of a better person to be associated with. When do
we start?'

There was frost in her voice. 'Not the kind of association
you are obviously thinking of, Mr Halloran.' She went off at
a tangent. 'I saw your . . . er . . . companions ashore. They
didn't see me – I wanted to talk to you alone.'

'We're alone,' I said briefly.

She gathered her thoughts, then said precisely, 'Mr
Halloran, you have come to Italy with Mr Coertze and
Mr Walker to remove something valuable from the country. You intend to do this illicitly and illegally, therefore
your whole plan depends on secrecy; you cannot – shall
we say 'operate' – if someone is looking over your shoulder. I intend to look over your shoulder.'

I groaned mentally. Metcalfe had the whole story.
Apparently the only thing he didn't know was where the

treasure was hidden. This girl was quite right when she said that it couldn't be lifted if we were under observation, so he was coming right out and asking for a cut. Walker really *must* have talked in Tangier if Metcalfe could pinpoint it as close as Rapallo.

I said, 'O.K., Contessa; how much does Metcalfe want?'

She raised her winged eyebrows. 'Metcalfe?'

'Yes, Metcalfe; your boss.'

She shook her head. 'I know of no Metcalfe, whoever he is. And I am my own boss, I assure you of that.'

I think I kept my face straight. The surprises were certainly piling up. If this Estrenoli woman was mixed up with Metcalfe, then why would she deny it? If she wasn't then who the devil was she – and how did she know of the treasure?'

I said, 'Supposing I tell you to jump over the side?'

She smiled. 'Then you will never get these valuables out of Italy.'

There seemed to be a concession there, so I said, 'And if I *don't* tell you to jump over the side, then we *will* get the stuff out of the country, is that it?'

'Some of it,' she compromised. 'But without my cooperation you will spend a long time in an Italian prison.'

That was certainly something to think about and when I had time. I said, 'All right; who are you, and what do you know?'

'I knew that the news was out on the waterfront to watch for the yacht *Sanford*. I knew that the yacht was owned by Mr Halloran and that Mr Coertze and Mr Walker were his companions. That was enough for me.'

'And what has the Contessa di Estrenoli got to do with waterfront rumours? What has an Italian aristocrat got to do with the jailbirds that news was intended for?'

She smiled and said, 'I have strange friends, Mr Halloran. I learn all that is interesting on the waterfront. I realize now that perhaps your Mr Metcalfe was responsible for the circulation of those instructions.'

'So you learned that a yacht and three men were coming to Rapallo, and you said to yourself, "Ah, these three men are coming to take something out of Italy illegally," ' I said with heavy irony. 'You'll have to do better than that, Contessa.'

'But you see, I know Mr Coertze and Mr Walker,' she said. 'The heavy and clumsy Mr Coertze has been to Italy quite often. I have always known about him and I always had him watched.' She smiled. 'He was like a dog at a rabbit hole who yelps because it is too small and he cannot get in. He always left Italy empty-handed.'

That did it. Coertze must have shown his hand on one of his periodic trips to Italy. But how the devil did she know Walker? He hadn't been to Italy recently – or had he?

She continued. 'So when I heard that Mr Coertze was returning with Mr Walker and the unknown Mr Halloran, then I knew that something big was going to happen. That you were ready to take away whatever was buried, Mr Halloran.'

'So you don't know exactly what we're after?'

'I know that it is very valuable,' she said simply.

'I might be an archaeologist,' I said.

She laughed. 'No, you are not an archaeologist, Mr Halloran; you are a boat-builder.' She saw the surprise in my eyes, and added, 'I know a lot about you.'

I said, 'Let's quit fencing; how do you know about whatever it is?'

She said slowly, 'A man called Alberto Corso had been writing a letter to my father. He was killed before the letter was finished, so there was not all the information that could be desired. But there was enough for me to know that Mr Coertze must be watched.'

I snapped my fingers. 'You're the Count's little daughter. You're . . . er . . . Francesca.'

She inclined her head. 'I am the daughter of a count.'

'Not so little now,' I said. 'So the Count is after the loot.'

Her eyes widened. 'Oh, no. My father knows nothing about it. Nothing at all.'

I thought that could do with a bit of explanation and was just going to query the statement when someone jumped on deck. 'Who is that?' asked the Contessa.

'Probably the others coming back,' I said, and waited. Perhaps there were to be some more surprises before the evening was out.

Walker came down the companionway and stopped when he saw her. 'Oh,' he said. 'I hope I'm not butting in.'

I said, 'This is the Contessa di Estrenoli – Mr Walker.' I watched him to see if he recognized her, but he didn't. He looked at her as one looks at a beautiful woman and said, in Italian, 'A pleasure, signora.'

She smiled at him and said, 'Don't you know me, Mr Walker? I bandaged your leg when you were brought into the hill camp during the war.'

He looked at her closely and said incredulously, 'Francesca!'

'That's right; I'm Francesca.'

'You've changed,' he said. 'You've grown up. I mean . . . er . . .' he was confused.

She looked at him. 'Yes, we've all changed,' she said. I thought I detected a note of regret. They chatted for a few minutes and then she picked up her shoes. 'I must go,' she said.

Walker said, 'But you've only just got here.'

'No, I have an appointment in twenty minutes.' She rose and went to the companionway and I escorted her on deck.

She said, 'I can understand Coertze, and now I can understand Walker; but I cannot understand you, Mr

Halloran. Why are you doing this? You are a successful man, you have made a name in an honourable profession. Why should you do this?'

I sighed and said, 'I had a reason in the beginning; maybe I still have it – I don't know. But having come this far I must go on.'

She nodded, then said, 'There is a café on the waterfront called the Three Fishes. Meet me there at nine tomorrow morning. Come alone; don't bring Coertze or Walker. I never liked Coertze, and now I don't think I like Walker any more. I would prefer not to talk to them.'

'All right,' I said. 'I'll be there.'

She jumped lightly on to the jetty and swayed a little as she put her shoes on. I watched her go away, hearing the sharp click of her heels long after the darkness had swallowed her. Then I went below.

Walker said, 'Where did she come from? How did she know we were here?'

'The gaff has been blown with a loud trumpeting noise,' I said. 'She knows all – or practically all – and she's putting the screws on.'

Walker's jaw dropped. 'She knows about the gold?'

'Yes,' I said. 'But I'm not going to talk about it till Coertze comes. No point in going over it twice.'

Walker protested, but swallowed his impatience when I made it clear that I wasn't going to talk, and sat wriggling on the settee. After half an hour we heard Coertze come on board.

He was affable – full of someone else's cooking for a change, and he'd had a few drinks. 'Man,' he said, 'these Italians can cook.'

'Francesca was here,' I said.

He looked at me, startled. 'The Count's daughter?'

'Yes.'

Walker said, 'I want to know how she found us.'

'What did the stuck-up bitch want?' asked Coertze.

I raised my eyebrows at that. Apparently the dislike between these two was mutual. 'She wants a cut of the treasure,' I said bluntly.

Coertze swore. 'How the hell did she get to know about it?'

'Alberto wrote a letter before he was killed.'

Coertze and Walker exchanged looks, and after a pregnant silence, Coertze said, 'So Alberto was going to give us away, after all.'

I said, 'He *did* give you away.'

'Then why is the gold still there?' demanded Coertze.

'The letter was incomplete,' I said. 'It didn't say exactly where the gold is.'

Coertze sighed windily. 'Well, there's not too much damage done.'

I fretted at his stupidity. 'How do you suppose we're going to get it out with half of Italy watching us?' I asked. 'She's been on to you all the time – she's watched you every time you've been in Italy and she's been laughing at you. And she knows there's something big under way now.'

'That bitch would laugh at me,' said Coertze viciously. 'She always treated me like dirt. I suppose the Count has been laughing like hell, too.'

I rubbed my chin thoughtfully. 'She says the Count knows nothing about it. Tell me about him.'

'The Count? Oh, he's an old no-good now. He didn't get his estates back after the war – I don't know why – and he's as poor as a church mouse. He lives in a poky flat in Milan with hardly enough room to swing a cat.'

'Who supports him?'

Coertze shrugged. 'I dunno. Maybe she does – she can afford it. She married a Roman count; I heard he was stinking rich, so I suppose she passes on some of the housekeeping money to the old boy.'

'Why don't you like her?'

'Oh, she's one of these stuck-up society bitches – I never did like that kind. We get plenty in Houghton, but they're worse here. She wouldn't give me the time of day. Not like her old man. I get on well with him.'

I thought perhaps that on one of his visits to Italy Coertze had made a pass at her and been well and truly slapped down. A pass from Coertze would be clumsy and graceless, like being propositioned by a gorilla.

I said, 'Was she around often during the times you were in Italy?'

He thought about that, and said, 'Sometimes. She turned up at least once on every trip.'

'That's all she'd need. To locate you, I mean. She seems to have a circle of pretty useful friends and apparently they're not the crowd you'd think a girl like that would mix with. She picked up Metcalfe's signals to the Mediterranean ports and interpreted them correctly, so it looks as though she has brains as well as beauty.'

Coertze snorted. 'Beauty! She's a skinny bitch.'

She *had* got under his skin. I said, 'That may be, but she's got us cold. We can't do a damn' thing while she's on our necks. To say nothing of Metcalfe, who'll be on to us next. Funny that he hasn't shown his hand in Rapallo yet.'

'I tell you he's scared off,' growled Coertze.

I let that pass. 'Anyway, we can't do any heavy thinking about it until we find out exactly what she wants. I'm seeing her tomorrow morning, so perhaps I'll be able to tell you more after that.'

'I'll come with you,' said Coertze instantly.

'She wants to see me, not you,' I said. 'That was something she specified.'

'The bloody little bitch,' exploded Coertze.

'And for God's sake, think up another word; I'm tired of that one,' I said irritably.

He glowered at me. 'You falling for her?'

I said wearily, 'I don't know the woman – I've seen her for just fifteen minutes. I'll be better able to tell you about that tomorrow, too.'

'Did she say anything about me?' asked Walker.

'No,' I lied. There wasn't any point in having both of them irritated at her – it was likely that we'd all have to work closely together, and the less friction the better. 'But I'd better see her alone.'

Coertze growled under his breath, and I said, 'Don't worry; neither she nor I know where the gold is. We still need you – she and I and Metcalfe. We mustn't forget Metcalfe.'

III

Early next morning I went to find the Three Fishes. It was just an ordinary dockside café, the kind of dump you find on any waterfront. Having marked it, I went for a stroll round the yacht basin, looking at the sleek sailing yachts and motor craft of the European rich. A lot were big boats needing a paid crew to handle them while the owner and his guests took it easy, but some were more to my taste – small, handy sailing cruisers run by their owners who weren't afraid of a bit of work.

After a pleasant hour I began to feel hungry so I went back to the Three Fishes for a late breakfast and got there on the dot of nine. She wasn't there, so I ordered breakfast and it turned out better than I expected. I had just started to eat when she slid into the seat opposite.

'Sorry I'm late,' she said.

'That's O.K.'

She was wearing slacks and sweater, the kind of clothes you see in the women's magazines but seldom in real life. The sweater suited her.

She looked at my plate and said, 'I had an early breakfast, but I think I'll have another. Do you mind if I join you?'

'It's your party.'

'The food is good here,' she said, and called a waiter, ordering in rapid Italian. I continued to eat and said nothing. It was up to her to make the first move. As I had said – it was her party.

She didn't say anything, either; but just watched me eat. When her own breakfast arrived she attacked it as though she hadn't eaten for a week. She was a healthy girl with a healthy appetite. I finished my breakfast and produced a packet of cigarettes. 'Do you mind?' I asked.

I caught her with her mouth full and she shook her head, so I lit a cigarette. At last she pushed her plate aside with a sigh and took the cigarette I offered. 'Do you know our *Espresso*?' she asked.

'Yes, I know it.'

She laughed. 'Oh, yes, I forgot that it must have penetrated even your Darkest Africa. It is supposed to be for after dinner, but I drink it all the time. Would you like some?'

I said that I would, so she called out to the waiter, '*Due Espressi*,' and turned back to me. 'Well, Mr Halloran, have you thought about our conversation last night?'

I said I had thought about it.

'And so?'

'And so,' I repeated. 'Or more precisely – so what? I'll need to know a lot more about you before I start confiding in you, Contessa.'

She seemed put out. 'Don't call me Contessa,' she said pettishly. 'What do you want to know?'

I flicked ash into the ashtray. 'For one thing, how did you intercept Metcalfe's message? It doesn't seem a likely thing for a Contessa to come across – just like that.'

'I told you I have friends,' she said coldly.

'Who are these friends?'

She sighed. 'You know that my father and I were rebels against the Fascist Government during the war?'

'You were with the partisans, I know.'

She gestured with her hand. 'All right, with the partisans, if you wish. Although do not let my friends hear you say that – the Communists have made it a dirty word. My friends were also partisans and I have never lost contact with them. You see, I was only a little girl at the time and they made me a sort of mascot of the brigade. After the war most of them went back to their work, but some of them had never known any sort of life other than killing Germans. It is a hard thing to forget, you understand?'

I said, 'You mean they'd had a taste of adventure, and liked it.'

'That is right. There was plenty of adventure even after the war. Some of them stopped killing Germans and started to kill Communists – Italian Communists. It was dreadful. But the Communists were too strong, anyway. A few turned to other adventures – some are criminals – nothing serious, you understand; some smuggling, some things worse, but nothing very terrible in most cases. Being criminals, they also know other criminals.'

I began to see how it had been worked; it was all very logical, really.

'There is a big man in Genoa, Torloni; he is a leader of criminals, a very big man in that sort of thing. He sent word to Savona, to Livorno, to Rapallo, to places as far south as Napoli, that he was interested in you and would pay for any information. He gave all your names and the name of your boat.'

That was the sort of pull Metcalfe would have. Probably this Torloni owed him a favour and was paying it off.

Francesca said, 'My friends heard the name – Coertze. It is very uncommon in Italy, and they knew I was interested in a man of that name, so I was told of this. When I also heard the name of Walker I was sure that something was happening.' She shrugged. 'And then there was this Halloran – you. I did not know about you, so I am finding out.'

'Has Torloni been told about us?'

She shook her head. 'I told my friends to see that Torloni was not told. My friends are very strong on this coast; during the war all these hills belonged to us – not to the Germans.'

I began to get the picture. Francesca had been the mascot and, besides, she was the daughter of the revered leader. She was the Lady of the Manor, the Young Mistress who could do no wrong.

It looked also as though, just by chance, Metcalfe had been stymied – temporarily, at least. But I was landed with Francesca and her gang of merry men who had the advantage of knowing just what they wanted.

I said, 'There's another thing. You said your father doesn't know anything about this. How can that be when Alberto Corso wrote him a letter?'

'I never gave it to him,' she said simply.

I looked at her quizzically. 'Is that how a daughter behaves to her father? Not only reading his correspondence, but withholding it as well.'

'It was not like that at all,' she said sharply. 'I will tell you how it was.' She leaned her elbows on the table. 'I was very young during the war, but my father made me work, everyone had to work. It was one of my tasks to gather together the possessions of those who were killed so that useful things could be saved and anything personal could be passed on to the family.

'When Alberto was killed on the cliff I gathered his few things and I found the letter. It was addressed to my father and there were two pages, otherwise it was unfinished.

I read it briefly and it seemed important, but how important it was I did not know because I was very young. I put it in my pocket to give to my father.

'But there was a German attack and we had to move. We sheltered in a farmhouse but we had to move even from there very quickly. Now, I carried my own possessions in a little tin box and that was left in the farmhouse. It was only in 1946 that I went back to the farm to thank those people – the first chance I had.

'They gave me wine and then the farmer's wife brought out the little box and asked it if was mine. I had forgotten all about it and I had forgotten what was in it.' She smiled. 'There was a doll – no, not a doll; what you call an . . . Eddy-bear?'

'A Teddy-bear.'

'That is right; a Teddy-bear – I have still got it. There were some other things and Alberto's letter was there also.'

I said, 'And you still didn't give it to your father. Why not?'

She thumped the table with a small fist. 'It is difficult for you to understand the Italy of just after the war, but I will try to explain. The Communists were very strong, especially here in the north, and they ruined my father after the war. They said he had been a collaborationist and that he had fought the Communist partisans instead of fighting the Fascists. My father, who had been fighting the Fascists all his life! They brought up false evidence and no one would listen to him.

'His estates had been confiscated by the Fascist Government and he could not get them back. How could he when Togliatti, the Vice-Premier of the Government, was the leader of the Italian Communist Party? They said, 'No, this man was a collaborator, so he must be punished. But even with all their false evidence they dared not bring him to trial, but he could not get back his estates, and today he is a poor man.'

Francesca's eyes were full of tears. She wiped them with a tissue and said, 'Excuse me, but my feeling on this is strong.'

I said awkwardly, 'That's all right.'

She looked up and said, 'These Communists with their fighting against the Fascists. My father fought ten times harder than any of them. Have you heard of the 52nd Partisan Brigade?'

I shook my head.

'That was the famous Communist Brigade which captured Mussolini. The famous Garibaldi Brigade. Do you know how many men were in this so-famous Garibaldi Brigade in 1945?'

I said, 'I know very little about it.'

'Eighteen men,' she said contemptuously. 'Eighteen men called themselves the 52nd Brigade. My father commanded fifty times as many men. But when I went to Parma for the anniversary celebrations in 1949 the Garibaldi Brigade marched through the street and there were hundreds of men. All the Communist scum had crawled out of their holes now the war was over and it was safe. They marched through the streets and every man wore a red scarf about his neck and every man called himself a partisan. They even painted the statue of Garibaldi so that it had a red shirt and a red hat. So my friends and I do not call ourselves partisans, and you must not call us by that word the Communists have made a mockery of.'

She was shaking with rage. Her fists were clenched and she looked at me with eyes bright with unshed tears.

'The Communists ruined my father because they knew he was a strong man and because they knew he would oppose them in Italy. He was a liberal, he was for the middle of the road – the middle way. He who is in the middle of the road gets knocked down, but he could not understand that,' she said sombrely. 'He thought it was an honourable fight – as though the Communists have ever fought honourably.'

It was a moving story and typical of our times. I also observed that it fitted with what Coertze had told me. I said, 'But the Communists are not nearly as strong today. Is it not possible for your father to appeal and to have his case reviewed?'

'Mud sticks, whoever throws it,' she said sadly. 'Besides, the war was a long time ago – people do not like to be reminded about those times – and people, especially officials, never like to admit their mistakes.'

She was realistic about the world and I realized that I must be realistic too. I said, 'But what has this got to do with the letter?'

'You wanted to know why I did not give the letter to my father after the war; is that so?'

'Yes.'

She smiled tightly. 'You must meet my father and then you would understand. You see, whatever you are looking for is valuable. I understood from Alberto's letter that there are papers and a lot of gold bars. Now, my father is an honourable man. He would return everything to the Government because from the Government it came. To him, it would be unthinkable to keep any of the gold for himself. It would be dishonourable.'

She looked down at the backs of her hands. 'Now, I am not an honourable woman. It hurts me to see my father so poor he has to live in a Milan slum, that he has to sell his furniture to buy food to eat. He is an old man – it is not right that he should live like that. But if I can get some money I would see that he had a happy old age. He does not need to know where the money comes from.'

I leaned back in my chair and looked at her thoughtfully. I looked at the expensive, fashion-plate clothing she was wearing, and she coloured under my scrutiny. I said softly,

'Why don't *you* send him money? I hear you made a good marriage; you ought to be able to spare a little for an old man.'

Her lips twisted in a harsh smile. 'You don't know anything about me, do you, Mr Halloran? I can assure you that I have no money and no husband, either – or no one that I would care to call my husband.' She moved her hands forward on the table. 'I sold my rings to get money to send to my father, and that was a long time ago. If it were not for my friends I would be on the streets. No, I have no money, Mr Halloran.'

There was something here I did not understand, but I didn't press it. The reason she wanted to cut in didn't matter; all that mattered was she had us over a barrel. With her connections we could not make a move in Italy without falling over an ex-partisan friend of hers. If we tried to lift the gold without coming to terms with her she would coolly step in at the right time and take the lot. She had us taped.

I said, 'You're as bad as Metcalfe.'

'That is something I wanted to ask you,' she said. 'Who is this Metcalfe?'

'He's up to the same lark that you are.'

Her command of English was not up to that. 'Lark?' she said in mystification. 'That is a bird?'

I said, 'He's one of our mutual competitors. He's after the gold, too.' I leaned over the table. 'Now, if we cut you in, we would want certain guarantees.'

'I do not think you are in a position to demand guarantees,' she said coldly.

'Nevertheless, we would want them. Don't worry, this is in your interest, too. Metcalfe is the man behind Torloni and he's quite a boy. Now, we would want protection against Metcalfe and anything he could throw against us. From what you've said, Torloni carries a bit of weight, and if he hasn't got enough, Metcalfe can probably drum up some more. What I want to know is – can you give us protection against that lot?'

'I can find a hundred men, any time I want,' she said proudly.

'What kind of men?' I asked bluntly. 'Old soldiers on pension?'

She smiled. 'Most of my wartime friends live quietly and go about their work. I would not want them to be mixed up in anything illegal or violent, although they would help if they had to. But my . . .' she hesitated for a word, '. . . my more unsavoury friends I would willingly commit to this affair. I told you they are adventurous and they are not old men – no older than you, Mr Halloran,' she ended sweetly.

'A hundred of them?'

She thought a little. 'Fifty, then,' she compromised. 'My father's hill fighters will be more than a match for those dockland gangsters.'

I had no doubt about that – if they fought man to man. But Metcalfe and Torloni could probably whip up every thug in Italy, and would do for a stake as large as this.

I said, 'I want further guarantees. How do I know we won't be double-crossed?'

'You don't,' she said meagrely.

I decided to go in for some melodramatics. 'I want you to swear that you won't double-cross us.'

She raised her hand. 'I swear that I, Francesca di Estrenoli, promise faithfully not to trick, in any way, Mr Halloran of South Africa.' She smiled at me. 'Is that good enough?'

I shook my head. 'No, it isn't enough. You said yourself that you were a dishonourable woman. No, I want you to swear on your father's name and honour.'

Pink anger spots burned on her cheeks and I thought for a moment that she was going to slap my face. I said gently, 'Do you swear?'

She dropped her eyes. 'I swear,' she said in a low voice.

'On your father's name and honour,' I persisted.

'On my father's name and on his honour,' she said, and looked up. 'Now I hope you are satisfied.' There were tears in her eyes again.

I relaxed. It wasn't much but it was the best I could do and I hoped it would hold her.

The man from behind the counter came over to the table slowly. He looked at me with dislike and said to Francesca, 'Is everything all right, madame?'

'Yes, Giuseppi, everything is all right.' She smiled at him. 'Nothing is wrong.'

Giuseppi smiled back at her, gave me a hard look and returned to the counter. I felt a prickle at the back of my neck. I had the feeling that if Francesca had said that everything was *not* all right I would have been a candidate for a watery dockside grave before the week was out.

I cocked my thumb at the counter. 'One of your soldier friends?'

She nodded. 'He saw you had hurt me, so he came over to see what he could do.'

'I didn't mean to hurt you,' I said.

'You shouldn't have come here. You shouldn't have come to Italy. What is it to you? I can understand Coertze and Walker; they fought the Germans, they buried the gold. But I cannot understand you.'

I said gently, 'I fought the Germans, too, in Holland, and Germany.'

'I'm sorry,' she said. 'I shouldn't have said that.'

'That's all right. As for the rest . . .' I shrugged. 'Somebody had to plan – Coertze and Walker couldn't do it. Walker is an alcoholic and Coertze is all beef and no – subtlety. They needed someone to get behind and push.'

'But why is it you who has to push?'

'I had a reason once,' I said shortly. 'Forget it. Let's get some things straightened out. What about the split?'

'The split?'

'How do we divide the loot?'

'I hadn't thought of that – it will need some thinking about.'

'It will,' I agreed. 'Now, there's the three of us, there's you and there's fifty of your friends – fifty-four in all. If you're thinking along the lines of fifty-four equal shares you can forget about it. We won't have it.'

'I can't see how we can work this out when we don't know how much money will be involved.'

'We work it on a percentage basis,' I said impatiently. 'This is how I see it – one share each for the three of us, one share for you and one share to be divided among your friends.'

'No,' she said firmly. 'That's not fair. You have done nothing about this, at all. You are just a plunderer.'

'I thought you'd take that attitude,' I said. 'Now, listen, and listen damned carefully because I'm not going to repeat this. Coertze and Walker are entitled to a share each. They fought for the gold and they disposed of it carefully. Besides, they are the only people who know where it is. Right?'

She nodded agreement.

I smiled grimly. 'Now we come to me whom you seem to despise.' She made a sudden gesture with her hand and I waved her down. 'I'm the brains behind this. I know a way of getting the stuff out of Italy and I've arranged a sale for it. Without me this whole plan would flop, and I've invested a lot of time and money in it. Therefore I think I'm entitled to an equal share.'

I stabbed my finger at her. 'And now you come along and blackmail us. Yes, blackmail,' I said as she opened her mouth to protest. 'You've done nothing constructive towards the plan and you complain about getting an equal share. As for your friends, as far as I'm concerned, they are hired muscle to be paid for. If you don't think they're being paid enough with one-fifth between them you can supplement it out of your own share.'

'But it will be so little for them,' she said.

'Little!' I said, and was shocked into speechlessness. I recovered my breath. 'Do you know how much is involved?'

'Not exactly,' she said cautiously.

I threw discretion to the winds. 'There's over £1,500,000 in gold alone – and there's probably an equal amount in cut gem-stones. The gold alone means £300,000 for a fifth share and that's £6,000 each for your friends. If you count the jewels you can double those figures.'

Her eyes widened as she mentally computed this into lire. It was an astronomical calculation and took her some time. 'So much,' she whispered.

'So much,' I said. I had just had an idea. The gems had been worrying me because they would be hot – in the criminal sense. They would need recutting and disguising and the whole thing would be risky. Now I saw the chance of doing an advantageous deal.

'Look here,' I said generously. 'I've just offered you and your friends two-fifths of the take. Supposing the jewels are worth more than two-fifths – and I reckon they are – then you can take the lot of them, leaving the disposal of the gold to the three of us. After all, gems are more portable and easily hidden.'

She fell for it. 'I know a jeweller who was with us during the war; he could do the valuation. Yes, that seems reasonable.'

It seemed reasonable to me, also, since I had been taking only the gold into my calculations all the time. Coertze, Walker and myself would still come out with half a million each.

'There's one other thing,' I said.

'What's that?'

'There's a lot of paper money in this hoard – lire, francs, dollars and so on. Nobody takes any of that – there'll be records of the numbers lodged with every bank in the world. You'll have to control your friends when it comes to that.'

'I can control them,' she said loftily. She smiled and held out her hand. 'It's a deal, then, as the Americans say.'

I looked at her hand but didn't touch it. I shook my head. 'Not yet. I still have to discuss it with Coertze and Walker. They'll take a hell of a lot of convincing – especially Coertze. What did you do to him, anyway?' She withdrew her hand slowly and looked at me strangely. 'Almost you convince me that you are an honest man.'

I grinned at her cheerfully. 'Out of necessity, that's all. Those two are the only ones who know where the gold is.'

'Oh, yes, I had forgotten. As for Coertze, he is a boor.'

'He'd be the first to agree with you,' I said. 'But it means something different in Afrikaans.' I had a sudden thought. 'Does anyone else know what you know – about Alberto's letter and all that?'

She started to shake her head but stopped suddenly, deciding to be honest. 'Yes,' she said. 'One man, but he can be trusted – he is a true friend.'

'O.K.,' I said. 'I just wanted to be sure that no one else will try to pull the same stunt that you've just pulled. The whole damn' Mediterranean seems to be getting into the act. I wouldn't tell your friends anything you don't have to – at least, not until it's all over. If they are criminals, as you say, they might get their own ideas.'

'I haven't told them anything so far, and I'm not going to tell them now.'

'Good. But you *can* tell them to watch for Torloni's men. They'll be keeping an eye on *Sanford* when they get round to finding where she is.'

'Oh, yes, Mr Halloran; I'll certainly tell them to keep a watch on your boat,' she said sweetly.

I laughed. 'I know you will. When you've got things organized drop in and see us anytime – but make it quick, there's a time limit on all this.'

I got up from the table and left her. I thought she might as well pay for the breakfast since we were partners – or, as she had put it, 'in association'.

IV

She came that afternoon, accompanied by a man even bigger than Coertze, whom she introduced as Piero Morese. He nodded civilly enough to me, ignored Walker and regarded Coertze watchfully.

I had had trouble with Coertze – he had taken a lot of convincing and had reiterated in a bass growl, 'I will not be cheated, I will not be cheated.'

I said wearily, 'O.K. The gold is up in those hills somewhere; you know where it is. Why don't you go and get it? I'm sure you can fight Torloni and Metcalfe and the Contessa and her cut-throats single-handed; I'm sure you can bring back the gold and take it to Tangier before April 19. Why don't you just go ahead and stop bothering me?'

He had calmed down but was not altogether happy and he rumbled like a volcano which does not know whether to erupt again or not. Now he sat in the cabin looking at the Contessa with contempt and the big Italian with mistrust.

Morese had no English so the meeting came to order in Italian, which I could understand if it was not spoken too quickly. The Contessa said, 'It is all right to speak in front of Piero, he knows everything that I know.'

'I know you: you were with Umberto,' said Coertze in mashed Italian.

Morese gave a quick nod but said nothing. The Contessa said, 'Here is where we talk seriously.' She looked at me. 'Have you talked this over?'

'We have.'

'Do they accept the terms?'

'They do.'

'Very well, where is the gold?'

There was a growl from Coertze which I covered with a quick burst of laughter. 'Contessa, you'll be the death of me,' I said. 'I'll die laughing. You don't suppose we'll tell you that, do you?'

She smiled acidly. 'No – but I thought I would try it. All right, how do we go about this?'

I said, 'First of all, there's a time limit. We'll want the gold delivered to Rapallo by the 1st of March at the latest. We also want a place where we can work undisturbed with this boat; either a private boat-shed or a boatyard. That must be arranged for now.'

Her eyes narrowed. 'Why the 1st of March?'

'That is of no consequence to you, but that is the way it must be.'

Morese said, 'That does not leave much time. The first of the month is in two weeks.'

'True,' I said. 'But that is the way it must be. The next thing is that only the five of us here will go to the gold. There must be no one else. We will unseal the place where it is hidden, pack what we want into strong boxes and move it out. Then we will seal the hidden place again. After that, and only after that, will we need the help of anyone else, and even then, only for lifting and transport to the coast. There is no need to have too many people knowing what we are doing.'

'That is well thought of,' said Morese.

I said, 'Everything will be brought to the boat-shed – everything, including the jewels. We five will live together for one month while my friends and I do what we have to do. If you want the jewels valued you must bring your valuer to the jewels – not vice versa. The final share-out will be decided when the stones have been valued, but will not take place until the boat is in the water.'

'You talk as though you do not trust us,' said Morese.

'I don't,' I said bluntly. I jerked my thumb at the Contessa. 'Your friend here is blackmailing us into all this, so I don't see where the trust comes in.'

His face darkened. 'That is unworthy of you.'

I shrugged. 'Say, rather, it is unworthy of her. She started all this and those are the facts.'

The Contessa put her hand on Morese's shoulder and he subsided. Coertze barked a short laugh. '*Magtig*, but you have taken her measure.' He nodded. 'You'll have to watch her, she a *slim meisie*.'

I turned to him. 'Now it's up to you. What will you need to get the gold?'

Coertze leaned forward. 'When I was here last year nothing had changed or been disturbed. The place is in the hills where no one goes. There is a rough road so we can take a lorry right up to the place. The nearest village is four miles away.'

'Can we work at night?' I asked.

Coertze thought about that. 'The fall of rocks looks worse than it is,' he said. 'I know how to blast and I made sure of that. Two men with picks and shovels will be able to get through in four hours – longer at night, perhaps – I would say six hours at night.'

'So we will be there at least one whole night and probably longer.'

'*Ja*,' he said. 'If we work at night only, it will take two nights.'

The Contessa said, 'Italians do not walk the hills at night. It will be safe to have lights if they cannot be seen from the village.'

Coertze said, 'No lights can be seen from the village.'

'All the same, we must have a cover,' I said. 'If we have to hang around in the vicinity for at least one day then we must have a sound reason. Has anyone got any ideas?'

There was a silence and suddenly Walker spoke for the first time. 'What about a car and a caravan? The English are noted for that kind of thing – camping and so on. The Italians don't even have a word for it, they use the English word. If we camp out for a couple of nights we'll be only another English crowd as far as the peasants are concerned.'

We all thought about that and it seemed a good idea. The Contessa said, 'I can arrange for the car and the caravan and a tent.'

I started to tick off all the things we would need. 'We want lights.'

'We use the headlights of the car,' said Coertze.

'That's for outside,' I said. 'We'll need lights for inside. We'll need torches – say a dozen – and lots of torch cells.' I nodded to Morese. 'You get those. We need picks and shovels, say four of each. We'll need lorries. How many to do the job in one haul?'

'Two three-tonners,' said Coertze with certainty. 'The Germans had four, but they were carrying a lot of stuff we won't want.'

'We'll have to have those standing by with the drivers,' I said. 'Then we'll need a lot of timber to make crates. The gold will need re-boxing.'

'Why do that when it's already in boxes?' objected Coertze. 'It's just a lot of extra work.'

'Think back,' I said patiently. 'Think back to the first time you saw those boxes in the German truck. You *recognized* them as bullion boxes. We don't want any snooper doing the same on the way back.'

Walker said, 'You don't have to take the gold out, and it wouldn't need much timber. Just nail thin pieces of wood on the outside of the bullion boxes to change their shape and make them look different.'

Walker was a real idea machine when he wasn't on the drink. He said, 'There must be plenty of timber down there we can use.'

'No,' I said. 'We use new wood. I don't want anything that looks or even smells as though it's come from a hole in the ground. Besides, there might be a mark on the wood we could miss which would give the game away.'

'You don't take any chances, do you?' observed the Contessa.

'I'm not a gambler,' I said shortly. 'The timber can go up in the trucks,' I looked at Morese.

'I will get it,' he said.

'Don't forget hammers and nails,' I said. I was trying to think of everything. If we slipped up on this job it would be because of some insignificant item which nobody had thought important.

There was a low, repeated whistle from the dockside. Morese looked at the Contessa and she nodded almost imperceptibly. He got up and went on deck.

I said to Coertze, 'Is there anything else we ought to know – anything you've forgotten or left out?'

'No,' he said. 'That's all.'

Morese came back and said to the Contessa, 'He wants to talk to you.'

She rose and left the cabin and Morese followed her on deck. Through the open port I could hear a low-voiced conversation.

'I don't trust them,' said Coertze violently. 'I don't trust that bitch and I don't trust Morese. He's a bad bastard;

he was a bad bastard in the war. He didn't take any prisoners – according to him they were all shot while escaping.'

'So were yours,' I said, 'when you took the gold.'

He bridled. 'That was different; they *were* escaping.'

'Very conveniently,' I said acidly. It galled me that this man, whom I had good reason to suspect of murdering at least four others, should be so mealy-mouthed.

He brooded a little, then said, 'What's to stop them taking it all from us when we've got it out? What's to stop them shooting us and leaving us in the tunnel when they seal it up again?'

'Nothing that you'd understand,' I said. 'Just the feeling of a girl for her father and her family.' I didn't elaborate on that; I wasn't certain myself that it was a valid argument.

The Contessa and Morese came back. She said, 'Two of Torloni's men are in Rapallo. They were asking the Port Captain about you not ten minutes ago.'

I said, 'Don't tell me that the Port Captain is one of your friends.'

'No, but the Chief Customs Officer is. He recognized them immediately. One of them he had put in jail three years ago for smuggling heroin; the other he has been trying to catch for a long time. Both of them work for Torloni, he says.'

'Well, we couldn't hope to hide from them indefinitely,' I said. 'But they mustn't connect you with us – not yet, anyway – so you'll have to wait until it's dark before you leave.'

She said, 'I am having them watched.'

'That's fine, but it's not enough,' I said. 'I want to do to Metcalfe what he's been doing to us. I want Torloni watched in Genoa; I want the docks watched all along this coast for Metcalfe's boat. I want to know when he comes to Italy.'

I gave her a detailed description of Metcalfe, of Krupke and the Fairmile. 'Can you do all that?'

'Of course. You will know all about this Metcalfe as soon as he sets foot in Italy.'

'Good,' he said. 'Then what about a drink?' I looked at Coertze. 'It seems you didn't scare Metcalfe off, after all.' He looked back at me with an expressionless face, and I laughed. 'Don't look so glum. Get out the bottle and cheer up.'

V

We didn't see the Contessa or Morese after that. They stayed out of sight, but next morning I found a note in the cockpit telling me to go to the Three Fishes and say that I wanted a watchman for *Sanford*.

I went, of course, and Giuseppi was more friendly than when I had last seen him. He served me personally and, as he put down the plate, I said, 'You ought to know what goes on on the waterfront. Can you recommend a watchman for my boat? He must be honest.'

'Ah, yes, signor,' he said. 'I have the very man – old Luigi there. It's a pity; he was wounded during the war and since then he has been able to undertake only light work. At present he is unemployed.'

'Send him over when I have finished breakfast,' I said.

Thus it was that we got an honest watchman and old Luigi became the go-between between the Contessa and *Sanford*. Every morning he would bring a letter in which the Contessa detailed her progress.

Torloni was being watched, but nothing seemed to be happening; his men were still in Rapallo watching *Sanford* and being watched themselves; the trucks had been arranged for and the drivers were ready; the timber was prepared and the tools had been bought; she had been offered a German caravan but she had heard of an English caravan for sale in Milan and thought it would be better – would I give her some money to buy it as she had none.

It all seemed to be working out satisfactorily.

The three of us from *Sanford* spent our time sightseeing, much to the disgust of Torloni's spies. I spent a lot of time in the Yacht Club and it was soon noised about that I intended to settle in the Mediterranean and was looking for a suitable boatyard to buy.

On our fifth day in Rapallo the morning letter instructed me to go to the boatyard of Silvio Palmerini and to ask for a quotation for the slipping and painting of *Sanford*. 'The price will be right,' wrote the Contessa. 'Silvio is one of my – our – friends.'

Palmerini's yard was some way out of Rapallo. Palmerini was a gnarled man of about sixty who ruled his yard and his three sons with soft words and a will of iron. I said, 'You understand, Signor Palmerini, that I am a boat-builder, too. I would like to do the job myself in your yard.'

He nodded. It was only natural that a man must look after his own boat if he could; besides, it would be cheaper.

'And I would want it under cover,' I said. 'I fastened the keel in an experimental way and I may want to take it off to see if it is satisfactory.'

He nodded again. Experimental ways were risky and a man should stick to the old traditional ways of doing things. It would be foolish, indeed, if milord's keel dropped off in the middle of the Mediterranean.

I agreed that I should look a fool, and said, 'My friends and I are capable of doing the work and we shall not need extra labour. All that is required is a place where we can work undisturbed.'

He nodded a third time. He had a large shed we could use and which could be locked. No one would disturb us, not

even himself – certainly no one outside his family – he
would see to that. And was milord the rich Englishman who
wanted to buy a boatyard? If so, then perhaps the milord
would consider the boatyard Palmerini, the paragon of
the Western Mediterranean.

That brought me up with a jerk. Another piece of polite
blackmail was under way and I could see that I would have
to buy the yard, probably at an exorbitant price – the price
of silence.

I said diplomatically, 'Yes, I am thinking of buying a yard,
but the wise man explores every avenue.' Dammit, I was
falling into his way of speech. 'I have been to Spain and
France; now I am in Italy and after Italy I am going to
Greece. I must look at everything.'

He nodded vigorously, his crab-apple head bobbing up
and down. Yes, the milord was indeed wise to look at everything, but in spite of that he was sure that the milord would
unfailingly return to the boatyard Palmerini because it was
certainly the best in the whole Mediterranean.

Pah, what did the Greeks know of fine building? All they
knew were their clumsy caiques. The price would be reasonable for milord since it appeared that they had mutual
friends, and such a price could be spread over a period
provided the proper guarantees could be given.

From this I understood the old rascal to say that he
would wait until the whole job was completed and I had
fluid capital, if I could prove that I would keep my word.

I went back to *Sanford* feeling satisfied that this part of the
programme was going well. Even if I had to buy Palmerini's
yard, it would not be a bad thing and any lengthening of the
price could be written off as expedition expenses.

On the ninth day of our stay in Rapallo the usual morning letter announced that all was now ready and we could
start at any time. However, it was felt that, since the next
day was Sunday, it would be more fitting to begin the

expedition inland on Monday. That gave an elevating tone to the whole thing, I thought; another crazy aspect of a crazy adventure.

The Contessa wrote: 'Torloni's men will be discreetly taken care of, and will not connect their inability to find you with any trickery on your part. They will have no suspicions. Leave your boat in the care of Luigi and meet me at nine in the morning at the Three Fishes.'

I put a match to the letter and called Luigi below. 'They say you are an honest man, Luigi; would you take a bribe?'

He was properly horrified. 'Oh no, signor.'

'You know this boat is being watched?'

'Yes, signor. They are enemies of you and Madame.'

'Do you know what Madame and I are doing?'

He shook his head. 'No, signor. I came because Madame said you needed my help. I did not ask any questions,' he said with dignity.

I tapped on the table. 'My friends and I are going away for a few days soon, leaving the boat in your charge. What will you do if the men who are watching want to bribe you to let them search the boat?'

He drew himself up. 'I would slap the money out of their hands, signor.'

'No, you won't,' I said. 'You will say it is not enough and you will ask them for more money. When you get it, you will let them search the boat.'

He looked at me uncomprehendingly. I said slowly, 'I don't mind if they search – there is nothing to be found. There is no reason why you should not make some money out of Madame's enemies.'

He laughed suddenly and slapped his thigh. 'That is good, signor; that is very good. You *want* them to search.'

'Yes,' I replied. 'But don't make it too easy for them or they will be suspicious.'

I wanted, as a last resort, to try to fool Metcalfe as I had fooled him in Barcelona, or rather, as I had hoped to fool him before Coertze put his foot in it. I wrote a letter to the Contessa telling her what I was doing, and gave it to Luigi to pass on.

'How long have you known Madame?' I asked curiously.

'Since the war, signor, when she was a little girl.'

'You would do anything for her, wouldn't you?'

'Why not?' he asked in surprise. 'She has done more for me that I can ever repay. She paid for the doctors after the war when they straightened my leg. It is not her fault they could not get it properly straight – but I would have been a cripple, otherwise.'

This was a new light on Francesca. 'Thank you, Luigi,' I said. 'Give the letter to Madame when you see her.'

I told Coertze and Walker what was happening. There was nothing else to do now but wait for Monday morning.

FIVE: THE TUNNEL

On Monday morning I again set the stage, leaving papers where they could easily be found. On the principle of the Purloined Letter I had even worked out a costing for a refit of *Sanford* at Palmerini's boatyard, together with some estimates of the probable cost of buying the yard. If we were seen there later we would have good reason.

We left just before nine, saying goodbye to Luigi, who gave me a broad wink, and arrived at the Three Fishes on time. The Contessa and Morese were waiting and we joined them for breakfast. The Contessa wore clothing of an indefinably English cut of which I approved; she was using her brain.

I said, 'How did you get rid of Torloni's boys?'

Morese grinned. 'One of them had an accident with his car. The other, who was waiting for him at the dock, got tired of waiting and unaccountably fell into the water. He had to get a taxi to his hotel so that he could change his clothes.'

'Your friend Metcalfe arrived in Genoa last night,' said the Contessa.

'You're sure.'

'I'm certain. He went straight to Torloni and stayed with him for a long time. Then he went to a hotel.'

That settled that. I had wondered for a long time if my suspicions of Metcalfe hadn't been just a fevered bit of imagination. After all, my whole case against Metcalfe had been built up of supposition and what I knew of his character.

'You're having him watched?'

'Of course.'

Breakfast arrived and all conversation stopped until Giuseppi went back to his counter. Then I said, 'All right, friend Kobus, this is where you tell us where the gold is.'

Coertze's head came up with a jerk. 'Not on,' he said. 'I'll take you there, but I'm not telling first.'

I sighed. 'Look, these good people have laid on transport. How can they tell the trucks to rendezvous unless we know where we're going?'

'They can telephone back here.'

'From where?'

'There'll be a phone in the village.'

'None of us is going anywhere near that village,' I said. 'Least of all one of us foreigners. And if you think I'll let one of these two go in alone, you're crazy. From now on we don't let either of them out of our sight.'

'Not very trusting, are you?' observed the Contessa.

I looked at her. 'Do you trust me?'

'Not much.'

'Then we're even.' I turned back to Coertze. 'Any telephoning the Contessa is going to do is from that telephone in the corner there – with me at her elbow.'

'Don't call me the Contessa,' she snapped.

I ignored her and concentrated on Coertze. 'So, you see, we have to know the spot. If you won't tell us, I'm sure that Walker will – but I'd rather it was you.'

He thought about it for quite a while, then he said, 'Magtig, but you'll argue your way into heaven one day. All right, it's about forty miles north of here, between Varsi and Tassaro.' He went into detailed explanations and Morese said, 'It's right in the hills.'

I said, 'Do you think you can direct the trucks to this place?'

Francesca said, 'I will tell them to wait in Varsi. We will not need them until the second night; we can go to Varsi and direct them from there tomorrow.'

'O.K.,' I said. 'Let's make that phone call.'

I escorted her to the corner and stood by while she gave the instructions, making sure she slipped nothing over. A trustful lot, we were. When we got back to the table, I said, 'That does it; we can start at any time.'

We finished breakfast and got up to go. Francesca said, 'Not by the front; Torloni's men will be back now and they can see this café. We go this way.'

She led us out by the back door into a yard where a car was standing with an Eccles touring caravan already coupled. She said, 'I stocked up with enough food for a week – it might be necessary.'

'It won't,' I said grimly. 'If we don't have the stuff out by tomorrow night we'll never get it – not with Metcalfe sniffing on our trail.'

I looked at our party and make a quick decision. 'We look English enough, all except you, Morese; you just don't fit. You travel in the caravan and keep out of sight.'

He frowned and looked at Francesca. She said, 'Get into the caravan, Piero; do as Mr Halloran says,' and then turned to me. 'Piero takes his instructions from no one but me, Mr Halloran. I hope you remember that in future.'

I shrugged and said, 'Let's go.'

Coertze was driving because he knew the way. Walker was also in front and Francesca and I shared the back seat. No one did much talking and Coertze drove very slowly because he was unaccustomed to towing a caravan and driving on the right simultaneously.

We left Rapallo and were soon ascending into the hills – the Ligurian Apennines. It looked poor country with stony soil and not much cultivation. What agriculture there was was scattered and devoted to vines and olives, the two trees which look as though they've been tortured to death. Within the hour we were in Varsi, and soon after that, we left the main road and bounced along a secondary country road, unmetalled and with a poor surface. It had not rained for some days and the dust rose in clouds.

After a while Coertze slowed down almost to a stop as he came to a corner. 'This is where we shot up the trucks,' he said.

We turned the corner and saw a long stretch of empty road. Coertze stopped the car and Walker got out. This was the first time he had seen the place in fifteen years. He walked a little way up the road to a large rock on the right, then turned and looked back. I guessed it was by that rock that he had stood while he poured bullets into the driver of the staff car.

I thought about the sudden and dreadful slaughter that had happened on that spot and, looking up the shaggy hillside, I visualized the running prisoners being hunted and shot down. I said abruptly, 'No point in waiting here, let's get on with it.'

Coertze put the car into gear and drove forward slowly until Walker had jumped in, then he picked up speed and we were on our way again. 'Not far now,' said Walker. His voice was husky with excitement.

Less than fifteen minutes later Coertze pulled up again at the junction of another road so unused that it was almost invisible. 'The old mine is about a mile and a half up there,' he said. 'What do we do now?'

Francesca and I got out of the car and stretched our stiffened legs. I looked about and saw a stream about a hundred yards away. 'That's convenient,' I said. 'The perfect camp site. One thing is certain – none of us so much as looks sideways at that side road during the hours of daylight.'

We pulled the caravan off the road and extended the balance legs, then we put up the tent. Francesca went into the caravan and talked to Morese. I said, 'Now, for God's sake, let's act like innocent tourists. We're mad Englishmen who prefer to live uncomfortably rather than stay at a hotel.'

It was a long day. After lunch, which Francesca made in the little galley of the caravan, we sat about and talked desultorily and waited for the sun to go down. Francesca stayed in the caravan most of the time keeping Morese company; Walker fidgeted; Coertze was apparently lost in contemplating his navel; I tried to sleep, but couldn't.

The only excitement during the afternoon was the slow approach of a farm cart. It hove into sight as a puff of dust at the end of the road and gradually, with snail-like pace, came near enough to be identified. Coertze roused himself enough to make a number of small wagers as to the time it would draw level with the camp. At last it creaked past, drawn by two oxen and looking like a refugee from a Breughel painting. A peasant trudged alongside and I mustered my worst Italian, waved and said, '*Buon giorno.*'

He gave me a sideways look, muttered something I did not catch, and went on his way. That was the only traffic on the road the whole time we were there.

At half past four I roused myself and went to the caravan to see Francesca. 'We'd better eat early,' I said. 'As soon as it's dark we'll be taking the car to the mine.'

'Everything is in cans,' she said. 'It will be easy to prepare. We will want something to eat during the night, so I got two of these big vacuum containers – I will cook the food before we go and it will keep hot all night. There are also some vacuum flasks for coffee.'

'You've been spending my money well,' I said.

She ignored that. 'I will need some water. Will you get me some from the stream?'

'If you will come with me,' I said. 'You need to stretch a bit.' I had a sudden urge to talk to her, to find out what made her tick.

'All right,' she said, and opening a cupboard, produced three canvas buckets. As we walked towards the stream, I said, 'You must have been very young during the war.'

'I was. We took to the hills, my father and I, when I was ten years old.' She waved at the surrounding mountains. 'These hills.'

'Not a very pleasant life for a little girl.'

She considered that. 'It was fun at first. Everyone likes a camping holiday and this was one long holiday for me. Yes, it was fun.'

'When did it stop being fun?'

Her face was quietly sad. 'When the men started to die; when the fighting began. Then it was not fun, it became a serious thing we were doing. It was a good thing – but it was terrible.'

'And you worked in the hospital?'

'Yes. I tended Walker when he came from the prison camp. Did you know that?'

I remembered Walker's description of the grave little girl who wanted him to get better so he could kill Germans. 'He told me,' I said.

We reached the stream and I looked at it doubtfully. It looked clear enough, but I said, 'Is it all right for drinking?'

'I will boil the water; it will be all right,' she said, and knelt to dig a hole in the shallows. 'We must have a hole deep enough to take a bucket; it is easier then.'

I helped her make a hole, reflecting that this was a product of her guerilla training. I would have tried to fill the buckets in drips and drabs. When the hole was big enough we sat on the bank waiting for the sediment to settle, and I said, 'Was Coertze ever wounded?'

'No, he was very lucky. He was never wounded beyond a scratch, although there were many times he could have been.'

I offered her a cigarette and lit it. 'So he did a lot of fighting?'

'All the men fought,' she said, and drew on the cigarette reflectively. 'But Coertze seemed to *like* fighting. He killed a lot of Germans – and Italians.'

'What Italians?' I said quickly. I was thinking of Walker's story.

'The Fascists,' she said. 'Those who stuck by Mussolini during the time of the Salo Republic. There was a civil war going on in these mountains. Did you know that?'

'No, I didn't,' I said. 'There's a lot about Italy that I don't know.'

We sat quietly for a while, then I said, 'So Coertze was a killer?'

'He was a good soldier – the kind of man we needed. He was a leader.'

I switched. 'How was Alberto killed?'

'He fell off a cliff when the Germans were chasing Umberto's section. I heard that Coertze nearly rescued him, but didn't get there in time.'

'Um,' I said. 'I heard it was something like that. How did Harrison and Parker die?'

She wrinkled her brow. 'Harrison and Parker? Oh yes, they were in what we called the Foreign Legion. They were killed in action. Not at the same time, at different times.'

'And Donato Rinaldi; how was he killed?'

'That was a funny thing. He was found dead near the camp with his head crushed. He was lying under a cliff and it was thought he had been climbing and had fallen off.'

'Why should he climb? Was he a mountaineer or something like that?'

'I don't think so, but he was a young man and young men do foolish things like that.'

I smiled, thinking to myself; not only the very young are foolish; and tossed a pebble into the stream. 'It sounds very like the song about the "Ten Little Niggers". "And then there were Two." Why did Walker leave?'

She looked up sharply. 'Are you saying that these men should not have died? That someone from the camp killed them?'

I shrugged. 'I'm not saying anything – but it was very convenient for someone. You see, six men hid this gold and four of them came to a sudden end shortly afterwards.' I tossed another pebble into the water. 'Who profits? There are only two – Walker and Coertze. Why did Walker leave?'

'I don't know. He left suddenly. I remember he told my father that he was going to try to join the Allied armies. They were quite close at that time.'

'Was Coertze in the camp when Walker left?'

She thought for a long time, then said, 'I don't know; I can't remember.'

'Walker says he left because he was frightened of Coertze. He still is, for that matter. Our Kobus is a very frightening man, sometimes.'

Francesca said slowly, 'There was Alberto on the cliff. Coertze could have . . .'

'. . . pushed him off? Yes, he could. And Walker said that Parker was shot in the *back* of the head. By all accounts, including yours, Coertze is a natural-born killer. It all adds up.'

She said, 'I always knew that Coertze was a violent man, but . . .'

'But? Why don't you like him, Francesca?'

She threw the stub of her cigarette into the water and watched it float downstream. 'It was just one of those things that happen between a man and a woman. He was . . . too pressing.'

'When was this?'

'Three years ago. Just after I was married.'

I hesitated. I wanted to ask her about that marriage, but she suddenly stood up and said, 'We must get the water.'

As we were going back to the caravan I said, 'It looks as though I'll have to be ready to jump Coertze – he could be dangerous. You'd better tell Piero the story so that he can be prepared if anything happens.'

She stopped. 'I thought Coertze was your friend. I thought you were on his side.'

'I'm on nobody's side,' I said shortly. 'And I don't condone murder.'

We walked the rest of the way in silence.

For the rest of the afternoon until it became dark Francesca was busy cooking in the caravan. As the light faded the rest of us began to make our preparations. We put the picks and shovels in the boot of the car, together with some torches. Piero had provided a Tilley pressure lamp together with half a gallon of paraffin – that would be a lot better than torches once we got into the tunnel. He also hauled a wheelbarrow out of the caravan, and said, 'I thought we could use this for taking the rock away; we must not leave loose rock at the entrance of the tunnel.'

I was pleased about that; it was something I had forgotten.

Coertze examined the picks with a professional air, but found no fault. To me, a pick is a pick and a spade is a bloody shovel, but I suppose that even pick-and-shovelling has its more erudite technicalities. As I was helping Piero put the wheelbarrow into the boot my foot turned on a stone and I was thrown heavily against Coertze.

'Sorry,' I said.

'Don't be sorry, be more careful,' he grunted.

We got the wheelbarrow settled – although the top of the boot wouldn't close – and I said to Coertze in a low voice, 'I'd like to talk to you . . . over there.'

We wandered a short distance from the rest of the party where we were hidden in the gathering darkness. 'What is it?' asked Coertze.

I tapped the hard bulge under the breast of his jacket, and said, 'I think that's a gun.'

'It is a gun,' he said.

'Who are you thinking of shooting?'

'Anyone who gets between me and the gold.'

'Now listen carefully,' I said in a hard voice. 'You're not going to shoot anyone, because you're going to give that gun to me. If you don't, you can get the gold yourself. I didn't come to Italy to kill anybody; *I'm* not a murderer.'

Coertze said, '*Klein man,* if you want this gun you'll have to take it from me.'

'O.K. You can force us all up to the mine at pistol point. But it's dark and you'll get a rock thrown at your head as soon as you turn your back – and I'd just as soon be the one who throws it. And if you get the gold out – at pistol point – what are you going to do besides sit on it? You can't get it to the coast without Francesca's men and you can't get it out of Italy without me.'

I had him cornered in the same old stalemate that had been griping him since we left South Africa. He was foxed and he knew it.

He said, 'How do we know the Contessa's partisans aren't hiding in these damned hills waiting to jump us as soon as the tunnel is opened?'

'Because they don't know where we are,' I said. 'The only instruction that the truck drivers had was to go to Varsi. Anyway, they wouldn't try to jump us; we have the Contessa as hostage.'

He hesitated, and I said, 'Now, give me the gun.'

Slowly he put his hand inside his jacket and pulled out the gun. It was too dark to see his eyes but I knew they were filled with hate. He held the gun pointed at me and I am sure he was tempted to shoot – but he relaxed and put it into my outstretched hand.

'There'll be a big reckoning between us when this is all over,' he said.

I remained silent and looked at the gun. It was a Luger, just like my own pistol which I had left in South Africa. I held it on him, and said, 'Now stand very still; I'm going to search you.'

He cursed me, but stood quietly while I tapped his pockets. Sure enough, in his jacket pocket I found a spare magazine. I took the clip from the Luger and snapped the action to see if he had a round up the spout. He had.

He said, 'Morese is sure to have a gun.'

'We'll see about that right now,' I said. 'I'll tackle him and you stand behind him ready to sock him.'

We walked back to the caravan and I called for Francesca and Piero and when they came Coertze unobtrusively stationed himself behind the big Italian. I said to Francesca, 'Has Piero got a gun?'

She looked startled. 'I don't know.' She turned to him. 'Are you carrying a gun, Piero?'

He hesitated, then nodded. I brought up the Luger and held it on him. 'All right, bring it out – slowly.'

He looked at the Luger and his brows drew down angrily, but he obeyed orders and slowly pulled a gun from a shoulder holster. I said, 'This is one time you take orders from me, Piero. Give it to Francesca.'

He passed the pistol to Francesca and I put the Luger away and took it from her. It was an army Beretta, probably a relic of his partisan days. I took the clip out, worked the action and put it in another pocket. Coertze passed two spare clips to me which he had taken from Piero's pockets.

I said to Walker, 'Are you carrying a gun?'

He shook his head.

'Come and be searched.' I was taking no chances.

Walker was bare of guns, so I said, 'Now search the car and see if anything is tucked away there.'

I turned to Francesca. 'Are you carrying anything lethal?'

She folded her arms. 'Are you going to search me, too?'

'No. I'll take your word, if you'll give it.'

She dropped her aggressive pose. 'I haven't a gun,' she said in a low voice.

I said, 'Now listen, everybody. I've taken a gun from Coertze and a gun from Morese. I hold in my hands the ammunition for those guns.' With a quick double jerk I threw the clips away into the darkness and they clattered on a rock. 'If there's going to be any fighting between us it will be with bare fists. Nobody gets killed, do you hear?'

I took the empty pistols from my pockets and gave them back to Coertze and Piero. 'You can use these as hammers to nail the crates up.'

They took them with bad grace and I said, 'We've wasted enough time with this nonsense. Is that car ready?'

'Nothing in here,' said Walker.

As the others were getting into the car, Francesca said to me, 'I'm glad you did that. I didn't know Piero had a gun.'

'I didn't know Coertze had one, either; although I should have guessed – knowing his record.'

'How did you take it from him?' she asked curiously.

'Psychology,' I said. 'He would rather have the gold than kill me. Once he gets the gold it might be a different matter.'

'You will have to be very careful,' she said.

'It's nice to know you care,' I said. 'Let's get in the car.'

II

Coertze drove slowly without lights along the overgrown road until we had turned a corner and were out of sight of the 'main' highway. I could hear the long grass swishing on the underside of the car. Once the first corner was turned he switched on the lights and picked up speed.

No one spoke. Coertze and Morese were mad at me and so was Francesca because of what I'd said. Walker was boiling with ill-suppressed excitement, but he caught the mood of the others and remained quiet. I said nothing because I had nothing to say.

It didn't take long to get to the mine and soon the headlights swept over the ruins of buildings – the shabby remnants of an industrial enterprise. There is nothing more ruinous-looking than derelict factory buildings and neglected machinery. Not that there was much left. The surrounding peasantry must have overrun the place like a swarm of locusts very soon after the mine was abandoned and carried off everything of value. What was left was worth about ten lire and would have cost a hundred thousand lire to take away.

Coertze stopped the car and we all got out. Piero said, 'What kind of mine was this?'

'A lead mine,' said Coertze. 'It was abandoned a long time ago – about 1908, I was told.'

'That was about the time they found the big deposits in Sardinia,' said Piero. 'It was easier to ship ore to the smeltery in Spezia than to rail it from here.'

'Where's your tunnel?' I asked.

Coertze pointed. 'Over there. There were four others besides the one I blocked.'

'We might as well get the car into position,' I said, so Coertze got into the driving seat and edged the car forward. The beams of light swept round and illuminated the caved-in mouth of the tunnel. It looked as though it would need a regiment of pioneers to dig that lot away and it would probably take them a month.

Coertze leaned out of the side window. 'I did a good job there,' he said with satisfaction.

I said, 'You're sure we can get through there in one night?'

'Easy,' he said.

I supposed he knew what he was about – he had been a miner. I went to help Piero and Walker get the tools from the boot and Coertze went to the rockfall and began to examine it. From this time on he took charge and I let him – I knew nothing about the job and he did. His commands were firm-voiced and we all jumped to it with a will.

He said, 'We don't have to dig the whole lot away. I set the charges so that the fall on this side would be fairly thin – not more than ten feet.'

I said, 'Ten feet sounds like a hell of a lot.'

'It's nothing,' he said, contemptuous of my ignorance. 'It isn't as though it was solid rock – this stuff is pretty loose.' He turned and pointed. 'Behind that building you'll find some baulks of timber I sorted out three years ago. You and Morese go and get them. Walker and I will start to dig this stuff out.'

'What can I do?' asked Francesca.

'You can load up the wheelbarrow with the stuff we dig out. Then take it away and scatter it so that it looks natural. Morese is right – we don't want to leave a pile of rocks here.'

Piero and I took torches and found the timber where Coertze had indicated. I thought of Coertze coming here every three or four years, frustrated by a problem he couldn't solve. He must have planned this excavating problem many times and spent hours sorting out this timber in readiness for a job which might never have happened. No wonder he was so touchy.

It took us about an hour to transfer all the timber and by that time Coertze and Walker had penetrated three feet into the rockfall. That was good going, and I said as much. Coertze said, 'It won't be easy as this all the way. We'll have to stop and shore the roof; that'll take time.'

The hole he was digging was not very big; about five feet high and two feet wide – just enough for one man to go through. Coertze began to select his timbers for the shoring and Piero and I helped Francesca to distribute the spoil.

Coertze was right. The shoring of the roof took a long time but it had to be done. It would be bad if the whole thing collapsed and we had to begin all over again; besides, someone might get hurt. A moon rose, making the distribution of the spoil easier, so the car lights were switched off and Coertze was working by the light of the Tilley lamp.

He would not let anyone work at the face except himself, so Walker, Piero and I took it in turns helping him, standing behind him and passing out the loose rocks to the entrance of the passage. After another three hours we had six feet of firmly shored passage drilled through the rockfall and at this stage we broke off for something to eat.

Piero had spoken to me about taking away his gun. He said, 'I was angry when you did it. I do not like to have guns pointed at me.'

'It was empty,' I said.

'That I found out, and it was that which made me angrier.' He chuckled suddenly. 'But I think it was well done, now I have thought about it. It is best if there is no shooting.'

We were some distance from the rockfall. I said, 'Did Francesca tell you about Coertze?'

'Yes. She told me what you said. It is something I have not thought of at all. I was surprised when Donato Rinaldi was found dead that time during the war, but I did not think anyone would have killed him. We were all friends.'

Gold is a solvent which dissolves friendships, I thought, but I could not put that into my limited Italian. Instead, I said, 'From what you know of that time, do you think that Coertze could have killed these four men?'

Piero said, 'He could not have killed Harrison because I myself saw Harrison killed. He was shot by a German and I killed the man who shot him. But the others – Parker, Corso and Rinaldi – yes, I think Coertze could have killed them. He was a man who thought nothing of killing.'

'He could have killed them, but did he?' I asked.

Piero shrugged. 'Who can tell? It was a long time ago and there are no witnesses.'

That was that, and there seemed no point in pressing it, so we returned to our work.

Coertze hurried over his meal so that he could get back to the rock face. His eyes gleamed brightly in the light of the lamp; the lust for gold was strong upon him, for he was within four feet of the treasure for which he had been waiting fifteen years. Walker was as bad; he scrambled to his feet as soon as Coertze made a move and they both hurried to the rockfall.

Piero and Francesca were more placid. They had not seen the gold and mere descriptive words have not that immediacy. Francesca leisurely finished her midnight snack and then collected the dishes and took them to the car.

I said to Piero, 'That is a very strange woman.'

'Any child who was brought up in a guerilla camp would be different,' he said. 'She has had a difficult life.'

I said carefully, 'I understand she has had an unfortunate marriage.'

He spat. 'Estrenoli is a degenerate.'

'Then why did she marry him?'

'The ways of the *aristos* are not our ways,' he said. 'It was an arranged marriage – or so everyone thinks. But that was not really the way of it.'

'What do you mean?'

He accepted a cigarette. 'Do you know what the Communists did to her father?'

'She told me something about it.'

'It was shameful. He was a man, a true man, and they were not fit to lick his boots. And now he is but a shell, an old broken man.' He struck a match and the flame lit up his face. 'Injustice can crush the life from a man even if his body still walks the streets,' he said.

'What has this to do with Francesca's marriage?'

'The old man was against it. He knew the Estrenoli breed. But Madame was insistent on it. You see, young Estrenoli wanted her. There was no love in him, only lust – Madame is a very beautiful woman – and so he wanted her, but he could not get her. She knew what he was.'

This was confusing. 'Then why the hell did she marry him?'

'That was where Estrenoli was clever. He has an uncle in the Government and he said that perhaps they would reconsider the case of her father. But, of course, there was a price.'

'I see,' I said thoughtfully.

'So she married him. I would as soon she married an animal.'

'And he found he could not keep his promise?'

'Could not?' said Piero disgustedly. 'He had no intention of keeping it. The Estrenolis have not kept a promise in the last five hundred years.' He sighed. 'You see, she is a good daughter of the Church and when she married him, Estrenoli knew that he had her for ever. And he was proud of her; oh yes, very proud. She was the most beautiful woman in Roma, and he bought her clothes and dressed her as a child will dress a doll. She was the most expensively dressed mannequin in Italy.'

'And then?'

'And then he got tired of her. He is an unnatural man and he went back to his little boys and his drugs and all the other vices of Roma. Signor Halloran, Roman society is the most corrupt in the world.'

I had heard something of that; there had been a recent case of a drowned girl which threatened to rip apart the whole shoddy mess. But it was said that the Italian Government was intent on hushing it up.

Piero said, 'At that time she helped her father and her old comrades. There were many cases of hardship and she did what she could. But Estrenoli found out and said he would not have his money squandered on a lot of filthy partisans, so he did not give her any more money – not one single lire. He tried to corrupt her, to bring her down to his level, but he could not – she is incorruptible. So then he threw her out on to the street – he had what he wanted, as much as he could get, and he was finished with her.'

'So she came back to Liguria.'

'Yes. We help her when we can because of what she is and because of her father. We also try to help him, but that is difficult because he refuses to accept what he calls charity.'

'And she is still married to Estrenoli?'

'There is no divorce in Italy and she follows the Church. But before God I say the Church is wrong when this can happen.'

I said, 'And so you are helping her in this venture.'

'I think it is wrong and I think she is mistaken,' he said. 'I think many lives will be lost because of this. But I am helping her.'

'This is what is puzzling me,' I said. 'Her father is an old man; this gold cannot help him much.'

'But it is not only for her father,' said Piero. 'She says that the money is for all the men who fought with her father and were cheated by the Communists. She says it will be used to send them to hospitals when that is necessary and to educate their children. It will be a good thing if there is no killing.'

'Yes, it will,' I said reflectively. 'I do not want killing, either, Piero.'

'I know, Signor Halloran; you have already shown that. But there are others – Torloni and this Metcalfe. And there is your friend Coertze.'

'You don't trust him, do you? What about Walker?'

'Pah – a nonentity.'

'And me? Do you trust me?'

He stood and put a foot on his cigarette deliberately. 'I would trust you in another place, Signor Halloran, such as in a boat or on a mountain. But gold is not good for the character.'

He had said in different words what I had thought earlier. I was going to reply when Coertze shouted irately, 'What the hell are you doing out there? Come and get this stuff away.'

So we went on with the work.

III

We broke through at three in the morning. Coertze gave a joyous shout as his pick point disappeared unresistingly into emptiness. Within ten minutes he had broken a hole big enough to crawl through and he went into it like a terrier after a rabbit. I pushed the Tilley lamp through the hole and followed it.

I found Coertze scrambling over fallen rocks which littered the floor of the tunnel. 'Hold on,' I said. 'There's no hurry.'

He took no notice but plunged on into the darkness. There was a clang and he started to swear. 'Bring that bloody light,' he shouted.

I moved forward and the circle of light moved with me. Coertze had run full tilt into the front of a truck. He had gashed his cheek and running blood was making runnels in the dust which coated his face, giving him a maniacal look which was accentuated by the glare of his eyes.

'Here it is,' he cackled. '*Magtig*, what did I tell you? I told you I had gold here. Well, here it is, as much gold as comes out of the Reef in a month.' He looked at me in sudden wonder. '*Christus*, but I'm happy,' he said. 'I never thought I'd make it.'

I could hear the others coming through the hole and I waited for them to come up. 'Kobus Coertze is going to give us a guided tour of his treasure cave,' I said.

Walker said, chattering, 'The gold is in the first truck, this one. Most of it, that is. There's some more, though, in the second one, but most of it is in this one. The jewels are in the second one; lots and lots of necklaces and rings, diamonds and emeralds and pearls and cigarette lighters and cases, all in gold, and there's lots of money, too, lire and dollars and pounds and stuff like that, and there's lots of papers but those are in the trucks right at the back with the bodies . . .' His voice trailed off. 'With the bodies,' he repeated vacantly.

There was a bit of a silence then as we realized that this was a mausoleum as well as a treasure cave. Coertze recovered his usual gravity and took the lamp from me. He held it up and looked at the first truck. 'I should have put it up on blocks,' he observed wryly.

The tyres were rotten and sagging, as flat as I've ever seen tyres. 'You know,' said Coertze, 'when we put this lot in here, my intention was to drive these trucks out some time. I never thought it would be fifteen years.'

He gave a short laugh. 'We'd have a job starting these engines now.'

Walker said impatiently, 'Well, let's get on with it.' He had apparently recovered from the scare he had given himself.

I said, 'We'd better do this methodically, truck by truck. Let's have a look in the first one.'

Coertze led the way, holding up the Tilley lamp. There was just enough room to squeeze between the truck and the side of the tunnel. I noticed the shattered windscreen where a burst of machine-gun fire had killed the driver and his mate. Everything was covered with a heavy layer of dust, most of which must have been deposited when Coertze originally blew in the front of the tunnel.

Coertze was hammering at the bolts of the tailboard with a piece of rock. 'The damn' things have seized solid,' he said. 'I'll need a hammer.'

'Piero,' I called. 'Bring a hammer.'

'I've got one,' said Francesca quietly, so close behind me that I jumped. I took it and passed it on to Coertze. With a few blows the bolt came free and he attacked the other and caught the tailboard as it dropped. 'Right,' he said, 'here we go for the gold,' and vaulted into the truck.

I handed him the lamp and then climbed up and turned to give Francesca a hand. Walker crowded past me, eager to see the gold, while Piero climbed in more sedately. We squatted on our haunches in a circle, sitting on the bullion boxes.

'Where's the one we opened?' asked Coertze. 'It must be at the back somewhere.'

Francesca gave a yelp. 'I've got a nail in my foot.'

'That's the box,' said Coertze with satisfaction.

Francesca moved and Coertze held up the lamp. The box on which Francesca had been sitting had been torn open and the cover roughly replaced. I stretched my hand

and lifted the lid slowly. In the light of the lamp there was the yellow gleam of metal, the dull radiance of gold which rusts not nor doth moth corrupt – rather like treasure laid up in heaven. This gold, however, had been laid up in hell.

Coertze sighed. 'There it is.'

I said to Francesca, 'Did you hurt your foot?'

She was staring at the gold, 'No, it's all right,' she said absently.

Piero lifted an ingot from the box. He misjudged the weight and tried to use one hand; then he got both hands to it and rested the ignot on his thighs. 'It *is* gold!' he said in wonder.

The ingot was passed round the circle and we all handled it and stroked it. I felt a sudden resurgence of the passion I had felt in Aristide's strong-room when I held the heavy gold Hercules in my fingers.

Walker had a kind of terror in his voice. 'How do we know that all these boxes have gold in them? We never looked.'

'I know,' said Coertze. 'I tested the weight of every box fifteen years ago. I made sure all right. There's about three tons of gold in this truck and another ton in the next one.'

The gold had an insidious fascination and we were reluctant to leave it. For Walker and Coertze this was the culmination of the battle which was fought on that dusty road fifteen years previously. For me, it was the end of a tale that had been told many years before in the bars of Cape Town.

I suddenly pulled myself together. It was *not* the end of the tale, and if we wanted the tale to have a happy ending there was still much to do.

'O.K., let's break it up,' I said. 'There's still a lot more to see and a hell of a lot to do.'

The golden spell broken, we went to the next truck and Coertze again hammered the tailboard free. The bullion boxes were hidden this time, lying on the floor of the truck with other boxes piled on top.

'That's the box with the crown in it,' said Walker excitedly.

We all climbed in, squashed at the back of the truck, and Coertze looked round. He suddenly glanced at Francesca and said, 'Open that box and take your pick.' He pointed to a stout case with a broken lock.

She opened the box and gasped. There was a shimmer of coruscating light, the pure white of diamonds, the bright green of emeralds and the dull red of rubies. She stretched forth her hand and picked out the first thing she encountered. It was a diamond and emerald necklace.

She ran it through her fingers. 'How lovely!'

There was a catch in Piero's voice. 'How much would that be worth?' he asked huskily.

'I don't know,' I said. 'Fifty thousand pounds, perhaps. That is, if the stones are real,' I ended sardonically.

Coertze said, 'Get this stuff out, then we can see what we have. I didn't have time when we put it in here.'

'That's a good idea,' I said. 'But you won't have too much time now. It'll be dawn pretty soon, and we don't want to be seen around here.'

We began to pull the boxes out. Coertze had thought-fully left plenty of room between the trucks so that it was easy enough. There were four boxes of jewellery, one filled with nothing else but wedding rings, thousands of them. I had a vague recollection that the patriotic women of Italy had given their wedding rings to the cause – and here they were.

There was the box containing the crown, a massive head-piece studded with jewels. There were eight large cases holding paper currency, neatly packeted and bound with rotting rubber bands. The lire had the original bank wrappers round each bundle. Then there were the remaining bullion boxes on the floor of the truck – another ton of gold.

Francesca went out to the car and brought in some flasks of coffee, and then we sat about examining the loot. The box from which Francesca had taken the necklace was the only one containing jewellery of any great value – but that was enough. I don't know anything about gems, but I conservatively estimated the value of that one box at well over a million pounds.

One of the other boxes was filled with various objects of value, usually in gold, such as pocket watches of bygone design, cigarette cases and lighters, gold medals and medallions, cigar cutters and all the other usual pieces of masculine jewellery. A lot of the pieces were engraved, but with differing names, and I thought that this must be the masculine equivalent of the wedding rings – sacrifices to the cause.

The third box contained the wedding rings and the last one was full of gold currency. There were a lot of British sovereigns and thousands of other coins which I identified as being similar to the coins shown to me by Aristide. There were American eagles and Austrian ducats and even some Tangier Hercules. That was a very heavy box.

Francesca picked up the necklace again. 'Beautiful, isn't it?' I said.

'It's the loveliest thing I've seen,' she breathed.

I took it from her fingers. 'Turn round,' I said, and fastened it round her neck. 'This is the only opportunity you'll have of wearing it; it's a pity to waste it.'

Her shoulders straightened and the triple line of diamonds sparkled against her black sweater. Womanlike, she said, 'Oh, I wish I had a mirror.' Her fingers caressed the necklace.

Walker laughed and staggered to his feet, clutching the crown in both hands. He placed it on Coertze's head, driving the bullet head between the broad shoulders. 'King Coertze,' he cried hysterically. 'All hail.'

Coertze braced under the weight of the crown. *'Nee, man,'* he said, 'I'm a Republican.' He looked straight at me and smiled sardonically. 'There's the king of the expedition.'

To an outsider it would have been a mad sight. Four dishevelled and dirty men, one wearing a golden crown and with drying blood streaking his face, and a not-too-clean woman wearing a necklace worth a queen's ransom. We ourselves were oblivious to the incongruity of the scene; it had been with us too long in our imaginations.

I said, 'Let's think of the next step.'

Coertze lifted his hands and took off the crown. The fun was over; the serious work was to begin again.

'You'll have to finish off the entrance,' I said. 'That last bit isn't big enough to take the loot out.'

Coertze said, *'Ja,* but that won't take long.'

'Nevertheless, it had better be done now; it'll soon be dawn.' I jerked my thumb at the third truck. 'Anything of value back there?'

'There's nothing there but boxes of papers and dead Germans. But you can have a look if you want.'

'I will,' I said, and looked about the tunnel. 'What I suggest is that Walker and I stay here today to get this stuff, sorted out and moved to the front where it'll be easier to get out. It'll save time when the trucks come; I don't want them hanging about here for a long time.'

I had thought out this move carefully. Coertze could be relied upon to keep a close watch on Piero and Francesca and would stand no nonsense from them when they went into Varsi.

But Coertze was immediately suspicious; he didn't want to leave me and Walker alone with the loot. I said, 'Dammit, you'll seal us in, and even if we did make a break the stuff we would carry in our pockets wouldn't be worth worrying about compared with the rest of the treasure. All I want to do is save time.'

After a glowering moment he accepted it, and he and Piero went to complete the entrance. I said to Walker, 'Come on, let's take a look farther back.'

He hesitated, and then said, 'No. I'm not going back there. I'm not.'

'I'll go with you,' said Francesca quietly. 'I'm not afraid of Germans, especially dead ones.' She gave Walker a look of contempt.

I picked up the Tilley lamp and Walker said hysterically, 'Don't take the light.'

'Don't be a damn' fool,' I said. 'Take this to Coertze; it'll suit him better than a torch. You can give him a hand, too.'

As he left I switched on my torch and Francesca did the same. I hefted the hammer and said, 'O.K. Let's frighten all those ghosts.'

The third truck was full of packing cases and weapons. There looked to be enough guns to start a war. I picked up a sub-machine-gun and cocked the action; it was stiff, but it worked and a round flew out of the breech. I thought that my gallant efforts at disarming Coertze and Piero were all wasted, or would have been if Coertze had remembered that all these guns were here. I wondered if the ammunition was still safe to use.

Francesca pushed some rifles aside and pulled the lid off one of the cases. It was full of files – dusty files with the *fasces* of the Fascist Government embossed on the covers. She pulled a file out and started to read, riffling the pages from time to time.

'Anything interesting?' I asked.

'It's about the invasion of Albania,' she said. 'Minutes of the meetings of the Army Staff.' She took another file and became absorbed in it. 'This is the same kind of thing, but it's the Ethiopian campaign.'

I left her to the dusty records of forgotten wars and went back to the fourth truck. It was not pretty. The tunnel was very dry and apparently there had been no rats. The bodies were mummified, the faces blackened and the skin drawn tight into ghastly grins – the rictus of death. I counted the bodies – there were fifteen in the truck, piled in higgledy-piggledy like so many sides of beef – and two in the staff car, one of which was the body of an S.S. officer. There was a wooden case in the back of the truck but I did not investigate it – if it contained anything of value, the dead were welcome to keep it.

I went back to the staff car because I had seen something that interested me. Lying in the back, half hidden by the motor-cycle, was a Schmeisser machine pistol. I picked it up and hefted it thoughtfully in my hand. I was thinking more of Coertze than of Metcalfe and my thoughts weren't pleasant. Coertze was suspected of having killed at least three men in order to get this treasure to himself. There was still the share-out to take place and it was on the cards that he would play the same game at some stage or other. The stake involved was tremendous.

The Schmeisser machine pistol is a very natty weapon which I had seen and admired during the war. It looks exactly like an ordinary automatic pistol and can be used as such, but there is a simple shoulder rest which fits into the holster and which clips into place at the back of the hand-grip so that you can steady the gun at your shoulder.

In principle, this is very much like the old Mauser pistol, but there the resemblance ends. Magazines for the

Schmeisser come in two sizes – one of eight rounds like an ordinary pistol clip – and the long magazine holding about thirty rounds. With the long magazine in place and the gun switched to rapid fire you have a very handy sub-machinegun, most effective at close range.

I had not fired a gun since the war and the thought of something which would make up for my lack of marksmanship by its ability to squirt out bullets was very appealing. I looked round to see if there were any spare clips but I didn't see any. Machine pistols were usually issued to sergeants and junior officers, so I prepared myself for an unpleasant task.

Ten minutes later I had got what I wanted. I had the holster and belt, stiff with neglect, but containing the shoulder rest, four long clips and four short clips. There was another machine pistol, but I left that. I put the gun in the holster and left it resting in a niche in the tunnel wall together with the clips of ammunition. Then I went back to Francesca.

She was still reading the files by the light of her torch. I said, 'Still reading history?'

She looked up. 'It's a pitiful record; all the arguments and quarrels in high places, neatly tabulated and set down.' She shook her head. 'It is best that these files stay here. All this should be forgotten.'

'It's worth a million dollars,' I said, 'if we could find an American university dishonest enough to buy it. Any historian would give his right arm for that lot. But you're right; we can't let it into the world outside – that would really give the game away.'

'What is it like back there?' she asked.

'Nasty.'

'I would like to see,' she said and jumped down from the truck. I remembered the little girl of the war years who hated Germans, and didn't try to stop her.

She came back within minutes, her face pale and her eyes stony, and would not speak of it. A long time afterwards she told me that she had vomited back there in sheer horror at the sight. She thought that the bodies ought to have been given decent burial, even though they were German.

When we got back to the front of the tunnel Coertze had finished his work and the entrance was now big enough to push the cases through. I sent Walker and Francesca back to the caravan to bring up food and bedding, then I took Coertze to one side, speaking in English so that Piero wouldn't understand.

'Is there any way to this mine other than by the road we came?' I asked.

'Not unless you travel cross-country,' he said.

I said, 'You'll stay with Piero and Francesca at the caravan until late afternoon. You'll be able to see if anyone goes up the road; if anyone does you'll have to cut across country damn' quick and warn us, because we may be making a noise here. We'll probably sleep in the afternoon, so it should be all right then.'

'That sounds fair enough,' he said.

'Piero will probably start to look for those ammunition clips I threw away,' I said. 'So you'll have to keep an eye on him. And when you go to Varsi to pick up the trucks, make sure that you all stick together and don't let them talk to anyone unless you're there.'

'*Moenie panik nie,*' he said. 'They won't slip anything over on me.'

'Good,' I said. 'I'm just going to slip out for a breath of fresh air. It'll be the last I'll get for a long time.'

I went outside and strolled about for a while. I thought that everything was going well and if it stayed that way I would be thankful. Only one thing was worrying me. By bringing Francesca and Piero with us, we had cut ourselves

off from our intelligence service and we didn't know what
Metcalfe and Torloni were up to. It couldn't be helped, but
it was worrying all the same.

After a while Piero came from the tunnel and joined me.
He looked at the sky and said, 'It will soon be dawn.'

'Yes,' I said. 'I wish Walker and Francesca would
come back,' I turned to him. 'Piero, something is worrying me.'

'What is it, Signor Halloran?'

I said, 'Coertze! He still has his gun, and I think he will
try to look for those ammunition clips I threw away.'

Piero laughed. 'I will watch him. He will not get out of
my sight.'

And that was that. Those two would be so busy watching
each other that they wouldn't have time to get up to mischief, and they would stay awake to watch the road. I rather
fancied myself as a Machiavelli. I was no longer worrying
too much about Francesca; I didn't think she would double-
cross anyone. Piero was different; as he had said himself –
gold has a bad effect on the character.

A few minutes later, Walker and Francesca came back in
the car bringing food and blankets and some upholstered
cushions from the caravan to use as pillows. I asked Walker
discreetly, 'Any trouble?'

'Nothing,' he said.

The first faint light of morning was in the east. I said,
'Time to go in,' and Walker and I went back into the tunnel.
Coertze began to seal up the entrance and I helped him
from the inside. As the wall of rock grew higher I began to
feel like a medieval hermit being walled up for the good of
his soul. Before the last rocks were put in place Coertze said,
'Don't worry about Varsi, it will be all right.'

I said, 'I'll be expecting you tomorrow at nightfall.'

'We'll be here,' he said. 'You don't think I trust you
indefinitely with all that stuff in there?'

Then the last rock sealed the entrance, but I heard him scuffling about for a long time as he endeavoured to make sure that it looked normal from the outside.

I went back into the tunnel to find Walker elbow deep in sovereigns. He was kneeling at the box, dipping his hands into it and letting the coins fall with a pleasant jingling sound. 'We might as well make a start,' I said. 'We'll get half of the stuff to the front, then have breakfast, then shift the other half. After that we'll be ready for sleep.'

The job had to be done so we might as well do it. Besides, I wanted to get Walker dead tired so that he would be heavily asleep, when I went to retrieve the Schmeisser.

The first thing we did was to clear the fallen rock from in front of the first truck. This would be our working space when we had to disguise the bullion boxes and recrate the other stuff. We worked quickly without chatting. There was no sound except our heavy breathing, the subdued roar of the Tilley lamp and the occasional clatter of a rock.

After an hour we had a clear space and began to bring the gold to the front. Those bullion boxes were damnably heavy and needed careful handling. One of them nearly fell on Walker's foot before I evolved the method of letting them drop from the lorry on to the piled-up caravan cushions. The cushions suffered but that was better than a broken foot.

It was awkward getting them to the front of the tunnel. The space between the lorry and the wall was too narrow for the two of us to carry a box together and the boxes were a little too heavy for one man to carry himself. I swore at Coertze for having reversed the trucks into the tunnel.

Eventually I hunted round among the trucks and found a long towing chain which we fastened round each box in turn so that we could pull it along the ground. The work went faster then.

After we had emptied all the gold from the first truck and had taken it to the front, I declared a breakfast break. Francesca had prepared a hot meal and there was plenty of coffee. As we ate we conversed desultorily.

'What will you do with your share?' I asked Walker curiously.

'Oh, I don't know,' he said. 'I haven't any real plans. I'll have a hell of a good time, I'll tell you that.'

I grimaced. The bookmakers would take a lot of it, I guessed, and the distillers would show a sudden burst in their profits for the first year, and then Walker would probably be dead of cirrhosis of the liver and delirium tremens.

'I'll probably do a lot of travelling,' he said. 'I've always wanted to travel. What will you do?'

I leaned my head back dreamily. 'Half a million is a lot of money,' I said. 'I'd like to design lots of boats, the experimental kind that no one in their right minds would touch with a barge pole. A big cruising catamaran, for instance; there's a lot of work to be done in that field. I'd have enough money to have any design tank-tested as it should be done. I might even finance a private entry for the America's Cup – I've always wanted to design a 12-metre, and wouldn't it be a hell of a thing if my boat won?'

'You mean you'd go on *working?* said Walker in horror.

'I like it,' I said. 'It's not work if you like it.'

And so we planned our futures, going from vision to wilder vision until I looked at my watch and said, 'Let's get cracking; the sooner we finish, the sooner we can sleep.' It was nine o'clock and I reckoned we would be through by midday.

We moved the gold from the third truck. This was a longer haul and so took more time. After that it was easy and soon there was nothing left except the boxes of paper currency. Walker looked at them and said hesitantly, 'Shouldn't we. . .?'

'Nothing doing,' I said sharply. 'I'd burn the lot if I was sure no one would see the smoke.'

He seemed troubled at the heresy of someone wanting to burn money and set himself to count it while I got my blankets together and prepared for sleep. As I lay down, he said suddenly, 'There's about a thousand million lire here – that's a hell of a lot of money. And there's any amount of sterling. Thousands of British fivers.'

I yawned. 'What colour are they?'

'White,' he said. 'The biggest notes I've ever seen.'

'You pass one of those and you're for the high jump,' I said. 'They changed the design of the fiver when they discovered that the Germans had forged God knows how many millions. Come to think of it, it's quite likely that those are of German manufacture.'

He seemed disappointed at that, and I said, 'Get some sleep; you'll be glad of it later.'

He gathered his blankets and settled himself down. I lay awake, fighting off sleep, until I heard the slow, regular breathing of deep slumber, then I got up and softly made my way down the tunnel. I retrieved the Schmeisser and the clips and brought them back. I didn't know where to put them at first, then I found that the cushion I was using as a pillow was torn and leaking stuffing. I tore out some more of the stuffing and put the gun and the clips inside. It made a hard pillow, but I didn't mind that – if people were going to wave guns at me, I wanted one to wave back.

IV

Neither of us slept very well – we had too much on our minds. I lay, turning restlessly, and hearing Walker doing the same until, at last, we could stand it no longer and we abandoned the pretence of sleep. It was four in the afternoon and I reckoned that the others should be starting for Varsi just about then.

We went up to the front of the tunnel and checked everything again, then settled to wait for nightfall. It could have been night then, if my watch hadn't told us otherwise, because there was no light in the tunnel except for the bright circle cast by the lamp, which quickly faded into darkness.

Walker was nervous. Twice he asked me if I heard a noise, not from the entance but from back in the tunnel. The bodies of the men he had killed were worrying him. I told him to go back and look at them, thinking the shock treatment might do him good, but he refused to go.

At last I heard a faint noise from the entrance. I took the hammer in my hand and waited – this might not be Coertze at all. A rock clattered and a voice said, 'Halloran?'

I relaxed and blew my cheeks out. It *was* Coertze.

Another rock clattered and I said, 'Is everything all right?'

'No trouble at all,' he said, furiously pulling down the screen of rocks. 'The trucks are here.'

Walker and I helped to push down the wall from the inside and Coertze shone a torch in my face. 'Man,' he said. 'But you need a clean-up, ay.'

I could imagine what I looked like. We had no water for washing and the dust lay heavily upon us. Francesca stood next to Coertze. 'Are you all right, Mr Halloran?'

'I'm O.K. Where are the trucks?'

She moved, barely distinguishable in the darkness. 'They are back there.'

'There are four Italians,' said Coertze.

'Do they know what they are doing here?' I asked swiftly.

Piero loomed up. 'They know that this is secret, and therefore certainly illegal,' he said. 'But otherwise they know nothing.'

I thought about that. 'Tell two of them to go down to the caravan, strike camp, and then wait there. Tell them to keep a watch on the road and to warn us if anyone comes up. The other two must go into the hills overlooking the mine, one to the left, the other to the right. They must watch for anyone coming across country. This is the tricky part and we don't want anyone surprising us when the gold is in the open.'

Piero moved away and I heard him giving quick instructions. I said, 'The rest of us will start work inside. Bring the timber from the trucks.'

The trucks were all right, bigger than we needed. One of them was loaded with lengths of rough boxwood and there were also some crude crates that would do for putting the loose stuff in. We hauled out the wood and took it into the tunnel, together with the tools – a couple of saws, four hammers and several packets of nails – and we started to nail covers on to the bullion boxes, changing their shape and character.

With four of us it went quickly and, as we worked, we developed an assembly-line technique. Walker sawed the wood into the correct lengths, Coertze nailed on the bottoms and the tops, I put on the sides and Piero put on the ends. Francesca was busy transferring the jewels and the gold trivia from the original boxes into the crates.

Within three hours we had finished and all there was left to do was to take the boxes outside and load them into the trucks.

I rolled my blankets and took my pillow outside and thrust them behind the driving-seat of one of the trucks – that disposed of the Schmeisser very nicely.

The boxes were heavy but Coertze and Piero had the muscle to hoist them vertically into the trucks and to stow them neatly. Walker and I used the chain again to pull the boxes through the narrow entrance. Francesca produced some flasks of coffee and a pile of cut sandwiches and we ate and drank while we worked. She certainly believed in feeding the inner man.

At last we were finished. I said, 'Now we must take away from the tunnel everything we have brought here. We mustn't leave a scrap of evidence that we have been here, not a thing that can be traced back to us.'

So we all went back into the tunnel and collected everything – blankets, cushions, tools, torches, flasks, even the discarded bent nails and the fragments of stuffing from the torn cushions. All this went outside to be stowed in the trucks and I stayed behind to take one last look round. I picked up a length of wood that had been forgotten and turned to leave.

Then it happened.

Coertze must have been hasty in shoring up the last bit of the entrance – he had seen the gold and his mind wasn't on his job. As I turned to leave, the piece of timber I was carrying struck the side of the entrance and dislodged a rock. There was a warning creak and I started to run – but it was too late.

I felt a heavy blow on my shoulder which drove me to my knees. There was a rumble of falling rock and then I knew no more.

V

I came round fuzzily, hearing a voice, 'Halloran, are you all right? Halloran!'

Something soft touched my cheek and then something cold and wet. I groaned and opened my eyes but everything was hazy. The back of my head throbbed and waves of pain washed forward into my eyes.

I must have passed out again, but the next time I opened my eyes things were clearer. I heard Coertze saying, 'Can you move your legs, man; can you move your legs?'

I tried. I didn't understand why I should move my legs but I tried. They seemed to move all right so, dizzily, I tried to get up. I couldn't! There was a weight on my back holding me down.

Coertze said, 'Man, now take it easy. We'll get you out of there, ay.'

He seemed to move away and then I heard Francesca's voice. 'Halloran, you must stay quiet and not move. Can you hear me?'

'I can hear you,' I mumbled. 'What happened?' I found it difficult to speak because the right side of my face was lying on something rough and hard.

'You are pinned down by a lot of rock,' she said. 'Can you move your legs?'

'Yes, I can move my legs.'

She went away and I could hear her talking to someone. My wits were coming back and I realized that I was lying prone with a heavy weight on my back and my head turned so that my right cheek was lying on rock. My right arm was by my side and I couldn't move it; my left arm was raised, but it seemed to be wedged tight.

Francesca came back and said, 'Now, you must listen carefully. Coertze says that if your legs are free then you are only held in your middle. He is going to get you out, but it will be very slow and you mustn't move. Do you understand?'

'I understand,' I said.

'How do you feel? Is there pain?' Her voice was low and gentle.

'I feel sort of numb,' I said. 'All I feel is a lot of pressure on my back.'

'I've got some brandy. Would you like some?'

I tried to shake my head and found it impossible. 'No,' I said. 'Tell Coertze to get cracking.'

She went away and Coertze came back. 'Man,' he said. 'You're in a spot, ay. But not to worry, I've done this sort of thing before. All you have to do is keep still.'

He moved and then I heard the scrape of rock and there was a scattering of dust on my face.

It took a long time. Coertze worked slowly and carefully, removing rocks one at a time, testing each one before he took it away. Sometimes he would go away and I would hear a low-voiced conversation, but he always came back to work again with a slow patience.

At last he said, 'It won't be long now.'

He suddenly started to shovel away rocks with more energy and the weight on my back eased. It was a wonderful feeling. He said, 'I'm going to pull you out now. It might hurt a bit.'

'Pull away,' I said.

He grasped my left arm and tugged. I moved. Within two minutes I was in the open air looking at the fading stars. I tried to get up, but Francesca said, 'Lie still.'

Dawn was breaking and there was enough light to see her face as she bent over me. The winged eyebrows were drawn down in a frown as her hands pressed gently on my body testing for broken bones. 'Can you turn over?' she asked.

It hurt, but I turned on to my stomach and heard the rip as she cut away my shirt. Then I heard the sudden hiss of her breath. 'Your back is lacerated badly,' she said.

I could guess how badly. Her hands were soft and gentle as they moved over my back. 'You haven't broken anything,' she said in wonderment.

I grinned. To me it felt as though my back was broken and someone had built a fire on it, but to hear that there were no broken bones was good. She tore some cloth and began to bind the wounds and when she had finished I sat up.

Coertze held out a baulk of six-by-six. 'You were damned lucky, man. This was across your back and kept the full weight of the rock off you.'

I said, 'Thanks, Kobus.'

He coloured self-consciously and looked away. 'That's all right – Hal,' he said. It was the first time he had ever called me Hal.

He looked at the sky. 'We had better move now.' He appealed to Francesca. 'Can he move?'

I got to my feet slowly. 'Of course I can move,' I said. Francesca made a sudden gesture which I ignored. 'We've got to get out of here.'

I looked at the tunnel. 'You'd better bring down the rest of that little lot and make a good job of it. Then we'll leave.'

Coertze went off towards the tunnel, and I said, 'Where's Walker?'

Piero said, 'He is sitting in a truck.'

'Send him down to the caravan, and whistle up your other two boys – they can go with him. They can all leave now for Rapallo.'

Piero nodded and went away. Francesca said, 'Hadn't you better rest a little?'

'I can rest in Rapallo. Can you drive one of those?' I nodded towards a truck.

'Of course.'

'Good. Coertze and Piero can take one; we'll take the other. I might not be able to manage the driving part, though.'

I didn't want Piero and Francesca alone, and I wanted Walker to keep a watch on the other Italians. Of course, I could have gone as passenger with Piero, but if he tried anything rough I was no match for him in my beat-up condition. Coertze could cope with him – so that left me with Francesca.

'I can manage,' she said.

There was a rumble from the tunnel as Coertze pulled in the entrance, sealing it for ever, I hoped. He came back and I said, 'You go with Piero in that truck; he'll be back in a minute. And don't tail me too close; we don't want to look like a convoy.'

He said, 'Think you'll be all right?'

'I'll be O.K.,' I said, and walked stiffly towards the truck in which I had left my gear. It was a painful business getting into the cab, but I managed in the end and rested gingerly in the seat, not daring to lean back. Francesca swung easily into the driving seat and slammed the door. She looked at me and I waved my hand. 'Off we go.'

She started the engine and got off badly by grinding the gears, and we went bouncing down the road from the mine, the rising sun shining through the wind-screen.

The journey back to Rapallo was no joy-ride for me. The truck was uncomfortable as only trucks can be at the best of times, and for me it was purgatory because I was unable to lean back in the seat. I was very tired, my limbs were sore and aching, and my back was raw. Altogether I was not feeling too bright.

Although Francesca had said that she could drive the truck, she was not doing too well. She was used to the synchromesh gears of a private car and had a lot of trouble in changing the gears of the truck. To take my mind off my troubles we slowed down and I taught her how to double-declutch and after that things went easier and we began to talk.

She said, 'You will need a doctor, Mr Halloran.'

'My friends call me Hal,' I said.

She glanced at me and raised her eyebrows. 'Am I a friend now?'

'You didn't kick me in the teeth when I was stuck in the tunnel,' I said. 'So you're my friend.'

She slanted her eyes at me. 'Neither did Coertze.'

'He still needs me. He can't get the gold out of Italy without me.'

'He *was* very perturbed,' she agreed. 'But I don't think he had the gold on his mind.' She paused while she negotiated a bend. 'Walker had the gold on his mind, though. He sat in a truck all the time, ready to drive away quickly. A contemptible little man.'

I was too bemused by my tiredness to take in the implications of all this. I sat watching the ribbon of road unroll and I lapsed into an almost hypnotic condition. One of the things which fleetingly passed through my mind was that I hadn't seen the cigarette case which Walker had spoken of many years previously – the cigarette case which Hitler was supposed to have presented to Mussolini at the Brenner Pass in 1940.

I thought of the cigarette case once and then it passed from my mind, not to return until it was too late to do anything about it.

SIX: METCALFE

The next day I felt better.

Everybody had got back to Palmerini's boatyard without untoward happenstance and we had moved into the big shed that was reserved for us. The trucks had been unloaded and returned to their owners with thanks, and the caravan stayed in a corner to provide cooking and sleeping space.

But I was in no shape to do much work, so Walker and Coertze went to bring *Sanford* from the yacht basin, after I had checked on Metcalfe and Torloni. Francesca spoke to Palmerini and soon a procession of Italians slipped into the yard to make their reports. They spoke seriously to Francesca and ducked out again, obviously delighting in their return to the role of partisans.

When she had absorbed all they could tell her, Francesca came to me with a set face. 'Luigi is in hospital,' she said unhappily. 'They broke his skull.'

Poor Luigi. Torloni's men had not bothered to bribe him, after all. The harbour police were searching for the assailants but had had no success; and they wanted to see me to find out what had been stolen. As far as they were concerned it was just another robbery.

Francesca had an icy coldness about her. 'We know who they were,' she said. 'They will not walk out of Rapallo on their own legs.'

'No,' I said. 'Leave them alone.' I didn't want to show my hand yet because, with any luck, Metcalfe and Torloni might have fallen for the story I had planted. And for some reason, not yet clearly defined in my mind, I didn't want Francesca openly associated with us – she would still have to live in Italy when we had gone.

'Don't touch them,' I said. 'We'll take care of them later. What about Metcalfe and Torloni?'

They were still in Genoa and saw each other every day. When they had found out that we had disappeared from Rapallo they had rushed up another three men, making five in all. Metcalfe had pulled the Fairmile from the water and Krupke was busy repainting the bottom. The Arab, Moulay Idriss, had vanished; no one knew where he was, but he was certainly not in Rapallo.

That all seemed satisfactory – except for the reinforcement of Torloni's men in Rapallo. I called Coertze and told him what was happening. 'When you go to get *Sanford* tell the police that I've had a climbing accident, and that I'm indisposed. Make a hell of a fuss about the burglary, just as though you were an honest man. Go to the hospital, see Luigi and tell him that his hospital bill will be paid and that he'll get something extra for damages.'

Coertze said, 'Let me *donner* those bastards. They needn't have hit that old man.'

'Don't go near them,' I said. 'I'll let you loose later, just before we sail.'

He grumbled but held still, and he and Walker went to see what damage had been done to *Sanford*. After they had gone I had a talk with Piero. 'You heard about Luigi?'

He pulled down his mouth. 'Yes, a bad business – but just like Torloni.'

I said, 'I am thinking we might need some protection here.'

'That is taken care of,' he said. 'We are well guarded.'

'Does Francesca know about this?'

He shook his head. 'Women do not know how to do these things – I will tell Madame when it is necessary. But this boatyard is well guarded; I can call on ten men within fifteen minutes.'

'They'll have to be strong and tough men to fight Torloni's gangsters.'

His face cracked into a grim smile. 'Torloni's men know nothing,' he said contemptuously. 'The men I have called are fighting men; men who have killed armed Germans with their bare hands. I would feel sorry for Torloni's gang were it not for Luigi.'

I felt satisfied at that. I could imagine the sort of dock rats Torloni would have working for him; they wouldn't stand a chance against disciplined men accustomed to military tactics.

I said, 'Remember, we want no killing.'

'There will be no killing if they do not start it first. After that . . .?' He shrugged. 'I cannot be responsible for the temper of the men.'

I left him and went into the caravan to clean and oil the Schmeisser. The tunnel had been dry and the gun hadn't taken much harm. I was more dubious about the ammunition; wondering if the charges behind the bullets had suffered chemical deterioration over the past fifteen years. That was something I would find out when the shooting started.

But perhaps there would be no shooting. There was a fair chance that Metcalfe and Torloni knew nothing of our connection with the partisans – I had worked hard enough to cover it. If Torloni attacked he would get the surprise of his life, but I hoped he wouldn't – I didn't want the Italians involved too much.

Coertze and Walker brought *Sanford* to the yard in the late afternoon and Palmerini's sons got busy slipping her and unstepping the mast. Coertze said, 'We were followed by a fast launch.'

'So they know we are here?'

'Ja,' he said, 'But we made them uncomfortable.'

Walker said, 'We took her out, and they had to follow us because they thought we were leaving. There was a bit of a lop outside the harbour and they were sea-sick – all three of them.' He grinned. 'So was Coertze.'

'Did they do much damage to *Sanford* when they broke in?'

'Not much,' replied Coertze. 'They turned everything out of the lockers, but the police had cleaned up after the pigs.'

'The furnaces?'

'All right; those were the first things I checked.'

That was a relief. The furnaces were now the king-pins of the plan and if they had gone the whole of our labour would have been wasted. There would have been no time to replace them and still meet the deadline of Tangier. As it was, we would have to work fast.

Coertze got busy getting the furnaces out of *Sanford*. It wasn't a long job and soon he was assembling them on a bench in the corner of the shed. Piero looked at them uncomprehendingly but said nothing.

I realized it would be pointless to try to conceal our plan from him and Francesca – it just couldn't be done. And in any case, I was getting a bit tired of the shroud of suspicion with which I had cloaked myself. The Italians had played fair with us so far and we were entirely at their mercy, anyway; they could take the lot any time they wanted if they felt so inclined.

I said, 'We're going to cast a new keel for *Sanford*.'

Piero said, 'Why? What is wrong with that one?'

'Nothing, except it's made of lead. I'm a particular man – I want a keel of gold.'

His face lit up in a delighted smile. 'I wondered how you were going to get the gold out of the country. I thought about it and could see no way, but you seemed so sure.'

'Well, that's how we're going to do it,' I said, and went over to Coertze. 'Look,' I said. 'I'm not going to be good for any heavy work over the next few days. I'll assemble these gadgets – it's a sitting job – you'd better be doing something else. What about the mould?'

'I'll get started on that,' he said. 'Palmerini has plenty of moulding sand.'

I unfastened my belt and, from the hidden pocket, I took the plan of the new keel I had designed many months previously. I said, 'I had Harry make the alterations to the keelson to go with the new keel. He thought I was nuts. All you've got to do is to cast the keel to this pattern and it'll fit sweetly.'

He took the drawing and went off to see Palmerini. I started to assemble the furnaces – it wasn't a long job and I finished that night.

II

I suppose that few people have had occasion to cut up gold ingots with a hacksaw. It's a devilish job because the metal is soft and the teeth of the saw blades soon become clogged. Walker said it was like sawing through treacle.

It had to be done because we could only melt a couple of pounds of gold at a time, and it was Walker's job to cut up the ingots into nice handy pieces. The gold dust was a problem which I solved by sending out for a small vacuum cleaner which Walker used assiduously, sucking up every particle of gold he could find.

And when he had finished sawing for the day he would sweep round his bench and wash the dust in a pan just like an old-time prospector. Even with all those precautions I reckon we must have wasted several pounds of gold in the sawing operation.

We all gathered round to watch the first melt. Coertze dropped the small piece of gold on to the graphite mat and switched on the machine. There was an intense white flare as the mat went incandescent and the gold drooped and flowed and, within seconds, was ready for pouring into the mould.

The three furnaces worked perfectly but as they were only laboratory instruments after all, and could only take a small amount at a time, it was going to be a long job. Inside the mould we put a tangle of wires which was to hold the gold together. Coertze was dubious about the method of pouring so little at a time and several times he stopped and removed gold already poured.

'This keel will be so full of faults and cracks I don't think it'll hold,' he said.

So we put in more and more wires and poured the gold round them, hoping they would bind the mass together.

I was stiff and sore and to bend was an agony, so there was not much I could do to help effectively. I discussed this with Coertze, and said, 'You know, one of us had better show his face in Rapallo. Metcalfe knows we're here and it'll look odd if we all stay in this shed and never come out. He'll know we're up to something.'

'You'd better wander round town then,' said Coertze. 'You can't do much here.'

So after Francesca had rebandaged my back, I went into town and up to the Yacht Club. The secretary commiserated with me on the fact that *Sanford* had been broken into and hoped that nothing had been stolen. 'It cannot have been done by men of Rapallo,' he said. 'We are very strict about that here.'

He also looked at my battered face in mute inquiry, so I smiled and said, 'Your Italian mountains seem to be made of harder rock than those in South Africa.'

'Ah, you've been climbing?'

'Trying to,' I said. 'Allow me to buy you a drink.'

He declined, so I went into the bar and ordered a Scotch, taking it to the table by the window where I could look over the yacht basin. There was a new boat in, a large motor yacht of about a hundred tons. You see many of those in the Mediterranean – the luxury boats of the wealthy. They put to sea in the calmest of weather and the large paid crews have the life of Reilly – hardly any work and plenty of shore time. Idly, I focused the club binoculars on her. Her name was *Calabria*.

When I left the club I spotted my watchers and took delight in leading them to innocent places which any tourist might have visited. If I had been fitter I would have walked their legs off, but I compromised by taking a taxi. Their staff-work was good, because I noticed a cruising car come up from nowhere and pick them up smoothly.

I went back and reported to Francesca. She said, 'Torloni has sent more men into Rapallo.'

That sounded bad. 'How many?'

'Three more – that makes eight. We think that he wants enough men to follow each of you, even if you split up. Besides, they must sleep sometimes, too.'

'Where's Metcalfe?'

'Still in Genoa. His boat was put into the water this morning.'

'Thanks, Francesca, you're doing all right,' I said.

'I will be glad when this business is finished,' she said sombrely. 'I wish I had never started it.'

'Getting cold feet?'

'I do not understand what you mean by that; but I am afraid there will be much violence soon.'

'I don't like it, either,' I said candidly. 'But the thing is under way; we can't stop now. You Italians have a phrase for it – *che sera, sera.*'

She sighed. 'Yes, in a matter like this there is no turning back once you have begun.'

I left her sitting in the caravan, thinking that she was beginning to realize that this was no light-hearted adventure she had embarked upon. This was deadly serious, a game for high stakes in which a few murders would not be boggled at, at least, not by the opposition – and I wasn't too sure about Coertze.

The keel seemed to be going well. Coertze and Piero were sweating over the hot furnaces, looking demoniacal in the sudden bursts of light. Coertze pushed up his goggles and said, 'How many graphite mats did we have?'

'Why?'

'They don't last long. I'm not getting more than four melts out of each, then they burn out. We might run out of mats before the job's finished.'

'I'll check on it,' I said, and went to figure with pencil and paper. After checking my calculations and recounting the stock of mats I went back to Coertze. 'Can you squeeze five melts out of a mat?'

He grunted. 'We'll have to be careful about it, which means we'll be slower. Can we afford the time?'

'If we burn out the mats before the job's done then the time won't matter – it'll be wasted anyway. We'll have to afford the time. How many melts a day can you do at five melts to a mat?'

He thought about that. 'It'll cut us down to twelve melts an hour, no more than that.'

I went away to do some more figuring. Taking the gold at 9000 pounds, that meant 4,500 melts of which Coertze had already done 500. Twelve melts an hour meant 340 working hours – at twelve hours a day, twenty-eight days.

Too long – start again.

Three hundred and forty hours working at sixteen hours a day – twenty-one days. But could he work sixteen hours

a day? I cursed my lacerated back which kept me from helping, but if anything happened and it got worse then I was
sure the plan would be torpedoed. Somebody had to take
Sanford out and I had an increasing distrust of Walker, who
had grown silent and secretive.

I went back to Coertze, walking stiffly because my back
was hurting like hell. 'You'll have to work long hours,'
I said. 'Time's running out.'

'I'd work twenty-four hours a day if I could,' he said.
'But I can't, so I'll work till I drop.'

I thought maybe I'd better go at it a different way, so
I stood back and watched how Coertze and Piero were
going about the job. Soon I had ideas about speeding
it up.

The next morning I took charge. I told Coertze to do
nothing but pour gold; he must not have anything to do
with loading the furnaces or cleaning mats – all he had to
do was pour gold. Piero I assigned to melting the gold and
to passing the furnace with the molten gold to Coertze. The
furnaces were light enough to be moved about so I arranged
a table so that they could move bodily along it.

Walker had sawn plenty of gold, so I pulled him from his
bench. He had to take a furnace from Coertze, replace the
mat with a new one and put a chunk of gold on it ready for
melting. Myself I set to the task of cleaning the used mats
ready for re-use – this I could do sitting down.

All in all, it was a simple problem in time and motion
study and assembly line technique. By the end of the day
we were doing sixteen melts an hour without too many
burnt-out mats.

So the days went by. We started by working sixteen
hours a day but we could not keep it up and gradually our
daily output dropped in spite of the increase in the hourly
output. Mistakes were made in increasing numbers and
the percentage of burnt-out mats went up sharply.

Working in those sudden bursts of heat from the furnaces was hellish; we all lost weight and our thirst was unquenchable.

When the output dropped below 150 melts a day with another 2000 to go I began to get really worried. I wanted a clear three weeks to sail to Tangier and it looked as though I was not going to get them.

Obviously something had to be done.

That evening, when we were eating supper after finishing work for the day, and before we turned exhaustedly into our berths, I said, 'Look, we're too tired. We're going to have a day off, tomorrow. We do nothing at all – we just laze about.'

I was taking a chance, gambling that the increased output by refreshed men would more than offset the loss of a day. But Coertze said bluntly. 'No, we work. We haven't the time to waste.'

Coertze was a good man if a bit bull-headed. I said, 'I've been right up to now, haven't I?'

He grudgingly assented to that.

'The output will go up if we have a rest,' I said. 'I promise you.'

He grumbled a little, but didn't press it – he was too tired to fight. The others agreed lacklustrely, and we turned in that night knowing that the next day would be a day of rest.

III

At breakfast, next morning, I asked Francesca, 'What's the enemy doing?'

'Still watching.'

'Any reinforcements?'

She shook her head, 'No, there's just the eight of them. They take it in turns.'

I said, 'We might as well give them some exercise. We'll split up and run them about town, or even outside it. They've been having it too easy lately.'

I looked at Coertze. 'But don't touch them – we're not ready to force a showdown yet, and the later it comes the better for us. We can't afford for any one of us to be put out of action now; if that happens we're sunk. It'll take all our time to cast the keel and meet the deadline as it is.'

To Walker I said, 'And you keep off the booze. You might be tempted, but don't do it. Remember what I said in Tangier?'

He nodded sullenly and looked down at his plate. He had been too quiet lately to suit me and I wondered what he was thinking.

I said to Francesca, 'I thought you were getting a jeweller to appraise the gems.'

'I will see him today,' she said. 'He will probably come tomorrow.'

'Well, when he comes, it must be in disguise or something. Once Torloni's men know that there are jewels involved there may be no holding them.'

Piero said, 'Palmerini will bring him hidden in a lorry.'

'Good enough.' I got up from the table and stretched. 'Now to confuse the issue and the enemy. We'll all leave in different directions. Piero, you and Francesca had better leave later; we don't want any connection to be made between us. Will this place be safe with us all gone?'

Francesca said, 'There'll be ten of our men in the yard all day.'

'That's fine,' I said. 'Tell them not to be too conspicuous.'

I felt fine as I walked into town. My back was healing and my face no longer looked like a battlefield. I was exhilarated at the prospect of a day off work and Coertze must have been feeling even better, I thought. He had not left

Palmerini's yard since he had brought *Sanford* in, while I had had several visits to town.

I spent the morning idling, doing a little tourist shopping in the Piazza Cavour where I found a shop selling English books. Then I had a lengthy stay at a boulevard café where I leisurely read a novel over innumerable cups of coffee, something I had not had time for for many months.

Towards midday I went up to the Yacht Club for a drink. The bar seemed noisier than usual and I traced the disturbance to an argumentative and semi-drunken group at the far end of the room. Most members were pointedly ignoring this demonstration but there were raised eyebrows at the more raucous shouts. I ordered a Scotch from the steward and said, 'Why the celebration?'

He sneered towards the end of the bar. 'No celebration, signor; just idle drunkenness.'

I wondered why the secretary didn't order the men from the club and said so. The steward lifted his shoulders helplessly. 'What can one do, signor? There are some men who can break all rules – and here is one such man.'

I didn't press it; it was no affair of mine and it wasn't my business to tell the Italians how to run the club in which I was their guest. But I did take my drink into the adjoining lounge where I settled down to finish the novel.

It was an interesting book, but I never did get it finished, and I've often wondered how the hero got out of the predicament in which the author placed him. I had not read half a dozen pages when a steward came up and said, 'There is a lady to see you, signor.'

I went into the foyer and saw Francesca. 'What the devil are you doing here?' I demanded.

'Torloni is in Rapallo,' she said.

I was going to speak when the club secretary came round the corner and saw us. I said, 'You'd better come inside; it's too damn' conspicuous here.'

The secretary hurried over, saying, 'Ah, Madame, we have not had the honour of a visit from you for a long time.'

I was a member of the club – if only honourary – so I said, 'Perhaps I could bring Madame into the club as my guest?'

He looked unaccountably startled and said nervously, 'Yes, yes, of course. No, there is no need for Madame to sign the book.'

As I escorted Francesca into the lounge I wondered what was agitating the secretary, but I had other things on my mind so I let it slide. I seated Francesca and said, 'You'd better have a drink.'

'Campari,' she said, and then quickly, 'Torloni brought a lot of men with him.'

'Relax,' I said, and ordered a Campari from the lounge steward. When he had left the table I said, 'What about Metcalfe?'

'The Fairmile left Genoa; we don't know where it is.'

'And Torloni? Where is he?'

'He booked into a hotel on the Piazza Cavour an hour ago.'

That was when I had been sitting in the pavement café. I might even have seen him. I said, 'You say he brought some men with him?'

'There are eight men with him.'

That was bad; it looked as though an attack was building up. Eight plus eight made sixteen, plus Torloni himself and possibly Metcalfe, Krupke, the Moroccan and what other crew the Fairmile might have. More than twenty men!

She said, 'We had to work quickly. There was a lot of reorganizing to do – that is why I came here myself, there was no one else.'

I said, 'Just how many men have *we* got?'

She furrowed her brow. 'Twenty-five – possibly more later. I cannot tell yet.'

That sounded better; the odds were still in our favour. But I wondered about Torloni's massing of force. He would not need so many men to tackle three presumably unsuspecting victims, therefore he must have got wind of our partisan allies, so perhaps we wouldn't have the advantage of surprise.

The steward came with the Campari and as I paid him Francesca looked from the window over the yacht basin. When the steward had gone, she said, 'What ship is that?'

'Which one?'

She indicated the motor yacht I had noticed on my earlier visit to the club. 'Oh, that! It's just some rich man's floating brothel.'

Her voice was strained. 'What is the name?'

I hunted in my memory. 'Er – *Calabria*, I think.'

Her knuckles were clenched white as she gripped the arms of her chair. 'It is Eduardo's boat,' she said in a low voice.

'Who is Eduardo?'

'My husband.'

A light dawned on me. So that was why the secretary had been so startled. It is not very usual for a stranger to ask a lady to be his guest when the lady's husband is within easy reach and possibly in the club at that very moment. I chuckled and said, 'I'll bet he's the chap who is kicking up such a shindy in the bar.'

She said, 'I must go.'

'Why?'

'I do not wish to meet him.' She pushed her drink to one side and picked up her handbag.

I said, 'You might as well finish your drink. It's the first drink I've ever bought you. No man is worth losing a drink over, anyway.'

She relaxed and picked up the Campari. 'Eduardo is not worth anything,' she said tightly. 'All right, I will be civilized and finish my drink; then I will go.'

But we did meet him, after all. Only an Estrenoli – from what I had heard of the breed – would have paused dramatically in the doorway, veered over to our table and have addressed Francesca as he did.

'Ah, my loving wife,' he said. 'I'm surprised to find you here in civilized surroundings. I thought you drank in the gutters.'

He was a stocky man, with good looks dissipated by red-veined eyes and a slack mouth. A wispy moustache disfigured his upper lip and his face was flushed with drink. He ignored me altogether.

Francesca looked stonily ahead, her lips compressed, and did not turn to face him even when he dropped heavily into a chair by her side.

I said, 'You weren't invited to sit with us, signor.'

He swung round and gave a short laugh, looking at me with an arrogant stare. He turned back to Francesca. 'I see that even the Italian scum is not good enough for you now; you must take foreign lovers.'

I stretched out my foot and hooked it behind the rung of his chair, then pulled hard. The chair slid from under him and he tumbled on to the floor and sprawled full length. I got up and stood over him. 'I said you weren't invited to sit down.'

He looked up at me, his face suffused with anger, and slowly scrambled to his feet. Then he glared at me. 'I'll have you out of the country within twenty-four hours,' he screamed. 'Do you know who I am?'

The chance was too good to miss. 'Scum usually floats on top,' I said equably, then I hardened my voice. 'Estrenoli, go back to Rome. Liguria isn't a healthy place for you.'

'What do you mean by that?' he said uneasily. 'Are you threatening me?'

'There are fifty men within a mile of here who would fight each other for the privilege of cutting your throat,'

I said. 'I'll tell you what; I'll give *you* twenty-four hours to get out of Liguria. After that I wouldn't give a busted lira for your chances.'

I turned to Francesca. 'Let's get out of here; I don't like the smell.'

She picked up her handbag and accompanied me to the door, walking proudly and leaving Estrenoli standing there impotently. I could hear a stifled buzz of comment in the lounge and there were a few titters at his discomfiture. I suppose there were many who had wanted to do the same thing but he was too powerful a man to cross. I didn't give a damn; I was boiling with rage.

The tittering was too much for Esternoli and he caught up with us as we were crossing the foyer. I felt his hand on my shoulder and turned my head. 'Take your hand off me,' I said coldly.

He was almost incoherent in his rage. 'I don't know who you are, but the British Ambassador will hear about this.'

'The name's Halloran, and take your goddamm hand off me.'

He didn't. Instead his hand tightened and he pulled me round to face him.

That was too much.

I sank three stiff fingers into his soft belly and he gasped and doubled up. Then I hit him with my fist as hard as I could. All the pent-up frustrations which had accumulated over the past weeks went into that blow; I was hitting Metcalfe and Torloni and all the thugs who were gathering like vultures. I must have broken Estrenoli's jaw and I certainly scraped my knuckles. He went down like a sack of meal and lay in a crumpled heap, blood welling from his mouth.

In the moment of hitting him I felt a fierce pain in my back. 'Christ, my back!' I groaned, and turned to Francesca. But she was not there.

Instead, I was face to face with Metcalfe.

'What a punch!' he said admiringly. 'That bloke's got a busted jaw for sure; I heard it go. Ever consider fighting light-heavyweight, Hal?'

I was too astounded to say anything, then I remembered Francesca and looked about wildly. She moved into sight from behind Metcalfe.

He said, 'Wasn't this character saying something about the British Ambassador?' He looked about the foyer. Luckily it was deserted and no one had seen the fracas. Metcalfe looked at the nearest door, which was the entrance to the men's room. He grinned. 'Shall we lug the guts into the neighbouring room?'

I saw his point and together we dragged Estrenoli into the lavatory and stuffed him into a cubicle. Metcalfe straightened and said, 'If this bird is on speaking terms with the British Ambassador he must be a pretty big noise. Who is he?'

I told him and Metcalfe whistled. 'When you hit 'em, you hit 'em big! Even I have heard of Estrenoli. What did you slug him for?'

'Personal reasons,' I said.

'Connected with the lady?'

'His wife.'

Metcalfe groaned. 'Brother you do get complicated. You're in a jam, for sure – you'll be tossed out of Italy on your ear within twelve hours.' He scratched behind his ear. 'But maybe not; maybe I can fix it. Wait here and don't let anyone use this john. I'll tell your girlfriend to stick around – and I'll be back in a couple of minutes.'

I leaned against the wall and tried to think coherently about Metcalfe, but I couldn't. My back was hurting like hell and there was a dull throbbing in the hand with which I had hit Estrenoli. It looked as though I had made a mess of everything. I had repeatedly warned Coertze not to get into brawls and now I was guilty of that same thing – and mixed up with Metcalfe to boot.

Metcalfe was as good as his word and was back within two minutes. With him was a squat, blue-jowled Italian dressed in a sharp suit. Metcalfe said, 'This is a friend of of mine, Guido Torloni. Guido, this is Peter Halloran.'

Torloni looked at me in quick surprise. Metcalfe said, 'Hal's in a jam. He's a broken a governmental jaw.' He took Torloni on one side and they spoke in low tones. I watched Torloni and thought that the mess was getting worse.

Metcalfe came back. 'Don't worry, Guido can fix it, he can fix anything.'

'Even Estrenoli?' I said incredulously.

Metcalfe smiled. 'Even Estrenoli. Guido is Mr Fixit himself in this part of Italy. Come, let's leave him to it.'

We went into the foyer and I did not see Francesca. Metcalfe said, 'Mrs Estrenoli is waiting in my car.'

We went out to the car and Francesca said, 'Is everything all right?'

'Everything is fine,' I said.

Metcalfe chuckled. 'Excepting your husband, Madame. He will be very sorry for himself when he wakes up.'

Francesca's hand was on the edge of the door. I put my hand over hers and pressed it warningly. 'I'm sorry,' I said. 'Francesca, this is Mr Metcalfe, an old friend of mine from South Africa.'

I felt her fingers tense. I said quickly, 'Mr Metcalfe's friend, Mr Torloni, is looking after your husband. I'm sure he'll be all right.'

'Oh yes,' agreed Metcalfe cheerfully. 'Your husband will be fine. He won't make trouble for anyone.' He suddenly frowned. 'How's your back, Hal? You'd better have it seen to right away. If you like I'll drive you to a doctor.'

'It doesn't matter,' I said. I didn't want to be driving anywhere with Metcalfe.

'Nonsense!' he said. 'Who is your doctor?'

It made a bit of difference if he would take us to a doctor of *our* choice. I looked at Francesca who said, 'I know a good doctor.'

Metcalfe clapped his hands together. 'Fine. Let's get cracking.'

So he drove us through the town and Francesca pointed out a doctor's rooms. Metcalfe pulled up and said, 'You two go in; I'll wait for you here and give you a lift to Palmerini's yard.'

That was another facer. Apparently Metcalfe didn't mind us knowing that he knew our whereabouts. There was something queer in the air and I didn't like it.

As soon as we got into the doctor's waiting-room Francesca said, 'Is *that* Metcalfe? He seems a nice man.'

'He is,' I said. 'But don't get in his way or you'll get run over.' I winced as my back gave a particularly nasty throb. 'What the hell do we do now?'

'Nothing has changed,' said Francesca practically. 'We knew they would be coming. Now they are here.'

That was true. I said, 'I'm sorry I hit your husband.'

'I'm not,' she said simply. 'The only thing I'm sorry for is that you got hurt doing it. And that it might cause trouble for you.'

'It won't,' I said grimly. 'Not while he's in Torloni's hands. And that's another thing I don't understand – why should Metcalfe and Torloni be interested in getting me out of trouble? It doesn't make sense.'

The doctor was ready for us then and he looked at my back. He said that I had torn a ligament and proceeded to truss me up like a chicken. He also bound up my hand, which was a bit damaged where the knuckles had been scraped on Estrenoli's teeth. When we came out Metcalfe waved at us from the car, and called, 'I'll take you down to the yard.'

There didn't seem to be much point in refusing under the circumstances so we climbed into the car. As we were pulling away I said casually, 'How did you know we were in Palmerini's yard?'

'I knew you were cruising in these waters so I asked the Port Captain if you'd shown up yet,' said Metcalfe airily. 'He told me all about you.'

It was logical enough, and if I hadn't known better I might have believed him. He said, 'I hear you're having trouble with your keel.'

That was cutting a bit near the bone. I said, 'Yes, I tried an experimental method of fastening but it doesn't seem to be working out. I might have to take the keel off and refasten it.'

'Make a good job of it,' he said. 'It would be a pity if it dropped off when you're off-shore. You'd capsize immediately.'

This was an uncomfortable conversation; it was reasonable small boat shop-talk, but with Metcalfe you never knew. To my relief he switched to something else. 'What did you do to your face? Been in another brawl lately?'

'I fell off a mountain,' I said lightly.

He made a sucking sound with his lips in commiseration. 'You want to take more care of yourself, Hal, my boy. I wouldn't want anything to happen to you.'

This was too much. 'Why the sudden solicitude?' I asked acidly.

He turned in surprise. 'I don't like seeing my friends get bashed about, especially you. You're quite a handsome feller, you know.' He turned to Francesca. 'Isn't he?'

'I think so,' she said.

I was surprised at that. 'I'll survive,' I said, as Metcalfe drew up at the gate of the boatyard. 'I'm getting to be an expert at it.'

Francesca and I got out of the car, and Metcalfe said, 'Not going to show me your new keel fastening, Hal?'

I grinned. 'Hell, I'm a professional designer; I never show my mistakes to anyone.' If he could play fast and loose in a hinting conversation, so could I.

He smiled. 'Very wise of you. I'll be seeing you around, I suppose?'

I stepped up to the car out of earshot of Francesca. 'What will happen to Estrenoli?'

'Nothing much, Guido will take him to a good, safe doctor and have him fixed up, then he'll dump him in Rome after throwing a hell of a scare into him. It's my guess that Estrenoli's not very brave and our Guido is a very scary character when he wants to be. There'll be no more trouble.'

I stepped back from the car, relieved. I had been afraid that Estrenoli would be dumped at the bottom of the bay in a concrete overcoat, and I didn't want anyone's life on my conscience, not even his. I said, 'Thanks. Yes, I'll be seeing you around. One can scarcely avoid it – in a town as small as this, can one?'

He put the car into gear and moved forward slowly, grinning from the side window. 'You're a good chap, Hal; don't let anybody put one over on you.'

Then he was gone and I was left wondering what the hell it was all about.

IV

The atmosphere in the shed was tense. As we walked through the yard I noticed that there were many more people about than usual; those would be Francesca's friends. When we got into the shed Piero strode up and said, 'What happened at the club?' His voice was shaking with emotion.

'Nothing happened,' I said. 'Nothing serious.' I saw a stranger in the background, a little man with bright, watchful eyes. 'Who the devil's that?'

Piero turned. 'That's Cariaceti, the jeweller – never mind him. What happened at the club? You went in and so did Madame; then this Metcalfe and Torloni went in; then you and Madame came out with Metcalfe. What is happening?'

I said, 'Take it easy; everything is all right. We bumped into Estrenoli and he got flattened.'

'Estrenoli?' said Piero in surprise, and looked at Francesca who nodded in confirmation. 'Where is he now?' he demanded fiercely.

'Torloni's got him,' I said.

That was too much for Piero. He sat on a trestle and gazed at the floor. 'Torloni?' he said blankly. 'What would Torloni want with Estrenoli?'

'Damned if I know,' I said. 'This whole thing is one of Metcalfe's devious plays. All I know is that I had a bust-up with Estrenoli and Metcalfe has removed him from circulation for a while – and don't ask me why.'

He looked up. 'It is said that you were very friendly with Metcalfe today.' His voice was heavy with suspicion.

'Why not? There's nothing to be gained by antagonizing him. If you want to know what happened, ask Francesca – she was there.'

'Hal is right,' said Francesca. 'His treatment of Metcalfe was correct. He was given much provocation and refused to be annoyed by it. Besides,' she said with a slight smile, 'Metcalfe would seem to be a difficult man to hate.'

'It is not difficult to hate Torloni,' growled Piero. 'And Metcalfe is his friend.'

This wasn't getting us anywhere, so I said, 'Where are Coertze and Walker?'

'In the town,' said Piero. 'We know where they are.'

'I think they had better come in,' I said. 'Things may start to move fast – we'd better decide what to do next.'

He silently got up and went outside. I walked over to the little jeweller. 'Signor Cariaceti,' I said. 'I understand that you have come here to look at some gems.'

'That is so,' he said. 'But I do not wish to remain here long.'

I went back to Francesca. 'You'd better turn Cariaceti loose among those jewels,' I said. 'There may not be much time.'

She went to talk to Cariaceti and I looked moodily at the keel, still lacking nearly two tons of weight. Things were at a low ebb and I felt pretty desperate. It would take eight more days working at high pressure to finish the keel, another day to fasten it in position and another to replace the glass-fibre cladding and to launch *Sanford*.

Ten days! Would Metcalfe and Torloni wait that long?

After a little while Francesca came back. 'Cariaceti is amazed,' she said. 'He is the happiest man I have ever seen.'

'I'm glad someone is happy,' I said gloomily. 'This whole thing is on the point of falling to pieces.'

She put her hand on my arm. 'Don't blame yourself,' she said. 'No one could have done more than you.'

I sat on the trestle. 'I suppose things *could* be worse,' I said. 'Walker could get stinking drunk just when we need him, Coertze could run amok like a mad bull and I could fall and break a few bones.'

She took my bandaged hand in hers. 'I have never said this to any man,' she said. 'But you are a man I could admire very much.'

I looked at her hand on mine. 'Only admire?' I asked gently.

I looked up to see her face colouring. She took her hand away quickly and turned from me. 'Sometimes you make me very annoyed, Mr Halloran.'

I stood up. 'It was "Hal" not very long ago. I told you that my friends called me Hal.'

'I am your friend,' she said slowly.

'Francesca, I would like you to be more than my friend,' I said.

She was suddenly very still and I put my hand on her waist. I said, 'I think I love you, Francesca.'

She turned quickly, laughing through tears. 'You only think so, Hal. Oh, you English are so cold and wary. I *know* that I love you.'

Something seemed to give at the pit of my stomach and the whole dark shed suddenly seemed brighter. I said, 'Yes, I love you; but I didn't know how to say it properly – I didn't know what you would say when I told you.'

'I say "bravo".'

'We'll have a good life,' I said. 'The Cape is a wonderful place – and there is the whole world besides.'

She saddened quickly. 'I don't know, Hal; I don't know. I am still a married woman; I can't marry you.'

'Italy isn't the world,' I said softly. 'In most other countries divorce is not dishonourable. The men who made the laws for divorce were wise men; they would never tie anyone to a man like Estrenoli for life.'

She shook her head. 'Here in Italy and in the eyes of my Church, divorce is a sin.'

'Then Italy and your Church are wrong. I say it; even Piero says it.'

She said slowly, 'What is going to happen to my husband?'

'I don't know,' I said. 'Metcalfe tells me that he will be taken back to Rome – under escort.'

'That is all? Torloni will not kill him?'

'I don't think so. Metcalfe said not – and I believe Metcalfe. He may be a scoundrel, but I've never caught him out in a black lie yet.'

She nodded. 'I believe him, too.' She was silent for a while, then she said, 'When I know that Eduardo is safe, then I will come away with you, to South Africa or any other place. I will get a foreign divorce and I will marry you, but Eduardo must be alive and well. I could not have that thing on my conscience.'

I said, 'I will see to it. I will see Metcalfe.' I looked at the keel. 'But I must also see this thing through. I have set my hand to it and there are others to consider – Coertze, Walker, Piero, all your men – I can't stop now. It isn't just the gold, you know.'

'I know,' she said. 'You must have been hurt by someone to start a thing like this. It is not your natural way.'

I said, 'I had a wife who was killed by a drunkard like Walker.'

'I know so little of your past life,' she said in wonder. 'I have so much to learn. Your wife – you loved her very much.' It was not a question, it was a statement.

I told her a little about Jean and more about myself and for a while we talked about each other in soft voices, the way that lovers do.

V

Then Coertze came in.

He wanted to know what all the hurry was and why his rest day had been broken into. For a man who didn't want to stop work he was most averse to being interrupted in his brief pleasures.

I brought him up to date on events and he was as puzzled as any of us. 'Why should Metcalfe want to help us?' he asked.

'I don't know, and I don't intend to ask him,' I said. 'He might tell me the truth and the truth might be worse than any supicions we might have.'

Coertze did as I had done and went to stare at the keel. I said, 'Another eight days of casting – at the least.'

'*Magtig*,' he burst out. 'No one is going to take this away from me now.' He took off his jacket. 'We'll get busy right now.'

'You'll have to do without me for an hour,' I said. 'I have an appointment.'

Coertze stared at me but did not say anything as I struggled into my jacket. Francesca helped me to put it on over the carapace of bandaging under my shirt. 'Where are you going?' she asked quietly.

'To see Metcalfe. I want to make things quite clear.'

She nodded. 'Be careful.'

On the way out I bumped into Walker who looked depressed. 'What's the matter with you?' I said. 'You look as though you've lost a shilling and found a sixpence.'

'Some bastard picked my pocket,' he said savagely.

'Lose much?'

'I lost my ci . . .' He seemed to change his mind. 'I lost my wallet.'

'I wouldn't worry about that,' I said. 'We're going to lose the gold if we aren't careful. See Coertze, he'll tell you about it.' I pushed past him, leaving him staring at me.

I went into Palmerini's office and asked if I could borrow his car. He didn't mind so I took his little Fiat and drove down to the yacht basin. I found the Fairmile quite easily and noted that it was not visible from the Yacht Club, which was why I hadn't spotted it earlier. Krupke was polishing the brightwork of the wheelhouse.

'Hi,' he said. 'Glad to see you. Metcalfe told me you were in town.'

'Is he on board? I'd like to see him.'

'Wait a minute,' said Krupke and went below. He came back almost immediately. 'He says you're to come below.'

I jumped on to the deck and followed Krupke below to the main saloon. Metcalfe was lying on a divan reading a book. 'What brings you here so soon?' he asked.

'I want to tell you something,' I said, and glanced at Krupke.

'O.K., Krupke,' said Metcalfe, and Krupke went out. Metcalfe opened a cupboard and produced a bottle and two glasses. 'Drink?'

'Thanks,' I said.

He poured out two stiff ones, and said, 'Mud in your eye.' We drank, then he said, 'What's your trouble?'

'That story you told me about Torloni taking care of Estrenoli – is it true?'

'Sure. Estrenoli's with a doctor now.'

'I just wanted to make sure,' I said. 'And to make certain, you can tell Torloni from me that if Estrenoli doesn't reach Rome safe and sound then I'll kill him personally.'

Metcalfe looked at me with wide eyes. 'Wow!' he said. 'Someone's been feeding you on tiger's milk. What's your interest in the safety of Estrenoli?' He looked at me closely, then laughed and snapped his fingers. 'Of course, the Contessa has turned chicken.'

'Leave her out of it,' I said.

Metcalfe smiled slyly, 'Ah, you young folk; there's no knowing what you'll get up to next.'

'Shut up.'

He held up his hands in mock terror. 'All right, all right.' He laughed suddenly. 'You damn' near killed Estrenoli yourself. If you'd have hit him a fraction harder he'd have been a dead man.'

'I couldn't hit him harder.'

'I wouldn't take any bets on that,' said Metcalfe. 'He's still unconscious. The quack has wired up his jaw and he won't be able to speak for a month.' He poured out another couple of drinks. 'All right, I'll see he gets to Rome not hurt any more than he is now.'

'I'll want that in writing,' I said. 'From Estrenoli himself – through the post in a letter from Rome datemarked not later than a week today.'

Metcalfe was still. 'You're pushing it a bit hard, aren't you?' he said softly.

'That's what I want,' I said stubbornly.

He looked at me closely. 'Someone's been making a man out of you, Hal,' he said. 'All right; that's the way it'll be.' He pushed the drink across the table. 'You know,' he said musingly, almost to himself, 'I wouldn't stay long in Rapallo if I were you. I'd get that keel fixed damn' quick and I'd clear out. Torloni's a bad man to tangle with.'

'I'm not tangling with Torloni; I only saw him for the first time today.'

He nodded. 'O.K. If that's the way you're going to play it, that's your business. But look, Hal; you pushed me just now and I played along because Estrenoli is no business of mine and you're by way of being a pal and maybe I don't mind being pushed in this thing. But don't try to push Torloni; he's bad, he'd eat you for breakfast.'

'I'm not pushing Torloni,' I said. 'Just as long as he doesn't push me.' I finished the drink and stood up. 'I'll see you around.'

Metcalfe grinned. 'You certainly will. As you said – it's a small town.'

He came up on deck to see me off and as I drove back to the yard I wondered greatly about Metcalfe. There had been some plain speaking – but not plain enough – and the whole mystery of Metcalfe's position was deepened. He had as much as said, 'Get clear before Torloni chops you,' and I couldn't understand his motives – after all, Torloni was *his* man.

It was beyond me.

When I got back to the boatyard work in the shed was continuing as though there had never been a break. There was a sudden glare as a chunk of gold melted and Coertze bent over the mould to pour it.

Francesca came up to me and I said, 'It's fixed; you'll hear from Eduardo within the week.'

She sighed. 'Come and have supper. You haven't eaten yet.'

'Thanks,' I said and followed her to the caravan.

SEVEN: THE GOLDEN KEEL

We worked, my God, how we worked.

The memory of that week remains with me as a dark and shadowed mystery punctuated by bright flashes of colour. We melted and poured gold for sixteen hours a day, until our arms were weary and our eyes sore from the flash of the furnaces. We dropped into our berths at night, asleep before we hit the pillows, and it would seem only a matter of minutes before we were called again to that damned assembly line I had devised.

I grew to hate the sight and the feel of gold, and the smell too – it has a distinctive odour when molten – and I prayed for the time when we would be at sea again with nothing more than a gale and a lee shore to worry about. I would rather have been alone in a small boat in a West Indies hurricane than undergo another week of that torture.

But the work got done. The mass of gold in the mould grew bigger and bigger and the pile of unmelted ingots became smaller. We were doing more than 250 melts a day and I calculated that we would gain half a day on my original ten-day schedule. A twelve-hour gain was not much, but it might mean the difference between victory and defeat.

Metcalfe and Torloni were keeping oddly quiet. We were watched – or rather, the boatyard was watched – and that was all. In spite of the reinforcements that Torloni had pushed into Rapallo, and in spite of the fact that he was personally supervising operations himself, there were no overt moves against us.

I couldn't understand it.

The only cheering aspect of the whole situation was Francesca. She cooked our food and did our housekeeping, received messages and issued instructions to the intelligence service and, although in the pace of work we had little time to be together, there was always something small like a hand's touch or a smile across the room to renew my will to go on.

Five days after I had seen Metcalfe she received a letter which she burned after reading it with a frown of pain on her brow. She came to me and said, 'Eduardo is safe in Rome.'

'Metcalfe kept his promise,' I said.

A brief smile touched her lips. 'So will I.' She grew serious. 'You must see the doctor tomorrow.'

'I haven't time,' I said impatiently.

'You must make time,' she insisted. 'You will have to sail *Sanford* very soon; you must be fit.'

She brought Coertze into the argument. He said, 'She's right. We don't want to depend on Walker, do we?'

That was another worry. Walker was deteriorating rapidly. He was moody and undependable, given to violent tempers and unpredictable fits of sulking. The gold was rotting him slowly but certainly, corrupting him far more surely than any alcohol.

Coertze said, 'Man, go to the doctor.' He smiled sheepishly. 'It's my fault you have a bad back, anyway. I could have shored up that passage better than I did. You go, and I'll see the work doesn't suffer.'

That was the first time that Coertze admitted responsibility for anything, and I respected him for it. But he had no sympathy for my scraped knuckles, maintaining that a man should learn how to punch without damaging himself.

So the next day Francesca drove me to see the doctor. After he had hissed and tutted and examined and reband-aged my back, he expressed satisfaction at my progress and said I must see him at the same time the following week. I said I would come, but I knew that by then we would be at sea on our way to Tangier.

When we were again seated in the car Francesca said, 'Now we go to the Hotel Levante.'

'I've got to get back,' I said.

'A drink will do you good,' she said. 'A few minutes won't hurt.'

So we went to the Hotel Levante, wandered into the lounge and ordered drinks. Francesca toyed with her glass and then said hesitantly, 'There's something else – another reason why I brought you here. I want you to meet someone.'

'Someone here? Who?'

'My father is upstairs. It is right that you see him.'

This was unexpected. 'Does he know about us?'

She shook her head. 'I told him about the gold and the jewels. He was very angry about that, and I don't know what he is going to do. I did not tell him about you and me.'

This looked as though it was going to be a difficult inter-view. It is not often that a prospective son-in-law has to admit that he is a gold smuggler before he asks for a hand in marriage – a hand that is already married to someone else, to make things worse.

I said, 'I would like very much to meet your father.'

We finished our drinks and went up to the old man's room. He was sitting in an armchair with a blanket across his knees and he looked up sharply when we appeared. He looked tired and old; his hair was white and his beard no longer bristled, as I had heard it described, but had turned wispy and soft. His eyes were those of a beaten man and had no fight in them.

'This is Mr Halloran,' said Francesca.

I walked across to him. 'I'm very glad to meet you, sir.'

Something sparked in his eyes. 'Are you?' he said, ignoring my outstretched hand. He leaned back in his chair. 'So you are the thief who is stealing my country's gold.'

I felt my jaw tightening. I said evenly, 'Apparently you do not know the laws of your own country, sir.'

He raised shaggy white eyebrows. 'Oh! Perhaps you can enlighten me, Mr Halloran.'

'This treasure falls under the legal heading of abandoned property,' I said. 'According to Italian law, whoever first takes possession of it thereafter is the legal owner.'

He mused over that. 'I dare say you could be right; but, in that case, why all this secrecy?'

I smiled. 'A lot of money is involved. Already the vultures are gathering, even with the secrecy we have tried to keep.'

His eyes snapped. 'I don't think your law is good, young man. This property was not abandoned; it was taken by force of arms from the Germans. It would make a pretty court case indeed.'

'The whole value would go in legal expenses, even if we won,' I said dryly.

'You have made your point,' he said. 'But I don't like it, and I don't like my daughter being involved in it.'

'Your daughter has been involved in worse things,' I said tightly.

'What do you mean by that?' he demanded sharply.

'I mean Estrenoli.'

He sighed and leaned back in his chair, the spark that had been in him burned out and he was once more a weary old man. 'Yes, I know,' he said tiredly. 'That was a shameful thing. I ought to have forbidden it, but Francesca . . .'

'I had to do it,' she said.

'Well you won't have to worry about him any more,' I said. 'He'll stay away from you now.'

The Count perked up. 'What happened to him?'

There was a ghost of a smile round Francesca's mouth as she said, 'Hal broke his jaw.'

'You did? You did?' The Count beckoned. 'Come here, young man; sit close to me. You really hit Estrenoli? Why?'

'I didn't like his manners.'

He chuckled. 'A lot of people don't like Estrenoli manners, but no one has hit an Estrenoli before. Did you hurt him?'

'A friend tells me that I nearly killed him.'

'Ah, a pity,' said the Count ambiguously. 'But you will have to be careful. He is a powerful man with powerful friends in the Government. You will have to leave Italy quickly.'

'I will leave Italy, but not because of Estrenoli. I imagine he is a very frightened man now. He will be no trouble.'

The Count said, 'Any man who can get the better of an Estrenoli must have my thanks – and my deepest respect.'

Francesca came over to me and put her hand on my shoulder. 'I also am going to leave Italy,' she said. 'I am going away with Hal.'

The Count looked at her for a long time then dropped his head and stared at the bony hands crossed in his lap. 'You must do what you think best, my child,' he said in a low voice. 'Italy has given you nothing but unhappiness; perhaps to find happiness you must go to another country and live under different laws.'

He raised his head. 'You will cherish her, Mr Halloran?'

I nodded, unable to speak.

Francesca went to him, kneeling at his side, and took his hand in hers. 'We must do it, Papa; we're in love. Can you give us your blessing?'

He smiled wryly. 'How can I give my blessing to some-thing I think is a sin, child? But I think that God is wiser than the churchmen and He will understand. So you have my blessing and you must hope that you have God's bless-ing too.'

She bent her head and her shoulders shook. He looked up at me. 'I was against this marriage to Estrenoli, but she did it for me. It is our law here that such a thing cannot be undone.'

Francesca dried her eyes. She said, 'Papa, we have little time and I must tell you something. Cariaceti – you remem-ber little Cariaceti – will come to you from time to time and give you money. You must . . .'

He broke in. 'I do not want such money.'

'Papa, listen. The money is not for you. There will be a lot of money and you must take a little for yourself if you need it, but most of it must be given away. Give some to Mario Pradelli for his youngest child who was born spastic; give some to Pietro Morelli for his son whom he cannot afford to send to university. Give it to those who fought with you in the war; those who were cheated by the Communists just like you were; those who need it.'

I said, 'My share of the gold is Francesca's to do with as she likes. That can be added, too.'

The Count thought deeply for a long time, then he said musingly, 'So something good may come out of this after all. Very well, I will take the money and do as you say.'

She said, 'Piero Morese will help you – he knows where all your old comrades are. I will not be here; I leave with Hal in a few days.'

'No,' I said. 'You stay. I will come back for you.'

'I am coming with you,' she declared.

'You're staying here. I won't have you on *Sanford*.'

The Count said, 'Obey him, Francesca. He knows what he must do, and perhaps he could not do it if you were there.'

She was rebellious, but she acquiesced reluctantly. The Count said, 'Now you must go, Francesca. I want to talk to your Hal – alone.'

'I'll wait downstairs,' she said.

The Count watched her go. 'I think you are an honourable man, Mr Halloran. So I was told by Piero Morese when he talked to me on the telephone last night. What are your exact intentions when you take my daughter from Italy?'

'I'm going to marry her,' I said. 'Just as soon as she can get a divorce.'

'You realize that she can never come back to Italy in those circumstances? You know that such a marriage would be regarded here as bigamous?'

'I know – and Francesca knows. You said yourself that she has had nothing but unhappiness in Italy.'

'That is true.' He sighed. 'Francesca's mother died when she was young, before the war. My daughter was brought up in a partisan camp in the middle of a civil war and she has seen both the heroism and degradation of men from an early age. She is not an ordinary woman because of this; some would have been made bitter by her experiences, but she is not bitter. Her heart is big enough to have compassion for all humanity – I would not like to see it broken.'

'I love Francesca,' I said. 'I will not break her heart, not wittingly.'

He said, 'I understand you are a ship designer and a shipbuilder.'

'Not ships – small boats.'

'I understand. After I talked to Piero I thought I would see what sort of a man you were, so a friend kindly asked some questions for me. It seems you have a rising reputation in your profession.'

I said, 'Perhaps in South Africa; I didn't know I was known here.'

'There has been some mention of you,' he said. 'The reason I bring this up is that I am pleased that it is so. This present venture in which you are engaged I discount entirely. I do not think you will succeed – but if you do, such wealth is like the gold of fairies, it will turn to leaves in your hands. It is good to know that you do fine work in the field of your choice.'

He pulled the blanket round him. 'Now you must go; Francesca will be waiting. I cannot give you more than my good wishes, but those you have wherever you may be.'

I took his proffered hand and said impulsively, 'Why don't you leave Italy, too, and come with us?'

He smiled and shook his head. 'No, I am old and the old do not like change. I cannot leave my country now, but thank you for the thought. Goodbye, Hal, I think you will make my daughter very happy.'

I said goodbye and left the room. I didn't see the Count ever again.

II

The time arrived when, incredibly, the keel was cast.

We all stood round the mould and looked at it a little uncertainly. It seemed impossible that all our sweat and labour should have been reduced to this inert mass of dull yellow metal, a mere eight cubic feet shaped in a particular and cunning way.

I said, 'That's it. Two more days and *Sanford* will be in the water.'

Coertze looked at his watch. 'We've got to do some more work today; we can't knock off just because the keel is finished – there's still plenty to do.'

So we got on with it. Walker began to strip the furnaces and I directed Coertze and Piero in stripping the glass-fibre cladding from *Sanford* preparatory to removing the lead keel. We were happy that night. The change of work and pace had done us good and we all felt rested.

Francesca reported that everything was quiet on the potential battle-front – Metcalfe was on the Fairmile and Torloni was in his hotel; the watch on the boatyard had not been intensified – in fact, everything was as normal as a thoroughly abnormal situation could be.

The trouble would come, if it had to come at all, when we launched *Sanford*. At the first sign of us getting away the enemy would be forced to make a move. I couldn't understand why they hadn't jumped us before.

The next day was pure joy. We worked as hard as ever and when we had finished *Sanford* was the most expensively built boat in the world. The keel bolts which Coertze had cast into the golden keel slipped smoothly into the holes in the keelson which Harry had prepared long ago in Cape Town, and as we let down the jacks *Sanford* settled comfortably and firmly on to the gold.

Coertze said, 'I can't see why you didn't use the exisiting holes – the ones drilled for the old keel.'

'It's the difference in weight distribution,' I said. 'Gold is half as heavy again as lead and so this keel had to be a different shape from the old one. As it is, I had to juggle with the centre of gravity. With the ballast being more concentrated I think *Sanford* will roll like a tub, but that can't be helped.'

I looked at *Sanford*. She was now worth not much short of a million and three-quarter pounds – the most expensive 15-tonner in history. I felt quite proud of her – not many yacht designers could boast of such a design.

When we had supper that night we were all very quiet and relaxed. I said to Francesca, 'You'd better get the jewels out tonight – it may be your last chance before the fireworks start.'

She smiled. 'That will be easy; Piero has cast them into concrete bricks – we are learning the art of disguise from you. They are outside near the new shed that Palmerini is building.'

I laughed. 'I must see this.'

'Come,' she said. 'I will show you.'

We went into the dark night and she flashed a torch on an untidy heap of bricks near the new shed. 'There they are; the valuable bricks are spotted with whitewash.'

'Not bad,' I said. 'Not bad at all.'

She leaned against me and I put my arms around her. It was not often we had time for this sort of thing, we were missing a lot that normal lovers had. After a moment she said quietly, 'When are you coming back?'

'As soon as I've sold the gold,' I said. 'I'll take the first plane out of Tangier.'

'I'll be waiting,' she said. 'Not here – I'll be in Milan with my father.'

She gave me the address which I memorized. I said, 'You won't mind leaving Italy?'

'No, not with you.'

'I asked your father to come with us, but he wouldn't.'

'Not after seventy years,' she said. 'It's too much to ask an old man.'

I said, 'I knew that, but I thought I'd make the offer.'

We talked for a long time there in the darkness, the small personal things that lovers talk about when they're alone.

Then Francesca said that she was tired and was going to bed.

'I'll stay and have another cigarette,' I said. 'It's pleasant out here.'

I watched her melt into the darkness and then I saw the gleam of light as she opened the door of the shed and slipped inside.

A voice whispered from out of the darkness, 'Halloran!'

I started, 'Who's that?' I flashed my torch about.

'Put out that damned light. It's me – Metcalfe.'

I clicked off the torch and stooped to pick up one of the concrete bricks. I couldn't see if it had spots of whitewash on it or not; if it had, then Metcalfe was going to be clobbered by a valuable brick.

A dark silhouette moved closer. 'I thought you'd never stop making love to your girlfriend,' said Metcalfe.

'What do you want, and how did you get here?'

He chuckled. 'I came in from the sea – Torloni's boys are watching the front of the yard.'

'I know,' I said.

There was surprise in his voice. 'Do you, now?' I saw the flash of his teeth. 'That doesn't matter, though; it won't make any difference.'

'It won't make any difference to what?'

'Hal, boy, you're in trouble,' said Metcalfe. 'Torloni's going to jump you – tonight. I tried to hold him in, but he's got completely out of hand.'

'Whose side are you on?' I demanded.

He chuckled. 'Only my own,' he said. He changed his tone. 'What are you going to do?'

I shrugged. 'What can I do except fight?'

'Be damned to that,' he said. 'You wouldn't have a chance against Torloni's cut-throats. Isn't your boat ready for launching?'

'Not yet. She still needs sheathing and painting.'

'What the hell?' he said angrily. 'What do you care if you get worm in your planking now? Is the new keel on?'

I wondered how he knew about that. 'What if it is?'

'Then get the stick put back and get the boat into the water, and do it now. Get the hell out of here as fast as you can.' He thrust something into my hand. 'I had your clearance made out. I told you I was a pal of the Port Captain.'

I took the paper and said, 'Why warn us? I thought Torloni was your boy.'

He laughed gently. 'Torloni is nobody's boy but his own. He was doing me a favour but he didn't know what was in the wind. I told him I just wanted you watched. I was sorry to hear about the old watchman – that was Torloni's thugs, it wasn't my idea.'

I said, 'I thought hammering old men wasn't your style.'

'Anyway,' he said. 'Torloni knows the score now. It was that damn' fool Walker who gave it away.'

'Walker! How?'

'One of Torloni's men picked his pocket and pinched his cigarette case. It wasn't a bad case, either; it was made of gold and had a nice tasteful inscription on the inside – 'Caro Benito da parte di Adolf – Brennero – 1940.' As soon as Torloni saw that he knew what was up, all right. People have been scouring Italy for that treasure ever since the war, and now Torloni thinks he has it right in his greasy fist.'

I damned Walker at length for an incompetent, crazy idiot.

Metcalfe said, 'I tried to hold Torloni, but he won't be held any longer. With what's at stake he'd as soon cut my throat as yours – that's why I'm giving you the tip-off.'

'When is he going to make his attack?'

'At three in the morning. He's going to move in with all his crowd.'

'Any guns?'

Metcalfe's voice was thoughtful. 'No, he won't use guns. He wants to do this quietly and he has to get the gold out. That'll take some time and he doesn't want the police breathing down his neck while he's doing it. So there'll be no guns.'

That was the only good thing I'd heard since Metcalfe had surprised me. I said, 'Where are his men now?'

'As far as I know they're getting some sleep – they don't like being up all night.'

'So they're in their usual hotels – all sixteen of them.'

Metcalfe whistled. 'You seem to know as much about it as I do.'

'I've known about it all the time,' I said shortly. 'We've had them tabbed ever since they moved into Rapallo – before that, too. We had your men spotted in every port in the Mediterranean.'

He said slowly, 'I wondered about that ever since Dino was beaten up in Monte Carlo. Was that you?'

'Coertze,' I said briefly. I gripped the brick which I was still holding. I was going to clobber Metcalfe after all – he played a double game too often and he might be playing one now. I thought we had better keep him where we could watch him.

He laughed. 'Yes, of course; that's just his mark.'

I lifted the brick slowly. 'How did you cotton on to us?' I asked. 'It must have been in Tangier, but what gave the game away?'

There was no answer.

I said, 'What was it, Metcalfe?' and raised the brick.

There was silence.

'Metcalfe?' I said uncertainly, and switched on my torch. He had gone and I heard a faint splashing from the sea and the squeak of a rowlock. I ought to have known better than to think I could outwit Metcalfe; he was too wise a bird for me.

III

As I went back to the shed I looked at my watch; it was ten o'clock – five hours to go before Torloni's assault. Could we replace the mast and all the standing rigging in time?

I very much doubted it. If we turned on the floodlights out-side the shed, then Torloni's watchers would know that something unusual was under way and he would move in immediately. If we worked in the dark it would be hell's own job – I had never heard of a fifty-five foot mast being stepped in total darkness and I doubted if it could be done.

It looked very much as though we would have to stay and fight.

I went in and woke Coertze. He was drowsy but he woke up fast enough when I told him what was happening. I omitted to mention Walker's part in the mess – I still needed Walker and I knew that if I told Coertze about it I would have a corpse and a murderer on my hands, and this was not time for internal dissension.

Coertze said suspiciously, 'What the hell is Metcalfe's game?'

'I don't know and I care less. The point is that he's given us the tip-off and if we don't use it we're fools. He must have fallen out with Torloni.'

'*Reg,*' said Coertze and swung himself out of his berth. 'Let's get cracking.'

'Wait a minute,' I said. 'What about the mast?' I told him my estimate of the chance of replacing the mast in darkness.

He rubbed his chin and the bristles crackled in the silence. 'I reckon we should take a chance and turn the lights on,' he said at last. 'That is, after we've made our preparations for Torloni. We know he's going to attack and whether he does it sooner or later doesn't matter as long as we're ready for him.'

This was the man of action – the military commander – speaking. His reasoning was good so I left him to it. He roused Piero and they went into a huddle while Walker and I began to clear the shed and to load up *Sanford.* Francesca heard the noise and got up to see what was going on and was drawn into Coertze's council of war.

Presently Piero slipped out of the shed and Coertze called me over. 'You might as well know what's going to happen,' he said.

He had a map of Rapallo spread out, one of the give-aways issued by the Tourist Office, and as he spoke he pointed to the salient features on the map. It was a good plan that he described and like all good plans it was simple.

I think that if Coertze had not been taken prisoner at Tobruk he would have been commissioned as an officer sooner or later. He had a natural grasp of strategy and his plan was the classic military design of concentration to smash the enemy in detail before they could concentrate.

He said, 'This is the holiday season and the hotels are full. Torloni couldn't get all his men into the same hotel, so they're spread around the town – four men here, six here, three here and the rest with Torloni himself.' As he spoke his stubby forefinger pointed to places on the map.

'We can call up twenty-five men and I'm keeping ten men here at the yard. There are four of Torloni's men out-side the yard right now, watching us, and we're going to jump them in a few minutes – ten men should clean them up easily. That means that when we turn on the lights there'll be no one to warn Torloni about it.'

'That seems a good idea,' I said.

'That leaves us fifteen men we can use outside the yard as a mobile force. We have two men outside each hotel excepting this one, here, where we have nine. There are four of Torloni's men staying here and when they come out they'll get clobbered. That ought to be easy, too.'

'You'll have already cut his force by half,' I said.

'That's right. Now, there'll be Torloni and eight men moving in on the yard. He'll expect to have sixteen, but he won't get them. This may make him nervous, but I think not. He'll think that there'll only be four men and a girl here and he'll reckon he can take us easily. But we'll have fourteen men in the yard – counting us – and I'll bring in another fifteen behind him as soon as he starts anything.'

He looked up. 'How's that, ay?'

'It's great,' I said. 'But you'll have to tell the Italians to move in fast. We want to nail those bastards quick before they can start shooting. Metcalfe said they wouldn't shoot, but they might if they see they're on the losing end.'

'They'll be quick,' he promised. 'Piero's on the blower now, giving instructions. The orders are to clean up the four watchers here at eleven o'clock.' He looked at his watch. 'That's in five minutes. Let's go and see the fun.'

Francesca said, 'I don't see how anything can go wrong.'

Neither could I – but it did!

We were leaving the shed when I noticed Walker tagging on behind. He had been keeping in the background, trying to remain inconspicuous. I let the others go and caught his arm. 'You stay here,' I said. 'If you move out of this shed I swear I'll kill you.'

His face went white. 'Why?'

'So you had your wallet stolen,' I said. 'You damn' fool, why did you have to carry that cigarette case?'

He tried to bluff his way out of it. 'Wh . . . what cigarette case?'

'Don't lie to me. You know what cigarette case. Now stay here and don't move out. I don't want you underfoot – I don't want to have to keep an eye on you all the time in case you make any more damn' silly mistakes.' I took him by the shirt. 'If you don't stay in here I'll tell Coertze just why Torloni is attacking tonight – and Coertze will dismember you limb from limb.'

His lower lip started to tremble. 'Oh, don't tell Coertze,' he whispered. 'Don't tell him.'

I let him go. 'O.K. But don't move out of this shed.'

I followed the others up to Palmerini's office. Coertze said, 'It's all set.'

I said to Piero, 'You'd better get Palmerini down here; we'll need his help in rigging the mast.'

'I have telephoned him,' said Piero. 'He will be coming at eleven-fifteen – after we have finished our work here.' He nodded towards the main gate.

'Fine,' I said. 'Do you think we shall see anything of what is happening?'

'A little. One of Torloni's men is not troubling to hide himself; he is under the street lamp opposite the main gate.'

We went up to the gate, moving quietly so as not to alarm the watchers. The gate was of wood, old, unpainted and warped by the sun; there were plenty of cracks through which we could see. I knelt down and through one of the cracks saw a man on the other side of the road, illuminated by the street lamp. He was standing there, idly smoking a cigarette, with one hand in his trouser-pocket. I could hear the faint click as he jingled money or keys.

Coertze whispered, 'Any time now.'

Nothing happened for a while. There was no sound to be heard except for the sudden harsh cry of an occasional seabird. Piero said in a low voice, 'Two have been taken.'

'How do you know?'

There was laughter in his voice. 'The birds – they tell me.'

I suddenly realized what had been nagging at my mind. Seagulls sleep at night and they don't cry.

There was a faint sound of singing which grew louder, and presently three men came down the street bellowing vociferously. They had evidently been drinking because they wavered and staggered and one of them had to be helped by the others. The man under the lamp trod on the butt of his cigarette and moved back to the wall to let them pass. One of them waved a bottle in the air and shouted, 'Have a drink, brother; have a drink on my first-born.'

Torloni's man shook his head but they pressed round him clamouring in drunken voices for him to drink. Suddenly the bottle came down sharply and I heard the thud even from across the street.

'God,' I said. 'I hope they haven't killed him.'

Piero said, 'It will be all right; they know the thickness of a man's skull.'

The drunken men were suddenly miraculously sober and came across the street at a run carrying the limp figure of Torloni's man. Simultaneously others appeared from the left and the right, also bearing unconscious bodies. A car came up the street and swerved through the gateway.

'That's four,' said Coertze with satisfaction. 'Take them into the shed.'

'No,' I said. 'Put them in that half-finished shed.' I didn't want them to get a glimpse of anything that might do us damage later. 'Tie them up and gag them; let two men watch them.'

Piero issued orders in rapid Italian and the men were carried away. We were surrounded by a group of Italians babbling of how easy it was until Piero shouted for silence. 'Are you veterans or are you green recruits?' he bawled. 'By God, if the Count could see you now he'd have you all shot.'

There was an abashed silence at this, and Piero said, 'Keep a watch outside. Giuseppi, go to the office and stay with the telephone; if it rings, call me. You others, watch and keep quiet.'

A car hooted outside the gate and I started nervously. Piero took a quick look outside. 'It is all right; it is Palmerini. Let him in.'

Palmerini's little Fiat came through the gateway and disgorged Palmerini and his three sons in a welter of arms and legs. He came up to me and said, 'I am told you are in a hurry to get your boat ready for sea. That will be extra for the overtime, you understand.'

I grinned. Palmerini was running true to form. 'How long will it take?'

'With the lights – four hours, if you help, too.'

That would be three-fifteen – just too late. We would probably have to fight, after all. I said, 'We may be interrupted, Signor Palmerini.'

'That is all right, but any damage must be paid for,' he answered.

Evidently he knew the score, so I said, 'You will be amply recompensed. Shall we begin?'

He turned and began to berate his sons. 'What are you waiting for, you lazy oafs; didn't you hear the signor? The good God should be ashamed for giving me sons so strong in the arm but weak in the head.' He chased them down to the shed and I began to feel happier about everything.

As the lights sprang up at the seaward end of the shed Francesca looked at the gate and said thoughtfully, 'If I was Torloni and I wanted to come in here quickly I would drive right through the gate in a car.'

'You mean ram it?'

'Yes, the gate is very weak.'

Coertze said jovially. '*Reg*, we can soon stop that. We've captured one of his cars; I'll park it across the gateway behind the gate. If he tries that trick he'll run into something heavier than he bargains for.'

'I'll leave you to it, then,' I said. 'I've got to help Palmerini.' I ran down to the shed and heard the car revving up behind me.

Palmerini met me at the door of the shed. He was outraged. 'Signor, you cannot put this boat into the water. There is no paint, no copper, nothing on the bottom. She will be destroyed in our Mediterranean water – the worms will eat her up entirely.'

I said, 'We have no time; she must go into the water as she is.'

His professional ethics were rubbed raw. 'I do not know whether I should permit it,' he grumbled. 'No boat has ever left my yard in such a condition. If anyone hears of it they will say, "Palmerini is an old fool; Palmerini is losing his mind – he is getting senile in his old age."'

In my impatience to get on with the job I suspected he wasn't far off the truth. I said, 'No one will know, Signor Palmerini. I will tell no one.'

We walked across to *Sanford*. Palmerini was still grumbling under his breath about the iniquity of leaving a ship's bottom unprotected against the small beasts of the sea. He looked at the keel and rapped it with his knuckles. 'And this, signor. Whoever heard of a brass keel?'

'I told you I was experimenting,' I said.

He cocked his head on one side and his walnut face looked at me impishly. 'Ah, signor, never has there been such a yacht as this in the Mediterranean. Not even the famous *Argo* was like this boat, and not even the Golden Fleece was so valuable.' He laughed. 'I'll see if my lazy sons are getting things ready.'

He went off into the lighted area in front of the shed, cackling like a maniac. I suppose no one could do anything in his yard without his knowing exactly what was going on. He was a great leg-puller, this Palmerini.

I called him back, and said, 'Signor Palmerini, if all goes well I will come back and buy your boatyard if you are willing to sell. I will give you a good price.'

He chuckled. 'Do you think I would sell my yard to a man who would send a boat out without paint on her bottom? I was teasing you, my boy, because you always look so serious.'

I smiled. 'Very well, but there is a lead keel I have no use for. I'm sure you can use it.' At the current price of lead the old keel was worth nearly fifteen hundred pounds.

He nodded judiciously. 'I can use it,' he said. 'It will just about pay for tonight's overtime.' He cackled again and went off to crack the whip over his sons.

Walker was still sullen and pale and when I began to drive him he became even more sulky, but I ignored that and drove him all the more in my efforts to get *Sanford* ready for sea. Presently we were joined by Coertze and Francesca and the work went more quickly.

Francesca said, 'I've left Piero in charge up there. He knows what to do; besides, he knows nothing about boats.'

'Neither do you,' I said.

'No, but I can learn.'

I said, 'I think you should leave now. It might get a bit dangerous round here before long.'

'No,' she said, stubbornly, 'I'm staying.'

'You're going.'

She faced me. 'And just how will you make me go?'

She had me there and she knew it. I hesitated, and she said, 'Not only am I staying, but I'm coming with you in *Sanford*.'

'We'll see about that later,' I said. 'At the moment I've no time to argue.'

We pulled *Sanford* out of the shed and one of Palmerini's sons ran the little crane alongside. He picked up the mast and hoisted it high above the boat, gently lowering it between the mast partners. I was below, making sure that the heel of the mast was correctly bedded on the butt plate. Old Palmerini came below and said, 'I'll see to the wedges. If you are in the hurry you say you are, you had better see that your engine is fit to run.'

So I went aft and had a look at the engine. When *Sanford* had been taken from the water I had checked the engine twice a week, turning her over a few revolutions to circulate the oil. Now, she started immediately, running sweetly, and I knew with satisfaction that once we were in the water we could get away at a rate of knots.

I checked the fuel tanks and the water tanks and then went on deck to help the Palmerini boys with the standing rigging. After we had been working for some time, Francesca brought us coffee. I accepted it with thanks, and she said quietly, 'It's getting late.'

I looked at my watch; it was two o'clock. 'My God!' I said. 'Only an hour before the deadline. Heard anything from Piero?'

She shook her head. 'How long will it be before you are finished?' she asked, looking round the deck.

'It looks worse than it is,' I said. 'I reckon we'll be nearly two hours, though.'

'Then we fight,' she said with finality.

'It looks like it.' I thought of Coertze's plan. 'It shouldn't come to much, though.'

'I'll stay with Piero,' she said. 'I'll let you know if anything happens.'

I watched her go, then went to Walker. 'Never mind the running rigging,' I said. 'We'll fix that at sea. Just reeve the halyards through the sheaves and lash them down. We haven't much time now.'

If we worked hard before, we worked harder then – but it was no use. Francesca came running down from the office. 'Hal, Hal, Piero wants you.'

I dropped everything and ran up the yard, calling for Coertze as I went. Piero was talking on the telephone when I arrived. After a minute he hung up and said, 'It's started.'

Coertze sat on at the desk upon which was spread the map. 'Who was that?'

Piero laid his finger on the map. 'These men. We have two men following.'

'Not the four we're tackling straight away?' I asked.

'No, I haven't heard of them.' He crossed to the window and spoke a few words to a man outside. I looked at my watch – it was half past two.

We sat in silence and listened to the minutes tick away. The atmosphere was oppressive and reminded me of the time during the war when we expected a German attack but didn't know just when or where it was going to come.

Suddenly the telephone rang and we all started.

Piero picked it up and as he listened his lips tightened. He put the telephone down and said, 'Torloni has got more men. They are gathering in the Piazza Cavour – there are two lorry loads.'

'Where the hell did *they* come from?' I demanded.

'From Spezia; he has called in another gang.'

My brain went into high gear. Why had Torloni done that? He didn't need so many men against four of us – unless he knew of our partisan allies – and it was quite evident that he did. He was going to overrun us by force of numbers.

'How many extra men?' asked Coertze.

Piero shrugged. 'At least thirty, I was told.'

Coertze cursed. His plan was falling to pieces – the enemy was concentrating and our own forces were divided.

I said to Piero, 'Can you get in touch with your men?'

He nodded. 'One watches – the other is near a telephone.'

I looked at Coertze. 'You'd better bring them in.'

He shook his head violently. 'No, the plan is still good. We can still engage them here and attack them in the rear.'

'How many men have we got altogether?'

Coertze said, 'Twenty-five Italians and the four of us.'

'And they've got forty-three at least. Those are bad odds.'

Francesca said to Piero, 'The men we have are those who can fight. There are others who cannot fight but who can watch. It is a pity that the fighters have to be watchers, too. Why not get some of the old men to do the watching so that you can collect the fighters together?'

Piero's hand went to the phone but stopped as Coertze abruptly said, 'No!' He leaned back in his chair. 'It's a good idea, but it's too late. We can't start changing plans now. And I want that phone free – I want to know what is happening to our mobile force.'

We waited while the leaden minutes dragged by. Coertze suddenly said, 'Where's Walker?'

'Working on the boat,' I said. 'He's of more use down there.'

Coertze snorted. 'That's God's truth. He'll be no use in a brawl.'

The telephone shrilled and Piero scooped it up in one quick movement. He listened intently, then began to give quick instructions. I looked at Coertze and said, 'Four down.'

'. . . and thirty-nine to go,' he finished glumly.

Piero put down the phone. 'That was the mobile force – they are going to the Piazza Cavour.'

The phone rang again under his hand and he picked it up. I said to Francesca, 'Go down to the boat and tell Walker to work like hell. You'd better stay down there, too.'

As she left the office, Piero said, 'Torloni has left the Piazza Cavour – two cars and two trucks. We had only two men there and they have already lost one truck. The other truck and the cars are coming straight here.'

Coertze thumped the table. 'Dammit, where did that other truck go?'

I said sardonically, 'I wouldn't worry about it. Things can't help but get better from now on; they can't get any worse, and we've nowhere to go but up.'

I left the office and stood in the darkness. Giuseppi said, 'What is happening, signor?'

'Torloni and his men will be here within minutes. Tell the others to be prepared.'

After a few moments Coertze joined me. 'The telephone line's been cut,' he said.

'That tops it,' I said. 'Now we don't know what's going on at all.'

'I hope our friends outside use their brains and concentrate into one bunch; if they don't, we're sunk,' he said grimly.

Piero joined us. 'Will Palmerini's sons fight?' I asked.

'Yes, if they are attacked.'

'You'd better go down and tell the old man to lie low. I wouldn't want him to get hurt.'

Piero went away and Coertze settled down to watch. The street was empty and there was no sound. We waited a long time and nothing happened at all. I thought that perhaps Torloni was disconcerted by finding his watchmen missing – that might put him off his stroke. And if he had a roll-call and discovered a total of eight men missing it was bound to make him uneasy.

I looked at my watch – three-fifteen. If Torloni would only hold off we might get the boat launched and away and the men dispersed. I prayed he would hold off at least another half-hour.

He didn't.

Coertze said suddenly, 'Something's coming.'

I heard an engine changing gear and the noise was suddenly loud. Headlights flashed from the left, approaching rapidly, and the engine roared. I saw it was a lorry being driven fast, and when it was abreast of the yard, it swerved and made for the gate.

I blessed Francesca's intuition and shouted in Italian, 'To the gates!'

The lorry smashed into the gates and there was a loud cracking and snapping of wood, overlaid by the crash as the lorry hit the car amidships and came to a jolting halt. We didn't wait for Torloni's men to recover but piled in immediately. I scrambled over the ruined car and got on to the bonnet of the lorry, whirling round to the passenger side. The man in the passenger seat was shaking his head groggily; he had smashed it against the windscreen, unready for such a fierce impact. I hit him with my fist and he slumped down to the floor of the cab.

The driver was frantically trying to restart his stalled engine and I saw Coertze haul him out bodily and toss him away into the darkness. Then things got confused. Someone from the back of the lorry booted me on the head and I slipped from the running-board conscious of a wave of our men going in to the attack. When I had recovered my wits it was all over.

Coertze dragged me from under the lorry and said, 'Are you all right?'

I rubbed my sore head. 'I'm O.K. What happened?'

'They didn't know what hit them – or they didn't know what they hit. The smash shook them up too much to be of any use; we drove them from the lorry and they ran for it.'

'How many of them were there?'

'They were jammed in the back of the lorry like sardines. I suppose they thought they could smash in the gates, drive into the yard and get out in comfort. They didn't get the chance.' He looked at the gateway. 'They won't be coming that way again.'

The gateway, from being our weakest point had become our strongest. The tangled mess of the lorry and the car completely blocked the entrance, making it impassable.

Piero came up and said, 'We have three prisoners.'

'Tie them up and stick them with the others,' I said. One commodity which is never in short supply in a boatyard is rope. Torloni was now missing eleven men – a quarter of his force. Perhaps that would make him think twice before attacking again.

I said to Coertze, 'Are you sure they can't attack us from the sides?'

'Positive. We're blocked in with buildings on both sides. He has to make a frontal attack. But, hell, I wish I knew where that other lorry went.'

The telephone began to ring shrilly.

I said, 'I thought you said the wire had been cut.'

'Piero said it had.'

We ran to the office and Coertze grabbed the phone. He listened for a second, then said, 'It's Torloni!'

'I'll speak to him,' I said, and took the phone. I held my hand over the mouthpiece. 'I've got an idea – get old Palmerini up here.' Then I said into the phone, 'What do you want?'

'Is that Halloran?' The English was good, if strongly tinged with an American accent.

'Yes.'

'Halloran, why don't you be reasonable? You know you haven't a chance.'

I said, 'This phone call of yours is proof that we *have* a chance. You wouldn't be speaking to me if you thought you could get what you want otherwise. Now, if you have a proposition, make it; if you haven't, shut up.'

His voice was softly ugly. 'You'll be sorry you spoke to me like that. Oh, I know all about the Estrenoli woman's old soldiers, but you haven't got enough of them. Now if you cut me in for half I'll be friendly.'

'Go to hell!'

'All right,' he said. 'I'll crush you and I'll like doing it.'

'Make one more attack and the police will be here.' I might as well try to pull a bluff.

He thought that one over, then said silkily, 'And how will you call them with no telephone?'

'I've made my arrangements,' I said. 'You've already run into some of them.' I rubbed it in. 'A lot of your men are mysteriously missing, aren't they?'

I could almost hear his brain click to a decision. 'You won't send for the police,' he said with finality. 'You want the police as little as I do. Halloran, I did you a favour once; I got rid of Estrenoli, didn't I? You could return the favour.'

'The favour was for Metcalfe, not me,' I said, and hung up on him. He wouldn't like that.

Coertze said, 'What did he want?'

'A half-share – or so he said.'

'I'll see him in hell first,' he said bluntly.

'Where's Palmerini?'

'Coming up. I sent Giuseppi for him.'

Just then Palmerini came into the office. I said, 'First, how's the boat getting on?'

'Give me fifteen minutes – just fifteen minutes, that's all.'

'I may not be able to,' I said. 'You've got some portable floodlights you use for working at night. Take two men and bring them up here quickly.'

I turned to Coertze. 'We want to be able to see what's happening. They'll have to come over the wall this time, and once they're over it won't be easy for them to get back. That means that the next attack will be final – make or break. Now here's what we do.'

I outlined what I wanted to do with the lights and Coertze nodded appreciatively. It took a mere five minutes to set them up and we used the Fiat and a truck to give added light by their headlamps. We placed the men and settled down to wait for the impending attack.

It wasn't long in coming. There were odd scraping noises from the wall and Coertze said, 'They're coming over.'

'Wait,' I breathed.

There were several thumps which could only be made by men dropping heavily to the ground. I yelled, *'Luce!'* and the lights blazed out.

It was like a frozen tableau. Several of the enemy were on our side of the wall, squinting forward at the light pouring on to them. Several others were caught lowering themselves, their head turned to see what was happening.

What they must have seen cannot have been reassuring – a blaze of blinding light behind which was impenetrable darkness heavy with menace, while they themselves were in the open and easily spotted – not a very comfortable thought for men supposedly making a surprise attack.

They hesitated uncertainly and in that moment we hit them on both flanks simultaneously, Piero leading from the right and Coertze from the left. I stayed with a small reserve of three men, ready to jump in if either flank party had bitten off more than it could chew.

I saw upraised clubs and the flash of knives and three of Torloni's men went down in the first ten seconds. We had caught them off balance and the flank attacks quickly rolled them up into the centre and there was a confused mob of shouting, fighting men. But more of the enemy were coming over the wall fast, and I was just going to move my little group into battle when I heard more shouting.

It came from *behind* me.

'Come on,' I yelled and ran down the yard towards *Sanford*. Now we knew what had happened to that other lorryload of men. They had come in from the seaward side and Torloni was attacking us front and rear.

Sanford was beseiged. A boat was drawn up on the hard and another boat full of men was just landing. There was a fight going on round *Sanford* with men trying to climb up on the deck and our working party valiantly trying to drive them off. I saw the small figure of old Palmerini; he had a rope with a block on the end of it which he whirled round his head like a medieval ball and chain. He whirled it once again and the block caught the attacker under the jaw and he toppled from the ladder he was climbing and fell senseless to the ground.

Palmerini's sons were battling desperately and I saw one go down. Then I saw Francesca wielding a boat-hook like a spear. She drove it at a boarder and the spike penetrated his thigh. He screamed shrilly and fell away, the boat-hook still sucking out of his leg. I saw the look of horror on Francesca's face and then drove home my little attack.

It was futile. We managed to relieve the beleaguered garrison on *Sanford*, but then we were outnumbered three to one and had to retreat up the yard. The attackers did not press us; they were so exultant at the capture of *Sanford* that they stayed with her and didn't follow us. We were lucky in their stupidity.

I looked around to see what was happening at the top of the yard. Coertze's party was closer than I had hoped – he had been driven back, too, but he was not under attack and I wondered why. If both enemy groups now made a concerted effort we were lost.

I said to Francesca, 'Duck under those sacks and stay quiet – you may get away with it.' Then I ran over to Coertze. 'What's happening?'

He grinned and wiped some blood from his cheek. 'Our outside boys concentrated and hit Torloni hard on the other side of the wall, all fifteen of them. He can't retreat now – anyone who tries to go back over the wall gets clobbered. I'm just getting my breath back before I hit 'em again.'

I said, 'They've got *Sanford*. They came in from the sea – we're boxed in, too.'

His chest heaved. 'All right; we'll hit 'em down there.'

I looked up the yard. 'No,' I said. 'Look, there's Torloni.'

We could see him under the wall, yelling at his men, whipping them up for another attack. I said, 'We attack up the yard – all of us – and we hope that the crowd at the back of us stay put for the time we need. We're going to snatch Torloni himself. Where's Piero?'

'I am here.'

'Good! Tell your boys to attack when I give the signal. You stay with Coertze and me, and the three of us will make for Torloni.'

I turned to find Francesca at my elbow. 'I thought I told you to duck out of sight.'

She shook her head stubbornly. Old Palmerini was behind her, so I said, 'See that she stays here, old friend.'

He nodded and put his arm round her. I said to Coertze, 'Remember, we want Torloni – we don't stop for anything else.'

Then we attacked up the yard. The three of us, Coertze, Piero and I, made a flying wedge, evading anyone who tried to stop us. We didn't fight, we just ran. Coertze had grasped the idea and was running as though he was on a rugby field making an effort for the final try.

The goal line was Torloni and we were on him before he properly realized what was happening. He snarled and blue steel showed in his hand.

'Spread out!' I yelled, and we separated, coming at him from three sides. The gun in his hand flamed and Coertze staggered; then Piero and I jumped him. I raised my arm and hit him hard with the edge of my hand; I felt his collar-bone break and he screamed and dropped the pistol.

With Torloni's scream a curious hush came over the yard. There was an uncertainty in his men as they looked back to see what was happening. I picked up the gun and held it to Torloni's head. 'Call off your dogs or I'll blow your brains out,' I said harshly.

I was as close to murder then as I have ever been. Torloni saw the look in my eyes and whitened. 'Stop,' he croaked.

'Louder,' ordered Piero and squeezed his shoulder.

He screamed again, then he shouted, 'Stop fighting – stop fighting. Torloni says so.'

His men were hirelings – they fought for pay and if the boss was captured they wouldn't get paid. There is not much loyalty among mercenaries. There was an uncertain shuffling and a melting away of figures into the darkness.

Coertze was sitting on the ground, his hand to his shoulder. Blood was oozing between his fingers. He took his hand away and looked at it with stupefied amazement. 'The bastard shot me,' he said blankly.

I went over to him. 'Are you all right?'

He held his shoulder again and got to his feet. 'I'm O.K.' He looked at Torloni sourly. 'I've got a bone to pick with you.'

'Later,' I said. 'Let's deal with the crowd at the bottom of the yard.'

We were being reinforced rapidly by men climbing over the wall. This was our mobile force which had taken Torloni's men in the rear and had whipped them. In a compact mass we marched down the yard towards *Sanford*, Torloni being frog-marched in front.

As we came near *Sanford* I poked the pistol muzzle into Torloni's fleshy neck. 'Tell them,' I commanded.

He shouted, 'Leave the boat. Go away. Torloni says that.'

The men around *Sanford* looked at us expressionlessly and made no move. Piero squeezed Torloni's shoulder again. 'Aaah. Leave the boat, I tell you,' he yelled.

They raised their eyes to the crowd behind us, realized they were outnumbered, and slowly began to drift towards the hard where their boats were drawn up. Piero said quietly, 'These are the men from La Spezia. That man in the blue jersey is their leader; Morlaix; he is a Frenchman from Marseilles.' He looked speculatively at their boats. 'You may have trouble with him yet. He does not care if Torloni lives or dies.'

I watched Morlaix's crowd push their boats into the water. 'We'll cross that bridge when we come to it,' I said. 'We've got to get out of here. Somebody might have notified the police about the brawl – we made enough noise, and there was a gunshot. Did we have many casualties?'

'I don't know; I will find out.'

Palmerini came pushing through the crowd with Francesca at his side. 'The boat is not harmed,' he said. 'We can put her into the water at any time.'

'Thanks,' I said. I looked at Francesca and made a quick decision. 'Still want to come?'

'Yes, I'm coming.'

'O.K. You won't have time to pack, though. We're leaving within the hour.'

She smiled. 'I have a small suitcase already packed. It has been ready for a week.'

Coertze was standing guard over Torloni. 'What do we do with this one?' he asked.

I said, 'We take him with us a little way. We may need him yet. Francesca, Kobus was shot; will you strap him up?'

'Oh, I didn't know,' she said. 'Where is the wound?'

'In the shoulder,' said Coertze absently. He was watching Walker on the deck of *Sanford*. 'Where was that *kêrel* when the trouble started?'

'I don't know,' I said. 'I never saw him from start to finish.'

IV

We put *Sanford* into the water very easily; there were plenty of willing hands. I felt better with a living, moving deck under my feet than I had for a long time. Before I went aboard for the last time I took Piero on one side.

'Tell the Count I've taken Francesca away,' I said. 'I think it's better this way – Torloni might look for revenge. You men can look after yourselves, but I wouldn't like to leave her here.'

'That is the best thing,' he said.

'If Torloni wants to start any more funny tricks you know what to do now. Don't go for his men – go for Torloni. He cracks easily under direct pressure. I'll make it clear to him that if he starts any of his nonsense he'll wind up floating somewhere in the bay. What did you find out about casualties?'

'Nothing serious,' said Piero. 'One broken arm, three stab wounds, three or four concussions.'

'I'm glad to see no one was killed,' I said. 'I wouldn't have liked that. I think Francesca would like to speak to you, so I'll leave you to it.'

We shook hands warmly and I went aboard. Piero was a fine man – a good man to have beside you in a fight.

He and Francesca talked together for a while and then she came on board. She was crying a little and I put my arms about her to comfort her. It's not very pleasant to leave one's native land at the best of times, and leaving in these circumstances the unpleasantness was doubled. I sat in the cockpit with my hand on the tiller and Walker started the engine. As soon as I heard it throb I threw it into gear and we moved away slowly.

For a long time we could see the little patch of light in front of the shed speckled with the waving Italians. They waved although they could not see us in the darkness and I felt sad at leaving them. 'We'll come back sometime,' I said to Francesca.

'No,' she said quietly. 'We'll never be back.'

V

We pressed on into the darkness at a steady six knots making our way due south to clear the Portovento headland. I looked up at the mast dimly outlined against the stars and wondered how long it would take to fix the running rigging. The deck was a mess, making nonsense of the term 'ship-shape,' but we couldn't do anything about that until it was light. Walker was below and Coertze was on the foredeck keeping guard on Torloni. Francesca and I conversed in low tones in the cockpit, talking of when we would be able to get married.

Coertze called out suddenly, 'When are we going to get rid of this garbage? He wants to know. He thinks we're going to put him over the side and he says he can't swim.'

'We'll slip inshore close to Portovento,' I said. 'We'll put him ashore in the dinghy.'

Coertze grumbled something about it being better to get rid of Torloni there and then, and relapsed into silence. Francesca said, 'Is there something wrong with the engine? It seems to be making a strange noise.'

I listened and there was a strange noise – but it wasn't *our* engine. I throttled back and heard the puttering of an outboard motor quite close to starboard.

'Get below quickly,' I said, and called to Coertze in a low voice, 'We've got visitors.'

He came aft swiftly. I pointed to starboard and, in the faint light of the newly risen moon, we could see the white feather of a bow wave coming closer. A voice came across the water. 'Monsieur Englishman, can you hear me?'

'It's Morlaix,' I said, and raised my voice. 'Yes, I can hear you.'

'We are coming aboard,' he shouted. 'It is useless to resist.'

'You stay clear,' I called. 'Haven't you had enough?'

Coertze got up with a grunt and went forward. I pulled Torloni's gun from my pocket and cocked it.

'There are only four of you,' shouted Morlaix. 'And many more of us.'

The bow wave of his boat was suddenly much closer and I could see the boat more clearly. It was full of men. Then it was alongside and, as it came close enough to bump gunwales, Morlaix jumped to the deck of *Sanford*. He was only four feet away from me so I shot him in the leg and he gave a shout and fell overboard.

Simultaneously Coertze rose, lifting in one hand the struggling figure of Torloni. 'Take this rubbish,' he shouted and hurled Torloni at the rush of men coming on deck. Torloni wailed and the flying body bowled them over and they fell back into their boat.

I took advantage of the confusion by suddenly bearing to port and the gap between the boats widened rapidly. Their boat seemed to be out of control – I imagine that the steersman had been knocked down.

They didn't bother us again. We could hear them shouting in the distance as they fished Morlaix from the water, but they made no further attack. They had no stomach for guns.

Our wake broadened in the moonlight as we headed for the open sea. We had a deadline to meet in Tangier and time was short.

BOOK THREE

The Sea

EIGHT: CALM AND STORM

We had fair winds at first and *Sanford* made good time. As I had suspected, the greater concentration of weight in the keel made her crotchety. In a following sea she rolled abominably, going through a complete cycle in two minutes. With the wind on the quarter, usually *Sanford*'s best point of sailing, every leeward roll was followed by a lurch in the opposite direction and her mast described wide arcs against the sky.

There was nothing to be done about it so it had to be suffered. The only cure was to have the ballast spread out more and that was the one thing we couldn't do. The violent motion affected Coertze most of all; he wasn't a good sailor at the best of times and the wound in his shoulder didn't help.

With the coming of dawn after that momentous and violent night we lay hove-to just out of sight of land and set to work on the running rigging. It didn't take long – Palmerini had done more in that direction than I'd expected – and soon we were on our way under sail. It was then that the crankiness of *Sanford* made itself evident, and I experimented for a while to see what I could do, but the cure was beyond me so I stopped wasting time and we pressed on.

We soon fell into our normal watchkeeping routine, modified by the presence of Francesca, who took over the

cooking from Coertze. During small boat voyages one sees
very little of the other members of the crew apart from
the times when the watch is changed, but Walker was
keeping more to himself than ever. Sometimes I caught
him watching me and he would start and roll his eyes like
a frightened horse and look away quickly. He was obviously terrified that I would tell Coertze about the cigarette
case. I had no such intention – I needed Walker to help
run *Sanford* – but I didn't tell him so. Let him sweat, I
thought callously.

Coertze's shoulder was not so bad; it was a clean flesh
wound and Francesca kept it well tended. I insisted that he
sleep in the quarter berth where the motion was least violent, and this led to a general post. I moved to the port pilot
berth in the main cabin while Francesca had the starboard
pilot berth. She rigged up a sailcloth curtain in front of it to
give her a modicum of privacy.

This meant that Walker was banished to the forecastle to
sleep on the hitherto unused pipe berth. This was intended
for a guest in port and not for use at sea; it was uncomfortable and right in the bows where the motion is most felt.
Serve him damn' well right, I thought uncharitably. But it
meant that we saw even less of him.

We made good time for the first five days, logging over a
hundred miles a day crossing the Ligurian Sea. Every day I
shot the sun and contentedly admired the course line on
the chart as it stretched even farther towards the Balearics.
I derived great pleasure from teaching Francesca how to
handle *Sanford*; she was an apt pupil and made no more
than the usual beginner's mistakes.

I observed with some amusement that Coertze seemed to
have lost his antipathy towards her. He was a changed man,
not as prickly as before. The gold was safe under his feet and
I think the fight in the boatyard had worked some of the
violence out of him. At any rate, he and Francesca got on

well together at last, and had long conversations about South Africa.

Once she asked him what he was going to do with his share of the spoil. He smiled. 'I'm going to buy a *plaas,*' he said complacently.

'A what?'

'A farm,' I translated. 'All Afrikaners are farmers at heart; they even call themselves farmers – boers – at least they used to.'

I think that those first five days after leaving Italy were the best sea days of the whole voyage. We never had better days before and we certainly didn't have any after- wards.

On the evening of the fifth day the wind dropped and the next day it kept fluctuating as though it didn't know what to do next. The strength varied between force three and dead calm and we had a lot of sail work to do. That day we only logged seventy miles.

At dawn the next day there was a dead calm. The sea was slick and oily and coming in long even swells. Our tempers tended to fray during the afternoon when there was noth- ing to do but watch the mast making lazy circles against the sky, while the precious hours passed and we made no way towards Tangier. I got tired of hearing the squeak of the boom in the gooseneck so I put up the crutch and we lashed down the boom. Then I went below to do some figuring at the chart table.

We had logged twenty miles, noon to noon, and at that rate we would reach Tangier about three months too late. I checked the fuel tank and found we had fifteen gallons left – that would take us 150 miles in thirty hours at our most economical speed. It would be better than sitting still and listening to the halyards slatting against the mast, so I started the engine and we were on our way again.

I chafed at the use of fuel – it was something we might need in an emergency – but this *was* an emergency, anyway, so I might as well use it; it was six of one and a half dozen of the other. We ploughed through the still sea at a steady five knots and I laid a course to the south of the Balearics, running in close to Majorca. If for some reason we had to put into port I wanted a port to be handy, and Palma was the nearest.

All that night and all the next morning we ran under power. There was no wind nor was there any sign that there was ever going to be any wind ever again. The sky was an immaculate blue echoing the waveless sea and I felt like hell. With no wind a sailing boat is helpless, and what would we do when the fuel ran out?

I discussed it with Coertze. 'I'm inclined to put in to Palma,' I said. 'We can fill up there.'

He threw a cigarette stub over the side. 'It's a damn' waste of time. We'd be going off course, and what if they keep us waiting round there?'

I said, 'It'll be a bigger waste of time if we're left without power. This calm could go on for days.'

'I've been looking at the Mediterranean Pilot,' he said. 'It says the percentage of calms at this time of year isn't high.'

'You can't depend on that – those figures are just averages. This could go on for a week.'

He sighed. 'You're the skipper,' he said. 'Do the best you can.'

So I altered course to the north and we ran for Palma. I checked on the fuel remaining and doubted if we'd make it – but we did. We motored into the yacht harbour at Palma with the engine coughing on the last of the fuel. As we approached the mooring jetty the engine expired and we drifted the rest of the way by momentum.

It was then I looked up and saw Metcalfe.

II

We cut the Customs formalities short by saying that we weren't going ashore and that we had only come in for fuel. The Customs officer commiserated with us on the bad sailing weather and said he would telephone for a chandler to come down and see to our needs.

That left us free to discuss Metcalfe. He hadn't said anything – he had just regarded us with a gentle smile on his lips and then had turned on his heel and walked away.

Coertze said, 'He's cooking something up.'

'Nothing could be more certain,' I said bitterly. 'Will we never get these bastards off our backs?'

'Not while we've got four tons of gold under our feet,' said Coertze. 'It's like a bloody magnet.'

I looked forward at Walker sitting alone on the foredeck. There was the fool who, by his loose tongue and his stupidities, had brought the vultures down on us. Or perhaps not – men like Metcalfe and Torloni have keen noses for gold. But Walker hadn't helped.

Francesca said, 'What do you think he will do?'

'My guess is a simple act of piracy,' I said. 'It'll appeal to his warped sense of humour to do some Spanish Main stuff.'

I lay on my back and looked at the sky. The club burgee at the masthead was lifting and fluttering in a light breeze. 'And look at that,' I said. 'We've got a wind, dammit.'

'I said we shouldn't have come in here,' grumbled Coertze. 'We'd have had the wind anyway, and Metcalfe wouldn't have spotted us.'

I considered Metcalfe's boat and his radar – especially the radar. 'No,' I said. 'It wouldn't have made any difference. He's probably known just where to put his hand on us ever since we left Italy.' I made a quick calculation on the basis of a 15-mile radar range. 'He can cover 700 square miles of sea with one pass of his radar. That Fairmile has probably been hovering hull-down on the horizon keeping an eye on us. We'd never spot it.'

'Well, what do we do now?' asked Francesca.

'We carry on as usual,' I said. 'There's not much else we can do. But I'm certainly not going to hand the gold to Mr Bloody Metcalfe simply because he shows up and throws a scare into us. We carry on and hope for the best.'

We refuelled and topped up the water tanks and were on our way again before nightfall. The sun was setting as we passed Cabo Figuera and I left the helm to Francesca and went below to study the chart. I had a plan to fox Metcalfe – it probably wouldn't work but it was worth trying.

As soon as it was properly dark I said to Francesca, 'Steer course 180 degrees.'

'South?' she said in surprise.

'That's right – south.' To Coertze I said, 'Do you know what that square gadget half-way up the mast is for?'

'*Nee, man,* I've never worried about it.'

'It's a radar reflector,' I said. 'A wooden boat gives a bad radar reflection so we use a special reflector for safety – it gives a nice big blip on a screen. If Metcalfe has been following us he must have got used to that blip by now – he can probably identify us sight unseen, just from the trace on the screen. So we're going to take the reflector away. He'll still get an echo but it'll be different, much fainter.'

I fastened a small spanner on a loop round my wrist and clipped a lifeline on to my safety belt and began to climb the mast. The reflector was bolted on to the lower spreaders and it was an uneasy job getting it down. *Sanford* was doing her new style dot-and-carry-one, and following the old-time sailor maxim of 'one hand for yourself and one hand for the ship' it was not easy to unfasten those two bolts. The trouble was that the bolts started to turn as well as the nuts, so I was getting nowhere fast. I was up the mast for over forty-five minutes before the reflector came free.

I got down to the deck, collapsed the reflector for stowage and said to Coertze, 'Where's Walker?'

'Dossing down; it's his watch at midnight.'

'I'd forgotten. Now we change the lights.' I went below to the chart table. I had a white light at the masthead visible all round which was coupled to a Morse key for signalling. I tied the key down so that the light stayed on all the time.

Then I called up to Coertze, 'Get a lantern out of the fo'c'sle and hoist it in the rigging.'

He came below. 'What's all this for?'

I said, 'Look, we're on the wrong course for Tangier – it's wasting time but it can't be helped because anything that puts Metcalfe off his stroke is good for us. We've altered our radar trace but Metcalfe might get suspicious and come in for a look at us, anyway. So we're festooned with lights in the usual sloppy Spanish fisherman fashion. We're line fishing and he won't see otherwise – not at night. So he just may give us the go-by and push off somewhere else.'

'You're a tricky bastard,' said Coertze admiringly.

'It'll only work once,' I said. 'At dawn we'll change course for Tangier.'

III

The wind got up during the night and we handed the light weather sails so that *Sanford* developed a fair turn of speed. Not that it helped much; we weren't making an inch of ground in the direction of Tangier.

At dawn it was blowing force five and we changed course so that the wind was on the quarter and *Sanford* began to stride out, her lee rail under and the bow wave showing white foam. I checked the log and saw that she was doing seven knots, which was close to her limit under sail. We were doing all right at last – on the right course for Tangier and travelling fast.

We kept a close watch on the horizon for Metcalfe but saw nothing. If he knew where we were he wasn't showing his hand. I didn't know whether to be glad or sorry about that; I would be glad if my stratagem had deceived him, but if it hadn't then I wanted to know about it.

The fresh breeze held all day and even tended to increase towards nightfall. The waves became larger and foam-crested, breaking every now and then on *Sanford*'s quarter. Every time that happened she would shudder and shake herself free to leap forward again. I estimated that the wind was now verging on force six and, as a prudent seaman, I should have been thinking of taking a reef in the mainsail, but I wanted to press on – there was not much time left, and less if we had to tangle with Metcalfe.

I turned in early, leaving Walker at the helm, and before I went to sleep I contemplated what I would do if I were Metcalfe. We had to go through the Straits of Gibraltar – the whole Mediterranean was a funnel with the Straits forming the spout. If Metcalfe took station there his radar could cover the whole channel from shore to shore.

On the other hand, the Straits were busy waters, so he'd have to zig-zag to check dubious boats visually. Then again, if he was contemplating piracy, it would be dangerous to try it where it could be spotted easily – there were some very fast naval patrol boats at Gibraltar and I didn't think that even Metcalfe would have the nerve to tackle us in daylight.

So that settled that – we would have to run through the Straits in daylight.

If – and I was getting tired of all these ifs – if he didn't nobble us before or after the Straits. I hazily remembered a case of piracy just outside Tangier in 1956 – two groups of smugglers had tangled with each other and one of the boats had been burned. Perhaps he wouldn't want to leave it as long as that; we would be close to home and we might give him the slip after all – once we were in the yacht harbour there wouldn't be a damn' thing he could do. No, I didn't think he would leave it as late as that.

But before the Straits? That was a different kettle of fish and that depended on another 'if'. If we had given him the slip on leaving Majorca – if he didn't know where we were now – then we might have a chance. But if he did know where we were, then he could close in any time and put a prize crew aboard. If – yet another if – the weather would let him.

As I drifted off to sleep I blessed the steadily rising wind which added wings to *Sanford* and which would make it impossible for the Fairmile to come alongside.

IV

Coertze woke me up. 'The wind's getting stronger; I think we should change sail or something.' He had to shout above the roar of the wind and the sea.

I looked at my watch as I pulled on my oilies; it was two o'clock and I had had six hours' sleep. *Sanford* was bucking a bit and I had a lot of trouble putting my trousers on. A sudden lurch sent me across the cabin and I carommed into the berth in which Francesca slept.

'What is wrong?' she asked.

'Nothing,' I said. 'Everything is fine; go back to sleep.'

'You think I can sleep in this?'

I grinned. 'You'll soon get used to it. It's blowing up a bit, but nothing to worry about.'

I finished dressing and went up into the cockpit. Coertze was right; we should do something about taking in sail. The wind was blowing at a firm force seven – what old-time sailormen referred to contemptuously as a 'yachtsman's gale' and what Admiral Beaufort temperately called a 'strong wind'.

Tattered clouds fled across the sky, making a baffling alteration of light and shade as they crossed the moon. The seas were coming up in lumps and the crests were being blown away in streaks of foam. *Sanford* was plunging her head into the seas and every time this happened she would stop with a jerk, losing speed. A reduction of sail would hold her head up and help her motion, so I said to Coertze, my voice raised in a shout, 'You're right; I'll reef her down a bit. Hold her as she is.'

I snapped a lifeline on to my safety belt and went forward along the crazily shifting deck. It took half an hour to take in two rolls round the bottom of the mainsail and to take in the jib, leaving the foresail to balance her head. As soon as I handed the jib I could feel the difference in motion; *Sanford* rode more easily and didn't ram her bows down as often.

I went back to the cockpit and asked Coertze, 'How's that?'

'Better,' he shouted. 'She seems to be going faster, though.'

'She is; she's not getting stopped.'

He looked at the piled-up seas. 'Will it get worse than this?'

'Oh, this is not so bad,' I replied. 'We're going as fast as we can, which is what we want.' I smiled, because from a small boat everything looked larger than life and twice as dangerous. However I hoped the weather wouldn't worsen; that would slow us down.

I stayed with Coertze for a time to reassure him. It was nearly time for my watch, anyway, and there was no point in going back to sleep. After some time I slipped down into the galley and made some coffee – the stove was rocking crazily in its gimbals and I had to clamp the coffee-pot, but I didn't spill a drop.

Francesca was watching me from her berth and when the coffee was ready I beckoned to her. If she came to the coffee instead of vice versa there was less chance of it spilling. We wedged ourselves in between the galley bench and the companionway, sipping hot coffee and talking about the weather.

She smiled at me. 'You like this weather, don't you?'

'It's fine.'

'I think it's a little frightening.'

'There's nothing to be frightened of,' I said. 'Or rather, only one thing.'

'What is that?'

'The crew,' I said. 'You see, small boat design has reached the point of perfection just about, as far as seaworthiness is concerned. A boat like this can take any weather safely if she's handled right – and I'm not saying this because I designed and built her – it applies to any boat of this general type. It's the crew that fails, rather than the boat. You get tired and then you make a mistake – and you only have to make one mistake – you can't play about with the sea.'

'How long does it take before the crew gets as tired as that?'

'We're all right,' I said cheerfully. 'There are enough of us, so that we can all get our sleep, so we can last indefinitely. It's the single-handed heroes who have the trouble.'

'You're very reassuring,' she said, and got up to take another cup from the shelf. 'I'll take Coertze some coffee.'

'Don't bother; it'll only get full of salt spray, and there's nothing worse than salted coffee. He'll be coming below in a few minutes – it's my watch.'

I buttoned my oilies and tightened the scarf round my neck. 'I think I'll relieve him now; he shouldn't really be up there in this weather with that hole in his shoulder. How's it doing, anyway?'

'Healing nicely,' she said.

'If he had to have a hole in him he couldn't have done better than that one,' I said. 'Six inches lower and he'd have been plugged through the heart.'

She said, 'You know, I'm changing my mind about him. He's not such a bad man.'

'A heart of gold beneath that rugged exterior?' I queried, and she nodded. I said, 'His heart is set on gold, anyway. We may have some trouble with him if we avoid Metcalfe – don't forget his history. But give the nice man some coffee when he comes below.'

I went up into the cockpit and relieved Coertze. 'There's coffee for you,' I shouted.

'Thanks, just what I need,' he answered and went below.

Sanford continued to eat up the miles and the wind continued to increase in force. Good and bad together. I still held on to the sail I had, but when Walker came to relieve me in a cloudy and watery dawn I took in another roll of the mainsail before I went below for breakfast.

Just before I descended the companionway, Walker said, 'It'll get worse.'

I looked at the sky. 'I don't think so; it rarely gets worse than this in the Mediterranean.'

He shrugged. 'I don't know about the Mediterranean, but I have a feeling it'll get worse, that's all.'

I went below feeling glum. Walker had previously shown an uncanny ability to detect changes in the weather on no visible evidence. He had displayed this weather sense before and had invariably been proved right. I hoped he was wrong this time.

He wasn't!

I couldn't take a noonday sight because of thick cloud and bad visibility. Even if I could have seen the sun I doubt if I could have held a sextant steady on that reeling deck. The log reading was 152 miles from noon to noon, *Sanford*'s best run ever.

Shortly after noon the wind speed increased gently to force eight verging on force nine – a strong gale. We handed the mainsail altogether and set the trysail, a triangular handkerchief-sized piece of strong canvas intended for heavy weather. The foresail we also doused with difficulty – it was becoming very dangerous to work on the foredeck.

The height of the waves had increased tremendously and they would no sooner break in a white crest than the wind would tear the foam away to blow it in ragged streaks across the sea. Large patches of foam were beginning to form until the sea began to look like a giant washtub into which some-one had emptied a few thousand tons of detergent.

I gave orders that no one should go on deck but the man on watch and that he should wear a safety line at all times. For myself, I got into my berth, put up the bunkboards so that I wouldn't be thrown out, and tried unsuccessfully to read a magazine. But I kept wondering if Metcalfe was out in this sea. If he was, I didn't envy him, because a power boat does not take heavy weather as kindly as a sailing yacht, and he must be going through hell.

Things got worse later in the afternoon so I decided to heave-to. We handed the trysail and lay under bare poles abeam to the seas. Then we battened down the hatches and all four of us gathered in the main cabin chatting desultorily when the noise would allow us.

It was about this time that I started to worry about sea room. As I had been unable to take a sight I didn't know our exact position – and while dead reckoning and log readings were all very well in their way, I was beginning to become perturbed. For we were now in the throat of the funnel between Almeria in Spain and Morocco. I knew we were safe enough from being wrecked on the mainland, but just about here was a fly-speck of an island called Alboran which could be the ruin of us if we ran into it in this weather.

I studied the Mediterranean Pilot. I had been right when I said that this sort of weather was not common in the Mediterranean, but that was cold comfort. Evidently the Clerk of the Weather hadn't read the Mediterranean Pilot – the old boy was certainly piling it on.

At five o'clock I went on deck for a last look round before nightfall. Coertze helped me take away the batten boards from the companion entrance and I climbed into the cockpit. It was knee-deep in swirling water despite the three two-inch drains I had built into it; and as I stood there, gripping a stanchion, another boiling wave swept across the deck and filled the cockpit.

I made a mental note to fit more cockpit drains, then looked at the sea. The sight was tremendous; this was a whole gale and the waves were high, with threatening overhanging crests. As I stood there one of the crests broke over the deck and *Sanford* shuddered violently. The poor old girl was taking a hell of a beating and I thought I had better do something about it. It would mean at least one man in the cockpit getting soaked and miserable and frightened and I knew that man must be me – I wouldn't trust anyone else with what I was about to do.

I went back below. 'We'll have to run before the wind,' I said. 'Walker, fetch that coil of 4-inch nylon rope from the fo'c'sle. Kobus, get into your oilskins and come with me.'

Coertze and I went back into the cockpit and I unlashed the tiller. I shouted, 'When we run her downwind we'll have to slow her down. We'll run a bight of rope astern and the drag will help.'

Walker came up into the cockpit with the rope and he made one end fast to the port stern bitts. I brought *Sanford* downwind and Coertze began to pay the rope over the stern. Nylon, like hemp and unlike manila, floats, and the loop of rope acted like a brake on *Sanford*'s wild rush.

Too much speed is the danger when you're running before a gale; if you go too fast then the boat is apt to trip just like a man who trips over his own feet when running. When that happens the boat is likely to capsize fore-and-aft – the bows dig into the sea, the stern comes up and the boat somersaults. It happened to *Tzu Hang* in the Pacific and it happened to Erling Tambs' *Sandefjord* in the Atlantic when he lost a man. I didn't want it to happen to me.

Steering a boat in those conditions was a bit hair-raising. The stern had to be kept dead in line with the overtaking wave and, if you got it right, then the stern rose smoothly and the wave passed underneath. If you were a fraction out then there was a thud and the wave would break astern; you would be drenched with water, the tiller would nearly be wrenched from your grasp and you would wonder how much more of that treatment the rudder would take.

Coertze had paid out all the nylon, a full forty fathoms, and *Sanford* began to behave a little better. The rope seemed to smooth the waters astern and the waves did not break as easily. I thought we were still going a little too fast so I told Walker to bring up some more rope. With another two lengths of twenty-fathom three-inch nylon also streamed astern I reckoned we had cut *Sanford*'s speed down to three knots.

There was one thing more I could do. I beckoned to Coertze and put my mouth close to his ear. 'Go below and get the spare can of diesel oil from the fo'c'sle. Give it to Francesca and tell her to put half a pint at a time into the lavatory then flush it. About once every two or three minutes will do.'

He nodded and went below. The four-gallon jerrycan we kept as a spare would now come in really useful. I had often heard of pouring oil on troubled waters – now we would see if there was anything in it.

Walker was busy wrapping sailcloth around the ropes streamed astern where they rubbed on the taffrail. It wouldn't take much of this violent movement to chafe them right through, and if a rope parted at the same moment that I had to cope with one of those particularly nasty waves which came along from time to time then it might be the end of us.

I looked at my watch. It was half past six and it looked as though I would have a nasty and frightening night ahead of me. But I was already getting the hang of keeping *Sanford* stern on to the seas and it seemed as though all I would need would be concentration and a hell of a lot of stamina.

Coertze came back and shouted, 'The oil's going in.'

I looked over the side. It didn't seem to be making much difference, though it was hard to tell. But anything that *could* make a difference I was willing to try, so I let Francesca carry on.

The waves were big. I estimated they were averaging nearly forty feet from trough to crest and *Sanford* was behaving like a roller-coaster car. When we were in a trough the waves looked frighteningly high, towering above us with threatening crests. Then her bows would sink as a wave took her astern until it seemed as if she was vertical and going to dive straight to the bottom of the sea. The wave would lift her to the crest and then we could see the stormtattered sea around us, with spume being driven from the waves horizontally until it was difficult to distinguish between sea and air. And back we would go into a trough with *Sanford*'s bows pointing to the skies and the monstrous waves again threatening.

Sometimes, about four times in an hour, there was a freak wave which must have been caused by one wave catching up with another, thus doubling it. These freaks

I estimated at sixty feet high – higher than *Sanford*'s mast! – and I would have to concentrate like hell so that we wouldn't be pooped.

Once – just once – we were pooped, and it was then that Walker went overboard. We were engulfed in water as a vast wave broke over the stern and I heard his despairing shout and saw his white face and staring eyes as he was washed out of the cockpit and over the side.

Coertze's reaction was fast. He lunged for Walker – but missed. I shouted, 'Safety line – pull him in.'

He brushed water out of his eyes and yelled, 'Wasn't wearing one.'

'The damned fool,' I thought. I think it was a thought – I might even have yelled it. Coertze gave a great shout and pointed aft and I turned and could see a dark shape rolling in the boiling waters astern and I saw white hands clutching the nylon rope. They say a drowning man will clutch at a straw – Walker was lucky – he had grabbed at something more substantial, one of the drag ropes.

Coertze was hauling the rope in fast. It couldn't have been easy with the drag of Walker in the water pulling on his injured shoulder, but he was hauling just as fast as though the rope was free. He pulled Walker right under the stern and then belayed the rope.

He shouted to me, 'I'm going over the counter – you'll have to sit on my legs.'

I nodded and he started to crawl over the counter stern to where Walker was still tightly gripping the rope. He slithered aft and I got up from my seat and hoisted myself out of the cockpit until I could sit on his legs. In the violent motion of the storm it was only my weight that kept Coertze from being hurled bodily into the sea.

Coertze grasped the rope and heaved, his shoulders writhing with the effort. He was lifting the dead weight of Walker five feet – the distance from the taffrail to the surface of the water. I hoped to God that Walker could hold on. If he let go then, not only would he be lost himself but the sudden release of tension would throw Coertze off balance and he would not have a hope of saving himself.

Walker's hands appeared above the taffrail and Coertze took a grip on the cuff of his coat. Then I looked aft and yelled, 'Hang on, for God's sake!'

One of those damnable freak seas was bearing on us, a terrifying monster coming up astern with the speed of an express train. *Sanford's* bows sank sickeningly and Coertze gave Walker another heave, and grasped him by the scruff of the neck, pulling him on to the counter.

Then the wave was upon us and away as fast as it had come. Walker tumbled into the bottom of the cockpit, unconscious or dead, I couldn't tell which, and Coertze fell on top of him, his chest heaving with the strain of his exertions. He lay there for a few minutes, then bent down to loosen Walker's iron grip on the rope.

As he prised the fingers away, I said, 'Take him below – and you'd better stay there yourself for a while.'

A great light had just dawned on me but I had not time to think about it just then – I had to get that bight of rope back over the stern while still keeping a grasp of the tiller and watching the next sea coming up.

It was nearly an hour before Coertze came back – a lonely and frightening hour during which I was too busy to think coherently about what I had seen. The storm seemed to be building up even more strongly and I began to have second thoughts about what I had told Francesca about the seaworthiness of small boats.

When he climbed into the cockpit he took over Walker's job of looking after the stern ropes, giving me a grin as he settled down. 'Walker's O.K.,' he bawled. 'Francesca's looking after him. I pumped the water out of him – the bilges must be nearly full.' He laughed and the volume of his great laughter seemed to overpower the noise of the gale.

I looked at him in wonder.

V

A Mediterranean gale can't last; there is not the power of a huge ocean to draw upon and a great wind soon dies. At four the next morning the storm had abated enough for me to hand over the tiller to Coertze and go below. When I sat on the settee my hands were shaking with the sudden release of tension and I felt inexpressibly weary.

Francesca said, 'You must be hungry; I'll get you something to eat.'

I shook my head. 'No, I'm too tired to eat – I'm going to sleep.' She helped me take off my oilies, and I said, 'How's Walker?'

'He's all right; he's asleep in the quarter berth.'

I nodded slowly – Coertze had put Walker into his own berth. That fitted in, too.

I said, 'Wake me in two hours – don't let me sleep any longer. I don't want to leave Coertze alone too long,' and I fell on to my berth and was instantly asleep. The last thing I remembered was a fleeting vision of Coertze hauling Walker over the stern by the scruff of the neck.

Francesca woke me at six-thirty with a cup of coffee which I drank gratefully. 'Do you want something to eat?' she asked.

I listened to the wind and analysed the motion of *Sanford*. 'Make breakfast for all of us,' I said. 'We'll heave to and have a rest for a bit. I think the time has come for a talk with Coertze, anyway.'

I went back into the cockpit and surveyed the situation. The wind was still strong but not nearly as strong as it had been, and Coertze had hauled in the two twenty-fathom ropes and had coiled them neatly. I said, 'We'll heave to now; it's time you had some sleep.'

He nodded briefly and we began to haul in the bight of rope. Then we lashed the tiller and watched *Sanford* take position broadside on to the seas – it was safe now that the wind had dropped. When we went below Francesca was in the galley making breakfast. She had put a damp cloth on the cabin table to stop things sliding about and Coertze and I sat down.

He started to butter a piece of bread while I wondered how to go about what I was going to say. It was a difficult question I was going to broach and Kobus had such a thorny character that I didn't know how he would take it. I said, 'You know, I never really thanked you properly for pulling me out of the mine – you know, when the roof caved in.'

He munched on the bread and said, with his mouth full, *'Nee, man,* it was my own fault, I told you that before. I should have shored the last bit properly.'

'Walker owes you his thanks, too. You saved his life last night.'

He snorted. 'Who cares what he thinks.'

I said carefully, getting ready to duck, 'Why did you do it, anyway? It would have been worth at least a quarter of a million *not* to pull him out.'

Coertze stared at me, affronted. His face reddened with anger. 'Man, do you think I'm a bloody murderer?'

I had thought so at one time but didn't say so. 'And you didn't kill Parker or Alberto Corso or Donato Rinaldi?'

His face purpled. 'Who said I did?'

I cocked my thumb at the quarter berth where Walker was still asleep. 'He did.'

I thought he would burst. His jaws worked and he was literally speechless, unable to say a damn' thing. I said, 'According to friend Walker, you led Alberto into a trap on a cliff and then pushed him off; you beat in the head of Donato; you shot Parker in the back of the head when you were both in action against the Germans.'

'The lying little bastard,' ground out Coertze. He started to get up. 'I'll ram those lies down his bloody throat.'

I held up my hand. 'Hold on – don't go off half-cocked. Let's sort it out first; I'd like to get your story of what happened at that time. You see, what happened last night has led me to reconsider a lot of things. I wondered why you should have saved Walker if you're the man he says you are. I'd like to get at the truth for once.'

He sat down slowly and looked down at the table. At last he said, 'Alberto's death was an accident; I tried to save him, but I couldn't.'

'I believe you – after last night.'

'Donato I know nothing about. I remember thinking that there was something queer about it, though. I mean, why should Donato go climbing for fun? He had enough of that the way the Count sent us all over the hills.'

'And Parker?'

'I couldn't have killed Parker even if I'd wanted to,' he said flatly.

'Why not?'

Slowly he said, 'We were with Umberto doing one of the usual ambushes. Umberto split the force in two – one group on one side of the valley, the other group on the other side. Parker and Walker were with the other group. The ambush was a flop, anyway, and the two parties went back to camp separately. It was only when I got back to camp that I heard that Parker had been killed.'

He rubbed his chin. 'Did you say that Walker told you that Parker had been shot in the back of the head?'

'Yes.'

He looked at his hands spread out on the table. 'Walker could have done it, you know. It would be just like him.'

'I know,' I said. 'You told me once that Walker had got you into trouble a couple of times during the war. When exactly did that happen? Before you buried the gold or afterwards?'

He frowned in thought, casting his mind back to faraway days. He said, 'I remember once when Walker pulled some men away from a ditch when he shouldn't have. He was acting as a messenger for Umberto and said he's misunderstood the instruction. I was leading a few chaps at the time and this left my flank wide open.' His eyes darkened. 'A couple of the boys copped it because of that and I nearly got a bayonet in my rump.' His face twisted in thought. 'It was *after* we buried the gold.'

'Are you sure?'

'I'm certain. We only joined Umberto's crowd after we'd buried the gold.'

I said softly, 'Maybe he could shoot Parker in the back of the head. Maybe he could beat in the back of Donato's head with a rock and fake a climbing accident. But maybe he was too scared of *you* to come at you front or rear – you're a bit of an awesome bastard at times, you know. Maybe he tried to arrange that the Germans should knock you off.'

Coertze's hands clenched on the table. I said, 'He's always been afraid of you – he still is.'

'*Magtig,* but he has reason to be,' he burst out. 'Donato got us out of the camp. Donato stayed with him on the hillside while the Germans were searching.' He looked at me with pain in his eyes. 'What kind of man is it who can do such a thing?'

'A man like Walker,' I said. 'I think we ought to talk to him. I'm getting eager to know what he's arranged for me and Francesca.'

Coertze's lips tightened. '*Ja,* I think we wake him up now out of that *lekker slaap.*'

He stood up just as Francesca came in loaded with bowls. She saw Coertze's face and paused uncertainly. 'What's the matter?'

I took the bowls from her and put them in the fiddles. 'We're just going to have a talk with Walker,' I said. 'You'd better come along.'

But Walker was already awake and I could see from his expression that he knew what was coming. He swung himself from the berth and tried to get away from Coertze, who lunged at him.

'Hold on,' I said, and grabbed Coertze's arm. 'I said we're going to talk to him.'

The muscles bunched in Coertze's arm and then relaxed and I let go. I said to Walker, 'Coertze thinks you're a liar – what do you say?'

His eyes shifted and he gave Coertze a scared glance, then he looked away. 'I didn't say he killed anybody. I didn't say that.'

'No, you didn't,' I agreed. 'But you damn' well implied it.'

Coertze growled under his breath but said nothing, apparently content to let me handle it for the moment. I said, 'What about Parker? You said that Coertze was near him when he was shot – Coertze said he wasn't. What about it?'

'I didn't say that either,' he said sulkily.

'You *are* a damned liar,' I said forcibly. 'You said it to me. I've got a good memory even if you haven't. I warned you in Tangier what would happen if you ever lied to me, so you'd better watch it. Now I want the truth – was Coertze near Parker when he was killed?'

He was silent for a long time. 'Well, was he?' I demanded.

He broke. 'No, he wasn't,' he cried shrilly. 'I made that up. He wasn't there; he was on the other side of the valley.'

'Then who killed Parker?'

'It was the Germans,' he cried frantically. 'It was the Germans – I told you it was the Germans.'

I suppose it was too much to expect him to confess to murder. He would never say outright that he had killed Parker and Donato Rinaldi – but his face gave him away. I had no intention of sparing him anything, so I said to Coertze, 'He was responsible for Torloni's attack.'

Coertze grunted in surprise. 'How?'

I told him about the cigarette case, then said to Walker, 'Coertze saved your life last night, but I wish to God he'd let you drown. Now I'm going to leave him down here alone with you and he can do what he likes.'

Walker caught my arm. 'Don't leave me,' he implored. 'Don't let him get at me.' What he had always feared was now about to happen – there was no one between him and Coertze. He had blackened Coertze in my eyes so that he would have an ally to fight his battles, but now I was on Coertze's side. He feared physical violence – his killing had been done from ambush – and Coertze was the apotheosis of violence.

'Please,' he whimpered, 'don't leave.' He looked at Francesca with a passionate plea in his eyes. She turned aside without speaking and went up the companionway into the cockpit. I shook off his hand and followed her, closing the cabin hatch.

'Coertze will kill him,' she said in a low voice.

'Hasn't he the right?' I demanded. 'I don't believe in private executions as a rule, but this is one time I'm willing to make an exception.'

'I'm not thinking of Walker,' she said. 'It will be bad for Coertze. No one can kill a man like that and be the same after. It will be bad for his . . . his spirit.'

I said, 'Coertze will do what he has to do.'

We lapsed into silence, just looking at the lumpy sea, and I began to think of the boat and what we had to do next.

The cabin hatch opened and Coertze came into the cockpit. There was a baffled expression on his face and he said in a hoarse voice, 'I was going to kill the little bastard. I was going to hit him – I did hit him once. But you can't hit anyone who won't fight back. You can't, can you?'

I grinned and Francesca laughed joyously. Coertze looked at us and his face broke into a slow smile. 'But what are we going to do with him?' he asked.

'We'll drop him at Tangier and let him shift for himself,' I said. 'We'll give him the biggest scare any man's ever had.'

We were sitting grinning at each other like a couple of happy fools when Francesca said sharply, 'Look!'

I followed the line of her outstretched arm. 'Oh, no!' I groaned. Coertze looked and cursed.

Coming towards us through the tossing seas and wallowing atrociously was the Fairmile.

NINE: SANFORD

I looked at it bitterly. I had been certain that Metcalfe must have lost us in the storm – he had the luck of the devil. He hadn't found us by radar either, because the storm had made a clean sweep of the Fairmile's upperworks – his radar antenna was gone, as also was the radio mast and the short derrick. It could only have been by sheer luck that he had stumbled upon us.

I said to Coertze, 'Get below and start the engine. Francesca, you go below, too, and stay there.'

I looked across at the Fairmile. It was about a mile away and closing at about eight knots – a little over five minutes to make what futile preparations we could. I had no illusions about Metcalfe. Torloni had been bad enough but all he knew was force – Metcalfe used his brains.

The Fairmile was in no better shape, either. She staggered and wallowed as unexpected waves hit her and I could imagine the tumult inside that hull. She was an old boat, being war surplus, and her hull must have deteriorated over the years despite the care Metcalfe had lavished on her. Then there was the fact that when she was built her life expectancy was about five years, and wartime materials weren't noted for their excessive quality.

I had the sudden idea that she couldn't move any faster, and that Metcalfe was driving her as fast as he dared in those heavy seas. Her engines were fine for twenty-six knots in calm water but if she was driven at much more than eight knots now she would be in danger of falling apart. Metcalfe might risk a lot for the gold, but he wouldn't risk that.

As I heard the engine start I opened the throttle wide and turned *Sanford* away from the Fairmile. We had a biggish engine and I could still get seven knots out of *Sanford,* even punching against these seas. Our five minutes' grace was now stretched to an hour, and maybe in that hour I'd get another bright idea.

Coertze came up and I handed the tiller over to him, and went below. I didn't bother to tell him what to do – it was obvious. I opened the locker under my berth and took out the Schmeisser machine pistol and all the magazines. Francesca looked at me from the settee. 'Must you do that?' she asked.

'I'll not shoot unless I have to,' I said. 'Not unless they start shooting first.' I looked round. 'Where's Walker?'

'He locked himself in the fo'c'sle. He's frightened of Coertze.'

'Good. I don't want him underfoot now,' I said, and went back to the cockpit.

Coertze looked incredulously at the machine pistol. 'Where the hell did you get that?'

'From the tunnel,' I said. 'I hope it works – this ammo is damned old.'

I put one of the long magazines into the butt and clipped the shoulder rest into place. I said, 'You'd better get your Luger; I'll take the helm.'

He smiled sourly. 'What's the use? You threw all the bullets away.'

'Damn! Wait a minute, though; there's Torloni's gun. It's in the chart table drawer.'

He went below and I looked back at the Fairmile. As I thought, Metcalfe didn't increase his speed when we turned away. Not that it mattered – he had the legs of us by about a knot and I could see that he was perceptibly closer.

Coertze came back with the pistol stuck in his trouser waistband. He said, 'How long before he catches up?'

'Less than an hour,' I said. I touched the Schmeisser. 'We don't shoot unless he does – and we don't shoot to kill.'

'Will he shoot to kill?'

'I don't know,' I said. 'He might.'

Coertze grunted and pulled out the gun and began to examine the action.

We fell into silence; there was nothing much to talk about, anyway. I ruminated on the firing of a sub-machine-gun. It had been a long time since I had fired one and I began to go over the training points that had been drilled into me by a red-faced sergeant. The big thing was that the recoil lifted the muzzle and if you didn't con-sciously hold it down most of your fire would be wasted in the air. I tried to think of other things I had learned but I couldn't think of anything else so that fragment of infor-mation would have to do.

After a while I said to Coertze, 'I could do with some coffee.'

'That's not a bad idea,' he said, and went below. An Afrikaner will never refuse the offer of coffee; their livers are tanned with it. In five minutes he was back with two steaming mugs, and said, 'Francesca wants to come up.'

I looked back at the Fairmile. 'No,' I said briefly.

We drank the coffee, spilling half of it as *Sanford* shud-dered to a particularly heavy sea, and when we had fin-ished the Fairmile was within a quarter of a mile and I could see Metcalfe quite clearly standing outside the wheelhouse.

I said, 'I wonder how he's going to go about it. He can't board us in this sea, there's too much danger of ramming us. How would you go about it, Kobus?'

'I'd lay off and knock us off with a rifle,' he grunted. 'Just like at a shooting gallery. Then when the sea goes down he can board us without a fight.'

That seemed reasonable but it wouldn't be as easy as in a shooting gallery – metal ducks don't shoot back. I handed the tiller to Coertze. 'We may have to do a bit of fancy manoeuvring,' I said. 'But you'll handle her well enough without sail. When I tell you to do something, you do it damn' quick.' I picked up the Schmeisser and held it on my knee. 'How many rounds are there in that pistol?'

'Not enough,' he said. 'Five.'

At last the Fairmile was only a hundred yards away on the starboard quarter and Metcalfe came out of the wheel-house carrying a Tannoy loud-hailer. His voice boomed across the water. 'What are you running away for? Don't you want a tow?'

I cupped my hands around my mouth. 'Are you claiming salvage?' I asked sardonically.

He laughed. 'Did the storm do any damage?'

'None at all,' I shouted. 'We can get to port ourselves.' If he wanted to play the innocent I was prepared to go along with him. I had nothing to lose.

The Fairmile was throttled back to keep pace with us. Metcalfe fiddled with the amplification of the loud-hailer and it whistled eerily. 'Hal,' he shouted, 'I want your boat – and your cargo.'

There it was – out in the open as bluntly as that.

The loud-hailer boomed, 'If you act peaceable about it I'll accept half, if you don't I'll take the lot, anyway.'

'Torloni made the same offer and look what happened to him.'

'He was at a disadvantage,' called Metcalfe. 'He couldn't use guns – I can.'

Krupke moved into sight – carrying a rifle. He climbed on top of the deck saloon and lay down just behind the wheelhouse. I said to Coertze, 'It looks as though you called that one.'

It was bad, but not as bad as all that. Krupke had been in the army; he was accustomed to firing from a steady position even though his target might move. I didn't think he could fire at all accurately from a bouncing platform like the Fairmile.

I saw the Fairmile edging in closer and said to Coertze, 'Keep the distance.'

Metcalfe shouted, 'What about it?'

'Go to hell!'

He nodded to Krupke, who fired immediately, I didn't see where the bullet went – I don't think it hit us at all. He fired again and this time he hit something forward. It must have been metal because I heard a 'spaang' as the bullet ricochetted away.

Coertze dug me in the ribs. 'Don't look back so that Metcalfe notices you, but I think we're in for some heavy weather.'

I changed position on the seat so that I could look astern from the corner of my eye. The horizon was black with a vicious squall – and it was coming our way. I hoped to God it would hurry.

I said, 'We'll have to play for time now.'

Krupke fired again and there was a slam astern. I looked over the side and saw a hole punched into the side of the counter. His aim was getting better.

I shouted, 'Tell Krupke not to hole us below the water-line. We might sink, and you wouldn't like that.'

That held him for a while. I saw him talking to Krupke, making gestures with his hand to indicate a higher elevation. I called urgently for Francesca to come on deck. Those nickel-jacketed bullets would go through *Sanford*'s thin planking as though it was tissue paper. She came up just as Krupke fired his next shot. It went high and didn't hit anything.

As soon as Metcalfe saw her he held up his hand and Krupke stopped firing. 'Hal, be reasonable,' he called. 'You've got a woman aboard.'

I looked at Francesca and she shook her head. I shouted, 'You're doing the shooting.'

'I don't want to hurt anybody,' pleaded Metcalfe.

'Then go away.'

He shrugged and said something to Krupke, who fired again. The bullet hit the gooseneck with a clang. I grinned mirthlessly at Metcalfe's curious morality – according to him it would be my fault if anyone was killed.

I looked astern. The squall was appreciably nearer and coming up fast. It was the last dying kick of the storm and wouldn't last long – just long enough to give Metcalfe the slip, I hoped. I didn't think that Metcalfe had seen it yet; he was too busy with us.

Krupke fired again. There was a thud forward and I knew the bullet must have gone through the main cabin. I had brought Francesca up just in time.

I was beginning to worry about Krupke. In spite of the difficulties of aiming, his shooting was getting better, and even if it didn't, then sooner or later he would get in a lucky shot. I wondered how much ammunition he had.

'Metcalfe,' I called.

He held up his hand but not soon enough to prevent Krupke pulling the trigger. The cockpit disintegrated into matchwood just by my elbow. We all ducked low into the cockpit and I looked incredulously at the back of my hand – a two-inch splinter of mahogany was sticking in it.

I pulled it out and shouted, 'Hey, hold it! That was a bit too close.'

'What do you want?'

I noticed that the Fairmile was crowding us again so I told Coertze to pull out.

'Well?' Metcalfe's voice was impatient.

'I want to make a deal,' I shouted.

'You know my terms.'

'How do we know we can trust you?'

Metcalfe was uncompromising. 'You don't.'

I pretended to confer with Coertze. 'How's that squall coming up?'

'If you keep stringing him along we might make it.'

I turned to the Fairmile. 'I'll make a counter-proposition. We'll give you a third – Walker won't be needing his share.'

Metcalfe laughed. 'Oh, you've found him out at last, have you?'

'What about it?'

'Nothing doing – half or all of it. Make your choice; you're in no position to bargain.'

I turned to Coertze. 'What do you think, Kobus?'

He rubbed his chin. 'I'll go along with anything you say.'

'Francesca?'

She sighed. 'Do you think this other storm coming up will help?'

'It's not a storm, but it'll help. I think we can lose Metcalfe if we can hold him off for another ten minutes.'

'Can we?'

'I think so, but it might be dangerous.'

Her lips tightened. 'Then fight him.'

I looked across at Metcalfe. He was standing by the door of the wheelhouse looking at Krupke who was pointing astern.

He had seen the squall!

I shouted, 'We've been having a conference and the general consensus of opinion is that you can still go to hell.'

He jerked his hand irritably and Krupke fired again – another miss.

I said to Coertze, 'We'll give him another two shots. Immediately after the second, starboard your helm as though you are going to ram him, but for God's sake don't ram him. Get as close as you can and come back on course parallel to him. Understand?'

As he nodded there was another shot from Krupke. That one hit *Sanford* just under the cockpit – Krupke was getting too good.

Metcalfe couldn't know that we had a machine-gun. *Sanford* had been searched many times and machine-guns – even small ones – aren't to be picked up on every street corner in Italy. There was the chance we could give him a fright. I said to Francesca, 'When we start to turn get down in the bottom of the cockpit.'

Krupke fired again, missed, and Coertze swung the tiller over. It caught Metcalfe by surprise – this was like a rabbit attacking a weasel. We had something like twenty seconds to complete the manoeuvre and it worked. By the time he had recovered enough to shout to the helmsman and for the helmsman to respond, we were alongside.

Krupke fired again when he saw us coming but the bullet went wild. I saw him aim at me and looked right into the muzzle of his gun. Then I cut loose with the Schmeisser.

I had only time to fire two bursts. The first one was for Krupke – I must get him before he got me. Two or three rounds broke the saloon windows of the Fairmile and I let the recoil lift the gun. Bullets smashed into the edge of the decking and I saw Krupke reel back with both hands clasped to his face and heard a thin scream.

Then I switched to the wheelhouse and hosed it. Glass flew but I was too late to catch Metcalfe who was already out of sight. The Schmeisser jammed on a defective round and I yelled at Coertze, 'Let's get out of here,' and he swung the helm over again.

'Where to?' he asked.

'Back to where we came from – into the squall.'

I looked back at the Fairmile. Metcalfe was on top of the deck saloon bending over Krupke and the Fairmile was still continuing on her original course. But her bows were swinging from side to side as though there was nobody at the helm. 'This might just work,' I said.

But after two or three minutes she started to turn and was soon plunging after us. I looked ahead and prayed we could get into the squall in time. I had never before prayed for dirty weather.

II

It was nip and tuck but we made it. The first gusts hit us when the Fairmile was barely two hundred yards behind, and ten seconds later she was invisible, lost in spearing rain and sea spume.

I throttled back the engine until it was merely ticking over; it would be suicide to try to butt our way through this. It was an angry bit of weather, all right, but it didn't have the sustained ferocity of the earlier storm and I knew it would be over in an hour or so.

In that short time we had to lose Metcalfe.

I left the tiller to Coertze and stumbled forward to the mast and hoisted the trysail. That would give us leeway and we could pick a course of sorts. I chose to beat to windward; that was the last thing Metcalfe would expect me to do in heavy weather, and I hoped that when the squall had blown out he would be searching to leeward.

Sanford didn't like it. She bucked and pitched more than ever and I cursed the crankiness caused by the golden keel, the cause of all our troubles. I said to Francesca, 'You and Kobus had better go below; there's no point in all of us getting soaked to the skin.'

I wondered what Metcalfe was doing. If he had any sense he would have the Fairmile lying head to wind with her engines turning just enough to keep position. But he wanted the gold and had guts enough to try anything weird as long as the boat didn't show signs of falling apart under him. He had shown his seamanship by coming through the big storm undamaged – this squall wouldn't hurt him.

Just then *Sanford* lurched violently and I thought for a moment that she was falling apart under *me*. There was a curious feel to the helm which I couldn't analyse – it was like nothing I had felt on a boat before. She lurched again and seemed to sideslip in the water and she swayed alarmingly even when she hadn't been pushed. I leaned on the helm tentatively and she came round with a rush.

Hastily I pulled the other way and she came back fast, overshooting. It was like riding a horse with a loose saddle and I couldn't understand it.

I had a sudden and dreadful thought and looked over the side. It was difficult to make out in the swirl of water but her boot-topping seemed to be much higher out of the water than it should have been, and I knew what had happened.

It was her keel – that goddamned golden keel.

Coertze had warned us about it. He had said that it would be full of flaws and cracks and that it would be structurally weak. *Sanford* had taken a hell of a hammering in the last couple of days and this last squall was the straw that broke the camel's back – or broke the ship's keel.

I looked over the side again, trying to estimate how much higher she was in the water. As near as I could judge three parts of the keel were gone. *Sanford* had lost three tons of ballast and she was in danger of capsizing at any moment.

I hammered on the cabin hatch and yelled at the top of my voice. Coertze popped his head out. 'What's wrong?' he shouted.

'Get on deck fast – Francesca, too. The bloody keel's gone. We're going to capsize.'

He looked at me blankly. 'What the hell do you mean?' His face flushed red as the meaning sank in. 'You mean the gold's gone?' he said incredulously.

'For Christ's sake, don't just stand there gaping,' I shouted. 'Get the hell up here – and get Francesca out of there. I don't know if I can hold her much longer.'

He whitened and his head vanished. Francesca came scrambling out of the cabin with Coertze on her heels. *Sanford* was behaving like a crazy thing and I shouted to Coertze, 'Get that bloody sail down quick or she'll be over.'

He lunged forward along the deck and wasted no time in unfastening the fall of the halyard from the cleat – instead he pulled the knife from his belt and cut it with one clean slice. As soon as the sail came down *Sanford* began to behave a little better, but not much. She slithered about on the surface of the water and it was by luck, not judgement, that I managed to keep her upright, because I had never had that experience before – few people have.

Coertze came back and I yelled, 'It's the mast that'll have us over if we're not careful.'

He looked up at the mast towering overhead and gave a quick nod. I wondered if he remembered what he had said the first time I questioned him about yachts in Cape Town. He had looked up at the mast of *Estralita* and said, 'She'll need to be deep to counterbalance that lot.'

The keel, our counterbalance, had gone and the fifty-five foot mast was the key to *Sanford*'s survival.

I pointed to the hatchet clipped to the side of the cockpit. 'Cut the shrouds,' I shouted.

He seized the hatchet and went forward again and swung at the after starboard shroud. It bounced off the stainless steel wire and I cursed myself for having built *Sanford* so stoutly. He swung again and again and finally the wire parted.

He went on to the forward shroud and I said, 'Francesca, I'll have to help him or it may be too late. Can you take the helm?'

'What must I do?'

'I think I've got the hang of it,' I said. 'She's very tender and you mustn't move the tiller violently. She swings very easily so you must be very gentle in your movements – otherwise it's the same as before.'

I couldn't stay with her long before I had to leave the cockpit and release both the backstay runners so that the stays hung loose. The mast now had no support from aft.

I went forward to the bows, clinging on for dear life, and crouched in the bow pulpit, using the marline-spike of my knife on the rigging screw of the forestay. The spike was not designed for the job and kept slipping out of the holes of the body, but I managed to loosen the screws appreciably in spite of being drenched every time *Sanford* dipped her bows. When I looked up I saw a definite curve in the stay to leeward which meant that it was slack.

I looked round and saw Coertze attacking the port shrouds before I bent to loosen the fore topmast stay. When I looked up again the mast was whipping like a fishing rod – but still the damn' thing wouldn't break.

It was only when I tripped over the fore hatch that I remembered Walker. I hammered on the hatch and shouted, 'Walker, come out; we're sinking.' But I heard nothing from below.

Damning his minuscule soul to hell, I went aft and clattered down the companionway and into the main cabin. I staggered forward, unable to keep my balance in *Sanford*'s new and uneasy motion and tried the door to the fo'c'sle. It was locked from the inside. I hammered on it with my fist, and shouted, 'Walker, come out; we're going to capsize.'

I heard a faint sound and shouted again. Then he called, 'I'm not coming out.'

'Don't be a damned fool,' I yelled. 'We're liable to sink at any minute.'

'It's a trick to get me out. I know Coertze's waiting for me.'

'You bloody idiot,' I screamed and hammered on the door again, but it was no use; he refused to answer so I left him there.

As I turned to go, *Sanford* groaned in every timber and I made a dash for the companionway, getting into the cockpit just in time to see the mast go. It cracked and split ten feet above the deck and toppled into the raging sea, still tethered by the back and fore stays.

I took the tiller from Francesca and tentatively moved it. *Sanford*'s motion was not much better – she still slid about unpredictably – but I felt easier with the top hamper gone. I kicked at a cockpit locker and shouted to Francesca, 'Life jackets – get them out.'

The solving of one problem led directly to another – the mast in the water was still held fore and aft and it banged rhythmically into *Sanford*'s side. Much of that treatment and she would be stove in and we would go down like a stone. Coertze was in the bows and I could see the glint of the hatchet as he raised it for another blow at the forestay. He was very much alive to the danger inherent in the mast.

I struggled into a life jacket while Francesca took the helm, then I grabbed the boathook from the coach roof and leaned over the side to prod the mast away when it swung in again for another battering charge. Coertze came aft and started to cut away the backstays; it was easier to cut them on the deck and within five minutes he had done it, and the mast drifted away and was lost to sight amid the sea spray.

Coertze dropped heavily into the cockpit, his face streaming with salt water, and Francesca gave him a life jacket. We fastened our safety lines and, on a sudden impulse, I battened down the main hatch – if Walker wanted to come out he could still use the fore hatch. I wanted to seal *Sanford* – if she capsized and filled with water she would sink within seconds.

Those last moments of the squall were pretty grim. If we could last them out we might stand a chance. *Sanford* would never sail again, but it might be possible to move her slowly by a judicious use of her engine. For the first time I hoped I had not misled Metcalfe and that he would be standing by.

But the squall had not done with us. A violent gust of wind coincided with a freak sea and *Sanford* tilted alarmingly. Desperately I worked the tiller, but it was too late and she heeled more and more until the deck was at an angle of forty-five degrees.

I yelled, 'Hang on, she's going,' and in that moment *Sanford* lurched right over and I was thrown into the sea.

I spluttered and swallowed salt water before the buoyancy of the jacket brought me to the surface, lying on my back. Frantically I looked round for Francesca and was relieved when her head bobbed up close by. I grabbed her safety line and pulled until we floated side by side. 'Back to the boat,' I spluttered.

We hauled on the safety lines and drew ourselves back to *Sanford*. She was lying on her starboard side, heaving sluggishly over the waves, and we painfully crawled up the vertical deck until we could grasp the stanchions of the port safety rail. I looked back over the rail and on to the new and oddly shaped upper deck – the port side of *Sanford*.

I helped Francesca over the rail and then I saw Coertze clinging to what was left of the keel – he had evidently jumped the other way. He was clutching a tangle of broken wires – the wires that were supposed to hold the keel together and which had failed in their purpose. I slid down the side and gave him a hand, and soon the three of us were uneasily huddled on the unprotected hull, wondering what the hell to do next.

That last flailing gust of wind had been the squall's final
crack of the whip and the wind dropped within minutes to
leave the hulk of *Sanford* tossing on an uneasy sea. I looked
around hopefully for Metcalfe but the Fairmile wasn't
in sight, although she could still come out of the dirty
weather left in the wake of the squall.

I was looking contemplatively at the dinghy which was
still lashed to the coach roof when Coertze said, 'There's still
a lot of gold down there, you know.' He was staring back at
the keel.

'To hell with the gold,' I said. 'Let's get this dinghy free.'

We cut the lashings and let the dinghy fall into the sea –
after I had taken the precaution of tying a line to it. It
floated upside down, but that didn't worry me – the buoyancy chambers would keep it afloat in any position. I went
down the deck and into the sea and managed to right it.
Then I took the baler which was still clipped in place and
began to bale out.

I had just finished when Francesca shouted, 'Metcalfe!
Metcalfe's coming.'

By the time I got back on top of the hull the Fairmile was
quite close, still plugging away at the eight knots which
Metcalfe favoured for heavy seas. We weren't trying to get
away this time, so it was not long before she was within
hailing distance.

Metcalfe was outside the wheelhouse. He bellowed, 'Can
you take a line?'

Coertze waved and the Fairmile edged in closer and
Metcalfe lifted a coil of rope and began to swing it. His first
throw was short, but Coertze caught the second and slid
down the deck to make the line fast to the stump of the
mast. I cut two lengths of line and tied them in loops round
the rope Metcalfe had thrown. I said, 'We'll go over in the
dinghy, pulling ourselves along the line. For God's sake,
don't let go of these loops or we might be swept away.'

We got into the dinghy and pulled ourselves across to the Fairmile. It wasn't a particularly difficult job but we were cold and wet and tired and it would have been easy to make a mistake. Metcalfe helped Francesca on board and Coertze went next. As I started to climb he threw me a line and said curtly, 'Make the dinghy fast; I might need it.'

So I made fast and climbed on deck. Metcalfe stepped up to me, his face contorted with rage. He grabbed me by the shoulders with both hands and yelled, 'You damn' fool – I told you to make certain of that keel. I told you back in Rapallo.'

He began to shake me and I was too tired to resist. My head lolled back and forward like the head of a sawdust doll and when he let me go I just sat down on the deck.

He swung round to Coertze. 'How much is left?' he demanded.

'About a quarter.'

He looked at the hulk of *Sanford,* a strained expression in his eyes. 'I'm not going to lose that,' he said. 'I'm not going to lose a ton of gold.'

He called to the wheelhouse and the Moroccan, Moulay Idriss, came on deck. Metcalfe gave quick instructions in Arabic and then dropped into the dinghy and pulled himself across to *Sanford.* The Arab attached a heavy cable to the line and when Metcalfe got to the hulk he began to pull it across.

Francesca and I were not taking much interest in this. We were exhausted and more preoccupied in being alive and together than with what happened to the gold. Coertze, however, was alive to the situation and was helping the Arab make the cable fast.

Metcalfe came back and said to Coertze, 'You were right, there's about a ton left. I don't know how that wreck will behave when it's towed, but we'll try.'

As the Fairmile turned and the cable tautened, a watery sun shone out over the heaving sea and I looked back at

Sanford as she moved sluggishly to the pull. The cockpit was half under water but the fore hatch was still free, and I said, 'My God! Walker's still in there!'

Coertze said, '*Magtig,* I'd forgotten him.'

He must have been knocked unconscious when *Sanford* capsized – otherwise we would have heard him. Francesca was staring back at *Sanford*. 'Look!' she exclaimed. 'There – in the cockpit.'

The main hatch was being forced open from the inside and I could see Walker's head as he tried to struggle out against the rush of water pouring into the boat. His hands grasped for the cockpit coaming – but it wasn't there – Krupke had shot it away. Then Walker disappeared as the force of the water pushed him back into the cabin.

If he had come out by the fore hatch he would have been safe, but even in death he had to make one of his inevitable mistakes. The main hatch was open, water was pouring into the hull and *Sanford* was sinking.

Metcalfe was in a rage. 'The damn' fool,' he cried. 'I thought you'd got rid of him. He's taking the bloody gold with him.'

Sanford was getting low in the water and as she did so, the water poured into her faster. Metcalfe stared at her in despair, his voice filled with fury. 'The stupid, bloody idiot,' he yelled. 'He's bitched things from the start.'

It wouldn't be long now – *Sanford* was going fast. The towing cable tightened as she sank lower in the water and the Fairmile went down by the stern as the pull on the cable became greater. *Sanford* gave a lurch as compressed air in the fo'c'sle blew out the forehatch and she began to settle faster as more water poured in through this new opening in her hull.

The downward drag on the stern of the Fairmile was becoming dangerous and Metcalfe took a hatchet from a clip and stood by the cable. He looked back at *Sanford*, his face twitching with indecision, then he brought the hatchet down on the cable with a great swing. It parted with a twang, the loose end snaked away across the sea and the Fairmile bobbed up her stern.

Sanford lurched again and turned over. As she went down and out of sight amid swirling waters a vagrant sunbeam touched her keel and we saw the glint of imperishable gold. Then there was nothing but the sea.

III

Metcalfe's anger was great but, like the squall, soon subsided and he became his usual saturnine self, taking the loss with a philosophical air. 'A pity,' he said. 'But there it is. It's gone and there isn't anything we can do about it now.'

We were sitting in the saloon of the Fairmile, on our way to Malaga where Metcalfe was going to drop us. He had given us dry clothing and food and we were all feeling better.

I said, 'What will you do now?'

He shrugged. 'Tangier is just about played out now the Moroccans are taking over. I think I'll pop down to the Congo – things seem to be blowing up down there.'

Metcalfe and a few others like him would be 'popping down to the Congo', I thought. Carrion crows flocking together – but he wasn't as bad as some. I said, 'I think you've got a few things to explain.'

He grinned. 'What do you want to know?'

'Well, the thing that's been niggling me is how you got on to us in the first place. What led you to suspect that we were after the gold?'

'Suspect, old boy? I didn't suspect, I *knew*.'

'How the devil did you know?'

'It was when I got Walker drunk. He spilled the whole story about the gold, the keel – everything.'

'Well, I'm damned.' I thought of all the precautions I'd taken to put Metcalfe off the scent; I thought of all the times I'd beaten my brains out to think up new twists of evasion. All wasted – he wasn't fooled at all!

'I thought you'd get rid of him,' Metcalfe said. 'He was a dead loss all the way through. I thought you'd put him over the side or something like that.'

I looked at Coertze, who grinned at me. I said, 'He was probably a murderer, too.'

'Wouldn't be surprised,' agreed Metcalfe airily. 'He was a slimy little rat.'

That reminded me – I had probably killed a man too. 'Where's Krupke?' I asked. 'I haven't seen him around.'

Metcalfe snickered. 'He's groaning in his bunk – he got a faceful of splinters.'

I held out the back of my hand. 'Well, he did the same to me.'

'Yes,' said Metcalfe soberly. 'But Krupke is probably going to lose an eye.'

'Serve him damn' well right,' I said viciously. 'He won't be too keen to look down rifle sights again.'

I hadn't lost sight of the fact that Metcalfe and his crew of ruffians had been doing their damnedest to kill us not many hours before. But there wasn't any advantage in quarrelling with Metcalfe about it – we were on his boat and he was going to put us ashore safely. Irritating him wasn't exactly the best policy just then.

He said, 'That machine-gun of yours was some surprise. You nearly plugged me.' He pointed to a battered loud-hailer on the sideboard. 'You shot that goddamn thing right out of my hand.'

Francesca said, 'Why were you so solicitous about my husband? Why did you take the trouble?'

'Oh, I felt real bad when I saw Hal slug him,' said Metcalfe seriously. 'I knew who he was, you see, and I knew he could make a stink. I didn't want anything like that. I wanted Hal to get on with casting the keel and get out of Italy. I couldn't afford to have the police rooting round.'

'That's why you tried to hold Torloni, too,' I said.

He rubbed his chin. 'That was *my* mistake,' he admitted. 'I thought I could use Torloni without him knowing it. But he's a bad bastard and when he got hold of that cigarette case the whole thing blew up in my face. I just wanted Torloni to keep an eye on you, but that damn' fool, Walker, had to go and give the game away. There was no holding Torloni then.'

'So you warned us.'

He spread his hands. 'What else could I do for a pal?'

'Pal nothing. You wanted the gold out.'

He grinned. 'Well, what the hell; you got away, didn't you?'

I had bitter thoughts of Metcalfe as the puppet master; he had manipulated all of us and we had danced to his tune. Not quite – one of his puppets had a broken string; if Walker had defeated us, he had also defeated Metcalfe.

I said, 'If you hadn't been so obvious about Torloni the keel wouldn't have broken. We had to cast it in a bloody hurry when he started putting the pressure on.'

'Yes,' said Metcalfe. 'And all those damned partisans didn't help, either.' He stood up. 'Well, I've still got to run this boat.' He hesitated, then put his hand in his pocket and pulled out a cigarette case. 'You might like this as a souvenir – Torloni mislaid it. There's something interesting inside.' He tossed it on the table and left the saloon.

I looked at Francesca and Coertze, then slowly put out my hand and picked it up. It had the heavy familiar feel of gold, but I felt no sudden twist to my guts as I had when Walker had put the gold Hercules into my hand. I was sick of the sight of gold.

I opened the case and found a letter inside, folded in two. It was addressed to me, care of the yacht *Sanford*, Tangier Harbour, and had been opened. I started to read it and began to laugh uncontrollably.

Francesca and Coertze looked at me in astonishment. I tried to control my laughter but it kept bursting out hysterically. 'We've . . . we've won . . . won a sweep . . . a lottery,' I gasped, and passed the letter to Francesca, who also started to laugh.

Coertze said blankly, 'What lottery?'

I said, 'Don't you remember? You insisted on buying a lottery ticket in Tangier – you said it was for insurance. It won!',

He started to smile. 'How much?'

'Six hundred thousand pesetas.'

'What's that in money?'

I wiped my eyes. 'A little over six thousand pounds. It won't cover expenses – what I've spent on this jaunt – but it'll help.'

Coertze looked sheepish. 'How much did you spend?'

I began to figure it out. I had lost *Sanford* – she had been worth about £12,000. I had covered all our expenses for nearly a year, and they had been high becaue we were supposed to be wealthy tourists; there had been the exorbitant rental of the Casa Saeta in Tangier; there was the outfitting and provisioning of the boat.

I said, 'It must run to about seventeen or eighteen thousand.'

His eyes twinkled and he put his hand to his fob pocket. 'Will these help?' he asked; and rolled four large diamonds on to the table.

'Well, I'm damned,' I said. 'Where did you get those?'

'They seemed to stick to my fingers in the tunnel.' He chuckled. 'Just like that machine pistol stuck to yours.'

Francesca started to giggle and put her hands to her breast. She produced a little wash-leather bag which was slung on a cord round her neck and emptied it. Two more diamonds joined those on the table and there were also four emeralds.

I looked at both of them and said, 'You damned thieves; you ought to be ashamed of yourselves. The jewels were supposed to stay in Italy.'

I grinned and produced my five diamonds and we all sat there laughing like maniacs.

IV

Later, when we had put the gems away safe from the prying eyes of Metcalfe, we went on deck and watched the hills of Spain emerge mistily from over the horizon. I put my arm round Francesca and said wryly, 'Well, I've still got a half-share in a boatyard in Cape Town. Will you mind being a boat-builder's wife?'

She squeezed my hand. 'I think I'll like South Africa.'

I took the cigarette case from my pocket and opened it with one hand. The inscription was there and I read it for the first time – *'Caro Benito da parte di Adolf – Brennero – 1940.'*

I said, 'This is a pretty dangerous thing to have around. Some other Torloni might see it.'

She shivered and said, 'Get rid of it, Hal; please throw it away.'

So I tossed it over the side and there was just one glint of gold in the green water and then it was gone for ever.

THE VIVERO LETTER

To that stalwart institution the British pub,
particularly the Kingsbridge Inn, Totnes,
and the Cott Inn, Dartington

I would like to thank Captain T. A. Hampton of the British Underwater Centre, Dartmouth, for detailed information about diving techniques.

My thanks also go to Gerard L'E. Turner, Assistant Curator of the Museum of the History of Science, Oxford, for information on certain bronze mirrors, Amida's Mirror in particular.

Theirs the credit for accuracy; mine the fault for inaccuracy.

ONE

I made good time on the way to the West Country; the road was clear and there was only an occasional car coming in the other direction to blind me with headlights. Outside Honiton I pulled off the road, killed the engine and lit a cigarette. I didn't want to arrive at the farm at an indecently early hour, and besides, I had things to think about.

They say that eavesdroppers never hear good of themselves. It's a dubious proposition from the logical standpoint, but I certainly hadn't disproved it empirically. Not that I had intended to eavesdrop – it was one of those accidental things you get yourself into with no graceful exit – so I just stood and listened and heard things said about myself that I would rather not have heard.

It had happened the day before at a party, one of the usual semi-impromptu lash-ups which happen in swinging London. Sheila knew a man who knew the man who was organizing it and wanted to go, so we went. The house was in that part of Golders Green which prefers to be called Hampstead and our host was a with-it whiz kid who worked for a record company and did a bit of motor racing on the side. His conversation was divided about fifty-fifty between Marshal MacLuhan waffle and Brand's Hatchery, all very wearing on the eardrums. I didn't know him personally and neither did Sheila – it was that kind of party.

One left one's coat in the usual bedroom and then drifted into the chatter, desperately trying to make human contact while clutching a glass of warm whisky. Most of the people were complete strangers, although they seemed to know each other, which made it difficult for the lone intruder. I tried to make sense of the elliptical verbal shorthand which passes for conversation on these occasions, and pretty soon got bored. Sheila seemed to be doing all right, though, and I could see this was going to be a long session, so I sighed and got myself another drink.

Halfway through the evening I ran out of cigarettes and remembered that I had a packet in my coat so I went up to the bedroom to get it. Someone had moved the coats from the bed and I found them dumped on the floor behind a large avant-garde screen. I was rooting about trying to find mine when someone else came into the room. A female voice said, 'That man you're with is pretty dim, isn't he?'

I recognized the voice as belonging to Helen Someone-or-other, a blonde who was being squired by a life-and-soul-of-the-party type. I dug into my coat pocket and found the cigarettes, then paused as I heard Sheila say, 'Yes, he is.'

Helen said, 'I don't know why you bother with him.'

'I don't know, either,' said Sheila. She laughed. 'But he's a male body, handy to have about. A girl needs someone to take her around.'

'You could have chosen someone more lively,' said Helen. 'This one's a zombie. What does he *do*?'

'Oh, he's some kind of an accountant. He doesn't talk about it much. A grey little man in a grey little job – I'll drop him when I find someone more interesting.'

I stayed very still in a ridiculous half crouch behind that screen. I certainly couldn't walk out into full view after hearing that. There was a subdued clatter from the dressing-table as the girls primped themselves. They chattered about hair styles for a couple of minutes, then Helen said, 'What happened to Jimmy What's-his-name?'

Sheila giggled. 'Oh, he was *too* wolfish – not at all safe to be with. Exciting, really, but his firm sent him abroad last month.'

'I shouldn't think you find this one too exciting.'

'Oh, Jemmy's all right,' said Sheila casually. 'I don't have to worry about my virtue with him. It's very restful for a change.'

'He's not a queer, is he?' asked Helen.

'I don't think so,' said Sheila. Her voice was doubtful. 'He's never appeared to be that way.'

'You never can tell; a lot of them are good at disguise. That's a nice shade of lipstick – what is it?'

They tailed off into feminine inconsequentialities while I sweated behind the screen. It seemed to be an hour before they left, although it probably wasn't more than five minutes, and when I heard the door bang I stood up cautiously and came out from under cover and went downstairs to rejoin the party.

I stuck it out until Sheila decided to call it a night and then took her home. I was in half a mind to demonstrate to her in the only possible way that I wasn't a queer, but I tossed the idea away. Rape isn't my way of having a good time. I dropped her at the flat she shared with two other girls and bade her a cordial good night. I would have to be very hard up for company before I saw her again.

A grey little man in a grey little job.

Was that how I really appeared to others? I had never thought about it much. As long as there are figures used in business there'll be accountants to shuffle them around, and it had never struck me as being a particularly grey job, especially after computers came in. I didn't talk about my work because it really isn't the subject for light conversation with a girl. Chit-chat about the relative merits of computer languages such as COBOL and ALGOL doesn't have the glamour of what John Lennon said at the last recording session.

So much for the job, but what about me? Was I dowdy and subfusc? Grey and uninteresting?

It could very well be that I was – to other people. I had never been one for wearing my heart on my sleeve, and maybe, judging by the peculiar mores of our times, I was a square. I didn't particularly like the 'swinging' aspect of mid-sixties England; it was cheap, frenetic and sometimes downright nasty, and I could do without it. Perhaps I was Johnny-out-of-step.

I had met Sheila a month before, a casual introduction. Looking back at that conversation in the bedroom it must have been when Jimmy What's-his-name had departed from her life that she had latched on to me as a temporary substitute. For various reasons, the principal one having to do with the proverb of the burnt child fearing the fire, I had not got into the habit of jumping into bed indiscriminately with female companions of short acquaintance, and if that was what Sheila had expected, or even wanted, she had picked the wrong boy. It's a hell of a society in which a halfway continent man is immediately suspected of homosexuality.

Perhaps I was stupid to take the catty chatter of empty-headed women so much to heart, but to see ourselves as others see us is a salutary experience and tends to make one take a good look from the outside. Which is what I did while sitting in the car outside Honiton.

A thumbnail sketch: Jeremy Wheale, of good yeoman stock and strong family roots. Went to university – but red-brick – emerging with a first-class pass in mathematics and economics. Now, aged 31, an accountant specializing in computer work and with good prospects for the future. Character: introverted and somewhat withdrawn but not overly so. When aged 25 had flammatory affaire which wrung out emotions; now cautious in dealings with women. Hobbies: indoors – recreational mathematics and fencing, outdoors – scuba diving. Cash assets to present minute: £102/18/4 in current bank account; stocks and shares to the market value of £940. Other assets: one overage Ford Cortina in which sitting brooding; one hi-fi outfit of superlative quality; one set of scuba gear in boot of car. Liabilities: only himself.

And what was wrong with that? Come to think of it – what was right with that? Maybe Sheila had been correct when she had described me as a grey man but only in a circumscribed way. She expected Sean Connery disguised as James Bond and what she got was me – just a good, old-fashioned, grey, average type.

But she had done one thing; she had made me take a good look at myself and what I saw wasn't reassuring. Looking into the future as far as I could, all I could see was myself putting increasingly complicated figures into increasingly complicated computers at the behest of the men who made the boodle. A drab prospect – not to mention that overworked word 'grey'. Perhaps I *was* getting into a rut and adopting middle-aged attitudes before my time.

I tossed the stub of the third cigarette from the window and started the car. There didn't seem to be much I could do about it, and I was quite happy and contented with my lot.

Although not perhaps as happy and contented as I was before Sheila had distilled her poison.

From Honiton to the farm, just short of Totnes, is a run of about an hour and a half if you do it early in the morning to avoid the holiday traffic on the Exeter by-pass, and dead on the minute I stopped, as I always did, on the little patch of ground by Cutter's Corner where the land fell away into the valley and where there was a break in the high hedge. I got out of the car and leaned comfortably on the fence.

I had been born in the valley thirty-one years earlier, in the farmhouse which lay snugly on the valley floor looking more like a natural growth than a man-made object. It had been built by a Wheale and Wheales had lived in it for over four hundred years. It was a tradition among us that the eldest son inherited the farm and the younger sons went to sea. I had put a crimp in the tradition by going into business, but my brother, Bob, held on to Hay Tree Farm and kept the land in good shape. I didn't envy Bob the farm because he was a better farmer than I ever would have been. I have no affinity with cattle and sheep and the job would have driven me round the twist. The most I had to do with it now was to put Bob right on his bookkeeping and proffer advice on his investments.

I was a sport among the Wheales. A long line of fox-hunting, pheasant-murdering, yeoman farmers had produced Bob and me. Bob followed the line; he farmed the land well, rode like a madman to hounds, was pretty good in a point-to-point and liked nothing better than a day's rough shooting. I was the oddity who didn't like massacring rabbits with an airgun as a boy, still less with a shotgun as a grown man. My parents, when they were alive, looked on me with some perplexity and I must have troubled their uncomplicated minds; I was not a *natural* boy and got into no mischief – instead I developed a most un-Whealeish tendency to book reading and the ability to make figures jump through hoops. There was much doubtful shaking of heads and an inolination to say 'Whatever will become of the lad?'

I lit a cigarette and a plume of smoke drifted away on the crisp morning air, then grinned as I saw no smoke coming from any of the farm chimneys. Bob would be sleeping late, something he did when he'd made a night of it at the Kingsbridge Inn or the Cott Inn, his favourite pubs. That was a cheerful practice that might end when he married. I was glad he was getting married at last; I'd been a bit worried because Hay Tree Farm without a Wheale would be unthinkable and if Bob died unmarried there was only me left, and I certainly didn't want to take up farming.

I got into the car, drove on a little way, then turned on to the farm road. Bob had had it graded and resurfaced, something he'd been talking about for years. I coasted along, past the big oak tree which, family legend said, had been planted by my great-grandfather, and around the corner which led straight into the farmyard.

Then I stamped on the brake pedal hard because someone was lying in the middle of the road.

I got out of the car and looked down at him. He was lying prone with one arm outflung and when I knelt and touched his hand it was stone cold. I went cold, too, as I looked at the back of his head. Carefully I tried to pull his head up but the body was stiff with rigor mortis and I had to roll him right over to see his face. The breath came from me with a sigh as I saw it was a perfect stranger.

He had died hard but quickly. The expression on his face showed that he had died hard; the lips writhed back from the teeth in a tortured grimace and the eyes were open and stared over my shoulder at the morning sky. Underneath him was a great pool of half-dried blood and his chest was covered with it. No one could have lost that much blood slowly – it must have gushed out in a sudden burst, bringing a quick death.

I stood up and looked around. Everything was very quiet and all I heard was the fluting of an unseasonable blackbird and the grating of gravel as I shifted my feet sounded unnaturally loud. From the house came the mournful howl of a dog and then a shriller barking from close by, and a young sheepdog flung round the corner of the house and yapped at me excitedly. He was not very old, not more than nine months, and I reckoned he was one of old Jess's pups.

I held out my hand and snapped my fingers. The aggressive barking changed to a delighted yelp and the young dog

wagged his tail vehemently and came forward in an ingratiat-
ing sideways trot. From the house another dog howled and
the sound made the hairs on my neck prickle.

I walked into the farmyard and saw immediately that the
kitchen door was ajar. Gently, I pushed it open, and called,
'Bob!'

The curtains were drawn at the windows and the light
was off, so the room was gloomy. There was a stir of movement and the sound of an ugly growl. I pushed the door
open wide to let in the light and saw old Jess stalking
towards me with her teeth bared in a snarl. 'All right, Jess,'
I said softly. 'It's all right, old girl.'

She stopped dead and looked at me consideringly, then
let her lips cover her teeth. I slapped the side of my leg.
'Come here, Jess.'

But she wouldn't come. Instead, she whined disconsolately and turned away to vanish behind the big kitchen
table. I followed her and found her standing drooping over
the body of Bob.

His hand was cold, but not dead cold, and there was a
faint flutter of a pulse beat at his wrist. Fresh blood oozed
from the ugly wound in his chest and soaked the front of his
shirt. I knew enough about serious injuries not to attempt
to move him; instead, I ran upstairs, stripped the blankets
from his bed and brought them down to cover him and
keep him warm.

Then I went to the telephone and dialled 999. 'This is
Jemmy Wheale of Hay Tree Farm. There's been a shooting
on the farm; one man dead and another seriously wounded.
I want a doctor, an ambulance and the police – in that order.'

II

An hour later I was talking to Dave Goosan. The doctor and
the ambulance had come and gone, and Bob was in hospital.

He was in a bad way and Dr Grierson had dissuaded me from going with him. 'It's no use, Jemmy. You'd only get in the way and make a nuisance of yourself. You know we'll do the best we can.'

I nodded. 'What are his chances?' I asked.

Grierson shook his head. 'Not good. But I'll be able to tell better when I've had a closer look at him.'

So I was talking to Dave Goosan who was a policeman. The last time I had met him he was a detective sergeant; now he was a detective inspector. I went to school with his young brother, Harry, who was also in the force. Police work was the Goosans' family business.

'This is bad, Jemmy,' he said. 'It's too much for me. They're sending over a superintendent from Newton Abbot. I haven't the rank to handle a murder case.'

I stared at him. 'Who has been murdered?'

He flung out his arm to indicate the farmyard, then became confused. 'I'm sorry,' he said. 'I didn't mean to say your brother had murdered anyone. But there's been a killing, anyway.'

We were in the living-room and through the window I could see the activity in the yard. The body was still there, though covered with a plastic sheet. There were a dozen coppers, some in plain clothes and others in uniform, a few seemed to be doing nothing but chat, but the others were giving the yard a thorough going over.

I said, 'Who was he, Dave?'

'We don't know.' He frowned. 'Now, tell me the story all over again – right from the beginning. We've got to get this right, Jemmy, or the super will blow hell out of me. This is the first killing I've worked on.' He looked worried.

So I told my story again, how I had come to the farm, found the dead man and then Bob. When I had finished Dave said, 'You just rolled the body over – no more than that?'

'I thought it was Bob,' I said. The build was the same and so was the haircut.'

'I'll tell you one thing,' said Dave. 'He might be an American. His clothes are American, anyway. Does that mean anything to you?'

'Nothing.'

He sighed. 'Ah, well, we'll find out all about him sooner or later. He was killed by a blast from a shotgun at close range. Grierson says he thinks the aorta was cut through – that's why he bled like that. Your brother's shotgun had both barrels fired.'

'So Bob shot him,' I said. 'That doesn't make it murder.'

'Of course it doesn't. We've reconstructed pretty well what happened and it seems to be a case of self defence. The man was a thief; we know that much.'

I looked up. 'What did he steal?'

Dave jerked his head. 'Come with me and I'll show you. But just walk where I walk and don't go straying about.'

I followed him out into the yard, keeping close to his heels as he made a circuitous approach to the wall of the kitchen. He stopped and said, 'Have you ever seen that before?'

I looked to where he indicated and saw the tray that had always stood on the top shelf of the dresser in the kitchen ever since I can remember. My mother used to take it down and polish it once in a while, but it was only really used on highdays and feast days. At Christmas it used to be put in the middle of the dining-table and was heaped with fruit.

'Do you mean to tell me he got killed trying to pinch a brass tray? That he nearly killed Bob because of that thing?'

I bent down to pick it up and Dave grabbed me hastily. 'Don't touch it.' He looked at me thoughtfully. 'Maybe you wouldn't know. That's not brass, Jemmy; it's gold!'

I gaped at him, then closed my mouth before the flies got in.

'But it's always been a brass tray,' I said inanely.

'So Bob thought,' agreed Dave. 'It happened this way. The museum in Totnes was putting on a special show of local bygones and Bob was asked if he'd lend the tray. I believe it's been in the family for a long time.'

I nodded. 'I can remember my grandfather telling me that *his* grandfather had mentioned it.'

'Well, that's going back a while. Anyway, Bob lent it to the museum and it was put on show with the other stuff. Then someone said it was gold, and by God, it was! The people at the museum got worried about it and asked Dave to take it back. It wasn't insured, you see, and there was a flap on about it might be stolen. It had been reported in the papers complete with photographs, and any wide boy could open the Totnes museum with a hairpin.'

'I didn't see the newspaper reports.'

'It didn't make the national press,' said Dave. 'Just the local papers. Anyway, Bob took it back. Tell me, did he know you were coming down this weekend?'

I nodded. 'I phoned him on Thursday. I'd worked out a scheme for the farm that I thought he might be interested in.'

'That might explain it. This discovery only happened about ten days ago. He might have wanted to surprise you with it.'

I looked down at the tray. 'He did,' I said bitterly.

'It must be very valuable just for the gold in it,' said Dave. 'Well worth the attention of a thief. And the experts say there's something special about it to add to the value, but I'm no antiquarian so I can't tell you what it is.' He rubbed the back of his head. There's one thing about all this that really worries me, though. Come and look at this – and don't touch it.'

He led me across the yard to the other side of the body where a piece of opaque plastic cloth covered something lumpy on the ground. 'This is what did the damage to your brother.'

He lifted the plastic and I saw a weapon – an antique horse pistol. 'Who'd want to use a thing like that?' I said.

'Nasty, isn't it?'

I bent down and looked closer and found I was wrong. It wasn't a horse pistol but a shotgun with the barrels cut very short and the butt cut off to leave only the hand grip. Dave said, 'What thief in his right mind would go on a job carrying a weapon like that? Just to be found in possession would send him inside for a year. Another thing – there were two of them.'

'Guns?'

'No – men. Two, at least. There was a car parked up the farm road. We found tracks in the mud and oil droppings. From what the weather's been doing we know the car turned in the road after ten o'clock last night. Grierson reckons that this man was shot before midnight, so it's a hundred quid to a pinch of snuff that the car and the man are connected. It can't have driven itself away, so that brings another man into the picture.'

'Or a woman,' I said.

'Could be,' said Dave.

A thought struck me. 'Where were the Edgecombes last night?' Jack Edgecombe was Bob's chief factotum on the farm, and his wife, Madge, did Bob's housekeeping. They had a small flat in the farmhouse itself; all the other farm workers lived in their own cottages.

'I checked on that,' said Dave. 'They're over in Jersey on their annual holiday. Your brother was living by himself.'

A uniformed policeman came from the house. 'Inspector, you're wanted on the blower.'

Dave excused himself and went away, and I stood and watched what was going on. I wasn't thinking much of anything; my mind was numbed and small, inconsequential thoughts chased round and round. Dave wasn't away long and when he came back his face was serious. I knew what he was going to say before he said it. 'Bob's dead,' I said flatly.

He nodded gravely. 'Ten minutes ago.'

'For God's sake!' I said. 'I wasted half an hour outside Honiton; it could have made all the difference.'

'Don't blame yourself, whatever you do. It would have made no difference at all, even if you had found him two hours earlier. He was too far gone.' There was a sudden snap to his voice. 'It's a murder case now, Jemmy; and we've got a man to look for. We've found an abandoned car the other side of Newton Abbot. It may not be the right one, but a check on the tyres will tell us.'

'Does Elizabeth Horton know of this yet?'

Dave frowned. 'Who's she?'

'Bob's fiancée.'

'Oh, God! He was getting married, wasn't he? No, she knows nothing yet.'

'I'd better tell her,' I said.

'All right,' he said. 'You've got a farm to run now, and cows don't milk themselves. Things can run down fast if there isn't a firm hand on the reins. My advice is to get Jack Edgecombe back here. But don't you worry about that; I'll find out where he is and send a telegram.'

'Thanks, Dave,' I said. 'But isn't that over and above the call of duty?'

'All part of the service,' he said with an attempt at lightness. 'We look after our own. I liked Bob very much, you know.' He paused. 'Who was his solicitor?'

'Old Mount has handled the family affairs ever since I can remember.'

'You'd better see him as soon as possible,' advised Dave. 'There'll be a will and other legal stuff to be handled.' He looked at his watch. 'Look, if you're here when the superintendent arrives you might be kept hanging around for hours. You'd better pop off now and do whatever you have to. Ill give your statement to the super and if he wants to see you he can do it later. But do me a favour and phone in in a couple of hours to let us know where you are.'

III

As I drove into Totnes I looked at my watch and saw with astonishment that it was not yet nine o'clock. The day that ordinary people live was only just beginning, but I felt I'd lived a lifetime in the past three hours. I hadn't really started to think properly, but somewhere deep inside me I felt the first stirring of rage tentatively growing beneath the grief. That a man could be shot to death in his own home with such a barbarous weapon was a monstrous, almost inconceivable, perversion of normal life. In the quiet Devon countryside a veil had been briefly twitched aside to reveal another world, a more primitive world in which sudden death was a shocking commonplace. I felt outraged that such a world should intrude on me and mine.

My meeting with Elizabeth was difficult. When I told her she became suddenly still and motionless with a frozen face. At first, I thought she was that type of Englishwoman to whom the exhibition of any emotion is the utmost in bad taste, but after five minutes she broke down in a paroxysm of tears and was led away by her mother. I felt very sorry for her. Both she and Bob were late starters in the Marriage Stakes and now the race had been scratched. I didn't know her very well but enough to know that she would have made Bob a fine wife.

Mr Mount, of course, took it more calmly, death being part of the stock-in-trade, as it were, of a solicitor. But he was perturbed about the manner of death. Sudden death was no stranger to him, and if Bob had broken his neck chasing a fox that would have been in the tradition and acceptable. This was different; this was the first murder in Totnes within living memory.

And so he was shaken but recovered himself rapidly, buttressing his cracking world with the firm assurance of the law. 'There is, of course, a will,' he said. 'Your brother was having talks with me about the new will. You may – or may not – know that on marriage all previous wills are automatically voided, so there had to be a new will. However, we had not got to the point of signing, and so the previous existing will is the document we have to consider.'

His face creased into a thin, legal smile. 'I don't think there is any point in beating about the bush, Jemmy. Apart from one or two small bequests to members of the farm staff and personal friends, you are the sole beneficiary. Hay Tree Farm is yours now – or it will be on probate. There will, of course, be death duties, but farm land gets forty-five per cent relief on valuation.' He made a note. 'I must see your brother's bank manager for details of his accounts.'

'I can give you most of that,' I said. 'I was Bob's accountant. In fact, I have all the information here. I was working on a suggested scheme for the farm – that's why I came down this weekend.'

'That will be very helpful,' said Mount. He pondered. 'I would say that the farm, on valuation, will prove to be worth something like £125,000. That is not counting live and dead stock, of course.'

My head jerked up. 'My God! So much?'

He gave me an amused look. 'When a farm has been in the same family for as long as yours the cash value of the land tends to be ignored – it ceases to be regarded as invested capital. Land values have greatly appreciated in recent years, Jemmy; and you have 500 acres of prime land on red soil. At auction it would fetch not less than £250 an acre. When you add the stock, taking into account the admirable dairy herd Bob built up and the amount of modernization he has done, then I would say that the valuation for the purposes of probate will be not much less than £170,000.'

I accepted this incredible thing he was telling me. Mount was a country solicitor and knew as much about local farm values as any hard-eyed unillusioned farmer looking over his neighbour's fields. He said, 'If you sold it you would have a sizeable fortune, Jemmy.'

I shook my head. 'I couldn't sell it.'

He nodded understandingly. 'No,' he said reflectively. 'I don't suppose you could. It would be as though the Queen were to sell Buckingham Palace to a property developer. But what do you intend to do? Run it yourself?'

'I don't know,' I said a little desperately. 'I haven't thought about it'

'There'll be time to think about it,' he said consolingly. 'One way would be to appoint a land agent. But your brother had a high opinion of Jack Edgecombe. You might do worse than make him farm manager; he can run the farming side, of which you know nothing – and you can operate the business side, of which *he* knows nothing. I don't think it would be necessary to interrupt your present career.'

'I'll think about that,' I said.

'Tell me,' said Mount. 'You said you had a scheme for the farm. Could I ask what it is?'

I said, 'The Government experimental farms have been using computers to work out maximum utilization of farm resources. Well, I have access to a computer and I put in all the data on Hay Tree Farm and programmed it to produce optimum profit.'

Mount smiled tolerantly. 'Your farm has been well worked for four hundred years. I doubt if you could find a better way of working it than the ways that are traditional in this area.'

I had come across this attitude many times before and I thought I knew how to handle it. 'Traditional ways *are* good ways, but nobody would say they are perfect. If you take all the variables involved in even a smallish farm – the right mix of arable and pasture, what animals to keep, how many animals and when to keep them, what feedstuffs to plant and what to buy – if you take all those variables and put them in permutation and combination you come up with a matrix of several million choices.

'Traditional ways have evolved to a pretty high level and it isn't worth a farmer's while to improve them. He'd have to be a smart mathematician and it would probably take him fifty years of calculation. But a computer can do it in fifteen minutes. In the case of Hay Tree Farm the difference between the traditional good way and the best way is fifteen per cent net increase on profits.'

'You surprise me,' said Mount interestedly. 'We will have to talk about this – but at a more appropriate time.'

It was a subject on which I could have talked for hours but, as he said, the time wasn't appropriate. I said, 'Did Bob ever talk to you about that tray?'

'Indeed he did,' said Mount. 'He brought it here, to this office, straight from the museum, and we discussed the insurance. It is a very valuable piece.'

'How valuable?'

'Now that is hard to say. We weighed it and, if the gold is pure, the intrinsic value will be about £2,500. But mere is also the artistic value to take into account – it's very beautiful – and the antiquarian value. Do you know anything of its history?'

'Nothing,' I said. 'It's just been something that's been around the house ever since I can remember.'

'It will have to be valued as part of the estate,' said Mount. 'Sotheby's might be best, I think.' He made another note. 'We will have to go very deeply into your brother's affairs. I hope there will be enough . . . er . . . loose money . . . available to pay the death duties. It would be a pity to have to sell off a part of the farm. Would you have any objection to selling the tray if it proved necessary?'

'No objection at all – if it helps to keep the farm in one piece.' I thought I would probably sell it anyway, it had too much blood on it for my liking. It would be an uncomfortable thing to have around.

'Well, I don't think there's more we can do now,' said Mount. 'I'll set the legal processes in motion – you can leave all that to me.' He stood up. 'I'm the executor of the estate, Jemmy, and executors have wide latitude, especially if they know the ins and outs of the law. You'll need ready money to run the farm – to pay the men, for example – and that can be drawn from the estate.' He grimaced. 'Technically speaking, *I'm* supposed to run the farm until probate, but I can appoint an expert to do it, and there's nothing to prevent me choosing you, so I think we'll let it go at that, shall we? Or would you rather I employed a land agent until probate?'

'Give me a couple of days,' I said. 'I want to think this over. For one thing, I'd like to talk to Jack Edgecombe.'

'Very well,' he said. 'But don't leave it much later than that.'

Before leaving Mount's office I telephoned the farm as I had promised Dave Goosan and was told that Detective-Superintendent Smith would be pleased if I would call at Totnes police station at three o'clock that afternoon. I said that I would and then went out into the street, feeling a little lost and wondering what to do next. Something was nagging at me and I couldn't pin it down, but suddenly I realized what it was.

I was hungry!

I looked at my watch and discovered it was nearly twelve o'clock. I had had no breakfast and only a very light snack the night before so it wasn't really surprising. Yet although I was hungry I didn't feel like facing a set meal, so I climbed into the car and headed towards the Cott where I could get a sandwich.

The saloon bar was almost empty with just an elderly man and woman sitting quietly in one corner. I went to the bar and said to Paula, 'I'll have a pint, please.'

She looked up. 'Oh, Mr Wheale, I'm so sorry to hear of what happened.'

It hadn't taken long for the news to get around, but that was only to be expected in a small town like Totnes. 'Yes,' I said. 'It's a bad business.'

She turned away to draw the beer, and Nigel came in from the other bar. He said, 'Sorry to hear about your brother, Jemmy.'

'Yes,' I said. 'Look, Nigel; I just want a beer and some sandwiches. I don't feel much like talking just now.'

He nodded, and said, 'I'll serve you in a private room if you like.'

'No, that doesn't matter; I'll have it here.'

He phoned the order through to the kitchen, then spoke to Paula who went into the other bar. I took a pull of beer and was aware of Nigel coming to the counter again. 'I know you don't want to talk,' he said. 'But there's something you ought to know.'

'What is it?'

He hesitated. 'Is it true that the dead man – the burglar – up at the farm was an American?'

'There's no certainty yet, but it's a probability,' I said.

He pursed his lips. 'I don't know if this is relevant, but Harry Hannaford told me a couple of days ago that an American had made Bob an offer for that tray – you know, the one they found was so valuable.'

'Where did this happen?'

Nigel flipped his hand. 'In here! I wasn't here at the time, but Harry said he heard the whole thing. He was having a drink with Bob at the time.'

I said, 'Do *you* know this American?'

'I don't think so. We get a lot of Yanks here – you run a place as old as the Cott and you're on the culture circuit. But we didn't have any Americans staying here just then. We have one here now, though; he arrived yesterday.'

'Oh! What kind of an American?'

Nigel smiled. 'Oldish – about sixty, I'd say. Name of Fallon. He must have a lot of money, too, judging by the telephone bill he's run up. But I wouldn't say he's a suspicious character.'

'Getting back to Hannaford and the other Yank,' I said. 'Can you tell me anything more?'

'There's nothing more to tell. Just that the Yank wanted to buy the tray – that's all Harry said.' He looked up at the clock. 'He'll be in soon, as like as not, for his midday pint. He usually comes in about now. Do you know him?'

'I can't place him.'

'All right,' said Nigel. 'When he comes in I'll tip you the wink.'

The sandwiches arrived and I took them to a corner table near the fireplace. When I sat down I felt suddenly tired, which wasn't surprising considering I'd been up all night and subject to a hell of a lot of tension. I ate the sandwiches slowly and drank some more beer. I was only now coming out of the shock that had hit me when I found Bob, and it was beginning to really hurt.

The pub started to fill up and I saw one or two faces I knew, but no one bothered me, although I intercepted some curious glances from eyes that were quickly averted. But there's a basic decency among countrymen which forbade them overt curiosity. Presently I saw Nigel talking to a big man in tweeds, then he crossed to me and said, 'Hannaford's here. Want to talk to him?'

I looked around the crowded bar. 'I'd rather it wasn't here. Have you a room I can use?'

'Take my office,' said Nigel promptly. 'I'll send Harry in after you.'

'You can send a couple of pints, too,' I said, and left the bar by the back door.

Hannaford joined me in a few minutes. 'Main sorry to hear about Bob,' he said in a deep voice. 'Many's the laugh we've had here. He was a good man.'

'Yes, Mr Hannaford; he was.' It was easy to see the relationship between Hannaford and Bob. When a man is a regular caller at a pub he strikes up an easy and casual acquaintanceship in those four walls. More often than not it goes no further than that and there may be no meeting outside the pub. But for all that there need be no shallowness to it – it's just uncomplicated and friendly.

I said, 'Nigel tells me there was an American wanting to buy the tray from Bob.'

'That there was – and more'n one. Bob had two offers to my knowledge, both from Americans.'

'Did he? Do you know anything about these men, Mr Hannaford?'

Hannaford pulled his ear. 'Mr Gatt was a real nice gentleman – not at all pushy like a lot of these Yanks. A middle-aged man he was, and well dressed. Very keen to buy that tray from Bob was Mr Gatt.'

'Did he offer a price – a definite price?'

'Not straight out he didn't. Your brother said it was no use him offering any price at all until he'd had the tray valued, and Mr Gatt said he'd give Bob the valuation price – whatever it was. But Bob laughed and said he might not sell it at all, that it was a family heirloom. Mr Gatt looked mighty put out when he heard that.'

'What about the other man?'

'The young chap? I didn't relish him much, he acted too high and mighty for me. He made no offer – not in my hearing – but he was disappointed when Bob said he wasn't set on selling, and he spoke pretty sharpish to Bob until his wife shut him up.'

'His wife!'

Hannaford smiled. 'Well, I wouldn't swear to that – he showed me no marriage lines – but I reckon it was his wife or, maybe his sister, perhaps.'

'Did he give a name?'

'That he did. Now, what was it? Hall? No, that's not it. Steadman? Nooo. Wait a minute and I'll get it.' His big red face contorted with the effort of remembering and suddenly smoothed out. 'Halstead – that was it. Halstead was the name. He gave your brother his card – I remember that. He said he'd get in touch again when the tray was valued. Bob said he was wasting his time and that's when he lost his temper.'

I said, 'Anything else you remember about it?'

Hannaford shook his head. That's about all there was to it. Oh, Mr Gatt did say he was a collector of pieces like that. One of these rich American millionaires, I expect.'

I thought that rich Americans seemed to be thick on the ground around the Cott. 'When did this happen?' I asked.

Hannaford rubbed his jaw. 'Let me see – it was after they printed about it in the *Western Morning News*; two days after, to my best recollection. That'ud make it five days ago, so it was Tuesday.'

I said, 'Thank you, Mr Hannaford. The police might be interested in this, you know.'

'I'll tell them all I've told you,' he said earnestly, and put his hand on my sleeve. 'When's the funeral to be? I'd like to be there to pay my respects.'

I hadn't thought of that; too much had happened in too short a time. I said, 'I don't know when it will be. There'll have to be an inquest first.'

'Of course,' said Hannaford. 'Best thing to do would be to tell Nigel as soon as you're sure, and he'll let me know. And others, too. Bob Wheale was well liked around here.'

'I'll do that.'

We went back into the bar and Nigel caught my eye. I put my tankard on the bar counter and he nodded across the room. 'That's the Yank who is staying here now. Fallon.'

I turned and saw a preternaturally thin man sitting near to the fire holding a whisky glass. He was abouty sixty years of age, his head was gaunt and fleshless and his skin tanned to the colour of well worn leather. As I watched he seemed to shiver and he drew his chair closer to the fire.

I turned back to Nigel, who said, 'He told me he spends a lot of time in Mexico. He doesn't like the English climate – he thinks it's too cold.'

IV

I spent that night alone at Hay Tree Farm. Perhaps I should have stayed at the Cott and saved myself a lot of misery, but I didn't. Instead I wandered through the silent rooms, peopled with the shadowy figures of memories, and grew more and more depressed.

I was the last of the Wheales – there was no one else. No uncles or aunts or cousins, no sisters or brothers – just me. This echoing, empty house, creaking with the centuries, had witnessed a vast procession down the years – a pageant of Wheales – Elizabethan, Jacobean, Restoration, Regency, Victorian, Edwardian. The little patch of England around the house had been sweated over by Wheales for more than four centuries in good times and bad, and now it all sharpened down to a single point – me. Me – a grey little man in a grey little job.

It wasn't fair!

I found myself standing in Bob's room. The bed was still dishevelled where I had whipped away the blankets to cover him and I straightened it almost automatically, smoothing down the counterpane. His dressing-table was untidy, as it always had been, and stuck in the crack up one side of the mirror was his collection of unframed photographs – one of our parents, one of me, one of Stalwart, the big brute of a horse that was his favourite mount, and a nice picture of Elizabeth. I pulled that one down to get a better look and something fluttered to the top of the dressing-table.

I picked it up. It was Halstead's card which Hannaford had spoken of. I looked at it listlessly. *Paul Halstead. Avenida Quintillana* 1534. *Mexico City.*

The telephone rang, startlingly loud, and I picked it up to hear the dry voice of Mr Mount. 'Hello, Jeremy,' he said. 'I just thought I'd tell you that you have no need to worry about the funeral arrangements. I'll take care of all that for you.'

'That's very kind of you,' I said, and then choked up.

'Your father and I were very good friends,' he said. 'But I don't think I've ever told you that if he hadn't married your mother, then I might have done so.' He rang off and the phone went dead.

I slept that night in my own room, the room I had always had ever since I was a boy. And I cried myself to sleep as I had not done since I was a boy.

TWO

It was only at the inquest that I found out the name of the dead man. It was Victor Niscemi, and he was an American national.

The proceedings didn't take long. First, there was a formal evidence of identification, then I told the story of how I had found the body of Niscemi and my brother dying in the farmhouse kitchen. Dave Goosan then stepped up and gave the police evidence, and the gold tray and the shotguns were offered as exhibits.

The coroner wrapped it up very quickly and the verdict on Niscemi was that he had been killed in self defence by Robert Blake Wheale. The verdict on Bob was that he had been murdered by Victor Niscemi and a person or persons unknown.

I saw Dave Goosan in the narrow cobbled street outside the Guildhall where the inquest had taken place. He jerked his head at two thick-set men who were walking away. 'From Scotland Yard,' he said. 'This is in their bailiwick now. They come in on anything that might be international.'

'You mean, because Niscemi was an American.'

'That's right. I'll tell you something else, Jemmy. He had form on the other side of the Atlantic. Petty thieving and robbery with violence. Not much.'

'Enough to do for Bob,' I said viciously.

Dave sighed in exasperated agreement. 'To tell you the truth, there's a bit of a mystery about this. Niscemi was never much of a success as a thief; he never had any money. Sort of working class, if you know what I mean. He certainly never had the money to take a trip over here – not unless he'd pulled off something bigger than usual for him. And nobody can see *why* he came to England. He'd be like a fish out of water, just the same as a Bermondsey burglar would be in New York. Still, it's being followed up.'

'What did Smith find out about Halstead and Gatt, the Yanks I turned up?'

Dave looked me in the eye. 'I can't tell you that, Jemmy. I can't discuss police work with you even if you are Bob's brother. The super would have my scalp.' He tapped me on the chest. 'Don't forget that you were a suspect once, lad.' The startlement must have shown on my face. 'Well, dammit; who has benefited most by Bob's death? All that stuff about the tray might have been a lot of flummery. *I* knew it wasn't you, but to the super you were just another warm body wandering about the scene of the crime.'

I let out a deep breath. 'I trust I'm not still on his list of suspects,' I said ironically.

'Don't give it another thought, although I'm not saying the super wont. He's the most unbelieving bastard I've ever come across. If he fell across a body himself he'd keep himself on his own list.' Dave pulled on his ear. 'I'll give you this much; it seems that Halstead is in the clear. He was in London and he's got an alibi for when he needs it.' He grinned. 'He was picked up for questioning in the Reading Room of the British Museum. Those London coppers must be a tactful lot.'

'Who is he? What is he?'

'He says he's an archeologist,' said Dave, and looked over my shoulder with mild consternation. 'Oh, Christ; here come those bloody reporters. Look, you nip into the church – they won't have the brazen nerve to follow you in there. I'll fight a rear-guard action while you leave by the side door in the vestry.'

I left him quickly and slipped into the churchyard. As I entered the church I heard the excited yelping as of hounds surrounding a stag at bay.

The funeral took place the day after the inquest. A lot of people turned up, most of whom I knew but a lot I didn't. All the people from Hay Tree Farm were there, including Madge and Jack Edgecombe who had come back from Jersey. The service was short, but even so I was glad when it was over and I could get away from all those sympathetic people. I had a word with Jack Edgecombe before I left. 'I'll see you up at the farm; there are things we must discuss.'

I drove to the farm with a feeling of depression. So that was that! Bob was buried, and so, presumably, was Niscemi, unless the police still had his body tucked away somewhere in cold storage. But for the loose end of Niscemi's hypothetical accomplice everything was neatly wrapped up and the world could get on with the world's futile business as usual.

I thought of the farm and what there was to do and of how I would handle Jack, who might show a countryman's conservative resistance to my new-fangled ideas. Thus occupied I swung automatically into the farmyard and nearly slammed into the back of a big Mercedes that was parked in front of the house.

I got out of the car and, as I did so, so did the driver of the Mercedes, uncoiling his lean length like a strip of brown rawhide. It was Fallon, the American Nigel had pointed out at the Cott. He said, 'Mr Wheale?'

'That's right.'

'I know I shouldn't intrude at this moment,' he said. 'But I'm pressed for time. My name is Fallon.'

He held out his hand and I found myself clutching skeletally thin fingers. 'What can I do for you, Mr Fallon?'

'If you could spare me a few minutes – it's not easy to explain quickly.' His voice was not excessively American.

I hesitated, then said, 'You'd better come inside.'

He leaned into his car and produced a briefcase. I took him into Bob's – my – study and waved him to a chair, then sat down facing him, saying nothing.

He coughed nervously, apparently not knowing where to begin, and I didn't help him. He coughed again, then said, 'I am aware that this may be a sore point, Mr Wheale, but I wonder if I could see the gold tray you have in your possession.'

'I'm afraid that is quite impossible,' I said flatly.

Alarm showed in his eyes. 'You haven't sold it?'

'It's still in the hands of the police.'

'Oh!' He relaxed and flicked open the catch of the briefcase. 'That's a pity. But I wonder if you could identify these photographs.'

He passed across a sheaf of eight by ten photographs which I fanned out. They were glossy and sharp as a needle, evidently the work of a competent commercial photographer. They were pictures of the tray taken from every conceivable angle; some were of the tray as a whole and there was a series of close-up detail shots showing the delicate vine leaf tracery of the rim.

'You might find these more helpful,' said Fallon, and passed me another heap of eight by tens. These were in colour, not quite as sharp as the black and whites but perhaps making a better display of the tray as it really was.

I looked up. 'Where did you get these?'

'Does it matter?'

'The police might think so,' I said tightly. 'This tray has figured in a murder, and they might want to know how you came by these excellent photographs of my tray.'

'Not your tray,' he said gently. 'My tray.'

'That be damned for a tale,' I said hotly. 'This tray has been used in this house for a hundred and fifty years that I am aware of. I don't see how the devil you can claim ownership.'

He waved his hand. 'We are talking at cross purposes. Those photographs are of a tray at present in my possession which is now securely locked in a vault. I came here to find out if your tray resembled mine at all. I think you have answered my unspoken question quite adequately.'

I looked at the photographs again, feeling a bit of a fool. This certainly looked like the tray I had seen so often, although whether it was an exact replica would be hard to say. I had seen the tray briefly the previous Saturday morning when Dave Goosan had shown it to me, but when had I seen it before that? It must have been around when I had previously visited Bob, but I had never noticed it. In fact, I had never examined it since I was a boy.

Fallon asked, 'Is it *really* like your tray?'

I explained my difficulty and he nodded understandingly, and said, 'Would you consider selling me your tray, Mr Wheale? I will give you a fair price.'

'It isn't mine to sell.'

'Oh? I would have thought you would inherit it.'

'I did. But it's in a sort of legal limbo. It won't be mine until my brother's will is probated.' I didn't tell Fallon that Mount had suggested selling the damned thing; I wanted to keep him on a string and find out what he was really after. I never forgot for one minute that Bob had died because of that tray.

'I see.' He drummed his fingers on the arm of the chair. 'I suppose the police will release it into your possession.'

'I don't see why they shouldn't.'

He smiled. 'Mr Wheale, will you allow me to examine the tray – to photograph it? It need never leave the house: I have a very good camera at my disposal.'

I grinned at him. 'I don't see why I should.'

The smile was wiped away from his face as though it had never been. After a long moment it returned in the form of a sardonic quirk of the corner of his mouth. 'I see you are . . . suspicious of me.'

I laughed. 'You're dead right. Wouldn't you be in my place?'

'I rather think I would,' he said. 'I've been stupid.' I once saw a crack chess player make an obviously wrong move which even a tyro should have avoided. The expression on his face was comical in its surprise and was duplicated on Fallon's face at that moment. He gave the impression of a man mentally kicking himself up the backside.

I heard a car draw up outside, so I got up and opened the casement. Jack and Madge were just getting out of their mini. I shouted, 'Give me a few more minutes, Jack; I'm a bit tied up.'

He waved and walked away, but Madge came over to the window. 'Would you like a cup of tea?'

'That seems a good idea. What about you, Mr Fallon – would you like some tea?'

'That would be very nice,' he said.

'Then that's it, Madge. Tea for two in here, please.' She went away and I turned back to Fallon. 'I think it would be a good idea if you told me what you are really getting at.'

He said worriedly, 'I assure you I have absolutely no knowledge of the events leading to your brother's death. My attention was drawn to the tray by an article and a photograph in the *Western Morning News* which was late in getting to me. I came to Totnes immediately, arriving rather late on Friday evening . . .'

'. . . and you booked in at the Cott Inn.'

He looked faintly surprised. 'Yes, I did. I intended going to see your brother on the Saturday morning but then I heard of the . . . of what had happened . . .'

'And so you didn't go. Very tactful of you, Mr Fallon. I suppose you realize you'll have to tell this story to the police.'

'I don't see why.'

'Don't you? Then I'll tell you. Don't you know that the man who killed my brother was an American called Victor Niscemi?'

Fallon seemed struck dumb and just shook his head.

'Didn't you read the report on the inquest this morning? It was in most of the papers.'

'I didn't read the newspaper this morning,' he said weakly.

I sighed. 'Look. Mr Fallon; an American kills my brother and the tray is involved. Four days before my brother is murdered two Americans try to buy it from him. And now you come along, an American, and also want to buy the tray. Don't you think you've got some explaining to do?'

He seemed to have aged five years and his face was drawn, but he looked up alertly. 'The Americans,' he said. 'The ones who wanted to buy the tray. What were their names?'

'Perhaps you can tell me,' I said.

'Was one of them Halstead?'

'Now you *have* got some explaining to do,' I said grimly. 'I think I'd better run you down to the police station right now. I think Superintendent Smith would be interested in you.'

He looked down at the floor and brooded for a while, then raised his head. 'Now I think you are being stupid, Mr Wheale. Do you really think that if I was implicated in this murder I would have come here openly today? I didn't know that Halstead had approached your brother, and I didn't know the housebreaker was an American.'

'But you knew Halstead's name.'

He flapped his hand tiredly. 'I've been crossing Halstead's trail all over Central America and Europe for the last three

years. Sometimes I'd get there first and sometimes he would.
I know Halstead; he was a student of mine some years ago.'

'A student of what?'

'I'm an archeologist,' said Fallon. 'And so is Halstead.'

Madge came in with the tea, and there were some scones
and strawberry jam and clotted cream. She put the tray on
the desk, smiled at me wanly and left the room. As I offered
the scones and poured the tea I reflected that it made a cosy
domestic scene very much at odds with the subject of discussion. I put down the teapot, and said, 'What about Gatt?
Did you know him?'

'I've never heard of the man,' said Fallon.

I pondered awhile. One thing struck me – I hadn't
caught out Fallon in a lie. He'd said that Halstead was an
archeologist, and that was confirmed by Dave Goosan.
He'd said he arrived at the Cott on Friday, and that was
confirmed by Nigel. I thought about that and made a long
arm to pull the telephone closer. Without saying anything
I dialled the Cott and watched Fallon drink his tea.

'Oh, hello, Nigel. Look, this chap Fallon – what time did
he arrive last Friday?'

'About half-past six in the evening. Why, Jemmy?'

'Just something that's come up. Can you tell me what he
did that night?' I stared unblinkingly at Fallon, who didn't
seem at all perturbed at the trend of the questions. He
merely spread some cream on a scone and took a bite.

'I can tell you everything he did that night,' said Nigel.
'We had a bit of an impromptu party which went on a bit.
I talked to Fallon quite a lot. He's an interesting old bird;
he was telling me about his experiences in Mexico.'

'Can you put a time on this?'

Nigel paused. 'Well, he was in the bar at ten o'clock – and
he was still there when the party broke up. We were a bit
late – say, quarter to two in the morning.' He hesitated. 'You
going to the police with this?'

I grinned. 'You weren't breaking the licensing laws, were you?'

'Not at all. Everyone there was staying at the Cott Guests' privileges and all that.'

'You're sure he was there continuously?'

'Dead sure.'

'Thanks, Nigel; you've been a great help.' I put down the phone and looked at Fallon. 'You're in the clear.'

He smiled and delicately dabbed his fingertips on a napkin. 'You're a very logical man, Mr Wheale.'

I leaned back in my chair. 'How much would you say the tray is worth?'

'That's a hard question to answer,' he said. 'Intrinsically not very much – the gold is diluted with silver and copper. Artistically, it's a very fine piece and the antiquarian value is also high. I daresay that at auction in a good saleroom it would bring about £7,000.'

'What about the archeological value?'

He laughed. 'It's sixteenth-century Spanish; where's the archeological value in that?'

'You tell me. All I know is that the people who want to buy it are archeologists.' I regarded him thoughtfully. 'Make me an offer.'

'I'll give you £7,000,' he said promptly.

'I could get that at Sotheby's,' I pointed out. 'Besides, Halstead might give me more or Gatt might'

'I doubt if Halstead could go that much,' said Fallon equably. 'But I'll play along, Mr Wheale; I'll give you £10,000.'

I said ironically, 'So you're giving me £3,000 for the archeological value it hasn't got. You're a very generous man. Would you call yourself a rich man?'

A slight smile touched his lips. 'I guess I would.'

I stood up and said abruptly, 'There's too much mystery involved in this for my liking. You know something about the tray which you're not telling. I think I'd better have a look at it myself before coming to any firm decision.'

If he was disappointed he hid it well. 'That would appear to be wise, but I doubt if you will find anything by a mere inspection.' He looked down at his hands. 'Mr Wheale, I have made you a most generous offer, yet I would like to go further. May I take an option on the tray? I will give you a thousand pounds now, on condition that you let no one else, particularly Dr Halstead, inspect it. In the event of your deciding to sell me the tray then the thousand pounds is in addition to my original offer. If you decide not to sell it then you may keep the thousand pounds as long as you keep your side of the bargain.'

I drew a deep breath. 'You're a real dog in the manger, aren't you? If you can't have it, then nobody else must. Nothing doing, Mr Fallon. I refuse to have my hands tied.' I sat down. 'I wonder what price you'd go to if I *really* pushed you.'

An intensity came into his voice. 'Mr Wheale, this is of the utmost importance to me. Why don't *you* state a price?'

'Importance is relative,' I said. 'If the importance is archeological then I couldn't give a damn. I know a fourteen-year-old girl who thinks the most important people in the world are the Beatles. Not to me they aren't.'

'Equating the Beatles with archeology hardly demonstrates a sensible scale of values.'

I shrugged. 'Why not? They're both concerned with people. It just shows that your scale of values is different from hers. But I just might state my price, Mr Fallon; and it may not be in money. I'll think about it and let you know. Can you come back tomorrow?'

'Yes, I can come back.' He looked me in the eye. 'And what about Dr Halstead? What will you do if he approaches you?'

'I'll listen to him,' I said promptly. 'Just as I've listened to you. I'm prepared to listen to anyone who'll tell me something I don't know. Not that it's happened noticeably yet.'

He did not acknowledge the jibe. Instead, he said, 'I ought to tell you that Dr Halstead is not regarded as being quite honest in some circles. And that is all I am going to say about him. When shall I come tomorrow?'

'After lunch; would two-thirty suit you?' He nodded, and I went on, 'I'll have to tell the police about you, you know. There's been a murder and you are one coincidence too many.' 'I see your point,' he said wearily. 'Perhaps it would be as well if I went to see them – if only to clear up a nonsense. I shall go immediately; where shall I find them?'

I told him where the police station was, and said, 'Ask for Detective-Inspector Goosan or Superintendent Smith.'

Inexplicably, he began to laugh. 'Goosan!' he said with a gasp, 'My God, but that's funny!'

I stared at him. I didn't see what was funny. 'It's not an uncommon name in Devon.'

'Of course not,' he said, choking off his chuckles. 'I'll see you tomorrow, then, Mr Wheale.'

I saw him off the premises, then went back to the study and rang Dave Goosan. 'There's someone else who wants to buy that tray,' I said. 'Another American. Are you interested?'

His voice was sharp. 'I think we might be very interested.'

'His name is Fallon and he's staying at the Cott. He's on his way to see you right now – he should be knocking on your door within the next ten minutes. If he doesn't it might be worth your while to go looking for him.'

'Point taken,' said Dave.

I said, 'How long do you intend holding on to the tray?'

'You can have it now if you like. I'll have to hold on to Bob's shotgun, though; this case isn't finished yet.'

'That's all right. I'll come in and pick up the tray. Can you do me a favour, Dave? Fallon will have to prove to you who and what he is; can you let me know, too? I'd like to know who I'm doing business with.'

'We're the police, not Dun and Bradstreet. All right, I'll let you know what I can, providing it doesn't run against regulations.'

'Thanks,' I said, and rang off. I sat motionless at the desk for a few minutes, thinking hard, and then got out the papers concerning the reorganization of the farm in preparation to doing battle with Jack Edgecombe. But my mind wasn't really on it.

II

Late that afternoon I went down to the police station to pick up the tray, and as soon as Dave saw me he growled, 'A fine suspect you picked.'

'He's all right?'

'He's as clean as a whistle. He was nowhere near your farm on Friday night. Four people say so – three of whom I know and one who is a personal friend of mine. Still, I don't blame you for sending him down here – you couldn't pass a coincidence like that.' He shook his head. 'But you picked a right one.'

'What do you mean?'

He grabbed a sheaf of flimsies from his desk and waved them under my nose. 'We checked him out – this is the telex report from the Yard. Listen to it and cry: John Nasmith Fallon, born Massachussetts, 1908; well educated – went to Harvard and Göttingen, with post-graduate study in Mexico City. He's an archeologist with all the letters in the alphabet after his name. In 1936 his father died and left him over 30 million dollars, which fortune he's more than doubled since, so he hasn't lost the family talent for making money.'

I laughed shortly. 'And I asked him if he considered himself a rich man! Is he serious about his archeology?'

'He's no dilettante,' said Dave. 'The Yard checked with the British Museum. He's the top man in his field, which is Central America.' He scrabbled among the papers. 'He publishes a lot in the scientific journals – the last thing he did was "Some Researches into the Calendar Glyphs of Dzi . . . Dzibi . . ." I'll have to take this one slowly . . . "Dzibilchaltun." God-almighty, he's investigating things I can't even pronounce! In 1949 he set up the Fallon Archeological Trust with ten million dollars. He could afford it since he apparently owns all the oil wells that Paul Getty missed.' He tossed the paper on to the desk. 'And that's your murder suspect.'

I said, 'What about Halstead and Gatt?'

Dave shrugged. 'What about them? Halstead's an archeologist, too, of course. We didn't dig too deeply into him.' He grinned. 'Pun not intended. Gatt hasn't been checked yet.'

'Halstead was one of Fallon's students. Fallon doesn't like him.'

Dave lifted his eyebrows. 'Been playing detective? Look, Jemmy; as far as I am concerned I'm off the case as much as any police officer can be. That means I'm not specifically assigned to it. Anything I'm told I pass on to the top coppers in London; it's their pigeon now, and I'm just a messenger boy. Let me give you a bit of advice. You can do all the speculating you like and there'll be no harm done but don't try to move in on the action like some half-baked hero in a detective story. The boys at Scotland Yard aren't damned fools; they can put two and two together a sight faster than you can, they've got access to more sources than you have, and they've got the muscle to make it stick when they decide to make a move. Leave it to the professionals; there are no Roger Sherringhams or Peter Wimseys in real life.'

'Don't get over-heated,' I said mildly.

'It's just that I don't want you making a bloody idiot of yourself.' He stood up. 'I'll get the tray – it's in the safe.'

He left the office and I picked up the telex message and studied it. It was in pretty fair detail but it more or less boiled down to what Dave had said. It seemed highly improbable that a man like Fallon could have anything in common with a petty criminal like Niscemi. And yet there was the tray – they were both interested in that, and so were Halstead and Gatt. Four Americans and the tray.

Dave came back carrying it in his hands. He put it on the desk. 'Hefty,' he said. 'Must be worth quite a bit if it really is gold.'

'It is.' I said. 'But not too pure.'

He flicked the bottom of the tray with his thumbnail. 'That's not gold – it looks like copper.'

I picked up the tray and examined it closely for, perhaps, the first time in twenty years. It was about fifteen inches in diameter and circular; there was a three-inch rim all the way round consisting of an intricate pattern of vine leaves, all in gold, and the centre was nine inches in diameter and of smooth copper. I turned it over and found the back to be of solid gold.

'You'd better have it wrapped,' said Dave. 'I'll find some paper.'

'Did you take any photographs of it?' I asked.

'Lots,' he said. 'And from every angle.'

'What about letting me have a set of prints?'

He looked pained. 'You seem to think the police are general dogsbodies for Jemmy Wheale. This isn't Universal Aunts, you know.' He shook his head. 'Sorry, Jemmy; the negatives were sent to London.'

He rooted around and found an old newspaper and began to wrap up the tray. 'Bob used to run his own darkroom. You have all the gear at home for taking your own snaps.'

That was true. Bob and I had been keen on photography as boys, he more than me. He'd stuck to it and I'd let it drop when I left home to go to university, but I thought I remembered enough to be able to shoot and develop a film and make some prints. I didn't feel like letting anyone else do it. In view of the importance Fallon had attached to examining the tray I wanted to keep everything under my own hand.

As I was leaving, Dave said, 'Remember what I said, Jemmy. If you feel any inclination to go off half-cocked come and see me first. My bosses wouldn't like it if you put a spoke in their wheel.'

I went home and found Bob's camera. I daresay he could have been called an advanced amateur and he had good equipment – a Pentax camera with a good range of lenses and a Durst enlarger with all the associated trimmings in a properly arranged darkroom. I found a spool of unexposed black and white film, loaded the camera and got to work. His fancy electronic flash gave me some trouble before I got the hang of it and twice it went off unexpectedly, but I finally shot off the whole spool and developed the film more or less successfully. I couldn't make prints before the film dried, so I went to bed early. But not before I locked the tray in the safe.

III

The next morning I continued the battle with Jack Edgecombe who was putting up a stubborn resistance to new ideas. He said unhappily, 'Eighty cows to a hundred acres is too many, Mr Wheale, sir; we've never done it like that before.'

I resisted the impulse to scream, and said patiently, 'Look, Jack: up to now this farm has grown its own feedstuff for the cattle. Why?'

He shrugged. 'It's always been like that.'

That wasn't an answer and he knew it. I said, 'We can buy cattle feed for less than it costs us to grow it, so why the devil should we grow it?' I again laid out the plan that had come from the computer, but giving reasons the computer hadn't. 'We increase the dairy herd to eighty head and we allocate this land which is pretty lush, and any extra feed we buy.' I swept my hand over the map. 'This hill area is good for nothing but sheep, so we let the sheep have it. I'd like to build up a nice flock of greyface. We *can* feed sheep economically by planting root crops on the flat by the river, and we alternate the roots with a cash crop such as malting barley. Best of all, we do away with all this market garden stuff. This is a farm, not an allotment; it takes too much time and we're not near enough to a big town to make it pay.'

Jack looked uncomprehendingly stubborn. It wasn't done that way, it never had been done that way, and he didn't see why it should be done that way. I was in trouble because unless Jack saw it *my* way we could never get on together.

We were interrupted by Madge. 'There's a lady to see you, Mr Wheale.'

'Did she give a name?'

'It's a Mrs Halstead.'

That gave me pause. Eventually I said, 'Ask her to wait a few minutes, will you? Make her comfortable – ask her if she'd like a cuppa.'

I turned back to Jack. One thing at a time was my policy. I knew what was the matter with him. If he became farm manager and the policy of the farm changed radically, he'd have to take an awful lot of joshing from the neighbouring farmers. He had his reputation to consider.

I said, 'Look at it this way, Jack: if we start on this thing, you'll be farm manager and I'll be the more-or-less absentee landlord. If the scheme falls down you can put all the blame on me because I'll deserve it, and you're only doing what I tell you to. If it's a success – which it will be if we both work hard at it – then a lot of the credit will go to you because you'll have been the one who made it work. You are the practical farmer, not me. I'm just the theoretical boy. But I reckon we can show the lads around here a thing or two.'

He contemplated that argument and brightened visibly – I'd offered him a way out with no damage to his self-esteem. He said slowly, 'You know, I like that bit about doing away with the garden produce; it's always been a lot of trouble – too much hand work, for one thing.' He shuffled among the papers. 'You know, sir, if we got rid of that I reckon we could work the farm with one less man.'

That had already been figured out – by the computer, not me – but I was perfectly prepared to let Jack take the credit for the idea. I said, 'Hey, so we could! I have to go now, but you stay here and go through the whole thing again. If you come up with any more bright ideas like that then let me know.'

I left him to it and went to see Mrs Halstead. I walked into the living-room and said, 'I'm sorry to have kept you waiting.' Then I stopped dead because Mrs Halstead was quite a woman – red hair, green eyes, a nice smile and a figure to make a man struggle to keep his hands to himself – even a grey little man like me.

'That's all right, Mr Wheale,' she said. 'Your housekeeper looked after me.' Her voice matched the rest of her; she was too perfect to be true.

I sat opposite her. 'What can I do for you, Mrs Halstead?'

'I believe you own a gold tray, Mr Wheale.'

'That is correct.'

She opened her handbag. 'I saw a report in a newspaper. Is this the tray?'

I took the clipping and studied it. It was the report that had appeared in the *Western Morning News* which I had heard of but not seen. The photograph was a bit blurred. I said, 'Yes, this is the tray.'

'That picture is not very good, is it? Could you tell me if your tray is anything like this one?'

She held out a postcard-size print. This was a better picture of a tray – but not my tray. It appeared to have been taken in some sort of museum because I could see that the tray was in a glass case and a reflection somewhat ruined the clarity of the picture. Everyone seemed to be pushing photographs of trays at me, and I wondered how many there were. I said cautiously, 'It might be something like this one. This isn't the best of pictures, either.'

'Would it be possible to see your tray, Mr Wheale?'

'Why?' I asked bluntly. 'Do you want to buy it?'

'I might – if the price were right.'

I pushed her again. 'And what would be a right price?'

She fenced very well. 'That would depend on the tray.'

I said deliberately, 'The going price has been quoted as being £7,000. Could you match that?'

She said evenly, 'That's a lot of money, Mr Wheate.'

'It is,' I agreed. 'It was, I believe, the amount offered by an American to my brother. Mr Gatt said he'd pay the price at valuation.'

Perhaps she was a little sad. 'I don't think that Paul . . . my husband . . . realized it would be as much as that.'

I leaned forward. 'I think I ought to tell you that I have had an even higher offer from a Mr Fallon.'

I watched her closely and she seemed to tighten, an almost imperceptible movement soon brought under control. She said quietly, 'I don't think we can compete with Professor Fallon when it comes to money.'

'No,' I said. 'He seems to have a larger share than most of us.'

'Has Professor Fallon seen the tray?' she asked.

'No, he hasn't. He offered me a very large sum, sight unseen. Don't you find that odd?'

'Nothing that Fallon does I find odd,' she said. 'Unscrupulous, even criminal, but not odd. He has reasons for everything he does.'

I said gently, 'I'd be careful about saying things like that, Mrs Halstead, especially in England. Our laws of slander are stricter than in your country.'

'Is a statement slanderous if it can be proved?' she asked. 'Are you going to sell the tray to Fallon?'

'I haven't made up my mind.'

She was pensive for a while, then she stirred. 'Even if it is not possible for us to buy it, would there be any objection to my husband examining it? It could be done here, and I assure you it would come to no harm.'

Fallon had specifically asked that Halstead should not be shown the tray. To hell with that! I said, 'I don't see why not.'

'This morning?' she said eagerly.

I lied in my teeth. 'I'm afraid not – I don't have it here. But it could be here this afternoon. Would that suit you?'

'Oh, yes,' she said, and smiled brilliantly. A woman has no right to be able to smile at a man like that, especially a man involved in tricking her into something. It tends to weaken his resolution. She stood up. 'I won't waste any more of your time this morning, Mr Wheale; I'm sure you're a busy man. What time should we come this afternoon?'

'Oh, about two-thirty,' I said casually. I escorted her to the door and watched her drive away in a small car. These archeological boffins seemed to be a queer crowd; Fallon had imputed dishonesty to Halstead, and Mrs Halstead had accused Fallon of downright criminality. The in-fighting in academic circles seemed to be done with very sharp knives.

I thought of the chemistry set I had when a boy; it was a marvellous set with lots of little bottles and phials containing powders of various hue. If you mixed the powders odd things were likely to happen, but if they were kept separate they were quite inert.

I was tired of meeting with inertness from Fallon and the Halsteads – no one had been forthright enough to tell why he wanted the tray. I wondered what odd things were likely to happen when I mixed them together at two-thirty that afternoon.

IV

I went back and had another go at Jack Edgecombe. If he hadn't actually caught fire, at least he was a bit luminous around the edges, which made arguing with him less of an uphill struggle. I chipped at him a bit more and managed to strike another spark of enthusiasm, and then packed him off to look at the farm with a new vision.

The rest of the morning was spent in the darkroom. I cut up the length of 35 mm film, which was now dry, and made a contact print just to see what I had. It didn't seem too bad and most of the stuff was usable, so I settled down and made a series of eight by ten prints. They weren't as professional as those that Fallon had shown me, but they were good enough for comparison with his.

I even printed out my failures including those that had happened when the electronic flash popped off unexpectedly. One of those was very interesting – to the point of being worthy of scrutiny under a magnifying glass. It was a real puzzler and I badly wanted to set up the tray and take more pictures, but there wasn't time to do it before my visitors arrived.

The Halsteads came fifteen minutes early, thus demonstrating their eagerness. Halstead was a man of about thirty-five who seemed to be living on his nerves. I suppose he was handsome in an odd sort of way if you go for the hawk-like visage; his cheekbones stood out prominently and his eyes were deep sunk in dark sockets so that he looked as though he were recovering from a week's binge. His movements were quick and his conversation staccato, and I thought he'd be a wearing companion if one had to put up with him for any length of time. Mrs Halstead seemed to manage all right and maintained a smooth outward serenity which shed a calmness over the pair of them and compensated for Halstead's nerviness. Maybe it was something she worked hard at.

She introduced her husband and there was the briefest of social chit-chat before a sudden silence. Halstead looked at me expectantly and twitched a bit. 'The tray?' he enquired in a voice which rose a bit more than was necessary.

I looked at him blandly. 'Oh, yes,' I said. 'I have some photographs here in which you might be interested.' I gave them to him and noted that his hands were trembling.

He flicked through them quickly, then looked up and said sharply, 'These are pictures of *your* tray?'

'They are.'

He turned to his wife. 'It's the right one – look at the vine leaves. Exactly like the Mexican tray. There's no doubt about it.'

She said doubtfully, 'It *seems* to be the same.'

'Don't be a fool,' he snapped. 'It·is the same. I studied the Mexican tray long enough, for God's sake! Where's our picture?'

Mrs Halstead produced it and they settled down to a comparison. 'Not an identical replica,' pronounced Halstead. 'But close enough. Undoubtedly made by the same hand – look at the veining in the leaves.'

'I guess you're right.'

'I *am* right,' he said positively, and jerked his head round to me. 'My wife said you'd let me see the tray.'

I didn't like his manner – he was too damned driving and impolite, and perhaps I didn't like the way he spoke to his wife. 'I told her there wasn't any reason why you shouldn't see it. At the same time there doesn't seem any reason why you should. Would you care to enlighten me?'

He didn't like resistance or opposition. 'It's a purely professional and scientific matter,' he said stiffly. 'It forms part of my present research; I doubt if you would understand it.'

'Try me,' I said softly, resenting his superior and condescending attitude. 'I can understand words of two syllables – maybe words of three syllables if you speak them very slowly.'

Mrs Halstead chipped in. 'We would be very grateful if We *could* see the tray. You would be doing us a great service, Mr Wheale.' She wouldn't apologize for her husband's unfortunate manner, but she was doing her best to drop some polite social oil into the works.

We were interrupted by Madge. 'There's a gentleman to see you, Mr Wheale.'

I grinned at Halstead. 'Thank you, Mrs Edgecombe; show him in, will you?'

When Fallon walked in Halstead gave a convulsive jerk. He turned to me and said in a high voice, 'What's he doing here?'

'Professor Fallon is here on my invitation, as you are,' I said sweetly.

Halstead bounced to his feet. 'I'll not stay here with that man. Come along, Katherine.'

'Wait a minute, Paul. What about the tray?'

That brought Halstead to a dead stop. He looked uncertainly at me, then at Fallon. 'I resent this,' he said in a trembling voice. 'I resent it very much.'

Fallon had been as astonished to see Halstead as Halstead had been to see him. He stood poised in the doorway and said, 'You think I don't resent it, too? But I'm not blowing my top about it like a spoiled child. You were always too explosive, Paul.' He advanced into the room. 'May I ask what you think you're doing, Wheale?'

'Maybe I'm holding an auction,' I said easily.

'Umph! You're wasting your time; this pair hasn't two cents to rub together.'

Katherine Halstead said cuttingly, 'I always thought you bought your reputation, Professor Fallon. And what you can't buy, you steal.'

Fallon whirled. 'Goddammit! Are you calling me a thief, young lady?'

'I am,' she said calmly. 'You've got the Vivero letter, haven't you?'

Fallon went very still. 'What do you know about the Vivero letter?'

'I know it was stolen from us nearly two years ago – and I know that you have it now.' She looked across at me. 'What conclusions would you draw from that, Mr Wheale?'

I looked at Fallon speculatively. The chemicals were mixing nicely and maybe they'd brew a little bit of truth. I was all for stirring up the broth. I said, 'Do you have this letter?'

Fallon nodded reluctantly. 'I do – I bought it quite legally in New York, and I have a receipt to prove it. But, hell, these are a fine pair to talk about theft. What about the papers you stole from me in Mexico, Halstead?'

Halstead's nostrils pinched in whitely. 'I stole nothing from you that wasn't mine. And what did you steal from me – just my reputation, that's all. There are too many thieving bastards like you in the profession, Fallon; incompetents who build their reputations on the work of others.'

'Why, you son of a bitch!' roared Fallon. 'You had your say in the journals and no one took any notice of you. Do you think anyone believes that poppycock?'

They were facing each other like fighting cocks and in another minute would have been at each other's throats had I not yelled at the top of my voice, 'Quiet!' They both turned, and I said in a calmer voice, 'Sit down both of you. I've never seen a more disgraceful exhibition by two grown men in my life. You'll behave yourselves in my house or I'll turn the lot of you out – and neither of you will ever get to see this bloody tray.'

Fallon said sheepishly, 'I'm sorry, Wheale, but this man got my goat.' He sat down.

Halstead also seated himself; he glared at Fallon and said nothing. Katherine Halstead's face was white and she had pink spots in her cheeks. She looked at her husband and tightened her lips and, when he maintained his silence, she said, 'I apologize for our behaviour, Mr Wheale.'

I said bluntly, 'You do your own apologizing, Mrs Halstead; you can't apologize for others – not even your husband.' I paused, waiting for Halstead to say something, but he maintained a stubborn silence, so I ignored him and turned to Fallon. 'I'm not particularly interested in the ins-and-outs of your professional arguments, although I must say I'm surprised at the charges that have been made here this afternoon.'

Fallon smiled sourly. 'I didn't start the mud-throwing.'

'I don't give a damn about that,' I said. 'You people are incredible. You're so wrapped up in your tuppenny-ha'penny professional concerns that you forget a man has been murdered because of that tray. Two men are already dead, for God's sake!'

Katherine Halstead said, 'I'm sorry if we appear so heartless; it must seem peculiar to you.'

'By God, it does! Now, listen to me carefully – all of you. I seem to have been dealt a high card in this particular game – I've got the tray that's so damned important. But nobody is going to get as much as a sniff at it until I'm told the name of the game. I'm not going to operate blindfolded. Fallon, what about it?'

He stirred impatiently. 'All right, it's a deal. I'll tell you everything you want to know – but privately. I don't want Halstead in on it.'

'Not a chance,' I said. 'Anything you want to tell me, you do it here and now in this room – and that applies to you, Halstead, too.'

Halstead said in a cold rage, 'This is monstrous. Am I to give away the results of years of research to this charlatan?'

'You'll put up or you'll shut up.' I stuck out a finger. The door's open and you can leave any time you like. Nobody is keeping you here. But if you go, that leaves Fallon with the tray.'

Indecision chased over his face and his knuckles whitened as he gripped the arms of the chair. Katherine Halstead took the decision from him. She said firmly, 'We accept your conditions. We stay.' Halstead looked at her with a sudden air of shock, and she said, 'It's all right, Paul; I know what I'm doing.'

'Fallon – what about you?'

'I guess I'm stuck with it,' he said, and smiled slowly. 'Halstead talks about years of research. Well, I've put in quite a few years myself. It wouldn't surprise me if we both know all there is to know about the problem. Heaven knows, I've been falling over this pair in every museum in Europe. I doubt if the pooling of information is going to bring up anything new.'

'I might surprise you,' said Halstead sharply. 'You have no monopoly on brains.'

'Cut it out,' I said coldly. 'This confessional is going to be run under my rules, and that means no snide comments from anyone. Do I make myself quite clear?'

Fallon said, 'You know, Wheale, when I first met you I didn't think much of you. You surprise me.'

I grinned. 'I surprise myself sometimes.' And so I did! Whatever had happened to the grey little man?

THREE

It was an astonishing, incredible and quite preposterous story, and, if I did not have a queer and inexplicable photograph up in the darkroom, I would have rejected it out of hand. And yet Fallon was no fool and he believed it – and so did Halstead, although I wouldn't have bet on the adequacy of *his* mental processes.

I ruled the proceedings firmly while the story was being told. Occasionally there were outbursts of temper, mostly from Halstead but with a couple of bitter attacks from Fallon, and I had to crack down hard. It was quite apparent that, while none of them liked what I was doing, they had no alternative but to comply. My possession of the tray was a trump card in this curious and involved game, and neither Fallon nor Halstead was prepared to let the other get away with it.

Fallon seemed to be the more sensible and objective of the two men so I let him open the account, asking him to begin. He pulled his ear gently, and said, 'It's hard to know where to start.'

I said, 'Begin at the beginning. Where did you come into it?'

He gave his ear a final tug, then folded one thin hand on top of the other. 'I'm an archeologist, working in Mexico mostly. Do you know anything about the Mayas?'

I shook my head.

'That's a great help,' he said acidly. 'But I don't suppose it matters at this stage because the preliminaries had nothing to do with the Mayas at all – superficially. I came across several references in my work to the de Vivero family of Mexico. The de Viveros were an old Spanish family – Jaime de Vivero, the founder, staked his claim in Mexico just after the time of Cortes; he grabbed a lot of land, and his descendants made it pay very well. They became big landowners, ranchers, owners of mines and, towards the end, industrialists. They were one of the big Mexican families that really ruled the roost. They weren't what you'd call a very public-spirited crowd and most of their money came from squeezing the peasants. They supported Maximilian in that damn-fool effort of the Hapsburgs to establish a kingdom in Mexico in the eighteen-sixties.

'That was their first mistake because Maximilian couldn't stand the pace and he went down. Still, that wasn't enough to break the de Viveros, but Mexico was in upheaval; dictator followed dictator, revolution followed revolution, and every time the de Viveros backed the wrong horse. It seems they lost their powers of judgement. Over a period of a hundred years the de Vivero family was smashed; if there are any of them still around they're lying mighty low because I haven't come across any of them.' He cocked an eye at Halstead. 'Have you come across a live de Vivero?'

'No,' said Halstead shortly.

Fallon nodded in satisfaction. 'Now, this was a very wealthy family in its time, even for Mexico, and a wealthy Mexican family was really something. They had a lot of possessions which were dispersed during the break-up, and one of these items was a golden tray something like yours, Wheale.' He picked up his briefcase and opened it. 'Let me read you something about it'

He pulled out a sheaf of papers. 'The tray was something of a family heirloom and the de Viveros looked after it; they didn't use it except at formal banquets and most of the time it was locked away. Here's a bit of gossip from the eighteenth century; a Frenchman called Murville visited Mexico and wrote a book about it. He stayed on one of the de Vivero estates when they threw a party for the governor of the province – this is the relevant bit.'

He cleared his throat. '"Never have I seen such a splendid table even in our French Court. The grandees of Mexico live like princes and eat off gold plate of which there was a profusion here. As a centrepiece to the table there was a magnificent array of the fruits of the country on golden trays, the most magnificent of which was curiously wrought in a pattern of vine leaves of exquisite design. I was informed by one of the sons of the family that this tray had a legend – that it was reputed to have been made by an ancestor of the de Viveros. This is unlikely since it is well known that the de Viveros have a noble lineage extending far back into the history of Old Spain and could not possibly have indulged in work of this nature, no matter how artful. I was told also that the tray is supposed to hold a secret, the discovery of which will make the recipient wealthy beyond measure. My informant smiled as he communicated this to me and added that as the de Viveros were already rich beyond computation the discovery of such a secret could not possibly make them effectively wealthier."'

Fallon dropped the papers back into the briefcase. That didn't mean much to me at the time, but I'm always interested in any secrets concerning Mexico so I copied it out as a matter of routine and filed it away. Incidentally, that bit about the noble lineage in Old Spain is phoney, the de Viveros were social climbers, men on the make – but we'll come to that later.

'Pretty soon after that I seemed to run into the de Viveros no matter which way I turned. You know how it is – you come across a strange word in a book, one which you've never seen before, and then you come across it again twice in the same week. It was like that with the de Viveros and their tray. Coming across references to the de Viveros is no trick in Mexico – they were a powerful family – but, in the next year I came across no less than seven references to the de Vivero tray, three of which mentioned this supposed secret. It appeared that the tray was important to the de Viveros. I just filed the stuff away; it was a minor problem of marginal interest and not really in my field.'

'Which is?' I asked.

'The pre-Columbian civilizations of Central America,' he answered. 'A sixteenth-century Spanish tray didn't mean much to me at the time. I was busy working on a dig in south Campeche. Halstead was with me then, among others. When the dig was finished for the season and we'd got back to civilization he picked a quarrel with me and left. With him went my de Vivero file.'

Halstead's voice was like a lash. 'That's a lie!'

Fallon shrugged. 'That's the way it was.'

So far we hadn't reached any point at which the tray was important, but here was the first mention of the deep-rooted quarrel between these two men, and that might be of consequence so I decided to probe. 'What was the quarrel about?'

'He stole my work,' said Halstead flatly.

'The hell I did!' Fallon turned to me. 'This is one of the things that crop up in academic circles, I'm sorry to say. It happens like this; young men just out of college work in the field with older and more experienced workers – I did the same myself with Murray many years ago. Papers get written and sometimes the younger fellow reckons he's not given due credit. It happens all the time.'

'Was it true in this case?'

Halstead was about to speak up but his wife put her hand on his knee and motioned him to silence. Fallon said, 'Most certainly not. Oh, I admit I wrote a paper on some aspects of the Quetzaecoatl legend which Halstead said I stole from him, but it wasn't like that at all.' He shook his head wearily. 'You've got to get the picture. You're on a dig and you work hard all day and at night you tend to relax and, maybe, drink a bit Now, if there's half a dozen of you then you might have a bull session – what you English call "talking shop". Ideas fly around thick and fast and nobody is ever certain who said what or when; these ideas tend to be regarded as common property. Now, it *may* be that the origin of the paper I wrote happened in such a way, and it *may* be that it was Halstead's suggestion, but I can't prove it and, by God, neither can he.'

Halstead said, 'You know damn well that I suggested the central idea of that paper.'

Fallon spread his hands and appealed to me. 'You see how it is. It might have gone for nothing if this young fool hadn't written to the journals and publicly accused me of theft. I could have sued the pants off him – but I didn't. I wrote to him privately and suggested that he refrain from entering into public controversy because I certainly wasn't going to enter into an argument of that nature in the pro-fessional prints. But he continued and finally the editors wouldn't print his letters any more.'

Halstead's voice was malevolent. 'You mean you bought the goddamn editors, don't you?'

'Think what you like,' said Fallon in disgust. 'At any rate, I found my de Vivero file had vanished when Halstead left. It didn't mean much at the time, and when it did start to mean something it wasn't much trouble to go back to the original sources. But when I started to bump into the Halsteads around every corner I put two and two together.'

'But you don't *know* he took your file,' I said. 'You couldn't prove it in a law court.'

'I don't suppose I could,' agreed Fallon.

'Then the less said about it the better.' Halstead looked pleased at that, so I added, 'You both seem free and easy in

throwing accusations about. This isn't my idea of professional dignity.'

'You haven't heard the whole story yet, Mr Wheale,' said
Mrs Halstead.

'Well, let's get on with it,' I said. 'Go ahead, Professor
Fallon – or do you have anything to say, Dr Halstead?'

Halstead gloomed at me. 'Not yet.' He said it with an air
of foreboding and I knew there were some more fireworks
ahead.

'Nothing much happened after that for quite a while,'
said Fallon. 'Then when I was in New York, I received a
letter from Mark Gerryson suggesting I see him. Gerryson is
a dealer whom I have used from time to time, and he said
he had some Mayan chocolate jugs – not the ordinary pottery jugs, but made of gold. They must have come from a
noble house. He also said he had part of a feather cloak and
a few other things.'

Halstead snorted and muttered audibly, 'A goddamn
feather cloak!'

'I know it was a fake,' said Fallon. 'And I didn't buy it.
But the chocolate jugs were genuine. Gerryson knew I'd be
interested – the ordinary Mayan specialist doesn't interest
Gerryson because he hasn't the money that Gerryson asks;
he usually sells to museums and rich collectors. Well, I run
a museum myself – among other things – and I've had some
good stuff from Gerryson in the past.

'We dickered for a bit and I told him what I thought of his
feather cloak; he laughed about that and said he was pulling
my leg. The chocolate jugs were genuine enough and I
bought those. Then he said he wanted my opinion on something that had just come in – it was a manuscript account by
a Spaniard who had lived among the Mayas in the early sixteenth century and he wanted to know if it was genuine.'

'He was consulting you as an expert in the field?' I said.
I saw Katherine Halstead lean forward intently.

Fallon nodded. 'That's right. The name of the Spaniard was de Vivero, and the manuscript was a letter to his sons.' He fell silent.

Halstead said, 'Don't stop now, Fallon – just when it's getting interesting.'

Fallon looked at me. 'Do you know anything about the conquest of Mexico?'

'Not much,' I said. 'I learned a bit about it at school – Cortes and all that – but I've forgotten the details, if I ever knew them.'

'Just like most people. Have you got a map of Mexico?'

I walked across the room and picked an atlas from the shelf. I drew up the coffee table and laid down the atlas turned to the correct page. Fallon hovered over it, and said, 'I'll have to give you some background detail or else the letter won't make sense.' He brought down his finger on to the map of Mexico close to the coast near Tampico. 'In the first couple of decades of the fifteen-hundreds the Spaniards had their eyes on what we now know as Mexico. There were rumours about the place – stories of unimaginable wealth – and they were poising themselves to go in and get it.'

His finger swept in an arc around the Gulf of Mexico. 'Hernandez de Cordoba explored the coast in 1517 and Juan de Grijalva followed in 1518. In 1519 Hernan Cortes took the plunge and mounted an expedition into the interior and we know what happened. He came up against the Aztecs and by a masterly mixture of force, statesmanship, superstition and pure confidence trickery he licked them – one of the most amazing feats any man has ever done.

'But having done it he found there were other worlds to conquer. To the south, covering what is now Yucatan, Guatemala and Honduras was another Amerind empire – that of the Mayas. He hadn't got as much gold from the Aztecs as he expected, but the Mayas were dripping with it if the reports that came up from the south were true. So in 1525 he marched against the Mayas. He left Tenochtitlan – now

Mexico City – and hit the coast here, at Coatzacualco, and then struck along the spine of the isthmus to Lake Peten and thus to Coban. He didn't get much for his pains because the main strength, of the Mayas wasn't on the Anahuac plateau at all but in the Yucatan Peninsula.'

I leaned over his shoulder and followed his exposition alertly. Fallon said, 'Cortes gave up personal direction at that point – he was pulled back to Spain – and the next expedition was led by Francisco de Montejo, who had already explored the coast of Yucatan from the sea. He had quite a respectable force but he found the Mayas a different proposition from the Aztecs. They fought back, and fought back hard, and Montejo was no Cortes – the Spaniards were trounced in the first few battles.

'With Montejo was Manuel de Vivero. I don't suppose Vivero was much more than a common foot soldier, but something funny happened to him. He was captured by the Mayas and they didn't kill him; they kept him alive as a sort of slave and as a mascot. Now, Montejo never did pacify Yucatan – he *never* got on top of the Mayas. Come to that, nobody ever did; they were weakened and absorbed to some extent, but they were never defeated in battle. In 1549, twenty-two years after he started out, Montejo was in control of barely half of the Yucatan Peninsula – and all this time Vivero was a captive in the interior.

'This was a rather curious time in the history of the Mayas and something happened which puzzled archeologists for a long time. They found that the Spaniards and the Mayas were living and working together side by side, each in his own culture; they found a Mayan temple and a Spanish church built next to each other and, what is more, contemporaneous – built *at the same time*. This was puzzling until the sequence of events had been sorted out as I've just described.

'In any event, there the Mayas and the Spaniards were, living cheek by jowl. They fought each other, but not continuously. The Spaniards controlled eastern Yucatan where the great Mayan cities of Chichen Itza and Uxmal are, but western Yucatan, the modern province of Quintana Roo, was a closed book to them. It's still pretty much of a closed book even now. However, there must have been quite a bit of trade going on between the two halves and Vivero, captive though he was, managed to write a letter to his sons and smuggle it out. That's the Vivero letter.'

He dug into his briefcase again. 'I have a transcription of it here if you want to read it.'

I flipped open the file he gave me – there was quite a lot of it. I said, 'Do you want me to read this now?'

'It would be better if you did,' he said. 'We'd be able to get on with the rest of our business a little faster. You can't understand anything until you read that letter.'

'All right,' I said. 'But I'll take it into my study. Can I trust you two not to kill each other in my absence?'

Katherine Halstead said coolly, 'There will be no trouble.'

I grinned at her cheerfully. 'I'll have Mrs Edgecombe bring you tea; that ought to keep the temperature down – no one kills over the teacups, it would be downright uncivilized.'

II

To my sons, Jaime and Juan,
greetings from Manuel de Vivero y Castuera, your father.

For many years my sons, I have been seeking ways by which I could speak to you to assure you of my safety in this heathen land. Many times have I sought escape and as many times I have been defeated and I know now that escape from my captivity cannot be, for I am watched continually. But by secret stratagems and the friendship of two men of the Mayas I am able to send you this missive in the hope that your hearts will be lightened and you will not grieve for me as for a dead man. But you must know,

my sons, that I will never come out of this land of the
Mayas nor out of this city called Uaxuanoc; like the
Children of Israel I shall be captive for as long as it pleases
the Lord, our God, to keep me alive.

In this letter I shall relate how I came to be here, how
God preserved my life when so many of my comrades
were slain, and tell of my life among those people, the
Mayas. Twelve years have I been here and have seen
many marvels, for this is the Great City of the Mayas, the
prize we have all sought in the Americas. Uaxuanoc is to
Tenochtitlan which Hernan Cortes conquered as Madrid is
to the meanest village in Huelva, the province of our family.
I was with Cortes in the taking of Tenochtitlan and saw
the puissant Montezuma and his downfall, but that mighty
king was as a mere peasant, a man poor in wealth, when
put against even the ordinary nobility of Uaxuanoc.

You must know that in the Year of Christ One
Thousand, Five Hundred and Twenty Seven I marched
with Francisco de Montejo into the Yucatan against the
Mayas. My position in the company was high and I led a
band of our Spanish soldiers. I had a voice with Cortes
when I was with that subtle soldier and I was high in the
councils of Francisco de Montejo, and so I know the inner
reasons for the many stratagems of the campaign. Since I
have lived with the Mayas I have come to know them, to
speak their words and to think their thoughts, and so I
know also why those stratagems came to naught.

Francisco de Montejo was – and, I hope, still is – my
friend. But friendship cannot blind me to his shortcomings
as a soldier and as a statesman. Brave he undoubtedly is,
but his is the bravery of the wild boar or of the bull of the
Basque country which charges straight without deceit or
evasion and so is easily defeated. Bravery is not enough
for a soldier, my sons: he must be wily and dishonest,
telling lies when appearing to speak truth, even to his men
when he finds this necessary, he must retreat to gain an

advantage, ignoring the ignorant pleadings of braver but lesser soldiers; he must lay traps to ensnare the enemy and he must use the strength of the enemy against himself as Cortes did when he allied, himself with the Tlascalans against the men of Mexico.

Hernan Cortes knew this most well. He spoke pleasantly to all and of all, but kept his counsel and went his own way. It may be that this use of lies and chicanes, the inventions of the Devil, is against the teachings of Holy Church and, indeed, would be reprehensible when fighting fellow Christians; but here we are fighting the Children of the Devil himself and turn his own weapons against him in the assurance that our cause is just and that with the help of our Lord, Jesus Christ, we can bring these ignorant savages to the One and True Faith.

Be that as it may, Francisco de Montejo was – and is – lacking in the qualities I have named and his efforts to subdue the Maya came to naught. Even now, twelve years after we marched so gaily on our Holy Crusade, the Maya is as strong as ever, though some of his cities are lost. Yet I would not lay all blame on Francisco, for this is as strange a land as any I have seen in all my journeyings in the Americas, where many strange and wondrous things are to be seen daily.

This I will tell you: the land of Yucatan is not like any other. When Hernan Cortes defeated the army of the Mayas on his journey to El Peten and the Honduras he was fighting on the uplands of Anahuac where the land is open and where all the noble resources of the art of war in which we are so advanced can be used. When we marched into Yucatan with de Montejo on the central strongholds of the enemy we found a green wilderness, a forest of trees so vast that it would cover all of Old Spain.

In this place, our horses, which so affright the ignorant savages, could not be used in battle; but we were not cast

down, thinking to use them as pack animals. To our sore
disappointment they were afflicted by disease and began to
die, more each day. And those that survived were of little
value, for the trees grew thickly and a man can go where a
horse cannot, and from being the most valued of our possessions, they stooped to become a hindrance to our expedition.

Another misfortune of this land is the lack of water,
which is very strange, for consider: how is it that there can
be a growth of strong trees and bushes of divers kind
where there is no water? But it is indeed so. When the
rain comes, which it does infrequently but more often at
certain times of year, then it is soaked direct into the solid
earth so that there are no streams and rivers in this land;
but sometimes there is a pool or well which the Maya calls
cenote and here the water is fresh and good although it is
fed not by running streams but rather issues forth from
the bowels of the earth.

Because these places are few in the forest they are
sacred to the Mayas who set up their temples here and give
praise to their idolatrous gods for the good water. Here also
they set up their castles and strong places, and so when we
marched with de Montejo we had to fight for the very
water for our bellies to give us strength to fight more.

The Mayas are a stubborn people who close their ears
to the Word of Christ. They would not listen to Francisco
de Montejo, nor to any of his captains, myself included,
nor even to the good priests of God in our train who
pleaded with them in the Name of our Saviour. They
rejected the Word of the Lamb of God and resisted us with
weapons although, in truth, since my captivity I have
found them a peaceful people, very slow to wrath but in
their anger terrible.

Although their weapons are poor, being wooden swords
with stone edges and spears with stone tips, they resisted us
mightily for their numbers were great and they knew the

secret paths of the land and laid snares for us, in which
ambuscades many of my comrades were slain and in one of
these affrays I, your father, was taken prisoner, to my shame.

I could not fight more for my sword was knocked from
my hand, nor could I run on their swords and die for I
was bound with ropes and helpless. I was carried, slung on
a pole, along many devious paths in the forest and so
came to the encampment of their army where I was questioned to some lengths by a great Cacique. The tongue of
these people is not so different from the Toltec tongue that
I could not understand but I dissimulated and gave no
knowledge of my understanding and so by this means was
I able to keep bidden from them the place of our main
force, nor could they wring it from me by means of torture
because of the confusion of tongues.

I think they were going to kill me but a priest among
them pointed to my hair which, as you know, is the colour
of ripe grain in summer, a strange thing for a Spaniard and
more natural in northern lands. And so I was taken from
that camp and sent under guard to the great city of
Chichen Itza. In this city there is a great cenote and
chichen in the Mayan tongue means the mouth of a well.
In this great pool are maidens thrown who go down to the
underworld and return to tell of the mysteries they have
seen in Hades. Surely these are the Devil's spawn!

In Chichen Itza I saw a Cacique even greater than the
first, a noble finely dressed in an embroidered kilt and
feather cloak and surrounded by papas or the priests of
these people. I was again questioned but to no avail and
much was made of my hair and a great cry arose among
the papas that surely I was Kukulkan, he whom you will
know in the Toltec tongue as Quetzaecoatl, the white god
who is to come from the West, a belief among the heathen
that has served us well.

In Chichen Itza I spent one month closely guarded in a
stone cell but other than that I was not harmed, being

served regularly with the corn of these people and some meat, together with that bitter drink called chocolatl. After one month I was sent again under guard to their main city which is Uaxuanoc and where I now am. But the guards were young nobles finely dressed in embroidered cotton armour and with good weapons of their kind. I do not think their armour as good as our iron armour, but no doubt it suffices well enough when they fight among themselves. I was fettered loosely but other than that no harm was offered and the chains were heavy, being of gold.

Uaxuanoc is a large city and there are many temples and big buildings the greatest of which is the temple to Kukulkan, decorated with the Feathered Serpent in his honour. Thither was I taken so that the papas of the temple could behold me and pass judgement whether I was indeed Kukulkan, their chief god. There was much argument among the papas: some said I was not Kukulkan because why would their chief god fight against them? Others among them asked why should not Kukulkan bring his warriors to chastise them with magical weapons if they had transgressed against the law of the gods; rather should they seek in their hearts where the transgression lay. Again, some said that this could not be Kukulkan because he spoke not their tongue, and others asked: why should the gods speak an earthly tongue when they undoubtedly spoke among themselves of things that could not be uttered by human lips?

I trembled before them but kept an outward calm, for was I not in evil straits? If I were not Kukulkan they would sacrifice me in the temple in the manner of the Aztecs of Tenochtitlan and tear the living heart from my body. But if they believed I was their god they would bow down before me and worship and I would be an abomination before Christ and damned thereafter to the pains of hell, for no mortal man is worthy of worship before God.

They resolved their disputation by taking me before their king for him to pass judgement between the divers parties in the manner of their law, he being the sole arbitrator in matters of high state and religion among them. He passed for a tall man among the Mayas though not as tall as would seem so in our eyes; he had a noble countenance and was dressed finely in a cloak of the bright feathers of humming birds and wore much gold about his person. He sat on a golden throne and above his head was a representation of the Feathered Serpent in gold and precious stones and fine enamels.

And he judged in this manner: that I should not be sacrificed but should be taken aside and taught the tongue of the Mayas so that I should be able to utter from my own lips and with their understanding what and who I was.

I was so overjoyed at the judgement of this Solomon that I nearly went on my knees before him but I caught myself up with the thought that indeed I did not know their tongue – or so they thought – and to learn it would take me many months or even years. By this stratagem I saved my life and my soul.

I was taken aside and put into the care of the eldest of the papas, who led me to the great temple where I was given lodging in the quarters of the papas. Soon I found I was free to come and go in the city as I wished although always accompanied by two noble guards and still clinking my golden fetters. Many years afterwards I discovered that the papas gave me this freedom for fear I was indeed Kukulkan and would exact vengeance at a later time if imprisoned. As for the golden chains: was not gold the metal of the gods? Perhaps Kukulkan would not be dishonoured by gold – if indeed this was Kukulkan. The king himself wore golden chains though they did not fetter him. Thus the papas reasoned in fear of disgrace should they be proved wrong in any way.

They taught me their tongue and I was slow to learn, my voice unready and my speech stumbling, and by this means passed many months to the great disappointment of the papas. During this time I saw many abominations in the great temple; young men sacrificed to Kukulkan, their bodies oiled and their heads garlanded with flowers going willingly to the bloodstained altar to have their hearts torn out by the papas and held in their sight before vision faded from their eyes. I was forced to attend these blasphemous ceremonies before the idol of the Feathered Serpent, my guards holding my arms so that I could not leave. Every time I closed my eyes and prayed to Christ and the Virgin for succour from the awful fate to which I found myself condemned.

There were other sacrifices at the great cenote in the midst of the city. A ridge of land splits the city from east to west and on the top of the ridge is the temple of Yum Chac, the god of rain, whose palace these foolish people believe to be at the bottom of the cenote. At ceremonies in honour of Yum Chac maidens are cast from the temple to the deep pool at the bottom of the cliff and disappear into the dark waters. These infidel wickednesses I did not attend.

It was during this time that I found my salvation from the terrible dilemma under which I laboured. You must know that the Mayas are great workers in stone and gold, although much of their labour is directed to making their heathen idols, a task unfitting for Christian hands. My sons, your grandfather and my father was a goldsmith in the city of Sevilla and when I was young I learned the trade at his knee. I observed that the Mayas were ignorant of the way of using wax which is common in Spain so I pleaded with the papas to give me gold and beeswax and to let me use a furnace to melt the gold.

They consulted among themselves and let me have the gold and beeswax and watched me closely to see what I did. There was a maiden, not above fourteen, who attended me in my lodging and saw to my wants, and I made a little model of her in the wax while the papas looked on and

frowned, for they were afraid of some bewitchment. The
Mayas have none of the Parisian plaster so I was constrained
to use well watered clay to put about the statue and to make
the funnel on the top for the pouring of the gold.

I was allowed to use the temple smithy and the papas
cried in wonder as the gold was poured into the funnel
and the hot wax spurted from the vent hole, the while I
sweated for fear that the clay mould would break, but it
did not and I was well satisfied with my little statue which
the papas took before the king and told him of its making.
Thereafter I made many objects in gold but would not
make idols for the temple nor any of the golden implements used therein. The king commanded I teach the
royal smiths this new art of working in gold, which I did,
and many of the great Caciques of the land came and had
me make jewellery for them.

The day came when I could no longer hide my knowledge of the Mayan tongue and the papas took me to the
king for judgement and he asked me to speak from my
mouth who or what I was. I spake plainly that indeed I
was not Kukulkan but a nobleman from lands to the east
and a faithful subject of the great Emperor Charles V of
Spain who had commanded me to come to the Mayas and
spread the Word of Christ among them.

The papas murmured among themselves and prevailed
upon the king, saying that the gods of the Mayas were
strong and they needed none other and that I should be
sacrificed in the temple of Kukulkan for blasphemy. I spake
boldly straight to the king, asking him would he kill such a
one as I who could teach his smiths many wonders so that
his kingdom should be ornamented beyond all others?

The king smiled on me and gave orders that indeed I
should not be sacrificed but should be given a house and
servants and should teach my arts to all the smiths of the
land to the benefit of the kingdom but that I should not
teach the Word of Christ on pain of death. This last he said

to please the papas of Kukulkan. And I was given a house with a smithy and many serving-maids and the smiths of the land came and sat at my feet and my chains were struck from me.

Twice thereafter I escaped and was lost in the great forest and the king's soldiers found me and took me back to Uaxuanoc and the king was lenient and punished me not. But the third time I escaped and was brought back again into the city he frowned like thunder and spoke to me, saying his patience was at an end and that if I escaped but once more I would be sacrificed in the temple of Kukulkan, so I perforce desisted and stayed in the city.

Here I have been for twelve long years, my sons, and am indeed counted now as one of their own save for the guards about my house and those that follow me when I go to the market place. I do not go to the temples but instead have made a chapel to Jesus and the Virgin in my house where I pray daily and am not hindered, for the king said: Let every man pray to the gods of his heart. But he will not let me preach the Word of Christ in the city and I do not for fear of death and am ashamed thereat.

Uaxuanoc is a great and fine city with much gold. Even the gutters which lead the rainwater from the temple roofs to the cisterns are gold and I myself use golden spoons in my kitchen, in which manner I am greater than any king in Christendom. I believe these people to have sprung from the loins of those Egyptians who kept the Israelites in captivity, for their temples are pyramids in the Egyptian manner as were described to me by a traveller who had been in those parts. But the king's palace is a square building, very great and plated with sheets of gold within and without even to the floors so that one walks on gold. And these people have the art of enamel such as I have never seen, but use the art in blasphemy to make their idols, although much fine jewellery is also made, even the common people wearing gold and enamel.

My life is easy, for I am held in much respect for my work in the smithy and because I have the friendship of the king who gives me many gifts when I please him with my work. But often in the nights I weep and wish I were back again in Spain even in a common tavern in Cadiz where there is music and singing, for these Mayas have but poor music, knowing only the pipe and drum and I have no knowledge of the musical art to teach them other.

But I say to you, my sons, God has touched this land with His Finger and surely intends it to be brought into the Fold of Christ for I have seen wonder upon wonder here and an even greater marvel which is a sign for all to behold that the gentle Hand of Christ encompasses the whole world and there is no corner which escapes Him. I have seen this sign written in burning gold upon a mountain of gold which lies not a step from the centre of the city and which shines in imperishable glory more brightly than the golden palace of the king of the Mayas; and surely this sign means that Christians shall possess this land for their own and the heathen shall be cast down and that men of Christ shall overturn the idols in the temples and shall strip the gold from the temple roofs and from the palace of the king and shall take possession of the golden mountain and the burning sign thereon which is a wonder for all eyes to see.

Therefore, my sons, Jaime and Juan, read carefully this letter for it is my wish that this glory shall come to the family of de Vivero which shall be exalted thereby. You know the de Viveros are of ancient lineage but were put upon in past time by the Moors in Spain so that the fortunes of the family were lost and the heads of the family were forced into common trade. My father was a goldsmith which, praise be to God, has been the saving of my soul in this land. When the infidel Moors were driven from Spain our family fortunes changed and by inheritance from my father I was able to buy land in the province of Huelva and became Alcalde. But I looked afar to the new lands in the

West and thought that a man might hew a greater inheritance to pass to his sons, who then might become governors of provinces under the king in these new lands. So I came to Mexico with Hernan Cortes.

Whoever takes this city of Uaxuanoc shall also possess that mountain of gold of which I have written and his name shall sound throughout all Christendom and he shall sit on the right hand of Christian kings and be honoured above all other men and it is my wish that this man should be called de Vivero. But it has grieved me that my sons should be quarrelsome as was Cain unto Abel, fighting the one with the other for little reason and bringing shame upon the name of de Vivero instead of uniting for the good of the family. Therefore I charge you under God to make your peace. You, Jaime, shall beg the forgiveness of your brother for the sins you have committed against him, and you, Juan, shall do likewise, and both shall live in amity and work towards the same end and that is to take this city and the mountain of gold with its wondrous sign.

So with this letter I send you gifts, one for each, made in that marvellous manner which my father learned of that stranger from the East which the Moors brought to Cordoba many years ago and of which I have spoken to you. Let the scales of enmity fall from your eyes and look upon these gifts with proper vision which shall join you together with strong bonds so that the name of de Vivero shall echo in Christendom for all time to come.

The men who shall bring you these gifts are Mayas whom I have secretly baptized in Christ against the wishes of the king and taught our Spanish tongue for their greater aid and safety in seeking you. Look upon them well and honour them, for they are brave men and true Christians and deserve much reward for their service.

Go with God, my sons, and fear not the snares laid in this forest land by your enemies. Remember what I have told you of the qualities of the true soldier, so that you shall prosper in battle and overcome the wickedness of the heathen to possess this land and the great wonder contained therein. So the name of de Vivero will be exalted for evermore.

It may be that when this is brought to pass I will be dead, for the king of the Mayas becomes old and he who will be king looks not upon me with favour, being corrupted by the papas of Kukulkan. But pray for me and for my soul, for I fear I shall spend long in purgatory for my pusillanimity in hesitating to convert this people to Christ for fear of my life. I am but a mortal man and much afraid, so pray for your father, my sons, and offer masses for his soul.

Written in the month of April in the year of Christ, One, Thousand, Five Hundred and Thirty Nine.

Manuel de Vivero y Castuera,
  Alcalde in Spain,
    Friend of Hernando Cortes
    and Francisco de Montejo.

III

I put the transcription of the Vivero letter back into the file and sat for a moment thinking of that long-dead man who had lived out his life in captivity. What had happened to him? Had he been sacrificed when the king died? Or had he managed to whip up a little more ingenuity and double-talk the Mayas into letting him live?

What a mixed-up man he was – according to our modern way of thinking. He regarded the Mayas as the man regarded the lion: 'This animal is dangerous; it defends itself when attacked.' That smacked of hypocrisy but de Vivero was educated in a different tradition; there was no dichotomy involved in converting the heathen and looting them of their gold simultaneously – to him it was as natural as breathing.

He was undoubtedly a brave and steadfast man and I hoped he had gone to his death unperturbed by the mental agonies of purgatory and hell.

There was an air of tension in the living-room and it was evident that the birdies in their little nest had not been agreeing. I tossed down the file, and said, 'All right; I've read it.'

Fallon said, 'What did you think of it?'

'He was a good man.'

'Is that all?'

'You know damn well that isn't all,' I said without heat. 'I see the point very well. Would I be correct if I said that this city of . . . Uax . . . Uaxua . . .' I stumbled.

'Wash-wan-ok,' said Fallon unexpectedly. 'That's how it's pronounced.'

'. . . Anyway, that this city hasn't been uncovered by you people?'

'Score one for you,' said Fallon. He tapped the file and said with intensity, 'On Vivero's evidence Uaxuanoc was bigger than Chichen Itza, bigger than Uxmal – and those places are pretty big. It was the central city of the Mayan civilization and the man who finds it will make a hell of a name for himself; he's going to be able to answer a lot of questions that are now unanswerable.'

I turned to Halstead. 'Do you agree?'

He looked at me with smouldering eyes. 'Don't ask damnfool questions. Of course I agree; it's about the only thing Fallon and I agree about.'

I sat down. 'And you're racing each other – splitting your guts to get there first. My God, what a commentary on science!'

'Wait a minute,' said Fallon sharply. 'That's not entirely true. All right; I agree that I'm trying to get in ahead of Halstead, but that's only because I don't trust him on something as important as this. He's too impatient, too thrusting for an important dig. He'll want to make a *quick* reputation – I know him of old – and that's the way evidence gets destroyed.'

Halstead didn't rise to the argument as I expected. Instead, he looked at me sardonically. 'There you have a fine example of professional ethics,' he said mockingly. 'Fallon is ready to run anyone's reputation into the ground if he can get what he wants.' He leaned forward and addressed Fallon directly. 'I don't suppose you want to add to your own reputation by the discovery of Uaxuanoc?'

'My reputation is already *made*,' said Fallon softly. 'I'm at the top already.'

'And you don't want anybody passing you,' said Halstead cuttingly.

I'd just about had enough of this bickering and was about to say so when Katherine Halstead interjected, 'And Professor Fallon has peculiar means of making sure he isn't passed.'

I raised my eyebrows and said, 'Could you explain that?'

She smiled. 'Well, he did steal the original of the Vivero letter.'

'So we're back at that again,' said Fallon disgustedly. 'I tell you I bought it from Gerryson in New York – and I can prove it.'

'That's enough of that,' I said. 'We've had enough of these counter-accusations. Let's stick to the point. From what I can gather old de Vivero sent the letter and gifts to his sons. You think that the gifts were two golden trays and that there is something about those trays that has a bearing on Uaxuanoc. Is that right?'

Fallon nodded and picked up the file. 'There was a hell of a lot of gold in Uaxuanoc – he mentions it time and again – and he made it quite clear that he wanted his sons to be leaders in sharing the loot. The one thing he didn't do that he might logically have been expected to do was to tell them where to find the city. Instead, he sent them gifts.'

Halstead broke in. 'I'm sure that I can figure this out just as well as Fallon. Vivero's family life wasn't too happy – it seems that his sons hated each other's guts, and Vivero didn't like that. It seems logical to me that he'd give each of them a piece of information, and the two pieces would have to be joined to make sense. The brothers would *have* to work together.' He spread his hands. 'The information wasn't in the letter so it must have been in the gifts – in the trays.'

'That's how I figured it, too,' said Fallon. 'So I went hunting for the trays. I knew the Mexican de Vivero tray was still in existence in 1782 because that's when Murville wrote about it, and I started to track it down from there.'

Halstead sniggered and Fallon said irascibly, 'All right; I made a goddamn fool of myself.' He turned to me and said with a weak grin, 'I chased all over Mexico and finally found it in my own museum – I'd owned it all the time!'

Halstead laughed loudly. 'And I'd beaten you to it; I knew it was there before you did.' The smile left his face. 'Then you withdrew it from public exhibition.'

I shook my head irritably. 'How the devil can you own something like that and not know about it?' I demanded.

'Your family did,' pointed out Fallon reasonably. 'But my case was a bit different. I established a trust, and, among other things, the trust runs a museum. I'm not responsible personally for everything the museum buys, and I don't know every item in stock. Anyway, the museum had the tray.'

'That's one tray. What about the other?'

'That was a bit more difficult, wasn't it, Paul?' He smiled across the room at Halstead. 'Manuel de Vivero had two sons, Jaime and Juan. Jaime stayed in Mexico and founded the Mexican branch of the de Viveros – you know about them already – but Juan had a bellyful of America and went back to Spain. He took quite a bit of loot with him and became an Alcalde like his father – that's a sort of country squire and magistrate. He had a son, Miguel, who prospered even more and became a wealthy shipowner.

'Came the time when trouble rubbed up between Spain and England and Philip II of Spain decided to end it once and for all and began to build the Armada. Miguel de Vivero contributed a ship, the *San Juan de Huelva*, and skippered her himself. She sailed with the Armada and never came back – neither did Miguel. His shipping business didn't die with Miguel, a son took over, and it lasted quite a long time – until the end of the eighteenth century. Fortunately they had a habit of keeping records and I dug out a juicy bit of information; Miguel wrote a letter to his wife asking her to send him "the tray which my grandfather had made in Mexico". It was with him on the ship when the Armada sailed for England. I thought then that the whole thing was finished.'

'I got to that letter before you did,' said Halstead with satisfaction.

'This sounds like a cross between a jigsaw puzzle and a detective story,' I said. 'What did you do then?'

'I came to England,' said Fallon. 'Not to look for the tray – I thought that was at the bottom of the sea – but just for a holiday. I was staying in Oxford at one of the colleges and I happened to mention my searches in Spain. One of the dons – a dry-as-dust literary character – said he vaguely remembered something about it in the correspondence of Herrick.'

I stared at Fallon. 'The poet?'

'That's right. He was rector of Dean Prior – that's not far from here. A man called Goosan had written a letter to him; Goosan was a local merchant, a nobody, his letter wouldn't have been preserved if it hadn't have been written to Herrick.'

Halstead was alert. 'I didn't know about this. Go on.'

'It doesn't really matter,' said Fallon tiredly. 'We know where the tray is now.'

'I'm interested,' I said.

Fallon shrugged. 'Herrick was bored to death with country life but he was stuck at Dean Prior. There wasn't much to do so I suppose he took more interest in his parishioners than the usual dull clod of a country priest He certainly took an interest in Goosan and asked him to put on paper what he had previously said verbally. To cut a long story short, Goosan's family name had originally been Guzman, and his grandfather had been a seaman on the *San Juan*. They'd had a hell of a time of it during the attack on England and, after one thing and another, the ship had gone down in a storm off Start Point. The captain, Miguel de Vivero, had died previously of ship fever – that's typhus – and when Guzman came ashore he carried that goddamn tray as part of his personal loot. Guzman's grandson – that's the Goosan who wrote to Herrick – even showed Herrick the tray. How your family got hold of it I don't know.'

I smiled as I said. 'That's why you laughed when I told you to see Dave Goosan.'

'It gave me something of a shock,' admitted Fallon.

'I didn't know anything about Herrick,' said Halstead. 'I was just following up on the Armada and trying to discover where the *San Juan* had sunk. I happened to be in Plymouth when I saw a photograph of the tray in the newspaper.'

Fallon raised his eyes to the ceiling. 'Sheer luck!' he commented.

Halstead grinned. 'But I was here before you.'

'Yes, you were,' I said slowly. 'And then my brother was murdered.'

He blew up. 'What the hell do you mean by that crack?'

'Just making a true observation. Did you know Victor Niscemi?'

'I'd never heard of him until the inquest. I don't know that I like the trend of your thinking, Wheale.'

'Neither do I,' I said sourly. 'Let's skip it – for the moment. Professor Fallon: I presume you've given your tray a thorough examination. What did you find?'

He grunted. 'I'm not prepared to discuss that in front of Halstead. I've been pushed far enough.' He was silent for a moment, then he sighed, 'All right; effectively, I found nothing. I assume that whatever it is will only come to light when the trays are examined as a pair.' He stood up. 'Now, I've had just about enough of this. A little while ago you told Halstead to put up or shut up – now I'm putting the same proposition to you. How much money will you take for the tray? Name your price and I'll write you a cheque right now.'

'You haven't enough money to pay my price,' I said, and he blinked in surprise. 'I told you my price might not necessarily be in cash. Sit down and listen to what I've got to say.'

Slowly Fallon lowered himself into his chair, not taking his eyes from me. I looked across at Halstead and at his wife who was almost hidden in the gathering shadows of evening. I said, 'I have three conditions for parting with the tray. *All* those conditions must be met before I do so. Is that clear?'

Fallon grunted and I accepted that as agreement. Halstead looked tense and then inclined his head stiffly.

'Professor Fallon has a lot of money which will come in useful. He will therefore finance whatever expedition is to be made to find this city of Uaxuanoc. You can't object to that, Fallon; it is something you would do in any event. But I will be a part of the expedition. Agreed?'

Fallon looked at me speculatively. 'I don't know if you could take it,' he said a little scornfully. 'It's not like a stroll on Dartmoor.'

'I'm not giving you a choice,' I said. 'I'm giving you an ultimatum.'

'All right,' he said. 'But it's your skin.'

'The second condition is that you help me as much as possible to find out why my brother was killed.'

'Won't that interfere with your jaunt in Yucatan?' he queried.

'I'm not so certain it will,' I said. 'I think that whoever wanted the tray enough to send a man armed with a sawn-off shotgun also knew that the tray had a secret. Possibly we'll meet him in Yucatan – who knows?'

'I think you're nuts,' he said. 'But I'll play along with you. I agree.'

'Good,' I said pleasantly, and prepared to harpoon him. 'The third condition is that Halstead comes with us.'

Fallon sat bolt upright and roared, I'll be damned if I'll take the son of a bitch.'

Halstead jumped from his chair. 'That's twice today you've called me that. I ought to knock your – '

'Belt up!' I yelled. Into the sudden silence that followed I said, 'You two make me sick. All afternoon you've been sniping at each other. You've both done very well in your investigations so far – you've arrived at the same point at the same time and honours ought to be even. And you've both made identical accusations about each other, so you're square there, too.'

Fallon looked stubborn, so I said, 'Look at it this way. If we two join forces, you know what will happen: Halstead will be hanging around anyway. He's as tenacious as you are and he'll follow the trail wherever we lead him. But the point doesn't arise, does it? I said that all *three* of my conditions must be met and, by God, if you don't agree to this I'll *give* my tray to Halstead. That way you'll have one each and be on an even footing for the next round of this academic dog-fight. Now, do you agree or don't you?'

His face worked and he shook his head sadly. 'I agree,' he said in a whisper.

'Halstead?'

'I agree.'

Then they both said simultaneously, 'Where's the tray?'

FOUR

Mexico City was hot and frenetic with Olympic Gamesmanship. The hotels were stuffed to bursting, but fortunately Fallon owned a country house just outside the city which we made our headquarters. The Halsteads also had their home in Mexico City but they were more often than not at Fallon's private palace.

I must say that when Fallon decided to move he moved fast. Like a good general, he marshalled his army close to the point of impact; he spent a small fortune on telephone calls and the end result was a concentration of forces in Mexico City. I had a fast decision to make, too; my job was a good one and I hated to give it up unceremoniously, but Fallon was pushing hard. I saw my boss and told him of Bob's death and he was good enough to give me six months' leave of absence. I bore down heavily on the farm management, so I suppose I deceived him in a way, yet I think that going to Yucatan *could* be construed as looking after Bob's estate.

Fallon also used the resources that only money can buy. 'Big corporations have security problems,' he said. 'So they run their own security outfits. They're as good as the police any time, and better in most cases. The pay is higher. I'm having Niscemi checked out independently.'

The thought of it made me a bit dizzy. Like most people, I'd thought of millionaires as just people who have a lot of money but I hadn't gone beyond that to the power and influence that money makes possible. That a man was able to lift a telephone and set a private police force in motion made me open my eyes and think again.

Fallon's house, was big and cool, set in forty acres of manicured grounds. It was quiet with unobtrusive service, which clicked into action as soon as the master set foot in it. Soft-footed servants were there when you wanted them and absent when not needed and I settled into sybaritic luxury without a qualm.

Fallon's tray had not yet come from New York, much to his annoyance, and he spent a lot of time arguing the archeological toss with Halstead. I was pleased to see that loss of temper was now confined to professional matters and did not take such a personal turn. I think much of that was due to Katherine Halstead, who kept her husband on a tight rein.

The morning after we arrived they were at it hammer and tongs. 'I think old Vivero was a damned liar,' said Halstead.

'Of course he was,' said Fallon crossly. 'But that's not the point at issue here. He says he was taken to Chichen Itza . . .'

'And I say he couldn't have been. The New Empire had fallen apart long before that – Chichen Itza was abandoned when Hunac Ceel drove out the Itzas. It was a dead city.'

Fallon made an impatient noise. 'Don't look at it from your viewpoint; see it as Vivero saw it. Here was an averagely ignorant Spanish soldier without the benefit of the hindsight we have. He *says* he was taken to Chichen Itza – he actually names it, and Chichen Itza is only one of two names he gives in the manuscript. He didn't give a damn whether *you* think Chichen Itza was occupied – he was taken there and he said so.' He stopped short. 'Of course, if you *are* right, it means that the Vivero letter is a modern fake, and we're all up the creek.'

'I don't think it's a fake,' said Halstead. 'I just think that Vivero was a congenital liar.'

'I don't think it's a fake, either,' said Fallon. 'I had it authenticated.' He crossed the room and pulled open a drawer. 'Here's the report on it.'

He gave it to Halstead, who scanned through it and dropped it on the table. I picked it up and found a lot of tables and graphs, but the meat was on the last page under the heading *Conclusions*. 'The document appears to be authentic as to period, being early sixteenth-century Spanish. The condition is poor – the parchment being of poor quality and, perhaps, of faulty manufacture originally. A radio-carbon dating test gives a date of 1534 A.D. with an error of plus or minus fifteen years. The ink shows certain peculiarities of composition but is undoubtedly of the same period as the parchment as demonstrated by radio-carbon testing. An exhaustive linguistic analysis displays no deviation from the norm of the sixteenth century Spanish language. While we refrain from judgement on the content of this document there is no sign from the internal evidence of the manuscript that the document is other than it purports to be.'

I thought of Vivero curing his own animal skins and making his own ink – it all fitted in. Katherine Halstead stretched out her hand and I gave her the report, then turned my attention back to the argument.

'I think you're wrong, Paul,' Fallon was saying. 'Chichen Itza was never wholly abandoned until much later. It was a religious centre even after the Spaniards arrived. What about the assassination of Ah Dzun Kiu? – that was in 1536, no less than nine years *after* Vivero was captured.'

'Who the devil was he?' I asked.

'The chief of the Tutal Kiu. He organized a pilgrimage to Chichen Itza to appease the gods; all the pilgrims were massacred by Nachi Cocom, his archenemy. But all that is immaterial – what matters is that we know *when* it happened, and that it's consistent with Vivero's claim to have been taken to Chichen Itza – a claim which Paul disputes.'

'All right. I grant you that one.' said Halstead. 'But there's a lot more about the letter that doesn't add up.'

I left them to their argument and walked over to the window. In the distance light reflected blindingly from the water of a swimming pool. I glanced at Katherine Halstead. 'I'm no good at this sort of logic chopping,' I said. 'It's beyond me.'

'It's over my head, too,' she admitted. 'I'm not an archeologist; I only know what I've picked up from Paul by a sort of osmosis.'

I looked across at the swimming pool again – it looked very inviting. 'What about a swim?' I suggested. 'I have some gear I want to test, and I'd like some company.'

She brightened. 'That's a good idea. I'll meet you out there in ten minutes.'

I went up to my room and changed into trunks, then unpacked my scuba gear and took it down to the pool. I had brought it with me because I thought there might be a chance of getting in some swimming in the Caribbean somewhere along the line and I wasn't going to pass up that chance. I had only swum in clear water once before, in the Mediterranean.

Mrs Halstead was already at the pool, looking very fetching in a one-piece suit. I dumped the steel bottles and the harness by the side of the pool and walked over to where she was sitting. A flunkey in white coat appeared from nowhere and said something fast and staccato in Spanish, and I shrugged helplessly and appealed to her. 'What's he saying?'

She laughed. 'He wants to know if we'd like something to drink.'

'That's not a bad idea. Something long and cold with alcohol in it.'

'I'll join you.' She rattled away in Spanish at the servant who went away. Then she said. 'I haven't thanked you for what you've done for Paul, Mr Wheale. Everything has happened so quickly – I really haven't had time to think.'

'There's nothing to thank me for,' I said. 'He just got his due.' I refrained from saying that the real reason I had brought Halstead into it was to keep him close where I could watch him. I wasn't too happy about husband Paul; he was too free with his accusations and his temper was trigger-quick. Somebody had been with Niscemi when Bob had been killed and though it couldn't have been Halstead that didn't mean he had nothing to do with it. I smiled pleasantly at his wife. 'Nothing to it,' I said.

'I think it was very generous – considering the way he behaved.' She looked at me steadily. 'Don't take any notice of him if he becomes bad-tempered again. He's had . . . had disappointments. This is his big chance and it plays on his nerves.'

'Don't worry,' I said soothingly. Privately I was certain that if Halstead became unpleasant he would get a quick bust on the snoot. If I didn't sock him then Fallon would, old as he was. It would be better if I did it, being neutral, then this silly expedition would be in less danger of breaking up.

The drinks arrived – a whitish concoction in tall frosted glasses with ice tinkling like silver bells. I don't know what it was but it tasted cool and soothing. Mrs Halstead looked pensive. She sipped from her glass, then said tentatively, 'When do you think you will leave for Yucatan?'

'Don't ask me. It depends on the experts up there.' I jerked my head towards the house. 'We still don't know where we're going yet.'

'Do you think the trays have a riddle – and that we can solve it?'

'They have – and we will,' I said economically. I didn't
tell her I thought I had the solution already. There was an
awful lot I wasn't telling Mrs Halstead – or anybody else.

She said, 'What do you think Fallon's attitude would be
if I suggested going with you to Yucatan?'

I laughed. 'He'd blow his top. You wouldn't have a
chance.'

She leaned forward and said seriously, 'It might be better
if I went. I'm afraid for Paul.'

'Meaning what?'

She made a fluttery gesture with her hand. 'I'm not the
catty kind of woman who makes derogatory statements
about her own husband to other men,' she said. 'But Paul is
not an ordinary man. There is a lot of violence in him which
he can't control – alone. If I'm with him I can talk to him:
make him see things in a different way. I wouldn't be a drag
on you – I've been on field trips before.'

She talked as though Halstead were some kind of a
lunatic needing a nurse around him all the time. I began to
wonder about the relationship between these two; some
marriages are awfully funny arrangements.

She said. 'Fallon would agree if you put it to him. You
could *make* him.'

I grimaced. 'I've already twisted his arm once. I don't
think I could do it again. Fallon isn't the man who likes to
be pushed around.' I took another pull at the drink and felt
the coolness at the back of my throat. 'I'll think about it,'
I said finally.

But I knew then that I'd put the proposition to Fallon –
and make him like it. There was something about Katherine
Halstead that got at me, something I hadn't felt about a
woman for many years. Whatever it was. I'd better keep it
bottled up, this was no time for playing around with a married woman – especially one married to a man like Paul
Halstead.

'Let's see what the water's like,' I suggested, and got up and walked to the edge of the pool.

She followed me. 'What have you brought that for?' she asked, indicating the scuba gear.

I told her, then said. 'I haven't used it for quite some time so I thought I'd check it. Have you done any scuba diving?'

Lots of times,' she said. 'I spent a summer in the Bahamas once, and spent nearly every day in the water. It's great fun.'

I agreed and settled down to checking the valves. I found that everything was working and put on the harness. As I was swilling the mask out with water she dived into the pool cleanly, surfaced and splashed at me. 'Come in,' she called.

'Don't tell me – the water's fine.' I sat on the edge of the pool and flopped in – you don't dive with bottles on your back. As usual, I found it difficult to get into the correct rhythm of breathing; it's something that requires practice and I was short of that. Because the demand valve is higher in the water than the lungs there is a difference of pressure to be overcome which is awkward at first. Then you have to breathe so as to be economical of air and that is a knack some divers never find. But pretty soon I had got it and was breathing in the irregular rhythm which feels, at first, so unnatural.

I swam around at the bottom of the pool and made a mental note to change the belt weights. I had put on a little flesh since the last time I wore the harness and it made a difference to flotation. Above, I could see Katherine Halstead's sun-tanned limbs and I shot upwards with a kick of the flippers and grabbed her ankles. As I pulled her under I saw the air dribbling evenly from her mouth in a regular line of bubbles rising to the surface. If I had surprised her it certainly didn't show; she had had sense enough not to gasp the air from her lungs.

She jack-knifed suddenly and her hands were on my air pipe. With a sudden twitch she pulled the mouthpiece away and I swallowed water and let go of her ankles. I rose to the surface gasping and treading water to find her laughing at me. I spluttered a bit and said, 'Where did you learn that trick?'

'The beach-bums in the Bahamas play rough,' she said. 'A girl learns to look after herself.'

'I'm going down again,' I said. 'I'm out of practice.'

'There'll be another drink waiting when you come out,' she said.

I dropped to the bottom of the pool again and went through my little repertoire of tricks – taking the mouth-piece out and letting the pipe fill with water and then clearing it, taking the mask off and, finally, taking off the whole harness and climbing into it again. This wasn't just a silly game; at one time or another I'd *had* to do every one of those things at a time when it would have been positively dangerous not to have been able to do them. Water at any depth is not man's natural element and the man who survives is the man who can get himself out of trouble.

I had been down about fifteen minutes when I heard a noise. I looked up and saw a splashing so I popped to the surface to see what was going on. Mrs Halstead had been smacking the water with the palm of her hand, and Fallon stood behind her. I climbed out, and he said, 'My tray has arrived – now we can compare them.'

I shucked off the harness and dropped the weight belt. 'I'll be up as soon as I've dried off.'

He regarded the scuba gear curiously. 'Can you use that – at depth?'

'It depends on what depth,' I said cautiously. 'The deepest I've been is a little over a hundred and twenty feet.'

'That would probably be enough,' he said. 'You might come in useful after all, Wheale; we might have to explore a cenote.' He dismissed the subject abruptly. 'Be as quick as you can.'

Near the pool was a long cabin which proved to be change-rooms. I showered and dried off, put on a terry-towelling

gown and went up to the house. As I walked in through
the French windows Fallon was saying '. . . thought it was in
the vine leaves so I gave it to a cryptographer. It could be the
number of veins on a leaf or the angle of the leaves to the
stem or any combination of such things. Well, the guy did a
run-through and put the results through a computer and
came up with nothing.'

It was an ingenious idea and completely wrong.
I joined the group around the table and looked down at
the two trays. Fallon said, 'Now we've got two trays, so
we'll have to go through the whole thing again. Vivero
might have alternated his message between them.'

I said casually, 'What trays?'

Halstead jerked up his head and Fallon turned and
looked at me blankly. 'Why, these two here.'

I looked at the table. 'I don't see any trays.'

Fallon looked baffled and began to gobble. 'Are . . . are
you nuts? What the hell do you think these are? Flying
saucers?'

Halstead looked at me irefully. 'Let's not have any
games,' he said. 'Murville called this one a tray, Juan de
Vivero called that one a tray, and so did Goosan in his letter
to Herrick.'

'I don't give a damn about that,' I said frankly. 'If everyone calls a submarine an aeroplane, it still can't fly. Old
Vivero didn't call them trays and he made them. He didn't
say, "Here, boys, I'm sending you a couple of nice trays."
Let's see what he *did* say. Where's the transcription?'

There was a glint in Fallon's eye as he held out the sheaf
of papers which were never far from him. 'You'd better
make this good.'

I flipped the sheets over to the last page. 'He said, "I send
you gifts made in that marvellous manner which my father
learned of that stranger from the East." He also said, "Let
the scales of enmity fall from your eyes and look upon these

gifts with proper vision." Doesn't that mean anything to you?'

'Not much,' said Halstead.

'These are mirrors,' I said calmly. 'And just because everyone has been using them as trays doesn't alter the fact.'

Halstead made a sound of irritation, but Fallon bent and examined them. I said, 'The bottom of that "tray" isn't copper – it's speculum metal – a reflective surface and it's slightly convex; I've measured it.'

'You could be right at that,' said Fallon. 'So they're mirrors! Where does that get us?'

'Take a closer look,' I advised.

Fallon picked up one of the mirrors and Halstead took the other. After a while Halstead said, 'I don't see anything except the reflection of my own face.'

'I don't do much better,' said Fallon. 'And it's not a good reflective surface, either.'

'What do you expect of a metal mirror that's had things dumped on it for the last four hundred years? But it's a neat trick, and I only came upon it by accident. Have you got a projection screen?'

Fallon smiled. 'Better than that – I have a projection theatre.'

He would have! Nothing small about millionaire Fallon. He led us into a part of the house where I had never been, and into a miniature cinema containing about twenty seats. 'I find this handy for giving informal lectures,' he said.

I looked around. 'Where's the slide projector?'

'In the projection room – back there.'

'I'll want it out here,' I said.

He looked at me speculatively, and shrugged. 'Okay, I'll have it brought in.'

There was a pause of about ten minutes while a couple of his servants brought in the projector and set it on a table in the middle of the room, acting under my instructions. Fallon

looked interested; Halstead looked bored; Mrs Halstead
looked beautiful. I winked at her. 'We're going to have a fine
show,' I said. 'Will you hold this mirror, Mrs Halstead?'

I puttered around with the projector. 'I'm using this as a
very powerful spotlight,' I said. 'And I'm going to bounce
light off the mirror and on to that screen up there. Tell me
what you see.'

I switched on the projector light and there was a sharp
intake of breath from Fallon, while Halstead lost his bore-
dom in a hurry and practically snapped to attention. I turned
and looked at the pattern on the screen. 'What do you think
it is?' I asked. 'It's a bit vague, but I think it's a map.'

Fallon said, 'What the hell! How does it . . .? Oh, never
mind. Can you rotate that thing a bit, Mrs Halstead?'

The luminous pattern on the screen twisted and flowed,
then steadied in a new orientation. Fallon clicked his tongue.
'I think you're right – it *is* a map. If that indentation on the
bottom right is Chetumal Bay – and it's the right shape – then
above it we have the bays of Espiritu Santo and Ascension.
That makes it the west coast of the Yucatan Peninsula.'

Halstead said. 'What's that circle in the middle?'

'We'll come to that in a minute,' I said, and switched off
the light. Fallon bent down and looked at the mirror still held
by Mrs Halstead and shook his head incredulously. He
looked at me enquiringly, and I said, 'I came across this bit of
trickery by chance. I was taking photographs of my tray – or
mirror – and I was a bit ham-handed; I touched the shutter
button by accident and the flash went off. When I developed
the picture I found that I'd got a bit of the mirror in the frame
but most of the picture was an area of wall. The light from the
flash had bounced off the mirror and there was something
bloody funny about its reflection on the wall, so I went into
it a bit deeper.'

Halstead took the mirror from his wife. 'This is impossible.
How can a reflection from a plane surface show a selectively

variable pattern?' He held up the mirror and moved it before his eyes. 'There's nothing here that shows.'

'It's not a plane mirror – it's slightly convex. I measured it; it has a radius of convexity of about ten feet. This is a Chinese trick.'

'Chinese!'

'Old Vivero said as much. ". . . that stranger from the East which the Moors brought to Cordoba." He was Chinese. That stumped me for a bit – what the hell was a Chinaman doing in Spain in the late fifteenth century? But it's not too odd, if you think about it. The Arab Empire stretched from Spain to India; it's not too difficult to imagine a Chinese metal worker being passed along the line. After all, there were Europeans in China at that date.'

Fallon nodded. 'It's a plausible theory.' He tapped the mirror. 'But how the hell is this thing done?'

'I was lucky,' I said. 'I went to the Torquay Public Library and there it was, all laid out in the ninth edition of the *Encyclopaedia Britannica*. I was fortunate that the Torquay Library is a bit old-fashioned because that particular item was dropped from later editions.'

I took the mirror from Halstead and laid it flat on the table. 'This is how it works. Forget the gold trimmings and concentrate on the mirror itself. All early Chinese mirrors were of metal, usually cast of bronze. Cast metal doesn't give a good reflective surface so it had to be worked on with scrapers to give a smooth finish. Generally, the scraping was done from the centre to the edge and that gave the finished mirror its slight convexity.'

Fallon took a pen from his pocket and applied it to the mirror, imitating the action of scraping. He nodded and said briefly, 'Go on.'

I said, 'After a while the mirrors began to become more elaborate. They were expensive to make and the manufacturers began to pretty them up a bit. One way of doing this was to put ornamentation on the *back* of the mirror. Usually it was a saying of Buddha cast in raised characters. Now, consider what might happen when such a mirror was scraped. It would be lying on its back on a solid surface, but only the raised characters would be in contact with that surface – the rest of the mirror would be supported by nothing. When scraper pressure was applied the unsupported parts would give a little and a fraction more metal would be removed over the supported parts.'

'Well, I'll be damned!' said Fallon. 'And that makes the difference?'

'In general you have a convex mirror which tends to diffuse reflected light,' I said. 'But you have plane bits where the characters are which reflects light in parallel lines. The convexity is so small that the difference can't be seen by the eye, but the short wavelengths of light show it up in the reflection.'

'When did the Chinese find out about this?' queried Fallon.

'Some time in the eleventh century. It was accidental at first, but later they began to exploit it deliberately. Then they came up with the composite mirror – the back would still have a saying of Buddha, but the mirror would reflect something completely different. There's one in the Ashmolean in Oxford – the back says "Adoration for Amida Buddha" and the reflection shows Buddha himself. It was just a matter of putting a false back on the mirror, as Vivero has done here.'

Halstead turned over the mirror and tapped the gold back experimentally. 'So under here there's a map cast in the bronze?'

'That's it. I rather think Vivero re-invented the composite mirror. There are only three examples known; the one in the Ashmolean, another in the British Museum, and one somewhere in Germany.'

'How do we get the back off?'

'Hold on,' I said. 'I'm not having that mirror ruined. If you rub a mercury amalgam into the mirror surface it improves the reflection a hundred per cent. But a better way would be to X-ray them.'

'I'll arrange it,' said Fallon decisively. 'In the meantime we'll have another look. Switch on that projector.'

I snapped on the light and we studied the vague luminous lines on the screen. After a while Fallon said, 'It sure looks like the coast of Quintana Roo. We can check it against a map.'

'Aren't those words around the edge?' asked Katherine Halstead.

I strained my eyes but it was a bit of a blurred mish-mash nothing was clear. 'Might be,' I said doubtfully.

'And there's that circle in the middle,' said Paul Halstead. 'What's that?'

'I think I've solved that one,' I said. 'Old Vivero wanted to reconcile his sons, so he gave them each a mirror. The puzzle can only be solved by using both mirrors. This one gives a general view, locating the area, and I'll lay ten to one that the other mirror gives a blown-up view of what's in that little circle. Each mirror would be pretty useless on its own.'

'We'll check on that,' said Fallon. 'Where's my mirror?'

The two mirrors were exchanged and we looked at the new pattern. It didn't mean much to me, nor to anyone else. 'It's not *clear* enough,' complained Fallon. 'I'll go blind if we have much more of this.'

'It's been knocked about after four hundred years,' I said. 'But the pattern on the back has been protected. I think that X-rays should give us an excellent picture.'

'I'll have it done as soon as possible.'

I turned off the light and found Fallon dabbing at his eyes with a handkerchief. He smiled at me. 'You're paying your way, Wheale,' he said. 'We might not have found this.'

'You would have found it,' I said positively. 'As soon as your cryptographer had given up in disgust you'd have started to wonder about this and that – such as what was concealed in the bronze-gold interface. What puzzles me is why Vivero's sons didn't do anything about it.'

Halstead said thoughtfully, 'Both branches of the family regarded these things as trays and not mirrors. Perhaps Vivero's rather obscure tip-off just went over their heads. They may have been told the story of the Chinese mirrors as children, when they were too young to really understand.'

'Could be,' agreed Fallon. 'It could also be that the quarrel between them – whatever it was – couldn't be reconciled so easily. Anyway, they didn't do anything about it. The Spanish branch lost their mirror and to the Mexican branch it was reduced to some kind of a legend.' He put his hands on the mirror possessively. 'But we've got them now – that's different.'

II

Looking back, I think it was about this time that Fallon began to lose his grip. One day he went into the city and when he came back he was gloomy and very thoughtful, and from that day on he was given to sudden silences and fits of absent-mindedness. I put it down to the worries of a millionaire – maybe the stock market had dropped or something like that – and I didn't think much about it at the time. Whatever it was it certainly didn't hamper his planning of the Uaxuanoc expedition into which he threw himself with a demoniac energy. I thought it strange that he should be devoting *all* his time to this; surely a millionaire must look after his financial interests – but Fallon wasn't worried about anything else but Uaxuanoc and whatever else it was that had made him go broody.

It was in the same week that I met Pat Harris. Fallon called me into his study, and said, 'I want you to meet Pat Harris – I borrowed him from an oil company I have an interest in. I'm fulfilling my part of the bargain; Harris has been investigating Niscemi.'

I regarded Harris with interest although, on the surface, there was little about him to excite it. He was average in every way; not too tall, not too short, not too beefy and not too scrawny. He wore an average suit and looked the perfect average man. He might have been designed by a statistician. He had a more than average brain – but that didn't show.

He held out his hand. 'Glad to meet you, Mr Wheale,' he said in a colourless voice.

'Tell Wheale what you found,' ordered Fallon.

Harris clasped his hands in front of his average American paunch. 'Victor Niscemi – small time punk,' he said concisely. 'Not much to say about him. He never was much and he never did much – except get himself rubbed out in England. Reform school education leading to bigger things – but not much bigger. Did time for rolling drunks but that was quite a while ago. Nothing on him in the last four years; he never appeared on a police blotter, I mean. Clean as a whistle as far as his police record goes.'

'That's his official police record, I take it. What about unofficially?'

Harris looked up at me approvingly. 'That's a different matter, of course,' he agreed. 'For a while he did protection for a bookie, then he got into the numbers racket – first as protection for a collector, then as collector himself. He was on his way up in a small way. Then he went to England and got himself shot up. End of Niscemi.'

'And that's all?'

'Not by a hell of a long way,' said Fallon abruptly. 'Go on, Harris.'

Harris moved in his chair and suddenly looked more relaxed. 'There's a thing you've got to remember about a guy like Niscemi – he has friends. Take a look at his record; reform school, petty assault and so on. Then suddenly, four years ago, no more police record. He was still a criminal and still small time, but he no longer got into trouble. He'd acquired friends.'

'Who were . . .?'

'Mr Wheale, you're English and maybe you don't have the problems we have in the States, so what I'm going to tell you now might seem extraordinary. You'll just have to take my word for it. Okay?'

I smiled. 'After meeting Mr Fallon there's very little I'll find unbelievable.'

'All right. I'm interested in the weapon with which Niscemi killed your brother. Can you describe it?'

'It was a sawn-off shotgun,' I said.

'And the butt was cut down. Right?' I nodded. 'That was a lupara; it's an Italian word and Niscemi was of Italian origin or, more precisely, Sicilian. About four years ago Niscemi was taken into the Organization. Organized crime is one of the worse facts of life in the United States, Mr Wheale; and it's mostly run by Italian Americans. It goes under many names – the Organization, the Syndicate, Cosa Nostra, the Mafia – although Mafia should strictly be reserved for the parent organization in Sicily.'

I looked at Harris uncertainly. 'Are you trying to tell me that the Mafia – the Mafia, for God's sake! – had my brother killed?'

'Not quite,' he said. 'I think Niscemi slipped up there. He certainly slipped up when he got *himself* killed. But I'd better describe what goes on with young punks like Niscemi when they're recruited into the Organization. The first thing he's told is to keep his nose clean – he keeps out of the way of the cops and he does what his capo – his boss – tells him, and nothing else. That's important, and it explains why Niscemi suddenly stopped figuring on the police blotter.' Harris pointed a finger at me. 'But it works the other way round, too. If Niscemi was up to no good with regard to your brother it certainly meant that he was acting under orders. The Organization doesn't stand for members who go in to bat on their own account.'

'So he was *sent?*'

'There's a ninety-nine per cent probability that he was.'

This was beyond me and I couldn't quite believe it. I turned to Fallon. 'I believe you said that Mr Harris is an employee of an oil company. What qualifications has he for assuming all this?'

'Harris was in the F.B.I.,' said Fallon.

'For fifteen years,' said Harris. 'I thought you might find this extraordinary.'

'I do,' I said briefly, and thought about it. 'Where did you get this information about Niscemi?'

'From the Detroit police – that was his stamping-ground.'

I said, 'Scotland Yard is interested in this. Are the American police collaborating with them?'

Harris smiled tolerantly. 'In spite of all the sensational stuff about Interpol there's not much that can be done in a case like this. Who are they going to nail for the job? The American law authorities are just glad to have got Niscemi out of their hair, and he was only small time, anyway.' He grinned and came up with an unexpected and parodied quotation. '"It was in another country and, besides, the guy is dead."'

Fallon said, 'It goes much further than this. Harris is not finished yet'

'Okay,' said Harris. 'We now come to the questions: Who sent Niscemi to England – and why? Niscemi's capo is Jack Gatt, but Jack might have been doing some other capo a favour. However, I don't think so.'

'Gatt!' I blurted out 'He was in England at the time of my brother's death.'

Harris shook his head. 'No, he wasn't. I checked him out on that. On the day your brother died he was in New York.'

'But he wanted to buy something from Bob,' I said. 'He made an offer in the presence of witnesses. He *was* in England.'

'Air travel is wonderful,' said Harris. 'You can leave London at nine a.m. and arrive in New York at eleven-thirty a.m. – local time. Gatt certainly didn't kill your brother.' He pursed his lips, then added, 'Not personally.'

'Who – and what – is he?'

'Top of the heap in Detroit,' said Harris promptly. 'Covers Michigan and a big slice of Ohio. Original name, Giacomo Gattini – Americanized to Jack Gatt. He doesn't stand very tall in the Organization, but he's a capo and that makes him important.'

'I think you'd better explain that.'

'Well, the Organization controls crime, but it's not a centralized business like, say, General Motors. It's pretty loose, in fact; so loose that sometimes pieces of it conflict with each other. That's called a gang war. But they're bad for business, attract too much attention from the cops, so once in a while all the capos get together in a council, a sort of board meeting, to iron out their difficulties. They allocate territory, slap down the hotheads and decide when and how to enforce the rules.'

This was the raw and primitive world that had intruded on Hay Tree Farm, so far away in Devon. I said, 'How do they do that?'

Harris shrugged. 'Suppose a capo like Gatt decided to ignore the top bosses and go it on his own. Pretty soon a young punk like Niscemi would blow into town, knock off Gatt and scram. If he failed then another would try it and, sooner or later, one would succeed. Gatt knows that, so he doesn't break the rules. But, while he keeps to the rules, he's capo – king in his own territory.'

'I see. But why should Gatt go to England?'

'Ah,' said Harris. 'Now we're coming to the meat of it. Let's take a good look at Jack Gatt This is a third-generation American mafioso. He's no newly arrived Siciliano peasant who can't speak English, nor is he a half-educated tough bum like Capone. Jack's got civilization; Jack's got culture. His daughter is at finishing school in Switzerland; one son is at a good college in the east and the other runs his own business – a legitimate business. Jack goes to the opera and ballet; in fact I hear that he's pretty near the sole support of one ballet group. He collects pictures, and when I say collects I don't mean that he steals them. He puts up bids at the Parke-Bernet Gallery in New York like any other millionaire, and he does the same at Sotheby's and Christie's in England. He has a good-looking wife and a fine house, mixes in the best society and cuts a fine figure among the best people, none of whom know that he's anything other than a legitimate businessman. He's that, too, of course; I wouldn't be surprised if he wasn't one of your biggest shareholders, Mr Fallon.'

'I'll check on it,' said Fallon sourly. 'And how does he derive his main income? The illegitimate part?'

'Gambling, drugs, prostitution, extortion, protection,' reeled off Harris glibly. 'And any combination or permutation. Jack's come up with some real dillies.'

'My God!' said Fallon.

'That's as maybe,' I said. 'But how did Niscemi suddenly pitch up at the farm? The photograph of the tray only appeared in the Press a few days before. How did Gatt get on to it so fast?'

Harris hesitated and looked at Fallon enquiringly. Fallon said glumly, 'You might as well have the whole story. I was upset at Halstead's accusation that I stole the Vivero letter from him, so I put Harris on to checking it.' He nodded to Harris.

'Gatt had men following Mr Fallon and probably Halstead, too,' said Harris. 'This is how it came about.

'Halstead *did* have the Vivero letter before Mr Fallon. He bought it here in Mexico for $200. Then he took it home to the States – he lived in Virginia at the time – and his house was burgled. The letter was one of the things that were stolen.' He put the tips of his fingers together and said. 'The way I see it, the Vivero letter was taken by sheer chance. It was in a locked briefcase that was taken with the other stuff.'

'What other stuff?' I asked.

'Household goods. TV set, radios, a watch, some clothing and a little money.'

Fallon cocked a sardonic eye at me. 'Can you see me interested in second-hand clothing?'

'I think it was a job done by a small-time crook,' said Harris. 'The easily saleable stuff would be got rid of fast – there are plenty of unscrupulous dealers who'd take it. I daresay the thief was disappointed by the contents of the briefcase.'

'But it got to the right man – Gerryson,' I said. 'How did he get hold of it?'

'I wondered about that myself,' said Harris. 'And I gave Gerryson a thorough going-over. His reputation isn't too good; the New York cops are pretty sure he's a high-class fence. One curious thing turned up – he's friendly with Jack Gatt. He stays at Jack's house when he's in Detroit.'

He leaned forward. 'Now, this is a purely hypothetical reconstruction. The burglar who did the Halstead residence found himself with the Vivero letter; it was no good to him because, even if he realized it had some value, he wouldn't know how much and he wouldn't know where to sell it safely. Well, there are ways and means. My guess is, it was passed along channels until it came to someone who recognized its value – and who would that be but Jack Gatt, the

cultured hood who owns a little museum of his own.
Now, I don't know the contents of this letter, but my guess
is that if Gatt was excited by it then he'd check back to the
source – to Halstead.'

'And what about Gerryson?'

'Maybe that was Gatt's way of getting a second opinion,'
said Harris blandly. 'Mr Fallon and I have been talking about
it, and we've come to some conclusions.'

Fallon looked sheepish. 'Er . . . it's like this . . . I . . .
er . . . I paid $2,000 to Gerryson for the letter.'

'So what,' I said.

He avoided my eyes. 'I knew the price was too low. It's
worth more than that.'

I grinned. 'You thought it might be . . . is the word *hot*,
Mr Harris?'

Harris winked. 'That's the word.'

'No,' said Fallon vehemently. 'I thought Gerryson
was making a mistake. If a dealer makes a mistake it's his
business – they take us collectors to the cleaners often
enough. I thought I was taking Gerryson, for a change.'

'But you've changed your mind since.'

Harris said, 'I think Mr Fallon got took. I think Gatt fed the
letter to him through Gerryson just to see what he'd do about
it. After all, he couldn't rely on Halstead who is only another
young and inexperienced archeologist. But if he gave the letter to Mr Fallon, who is the top man in the business, and then
Mr Fallon started to run around in the same circles as
Halstead, Gatt would be certain he was on the right track.'

'Plausible, but bloody improbable,' I said.

'Is it? Jack Gatt is no dumb bunny,' said Harris earnestly.
'He's highly intelligent and educated enough to see a profit
in things that would be right over any other hood's head. If
there's any dough in this Gatt will be after it.'

I thought of the golden gutters of the roofs of Uaxuanoc
and of the king's palace plated with gold within and without.

I thought of the mountain of gold and the burning sign of gold which Vivero had described. Harris could very well be right.

He said, 'I think that Halstead and Mr Fallon have been trailed wherever they've been. I think that Niscemi was one of the trailers, which is why he was on the spot when your golden tray was discovered. He tipped off Gatt, and Gatt flew across and made your brother an offer for it. I've investigated his movements at the time and it all checks out. When your brother turned him down flat he told Niscemi to get the tray the hard way. That wasn't something that would worry Jack Gatt, but he made damned sure that he wasn't even in the country when the job was pulled. And then Niscemi – and whoever else was with him – bungled it, and he got himself killed.'

And Gatt was the man whom that simple Devonshire farmer, Hannaford, had liked so much. I said, 'How can we get at the bastard?'

'This is all theoretical,' said Harris. 'It wouldn't stand up in a law court.'

'Maybe it's too theoretical,' I said. 'Maybe it didn't happen like that at all.'

Harris smiled thinly, and said, 'Gatt has this house under observation right now – and Halstead's house in the city. I can show you the guys who are watching you.'

I came to attention at that and looked at Fallon, who nodded. 'Harris is having the observers watched.'

That put a different complexion on things. I said, 'Are they Gatt's men?'

Harris frowned. 'Now that's hard to say. Let's say that someone in Mexico is doing Gatt a favour – the Organization works like that; they swap favours all the time.'

Fallon said, 'I'll have to do something about Gatt.'

Harris asked curiously, 'Such as?'

'I swing a lot of weight,' said Fallon. 'A hundred million dollars' worth.' He smiled confidently. 'I'll just lean on him.'

Harris looked alarmed. 'I wouldn't do that – not to Jack Gatt. You might be able to work that way with an ordinary business competitor, but not with him. He doesn't like pressure.'

'What could he do about it?' asked Fallon contemptuously.

'He could put you out of business – permanently. A bullet carries more weight than a hundred million dollars, Mr Fallon.'

Fallon suddenly looked shrunken. For the first time he had run into a situation in which his wealth didn't count, where he couldn't buy what he wanted. I had given him a slight dose of the same medicine but that was nothing to the shock handed him by Harris. Fallon wasn't a bad old stick but he'd had money for so long that he tended to handle it with a casual ruthlessness – a club to get what he wanted. And now he had come up against a man even more ruthless who didn't give a damn for Fallon's only weapon. It seemed to take the pith out of him.

I felt sorry for him and, more out of pity than anything else, I made conversation with Harris in order to give him time to pull himself together. 'I think it's time you were told what's at stake here,' I said. 'Then you might be able to guess what Gatt will do about it. But it's a long story.'

'I don't know that I want to know,' said Harris wryly. 'If it's big enough to get Jack Gatt out of Detroit it must be dynamite.'

'Is he out of Detroit?'

'He's not only out of Detroit – he's in Mexico City.' Harris spread his hands. 'He says he's here for the Olympic Games – what else?' he said cynically.

FIVE

As I dressed next morning I reflected on the strange turns a man's life can take. Four weeks previously I had been a London accountant – one of the bowler hat brigade – and now I was in exotic Mexico and preparing to take a jump into even more exotic territory. From what I could gather from Fallon the mysteriously named Quintana Roo was something of a hell hole. And why was I going to Quintana Roo? To hunt for a lost city, for God's sake! If, four weeks before, anyone had offered that as a serious prediction I would have considered him a candidate for the booby-hatch.

I knotted my tie and looked consideringly at the man facing me in the mirror: Jemmy Wheale, New Elizabethan, adventurer at large – *have gun, will travel*. The thought made me smile, and the man in the mirror smiled back at me derisively. I didn't have a gun and I doubted whether I could use one effectively, anyway. I suppose a James Bond type would have unpacked his portable helicopter and taken off after Jack Gatt long ago, bringing back his scalp and a couple of his choicest blondes. Hell, I didn't even look like Sean Connery.

So what was I supposed to do about Jack Gatt? From what Pat Harris had said Gatt was in an unassailable position from the legal point even if he had given the word to Niscemi. There wasn't a single charge to be brought against him that would stick. And for me to tackle Gatt on his own terms would be unthinkably stupid – the nearest analogy I could think of was Monaco declaring war on Russia and the United States.

What the devil was I doing in Mexico, anyway? I looked back on the uncharacteristic actions of my recent past and decided that the barbed words of that silly little bitch, Sheila, had probably set me off. Many men have been murdered in the past, but their brothers haven't run around the world thirsting for vengeance. Sheila's casual words had stabbed me in the ego and everything I had done since then had been to prove to myself that what she had said wasn't true. Which only went to show I was immature and probably a bit soft in the head.

Yet I had taken those actions and now I was stuck with the consequences. If I quit now and went back to England, then I suppose I'd regret it for the rest of my life. There would always be the nagging suspicion that I had run out on life and somehow betrayed myself, and that was something I knew I couldn't live with. I wondered how many other men did stupidly dangerous things because of a suspected assault on their self-respect.

For a short period I had talked big. I had browbeaten a millionaire into doing what I wanted him to do, but that was only because I had a supreme bargaining counter – the Vivero mirror. Now Fallon had the mirror and its secret and I was thrown back on my own resources. I didn't think he'd break his promises, but there wasn't a thing I could do if he reneged.

The grey little man was still around. He was dressed in some pretty gaudy and ill-fitting clothes and he wore his disguise with panache, but he wished to God he wore his conservative suit and his bowler hat and carried his rolled umbrella instead of this silly lance. I pulled a sour face at the man in the mirror; Jemmy Wheale – sheep in wolf's clothing.

My mood was uncertain and ambivalent as I left the room.

I found Pat Harris downstairs wearing a stethoscope and carrying a little black box from which protruded a shiny telescopic antenna. He waggled his hand at me frantically and put his finger to his lips, elaborately miming that I should be quiet. He circled the room like a dog in a strange place, crisscrossing back and forwards, and gradually narrowed his attention to the big refectory table of massive Spanish oak.

Suddenly he got down on to his hands and knees and disappeared beneath the table, completing his resemblance to a dog. All I could see were the seat of his pants and the soles of his shoes; his pants were all right, but his shoes needed repairing. After a while he backed out, gave me a grin, and put his finger to his lips again. He beckoned, indicating that I should join him, so I squatted down, feeling a bit silly. He flicked a switch and a narrow beam of light shot from the little torch he held. It roamed about the underside of the table and then held steady. He pointed, and I saw a small grey metal box half hidden behind a crossbeam.

He jerked his thumb and we climbed out from under the table and he led me at a quick walk out of the room, down the passage, and into Fallon's study which was empty. 'We've been bugged,' he said.

I gaped at him. 'You mean, that thing is . . .'

'. . . a radio transmitter.' He took the stethoscope from his ears with the air of a doctor about to impart bad news. 'This gadget is a bug finder. I sweep the frequencies and if there's a transmitter working close by this thing howls at me through the earphones. Then, to find it, all I have to do is watch the meter.'

I said nervously, 'Hadn't you better shut up about it?' I looked about the study. 'This place . . .'

'It's clean,' he said abruptly. 'I've checked it out.'

'Good God!' I said. 'What made you think there even might be anything like that?'

He grinned. 'A nasty suspicious mind and a belief in human nature. I just thought what I'd do if I were Jack Gatt and wanted to know what goes on in this house. Besides, it's standard procedure in my business.' He rubbed his chin. 'Was anything said in that room – anything important?'

I said cautiously, 'Do you know anything about what we're trying to do?'

'It's all right – Fallon filled me in on everything. We stayed up pretty late last night.' His eyes lit up. 'What a hell of a story – if true!'

I cast my mind back. 'We were all standing around that table talking about the trays. It was then I broke the news that they were really mirrors.'

'That's not too good,' said Harris.

'But then we went into the projection room,' I said. 'And I demonstrated what would happen when you bounced a light off the mirrors. Everything else was said in there.'

'Show me this projection room,' said Harris. So I showed him, and he donned his stethoscope and spent a few minutes twiddling the knobs on his gadget. At last he unclipped the earphones. 'Nothing here; so there's a good chance that Gatt knows only that these things are mirrors but can't know the particular significance.'

We went back into the study and found both Fallon and Halstead. Fallon was unsealing a large envelope, but stopped dead when he heard what Harris had to say. 'The conniving bastard!' he said in some wonder. 'Rip out the goddamn thing.'

'Hell, no!' objected Harris. 'I want that transmitter left where it is. It will be useful.' He looked at us with a slow smile. 'Do any of you gentlemen fancy yourselves as radio actors? I think we can feed Jack Gatt quite a line. All you have to remember is to say nothing important in that room.'

Fallon laughed. 'You're quite a conniver yourself, Harris.'

'I'm a professional,' said Harris easily. 'I don't think we'll make it a live show; there'd be too much chance of a slip-up. This calls for a nicely edited tape which we can feed into that microphone.' He paused. 'I'll keep an eye on that room. Someone will have to change the batteries; they won't last for ever.'

'But where is it transmitting to?' asked Halstead.

'Probably the car that's parked up the road a piece. Those two guys have been staked out there for a couple of days now. My guess is that they have a receiver linked to a tape-recorder. I won't bother them until they've swallowed the story we're going to concoct, and maybe not even then. It's one thing knowing something, but it's even better when the opposition doesn't know that you know it. My advice is to come the innocent bit. You're not supposed to know that Jack Gatt even exists.'

Fallon was right about Harris; he was the most deceitful man I've ever met, and an accountant is no stranger to wool-pulling. When I came to know him better I'd trust him with my life, but I wouldn't trust him not to know more about me than I did myself. His business was information and he gathered it assiduously, on the job and off it. He had a mind like a well-organized computer memory but, unlike a good computer, he tended to play tricks with what he knew.

Fallon ripped open the envelope. 'Let's get down to business. These are the X-ray prints – life size.' He sorted them out and gave us each two prints, one of each mirror.

They were very good, startling in clarity of details that had only been hinted at in the screened reflections. I said, 'Mrs Halstead was right; these are words around the cir-cumference.' I looked closer. 'I can't read Spanish.'

Fallon took a reading glass and mumbled a bit to himself. 'As near as I can make out it goes something like this. On your mirror it says: "The path to true glory leads through the portals of death." And on my mirror: "Life everlasting lies beyond the grave."'

'Morbid!' commented Harris.

'Not very precise instructions,' said Halstead ironically.

'It *may* mean something,' said Fallon doubtfully. 'But one thing is certain; this is definitely the coast of Quintana Roo.' He moved the magnifying glass over the print. 'And, by God, cities are indicated. See those square castle-like things?'

I sensed the air of rising excitement. 'Those two at the top must be Coba and Tulum,' said Halstead tensely. 'With Chichen Itza to the west.'

'And there's Ichpatuun on Chetumal Bay. And what's that south of Tulum? Would that be Chunyaxche?' Fallon lifted his head and stared into the middle distance. 'A city was discovered there not long ago. There's a theory it was the centre of the seaboard trade on the coast.'

Halstead's hand stabbed down. 'There's another city indicated just inland of it – and another here.' His voice cracked. 'And here's another. If this map is accurate we'll be discovering lost cities by the bushel.'

'Take it easy,' said Fallon and laid the print aside. 'Let's have a look at Uaxuanoc.' He took the other print and stared at it. 'If this corresponds to the small circle on the large-scale map then we ought to be able to pinpoint the position.'

I looked at my copy. Hills were indicated but there was no scale to tell how high they were. Scattered over the hills were crude representations of buildings. I remembered that Vivero had said in his letter that the city was built on a ridge lying east and west.

Halstead said, 'The layout looks like a mixture of Chichen Itza and Coba – but it's bigger than either. A lot bigger.'

'There's the cenote,' said Fallon. 'So this place would be the temple of Yum Chac – if Vivero is to be believed.

I wonder which is the king's palace?' He turned and grasped a large cardboard tube from which he took a map. 'I've spent a lot of time on this map,' he said. 'A lifetime.'

He unrolled it and spread it on the desk, weighing down the corners with books. 'Everything the Mayas ever built is marked here. Do you notice anything odd about it, Wheale?'

I contemplated the map and said at last, 'It looks crowded in the south.'

'That's the Peten – but that was the Old Empire which collapsed in the eleventh century. The Itzas moved in later – new blood which gave the Mayas a shot in the arm like a transfusion. They reoccupied some of the old cities like Chichen Itza and Coba, and they built some new ones like Mayapan. Forget the south; concentrate on the Yucatan Peninsula itself. What looks funny about it?'

'This blank space on the west. Why didn't they build there?'

'Who says they didn't?' asked Fallon. 'That's the Quintana Roo. The local inhabitants have a rooted objection to archeologists.' He tapped the map. 'They killed an archeologist here, and built his skeleton into a wall facing the sea as a sort of decoration – and as a warning to others.' He grinned. 'Still want to come along?'

The grey little man inside me made a frightened squawk but I grinned back at him. 'I'll go where you go.'

He nodded. 'That was a while ago. The indios sublevados have shot their bolt. But it's still not a pleasure trip. The inhabitants tend to be hostile – both the chicleros and the Chan Santa Rosa Indians; and the land itself is worse. 'That's the reason for this big blank space – and Uaxuanoc is plumb in the middle.'

He bent over the map, and compared it with the print 'I'd put it about there – give or take twenty miles. Vivero didn't have the benefit of a trigonometric survey when he did this scrawl; we can't rely on it too much.'

Halstead shook his head. 'It's going to be one hell of a job.' He looked up and found me smiling. I couldn't see what was going to be difficult about it. I'd been browsing through Fallon's library and studying the pictures of Mayan cities; there were pyramids the size of the Washington Pentagon, and I didn't see how you could miss seeing one of those.

Halstead said coldly, 'Take a circle twenty miles across — that's over three hundred square miles to search. You can walk within ten feet of a Mayan structure and not see it.' His lips drew back in a humourless smile. 'You can even be walking *on* it and not know it. You'll learn.'

I shrugged and let it pass. I didn't believe it was as bad as that.

Fallon said worriedly, 'What I don't know is why this man Gatt should be so interested. I can't see any conceivable motive for his interference.'

I regarded Fallon in astonished silence, then said, 'The gold, of course! Gatt is a treasure hunter.'

Fallon had a baffled look on his face. 'What gold?' he said dimly.

It was my turn to be baffled. 'You've read the Vivero letter, damn it! Doesn't he describe the king's palace as being plated with gold? Doesn't he go on and on about gold? He even mentions a mountain of gold!'

Halstead gave a shout of laughter and Fallon looked at me as though I had gone out of my mind. 'Where would the Mayas get the gold to cover a building?' he demanded. 'Use a bit of common sense, Wheale.'

For a moment I thought I *had* gone crazy. Halstead was laughing his head off and Fallon was looking at me with an air of concern. I turned to Harris who spread his hands and shrugged elaborately. 'It beats me,' he said.

Halstead was still struggling to contain himself. It was the first time I'd seen him genuinely amused at anything. 'I don't see what's funny,' I said acidly.

'Don't you?' he said, and wiped his eyes. He broke into chuckles. 'It's the funniest thing I've heard in years. Tell him, Fallon.'

'Do you really think Uaxuanoc is dripping in gold – or that it ever was?' Fallon asked. He too was smiling as though an infection had spread to him from Halstead.

I began to get angry. 'Vivero said so, didn't he?' I picked up the prints and thrust them under Fallon's nose. 'You believe in these, don't you? Vivero placed cities where you *know* there are cities, so you believe him that far. What's so bloody funny about the rest of his story?'

'Vivero was the biggest liar in the western hemisphere,' said Fallon. He looked at me in wonder. 'I thought you knew. I told you he was a liar. You've heard us discussing it.'

I told myself to relax, and said slowly, 'Would you mind spelling it out again in words of one syllable?' I glanced at Harris who, by his expression, was as puzzled as I was. 'I'm sure that Mr Harris would like to be let in on the joke, too.'

'Oh, I see,' said Fallon. 'You really took the Vivero letter at its face value.' Halstead again broke into laughter; I was getting pretty tired of that.

Fallon said, 'Let's take one or two points in the letter. He said the de Viveros were of ancient lineage and had been hammered by the Moors so that the family fortunes were lost. He was a goddamn liar. His father was a goldsmith – that's true enough – but his grandfather was a peasant who came from a long line of peasants – of nobodies. His father's name was Vivero, and it was Manuel himself who added on the aristocratic prefix and changed it to de Vivero. He did that in Mexico – he would never have got away with it in Spain. By the time Murville visited the Mexican branch of the family the myth had really taken hold. 'That's why he couldn't believe that a de Vivero had actually made the tray.'

'So he was a liar on that point. Lots of people lie about themselves and their families. But how do you know he was lying about the gold? And why should he spin a yarn like that?'

'All the gold the Mayas ever had was imported,' said Fallon. 'It came from Mexico, from Panama and from the Caribbean islands. These people were neolithic, they weren't metal workers. Look at Vivero's description of their weapons – wooden swords with stone edges. He was right there, but the stone would be obsidian.'

'But the Mayas *had* gold,' I objected. 'Look what they found when the cenote at Chichen Itza was dredged.' I'd read about that.

'So what did they find? A hell of a lot of gold objects – all imported,' said Fallon. 'Chichen Itza was an important religious centre and the cenote was sacred. You find sacred wells all over the world in which offerings are made, and cenotes are particularly important in Yucatan because water is so precious. There were pilgrimages made to Chichen Itza over a period of hundreds of years.'

Harris said, 'You can't put up a public fountain in New York without people throwing money into it.'

'Exactly,' said Fallon in a pleased voice. 'There seems to be a primitive attraction to water in that sense. Three Coins in the Fountain – and all that kind of thing. But the Mayas had no gold of their own.'

I was confused. 'Then why the hell should Vivero say they had?'

'Ah, that puzzled me at first, but Halstead and I discussed it and we've come up with a theory.'

'I'd be pleased to hear it,' I said sourly.

'Vivero found *something* – there's no doubt about that. But what it was, we don't know. He was cryptic about it because no doubt, he didn't want to give the secret away to anyone who might read that letter. The one thing he was quite clear about was that he wanted to reserve the honour of discovery for his sons – for the de Vivero family. So if he

couldn't actually tell his sons this mysterious secret then he
had to find some other way of attracting them – and that
was what they would confidently expect to find. Gold!'

I slumped in my chair dejectedly. 'And why would the
Spaniards be expecting to find gold where there wasn't
any? You've got me going round in circles.'

'It's simple enough. The Spaniards came to Mexico looking for plunder – and they found it. They raided the Aztecs
and found gold in plenty in the temple treasuries and in
Montezuma's palace. What they failed to realize was that it
wasn't a *continuing* supply. They weren't deep-thinking men
and it never occurred to them that this hoard of gold which
they had looted from the Aztecs had been built up over centuries, a little year by year. They thought there must be a
major source, a huge mine, perhaps. They gave it a name,
They called it Eldorado – and they never stopped looking for
it. It didn't exist.

'Consider these Spanish soldiers. After they had looted the
Aztecs, Cortes divided the spoils. When he had received and
swindled his captains, and the captains had put their sticky
fingers into what was left, there was little enough for the common soldiers. A gold chain, perhaps – or a wine cup. These
men were soldiers, not settlers, and always on the other side
of the hill was Eldorado. So they attacked the Mayas, thinking this was Eldorado and, after the Mayas, Pizarro attacked
the Incas of Peru. They brought down whole civilizations
because they weren't prepared to sweat and dig the gold from
the ground themselves. It was there, right enough, but it
certainly wasn't in Yucatan. The Mayas, like the Aztecs, certainly had plenty of gold, but not in such quantities that they
could cover buildings or make rainwater gutters from the
stuff. The nobles wore small pieces of gold jewellery and the
temple priests used certain gold implements.'

Harris said, 'So all this talk about gold by Vivero was just
a come-on to get his boys moving?'

'It seems so,' said Fallon. 'Oh, I daresay he did surprise the Mayas by melting gold and casting it. That was something they hadn't seen before. I'll show you a piece of genuine Mayan goldwork and you'll see what I mean.' He went to a safe, unlocked it, and returned with a small gold disk. 'This is a plate, probably used by a noble. You can see it's very nicely chased.'

It was very thin and flimsy looking. The design was of a warrior holding a spear and a shield with other figures bearing odd shaped objects. Fallon said. 'That probably started out as a nugget found in a mountain stream a long way from Yucatan. The Mayas beat it flat into its present shape and incised that design with stone tools.'

I said, 'What about the mountain of gold? Was that another of Vivero's lies? Couldn't there have been a mine?'

'Not a chance,' said Fallon decisively. 'The geology is dead against it. The Yucatan Peninsula is a limestone cap – not auriferous at all. No other metals, for that matter – that's why the Mayas never got out of the Stone Age, smart though they were.'

I sighed. 'All right, I accept it. No gold.'

'Which brings us back to Gatt,' said Fallon. 'What the hell is he after?'

'Gold,' I said.

'But I've just told you there is no gold,' said Fallon exasperatedly.

'So you did,' I said. 'And you convinced me. You convinced Harris, too.' I swung round to face Harris. 'Before you heard this explanation did you believe there was gold in Yucatan?'

'I thought that was what this was all about,' he said. 'Buried treasure in ruined cities.'

'There you are,' I said. 'What makes you think Gatt believes any different? He may be an educated man, but he's no archeological expert. I'm not an illiterate myself,

and I believed in buried treasure. I didn't have the technical
knowledge to know Vivero was lying, so why should Gatt?
Of course he's after the gold. He has the same mentality as
the Conquistadores – just another gangster unwilling to
sweat for his money.'

Fallon looked surprised. 'Of course. I hadn't allowed for
the lay mind. He must be told the truth.'

Harris wore a crooked smile. 'Do you think he'd believe
you?' he asked sardonically. 'Not after reading the Vivero
letter, he wouldn't. Hell, I can still see that king's palace all
shiny in the sun, even though I know it's not true. You'd
have a whale of a job convincing Gatt.'

'Then he must be a stupid man,' said Fallon.

'No, Gatt's not stupid,' said Harris. 'He just believes that
men who spend as much time as you have on this thing,
men who are willing to spend time in the jungle looking for
something, are looking for something very valuable. Gatt
doesn't believe that scientific knowledge is particularly
valuable, so it must be dough. He just measures you by his
own standards, that's all.'

'Heaven forbid!' said Fallon fervently.

'You're going to have trouble with Jack,' said Harris. 'He
doesn't give up easily.' He nodded to the prints on the table.
'Where did you have those made?'

'I have an interest in an engineering company in
Tampico. I had the use of a metallurgical X-ray outfit.'

'I'd better check up on that,' said Harris. 'Gatt might get
on to it.'

'But I've got the negatives here.'

Harris looked at him pityingly. 'What makes you think
those are the only negatives? I doubt if they'd get it right
first time – they'd give you the best of a series. I want to see
what has happened to the others and have them destroyed
before Gatt starts spreading palm-oil among your ill-paid
technicians.'

Harris was a professional and never gave up. He had a total disbelief in the goodness of human nature.

II

Fallon's way of organizing an archeological expedition was to treat it like a military operation – something on the same scale as the landing on Omaha Beach. This was no penurious egghead scratching along on a foundation grant and stretching every dollar to cover the work of two. Fallon was a multimillionaire with a bee in his bonnet and he could, and did, spend money as though he had a personal pipeline to Fort Knox. The money he spent to find Uaxuanoc would have been enough to build the damn place.

His first idea was to go in by sea, but the coast of Quintana Roo is cluttered up with islands and uncharted shoals and he saw the difficulties looming ahead so he abandoned the idea. He wasn't troubled about it; he merely chartered a small fleet of air freighters and flew his supplies in. To do this he had to send in a construction crew to build an airstrip at the head of Ascension Bay. This eventually became his base camp.

As soon as the airstrip was usable he sent in a photographic reconnaissance aircraft which operated from the base and which did an aerial survey, not only of the area in which Uaxuanoc was suspected to be, but of the entire provinces of Quintana Roo and Yucatan. This seemed a bit extravagant so I asked him why he did it. His answer was simple: he was co-operating with the Mexican Government in return for certain favours – it seemed that the cartographic department of the State Survey was very short on information about those areas and Fallon had agreed to supply a photo-mosaic.

'The only person who ever took aerial photographs of Quintana Roo was Lindbergh,' he said. 'And that was a long time ago. It will all come in very useful professionally.'

From Ascension Bay helicopters set up Camp Two in the interior. Fallon and Halstead spent quite a lot of time debating where to set up Camp Two. They measured the X-ray prints to the last millimetre and transferred reading to Fallon's big map and eventually came to a decision. Theoretically, Camp Two should have been set up smack on the top of the temple of Yum Chac in Uaxuanoc. It wasn't, of course; but that surprised nobody.

Halstead favoured me with one of his rare smiles, but there didn't seem to be much real humour in it. 'A field trip is like being in the army,' he said. 'You can use all the mechanization you like, but the job gets done by guys using their own feet. You're still going to regret coming on this jaunt, Wheale.'

I had the distinct impression that he was waiting for me to fall flat on my face when we got out in the field. He was the kind of man who would laugh himself silly at someone slipping on a banana skin and breaking his leg. A primitive sense of humour! Also, he didn't like me very much.

While all this was going on we stayed at Fallon's place outside Mexico City. The Halsteads had given up their own place and had moved in, so we were all together. Pat Harris was around from time to time. He departed upon mysterious trips without warning and came back just as unexpectedly. I suppose he reported to Fallon but he said nothing to the rest of us for the quite simple reason that everyone was too busy to ask him.

Fallon came to me one day, and said, 'About your skin-diving experience. Were you serious?'

'Quite serious. I've done a lot of it.'

'Good,' he said. 'When we find Uaxuanoc we'll want to investigate the cenote.'

'I'll need more equipment,' I said. 'The stuff I have is good enough for an amateur within reach of civilization but not for the middle of Quintana Roo.'

'What kind of equipment?'

'Oh, an air compressor for recharging bottles is one of the biggest items.' I paused. 'If the dives are more than a hundred and fifty feet I'd like a stand-by recompression chamber in case anyone gets into trouble.'

He nodded. 'Okay; get your equipment.'

He turned away and I said gently, 'What do I use in place of money?'

He stopped. 'Oh, yes. I'll ask my secretary to arrange all that. See him tomorrow.'

'Who is going down with me?'

'You need someone else?' he asked in surprise.

'That's a cardinal rule – you don't dive alone. Especially into the murky depths of a hole in the ground. Too many things can go wrong underwater.'

'Well, hire somebody,' he said a little irritably. This was a minor part of the main problem and he was only too eager to get rid of it.

So I went shopping and bought some lovely expensive equipment. Most of it was available locally, but the recompression chamber was more difficult. I saw Fallon's secretary about that and a few telephone calls to the States produced a minor flap in the far-flung Fallon empire; it also produced a recompression chamber on the first available air freighter. Maybe that piece of equipment was an extravagance, but it's one thing getting the bends in England where the port hospitals are equipped to handle it and where the Navy will give a hand in an emergency, and it's quite another thing to have nitrogen bubbling in your blood like champagne in the middle of a blasted wilderness. I preferred to play safe. Besides, Fallon could afford it.

I ended up with enough gear to outfit an average aqualung club, and normally I should have been full of gloating at the opportunity to handle and use all those efficient and well-designed tools of the diver's trade – but I wasn't. It had come too easy. This wasn't something I'd

sweated for, something I'd saved up to buy, and I began to
see why rich people became bored so easily and began to
indulge in way-out entertainments. Not that Fallon was like
that, to give him his due; he was all archeologist and very
professional.

Then I rounded up Katherine Halstead and took her
down to the pool. 'All right,' I said. 'Show me.'

She looked at me in surprise. 'Show you what?'

I pointed to the scuba harness I had brought down.
'Show me that you can use that thing.'

I watched her as she put it on and made no attempt to
help her. She seemed familiar enough with it and chose the
belt weights with care, and when she went into the water
she did it the right way without any fuss. I put on my own
gear and followed her and we drifted around the bottom of
the pool while I tested her on the international signals
which she seemed to understand. When we came out, I
said, 'You're hired.'

She looked puzzled. 'Hired for what?'

'As second string diver on the Uaxuanoc Expedition.'

Her face lit up. 'You really mean that?'

'Fallon told me to hire someone – and you can't come
along as a passenger. I'll tell him the bad news.'

He blew up as predicted, but I argued him into it by saying that Katherine at least knew something about archeology and that he wouldn't get an archeological diver this
side of the Mediterranean.

She must have worked on her husband because he didn't
object, but I caught him looking at me speculatively. I think
it was then that he was bitten by the bug of jealousy and
began to have the idea that I was up to no good. Not that I
cared what he thought; I was too busy drilling his wife into
the routine of learning how to use the air compressor and
the recompression chamber. We got pretty matey and soon
we were on first name terms. Up to then I'd always called

her Mrs Halstead, but you can hardly stick to that kind of thing when you're both ducking in and out of a pool. But I never laid a finger on her.

Halstead never called me anything but Wheale.

III

I liked Pat Harris. As a person he was slow and easy-going, no matter how mistrustful and devious he was when on the job. Just before we were due to leave for Quintana Roo he seemed to be spending more time at the house and we got into the habit of having a noggin together late at night. Once I asked him, 'What exactly is your job, Pat?'

He ran his finger down the outside of his beer glass. 'I suppose you could call me Fallon's trouble-shooter. When you have as much dough as he's got you find an awful lot of people trying to part you from it. I run checks on guys like that to see if everything is on the up and up.'

'Did you run a check on me?'

He grinned, and said easily, 'Sure! I know more about you than your own mother did.' He drank some cold beer. 'Then one of his corporations sometimes has security trouble and I go and see what's going on.'

'Industrial espionage?' I queried.

'I guess you'd call it that,' he agreed. 'But only from the security angle. Fallon doesn't play dirty pool, so I stick to counter-espionage.'

I said, 'If you investigated me, then you must have done the same with Halstead. He seems a pretty odd type.'

Pat smiled into his beer. 'You can say that again. He's a guy who thought he had genius and who has now found out that all he has is talent. That really disappoints a man – settling for second best. The trouble with Halstead is that he hasn't come to terms with it yet; it's really griping him.'

'You'll have to spell it out for me,' I said.

Pat sighed. 'Well, it's like this. Halstead started out as a boy wonder – voted the graduate most likely to succeed and all that kind of crap. You know, it's funny how wrong guys can be about other guys; every corporation is stuffed full to the brim with men who were voted most likely to succeed, and they're all holding down second-rate jobs. The men at the top – the guys who really have the power – got there the hard way by clawing their way up and wielding a pretty sharp knife. There are a hell of a lot of corporation presidents who never went to college. Or you have guys like Fallon – he started at the top.'

'In his business,' I said. 'But not in archeology.'

'I'll give you that,' said Pat. 'Fallon would succeed in anything he put his hand to. But Halstead is a second-rater; he knows it but he won't admit it, even to himself, and it's sticking in his craw. He's eaten up with ambition – that's why he was going solo on this Uaxuanoc thing. He wanted to be the man who discovered Uaxuanoc; it would make his name and he'd salvage his self-respect. But you twisted his arm and forced him in with Fallon and he doesn't like that. He doesn't want to share the glory.'

I contemplated that, then said cautiously, 'Both Fallon and Halstead were free in throwing accusations at each other. Halstead accused Fallon of stealing the Vivero letter. Well, we seem to have cleared up that one, and Fallon is in the clear. But what about Fallon's charge that Halstead pinched the file he'd built up?'

'I think Halstead is guilty of that,' said Pat frankly. 'Look at the timetable. Fallon, out of interest's sake, built up a dossier of references to the Vivero secret; Halstead knew about it because Fallon told him – there wasn't any need to keep it under wraps because it didn't seem all that important. Fallon and Halstead came back to civilization after a dig, and Halstead found the Vivero letter. He bought it up in Durango for two hundred dollars from an old guy who didn't know its value. But Halstead did – he knew it could be the key to the Vivero secret, whatever that was. And apart from that it was archeological dynamite – a city no one had even heard of.'

He reached out and opened another bottle of beer. 'I checked on the date he bought it. A month later he picked a quarrel with Fallon and went off in a huff, and Fallon's Vivero dossier disappeared. Fallon didn't think much of it at the time. As I say, the Vivero file didn't seem so important, and he thought Halstead might have made a genuine error and mixed up some of Fallon's papers with his own. And he didn't think it worth his while to add to the grief that Halstead was stirring up just about that time. He thinks differently now.'

I said slowly, 'It's all very circumstantial.'

'Most evidence is,' said Pat. 'Crimes are usually committed without witnesses. Another thing that inclines me to think he did it is his general reputation in the profession.'

'Not good?'

'A bit smelly. He's under suspicion of faking some of his results. Nothing that anyone can pin on him, and certainly not enough to justify him being drummed out of the profession publicly. But certainly enough for anything he produces in the future to be inspected mighty carefully. There's nothing new in that, of course; it's been done before. You had a case in England, didn't you?'

'That was in anthropology,' I said. 'The Piltdown man. Everyone wondered why it didn't fit in to the main sequence and there was a lot of theory-twisting to jam it in. Then science caught up with it when they developed radiocarbon date testing and discovered it was a fake.'

Pat nodded. 'Some guys do that kind of thing. If they can't make a reputation the straight way, they'll make it the crooked way. And they're usually like Halstead – second-raters who want to make a quick name.'

'But it's still circumstantial,' I said stubbornly. I didn't want to believe this. To me, science was equated with truth, and I didn't want to believe that any scientist would stoop to fraud. And maybe I didn't want to believe that Katherine Halstead was the kind of woman who would marry a man like that.

'Oh, he hasn't been found with dirty hands,' said Pat. 'But I guess it's just a matter of time.'

I said, 'How long have they been married?'

'Three years.' The hand holding his glass suddenly hovered halfway to his lips. 'If you're thinking what I think you're thinking, my advice is – don't! I know she's quite a dish, but keep your hands off. Fallon wouldn't like it.'

'Quite a thought-reader, aren't you?' I said sarcastically. 'Mrs Halstead is safe from me, I assure you.' Even as I said it I wondered how far that was true. I was also amused at the way Harris had put it – *Fallon wouldn't like it.* Pat's first loyalty was to his boss and he didn't give a damn about how Halstead might react. I said, 'Do you think she knows what you've told me – about her husband's reputation?'

'Probably not,' said Pat. 'I can't see anyone going up to her and saying, "Mrs Halstead, I have to tell you your husband's reputation is lousy." She'd be the last person to find out.' He regarded me with interest. 'What made you push her on to Fallon in this diving caper? That's twice you've made the boss eat crow. Your credit's running out fast.'

I said slowly, 'She can control her husband where other people can't. You know the foul temper he has. I've no intention of spending my time in Quintana Roo keeping those two from assaulting each other. I'll need some help.'

Pat cocked his head on one side, then nodded abruptly. 'You just might be right. Trouble won't come from Fallon, but Halstead might stir something up. I'm not saying he's nuts, but he's very unstable. You know what I think? I think if he gets a fraction too much pressure on him one

of two things will happen – either he'll split right open like
a rotten egg, or he'll blow up like a bomb. Now, if you're in
a pressure situation, either way brings you grief. I wouldn't
rely on him in a jam, and I'd trust him as far as I could
throw the Empire State Building.'

'Quite a recommendation. I'd hate to have you write out
a testimonial for me, Pat.'

He grinned. 'Yours might be a bit better. All you have to
do, Jemmy, to get a hundred per cent score is to stop being
so goddamn unobtrusive and neutral. I know you English
have a reputation for being quiet, but you push it too far. Do
you mind if I speak frankly?'

'Can I stop you?'

He snorted with laughter. 'Probably not.' He lifted his
glass. 'I'm probably just cut enough to tell the truth – it's a
failing of mine which has earned me a couple of black eyes
in my time.'

'You'd better go ahead and tell me the worst. I promise
not to sock you.'

'Okay. You've got some iron in you somewhere, or you
wouldn't have been able to strongarm Fallon the way you
have. He can be a tough guy to handle. But what have
you done since? Fallon and Halstead are running things now
and you're sitting on the sidelines. You've twisted Fallon's
arm again over Mrs Halstead – something that doesn't
matter a damn, and he'll remember it. What the hell are you
doing on this jaunt, anyway?'

'I had a crazy idea I might be able to do something about
my brother.'

'That you can forget,' said Pat briefly.

'So I've found out,' I said gloomily.

'I'm glad you realize it,' he said. 'Gatt would swat you
like a fly and never give it another thought. Why don't you
quit and go home, Jemmy; go back to that little farm of
yours? You've found out there's no treasure to be hunted,

and you don't give two cents for all the lost cities in Latin America, do you? Why stick around?'

'I'll stick around as long as Gatt does,' I said. 'He might leave himself open long enough for me to get at him.'

'Then you'll wait until hell freezes over. Look, Jemmy: I've got fifteen operatives on to him now, and I'm no nearer finding out what he's up to than when I started. He's a smart cookie and he doesn't make mistakes – not those kind of mistakes. He keeps himself covered all the time – it's a reflex with him.'

'You'll agree he'll be interested in what we'll be doing in Quintana Roo?'

'Apparently so,' said Pat. 'He's certainly keeping tabs on this operation.'

'Then he'll have to follow us there,' I said. 'He can't do anything from Mexico City. If he's so bloody interested in hypothetical treasure in Uaxuanoc, he'll have to go to Uaxuanoc to pick up the loot. Do you agree with that?'

'It's feasible,' said Pat judiciously. 'I can't see Jack being so trusting as to send anyone else – not with what he thinks is at stake.'

'He won't be on his home ground, Pat. He's a civilized city type – he'll be out of his depth. From what I can gather Quintana Roo is as unlike New York City as Mars is. He might make a mistake.'

Pat looked at me in astonishment. 'And what makes you think you're any different? I grant you that Gatt is a city type, but civilized he is not. Whereas you are a city type *and* civilized. Jemmy, you're a London accountant; you'll be just as much out of your depth in the Quintana Roo as Gatt.'

'Exactly,' I said. 'We'll be on equal terms – which is more than can be said right now.'

He drained his glass and slammed it down on to the table with a bang. 'I think you're nuts,' he said disgustedly. 'You talk a weird kind of sense, but I still think you're nuts.

You're as batty as Halstead.' He looked up. 'Tell me, can you handle a gun?'

'I've never tried,' I said. 'So I don't know.'

'For Christ's sake!' he said. 'What are you going to do if you do come up against Gatt on even terms, as you call it? Kiss him to death?'

'I don't know,' I said. 'I'll see when the time comes. I believe in handling situations as they happen.'

He passed his hand over his face in a bemused way and looked at me for a long time without saying anything. He took a deep breath. 'Let me outline a hypothetical situation,' he said mildly. 'Let us suppose that you've managed to separate Jack from his bodyguards, and that's a pretty foolish supposition in the first place. And let us suppose that there the two of you are, a pair of city slickers, babes in the wood.' He stuck out a rigid finger. 'The first – and last – thing you'd know was that Jack had bush-whacked you with a lupara, and you'd be in no condition to handle *any* situation.'

'Has Gatt ever killed anyone himself?' I asked.

'I'd guess so. He came up through the ranks in the Organization. Served his apprenticeship, you might say. He'll have done a killing or two in his younger days.'

'That's a long time ago,' I observed. 'Maybe he's out of practice.'

'Agh, there's no talking to you,' said Pat in a choked voice. 'If you have any brains you'll go back where you came from. I *have* to stick around, but at least I know what the score is, and I get paid for it. But you're the kind of guy that Kipling wrote about – "If you can keep your head while all about you are losing theirs, then maybe you don't know what the hell is going on."'

I laughed. 'You have quite a talent for parody.'

'I'm not as good as Fallon,' he said gloomily. 'He's turned this whole operation into a parody of security. I used the bug Gatt planted on us to feed him a queer line, and what does Fallon do? He stages a goddamn TV spectacular, for God's sake! I wouldn't be surprised, when you fly down to that airstrip he's built, if you don't find the CBS cameras already rolling and hooked up into a coast-to-coast broadcast – and a line of Rockettes from Radio City to give added interest. Every paisano in Mexico knows what's going on. Gatt doesn't have to bug us to find out what we're doing; all he has to do is to ask at any street corner.'

'It's a tough life,' I said sympathetically. 'Does Fallon usually behave like this?'

Harris shook his head. 'I don't know what's got into him. He's turned over control of his affairs to his brother – given him power of attorney. His brother's a nice enough guy, but I wouldn't trust *anyone* that far with a hundred million bucks. He's thinking of nothing else but finding this city.'

'I don't know about that,' I said thoughtfully. 'He seems to be worried about something else. He goes a bit dreamy at unexpected moments.'

'I've noticed that, too. Something's bugging him, but he hasn't let me in on it.' Harris seemed resentful at the idea that something was being kept from him. He rose to his feet and stretched. 'I'm going to bed – there's work to do tomorrow.'

IV

So there it was again!

First Sheila, and now Pat Harris. He hadn't said it as bluntly as Sheila, but he'd said it nevertheless. Apparently, my exterior appearance and mannerisms gave a good imitation of Caspar Milquetoast – the nine-to-fiver, the commuter par excellence. The trouble was that I wasn't at all sure that the interior didn't match the exterior.

Gatt, from Pat's description, was lethal. Maybe he wouldn't shoot anyone just to make bets on which way he'd fall, but he might if there was a dollar profit in it. I began to feel queasy at the thought of going up against him, but I knew I couldn't turn back now.

Pat's assessment of Halstead was quite interesting, too, and I wondered how much Katherine knew about her husband. I think she loved him – in fact, I was sure of it. No woman in her right mind would tolerate such a man otherwise, but maybe I was prejudiced. At any rate, she consistently took his side in any argument he had with Fallon. The very picture of a faithful wife. I went to sleep thinking about her.

SIX

We went to Camp One in Fallon's flying office – a Lear executive jet. Pat Harris didn't come with us – his job was to keep tabs on Gatt – so there were just four passengers, Fallon, the Halsteads and myself. Fallon and Halstead engaged in another of their interminable professional discussions, and Katherine Halstead read a magazine. Halstead had done a bit of manoeuvring when we entered the plane and Katherine was sitting on the other side of him and as far from me as it was possible to get. I couldn't talk to her without shouting across a technical argument so I turned my attention to the ground.

Quintana Roo, seen from the air, looked like a piece of mouldy cheese. The solid vegetative cover was broken only occasionally by a clearing which showed as a dirty whitish-grey among the virulent green of the trees. I did not see a single water-course, no rivers and not even a stream, and I began to appreciate Halstead's point of view about the difficulties of archeological exploration in the tropics.

At one point Fallon broke off his discussion to speak with the pilot on the intercom, and the plane wheeled slowly and began to descend. He turned to me and said, 'We'll have a look at Camp Two.'

Even from a thousand feet the forest looked solid enough to walk on without touching ground. There could have been a city the size of London under that sea of green and you'd never see it. I reminded myself not to be so bloody cocky in the future about things I knew nothing about. Halstead might be a faker, if what Pat Harris said was true, but a faker, of all people, must have a knowledge of his field. He had been right when he had said that this was going to be a tough job.

Camp Two came and went before I had a chance to get a good look at it, but the plane banked, and turned and we orbited the site, standing on one wingtip. There wasn't much to see: just another clearing with half a dozen prefab-ricated huts and some minuscule figures which waved their arms. The jet couldn't land there, but that wasn't the inten-tion. We straightened on course and rose higher, heading for the coast and Camp One.

About twenty minutes and eighty miles later we were over the sea and curving back over the white surf and gleaming beaches to touch down at the airstrip at Camp One. The jet bumped a bit in the coastal turbulence but put down gently and rolled to a stop at the further end of the strip, then wheeled and taxied to a halt in front of a hangar. As I left the plane the heat, after the air-conditioned com-fort of the flight, was like the sudden blow of a hammer.

Fallon didn't seem to notice the heat at all. Years of put-tering about in this part of the world had already dried the juices from him and he had been thoroughly conditioned. He set off at a brisk walk along the strip, followed by Halstead, who also didn't seem to mind. Katherine and I fol-lowed along more slowly and, by the time we got to the hut into which Fallon had disappeared she was looking defi-nitely wilted and I felt a bit brown around the edges myself.

'My God!' I said. 'Is it always like this?'

Halstead turned and gave me a smile which had all the elements of a sneer. 'You've been spoiled by Mexico City,' he said. 'The altitude up there takes the edge off. It's not really hot here on the coast. Wait until we get to Camp Two.' His tone implied that I'd feel bloody sorry for myself.

It was cooler in the hut and there was the persistent throb of an air-conditioning unit. Fallon introduced us to a big, burly man. 'This is Joe Rudetsky; he's the boss of Camp One.'

Rudetsky stuck out a meaty hand. 'Glad to meet you, Mr Wheale,' he boomed.

I later found out how Fallon had managed to organize the whole operation so quickly. He had merely appropriated the logistics unit from one of his oil exploration teams. Those boys were used to operating in rough country and under tropical conditions, and this job was very little different from a score of others they had done in North Africa, Saudi Arabia and Venezuela. When I explored the camp I admired the sheer efficiency of it all. They certainly knew how to make themselves comfortable – even to ice-cold Coca-Cola.

We stayed in Camp One all that day and slept there the night. Fallon and Halstead checked the mountain of equipment they evidently thought they needed, so Katherine and I did the same with the scuba gear. We weren't going to take it to Camp Two because that would be pointless; Camp Two was a mere centre of exploration and if and when we discovered Uaxuanoc it would be abandoned and Camp Three would be set up on the city site.

We worked until lunchtime and then stopped for something to eat. I wasn't very hungry – the heat affected my appetite – but I relished the bottle of cold lager that Rudetsky thrust into my hand. I'd swear it hissed going down.

Katherine and I had completed our inspection and found everything present and in working order, but Fallon and Halstead still had quite a way to go. I offered to give them a hand, but Fallon shook his head. 'It's mostly instrument checking now,' he said. 'You wouldn't know how to do that.'

His gaze wandered over my shoulder. 'If you turn round you'll see your first Maya.'

I twisted in my chair and looked across the strip. On the other side of the flattened ground and standing within easy running distance of the trees were two men. They were dressed in rather baggy trousers and white shirts and stood quite still. They were rather too far away for me to distinguish their features.

Fallon said, 'They don't know what to make of us, you know. This is an unprecedented invasion.' He looked across at Rudetsky. 'Have they given you any trouble, Joe?'

'The natives? No trouble at all, Mr Fallon. Those guys are from up the coast; they have a two-bit coconut plantation.'

'A cocal,' said Fallon. 'These people live entirely isolated lives, cut off from everything. The sea on one side – the forest on the other. There'll be just the one family – the cocal won't support two – and they're dependent entirely on their own resources.'

That seemed a grim life. 'What do they live on?' I asked.

Fallon shrugged. 'Fish, turtles, turtle eggs. Sometimes they're lucky enough to shoot a wild pig. Then twice a year they'll sell their copra and that gives them a little ready money to buy clothing and needles and a few cartridges.'

'Are those the indios sublevados you talked about?'

Fallon laughed. 'These boys aren't rebels – they wouldn't know how to start. We'll meet the indios sublevados in the interior, and the chicleros, too.' He switched to Rudetsky. 'Have you had any chicleros round here?'

Rudetsky nodded grimly. 'We ran the bastards off. They were stealing us blind.' He looked across at Katherine who was talking to Halstead, and lowered his voice. 'They murdered a native last week; we found his body on the beach.'

Fallon didn't seem perturbed. He merely picked up his pipe and said, 'You'd better keep a good watch, and don't let them in the camp on any account. And you'd better have the men stay in the camp and not go wandering around.'

Rudetsky grinned. 'Where is there to go?' he asked.

I began to wonder what kind of a country I was in where a murder could be taken so casually. Hesitantly, I said, 'Who or what are chicleros?'

Fallon pulled a sour face. 'The result of an odd penal system they have here. There's a tree which grows in the forest, the zapote; it grows only here, in Guatemala and in British Honduras. The tree is tapped for its sap and that's called chicle – it's the basic material of chewing gum. Now, no man in his right mind will go into the forest to gather chicle; the Maya certainly won't because he's too intelligent to risk his skin. So the government dumps its convicts in here to do the job. It's a six months' season but a lot of the chicleros stay all the year round. They're a local scourge. Mostly they kill each other off, but occasionally they'll knock off an outsider or an Indian.' He drew on his pipe. 'Human life isn't worth much in Quintana Roo.'

I thought that over. If I heard Fallon aright then this forest was deadly. If the Mayas whose native land it was wouldn't work in the forest then it must be positively lethal. I said, 'Why the devil don't they grow the trees in plantations?'

His face twisted into a wry grin. 'Because of the same argument that's been used for slavery ever since one man put a yoke on another. It's cheaper to continue using convicts than to start plantations. If the people who chew gum knew how it was produced, every stick would make them sick to their stomachs.' He pointed the stem of his pipe at me. 'If you ever meet any chicleros, don't do a damn thing. Keep your hands to your sides, don't make any sudden moves and like as not they'll just pass you by. But don't bet on it.'

I began to wonder if I was still in the twentieth century. 'And where do the indios sublevados come into all this?'

'That's quite a story,' said Fallon. 'The Spaniards took two hundred years to get on top of the Mayas, and the Lakondon tribe they never licked. The Mayas were kept down until 1847 when they rose in rebellion here in Quintana Roo. It was more populated in those days and the Mayas gave the Mexicans, as they now were, a hell of a trouncing in what was known as the War of the Castes. Try as they might the Mexicans could never get back in again. In 1915 the Mayas declared an independent state; they dealt with British Honduras and made business deals with British firms. The top Maya then was General Mayo; he was a really tough old bird; but the Mexicans got at him through his vanity. They signed a treaty with him in 1935, made him a general in the official Mexican army and invited him to Mexico City where they seduced him with civilization. He died in 1952. After 1935 the Mayas seemed to lose heart. They'd had a tough time since the War of the Castes and the land was becoming depopulated. On top of famine, which hit them hard, the Mexicans started to move colonists into Chan Santa Cruz. There are not more than a few thousand of the indios sub-levados left now, yet they still rule the roost in their own area.' He smiled. 'No Mexican tax collectors allowed.'

Halstead had broken off his conversation with his wife. 'And they don't like archeologists much, either,' he observed.

'Oh, it's not as bad as it was in the old times,' said Fallon tolerantly. 'In the early days of General Mayo any foreigner coming into Quintana Roo was automatically a dead man. Remember the story I told of the archeologist whose bones were built into a wall? But they've lost a lot of steam since then. They're all right if they're left alone. They're better than the chicleros.'

Halstead looked at me and said, 'Still glad to be along with us, Wheale?' He had a thin smile on his face.

I ignored him. 'Why isn't all this common knowledge?' I asked Fallon. 'A government running a species of slavery and a whole people nearly wiped out surely calls for comment.'

Fallon knocked out his pipe on the leg of the table. 'Africa is popularly known as the Dark Continent,' he said. 'But there are some holes and corners of Central and South America which are pretty black. Your popular journalist sitting in his office in London or New York has very limited horizons; he can't see this far and he won't leave his office.'

He put the pipe in his pocket. 'But I'll tell you something. The trouble with Quintana Roo isn't the Indians or the chicleros; they're people, and you can always get along with people somehow.' He stretched out his arm and pointed. 'There's your trouble.'

I looked to where he was pointing and saw nothing unusual – just the trees on the other side of the strip.

'You still don't understand?' he asked, and swung round to Rudetsky. 'What kind of a job did you have in clearing this strip?'

'The hardest work I've ever done,' said Rudetsky. 'I've worked in rain forest before – I was an army engineer during the war – but this one beats all hell.'

'That's it,' said Fallon flatly. 'Do you know how they classify the forest here? They say it's a twenty-foot forest, or a ten-foot forest, or a four-foot forest. A four-foot forest is getting pretty bad – it means that you can't see more than four feet in any direction – but there are worse than that. Add disease, snakes and shortage of water and you realize why the chicleros are among the toughest men in the world – those of them that survive. The forest is the enemy in Quintana Roo, and we'll have to fight it to find Uaxuanoc.'

II

We went to Camp Two next day, travelling in a helicopter which flew comparatively slowly and not too high. I looked down at the green tide which flowed beneath my feet and thought back to the conversation I'd had with Pat Harris about Jack Gatt and our hypothetical encounter in Quintana Roo. While I had envisaged something more than Epping Forest I certainly hadn't thought it would be this bad.

Fallon had explained the peculiarities of the Quintana Roo forest quite simply. He said, 'I told you the reason why there is no native gold in Yucatan is because of the geology of the area – there's just a limestone cap over the peninsula. That explains the forest, too, and why it's worse than any other.'

'It doesn't explain it to me,' I said. 'Or maybe I'm particularly stupid.'

'No; you just don't have the technical knowledge,' he said. 'The rainfall is quite heavy, but when it falls it sinks right into the ground until it meets an impermeable layer. Thus there is a vast reservoir of fresh water under Yucatan, but a shortage of water because there are no rivers. The water is quite close to the surface; on the coast you can dig a hole on the beach three feet from the sea and you'll get fresh water. In the interior sometimes the limestone cap collapses to reveal the underground water – that's a cenote. But the point is that the trees always have water available at their roots. In any other rain forest, such as in the Congo, most of the water is drained away into rivers. In Quintana Roo it's available to the trees and they take full advantage.'

I looked down at the forest and wondered if it was a twenty-foot forest or a four-footer. Whatever it was, I couldn't see the ground and we were less than five hundred feet high. If Jack Gatt had any sense he wouldn't come anywhere near Quintana Roo.

Camp Two was much simpler than Camp One. There was a rough hangar for the helicopter – a wall-less structure looking something like a Dutch barn; a dining-room-cum-lounge, a store hut for equipment and four huts for sleeping quarters. All the huts were factory-made prefabs and all had been flown in by helicopter. Simpler it might have been but there was no lack of comfort; every hut had an air-conditioning unit and the refrigerator was full of beer. Fallon didn't believe in roughing it unless he had to.

Apart from the four of us there were the cook and his helper to do the housekeeping and the helicopter pilot. What he was going to do, apart from flying us back and forward between camps, I didn't know; in the search for Uaxuanoc the helicopter would be about as much use as a bull's udder.

All around lay the forest, green and seemingly impenetrable. I walked to the edge of the clearing and inspected it, trying to assess it by the rating Fallon had given. As near as I could tell this would be a fifteen-foot forest – a rather thin growth by local standards. The trees were tall, pushing and fighting in a fiercely competitive battle for light, and were wreathed and strangled by an incredible variety of parasitic plant life. And apart from the purely human sounds which came from the huts everything was deathly silent.

I turned to find Katherine standing near me. 'Just inspecting the enemy,' I said. 'Have you been here before – in Quintana Roo, I mean?'

'No,' she said. 'Not here. I was on digs with Paul in Campeche and Guatemala. I've never seen anything like this before.'

'Neither have I,' I said. 'I've lived a sheltered life. If Fallon had taken the trouble to explain things when we were back in England as he explained them at Camp One I doubt if I'd be here at all. This is a wild-goose chase if ever there was one.'

'I think you underestimate Fallon – and Paul,' she said. 'Don't you think we'll find Uaxuanoc?'

I jerked my thumb at the green wall. 'In this? I wouldn't trust myself to find the Eiffel Tower if someone dumped it down here.'

'That's just because you don't know how to look and where to look,' she said. 'But Paul and Fallon are professionals; they've done this before.'

'Yes, there are tricks to every trade,' I admitted. 'I know there are plenty in mine, but I can't see much use for an accountant here. I feel as out of place as a Hottentot at a Buck House garden party.' I looked into the forest. 'Talk about not being able to see the wood for the trees – I'll be interested to see how the experts go about this.'

I soon found out because Fallon called a conference in the big hut. There was a huge photo-mosaic pinned to a cork board on the wall and the table was covered with maps. I was curious to know why the helicopter pilot, a Texan called Harry Rider, was included in the discussion, but it soon became clear.

Fallon broke open the refrigerator and served beer all round, then said succinctly, 'The key to this problem is the cenotes. We know Uaxuanoc was centred on a cenote because Vivero said so, and there was no reason for him to lie about *that*. Besides, it's the most likely occurrence – a city must have water and the only water is at the cenotes.'

He took a pointer and stepped up to the photo-mosaic. He laid the tip of the pointer in the centre, and said, 'We are here, next to a very small cenote on the edge of the clearing.' He turned to me. 'If you want to see your first Mayan structure you'll find it next to the cenote.'

I was surprised. 'Aren't you going to investigate it?'

'It's not worth it; it won't tell me anything I don't know already.' He swept the pointer around in a large circle. 'Within ten miles of this point there are fifteen cenotes, large and small, and around one of them *may* be the city of Uaxuanoc.'

I was still trying to clarify in my mind the magnitude of the problem. 'How big would you expect it to be?' I asked.

Halstead said, 'Bigger than Chichen Itza – if we can believe Vivero's map.'

'That doesn't mean much to me.'

'The centre of Copan is over seventy-five acres,' said Fallon. 'But you mustn't confuse a Mayan city with any other city you've seen. The centre of the city – the stone structures we are looking for – was the religious and administrative centre, and probably the market-place. Around it, for several square miles, lived the Mayas of the city. They didn't live in neat little houses built into streets as we do but in an immense system of small-holdings. Each family would have its own little farm, and the household buildings were very little different from the huts that the Mayas now build, although probably more extensive. There's nothing wrong with the Mayan hut – it's ideally suited to this climate.'

'And the population?'

'Chichen Itza was about 200,000 according to Morley,' said Halstead. 'Uaxuanoc might run upwards of a quarter-million.'

'That's a devil of a lot of people,' I said in astonishment.

'To build the immense structures they did require a lot of hands,' said Fallon. 'These were a neolithic people, remember, using stone tools to carve stone. I expect the centre of Uaxuanoc will be about one hundred acres, if we can rely on Vivero's map, so the outer city would have been populous, with more people in it than in the whole of Quintana Roo now. But there'll be no trace left of the outer city; timber buildings don't last in this climate.'

He tapped with the pointer again. 'Let's get on with it. So we have fifteen cenotes to look at, and if we don't find what we're looking for we'll have to go further afield. That will be unfortunate, because within twenty miles of here there are another forty-nine cenotes and it's going to take a long time if we have to investigate them all.'

He waved the pointer at the pilot. 'Fortunately we have Harry Rider and his helicopter so we can do it in reasonable comfort. I'm getting too old to tackle the forest.'

Rider said, 'I've already had a look at some of those water-holes, Mr Fallon; in most of them there's no place to put down – not even my chopper. It's real thick.'

Fallon nodded. 'I know; I've been here before and I know what it's like. We'll run a preliminary photo survey. Colour film might show up differences in vegetation due to underlying structures, and infrared might show more. And I'd like to do some flights early morning and late evening – we might get something out of the shadows.'

He turned and regarded the photo-mosaic. 'As you can see, I've numbered the cenotes under consideration. Some are more likely than others. Vivero said there was a ridge running through Uaxuanoc with a temple at the top and a cenote at the bottom. Cenotes and ridges seem to be associated in this area, which is bad luck; but it cuts the possibles down to eleven. I think we can forget numbers four, seven, eight and thirteen for the time being.' He turned to Rider. 'When can we start?'

'Any time you like – I'm fuelled up,' said Rider.

Fallon consulted his watch. 'We'll fix up the cameras, and leave directly after lunch.'

I helped to load the cameras into the helicopter. There was nothing amateurish or snapshottery about this gear; they were professional aerial cameras and I noticed that the helicopter was fitted with all the necessary brackets to receive them. My respect for Fallon's powers of organization grew even more. Allowing for the fact that he had more money to chuck about than appeared decent, at least he knew how to spend it to the best advantage. He was no playboy of the jet-set circuit spilling his wealth into some casino owner's pocket.

After a quick lunch Fallon and Halstead made for the helicopter. I said, 'What do I do?'

Fallon rubbed his chin. 'There doesn't seem to be anything you can do,' he said, and over his shoulder I saw

Halstead grinning widely. 'You'd better rest up this afternoon. Stay out of the sun until you're used to this heat.
We'll be back in a couple of hours.'

I watched the helicopter take off and disappear over the
trees feeling a little silly and like an unwanted spare part.
Katherine was nowhere to be seen – I think she'd gone into
the hut she shared with Halstead to unpack their personal
gear. I wondered what to do and wandered disconsolately to
the far end of the clearing to look at the Mayan building
Fallon had mentioned.

The cenote was about thirty feet in diameter and the
water lay about fifteen feet down in the pit. The sides of the
pit were almost sheer, but someone had cut rough steps so
as to get to the water. I was startled by the sudden noisy
throb of an engine close by and found a small pump run by
a petrol engine which had apparently come into operation
automatically. It was pumping water from the cenote up to
the camp – another bit of Fallonese efficiency.

I didn't find a building although I looked hard enough,
and after half an hour of futile searching I gave up. I was
about to go back to the camp when I saw two men on the
other side of the cenote looking at me. All they wore were
ragged white trousers and they stood as still as statues. They
were small, sinewy and brown, and a stray sunbeam falling
through the leaves reflected in a coppery sheen from the
naked chest of the nearest man. They regarded me solemnly
for the space of thirty seconds and then turned and vanished
into the forest.

III

The helicopter came back and Fallon dumped a load of film
spools on the table in the big hut. 'Know anything about
film processing?' he asked.

'In an amateur sort of way.'

'Umph! That might not be good enough. But we'll do the best we can. Come with me.' He led me into another hut and showed me his photographic department. 'You should be able to get the hang of this,' he said. 'It's not too difficult.'

There was no dabbling in trays of hypo for Fallon; he had the neatest darkroom set-up I'd ever seen – and he didn't need a darkroom. I watched him as he demonstrated. It was a big box with a sliding, light-tight door at one side and a slot at the other. He slid open the door, put a spool of undeveloped film into a receptacle and threaded the leader through sprockets. Then he closed the door and pressed a button. Fifteen minutes later the developed colour film uncoiled through the slot on the other side, dry and ready for screening.

He took the cover off the box and showed me the innards – the sets of slowly turning rollers and baths of chemicals, and the infra-red dryer at the end – and he explained which chemicals went where. 'Think you can handle it? It will save time if we have someone who can process the film as quickly as possible.'

'I don't see why not,' I said.

'Good! You can carry on with these, then. There's something I want to talk over with Paul.' He smiled. 'You can't really carry on a sensible conversation in a whirlybird – too noisy.' He held up a spool. 'This one consists of stereo pairs; I'll show you how to cut it and register it accurately into frames when it's developed.'

I got stuck in to developing the films, pleased that there was something I could do. All it took was time – the job itself was so simple it could have been contracted out to child labour. I developed the last spool – the stereos – and took it to Fallon, and he showed me how to fit the images into the double frames, which was easy if finicky.

That evening we had a magic-lantern show in the big hut. Fallon put a spool into the film strip projector and switched on. There was just a green blur on the screen and he chuckled. 'I seem to have got the focus wrong on that one.'

The next frame was better and the screen showed an area of forest and a cenote reflecting the blue of the sky. It just looked like any other bit of forest to me, but Fallon and Halstead discussed it for quite a while before moving on to the next frame. It was a good two hours before all the pictures were shown and I'd lost interest long before that, especially when it seemed that the first cenote had proved a bust.

Fallon said at last, 'We still have the stereo pictures. Let's have a look at those.'

He changed the projectors and handed me a pair of polaroid glasses. The stereo pictures were startlingly three-dimensional; I felt that all I had to do was lean forward to pluck the topmost leaf from a tree. Being aerial shots, they also gave a dizzying sense of vertigo. Fallon ran through them all without result. 'I think we can chalk that one off our list,' he said. 'We'd better go to bed – we'll have a heavy day tomorrow.'

I yawned and stretched, then I remembered the men I had seen. 'I saw two men down at the cenote.'

'Chicleros?' asked Fallon sharply.

'Not if chicleros are little brown men with big noses.'

'Mayas,' he decided. 'They'll be wondering what the hell we're doing.'

I said, 'Why don't you ask them about Uaxuanoc? Their ancestors built the place, after all.'

'They wouldn't know about it – or if they did, they wouldn't tell us. The modern Maya is cut off from his history. As far as he is concerned the ruins were made by giants or dwarfs and he steers clear of them. They're magical places and not to be approached by men. What did you think of that building down there?'

'I couldn't find it,' I said.

Halstead gave a suppressed snort, and Fallon laughed. 'It's not so hidden; I spotted it straightaway. I'll show you tomorrow – it will give you some idea of what we're up against here.'

IV

We established a routine. Fallon and Halstead made three flights a day – sometimes four. After each flight they would hand me the films and I would get busy developing them and every night we would screen the results. Nothing much came of that except the steady elimination of possibilities.

Fallon took me down to the cenote and showed me the Mayan building and I found that I had passed it half a dozen times without seeing it. It was just by the side of the cenote in thick vegetation, and when Fallon said, 'There it is!' I didn't see a thing except another bit of forest.

He smiled, and said, 'Go closer,' so I walked right to the edge of the clearing and saw nothing except the dappled dazzle-pattern of sun, leaves and shadows. I turned around and shrugged, and he called, 'Push your hand through the leaves.' I did as he said and rammed my fist against a rock with an unexpected jolt.

'Now step back a few paces and have another look,' said Fallon.

I walked back, rubbing my skinned knuckles and looked again at the vegetation through narrowed eyes. It's a funny thing – one moment it wasn't there and a split second later it was, like a weird optical illusion, but even then it was only the ghostly hint of a building made up imperfectly of shadows. I lifted my hand and said uncertainly, 'It starts there – and ends . . . there?'

'That's right; you've got it.'

I stared at it, afraid it would go away again. If any army staff in the world wants to improve its camouflage units I would strongly advise a course in Quintana Roo. This natural camouflage was just about perfect. I said. 'What do you think it was?'

'Maybe a shrine to Chac, the Rain God; they're often associated with cenotes. If you like you can strip the vegetation from it. We might find something of minor interest. But watch out for snakes.'

'I might do that, if I can ever find it again.'

Fallon was amused. 'You'll have to develop an eye for this kind of thing if you contemplate archeological research in these parts. If not, you'll walk right through a city and not know it's there.'

I could believe him.

He consulted his watch. 'Paul will be waiting for me,' he said. 'We'll be back with some film in a couple of hours.'

The relationship between the four of us was odd. I felt left out of things because I didn't really know what was going on. The minutiae of research were beyond me and I didn't understand a tenth of what Fallon and Halstead were talking about when they conversed on professional matters, which is all they ever spoke to each other about.

Fallon rigidly confined his relationship with Halstead to the matter in hand and would not overstep it by an inch. It was obvious to me that he did not particularly like Paul Halstead, nor did he trust him overmuch. But then, neither did I, especially after that conversation with Pat Harris. Fallon would have received an even more detailed report on Halstead from Harris and so I understood his attitude.

He was different with me. While regarding my ignorance of archeological fieldwork with a tolerant amusement, he did not try to thrust his professional expertise down my throat. He patiently answered my questions which, to him, I suppose, were simple and often absurd, and let it go at that. We got into the habit of sitting together in the evening for an hour before going to bed, and we yarned on a wide variety of topics. Apart from his professional work he was well read and a man of wide erudition. Yet I was able to interest him in the application of computers to farming practice and I detailed what I was doing to Hay Tree Farm. It seemed that he owned a big ranch in Arizona and he saw the possibilities at once.

But then he shook his head irritably. 'I'll pass that on to my brother,' he said. 'He's looking after all that now.' He stared blindly across the room. 'A man has so little time to do what he really wants to do.'

Soon thereafter he became abstracted and intent on his own thoughts and I excused myself and went to bed.

Halstead tended to be morose and self-contained. He ignored me almost completely, and rarely spoke to me unless it was absolutely necessary. When he did volunteer any remarks they were usually accompanied by an ill-concealed sneer directed at my abysmal ignorance of the work. Quite often I felt like taking a poke at him, but I bottled up my temper for the sake of the general peace. In the evenings, after our picture show and discussion, he and his wife would withdraw to their hut.

And that leaves Katherine Halstead, who was tending to become a tantalizing mystery. True, she was doing what she said she would, and kept her husband under tight control. Often I saw him on the edge of losing his temper with Fallon – he didn't lose his temper with me because I was beneath his notice – and be drawn back into semi-composure by a look or a word from his wife. I thought I understood him and what made him tick, but I'm damned if I could understand her.

A man often sees mystery in a woman where there is nothing but a yawning vacuity, the so-called feminine mystery being but a cunning façade behind which lies nothing worthwhile. But Katherine wasn't like that. She was amusing, intelligent and talented in a number of ways; she sketched competently in a better than amateur way, she cooked well and alleviated our chuckwagon diet, and she knew a hell of a lot more about the archeological score than I did, although she admitted she was but a neophyte. But she would never talk about her husband in any way at all, which is a trait I'd never come across in a married woman before.

Those I had known – not a few – always had something to say about their mates, either in praise or blame. Most would be for their husbands, with perhaps a tolerant word for their weaknesses. A few would praise incessantly and not hear a word against the darling man, and a few, the regrettable bitches, would be acid in esoteric asides meant for one pair of ears but understood by all – sniping shots in the battle of the sexes. But from Katherine Halstead there was not a cheep, one way or the other. She just didn't talk about him at all. It was unnatural.

Because Fallon and Halstead were away most of the day we were thrown together a lot. The camp cook and his assistant were very unobtrusive; they cooked the grub, washed the dishes, repaired the generator when it broke down, and spent the rest of their time losing their wages to each other at gin rummy. So Katherine and I had each other for company during those long hot days. I soon got the film developing taped and had plenty of time on my hands, so I suggested we do something about the Mayan building.

'We might come up with an epoch-making discovery,' I said jocularly. 'Let's give it a bash. Fallon said it would be a good idea.'

She smiled at the idea that we might find anything of importance, but agreed that it would be something semi-constructive to do, so we armed ourselves with machetes and went down to the cenote to hew at the vegetation.

I was surprised to see how well preserved the building was once it was denuded of its protective cover. The limestone blocks of which it was built were properly cut and shaped, and laid in a workmanlike manner. On the wall nearest the cenote we found a doorway with a sort of corbelled arch, and when we looked inside there was nothing but darkness and an angry buzz of disturbed wasps.

I said, 'I don't think we'd better go in there just yet; the present inhabitants might not like it.'

We withdrew back into the clearing and I looked down at myself. It had been hard work cutting the creepers away from the building and I'd sweated freely, and my chest was filthy with bits of earth turned into mud by the sweat. I was in a mess.

'I'm going to have a swim in the cenote,' I said. 'I need cleaning up.'

'What a good idea,' she said. 'I'll get my costume.'

I grinned. 'I won't need one – these shorts will do.'

She went back to the huts and I walked over to the cenote and looked down into the dark water. I couldn't see bottom and it could have been anything between six inches and sixty feet deep, so I thought it was inadvisable to dive in. I climbed down to water level by means of the steps, let myself into the water and found it pleasantly cool. I splashed about for a bit but I didn't find bottom, so I dived and went down to look for it. I must have gone down thirty feet and I still hadn't found it. It was bloody dark down there, which gave me a good indication of conditions if I had to dive for Fallon. I let myself up slowly, dribbling air from my mouth, and came up to sunlight again.

'I wondered where you were,' Katherine called, and I looked up to see her poised on the edge of the cenote, silhouetted against the sun fifteen feet above my head. 'Is it deep enough for diving?'

'Too deep,' I said. 'I couldn't find bottom.'

'Good!' she said, and took off in a clean dive. I swam slowly around the cenote and became worried when she didn't come up, but suddenly I felt my ankles grabbed and I was pulled under.

We surfaced laughing, and she said. 'That's for pulling me under in Fallon's pool.' She flicked water at me with the palm of her hand, and for two or three minutes we had a splashing match like a couple of kids until we were breathless and had to stop. After that we just floated around feeling the difference between the coolness of the water and the heat of the direct sun.

She said lazily, 'What's it like down there?'

'Down where?'

'At the bottom of this pool.'

'I didn't find it; I didn't go down too far. It was a bit cold.'

'Weren't you afraid of meeting Chac?'

'Does he live down there?'

'He has a palace at the bottom of every cenote. They used to throw maidens in, and they'd sink down to meet him. Some of them would come back with wonderful stories.'

'What about those who didn't come back?'

'Chac kept them for his own. Sometimes he'd keep them all and the people would become frightened and punish the cenote. They'd throw stones into it and flog it with branches. But none of the maidens would ever come back because of that.'

'You'd better be careful, then,' I said.

She splashed water at me. 'I'm not exactly a maiden.'

I swam over to the steps. 'The chopper should be coming back soon. Another batch of film to be processed.' I climbed halfway up and stopped to give her a hand.

At the top she offered me a towel but I shook my head. 'I'll dry off quickly enough in the sun.'

'Suit yourself,' she said. 'But it's not good for your hair.' She spread the towel on the ground, sat on it, and started to rub her hair with another towel.

I sat down beside her and started to flip pebbles into the cenote. 'What are you *really* doing here, Jemmy?' she asked.

'I'm damned if I know,' I admitted. 'It just seemed a good idea at the time.'

She smiled. 'It's a change from your Devon, isn't it? Don't you wish you were back on your farm – on Hay Tree Farm? Incidentally, do you always make hay from trees in Devon?'

'It doesn't mean what you think. It's a dialect word meaning a hedge or enclosure.' I flicked another pebble into the pool. 'Do you think that annoys Chac?'

'It might, so I wouldn't do it too often – not if you have to dive into a cenote. Damn! I don't have any cigarettes.'

I got up and retrieved mine from where I had left them and we sat and smoked in silence for a while. She said, 'I haven't played about like that in the water for years.'

'Not since the carefree days of the Bahamas?' I asked.

'Not since then.'

'Is that where you met Paul?'

There was the briefest pause before she said, 'No. I met Paul in New York.' She smiled slightly. 'He isn't the type you find on the beach in the Bahamas.'

I silently agreed; it was impossible to equate him with one of those Travel Association carefree holiday advertisements – all teeth, sun glasses and suntan. I probed deeper, but went about it circuitously. 'What were you doing before you met him?'

She blew out a plume of smoke. 'Nothing much; I worked at a small college in Virginia.'

'A school teacher!' I said in surprise.

She laughed. 'No – just a secretary. My father teaches at the same college.'

'I thought you didn't look like a schoolmarm. What does your father teach? Archeology?'

'He teaches history. Don't imagine I spent *all* my time in the Bahamas. It was a very short episode – you can't afford more on a secretary's salary. I saved up for that vacation for a long time.'

I said, 'When you met Paul – was that before or after he'd started on this Vivero research?'

'It was before – I was with him when he found the Vivero letter.'

'You were married then?'

'We were on our honeymoon,' she said lightly. 'It was a working honeymoon for Paul, though.'

'Has he taught you much about archeology?'

She shrugged. 'He's not a very good teacher, but I've picked up quite a lot. I've tried to help him in his work – I think a wife should help her husband.'

'What do you think of this Vivero thing – the whole caper?'

She was silent for a time, then said frankly, 'I don't like it, Jemmy. I don't like anything about it. It's become an obsession with Paul – and not only him. Look at Fallon. My God, take a good look at yourself!'

'What about me?'

She threw her cigarette away half-smoked. 'Don't you think it's ridiculous that you should have been jerked out of a peaceful life in England and dumped in this wilderness just because of what a Spaniard wrote four hundred years ago? Too many lives are being twisted, Jemmy.'

I said carefully, 'I wouldn't say I'm obsessional about it. I don't give a damn about Vivero or Uaxuanoc. My motives are different. But you say that Paul is obsessed by it. How does his obsession take him?'

She plucked nervously at the towel in her lap. 'You've seen him. He can think or talk of nothing else. It's changed him; he's not the man I knew when we were married. And he's not only fighting Quintana Roo – he's fighting Fallon.'

I said shortly, 'If it weren't for Fallon he wouldn't be here now.'

'And that's a part of what he's fighting,' she said passionately. 'How can he compete with Fallon's reputation, with Fallon's money and resources? It's driving him crazy.'

'I wasn't aware that this was any kind of competition. Do you think Fallon will deny him any credit that's due to him?'

'He did before – why shouldn't he do it again? It's really Fallon's fault that Paul is in such a bad state.'

I sighed. Pat Harris was dead right. Katherine didn't know about Halstead's bad reputation in the trade. The advertising boys had got it down pat – *even her best friend wouldn't tell her!* I debated for a moment whether or not to tell her all about Pat Harris's investigations, but to tell a woman that her husband was a liar and a faker was certainly not the best way of making friends and influencing people. She would become more than annoyed and would probably tell Halstead – and what Halstead would do in his present frame of mind might be highly dangerous.

I said. 'Now, look, Katherine: if Paul has an obsession it has nothing to do with Fallon. I think Fallon is eminently fair, and will give Paul all the credit that's coming to him. That's just my own personal opinion, mind you.'

'You don't know what that man has done to Paul,' she said sombrely.

'Maybe he had it coming to him,' I said brutally. 'He doesn't make it easy for anyone working with him. I'm not too happy about his attitude to me, and if he keeps it up he's going to get a thick ear.'

'That's an unfair thing to say,' she burst out.

'What the hell's unfair about it? You asked to come on this jaunt on the grounds that you could control him. Well, you just do that, or I'll do a bit of controlling in my own way.'

She scrambled to her feet. 'You're against him, too. You're siding with Fallon.'

'I'm not siding with anyone,' I said tiredly. 'I'm just sick to death of seeing a piece of scientific research being treated as though it were a competitive sporting event – or a war. And I might tell you that *that* attitude is one sided – it doesn't come from Fallon.'

'It doesn't have to,' she said viciously. 'He's on top.'

'On top of what, for God's sake? Both Fallon and Paul are here doing a job of work, and why Paul doesn't get on with it and await the outcome is beyond me.'

'Because Fallon will . . .' She stopped. 'Oh, what's the use of talking? You wouldn't understand.'

'That's right,' I said sarcastically. 'I'm so dumb and stupid I can't put two and two together. Don't be so bloody patronizing.'

It's said that some women appear more beautiful when angry, but for my money it's a myth probably bruited about by constitutionally angry women. Katherine was in a rage and she looked ugly. With one quick movement she brought up her hand and slapped me – hard. She must have played a lot of tennis in her time because that forehand swing of hers really jolted me.

I just looked at her. 'Of course that solves a lot of problems.' I said quietly, 'Katherine, I admire loyalty in a wife, but you're not just loyal – you've been brainwashed.'

There was a sudden throb in the air and then a roar as the helicopter appeared over the trees and passed overhead. I looked up and saw Paul Halstead's head twist around to watch us.

SEVEN

Every three days a big helicopter came in from Camp One bringing drums of fuel for the diesel generators and cylinders of gas for the camp kitchen as and when necessary. It also brought in the mail which had been flown from Mexico City by Fallon's jet, so I could keep in touch with England. Mount wrote to me telling me that probate was going through without much difficulty, and Jack Edgecombe had taken fire at last and was enthusiastic about the new plan for the farm. He was going ahead in spite of acid comments from the locals and was sure we were on to a good thing.

Reading those letters from Devon while in that stinking hot clearing in the middle of Quintana Roo made me home-sick and I debated once again whether or not to quit. This business had got nothing to do with me and I was feeling more on the outside than ever because there was a distinct coolness now between Katherine and myself.

On the day of the quarrel there had been raised voices from the Halsteads' hut quite late into the night and, when Katherine appeared next morning, she wore a shirt with a high collar. It wasn't quite high enough to hide the bruise on the side of her throat and I felt an odd tension in the pit of my stomach. But how a man and his wife conducted their marriage had nothing to do with me, so I left it at that.

Katherine, for her part, pointedly ignored me, but Halstead didn't change at all – he just went on his usual bastardly way.

I was just on the point of quitting when Fallon showed me a letter from Pat Harris who had news of Gatt. *'Jack is making the rounds of Yucatan'* he wrote. *He has been to Merida, Valladolid and Vigio Chico, and is now in Felipe Carillo Puerto. He seems to be looking for something or someone – my guess is someone, because he's talking to some of the weirdest characters. Since Jack prefers to spend his vacations in Miami and Las Vegas I think this is a business trip – but it sure is funny business. It's not like him to sweat when there is no need, so whatever he is doing must be important.'*

'Felipe Carillo Puerto used to be called Chan Santa Cruz,' said Fallon. 'It was the heart of the Mayan revolt, the capital of the indios sublevados. The Mexicans changed the name of the town when they got on top of the rebels in 1935. It's not very far from here – less than fifty miles.'

'It's obvious that Gatt's up to something,' I said.

'Yes,' agreed Fallon pensively. 'But what? I can't understand the man's motives.'

'I can,' I said, and laid it all out for Fallon's inspection – gold, gold, and again gold. 'Whether or not there is any gold doesn't matter as long as Gatt thinks there is.' I had another thought. 'You once showed me a plate of Mayan manufacture. How much would the gold in that be worth?'

'Not much,' he said derisively. 'Maybe fifty or sixty dollars.'

'How much would the plate be worth at auction?'

'That's hard to say. Most of those things are in museums and don't come on the open market. Besides, the Mexican Government is very strict on the export of Mayan antiquities.'

'Make a guess?' I urged.

He looked irritated, and said, 'These things are priceless – no one has ever tried to put a price on them. Any unique work of art is worth what someone is willing to pay.'

'How much did you pay for that plate?'

'Nothing – I found it.'

'How much would you sell it for?'

'I wouldn't,' he said definitely.

It was my turn to get exasperated. 'For God's sake! How much would you be willing to pay for that plate if you didn't have it already? You're a rich man and a collector.'

He shrugged. 'Maybe I'd go up to $20,000 – maybe more, if pushed.'

'That's good enough for Gatt, even if he is clued up on the gold fallacy – which I don't think he is. Would you expect to find any similar objects in Uaxuanoc?'

'It's likely,' said Fallon. He frowned. 'I think I'd better have a word with Joe Rudetsky about this.'

'How are things coming along?' I asked.

'We can't get anything more out of the air survey,' he said. 'Now we've got to get down on the ground.' He pointed to the photo-mosaic. 'We've cut down the probables to four.' He looked up. 'Ah, here's Paul.'

Halstead came into the hut, the usual glower on his face. He dumped two belts on the table, complete with scabbarded machetes. 'These are what we'll need now,' he said. His tone implied – *I told you so!*

'I was just talking about that,' said Fallon. 'Will you ask Rider to come in?'

'Am I a messenger boy now?' asked Halstead sourly.

Fallon's eyes narrowed. I said quickly, 'I'll get him.' It wasn't to anyone's advantage to bring things to a boil, and *I* was quite willing to be a messenger boy – there are less dignified professions.

I found Rider doing a polishing job on his beloved chopper. 'Fallon's calling a conference,' I said. 'You're wanted.'

He gave a final swipe with a polishing rag. 'Right away.' As he walked with me to the hut, he asked, 'What's with that guy, Halstead?'

'What do you mean?'

'He's been trying to order me around; so I told him I work for Mr Fallon. He got quite sassy about it.'

'He's just like that,' I said. 'I wouldn't worry about it.'

'I'm not worried about it,' said Rider with elaborate unconcern. 'But he'd better worry. He's liable to get a busted jaw.'

I put my hand on Rider's arm. 'Not so fast – you wait your turn.'

He grinned. 'So it's like that? Okay, Mr Wheale; I'll fall in line right behind you. But don't wait too long.'

When Rider and I walked into the hut there seemed to be some tension between Fallon and Halstead. I thought that maybe Fallon had been tearing into Halstead for his unco-operative attitude – he wasn't the man to mince his words – and Halstead looked even more bloody-minded than ever. But he kept his mouth shut as Fallon said shortly, 'Let's get to the next step.'

I leaned against the table. 'Which do you tackle first?'

'That's obvious,' said Fallon. 'We have four possibles, but there's only one at which we can put down the helicopter. That's the one we explore first.'

'How do you get to the others?'

'We winch a man down,' said Fallon. 'I've done it before.'

So he might have, but he wasn't getting any younger. 'I'll give that a go,' I offered.

Halstead snorted. 'With what object in mind?' he demanded. 'What do *you* think you could do when you got on the ground? This needs a man with eyes in his head.'

Regardless of the unpleasant way in which he phrased it, Halstead was probably right. I had already seen how difficult it was to spot a Mayan ruin which Fallon had seen casually, and I could certainly miss something which might prove of the utmost importance.

Fallon made a quick gesture with his hand. 'I'll go down – or Paul will. Probably both of us.'

Rider said hesitantly, 'What about Number Two – that one's real tricky?'

'We'll consider that if and when it's necessary,' said Fallon. 'We'll save it until the last. When will you be ready to leave?'

'I'm ready now, Mr Fallon.'

'Let's go, then. Come on, Paul.'

Fallon and Rider walked out and I was about to follow when Halstead said. 'Just a minute, Wheale; I want to talk to you.'

I turned. There was something in his voice that made my short hairs prickly. He was buckling a belt around his middle and adjusting the machete at his side. 'What is it?'

'Just this,' he said in a strained voice. 'Stay away from my wife.'

'What the hell do you mean by that?'

'Exactly what I said. You've been hanging around her like a dog around a bitch in heat. Don't think I haven't seen you.' His deeply sunken eyes looked manic and his hands were trembling slightly.

I said, 'The choice of phrase was yours – you called her a bitch, not me.' His hand clutched convulsively at the hilt of the machete, and I said sharply, 'Now just listen to me. I haven't touched Katherine, nor do I intend to – nor would she let me if I tried. All that's gone on between us is all that goes on between reasonable people in our position, and that's conversation of varying degrees of friendliness. And I must say we're not too friendly right at this minute.'

'Don't try to pull that on me,' he said savagely. 'What were you doing with her down at the pool three days ago?'

'If you want to know, we were having a flaming row,' I said. 'But why don't you ask her?' He was silent at that, and looked at me hard. 'But, of course, you did ask her, didn't you? You asked her with your fist. Why don't you try asking me that way, Halstead? With your fists or with that oversized carving knife you have there? But watch it – you can get hurt.'

For a moment I thought he was going to pull the machete and cleave my skull, and my fingers closed around one of the stones that Fallon used to weigh the maps on the table. At last he expelled his breath in a whistling sound and he thrust home the machete into its sheath the half inch he had withdrawn it. 'Just stay away from her,' he said hoarsely. 'That's all.'

He shouldered past me and left the hut to disappear into the blinding sunlight outside. Then came the sudden rhythmical roar from the chopper and it took off, and the sound faded quickly as it went over the trees, just as it always did.

I leaned against the table and felt the sweat break out on my forehead and at the back of my neck. I looked at my hands. They were trembling uncontrollably, and when I turned them over I saw the palms were wet. What the flaming hell was I doing in a set-up like this? And what had possessed me to push at Halstead so hard? The man was obviously a little loose in the brainbox and he could very well have cut me down with that damned machete. I had a sudden feeling that this whole operation was sending me as crazy as he obviously was.

I pushed myself away from the table and walked outside. There was no one to be seen. I strode over to the Halsteads' hut and knocked on the door. There was no reply, so I knocked again, and Katherine called, 'Who is it?'

'Who were you expecting? It's Jemmy, damn it!'

'I don't want to talk to you.'

'You don't have to,' I said. 'All you have to do is listen. Open the door.'

There was a long pause and then a click as the door opened not too widely. She didn't look very well and there were dark smudges below her eyes. I leaned on the door and swung it open wider. 'You said you could control your husband,' I said. 'You'd better start hauling on the reins because he seems to think that you and I are having a passionate affair.'

'I know,' she said tonelessly.

I nodded. 'You know, of course. I wonder how he could have got that impression? You couldn't have led him on a bit – some women do.'

She flared. 'That's a despicable thing to say.'

'Very likely it is; I'm not feeling too spicable right now. That nutty husband of yours and I nearly had a fight not five minutes ago.'

She looked alarmed. 'Where is he?'

'Where do you think he is? He's gone with Fallon in the chopper. Look, Katherine; I'm not too sure that Paul shouldn't pull out of this expedition.'

'Oh, no,' she said quickly. 'You couldn't do that.'

'I could – and I will – if he doesn't bloody well behave himself. Even Rider is threatening to hammer him. You know that he is only here because of my say-so; that I forced him down Fallon's throat. One word from me and Fallon will be only too glad to get rid of him.'

She grabbed my hand. 'Oh, please, Jemmy; please don't do that.'

'Get up off your knees,' I said. 'Why the hell should you have to plead for him? I told you a long time ago, back in England, that you can't apologize for another person – not even your husband.' She was looking very blue, so I said, 'All right, I won't push him out – but see that he stays off my neck.'

'I'll try,' she said. 'I really will try. Thanks, Jemmy.'

I blew out my cheeks. 'If I'm accused of it, and if I'm going to get into a fight because of it, this passionate affair might not be such a bad idea. At least I'll get myself half-killed because of something I did.'

She stiffened. 'I don't think that's funny.'

'Neither do I,' I said wearily. 'With me the girl has to be willing – and you're not exactly panting hotly down the back of my neck. Forget it. Consider I made a pass and got slapped down. But Katherine, how you stand that character, I don't know.'

'Maybe it's something you wouldn't understand.'

'Love?' I shrugged. 'Or is it misplaced loyalty? But if I were a woman – and thank God I'm not – and a man hit me, I'd walk right out on him.'

Pink spots showed in her cheeks. 'I don't know what you mean.'

I lifted a finger and smoothed down her collar. 'I suppose you got that bruise walking into a door.'

She said hotly, 'How I get my bruises is none of your damned business.'

The door slammed in my face.

I contemplated the sun-seared woodwork for quite a while, then sighed and turned away. I went back to the big hut and opened the refrigerator and looked at the serried rows of beer cans, all nicely frosted. Then I slammed it shut and went into Fallon's hut where I confiscated a bottle of his best Glenlivet whisky. I needed something stronger than beer right then.

An hour later I heard the chopper coming back. It landed and taxied into the hangar and out of the sun and, from where I was sitting, I could see Rider refuelling and I heard the rhythmic clank of the hand pump. I suppose I should have gone to help him but I didn't feel like helping anyone, and after three stiff whiskies the idea of going into the sun struck me as being definitely unwise.

Presently Rider came into the hut. 'Hot!' he said, stating the obvious.

I looked up at him. 'Where are the brains?'

'I dropped them at the site. I'll go back in four hours to pick them up.' He sat down and I pushed the whisky bottle at him. He shook his head. 'Uh-uh – that's too strong for this time of day. I'll get me a cold beer.'

He stood up, got his beer, and came back to the table. 'Where's Mrs Halstead?'

'Sulking in her tent.'

He frowned at that, but his brow cleared as he drank his beer. 'Ah, that's good!' he sat down. 'Say, what happened between you and Halstead? When he climbed into the chopper he looked as though someone had rammed a pineapple up his ass.'

'Let's say we had a slight altercation.'

'Oh!' He pulled a pack of cards from his shirt pocket and riffled them. 'What about a game to pass the time?'

'What would you suggest?' I enquired acidly. 'Happy Families!'

He grinned. 'Can you play gin?'

He beat the pants off me.

II

There was nothing at the site. Fallon came back looking tired and drawn and I thought that his years were catching up with him. The forest of Quintana Roo was no place for a man in his sixties, or even for a man in his thirties as I had recently discovered. I had taken a machete and done a bit of exploring and I hadn't left the clearing for more than ten minutes before I was totally lost. It was only because I had the sense to take a compass and to make slash marks on trees that I managed to get back.

I gave him a glass of his own whisky which he accepted with appreciation. His clothes were torn and blood caked cuts in his hands. I said, 'I'll get the first-aid kit and clean that up for you.'

He nodded tiredly. As I cleaned the scratches, I said, 'You ought to leave the dirty work to Halstead.'

'He works hard enough,' said Fallon. 'He's done more than me today.'

'Where is he?'

'Getting cleaned up. I suppose Katherine is doing the same to him as you've done to me.' He flexed his fingers against the adhesive dressings. 'It's better when a woman does it, somehow. I remember my wife bandaging me up quite often.'

'I didn't know you are married.'

'I was. Very happily married. That was many years ago.' He opened his eyes. 'What happened between you and Halstead this morning?'

'A difference of opinion.'

'It often happens with that young man, but it's usually of a professional nature. This wasn't, was it?'

'No, it wasn't,' I said. 'It was personal and private.'

He caught the implication – that I was warning him off – and chose to ignore it. 'For anyone to interfere between man and wife is very serious,' he said.

I drove the cork into the bottle of antiseptic. 'I'm not interfering; Halstead just thinks I am.'

'I have your word for that?'

'You have my word – not that it's any business of yours,' I said. As soon as I had said it I was sorry. 'It is your business, of course; you don't want this expedition wrecked.'

'That wasn't in my mind,' he said. 'At least, not as far as you are concerned. But I am becoming perturbed about Paul; he is proving very awkward to work with. I was wondering if I could ask you to release me from my promise. It's entirely up to you.'

I pounded at the cork again. I had just promised Katherine that I wouldn't get Halstead tossed out on his ear, and I couldn't go back on that. 'No,' I said. 'Other promises have been made.'

'I understand,' said Fallon. 'Or, at least, I think I do.' He looked up at me. 'Don't make a fool of yourself, Jemmy.'

That piece of advice was coming a bit too late. I grinned and put down the antiseptic bottle. 'It's all right; I'm not a home wrecker. But Halstead had better watch himself or he'll be in trouble.'

'Pour me another whisky,' said Fallon. He picked up the antiseptic bottle, and said mildly, 'We're going to have trouble getting that cork out again.'

The Halsteads had another quarrel that night. Neither of them appeared for supper and, after dark, I listened to the raised voices coming from their hut, rising and falling but never distinguishable enough to make sense. Just raw anger coming from the darkness.

I half expected Halstead to stomp over to my hut and challenge me to a duel, but he didn't and I thought that maybe Katherine must have argued him out of it. More probably, the argument I had put up had a lot of weight behind it. Halstead couldn't afford to be ejected from the expedition at this stage. It might be a good idea to pass on Fallon's attitude to Katherine just to make sure that Halstead realized that I was the only person who could prevent it.

As I went to sleep it occurred to me that if we did find Uaxuanoc I'd better start guarding my back.

III

Four days later there was only one site to be investigated. Fourteen out of the fifteen in Fallon's original list had proved to be barren; if this last one proved a bust then we would have to extend our radius of exploration and take in another forty-seven sites. That would be a bind, to say the least of it.

We had an early-morning conference before the last site was checked and nobody was happy about it. The cenote lay below a ridge which was thickly covered in trees and Rider was worried about the problem of getting in while coping with air currents. Worse still, there was no possible place for a man to drop from the winch; the vegetation was thick and extended right to the edge of the cenote without thinning in any way.

Fallon studied the photographs and said despondently, 'This is the worst I've seen anywhere. I don't think there's a chance of getting in from the air. What do you think, Rider?'

'I can drop a man,' said Rider. 'But he'd probably break his neck. Those trees are running to 140 feet and tangled to hell. I don't think a man could reach the ground.'

'The forest primeval,' I commented.

'No,' contradicted Fallon. 'If it were, our work would be easier. All this ground has been cultivated at one time – all over Quintana Roo. What we have here is a second growth; that's why it's so goddamn thick.' He switched off the projector and walked over to the photo-mosaic. 'It's very thick for a long way around this cenote – which is archeologically promising but doesn't help us in getting in.' He laid his finger on the photograph. 'Could you put us down there, Rider?'

Rider inspected the point Fallon indicated, first with the naked eye and then through a magnifying glass. 'It's possible,' he said.

Fallon applied a ruler. 'Three miles from the cenote. In that stuff we couldn't do more than half a mile an hour – probably much less. Say a full day to get to the cenote. Well, if it must be done, we'll do it.' He didn't sound at all enthusiastic.

Halstead said, 'We can use Wheale now. Are you good with a machete, Wheale?' He just couldn't get out of the habit of needling me.

'I don't have to be good,' I said. 'I use my brains instead. Let me have another look at those photographs.'

Fallon switched on the projector and we ran through them again. I stopped at the best one which showed a very clear view of the cenote and the surrounding forest. 'Can you get down over the water?' I asked Rider.

'I guess I could,' said Rider. 'But not for long. It's goddamn close to that hillside at the back of the pool.'

I turned to Fallon. 'How did you make this clearing we have here?'

'We dropped a team in with power saws and flame-throwers,' he said. 'They burned away the ground vegetation and cut down the trees – then blasted out the stumps with gelignite.'

I stared at the photograph and estimated the height from water-level to the edge of the pit of the cenote. It appeared to be about thirty feet. I said, 'If Rider can drop me in the water, I can swim to the edge and climb out.'

'So what?' said Halstead. 'What do you do then? Twiddle your thumbs?'

'Then Rider comes in again and lowers a chain saw and a flame-thrower on the end of the winch.'

Rider shook his head violently. 'I couldn't get them anywhere near you. Those trees on the edge are too tall. Jesus, if I get the winch cable tangled in those I'd crash for sure.'

'Supposing when I went into the water I had a thin nylon cord, say about a couple of hundred yards, with one end tied to the winch cable. I pay it out as I swim to the side, then you haul up the cable and I pay out some more. Then you take up the chopper, high enough to be out of trouble, and I pay out even more line. When you come down again over the cenote with the stuff dangling on the end of the cable, I just haul it in to the side. Is that possible?'

Rider looked even more worried. 'Hauling a heavy weight to one side like that is going to have a hell of an effect on stability.' He rubbed his chin. 'I reckon I could do it though.'

'What would you reckon to do once you got down?' asked Fallon.

'If Rider will tell me how much clear ground he needs to land the chopper. I'll guarantee to clear it. There might be a few stumps, but he'll be landing vertically, so they shouldn't worry him too much. I'll do it – unless someone else wants to volunteer. What about you, Dr Halstead?'

'Not me,' he said promptly. He looked a bit shamefaced for the first time since I'd met him. 'I can't swim.'

'Then I'm elected,' I said cheerfully, although why I was cheerful is hard to say. I think it was the chance of actually doing something towards the work of the expedition that did it. I was tired of being a spare part.

I checked on the operation of the saw and the flame-thrower and saw they were fully fuelled. The flame-thrower produced a satisfactory gout of smoky flame which shrivelled the undergrowth very nicely. 'I'm not likely to start a forest fire, am I?' I asked.

'Not a chance,' said Fallon. 'You're in a rain forest and these aren't northern conifers.'

Halstead was coming with me. There was so much weight to be put into the helicopter that there could be only two passengers, and since it was going to be a job for a strongish man to attach the gear to the winch cable and get it out of the helicopter Halstead was chosen in preference to Fallon.

But I wasn't too happy about it. I said to Rider, 'I know you'll be busy jockeying this chopper at the critical moment, but I'd be obliged if you'd keep half an eye on Halstead.'

He caught the implication without half trying. 'I operate the winch. You'll get down safely.'

We took off and were over the site within a very few minutes. I waggled my hand in a circle to Rider and he orbited the cenote at a safe height while I studied the situation. It's one thing to look at photographs on solid ground, and quite another to look at the real thing with the prospect of dangling over it on the end of a line within the next five minutes.

At last I was satisfied that I knew where to aim for once I was in the water. I checked the nylon cord which was the hope of the whole operation and stepped into the canvas loops at the end of the cable. Rider brought the helicopter lower, and I went cautiously through the open door and was only supported by the cable itself.

The last thing I saw of Rider was his hand pulling on a lever and then I was dropping away below the helicopter and spinning like a teetotum. Every time I made a circuit I saw the green hillside behind the cenote coming closer until it was too damned close altogether and I thought the blades of the rotor were going to chop into projecting branches.

I was now a long way below the helicopter, as far as the winch cable would unreel, and my rate of spin was slowing. Rider brought the chopper down gently into the chimney formed by the surrounding trees and I touched the water. I hammered the quick-release button and the harness fell away and I found myself swimming. I trod water and organized the nylon cord, then struck out for the edge of the cenote, paying out the cord behind me, until I grasped a tree root at water-level.

The sides of the cenote were steeper than I had thought and covered with a tangle of creeper. I don't know how long it took me to climb the thirty feet to the top but it was much longer than I had originally estimated and must have seemed a lifetime to Rider, who had a very delicate bit of flying to do. But I made it at last, bleeding from a score of cuts on my arms and chest, yet still holding on to that precious cord.

I waved to Rider and the helicopter began to inch upwards, and slowly the cable was reeled in. I paid out the cord, and when the helicopter was hovering at a safe height, five hundred feet of cord hung down in a graceful catenary curve. While Halstead was no doubt struggling to get the load on to the end of the winch cable I got my breath back and prepared for my own struggle.

It was not going to be an easy task to haul over a hundred pounds of equipment sixty feet sideways. I took off the canvas belt that was wrapped around my middle and put it about a young tree. It was fitted with a snap hook with a quick release in case of emergencies. There was very little room to move on the edge of the cenote because of the vegetation – there was one tree that must have been ninety feet high whose roots were exposed right on the rim. I took the machete and swung at the undergrowth, clearing space to move in.

There was a change in the note of the chopper's engine, the pre-arranged signal that Rider was ready for the next stage of the operation, and slowly it began to descend again with the bulk of the cargo hanging below on the winch cable. Hastily I began to reel in the cord hand over hand until the shapeless bundle at the end of the winch cable was level with me, but sixty feet away and hanging thirty feet above the water of the cenote.

I wrapped three turns of the cord around the tree to serve as a friction brake and then began to haul in. At first it came easily but the nearer it got the harder it was to pull it in. Rider came lower as I pulled which made it a bit easier, but it was still back-breaking. Once the chopper wobbled alarmingly in the air, but Rider got it under control again and I continued hauling.

I was very glad when I was able to lean over and snap the hook of the canvas belt on to the end of the winch cable.

A blow at the quick-release button let the cargo fall heavily to the ground. I looked up at the chopper and released the cable, which swung in a wide arc right across the cenote. For a moment I thought it was going to entangle in the trees on the other side, but Rider was already reeling it in fast and the chopper was going up like an express lift. It stopped at a safe height, then orbited three times before leaving in the direction of Camp Two.

I sat on the edge of the cenote with my feet dangling over the side for nearly fifteen minutes before I did anything else. I was all aches and pains and felt as though I'd been in a wrestling match with a bear. At last I began to unwrap the gear. I put on the shirt and trousers that had been packed, and also the calf-length boots, then lit a cigarette before I went exploring.

At first I chopped around with the machete because the tank of the flame-thrower didn't hold too much fuel and the thing itself was bloody wasteful, so I wanted to save the fire for the worst of the undergrowth. As I chopped my way through that tangle of leaves I wondered how the hell Fallon had expected to travel half a mile in an hour; the way I was going I couldn't do two hundred yards an hour. Fortunately I didn't have to. All I had to do was to clear an area big enough for the helicopter to drop into.

I was flailing away with the machete when the blade hit something with a hell of a clang and the shock jolted up my arm. I looked at the edge and saw it had blunted and I wondered what the devil I'd hit. I swung again, more cautiously, clearing away the broad-bladed leaves, and suddenly I saw a face staring at me – a broad, Indian face with a big nose and slightly crossed eyes.

Half an hour's energetic work revealed a pillar into which was incorporated a statue of sorts of a man elaborately dressed in a long belted tunic and with a complicated head-dress. The rest of the pillar was intricately carved with a design of leaves and what looked like over-sized insects.

I lit a cigarette and contemplated it for a long time. It began to appear that perhaps we had found Uaxuanoc, although being a layman I couldn't be certain. However, no one would carve a thing like that just to leave it lying about in the forest. It was a pity in a way, because now I'd have to go somewhere else to carve my helicopter platform – the chopper certainly couldn't land on top of this cross-eyed character who stood about eight feet tall.

I went back to the edge of the cenote and started to carve a new path delimiting the area I wanted to clear, and a few random forays disclosed no more pillars, so I got busy. As I expected, the flame-thrower ran out of juice long before I had finished but at least I had used it to the best advantage to leave the minimum of machete work. Then I got going with the chain saw, cutting as close to the ground as I could, and there was a shriek as the teeth bit into the wood.

None of the trees were particularly thick through the trunk, the biggest being about two and a half feet. But they were tall and I had trouble there. I was no lumberjack and I made mistakes – the first tree nearly knocked me into the cenote as it fell, and it fell the wrong way, making a hell of a tangle that I had to clean up laboriously. But I learned and by the time darkness came I had felled sixteen trees.

I slept that night in a sleeping-bag which stank disgustingly of petrol because the chain saw around which it had been wrapped had developed a small leak. I didn't mind because I thought the smell might keep the mosquitoes away. It didn't.

I ate tinned cold chicken and drank whisky from the flask Fallon had thoughtfully provided, diluting it with warmish water from a water-bottle, and I sat there in the darkness thinking of the little brown people with big noses who had carved that big pillar and who had possibly built a city on this spot. After a while I fell asleep.

*   *   *

Morning brought the helicopter buzzing overhead and a man dangling like a spider from the cable winch. I still hadn't cleared up enough for it to land but there was enough manoeuvring space for Rider to drop a man by winch, and the man proved to be Halstead. He dropped heavily to the ground at the edge of the cenote and waved Rider away. The helicopter rose and slowly circled.

Halstead came over to me and then looked around. 'This isn't where you'd intended to clear the ground. Why the change?'

'I ran into difficulties,' I said.

He grinned humourlessly. 'I thought you might.' He looked at the tree stumps. 'You haven't got on very well, have you? You should have done better than this.'

I waved my arm gracefully. 'I bow to superior knowledge. Be my guest – go right ahead and improve the situation.'

He grunted but didn't take me up on the offer. Instead he unslung the long box he carried on his shoulder, and extended an antenna. 'We had a couple of walkie-talkies sent up from Camp One. We can talk to Rider. What do we need to finish the job?'

'Juice for the saw and the flamer; dynamite for the stumps – and a man to use it, unless you have the experience. I've never used explosives in my life.'

'I can use it,' he said curtly, and started to talk to Rider. In a few minutes the chopper was low overhead again and a couple of jerrycans of fuel were lowered to us. Then it buzzed off and we got to work.

To give Halstead his due, he worked like a demon. Two pairs of hands made a difference, too, and we'd done quite a lot before the helicopter came back. This time a box of gelignite came down, and after it Fallon descended with his pockets full of detonators. He turned them over to Halstead, and looked at me with a twinkle in his eye. 'You look as though you've been dragged through a bush backwards.' He looked about him. 'You've done a good job.'

'I have something to show you,' I said and led him along the narrow path I had driven the previous day. 'I ran across Old-Cross-eyes here; he hampered the operation a bit.'

Fallon threw a fit of ecstatics and damned near clasped Cross-eyes to his bosom. 'Old Empire!' he said reverently, and ran his hands caressingly over the carved stone.

'What is it?'

'It's a stele – a Mayan date stone. In a given community they erected a stele every katun – that's a period of nearly twenty years.' He looked back along the path towards the cenote. 'There should be more of these about; they might even ring the cenote.'

He began to strip the clinging creepers away and I could see he'd be no use anywhere else. I said, 'Well, I'll leave you two to get acquainted. I'll go help Halstead blow himself up.'

'All right,' he said absently. Then he turned. 'This is a marvellous find. It will help us date the city right away.'

'The city?' I waved my hand at the benighted wilderness. 'Is *this* Uaxuanoc?'

He looked up at the pillar. 'I have no doubt about it. Stelae of this complexity are found only in cities. Yes, I think we've found Uaxuanoc.'

IV

We had a hell of a job getting Fallon away from his beloved pillar and back to Camp Two. He mooned over it like a lover who had just found his heart's desire, and filled a notebook with squiggly drawings and pages of indecipherable scribblings. Late that afternoon we practically had to carry him to the helicopter, which had landed precariously at the edge of the cenote, and during the flight back he muttered to himself all the way.

I was very tired, but after a luxurious hot bath I felt eased in body and mind, eased enough to go into the big hut and join the others instead of falling asleep. I found Fallon and Halstead hot in the pursuit of knowledge, with Katherine hovering on the edge of the argument in her usual role of Halstead-quietener.

I listened in for a time, not understanding very much of what was going on and was rather surprised to find Halstead the calmer of the two. After the outbursts of the last few weeks, I had expected him to blow his top when we actually found Uaxuanoc, but he was as cold as ice and any discussion he had with Fallon was purely intellectual. He seemed as uninterested as though he'd merely found a sixpence in the street instead of the city he'd been bursting a gut trying to find.

It was Fallon who was bubbling over with excitement. He was as effervescent as a newly opened bottle of champagne and could hardly keep still as he shoved his sketches under Halstead's nose. 'Definitely Old Empire,' he insisted. 'Look at the glyphs.'

He went into a rigmarole which seemed to be in a foreign language. I said, 'Ease up, for heaven's sake! What about letting me in on the secret?'

He stopped and looked at me in astonishment. 'But I'm telling you.'

'You'd better tell me in English.'

He leaned back in his chair and shook his head sadly. 'To explain the Mayan calendar would take me more time than I have to spare, so you'll have to take my word for a lot of this. But look here.' He pushed over a set of his squiggles which I recognized as the insects I had seen sculpted on the pillar. 'That's the date of the stele – it reads: "9 Cycles, 12 Katuns, 10 Tuns, 12 Kins, 4 Eb, 10 Yax", and that's a total of

1,386,112 days, or 3,797 years. Since the Mayan datum from which all time measurement started was 3113 B.C., then that gives us a date of 684 A.D.'

He picked up the paper. 'There's a bit more to it – the Mayas were very accurate – it was 18 days after the new moon in the first cycle of six.'

He had said all that very rapidly and I felt a bit dizzy. 'I'll take your word for it,' I said. 'Are you telling me that Uaxuanoc is nearly thirteen hundred years old?'

'That stele is,' he said positively. 'The city is older, most likely.'

'That's a long time before Vivero,' I said thoughtfully. 'Would the city have been occupied that long?'

'You're confusing Old Empire with New Empire,' he said. 'The Old Empire collapsed about 800 A.D. and the cities were abandoned, but over a hundred years later there was an invasion of Toltecs – the Itzas – and some of the cities were rehabilitated like Chichen Itza and a few others. Uaxuanoc was one of them, very likely.' He smiled. 'Vivero referred often to the Temple of Kukulkan in Uaxuanoc. We have reason to believe that Kukulkan was a genuine historical personage; the man who led the Toltecs into Yucatan, very much as Moses led the Children of Israel into the Promised Land. Certainly the Mayan-Toltec civilization of the New Empire bore very strong resemblances to the Aztec Empire of Mexico and was rather unlike the Mayan Old Empire. There was the prevalence of human sacrifice, for one thing. Old Vivero wasn't wrong about that.'

'So Uaxuanoc was inhabited at the time of Vivero? I mean, ignoring his letter and going by the historical evidence.'

'Oh, yes. But don't get me wrong when I talk of empires. The New Empire had broken up by the time the Spaniards arrived. There were just a lot of petty states and warring provinces which banded together into an uneasy alliance to resist the Spaniards. It may have been the Spaniards who gave the final push, but the system couldn't have lasted much longer in any case.'

Halstead had been listening with a bored look on his face. This was all old stuff to him and he was becoming restive. He said, 'When do we start on it?'

Fallon pondered. 'We'll have to have quite a big organization there on the site. It's going to take a lot of men to clear that forest.'

He was right about that. It had taken three man-days to clear enough ground for a helicopter to land, piloted by a very skilful man. To clear a hundred acres with due archeological care was going to take a small army a hell of a long time.

He said, 'I think we'll abandon this camp now and pull back to Camp One. I'll get Joe Rudetsky busy setting up Camp Three on the site. Now we can get a helicopter in it shouldn't prove too difficult. We'll need quarters for twenty men to start with, I should think. It will take at least a fortnight to get settled in.'

'Why wait until then?' asked Halstead impatiently. 'I can get a lot of work done while that's going on. The rainy season isn't far off.'

'We'll get the logistics settled first,' said Fallon sharply. 'It will save time in the long run.'

'The hell with that!' said Halstead. 'I'm going to go up there and have a look round anyway. I'll leave you to run your goddamn logistics.' He leaned forward. 'Can't you see what's waiting to be picked up there – right on the ground? Even Wheale stumbled over something important first crack out of the box, only he was too dumb to see what it was.'

'It's been there thirteen hundred years,' said Fallon. 'It will still be there in another three weeks – when we can go about the job properly.'

'Well, I'm going to do a preliminary survey,' said Halstead stubbornly.

'No, you're not,' said Fallon definitely. 'And I'll tell you why you're not. Nobody is going to take you – I'll see to that. Unless you're prepared to take a stroll through the forest.'

'Damn you!' said Halstead violently. He turned to his wife. 'You wouldn't believe me, would you? You've been hypnotized by what Wheale's been telling you. Can't you see he wants to keep it to himself; that he wants first publication?'

'I don't give a damn about first publication,' said Fallon energetically. 'All I want is for the job to be done properly. You don't start excavating a city in the manner of a grave-robber.'

Their voices were rising, so I said, 'Let's keep this quiet, shall we?'

Halstead swung on me, and his voice cracked. 'You keep out of this. You've been doing me enough damage as it is – crawling to my wife behind my back and turning her against me. You're all against me – the lot of you.'

'Nobody's against you,' said Fallon. 'If we were against you, you wouldn't be here at all.'

I cut in fast. 'And any more of this bloody nonsense and you'll be out right now. I don't see why we have to put up with you, so just put a sock in it and act like a human being.'

I thought he was going to hit me. His chair went over with a crash as he stood up. 'For Christ's sake!' he said furiously, and stamped out of the hut.

Katherine stood up. 'I'm sorry,' she said.

'It's not your fault,' said Fallon. He turned to me. 'Psychiatry isn't my forte, but that looks like paranoia to me. That man has a king-size persecution complex.'

'It looks very like it.'

'Again I ask you to release me from my promise,' he said.

Katherine was looking very unhappy and disturbed. I said slowly, 'I told you there had been other promises.'

'Maybe,' said Fallon. 'But Paul, being in the mood he is, could endanger all of us. This isn't a good part of the world for personal conflicts.'

I said slowly, 'Katherine, if you can get Paul to see sense and come back and apologize, then he can stay. Otherwise he's definitely out – and I mean it. That puts it entirely in your hands, you understand.'

In a small voice she said, 'I understand.'

She went out and Fallon looked at me. 'I think you're making a mistake. He's not worth it.' He pulled out his pipe and started to fill it. After a moment he said in a low voice, 'And neither is she.'

'I've not fallen for her,' I said. 'I'm just bloody sorry for her. If Halstead gets pushed out now, her life won't be worth living.'

He struck a match and looked at the flame. 'Some people can't tell the difference between love and pity,' he said obscurely.

V

We flew down to the coast and Camp One early next morning. Halstead had slept on it, but not much, because the connubial argument had gone on long into the night. But she had evidently won because he apologized. It wasn't a very convincing apology and came as haltingly as though it were torn from him by hot pincers, but I judged it politic to accept it. After all, it was the first time in my experience that he had apologized for anything, so perhaps, although it came hesitantly, it was because it was an unaccustomed exercise. Anyway, it was a victory of sorts.

We landed at Camp One, which seemed to have grown larger in our absence; there were more huts than I remembered. We were met by Joe Rudetsky who had lost some of his easy imperturbability and looked a bit harried. When Fallon asked him what was the matter, he burst into a minor tirade.

'It's these goddamn poor whites – these chiclero bastards! They're the biggest lot of thieves I've ever seen. We're losing equipment faster than we can fly it in.'

'Do you have guards set up?'

'Sure – but my boys ain't happy. You jump one of those chicleros and he takes a shot at you. They're too goddamn trigger-happy and my boys don't like it; they reckon this isn't the job they're paid for.'

Fallon looked grim. 'Get hold of Pat Harris and tell him to ship in some of his security guards – the toughest he can find.'

'Sure, Mr Fallon, I'll do that.' Rudetsky looked relieved because someone had made a decision. He said, 'I didn't know what to do about shooting back. We thought we might wreck things for you if we got into trouble with the local law.'

'There isn't much of that around here,' said Fallon. 'If anyone shoots at you, then you shoot right back.'

'Right!' said Rudetsky. 'Mr Harris said he'd be coming along today or tomorrow.'

'Did he?' said Fallon. 'I wonder why.'

'There was a droning noise in the sky and I looked up. 'That sounds like a plane. Maybe that's him.'

Rudetsky cocked his head skywards. 'No,' he said. 'That's the plane that's been flying along the coast all week – it's back and forward all the time.' He pointed. 'See – there it is.'

A small twin-engined plane came into sight over the sea and banked to turn over the airstrip. It dipped very low and howled over us with the din of small engines being driven hard. We ducked instinctively, and Rudetsky said, 'It's the first time he's done that.'

Fallon watched the plane as it climbed and turned out to sea. 'Have you any idea who it is?'

'No,' said Rudetsky. He paused. 'But I think we're going to find out. It looks as though it's coming in for a landing.'

The plane had turned again over the sea and was coming in straight and level right at the strip. It landed with a small bounce and rolled to a stop level with us, and a man climbed out and dropped to the ground. He walked towards us and, as he got nearer, I saw he was wearing tropical whites, spotlessly cleaned and pressed, and an incongruous match to the clothing worn by our little party after the weeks at Camp Two.

He approached and raised his Panama hat. 'Professor Fallon?' he enquired.

Fallon stepped forward. 'I'm Fallon.'

The man pumped his hand enthusiastically. 'Am I glad to meet you, Professor! I was in these parts and I thought I'd drop in on you. My name is Gatt – John Gatt.'

EIGHT

Gatt was a man of about fifty-five and a little overweight. He was as smooth as silk and had the politician's knack of talking a lot and saying nothing. According to him, he had long admired Professor Fallon and had regretted not being able to meet him before. He was in Mexico for the Olympic Games and had taken the opportunity of an excursion to Yucatan to visit the great Mayan cities – he had been to Uxmal, Chichen Itza and Coba – and, hearing that the great Professor Fallon was working in the area, he had naturally dropped in to pay his respects and to sit at the feet of genius. He name-dropped like mad – apparently he knew everyone of consequence in the United States – and it soon turned out that he and Fallon had mutual acquaintances.

It was all very plausible and, as he poured out his smoke-screen of words, I became fidgety for fear Fallon would be too direct with him. But Fallon was no fool and played the single-minded archeologist to perfection. He invited Gatt to stay for lunch, which invitation Gatt promptly accepted, and we were all set for a cosy chat.

As I listened to the conversation of this evidently cultured man I reflected that, but for the knowledge gained through Pat Harris, I could have been taken in completely. It was almost impossible to equate the dark world of drugs, prostitution and extortion with the pleasantry spoken Mr

John Gatt, who talked enthusiastically of the theatre and the ballet and even nicked Fallon for a thousand dollars as a contribution to a fund for underprivileged children. Fallon made out a cheque without cracking a smile – a tribute to his own acting ability but even more a compliment to the fraudulent image of Gatt.

I think it was this aura of ambivalence about Gatt that prevented me from lashing out at him there and then. After all, this was the man who had caused the death of my brother and I ought to have tackled him, but in my mind there lurked the growing feeling that a mistake had been made, that this could not be the thug who controlled a big slice of the American underworld. I ought to have known better. I ought to have remembered that Himmler loved children dearly and that a man may smile and be a villain. So I did nothing – which was a pity.

Another thing which puzzled me about Gatt and which was a major factor contributing to my indecision was that I couldn't figure out what he was after. I would have thought that his reason for 'dropping in' would be to find out if we had discovered Uaxuanoc, but he never even referred to it. The closest he got to it was when he asked Fallon, 'And what's the subject of your latest research, Professor?'

'Just cleaning up some loose ends,' said Fallon noncommittally. 'There are some discrepancies in the literature about the dating of certain structures in this area.'

'Ah, the patient spadework of science,' said Gatt unctuously. 'A never-ending task.' He dropped the subject immediately and went on to say how impressed he had been by the massive architecture of Chichen Itza. 'I have an interest in city planning and urban renewal,' he said. 'The Mayas certainly knew all about pedestrian concourses. I've never seen a finer layout.'

I discovered later that his interest in city planning and urban renewal was confined to his activities as a slum landlord and the holding up of city governments to ransom over development plans. It was one of his most profitable sidelines.

He didn't concentrate primarily on Fallon; he discussed with Halstead, in fairly knowledgeable terms, some aspects of the Pueblo Indians of New Mexico, and talked with me about England. 'I was in England recently,' he said. 'It's a great country. Which part are you from?'

'Devon,' I said shortly.

'A very beautiful place,' he said approvingly. 'I remember when I visited Plymouth I stood on the very spot from which the Pilgrim Fathers set sail so many years ago to found our country. It moved me very much.'

I thought that was a bit thick coming from a man who had started life as Giacomo Gattini. 'Yes, I rather like Plymouth myself,' I said casually, and then sank a barb into him. 'Have you ever been to Totnes?'

His eyes flickered, but he said smoothly enough, 'I've never had the pleasure.' I stared at him and he turned away and engaged Fallon in conversation again.

He left soon after lunch, and when his plane had taken off and headed north, I looked at Fallon blankly and said, 'What the devil do you make of that?'

'I don't know what to make of it,' said Fallon. 'I expected him to ask more questions than he did.'

'So did I. If we didn't know he was up to something I'd take that visit as being quite above board. Yet we know it wasn't – he must have been after *something*. But what was it? And did he get it?'

'I wish I knew,' said Fallon thoughtfully.

II

Pat Harris turned up in the jet during the afternoon and didn't seem surprised that we had had a visit from Gatt.

He merely shrugged and went off to have a private talk with Fallon, but when he came back he was ruffled and exasperated. 'What's wrong with the Old Man?' he asked.

'Nothing that I know of,' I said. 'He's just the same as always.'

'Not from where I stand,' said Pat moodily. 'I can't get him to listen to me. All he's concerned with is pushing Rudetsky. Anything I say just bounces off.'

I smiled. 'He's just made the biggest discovery of his life. He's excited, that's all; he wants to get moving fast before the rains break. What's worrying you, Pat?'

'What do *you* think?' he said, staring at me. 'Gatt worries me – that's who. He's been holed up in Merida, and he's collected the biggest crowd of cut-throats assembled in Mexico since the days of Pancho Villa. He's brought in some of his own boys from Detroit, and borrowed some from connections in Mexico City and Tampico. And he's been talking to the chicleros. In my book that means he's going into the forest – he must have the chicleros to help him there. Now you tell me – if he goes into the forest, where would he be going?'

'Camp Three,' I said. 'Uaxuanoc. But there'll be nothing there for him – just a lot of ruins.'

'Maybe,' said Pat. 'But Jack evidently thinks differently. The thing that gripes me is that I can't get Fallon to do anything about it – and it's not like him.'

'Can't you do anything yourself? What about the authorities – the police? What about pointing out that there's a big build-up of known criminals in Merida?'

Pat looked at me pityingly. 'The fix is in,' he said patiently, as though explaining something to a small child. 'The local law has been soothed.'

'Bribed!'

'For Christ's sake, grow up!' he yelled. 'These local cops aren't as upright as your London bobbies, you know. I did what I could – and you know what happened? I got tossed in the can on a phoney charge, that's what! I only got out yesterday by greasing the palm of a junior cop who hadn't been lubricated by the top brass. You can write off the law in this part of the world.'

I took a deep breath. 'Accepting all this – what the hell would you expect Fallon to do about it?'

'He has high-level connections in the government; he's well respected in certain circles and can set things going so that the local law is short-circuited. But they're personal connections and he has to do it himself. I don't swing enough weight myself – I can't reach up that high.'

'Would it do any good if I talked to him?' I asked.

Pat shrugged. 'Maybe.' He shook his head dejectedly. 'I don't know what's got into him. His judgement is usually better than this.'

So I talked to Fallon and got a fast brush-off. He was talking to Rudetsky at the time, planning the move to Camp Three, and all his attention was on that. 'If you find anything in the preliminary clean-up, don't touch it,' he warned Rudetsky. 'Just leave it and clear round it.'

'I won't mess around with any stones,' said Rudetsky reassuringly.

Fallon looked tired and thinner than ever, as though the flesh was being burned from his bones by the fire glowing within him. Every thought he had at that time was directed solely to one end – the excavation of the city of Uaxuanoc – nothing else was of the slightest importance. He listened to me impatiently and then cut me off halfway through a sentence. 'All this is Harris's job,' he said curtly. 'Leave it to him.'

'But Harris says he can't do anything about it.'

'Then he's not worth the money I'm paying him,' growled Fallon, and walked away, ignoring me, and plunged again into the welter of preparations for the move to Camp Three.

I said nothing of this to the Halsteads; there was no point in scaring anyone else to death. But I did have another conversation with Pat Harris before he left to find out what Gatt was doing. I told him of my failure to move Fallon and he smiled grimly at Fallon's comment on his worth, but let it go.

'There's one thing that puzzles me,' he said. 'How in hell did Gatt know when to pitch up here? It's funny that he arrived just as soon as you'd discovered the city.'

'Coincidence,' I suggested.

But Pat was not convinced of that. He made me tell him of everything that had been said and was as puzzled as I had been about Gatt's apparent disinterest in the very thing we knew he was after. 'Did Gatt have the chance to talk to anyone alone?' he asked.

I thought about it and shook my head. 'He was with all of us all the time. We didn't let him wander around by himself, if that's what you mean.'

'He wasn't alone with anyone – not even for a minute?' Pat persisted.

I hesitated. 'Well, before he went to his plane he shook hands all round.' I frowned. 'Halstead had lagged behind and Gatt went back to shake hands. But it wasn't for long – not even fifteen seconds.'

'Halstead, by God!' exclaimed Pat. 'Let me tell you something. You can pass along a hell of a lot of information in a simple handshake. Bear that in mind. Jemmy.'

With that cryptic remark he left, and I began to go over all the things I knew about Halstead. But it was ridiculous to suppose he had anything to do with Gatt. Ridiculous!

III

Harry Rider was a very busy man during the next few days. He flew Rudetsky and a couple of his men to Camp Three at

Uaxuanoc, dropped them and came back for equipment. Rudetsky and his team hewed a bigger landing area out of the forest, and then the big cargo-carrying helicopter could go in and things really got moving. It was like a well-planned military operation exploiting a beach-head.

It would have been a big disappointment all round if this wasn't the site of Uaxuanoc, but Fallon showed no worry. He urged Rudetsky on to greater efforts and complacently watched the helicopters fly to and fro. The cost of keeping a big helicopter in the air is something fantastic and, although I knew Fallon could afford it, I couldn't help but point it out.

Fallon drew his pipe from his mouth and laughed. 'Damn it, you're an accountant,' he said. 'Use your brains. It would cost a lot more if I didn't use those choppers. I have to pay a lot of highly skilled men a lot of money to clear that site for preliminary investigation, and I'm damned if I'm going to pay them for hacking their way through the forest to get to the site. It's cheaper this way.'

And so it was from a cost-effectiveness point of view, as I found out when I did a brief analysis. Fallon wasn't wasting his money on that score, although some people might think that the excavation of a long-dead city was a waste of money in the first place.

Four more archeologists arrived – young men chock-full of enthusiasm. For three of them this was their first experience of a big dig and they fairly worshipped at the feet of Fallon, although I noticed they all tended to walk stiff-legged around Halstead. If his notoriety had spread down to the lower ranks of the profession then he was indeed in a bad way. I'm surprised Katherine didn't see it, although she probably put it down to the general effect of his prickly character on other people. But what a hell of a thing to have to live with!

Ten days after Fallon had made the big decision we went up to Camp Three and, circling over the cenote, I looked down upon a transformed scene quite different from what I had seen when dangling on the end of that cable. There was a little village down there – the huts were laid out in neat lines and there was a landing area to one side with hangars for the aircraft. All this had been chopped out of dense forest, in just over a week; Rudetsky was evidently something of a slave driver.

We landed and, as the rotor flapped into silence, I heard the howl of power saws from near by as the assault on the forest went on. And it was hot – hotter even than Camp Two; the sun, unshielded by the cover of trees, hammered the clearing with a brazen glare. Perspiration sprang out all over my body and by the time we had reached the shelter of a hut I was dripping.

Fallon wasted no time. 'This is not a very comfortable place,' he said. 'So we might as well get on with the job as quickly as we can. Our immediate aim is to find out what we have here in broad detail. The finer points will have to wait for the years to come. I don't intend to excavate any particular buildings at this time. Our work now is to delimit the area, to identify structures and to clear the ground for our successors.'

Halstead stirred and I could see he wasn't happy about that, but he said nothing.

'Joe Rudetsky has been here for nearly two weeks,' said Fallon. 'What have you found, Joe?'

'I found eight more of those pillars with carvings,' said Rudetsky. 'I did like you said – I just cleared around them and didn't go monkeying about.' He stood up and went to the map on the wall. Most of it was blank but an area around the cenote had been inked in. 'Here they are,' he said. 'I marked them all.'

'I'll have a look at them,' said Fallon. 'Gentlemen, Mr Rudetsky is not an archeologist, but he is a skilled surveyor and he will be our cartographer.' He waved his hand.

'As the work goes on I hope this map will become filled in and cease to be terra incognita. Now, let's get on with it.'

He set up five teams, each headed by an archeologist who would direct the Work, and to each team he gave an area. He had had the Vivero map from the mirror redrawn and used it as a rough guide. Then he turned to me. 'You will be an exception, Jemmy,' he said. 'I know we aren't going for detailed exploration at this time, but I think the cenote might provide some interesting finds. The cenote is yours.' He grinned. 'I think you're very lucky to be able to splash about in cool water all day while the rest of us sweat in the heat.'

I thought it was a good idea, too, and winked at Katherine. Halstead caught that and favoured me with a stony glare. Then he turned to Fallon, and said, 'Dredging would be quicker – as Thompson did at Chichen Itza.'

'That was a long time ago,' said Fallon mildly. 'Dredging tends to destroy pottery. It would be a pity not to use the advanced diving techniques that have been developed since Thompson's day.'

This was so true archeologically that Halstead could not object further without looking a damned fool, and he said no more; but he spoke in a low tone to Katherine and shook his head violently several times. I had a good idea what he was telling her but I didn't interrupt – I'd find out soon enough.

The discussion continued for another half hour and then the meeting broke up. I went along with Rudetsky who was going to show me where the diving gear was and he led me to a hut that had been erected right on the edge of the cenote. 'I thought you'd like to be on the spot,' he said.

Half of the hut was to be my living quarters and contained a bed with mosquito netting, a table and chair and a small desk. The other half of the hut was filled with gear. I looked at it and scratched my head. 'I'd like to get that air compressor out of here,' I said. 'And all the big bottles. Can you build a shack by the side of the hut?'

'Sure: that's no trouble at all. I'll have it fixed by tomorrow.'

We went outside and I looked at the cenote. It was roughly circular and over a hundred feet in diameter. Behind it, the ridge rose sharply in almost a cliff, but easing off in steepness towards the top where Vivero had placed the Chac temple. I wondered how deep it was. 'I'd like a raft,' I said. 'From that we can drop a shot line and anchor it to the bottom – if we can get down that far. But that can wait until I've done a preliminary dive.'

'You just tell me what you want and I'll fix it,' said Rudetsky. 'That's what I'm here for – I'm Mr Fixit in person.'

He went away and I tossed a pebble into the dark pool. It plopped in the middle of the still water and sent out a widening circle of ripples which lapped briefly at the edge, thirty feet below. If what I had been told was correct, many people had been sacrificed in this cenote and I wondered what I'd find at the bottom.

I went back to the hut and found Katherine waiting for me. She was looking dubiously at the pile of equipment and seemed appalled at the size of it. 'It's not as bad as that,' I said. 'We'll soon get it sorted out. Are you ready to go to work?'

She nodded. 'I'm ready.'

'All the air bottles are full,' I said. 'I saw to that at Camp One. There's no reason why we shouldn't do a dive right now and leave the sorting until later. I wouldn't mind a dip – it's too bloody hot here.'

She unbuttoned the front of her shirt 'All right. How deep do you think it is?'

'I wouldn't know – that's what we're going to find out. What's the deepest you've ever gone?'

'About sixty-five feet.'

'This might be deeper,' I said. 'When we find out how deep I'll make out a decompression table. You stick to it and you'll be all right.' I jerked my thumb at the recompression chamber. 'I don't want to use that unless I have to.'

I tested it. Rudetsky's electricians had wired it up to the camp supply and it worked all right. I pumped it up to the test pressure of ten atmospheres and the needle held steady. It was highly unlikely that we'd ever have to use it at more than five atmospheres though.

When one is making a dive into an unknown hole in the ground you find you need an awful amount of ancillary equipment. There was the scuba gear itself – the harness, mask and flippers; a waterproof watch and compass on the left wrist – I had an idea it would be dark down there and the compass would serve for orientation: and a depth meter and a decompression meter on the right wrist. A knife went in the belt and a light mounted on the head – by the time we were through kitting ourselves out we looked like a couple of astronauts.

I checked Katherine's gear and she checked mine, then we clumped heavily down the steps Rudetsky had cut in the sheer side of the cenote and down to the water's edge. As I dipped my mask into the water, I said, 'Just follow me, and keep your light on all the time. If you get into trouble and you can't attract my attention make for the surface, but try to stay a few minutes at the ten-foot level if you can. But don't worry – I'll be keeping an eye on you.'

'I'm not worried,' she said. 'I've done this before.'

'Not in these conditions,' I said. 'This isn't like swimming in the Bahamas. Just play it safe, will you?'

'I'll stick close,' she said.

I gave the mask a final swish in the water. 'Paul didn't seem too happy about this. Why did he want to dredge?'

She sighed in exasperation. 'He still has the same stupid idea about you and me. It's ridiculous, of course.'

'Of course,' I said flatly.

She laughed unexpectedly and indicated the bulky gear we were wearing. 'Not much chance, is there?'

I grinned at the idea of underwater adultery as I put on the mask. 'Let's call on Chac,' I said, and bit on the mouthpiece. We slipped into the water and swam slowly to the middle of the cenote. The water was clear but its depth made it dark. I dipped my head under and stared below and could see nothing, so I surfaced again and asked Katherine, by sign, if she was all right. She signalled that she was, so I signed that she was to go down. She dipped below the surface and vanished and I followed her, and just before I went down I saw Halstead standing on the edge of the cenote staring at me. I could have been wrong, though, because my mask was smeared with water – but I don't think I was.

It wasn't so bad at first. The water was clear and light filtered from the surface, but as we went deeper so the light failed rapidly. I had dived often off the coast of England and it is quite light at fifty feet, but diving into a comparatively small hole is different; the sheer sides of the cenote cut off the light which would otherwise have come in at an angle and the general illumination dropped off sharply.

I stopped at fifty feet and swam in a circle, checking to see if the compass was in order. Katherine followed, her flippers kicking lazily and the stream of bubbles from her mask sparkling in the light of the lamps like the fountaining eruption of a firework. She seemed all right, so I kicked off again and went down slowly, looking behind from time to time to see if she followed.

We hit bottom at sixty-five feet, but that was at the top of a slope which dropped into darkness at an angle of about twenty degrees. The bottom consisted of a slimy ooze which stirred as I casually handled it and rose into a smokescreen of sorts. I saw Katharine's light shining through the haze dimly, and thought that this was going to make excavation difficult.

It was cold down there, too. The hot sun merely warmed the surface of the water and, since the warm water was less dense, it stayed at the top of the pool. The water at the bottom came from the pores in the limestone all about, and was never exposed to the sun. I was beginning to get chilled as it sucked the heat from my body.

I signalled to Katherine again, and cautiously we swam down the slope to find that it ended in a solid wall. That was the absolute bottom of the cenote and I checked it at ninety-five feet. We swam about for a while, exploring the slope. It was smooth and level and nothing broke its surface. The ooze of which it was composed was the accumulated detritus of hundreds of years of leaf droppings from the surface and anything that was to be found would have to be discovered by digging.

At last I signalled that we were going up, and we rose from the bottom of the slope up past the vertical wall of limestone. About thirty feet up from the bottom I discovered a sort of cave, an opening in the sheer wall. That deserved to be explored, but I didn't feel like doing it then. I was cold and wanted to soak some hot sun into my bones.

We bad been underwater for half an hour and had been down nearly a hundred feet, and so we had to decompress on the way up. That meant a five-minute wait at twenty feet, and another five-minute wait at ten feet. When we began diving in earnest we'd have the shot line to hold on to at these decompression stops, but as it was we just circled in the water while I kept an eye on the decompression meter at my wrist.

We surfaced in the welcome sun and swam to the side. I heaved myself out and gave Katherine a hand, then spat out the mouthpiece and took off the mask. As I closed down the valve on the tank, I said, 'What did you think of that?'

Katherine shivered. 'You're right; it's not like the Bahamas. I didn't think I could feel so cold in Quintana Roo.'

I took off the harness and felt the hot sun striking my back. 'It seems bloody silly, but we're going to have to wear thermal suits, otherwise we'll freeze to death. What else struck you about it?'

She pondered. 'The ooze down there is going to be bad. It's dark enough without having to work in the muck we're going to stir up.'

I nodded. 'A suction pump is going to come in useful. The pump itself can be at the surface and we'll pump the mud ashore – with a filter in the line to catch any small objects. That'll cut down on the fog down there.' Now that I'd seen the situation, ideas were beginning to come thick and fast. 'We can drop our shot line from the raft, and anchor it to the bottom with a big boulder. We're going to have to have two lines to the bottom, because one will have to be hauled up every day.'

She frowned. 'Why?'

'Come up to the hut and I'll show you.'

We arrived at the hut to find Rudetsky and a couple of his men building a lean-to shelter against one end of it 'Hi!' he said. 'Have a nice dip?'

'Not bad. I'd like that raft now if you can do it.'

'How big?'

'Say, ten feet square.'

'Nothing to it' he said promptly. 'Four empty oil drums and some of that lumber we're cutting will make a dandy raft. Will you be using it in the evenings?'

'It's not very likely,' I said.

'Then you won't mind if the boys use it as a diving raft. It's nice to have a swim and cool off nights.'

I grinned. 'It's a deal.'

He pointed to the air compressor. 'Will that be all right just there?'

'That's fine. Look, can you lead that exhaust pipe away – as far away from the intake of the air pump as possible. Carbon monoxide and diving don't go together.'

He nodded. 'I'll get another length of hose and lead it round the other side of the hut.'

I joined Katherine in the hut and dug out my tattered copy of the Admiralty diving tables. 'Now I'll tell you why we have to have two lines to the bottom,' I said. I sat down at the table and she joined me, rubbing her hair with a towel. 'We're going down about a hundred feet and we want to spend as much time as possible on the bottom. Right?'

'I suppose so.'

'Say we spend two hours on the bottom – that means several decompression stops on the way up. Five minutes at fifty feet, ten at forty feet, thirty at thirty feet, forty at twenty feet and fifty at ten feet – a total of . . . er . . . one hundred and thirty-five minutes – two and a quarter hours. It's going to be a bit of a bind just sitting around at these various levels, but it's got to be done. Besides the weighted shot rope from the raft, we'll have to have another with slings fitted at the various levels to sit in, and with air bottles attached, because your harness bottles will never hold enough. And the whole lot will have to be pulled up every day to replenish the bottles.'

'I've never done this kind of thing before,' she said. 'I've never been so deep nor stayed so long. I hadn't thought of decompression.'

'You'd better start thinking now,' I said grimly. 'One slipup and you'll get the bends. Have you ever seen that happen to anyone?'

'No, I haven't.'

'Fizzy blood doesn't do you any good. Apart from being terrifyingly painful, once a nitrogen embolism gets to the heart you're knocking at the Pearly Gates.'

'But it's so long,' she complained. 'What do you *do* sitting at ten feet for nearly an hour?'

'I haven't done this too often myself,' I confessed. 'But I've used it as an opportunity to compose dirty limericks.'

I looked across at the recompression chamber. 'I'd like to have that thing a bit nearer the scene of the accident – maybe on the raft. I'll see what Rudetsky can do.'

IV

The work went on, week after week, and I nearly forgot about Gatt. We were in radio contact with Camp One which relayed messages from Pat Harris and everything seemed to be calm. Gatt had gone back to Mexico City and was living among the fleshpots, apparently without a care in the world, although his band of thugs was still quartered in Merida. I didn't know what to make of it, but I really didn't have time to think about it because the diving programme filled all my time. I kept half an eye on Halstead and found him to be working even harder than I was, which pleased Fallon mightily.

Every day discoveries were made – astonishing discoveries. This was indeed Uaxuanoc. Fallon's teams uncovered building after building – palaces, temples, games arenas and a few unidentifiable structures, one of which he thought was an astronomical observatory. Around the cenote was a ring of stelae – twenty-four of them – and there was another line of them right through the centre of the city. With clicking camera and busy pen Fallon filled book after book with data.

Although no one was trades-union inclined, one day in every week was a rest day on which the boffins usually caught up with their paper work while Rudetsky's men skylarked about in the cenote. Because safe diving was impossible under those conditions I used the free day to rest and to drink a little more beer than was safe during the working week.

On one of those days Fallon took me over the site to show me what had been uncovered. He pointed to a low hill which had been denuded of its vegetation. 'That's where Vivero nearly met his end,' he said. 'That's the Temple of Kukulkan – you can see where we're uncovering the steps at the front.'

It was a bit hard to believe. '*All* that hill?'

'All of it. It's one big building. In fact, we're standing on a part of it right now.'

I looked down and scuffled the ground with my foot. It didn't look any different from any other ground – there was just thin layer of humus. Fallon said, 'The Mayas had a habit of building on platforms. Their huts were built on platforms to raise them from the ground, and when they built larger structures they carried on the same idea. We're standing on a platform now, but it's so big you don't realize it.'

I looked at the ground stretching levelly to the hill which was the Temple of Kukulkan. 'How big?'

Fallon grinned cheerfully. 'Rudetsky went around it with a theodolite and transit. He reckons it's fifteen acres and averages a hundred and thirty feet high. It's an artificial acropolis – 90 million cubic feet in volume and containing about six and a half million tons of material.' He produced his pipe. 'There's one something like it at Copan, but not quite as big.'

'Hell's teeth!' I said. 'I didn't realize it would be anything like this.'

Fallon struck a match. 'The Mayas . . .' puff – puff '. . . were an . . .' puff '. . . industrious crowd.' He looked into the bowl of his pipe critically. 'Come and have a closer look at the temple.'

We walked over to the hill and looked up at the partly excavated stairway. The stairs were about fifty feet wide. Fallon pointed upwards with the stem of his pipe. 'I thought I'd find something up there at the top, so I did a bit of digging, and I found it all right. You might be interested.'

Climbing the hill was a heavy pull because it was very steep. Imagine an Egyptian pyramid covered with a thin layer of earth and one gets the idea. Fallon didn't seem unduly put out by the exertion, despite his age, and at the top he pointed. 'The edge of the stairway will come there – and that's where I dug.'

I strolled over to the pit which was marked by the heap of detritus about it, and saw that Fallon had uncovered a fearsome head, open-mouthed and sharp-toothed, with the lips drawn back in a snarl of anger. 'The Feathered Serpent,' he said softly. 'The symbol of Kukulkan.' He swept his arm towards a wall of earth behind. 'And that's the temple itself – where the sacrifices were made.'

I looked at it and thought of Vivero brought before the priests on this spot, and shivering in his shoes for fear he'd have the heart plucked out of him. It was a grim thought.

Fallon said objectively, 'I hope the roof hasn't collapsed; it would be nice to find it intact.'

I sat down on a convenient tree stump and looked over the site of the city. About a fifth of it had been cleared, according to Fallon, but that was just the vegetation. There were great mounds, like the one we were on then, waiting to be excavated. I said, 'How long do you think it will take? When will we see what it was really like?'

'Come back in twenty years,' he said. 'Then you'll get a fair idea.'

'So long?'

'You can't hurry a thing like this. Besides, we won't excavate it all. We must leave something for the next generation – they might have better methods and find things that we would miss. I don't intend uncovering more than half the city.'

I looked at Fallon thoughtfully. This was a man of sixty who was quite willing to start something he knew he would never finish. Perhaps it was because he habitually thought in terms of centuries, of thousands of years, that he attained a cosmic viewpoint. He was very different from Halstead.

He said a little sadly, 'The human lifespan is so short, and man's monuments outlast him generation after generation, more enduring than man himself. Shelley knew about that, and about man's vanity. "My name is Ozymandias, king of kings: Look on my works, ye Mighty, and despair!"' He waved his hand at the city. 'But do we despair when we see this? I know that I don't. I regard it as the glory of short-lived men.' He held out his hands before him, gnarled and blue-veined and trembling a little. 'It's a great pity that this flesh should rot so soon.'

His conversation was becoming too macabre for my taste, so I changed the subject. 'Have you identified the King's Palace yet?'

He smiled. 'Still hoping for plated walls of gold?' He shook his head. 'Vivero was mixed up, as usual. The Mayas didn't have kings, in the sense that we know them, but there was an hereditary chief among them called Halach uinic whom I suppose Vivero called king. Then there was the nacom, the war chief, who was elected for three years. The priesthood was hereditary, too. I doubt if the Halach uinic would have a palace, but we have found what we think is one of the main administrative buildings.' He pointed to another mound. 'That's it.'

It was certainly big, but disappointing. To me it was just another hill and it took a great deal of imagination to create a building in the mind's eye. Fallon said tolerantly, 'It isn't easy, I know. It takes a deal of experience to see it for what it is. But it's likely that Vivero was taken there for the judgement of the Halach uinic. He was also the chief priest but that was over Vivero's head – he hadn't read Frazer's *Golden Bough*.'

Neither had I, so I was as wise as Vivero. Fallon said. 'The next step is to get rid of these tree boles.' He kicked gently at the one on which I was sitting.

'What do you do? Blast them out?'

He looked shocked. 'My God, no! We burn them, roots and all. Fortunately the rain forest trees are shallow-rooted – you can see that much of the root system on this platform is above ground. When we've done that there is a system of tubes in the structure where the roots were, and we fill those with cement to bind the budding together. We don't want it falling down at this late stage.'

'Have you come across the thing Vivero was so excited about? The golden sign – whatever it was?'

He wagged his head doubtfully. 'No – and we may never do so. I think that Vivero – after twelve years as a captive – may have been a little bit nuts. Religious mania, you know. He could have had a hallucination.'

I said, 'Judging by today's standards any sixteenth-century Spaniard might be said to have had religious mania. To liquidate whole civilizations just because of a difference of opinion about God isn't a mark of sanity.'

Fallon cocked an eye at me. 'So you think sanity is comparative? Perhaps you're right; perhaps our present wars will be looked on, in the future, as an indication of warped minds. Certainly the prospect of an atomic war isn't a particularly sane concept.'

I thought of Vivero, unhappy and with his conscience tearing him to bits because he was too afraid to convert the heathen to Christianity. And yet he was quite prepared to counsel his sons in the best ways of killing the heathen, even though he admitted that the methods he advised weren't Christian. His attitude reminded me of Mr Puckle, the inventor of the first machine-gun, which was designed to fire round bullets at Christians and square bullets at Turks.

I said, 'Where did Vivero get the gold to make the mirrors? You said there was very little gold here.'

'I didn't say that,' contradicted Fallon. 'I said it had been accumulated over the centuries. There was probably quite a bit of gold here in one way and another, and a goldsmith can steal quite a lot over a period of twelve years. Besides, the mirrors aren't pure gold, they're tumbago – that's a mixture of gold, silver and copper, and quite a lot of copper, too. The Spaniards were always talking about the red gold of the Indies, and it was copper that gave it the colour.'

He knocked his pipe out. 'I suppose I'd better get back to Rudetsky's map and plot out next week's work schedule.' He paused. 'By the way, Rudetsky tells me that he's seen a few chicleros in the forest. I've given instructions that everyone must stay in camp and not go wandering about. That includes you.'

That brought me back to the twentieth century with a bang. I went back to camp and sent a message to Pat Harris via the radio at Camp One to inform him of this latest development. It was all I could do.

V

Fallon was a bit disappointed by my diving programme. 'Only two hours a day,' he said in disgust.

So I had to put him through a crash course of biophysics as it relates to diving. The main problem, of course, is the nitrogen. We were diving at a depth of about a hundred feet, and the absolute pressure at the depth is four atmospheres – about sixty pounds a square inch. This doesn't make any difference to breathing because the demand valve admits air to the lungs at the same pressure as the surrounding water, and so there is no danger of being crushed by the difference of pressure.

The trouble comes with the fact that with every breath you're taking four times as much of everything. The body can cope quite handily with the increase of oxygen, but the extra nitrogen is handled by being dissolved in the blood and stored in the tissues. If the pressure is brought back to normal *suddenly* the nitrogen is released quickly in the form of bubbles in the bloodstream – one's blood literally boils – a quick way to the grave.

And so one reduces the pressure slowly by coming to the surface very carefully and with many stops, all carefully calculated by Admiralty doctors, so that the stored nitrogen is released slowly and at a controlled safe rate.

'All right,' said Fallon impatiently. 'I understand that. But if you spend two hours on the bottom, and about the same time coming up, that's only half a day's work. You should be able to do a dive in the morning and another in the afternoon.'

'Not a chance,' I said. 'When you step out of the water, the body is still saturated with nitrogen at normal atmospheric pressure, and it takes at least six hours to be eliminated from the system. I'm sorry, but we can do only one dive a day.'

And he had to be satisfied with that.

The raft Rudetsky made proved a godsend. Instead of my original idea of hanging small air bottles at each decompression level, we dropped a pipe which plugged directly into the demand valve on the harness and was fed from big air bottles on the raft itself. And I explored the cave in the cenote wall at the seventy-foot level. It was quite large and shaped like an inverted sack and it occurred to me to fill it full of air and drive the water from it. A hose dropped from the air pump on the raft soon did the job, and it seemed odd to be able to take off the mask and breathe normally so deep below the surface. Of course, the air in the cave was at the same pressure as the water at that depth and so it would not help in decompression, but if either Katherine or myself got into trouble the cave could be a temporary shelter with an adequate air supply. I hung a light outside the entrance and put another inside.

Fallon stopped complaining when he saw what we began to bring up. There was an enormous amount of silt to be cleared first, but we did that with a suction pump, and the first thing I found was a skull, which gave me a gruesome feeling.

In the days that followed we sent up many objects – masks in copper and gold, cups, bells, many items of jewellery such as pendants, bracelets, rings both for finger and ear, necklace beads, and ornamental buttons of gold and jade. There were also ceremonial hatchets of flint and obsidian, wooden spear-throwers which had been protected from decay by the heavy overlay of silt, and no less than eighteen plates like that shown to me by Fallon in Mexico City.

The cream of the collection was a small statuette of gold, about six inches high, the figure of a young Mayan girl. Fallon carefully cleaned it, then stood it on his desk and regarded it with a puzzled air. 'The subject is Mayan,' he said. 'But the execution certainly isn't – they didn't work in this style. But it's a Mayan girl, all right. Look at that profile.'

Katherine picked it up. 'It's beautiful, isn't it?' She hesitated. 'Could this be the statue Vivero made which so impressed the Mayan priests?'

'Good God!' said Fallon in astonishment. 'It *could* be – but that would be a hell of a coincidence.'

'Why should it be a coincidence?' I asked, I waved my hand at the wealth of treasure stacked on the shelves. 'All these things were sacrificial objects, weren't they? The Mayas gave to Chac their most valued possessions. I don't think it unlikely that Vivero's statue could be such a sacrifice.'

Fallon examined it again. 'It *has* been cast,' he admitted. 'And that wasn't a Mayan technique. Maybe it is the work of Vivero, but it might not be the statue he wrote about. He probably made more of them.'

'I'd like to think it is the first one,' said Katherine.

I looked at the rows of gleaming objects on the shelves. 'How much is all this worth?' I asked Fallon. 'What will it bring on the open market?'

'It won't be offered,' said Fallon grimly. 'The Mexican Government has something to say about that – and so do I.'

'But assuming it did appear on the open market – or a black market. How much would this lot be worth?'

Fallon pondered. 'Were it to be smuggled out of the country and put in the hands of a disreputable dealer – a man such as Gerryson, for instance – he could dispose of it, over a period of time, for, say, a million and a half dollars.'

I caught my breath. We were not halfway through in the cenote and there was still much to be found. Every day we were finding more objects and the rate of discovery was consistently increasing as we delved deeper into the silt. By Fallon's measurement the total value of the finds in the cenote could be as much as four million dollars – maybe even five million.

I said softly, 'No wonder Gatt is interested. And you were wondering why, for God's sake!'

'I was thinking of finds in the ordinary course of excavation,' said Fallon. 'Objects of gold on the surface will have been dispersed long ago, and there'll be very little to be found. And I was thinking of Gatt as being deceived by Vivero's poppycock in his letter. I certainly didn't expect the cenote to be so fruitful.' He drummed his fingers on the desk. 'I thought of Gatt as being interested in gold for the sake of gold – an ordinary treasure hunter.' He flapped his hand at the shelves. 'The intrinsic value of the gold in that lot isn't more than fifteen to twenty thousand dollars.'

'But we know Gatt isn't like that,' I said. 'What did Harris call him? An educated hood. He isn't the kind of stupid thief who'll be likely to melt the stuff down; he knows its anti-quarian value, and he'll know how to get rid of it. Harris has already traced a link between Gatt and Gerryson, and you've just said that Gerryson can sell it unobtrusively. My advice is to get the stuff out of here and into the biggest bank vault you can find in Mexico City.'

'You're right, of course,' said Fallon shortly. 'I'll arrange it. And we must let the Mexican authorities know the extent of our discoveries here.'

VI

The season was coming to an end. The rains would soon be breaking and work on the site would be impossible. I daresay it wouldn't have made any difference to my own work in the cenote – you can't get wetter than wet – but we could see that the site would inevitably become a churned-up sea of mud if any excavations were attempted in the wet season, so Fallon reluctantly decided to pack it in.

This meant a mass evacuation back to Camp One. Rudetsky looked worriedly at all the equipment that had to be transported, but Fallon was oddly casual about it. 'Leave it here,' he said carelessly. 'We'll need it next season.'

Rudetsky fumed about it to me. 'There won't be a goddamn thing left next season,' he said passionately. 'Those chiclero vultures will clean the lot out.'

'I wouldn't worry,' I said. 'Fallon can afford to replace it.'

But it offended Rudetsky's frugal soul and he went to great lengths to cocoon the generators and pumps against the weather in the hopes that perhaps the chicleros would not loot the camp. 'I'm wasting my time,' he said gloomily as he ordered the windows of the huts to be boarded up. 'But, goddamn it, I gotta go through the motions!'

So we evacuated Uaxuanoc: The big helicopter came and went, taking with it the men who had uncovered the city. The four young archeologists went after taking their leave of Fallon. They were bubbling over with enthusiasm and promised fervently to return the following season when the real work of digging into the buildings was to begin. Fallon, the father figure, smiled upon them paternally and waved them goodbye, then went back to his work with a curiously grave expression on his face.

He was not taking any part in the work of the evacuation and refused to make decisions about anything, so Rudetsky tended to come to me for answers. I did what I thought was right, and wondered what was the matter with Fallon. He had withdrawn into the hut where the finds were lined up on the shelves and spent his time painstakingly cleaning them and making copious notes. He refused to be disturbed and neither would he allow the precious objects to be parted from him. 'They'll go when I go,' he said. 'Carry on with the rest of it and leave me alone.'

Finally the time came for us all to go. The camp was closed down but for three or four huts and all that was left would just make a nice load for the two helicopters. I was walking to Fallon's hut to announce the fact when Rudetsky came up at a dead run. 'Come to the radio shack,' he said breathlessly. 'There's something funny going on at Camp One.'

I went with him and listened to the tale of woe. They'd had a fire and the big helicopter was burned up – completely destroyed. 'Anyone hurt?' barked Rudetsky.

According to the tinny voice issuing waveringly from the loudspeaker no one had been seriously injured; a couple of minor burns was all. But the helicopter was a write-off.

Rudetsky snorted. 'How in hell did it happen?'

The voice wavered into nothingness and came back again, hardly more strongly. '. . . don't know . . . just happened . . .'

'It just happened,' said Rudetsky in disgust.

I said, 'What's the matter with that transmitter? It doesn't seem to have any power.'

'What's the matter with your transmitter?' said Rudetsky into the microphone. Turn up the juice.'

'I receive you loud and clear,' said the voice weakly. 'Can't you hear me?'

'You're damned right we can't,' said Rudetsky. 'Do something about it.'

The transmission came up a little more strongly. 'We've got everyone out of here and back to Mexico City. There are only three of us left here – but Mr Harris says there's something wrong with the jet.'

I felt a little prickling feeling at the nape of my neck, and leaned forward over Rudetsky's shoulder to say into the microphone, 'What's wrong with it?'

'. . . doesn't know . . . grounded . . . wrong registration . . . can't come until . . .' The transmission was again becoming weaker and hardly made sense. Suddenly it cut off altogether and there was not even the hiss of a carrier wave. Rudetsky fiddled with the receiver but could not raise Camp One again.

He turned to me and said, 'They're off the air completely.'

'Try to raise Mexico City,' I said.

He grimaced. 'I'll try, but I don't think there's a hope in hell. This little box don't have the power.'

He twiddled his knobs and I thought about what had happened. The big transport helicopter was destroyed, the jet was grounded in Mexico City for some mysterious reason and Camp One had gone off the air. It added up to one thing – isolation – and I didn't like it one little bit. I looked speculatively across the clearing towards the hangar where Rider was polishing up his chopper as usual. At least we had the other helicopter.

Rudetsky gave up at last. 'Nothing doing,' he said, and looked at his watch. 'That was Camp One's last transmission of the day. If they fix up their transmitter they'll be on the air again as usual at eight tomorrow morning. There's nothing we can do until then.'

He didn't seem, unduly worried, but he didn't know what I knew. He didn't know about Jack Gatt. I said, 'All right; we'll wait until then. I'll tell Fallon what's happened.'

That proved to be harder than I anticipated. He was totally wrapped up in his work, brooding over a golden plate and trying to date it while he muttered a spate of Mayan numbers. I tried to tell him what had happened but he said irritably, 'It doesn't sound much to me. They'll be on the air tomorrow with a full explanation. Now go away and don't worry me about it.'

So I went away and did a bit of brooding on my own. I thought of talking about it to Halstead but the memory of what Pat Harris had said stopped me; and I didn't say anything to Katherine because I didn't want to scare her, nor did I want her to pass anything on to her husband. At last I went to see Rider. 'Is your chopper ready for work?' I asked.

He looked surprised and a little offended. 'It's always ready,' he said shortly.

'We may need it tomorrow,' I said. 'Get ready for an early start.'

VII

That night *we* had a fire – in the radio shack!

I woke up to hear distant shouts and then the closer thudding of boots on the hard ground as someone ran by outside the hut. I got up and went to see what was happening and found Rudetsky in the shack beating out the last of the flames. I sniffed the air. 'Did you keep petrol in here?'

'No!' he grunted. 'We had visitors. A couple of those goddamn chicleros got in here before we chased them off.' He looked at the charred remains of the transmitter. 'Now why in hell would they want to do that?'

I could have told him but I didn't. It was something else to be figured into the addition which meant isolation. Has anything else been sabotaged?' I asked.

'Not that I know of,' he said.

It was an hour before dawn. 'I'm going down to Camp One,' I said. 'I want to know what's happened down there.'

Rudetsky looked at me closely. 'Expecting to find trouble?' He waved his hand. 'Like this?'

'I might be,' I admitted. 'There may be trouble here, too. Keep everyone in camp while I'm away. And don't take any backchat from Halstead; if he makes trouble you know what to do about it.'

'It'll be a pleasure,' said Rudetsky feelingly. 'I don't suppose you'd like to tell me what's really going on?'

'Ask Fallon,' I said. 'It's a long story and I have no time now. I'm going to dig out Rider.'

I had a bite to eat and then convinced Rider he had to take me to Camp One. He was a bit uncertain about it, but since Fallon had apparently abdicated all responsibility and because I was backed up by Rudetsky he eventually gave way and we were ready for takeoff just as the sun rose. Katherine came to see me off, and I leaned down and said, 'Stick close to the camp and don't move away. I'll be back before long.'

'All right,' she promised.

Halstead came into view from somewhere behind the helicopter and joined her. 'Are you speeding the hero?' he asked in his usual nasty way. He had been investigating the Temple of Yum Chac above the cenote and was chafing to really dig into it instead of merely uncovering the surface, but Fallon wouldn't let him. The finds Katherine and I had been making in the cenote had put his nose out of joint. It irked him that non-professionals were apparently scooping the pool – to make a bad pun – and he was irritable about it, even to the point of picking quarrels with his wife.

He pulled her away from the helicopter forcibly, and Rider looked at me and shrugged. 'We might as well take off,' he said. I nodded, and he fiddled with the controls and up we went.

I spoke to Rider and he merely grinned and indicated the intercom earphones, so I put them on, and said into the microphone 'Circle around the site for a bit, will you? I want to see what it looks like from the air.'

'Okay,' he said, and we cast around in a wide sweep over Uaxuanoc. It actually looked like a city from the air, at least the part that had been cleared did. I could see quite clearly the huge platform on which was built the Temple of Kukulkan and the building which Fallon referred to jocularly as 'City Hall'. And there was the outline of what seemed to be another big platform to the east along the ridge, but that had only been partially uncovered. On the hill above the cenote Halstead had really been working hard and the Temple of Yum Chac was unmistakable for what it was – not just a mound of earth, but a huge pyramid of masonry with, a pillared hall surmounting it.

We made three sweeps over the city, then I said. 'Thanks, Harry; we'd better be getting on. Do you mind keeping low – I'd like to take a closer look at the forest.'

'I don't mind, as long as you don't want to fly too low. I'll keep the speed down so you can really see.'

We headed east at a height of about three hundred feet and at not more man sixty miles an hour. The forest unreeled below, a green wilderness with the crowns of trees victorious in their fight for light spreading a hundred and sixty feet and more from the ground. Those crowns formed scattered islands against the lower mass of solid green, and nowhere was the ground to be seen.

'I'd rather fly than walk,' I said.

Harry laughed. 'I'd be scared to death down there. Did you hear those goddamn howler monkeys the other night?

It sounded as though some poor guy was having his throat cut – slowly.'

'The howlers wouldn't worry me,' I said. 'They just make a noise, nerve-racking though it is. The snakes and pumas would worry me more.'

'And the chicleros,' said Harry. 'I've been hearing some funny stories about those guys. Just as soon kill a man as spit from what I hear.' He looked down at the forest. 'Christ what a place to work in! No wonder the chicleros are tough. If I was working down there I wouldn't give a damn if I lived or died – or if anyone else did, either.'

We crossed a part of the forest that was subtly different from the rest. I said, 'What happened here?'

'I don't know,' said Harry, and sounded as puzzled as I was. 'That tree looks dead. Let's have a closer view.'

He manipulated the controls, and the chopper slowed and wheeled around the treetop. It was one of the big ones whose crown had broken free of the rest to spread luxuriantly in the upper air, but it was definitely leafless and dead, and there were other dead trees all about. 'I think I get it,' he said. 'Something has happened here, probably a tornado. The trees have been uprooted, but they're so damned close packed they can't fall, so they've just died where they are. What a hell of a place – you gotta die standing up!'

We rose and continued on course. Harry said, 'It must have been a tornado: the dead trees are in a straight line. The tornado must have cut a swathe right through. It's too localized to have been a hurricane – that would have smashed trees over a wider area.'

'Do they have hurricanes here?'

'Christ, yes! There's one cutting up ructions in the Caribbean right now. I've been getting weather reports on it just in case it decides to take a swing this way. It's not likely, though.'

The helicopter lurched in the air suddenly and he swore. 'What's wrong?' I asked.

'I don't know.' He was rapidly checking his instruments. After a while he said, 'Everything seems okay.'

No sooner had he said it than there was a hell of a bang from astern and the whole fuselage swung around violently. The centrifugal force threw me against the side of the cockpit and I was pinned there, while Harry juggled frantically with the controls.

The whole world was going around in a cock-eyed spin; the horizon rose and fell alarmingly and the forest was suddenly very close – too damned close. 'Hold on!' yelled Harry, and slammed at switches on the instrument panel.

The noise of the engine suddenly stopped, but we continued to spin. I saw the top of a tree athwart our crazy path and knew we were going to crash. The next thing – and last thing – I heard was a great crackling noise ending in a smash. I was thrown forward and my head connected violently with a metal bar.

And that was all I remember.

NINE

My head hurt like hell. At first it was a distant throb, no worse than someone else's hangover, but it grew in intensity until it felt as though someone was using my skull for a snaredrum. When I moved something seemed to explode inside and everything went blank.

The next time I came round was better – but not much. I was able to lift my head this time but I couldn't see. Just a lot of red lights which danced in front of my eyes. I leaned back and rubbed at them, and then was aware of someone groaning. It was some time before I could see properly and then everything was green instead of red – a dazzle of moving green something-or-other showing through the transparent canopy.

I heard the groan again and turned to see Harry Rider slumped forward in his seat, a trickle of blood oozing from the side of his mouth. I was very weak and couldn't seem to move; besides which, my thought processes seemed to be all scrambled and I couldn't put two consecutive thoughts together. All I managed to do was to flop my head to the other side and stare through the window.

I saw a frog! He was sitting on a broad leaf staring at me with beady and unwinking eyes, and was quite still except for the rapid pulsation of his throat. We looked at each other for a very long time, long enough for me to repeat to myself twice over that poem about the frog who would a-wooing go – *Heigh Ho, says Rowley.* After a while he blinked his eyes once, and that broke the spell, and I turned my head again to look at Harry.

He stirred slightly and moved his head. His face was very pale and the trickle of blood from his mouth disturbed me because it indicated an internal injury. Again I tried to move but I felt so damned weak. *Come on,* I said; *don't be so grey and dim. Bestir yourself, Wheale; act like a man who knows where he's going!*

I tried again and managed to sit up. As I did so the whole fabric of the cabin trembled alarmingly and swayed like a small boat in a swell. 'Christ!' I said aloud. 'Where *am* I going?' I looked at the frog. He was still there, but the leaf on which he sat was bobbing about. It didn't seem to worry him, though, and he said nothing about it.

I spoke again, because the sound of my voice had comforted me. 'You must be bloody mad,' I said. 'Expecting a frog to talk back! You're delirious, Wheale; you're concussed.'

'Wha . . . wha . . .' said Harry.

'Wake up, Harry boy!' I said. 'Wake up, for Christ's sake! I'm bloody lonely.'

Harry groaned again and his eye opened a crack. 'Wa . . . wat . . .'

I leaned over and put my ear to his mouth. 'What is it, Harry?'

'Wa . . . ter,' he breathed. 'Water be . . . hind seat.'

I turned and felt for it, and again the helicopter trembled and shuddered. I found the water-bottle and held it to his lips, uncertain of whether I was doing right. If he had a busted gut the water wouldn't do him any good at all.

But it seemed all right. He swallowed weakly and dribbled a bit, and a pink-tinged foam ran down his jaw. Then he came round fast, much faster than I had done. I took a sip of water myself, and that helped a lot. I offered Harry the bottle and he swilled out his mouth and spat. Two broken teeth clattered on the instrument panel. 'Aagh!' he said. 'My mouth's cut to bits.'

'Thank God for that,' I said. 'I thought your ribs were driven into your lungs.'

He levered himself up, and then paused as the helicopter swayed. 'What the hell!'

I suddenly realized where we were. 'Take it easy,' I said tightly. 'I don't think we're at ground level. This is a case of "Rock-a-bye baby, on the tree top".' I stopped and said no more. I didn't like the rest of that verse.

He froze in his seat and then sniffed. 'A strong smell of gas. I don't particularly like that.'

I said, 'What happened – up there in the sky?'

'I think we lost the rear rotor,' he said. 'When that happened the fuselage started to spin in the opposite direction to the main rotor. Thank God I was able to declutch and switch off.'

'The trees must have sprung our landing,' I said. 'If we'd have hit solid ground we'd have cracked like an eggshell. As it is, we seem to be intact.'

'I don't understand it,' he said. 'Why should the rear rotor come off?'

'Maybe a fatigue flaw in the metal,' I said.

'This is a new ship. It hasn't had time to get fatigued.'

I said delicately, 'I'd rather discuss this some other time. I propose to get the hell out of here. I wonder how far off the ground we are?' I moved cautiously. 'Stand by for sudden action.'

Carefully I pressed on the handle of the side door and heard the click as the catch opened. A little bit of pressure on the door swung it open about nine inches and then something stopped it, but it was enough open for me to look down. Directly below was a branch, and beyond that just a lot of leaves with no sign of the ground. I looked up and saw bits of blue sky framed between more leaves.

Fallon had wandered about in the forest for many years and, although he wasn't a botanist, he'd taken an interest in it and on several occasions he had discussed it with me. From what he had told me and from what I was able to see I thought that we were about eighty feet up. The main run of rain forest is built in three levels, the specialists call them galleries; we had bust through the top level and got hooked up on the thicker second level.

'Got any rope?' I asked Harry.

'There's the winch cable.'

'Can you unwind it all without too much moving about?'

'I can try,' he said.

There was a clutch on the winch drum which he was able to operate manually, and I helped him unreel the cable, coiling it as neatly as I could and putting it behind the front seat out of the way. Then I said, 'Do you know where we are?'

'Sure!' He pulled out a clipboard to which was attached a map. 'We're about there. We hadn't left the site more than ten minutes and we weren't moving fast. We're about ten miles from the camp. That's going to be a hell of a walk.'

'Do you have any kind of survival kit in here?'

He jerked his thumb. 'Couple of machetes, first aid kit, two water-bottles – a few other bits and pieces.'

I took the water-bottle that was lying between the seats and shook it experimentally. 'This one's half empty – or half full – depending on the way you look at things. We'd better go easy on the water.'

'I'll get the rest of the stuff together,' said Harry, and turned in his seat. The helicopter sagged and there was the rending cry of torn metal. He stopped instantly and looked at me with apprehensive eyes. There was a film of sweat on his upper lip. When nothing else happened he leaned over gently and stretched his hand for the machetes.

We got all we needed into the front, and I said, 'The radio! Is it working?'

Harry put his hand out to a switch and then drew it back. 'I don't know that I want to try it,' he said nervously. 'Can't you smell gas? If there's a short in the transmitter, one spark might blow us sky high.' We looked at each other in silence for some time, then he grinned weakly. 'All right; I'll try it.'

He snapped down the switch and listened in on an earphone. 'It's dead! No signal going out or coming in.'

'We won't have to worry any more about that, then.' I opened the door as far as it would go, and looked down at the branch. It was about nine inches thick and looked very solid. 'I'm getting out now. I want you to drop the cable to me when I shout.'

Squeezing out was not much of a problem for me, I'm fairly slim, and I eased myself down towards the branch. Even going as far as I could, my toes dangled in air six inches above it, and I'd have to drop the rest of the way. I let go, hit the branch squarely with my feet, teetered sickeningly and then dropped forward, wrapping my arms about it and doing a fair imitation of a man on a greasy pole. When I got in an upright position astride the branch I was breathing heavily.

'Okay – drop the cable.'

It snaked down and I grabbed it. Harry had tied the waterbottles and the machetes on to the harness at the end. I left them where they were, for safety, and snapped the harness around the branch. 'You can come out now,' I yelled.

More cable was paid out and then Harry appeared. He had tied a loop of cable around his waist, and instead of coming down to the branch he began to climb up on top of the helicopter canopy. 'What the hell are you doing?' I shouted.

'I want to look at the tail assembly,' he said, breathing heavily.

'For Christ's sake! You'll have the whole bloody thing coming down.'

He ignored me and climbed on hands and knees towards the rear. As far as I could see, the only thing holding the helicopter in position was one of the wheels which was jammed into the crotch formed by a branch and the trunk of a tree and, even as I looked, I saw the wheel slipping forward infinitesimally slowly.

When I looked up Harry had vanished behind a screen of leaves. 'It's going!' I yelled. 'Come back!'

There was only silence. The helicopter lurched amid a crackle of snapping twigs, and a few leaves drifted down. I looked at the wheel and it had slipped forward even more. Another two inches and all support would be gone.

Harry came into view again, sliding head first back towards the canopy. He climbed down skilfully and let himself drop on to the branch. It whipped as his boots struck it, and I caught him around the waist. We'd have made a good circus turn between us.

He manoeuvred until he, too, was astride the branch facing me. I pointed to the wheel which had only an inch to go. His face tautened. 'Let's get out of here.'

We untied the machetes and water-bottles and put the sling around our shoulders, then hauled the rest of the winch cable out of the chopper. 'How long is it?'

'A hundred feet.'

'It ought to be enough to reach the ground.' I started to pay it out until it had all gone. I went first, going down hand over hand. It wasn't so bad because there were plenty of branches lower down to help out. I had to stop a couple of times to disentangle the cable where it had caught up, and on one of those stops I waited for Harry.

He came down and rested on a branch, breathing heavily. 'Imagine me making like Tarzan!' he gasped. His face twisted in a spasm of pain.

'What's the matter?'

He rubbed his chest. 'I think maybe I cracked a couple of ribs. I'll be all right.'

I produced the half-empty water-bottle. 'Take a good swallow. Half for you and half for me.'

He took it doubtfully. 'I thought you said go easy on the water.'

'There's some more here.' I jerked my thumb at the scum-covered pool in the recess of a rotting tree. 'I don't know how good it is, so I don't want to mix it with what's in the bottle. Besides, water does you more good in your stomach than in the bottle – that's the latest theory.'

He nodded, and swallowed water convulsively, his Adam's apple jerking up and down. He handed the bottle to me and I finished it. Then I dipped it into the murky pool to refill it. Tadpoles darted away under the surface; the tree frogs bred up here in the high forest galleries, and lived from birth to death without ever seeing ground. I rammed the cork home, and said, 'I'll have to be *really* thirsty before I'll want to drink that. Are you ready?'

He nodded, so I grasped the cable and started down again, getting a hell of a fright when I startled a spider monkey who gave a squawk and made a twenty-foot leap to another tree, then turned and gibbered at me angrily. He was a lot more at home in the forest than I was, but he was built for it.

At last we reached bottom and stood in the humid greenness with firm ground underfoot. I looked up at the cable. Some Maya or chiclero would come along and wonder at it, and then find a use for it. Or maybe no human eyes would ever see it again. I said, 'That was a damnfool stunt you pulled up there. What the devil were you doing?'

He looked up. 'Let's get out from under the chopper. It's not too safe here.'

'Which way?'

'Any goddamn way,' he said violently. 'Just let's get out from under, that's all.' He drew his machete and swung it viciously at the undergrowth and carved a passage through it. It wasn't too bad – what Fallon would call a twenty-foot forest, perhaps, and we didn't have to work very hard at it.

After going about two hundred yards Harry stopped and turned to me. 'The chopper was sabotaged,' he said expressionlessly.

'What!'

'You heard me. That crash was rigged. I wish I could get my hands on the bastard who did it.'

I stuck my machete in the earth so that it remained upright. 'How do you know this?'

'I did the day-to-day maintenance myself, and I knew every inch of that machine. Do you know how a helicopter works?'

'Only vaguely,' I said.

He squatted on his heels and drew a diagram in the humus with a twig. 'There's the big rotor on top that gives lift. Newton's law says that for every action there's an equal and opposite reaction, so, if you didn't stop it, the whole fuselage would rotate in the opposite direction to the rotor. The way you stop it is to put a little propeller at the back which pushes sideways. Got that?'

'Yes,' I said.

'This helicopter had one engine which drove both rotors. The rear rotor is driven by a long shaft which runs the length of the fuselage – and there's a universal coupling here. Do you remember that bang we heard just before the crash? I thought it was the rear rotor flying off. It wasn't. It was this coupling giving way so that the shaft flailed clean through the side of the fuselage. Of course, the rear rotor stopped and we started to spin.'

I patted my pockets and found a half-empty packet of cigarettes. Harry took one, and said, 'I had a look at that coupling. The retaining screws had been taken out.'

'Are you sure about that? They couldn't have broken out?'

He gave me a disgusted look. 'Of course I'm goddamn sure.'

'When did you last inspect that coupling?'

'Two days ago. But the sabotage was done after that, because I was flying yesterday. My God, we were lucky to get ten minutes' flying without those screws.'

There was a noise in the forest – a dull boom from overhead – and a bright glare reflected through the leaves. 'There she goes,' said Harry. 'And we're damned lucky not to be going with her.'

II

'Ten miles,' said Harry. 'That's a long way in the forest. How much water have we got?'

'A quart of good, and a quart of doubtful.'

His lips tightened. 'Not much for two men in this heat, and we can't travel at night.' He spread out his map on the ground, and took a small compass from his pocket. 'It's going to take us two days, and we can't do it on two quarts of water.' His finger traced a line on the map. 'There's another cenote – a small one – just here. It's about three miles off the direct track, so we'll have to make a dog-leg.'

'How far from here is it?'

He spread his fingers on the map and estimated the distance.

'About five miles.'

'That's it, then,' I said. 'It's a full day's journey. What time is it now?'

'Eleven-thirty. We'd better get going; I'd like to make it before nightfall.'

The rest of that day was compounded of insects, snakes, sweat and a sore back. I did most of the machete work because Harry's chest was becoming worse and every time he lifted an arm he winced with pain. But he carried both water-bottles and the spare machete, which left me unencumbered.

At first, it wasn't too bad; more of a stroll through pleasant glades than anything else, with but the occasional tussle with the undergrowth. Harry navigated with the compass and we made good time. In the first hour we travelled nearly two miles, and my spirits rose. At this rate we'd be at the cenote by two in the afternoon.

But suddenly the forest closed in and we were fighting through a tangled mass of shrubbery. I don't know why the forest changed like that; maybe it was a difference in the soil which encouraged the growth. But there it was, and it slowed us up painfully. The pain came not only from the knowledge that we wouldn't get to water as quickly as we expected, but also very physically. Soon I was bleeding from a dozen cuts and scratches on my arms. Try as I would I couldn't help it happening; the forest seemed imbued with a malevolent life of its own.

We had to stop frequently to rest. Harry started to become apologetic because he couldn't take his turn with the machete, but I soon shut him up. 'You concentrate on keeping us on course,' I said. 'How are we doing for water?'

He shook a bottle. 'Just a swallow of the good stuff left.' He thrust it at me. 'You might as well have it.'

I uncorked the bottle, then paused. 'What about you?'

He grinned. 'You need it more. You're doing all the sweating.'

It sounded reasonable but I didn't like it. Harry was looking very drawn and his face had a greyish pallor under the dirt. 'How are you doing?'

'I'm okay,' he said irritably. 'Drink the water.'

So I finished off the bottle, and said wearily, 'How much further?'

'About two miles.' He looked at his watch. 'It's taken us three hours to do the last mile.'

I looked at the thick green tangle. This was Fallon's four-foot forest, and it had been steadily getting worse. At this rate it would take us at least six hours to get to the cenote, and possibly longer. 'Let's get on with it,' I said. 'Give me your machete; this one is bloody blunt.'

An hour later Harry said, 'Stop!' The way he said it made the hairs on the back of my neck prickle, and I stood quite still. 'Easy now!' he said. 'Just step back – very quietly and very slowly.'

I took a step backwards, and then another. 'What's the matter?'

'Back a bit more,' he said calmly. 'Another couple of steps.'

So I went back, and said, 'What the hell's wrong?'

I heard the sigh of his pent-up breath expelled. 'There's nothing wrong – now,' he said. 'But look there – at the base of that tree.'

Then I saw it, just where I had been standing – a coiled-up horror with a fiat head and unwinking eyes. One more step and I'd have trodden on it.

'That's a bushmaster,' said Harry. 'And God help us if we get bitten by one of those.'

The snake reared its head, then slid into the under-growth and vanished. I said, 'What a hell of a place this is,' and wiped the sweat from my forehead. There was a bit more wetness there than my exertions had called for.

'We'll take a rest,' said Harry. 'Have some water.'

I groped in my pocket. 'I'll have a cigarette instead.'

'It'll dry your throat,' Harry warned.

'It'll calm my nerves,' I retorted. I inspected the packet and found three left. 'Have one?'

He shook his head. He held up a flat box. 'This is a snake-bite kit. I hope we don't have to use it. The guy that gets bitten won't be able to travel for a couple of days, serum or no serum.'

I nodded. Any hold-up could ruin us. He took a bottle from his pocket. 'Let me put some more of this stuff on those scratches.' Harry cleaned up the blood and disinfected the scratches while I finished the cigarette. Then again I hefted the machete but a little more wearily this time, and renewed the assault on the forest.

The palm of my hand was becoming sore and calloused because sweat made the skin soft and it rubbed away on the handle of the machete. This was bladework of a different order than I was used to; the machete was much heavier than any sporting sabre I had used in the salle d'armes, and although the technique was cruder more sheer muscle was needed, especially as the blade lost its edge. Besides, I had never fenced continually for hours at a time – a sabre bout is short, sharp and decisive.

We continued until it was too dark to see properly, and then found a place to rest for the night. Not that we got much rest. I didn't feel like sleeping at ground level – there were too many creepie-crawlies – so we found a tree with out-spreading branches that were not too high, and climbed up. Harry looked inexpressibly weary. He folded his hands over his chest and, in the dimming light, again I saw a dark trickle of blood at the corner of his mouth.

'You're bleeding again,' I said, worriedly.

He wiped his mouth, and said, 'That's nothing. Just the cuts in my mouth where the teeth broke.' He lapsed into silence.

The forest at night was noisy. There were odd rustlings all about, and curious snufflings and snortings at the foot of the tree. Then the howler monkeys began their serenade and I awoke from a doze with a sense of shock, nearly falling out of the tree. It's a fearsome sound, like a particularly noisy multiple murder, and it sets the nerves on edge. Fortunately, the howlers are harmless enough, despite their racket, and even they could not prevent me from falling asleep again.

As I dozed off I had a hazy recollection of hearing voices far away, dreamlike and inconsequential.

III

The next day was just a repetition. We breakfasted on the last of the water and I drank the noisome dregs with fervent appreciation. I was hungry, too, but there was nothing we could do about that. A man can go a long time without food, but water is essential, especially in tropic heat.

'How far to the cenote?' I asked.

Harry gropingly found his map. All his movements were slow and seemed to pain him. 'I reckon we're about here,' he said croakingly. 'Just another mile.'

'Cheer up,' I said. 'We ought to make it in another three hours.'

He tried to smile and achieved a feeble grin. 'I'll be right behind you,' he said.

So we set off again, but our pace was much slower. My cuts with the machete didn't have the power behind them and it was a case of making two chops when only one had been necessary before. And I stopped sweating, which I knew was a bad sign.

Four hours later we were still not in sight of the cenote, and the bush was thick as ever. Yet even though I was leading and doing the work I was still moving faster than Harry, who stopped often to rest. All the stuffing seemed to be knocked out of him, and I didn't know what was the matter. I stopped and waited to let him catch up, and he came into view almost dropping with exhaustion and sagged to the ground at my feet.

I knelt beside him. 'What's wrong, Harry?'

'I'm all right,' he said with an attempt at force in his voice. 'Don't worry about me.'

'I'm worried about both of us,' I said. 'We should have reached the cenote by now. Are you sure we're heading the right way?'

He pulled the compass from his pocket 'Yes; we're all right.' He rubbed his face. 'Maybe we should veer a bit to the north.'

'How far, Harry?'

'Christ I don't know! The cenote's not very big. We could quite easily miss it.'

It dawned upon me that perhaps we were lost. I had been relying on Harry's navigation, but perhaps he wasn't in a fit state to make decisions. We could even have overshot the cenote for all I knew. I could see that it would be up to me to make the decisions in the future.

I made one. I said, 'We'll head due north for two hundred yards, then we'll take up a track parallel to this one.' I felt the edge of the machete; it was as dull as the edge of a poker and damned near useless for cutting anything. I exchanged it for the other, which wasn't much better, and said, 'Come on, Harry; we've got to find water.'

I carried the compass this time and changed direction sharply. After a hundred yards of hewing, much to my surprise I came to an open space, a sort of passage through the bush – a trail. I looked at it in astonishment and noted that it had been cut fairly recently because the slash marks were fresh.

I was about to step on to the trail when I heard voices and drew back cautiously. Two men passed within feet of me; both were dressed in dirty whites and floppy hats, and both carried rifles. They were speaking in Spanish, and I listened to the murmur of their voices fade away until all was quiet again.

Harry caught up with me, and I put my finger to my lips. 'Chicleros,' I said. 'The cenote must be quite near.'

He leaned against a tree. 'Perhaps they'll help us,' he said.

'I wouldn't bet on it. No one I ever heard has a good opinion of chicleros.' I thought about it a bit 'Look, Harry: you make yourself comfortable here, and I'll follow those two lads. I'd like to know a bit more about them before disclosing myself.'

He let himself slip to a sitting position at the bottom of the tree. 'That's okay with me,' he said tiredly. 'I could do with a rest.'

So I left him and entered the trail. By God, it was a relief to be able to move freely. I went fast until I saw a disappearing flick of white ahead which was the hindermost of the chicleros, then I slowed down and kept a cautious distance. After I'd gone about a quarter of a mile I smelled wood smoke and heard more voices, so I struck off the trail, and found that the forest had thinned out and I could move quite easily and without using the machete.

Then, through the trees, I saw the dazzle of sun on water, and no Arab, coming across an oasis in the desert, could have been more cheered than I was. But I was still careful and didn't burst into the clearing by the cenote; instead I sneaked up and hid behind the trunk of a tree and took a good look at the situation.

It was just as well I did because there were about twenty men camped there around a blue and yellow tent which looked incongruously out of place and seemed more suited to an English meadow. In front of the tent and sitting on a camp stool was Jack Gatt, engaged in pouring himself a drink. He measured a careful amount of whisky and then topped it with soda-water from a siphon. My throat tightened agonizingly as I watched him do it.

Immediately around Gatt and standing in a group were eight men listening attentively to what he was saying as he gestured at the map on the camp table. Four of them were obviously American from the intonation of their voices and from their clothing; the others were probably Mexican, although they could have come from any Central American country. To one side, and not taking part in Gatt's conference, were about a dozen chicleros lounging by the edge of the cenote.

I withdrew from my position and circled about the cenote, then went in again to get a view from a different angle. I had to get at that water somehow, without drawing attention to myself, but I saw that anyone going to the cenote would inevitably be spotted. Fortunately, this cenote was different from the others I'd seen in that it wasn't like a well, and the water was easily accessible. It was more like an ordinary pond than anything else.

I watched the men for a long time. They weren't doing anything in particular; just sitting and lying about and talking casually. I had the idea they were waiting for something. Gatt, sitting with his men under the awning in front of his elegant tent, seemed quite out of place among these chicleros, although if Harris was to be believed, he was worse than any of them.

There was nothing I could do there and then, so I drew away and continued to make the full circle around the cenote and so back to the trail. Harry was asleep and moaning a little, and when I woke him up he gave a muffled shout.

'Quiet, Harry!' I said. 'We're in trouble.'

'What is it?' He looked around wildly.

'I found the cenote. There's a crowd of chicleros there – and Jack Gatt.'

'Who the hell is Jack Gatt?'

Fallon, of course, hadn't told him. After all, he was only a chopper jockey in Fallon's employ and there was no reason why he should know about Gatt. I said, 'Jack Gatt is big trouble.'

'I'm thirsty,' said Harry. 'Can't we go along there and get water?'

'Not if you don't want your throat cut.' I said grimly. 'Look, Harry: I think Gatt is ultimately responsible for the sabotage to the helicopter. Can you stick it out until nightfall?'

'I reckon so. As long as I don't have to keep putting one foot in front of the other.'

'You won't have to do that,' I said. 'You just lie here.' I was becoming more and more worried about Harry. There was something wrong with him but I didn't know what it was. I put my hand to his forehead and found it burning hot and very dry. 'Take it easy,' I said. 'The time will soon pass.'

The afternoon burned away slowly. Harry fell asleep again or, at least, into a good imitation of sleep. He was feverish and moaned deliriously, which wasn't at all a good sign for the future. I sat next to him and tried to hone the machetes with a pebble I picked up. It didn't make much difference and I'd have given a lot for a proper whetstone.

Just before nightfall I woke Harry. 'I'm going down to the cenote now. Give me the water-bottles.' He leaned away from the tree and unslung them. 'What else have you got that will hold water?' I asked.

'Nothing.'

'Yes, you have. Give me that bottle of disinfectant. I know it will only hold a couple of mouthfuls, but water is important right now.'

I slung the water-bottles over my shoulder and got ready to go. 'Stay awake if you can, Harry,' I said. 'I don't know how long I'll be away, but I'll make it as quick as I can.'

I wanted to get down to the cenote before nightfall. It was quicker moving when you could see where you were going, and I wanted to get into a good position while the light held. As I came out on to the trail I took a scrap of paper from my pocket and spiked it on a twig as an indication of where to find Harry.

The chicleros had lit a fire and were cooking their evening meal. I manoeuvred into a strategic place – as close to the water as I could get yet as far from the camp as possible. The fire was newly built and the leaping flames illuminated the whole of the cenote and I settled down to a long wait.

The fire burned down to a red glow and the men clustered around it, some cooking meat held on sticks, and others making some sort of flapjacks. Presently the scent of coffee drifted tantalizingly over the cenote and my stomach tightened convulsively. I hadn't eaten for nearly two days and my guts were beginning to resent the fact.

I waited for three hours before the chicleros decided to turn in for the night although it was still quite early by city standards. Gatt, the city man, stayed up late, but he remained in his tent, no doubt under mosquito netting, and I could see the glow of a pressure lantern through the fabric. It was time to go.

I went on my belly like a snake, right to the water's edge. I had already taken the corks from the bottles and held them in my teeth, and when I put the first bottle in the water it gurgled loudly. Just then the first howler monkey let loose his bloodcurdling cry, and I praised God for all his creations, however weird. I withdrew the bottle and put it to my lips and felt the blessed water at the back of my parched throat. I drank the full quart and no more, although it took a lot of willpower to refrain. I filled both bottles and corked them, and then washed out the disinfectant bottle and filled that.

I daresay that anyone with keen eyes could have seen me from the chiclero camp. The sky was clear and the moon was full, and a man, especially a moving man, would be easily spotted. But I managed to get back into the cover of the forest without any outcry, so probably the chicleros hadn't a guard.

I found my way back to Harry without much difficulty and gave him a bottle of water which he drank thirstily. I had a problem – we had to get on the other side of the cenote under cover of darkness and that meant that Harry would have to move immediately, and I didn't know if he was up to it. I waited until he had satisfied his thirst, and said, 'We'll have to move now. Are you fit?'

'I'm okay, I guess,' he said. 'What's the hurry?'

'This cenote lies between us and Uaxuanoc and we want to get around it without being seen. I've discovered a trail on the other side which heads the right way. We'll be able to make better time tomorrow.'

'I'm ready,' he said, and hoisted himself slowly to his feet. But he had to clutch the tree trunk for support and that I didn't like. Still, he moved fast enough when we got going, and stuck close on my heels. I think the water had done him a lot of good.

I had a choice of making a wide sweep around the cenote and going through thick forest, or going straight down the trail and crawling around the chiclero camp. I chose the latter because it would be less strain on Harry, but I hoped he'd be able to keep quiet. We managed it without trouble – the dying embers of the camp fire gave good orientation – and I picked up the trail on the other side of the cenote. Once out of sight of the camp I checked the map and the compass and it seemed that the trail led pretty much in the direction of Uaxuanoc, which was all to the good.

After a mile of stumbling in the darkness Harry began to flag, so I made the decision to stop, and we pulled off the side of the trail and into the forest. I got Harry bedded down – he wasn't in any shape to climb a tree – and said, 'Have some more water.'

'What about you?'

I thrust the bottle into his hands. 'Fill up; I'm going back to get some more.' It had to be done – if we didn't get more water we'd never make it to Uaxuanoc, and since we only had the two bottles we might as well drink what we had.

I left him again and marked the place by thrusting a machete into the middle of the trail. Anyone moving along the trail would be certain of falling over it, including me. I didn't think anyone else would be moving around at night. It took me an hour and a half to get to the cenote, fifteen minutes to fill up, and another hour to get back and bark my shins on that damned machete. I swore at it but at least I was certain that Harry hadn't been discovered.

He was asleep and I didn't wake him, but dropped into an uneasy doze beside him.

Harry woke me at daybreak. He seemed cheerful enough but I felt as though I had been doped. My limbs were stiffened and I was one big ache from head to foot. I had never been a hearty camping type and this sleeping on the ground didn't agree with me. Besides, I hadn't had too much sleep at all and had been stumbling around in the forest for most of the hours of darkness.

I said, 'We have a decision to make. We can stick to the forest, which is safer – but slow. Or we can go up that trail with the likelihood of meeting one of Gatt's chicleros. What do you say, Harry?'

He was brighter this morning and not so disposed to mere acceptance. 'Who is this guy, Gatt?' he asked. 'I've never heard of him before.'

'It's a bit too involved to go into right now, but as far as we're concerned, he's sudden death. From what I've seen, he's allied himself with the chicleros.'

He shook his head. 'Why should a guy I've never heard of want to kill me?'

'He's a big-time American ganster,' I said. 'He's after the loot from Uaxuanoc. It's a long story, but that's the gist of it. There's a lot of money involved, and I don't think he'll stop at much to get it. He certainly won't stop short of killing us. In fact, he's already had a damned good try at it. I can't think of anyone else who'd sabotage your chopper.'

Harry grimaced. 'I'll take your word for it, but I hate like hell the idea of tackling the forest.'

So did I. An inspection of the map showed that we were a little more than five miles from Uaxuanoc. As we already knew, the forest in the immediate vicinity of Uaxuanoc was exceptionally thick and, in our present condition, it might take us two days to hack our way through. We couldn't afford two days, not on our limited supply of water. True, we had filled ourselves up, but that would be soon expended in sweat, and we only had the two quarts' reserve.

Then there was Harry. Whatever was wrong with him wasn't getting any better. The trail was easy travelling and we could do at least a mile an hour, or even more. At that rate we could be in Uaxuanoc in about five hours. It was very tempting.

Against it was the fact that the trail existed in the first place. The only place Gatt could comfortably camp was at the cenote we had just left – he had to stick near a water supply. So it followed that if he were keeping an eye on Uaxuanoc then the trail must have been made by his chicleros, and the likelihood of bumping up against one was high. I didn't know what would happen if we did, but all those I had seen were armed and, from Fallon's account, they were quite prepared to use their weapons.

It was a hell of a decision to make, but finally I opted for the trail. The forest was impossible and we *might* not encounter a chiclero. Harry sighed in satisfaction and nodded his head in agreement. 'Anything but the forest,' he said.

We entered the trail cautiously, found nothing to worry us, and went along it away from Gatt's camp. I kept my eyes down and found plenty of evidence that the trail was in frequent use. There were footprints on patches of soft earth; twice I found discarded cigarette butts, and once an empty corned beef can which had been casually tossed aside. All that was in the first hour.

It worried me very much, but what worried me even more was Harry's slow pace. He started off chirpily enough, but he couldn't keep it up, and he lagged behind more and more. And so I had to go along more slowly because I didn't feel like getting too far ahead of him. It was evident that his condition was deteriorating very rapidly; his eyes were sunk deep into his head, and his face was white under the dark bristle of his beard. All his movements were slow and he kept one arm across his chest as he staggered along as though to stop himself from falling apart.

The trail was just as wide as was necessary for the passage of men in single file, otherwise I would have helped him along, but it was impossible for us to walk side by side and he had to make his own way, stumbling blindly behind me. In that first hour we only went about three-quarters of a mile and I began to get perturbed. It seemed that we would be a long time getting to Uaxuanoc by trail or forest.

It was because of our slowness that we were caught. I had expected to encounter a chiclero head on – one coming down the trail the other way – and I kept a very good lookout. Every time the trail bent in a blind corner I stopped to check the trail ahead and to confirm that we weren't going to run into trouble.

We didn't run into trouble – it caught up with us. I suppose a chiclero had left Gatt's camp at daybreak just about the time we had set out on the trail. He wasn't weak with hunger and sickness and so he made good time and came up on us from behind. I couldn't blame Harry for not keeping a good watch on our back trail; he had enough difficulty in just putting one foot in front of the other. And so we were surprised.

There was a shout, 'He, compañero!' and then a startled oath as we turned round, which was accompanied by the ominous rattle of a rifle bolt. He wasn't a very big man, but his rifle made him ten feet tall. He had put a bullet up the spout and was regarding us warily. I don't think he knew who we were – all he knew was that we were strangers in a place where no strangers should be.

He rattled out a few words and brought the muzzle of the rifle to bear on us. 'Aguarde acqui! Tenga cuidado!'

It all happened in a split second. Harry turned and cannoned into me. 'Run!' he said hoarsely, and I turned and took off up the trail. There was a shot which clipped a splinter from a tree and ricocheted across the trail in front, and a shout of warning.

I was suddenly aware that I could only hear the thud of my own boots and I turned to see Harry sprawled on the ground and the chiclero running up to him with upraised gun. Harry tried weakly to struggle to his feet but the chiclero stood over him and raised the rifle to ram the butt at his skull.

There wasn't anything else I could do. I had the machete in my hand, so I threw it. If the machete had hit with the hilt or the flat of the blade, or even with that damned blunt edge, it would have served enough to knock the man off balance. But it struck point first, penetrating just under his rib cage, sinking in deep.

His mouth opened in surprise and he looked down at the broad blade protruding from his body with shock in his eyes. He made a choked sound which throttled off sharply and the upraised rifle slipped from his hands. Then his Knees buckled under him and he fell on top of Harry, arms outstretched and scrabbling at the rotting leaves on the ground.

I didn't mean to kill him – but I did. When I ran back he was already dead and blood was spurting from the wound with the last dying beats of his heart, reddening Harry's shirt. Then it stopped and there was just an oozing trickle. I rolled him away and bent down to help Harry. 'Are you all right?'

Harry wrapped his arms about his chest. 'Christ!' he said. 'I'm beat!'

I looked up and down the trail, wondering if anyone had heard the shot, then said, 'Let's get off this trail – quickly!' I grabbed the machete which Harry had dropped and slashed at the bush by the side of the trail, penetrating about ten yards into the forest, then I helped Harry, and he collapsed helplessly on to the ground.

His mouth was opening and closing and I bent down to hear him whisper, 'My chest – it hurts like hell!'

'Take it easy,' I said. 'Have some water.' I made him as comfortable as I could, then went back to the trail. The chiclero was indubitably dead and was lying in a puddle of rapidly clotting blood. I put my hand under his armpits and hauled the body off the trail and into cover, then went back and tried to disguise the evidence of death, scuffing up earth to cover the blood. Then I picked up the rifle and went back to Harry.

He was sitting with his back against a tree and his arms still hugged about his chest. He lifted lacklustre eyes, and said, 'I think this is it.'

I hunkered down next to him. 'What's wrong?'

'That fall – it's finished me. You were right; I think my ribs have got into my lungs.' A trickle of blood oozed from his mouth.

I said, 'For Christ's sake! Why didn't you tell me? I thought you were just bleeding from the mouth.'

He gave a twisted grin. 'Would it have made any difference?'

Probably it wouldn't have made any difference. Even if I had known about it I couldn't see that we could have done any different than we had. But Harry must have been in considerable pain marching through the forest with punctured lungs.

His breath came with a curious spasmodic whistling sound. 'I don't think I can make it to Uaxuanoc,' he whispered. 'You get out of here.'

'Wait!' I said, and went back to the body of the dead man. He was carrying a big water-bottle that held about a half-gallon, and he had a knapsack. I searched the pockets and came up with matches, cigarettes, a wicked-looking switch-blade knife and a few other odds and ends. The knapsack contained a few items of clothing, not very clean, three tins of bully beef, a round, flat loaf about the size of a dinner plate, and a hunk of dried beef.

I took all this stuff back to Harry. 'We can eat now,' I said.

He shook his head slowly. 'I'm not hungry. Get out of here, will you? While you still have time.'

'Don't be a damned fool,' I said. 'I'm not going to leave you here.'

His head dropped on one side. 'Please yourself,' he said, and coughed convulsively, his face screwed up in agony.

It was then I realized he was dying. The flesh on his face had fallen in so that his head looked like a skull and, as he coughed, blood spurted from his mouth and stained the leaves at his side. I couldn't just walk away and leave him, no matter what the danger from the chicleros, so I stayed at his side and tried to encourage him.

He would take no food or water and, for a time, he was delirious; but he rallied after about an hour and could speak rationally. He said, 'You ever been in Tucson, Mr Wheale?'

'No, I haven't,' I said. 'And my name is Jemmy.'

'Are you likely to be in Tucson?'

I said, 'Yes, Harry, I'll be in Tucson.'

'See my sister,' he said. 'Tell her why I'm not going back.'

'I'll do that,' I said gently.

'Never had a wife,' he said. 'Nor girl-friends – not seriously. Moved around too much, I guess. But me and my sister were real close.'

'I'll go and see her,' I said. 'I'll tell her all about it.'

He nodded and closed his eyes, saying no more. After half an hour he had a coughing fit and a great gout of red blood poured from his mouth.

Ten minutes later he died.

TEN

They chased me like hounds chase the fox. I've never been much in favour of blood sports and this experience reinforced my distaste because it gave me a very good idea of what it's like to be on the wrong end of a hunt. I also had the disadvantage of not knowing the country, while the hounds were hunting on their home ground. It was a nerve-racking and sweaty business.

It began not long after Harry died. I couldn't do much about Harry although I didn't like just leaving him there for the forest scavengers. I began to dig a grave, using Harry's machete, but I came across rock close to the surface and had to stop. In the end I laid him out with his arms folded across his chest and said goodbye.

That was a mistake, of course, and so was the attempt at a grave. If I had left Harry as he was when he died, just a tumbled heap at the foot of a tree, then I might have got clean away. The body of the dead chiclero was found, and so was Harry's body, a little further in the forest; if I had left him alone then Gatt's men might not even have suspected that I existed. But dead men don't attempt to dig their own graves, nor do they compose themselves for their end in such a neat manner, and the hunt was on.

But maybe I'm wrong, because I did take as much loot from the dead chiclero as I could. It was too precious to leave behind. I took his rifle, his pack, the contents of his pockets, a bandolier stuffed with cartridges and a nice new machete, as sharp as a razor and much better than those I had been using. I would have taken his clothing too, for use as a disguise, had I not heard voices on the trail. That scared me off and I slipped away into the forest, intent on putting as much distance between me and those voices as I could.

I don't know if they discovered the bodies then or at a later time because, in my hurry to get away, I got thoroughly lost for the rest of the day. All I knew was that Gatt's trail to Uaxuanoc was somewhere to the west, but by the time I'd figured that out it was too dark to do anything about it, and I spent the night up a tree.

Oddly enough, I was in better shape than at any time since the helicopter crashed. I had food and nearly three quarts of water, I was more accustomed to moving in the forest and did not have to do as much useless chopping with the machete, and one man can go where two men can't – especially when one of the two is sick. Without poor Harry I was more mobile. Then again, I had the rifle. I didn't know what I was going to do with it, but I stuck to it on general principles.

The next morning, as soon as it was light enough to see, I headed west, hoping to strike the trail. I travelled a hell of a long way and I thought I'd made a terrible mistake. I knew if I didn't find that trail then I'd never find Uaxuanoc, and I'd probably leave my bones somewhere in the forest when my food and water ran out, so I was justifiably anxious. I didn't find the trail, but I nearly ran into a bullet as someone raised a shout and took a shot at me.

The bullet went high and clipped leaves from a bush, and I took to my heels and got out of there fast. From then on there was a strange, slow-motion chase in the humid green dimness of the forest floor. The bush was so thick that you could be standing right next to a man and not know he was there if he were quiet enough. Imagine putting the Hampton Court maze into one of the big tropical houses at Kew, populating it with a few armed thugs with murder in their hearts, and you in the middle, the object of their unloving attentions.

I tried to move as quietly as I could, but my knowledge of woodcraft dates back to Fenimore Cooper and I wasn't so good at the Silent Savage bit. But then, neither were the chicleros. They crashed about and shouted one to the other, and a couple of shots were loosed off at random but nowhere near me. After a while I began to get over my immediate fright and the conviction grew upon me that if I chose a thickish bit of forest and just stood still I was as likely to get away with it as if I kept on running.

So I did that and stood screened by leaves with my hands sweaty on the rifle until the noise of pursuit disappeared. I didn't move out immediately, either. The greatest danger was the man more brainy than the others who would be doing the same as me – just standing quietly and waiting for me to come into view. So I waited a full hour before moving, and then, again, I headed west.

This time I found the trail. I burst into it unexpectedly, but luckily there wasn't anyone in sight. I hastily withdrew and looked at my watch to find it was after five in the afternoon, not far from nightfall. I debated with myself whether or not to take a chance and use the trail. I was tired, and perhaps my judgement wasn't as keen as it ought to have been, because I said out loud, 'The hell with it!' and boldly stepped out. Again it was a relief to have unhampered freedom of movement. There was no need for the machete, so I unslung the rifle and took it in both hands, and made good time, conscious that every step brought me nearer Uaxuanoc and safety.

This time *I* surprised a chiclero. He was standing in the trail with his back to me and I could smell the smoke of the

foul cigarette he was puffing. I was retreating cautiously
when, apparently by some sixth sense, he became aware of
me and turned fast. I popped off a shot at him and he
promptly fell flat and rolled into cover. The next thing was
an answering shot, so close that I felt the thrill of air on my
cheek.

I ducked for cover and, hearing shouts, pushed into the
forest. Again, there was a fantastic game of hide-and-seek. I
found another hidey-hole and froze in it like a hare in its
form, hoping that the hunt would go around me. I listened
to the chicleros plunging about and shouting to each other
and there was something about the quality in their voices
which made me think their hearts weren't in it. After all,
one of their number was dead, stabbed in a very nasty way,
and I had just taken a pot-shot at another. It can't have been
very encouraging; after all, I'd shown definitely murderous
tendencies, they didn't know who I was and I could be
standing in wait to garrotte any one of them. No wonder
they stuck together and shouted at each other – there was
comfort in numbers.

They gave up at nightfall and retreated to wherever they
had come from. I stayed where I was and put in a bit of solid
thought on the problem, something which I'd been neglect-
ing to do in the hurry-scurry of the day's events. I'd run into
two lots of them during the day, and as far as I could make
out, they were moving in groups of three or four. Whereas
the first chiclero – the one I had killed – had been alone.

Again, this last lot was neither spying on Uaxuanoc nor
staying at Gatt's camp, and it seemed to me that its sole purpose was to hunt for me, otherwise why would they have
been staked out on the trail? It was very likely that Gatt had
identified the body of Harry Rider and he had a shrewd suspicion of who Rider's companion was. Anyway, every time
I tried to make a break for Uaxuanoc there had been some
one placed to stop me.

Apart from all that, I had no illusions about what would happen to me if I were caught. The man I had killed would have friends, and it would be useless to expostulate that I hadn't intended killing him and that I was merely dissuading him from splitting Harry's skull. The fact was that I *had* killed him and there was no getting away from it.

Remembering how he had looked with the machete obscenely sticking from his body made me feel sick. I had killed a man and I didn't even know who he was or what he thought. Still, he had started it by shooting at us and he had got what he deserved, yet, oddly, that didn't make me feel any better about it. This primitive world of kill or be killed was a long way from Cannon Street and the bowler-hatted boys. What the hell was a grey little man like me doing here?

But this was no time for indulging in philosophy and I wrenched my mind back to the matter at hand. How in hell was I going to get back to Uaxuanoc? The idea came to me that I could move along the trail at night – that I had already proved. But would the chicleros be watching at night? There was only one thing to do and that was to find out the hard way.

It was not yet dark and I had just time to get back to the trail before the light failed. Moving in the forest at night was impossible, and movement on the trail wasn't much better but I persevered and went slowly and as quietly as I could. It was very depressing to see the fire. They had hewn out a little clearing, and the fire itself was built right in the middle of the trail. They sat around it talking and obviously wide awake. To go round was impossible at night, so I withdrew regretfully and, as soon as I thought I was out of hearing, I hacked into the forest and found myself a tree.

The next morning the first thing I did was to go further into the forest away from the trail and find myself another tree. I chose it very carefully and established myself on a sort of platform forty feet above the ground with leaf cover beneath so thick that I couldn't see the ground at all and no one on the ground could see me. One thing was certain – these boys couldn't possibly climb every tree in the forest to see where I was hiding, and I thought I'd be safe.

I was tired – tired to death of running, and fighting this bloody forest, tired of being shot at and of shooting at other people, tired because of lack of sleep and because too much adrenalin had been pumped into my system, tired above all, of being consistently and continually frightened.

Maybe the grey little man inside me was intent on running away. I don't know – but I rationalized it by saying to myself that I wanted a breathing space. I was staking everything on one last throw. I had a quart of water left, and a little food – enough for a day if I didn't have to run too much. I was going to stay in that tree for twenty-four hours – to rest and sleep and get my wind back. By that time I'd have eaten all the food and drunk all the water, and I'd bloody well have to make a move, but until then I was going to take it easy.

Maybe it's a trait of little grey men that they only go into action when pushed hard enough, and perhaps I was unconsciously putting myself into such a position that hunger and thirst would do the pushing; but what I consciously thought was that if the chicleros saw neither hair nor hide of me for the next twenty-four hours then they might assume that I'd either quit cold or gone elsewhere. I hoped, rather futilely, than when I came down out of that tree they'd have gone away.

So I made myself comfortable, or as comfortable as I could, and rested up. I split the food up into three meals and marked the water-bottle into three portions. The last lot was for breakfast just before I left. I slept, too, and I remember thinking just before I dozed off that I hoped I didn't snore.

Most of the time I spent in a somnolent condition, not thinking about anything much. All the affairs of Fallon and Uaxuanoc seemed very far away, and Hay Tree Farm could just as well have been on another planet. There was just the clammy green heat of the forest enfolding me, and even the ever-present danger from the chicleros seemed remote. I daresay if a psychiatrist could have examined me then he'd have diagnosed a case of schizophrenic retreat. I must have been in a bad way and I think that was my nadir.

Night came and I slept again, this time more soundly, and I slept right through until daybreak and awoke refreshed. I think that night's sleep did me a lot of good because I felt remarkably cheerful as I munched the tough dried beef and ate the last of the bread. I felt devilish reckless as I washed it down with the last of the water from the bottle. Today was going to be make or break for Jemmy Wheale – I had nothing left to fall back on, so I might as well push right ahead.

I abandoned the water-bottles and the knapsack and all I retained were the switchblade knife in my pocket, the machete and the rifle. I was going to travel light and fast. I didn't even take the bandolier, but just put a half-dozen rounds in my pocket. I didn't see myself fighting a pitched battle, and all the ammunition in the world wouldn't help me if I had to. I suppose the bandolier and the water-bottles are still up in that tree – I can't imagine anyone finding them.

I came out of the tree and dropped on to the ground, not worrying too much whether anyone saw or heard me or not, and made my way through the forest to the trail. When I got to it I didn't hesitate at all, but just turned and walked along as though I hadn't a care in the world. I carried the rifle at the trail and held the machete in the other hand, and I didn't bother to slow at the corners but just carried straight on.

When I arrived at the clearing the chicleros had chopped out for their little camp I stopped and felt the embers of the fire. It never occurred to me to be cautious in my approach; I just marched into the clearing, found no one there, and automatically bent to feel the heat of the embers. They were still warm and, as I turned them over with the point of the machete, there was a glow of red. It was evident that the chicleros were not long gone.

But which way? Up-trail or down-trail? I didn't particularly care and set off again at the same pace, striding out and trying to make good time. And I did make good time. I had examined the map and tried to trace the course of my wanderings during the days I had been harried. It was something of an impossibility, but as near as I could reckon I thought I was within three miles of Uaxuanoc, and I was damned well going to keep to that trail until I got there.

Fools may rush in where angels fear to tread, but there is also something called Fool's Luck. All the time those bastards had been chasing me and I'd been scared out of my wits, I had run into them, twist and turn as I would. Now, when I didn't give a damn, it was I who saw them first. Rather, I heard them nattering away in Spanish as they came up the trail, so I just stepped aside into the forest and let them pass.

There were four of them, all armed and all pretty villainous-looking, unshaven and dressed in the universal dirty whites of the chicleros. As they passed I heard a reference to Señor Gatt and there was a burst of laughter. Then they were gone up the trail and I stepped out of cover. If they'd had their wits about them they could easily have spotted me because I hadn't gone far into cover, but they didn't even turn their heads as they went by. I'd reached the stage when I didn't give a damn.

But I was heartened as I went on. It was unlikely that any more of them would be coming up the trail and I lengthened my stride to move faster so that I'd outpace any possible chicleros coming up behind. It was hot and strenuous work and the precious water I had drunk filmed my body in the form of sweat, but I drove myself on and on without relenting and kept up a lulling pace for the next two hours.

Suddenly the trail took a sharp turn to the left, went on a hundred yards, and petered out. I stopped, uncertain of where to go, and suddenly became aware of a man lying on top of a hillock to my right. He was staring at something through field glasses, and as I convulsively brought up the rifle, he half-turned his head and said casually, 'Es usted, Pedro?'

I moistened my lips, 'Si!' I said hoping that was the right answer.

He put the glasses to his eyes again and resumed his contemplation of whatever was on the other side of the hillock. 'Tiene usted fosforos y cigarrillos?'

I didn't know what he was saying, but it was obviously a question, so I repeated again, 'Si!' and climbed up the hillock boldly until I was standing over him, just a little behind.

'Gracias,' he said. 'Que hora es?' He put down the glasses and turned to look at me just as I brought the rifle butt down on his head. It hit him just above the right eye and his face creased in sudden pain. I lifted the rifle and slammed it down harder in a sudden passion of anger. This is what would have happened to Harry. The sound that came from him was midway between a wail and a grunt, and he rolled over down the hillock and was still.

I gave him a casual glance and stirred him with my foot. He did not move, so I turned to see what he had been looking at. Spread out below was Uaxuanoc and Camp Three, not a quarter of a mile away across open ground. I looked at it as the Israelites must have looked upon the Promised

Land; tears came to my eyes and I took a few stumbling steps forward and shouted in a hoarse croak at the distant figures strolling about the huts.

I began to run clumsily and found that all the strength seemed to have suddenly drained from my body. I felt ridiculously weak and at the same time, airy and buoyant and very light-headed. I don't know if the man I had stunned – or killed for all I knew – was the only chiclero overlooking the camp, or whether he had companions. Certainly it would have been a simple matter for a man with a rifle to shoot me in the back as I stumbled towards the huts, but there was no shot.

I saw the big figure of Joe Rudetsky straighten as he turned to look at me and there was a faint shout. Then there was a bit of a blankness and I found myself lying on the ground looking up at Fallon, who wore a concerned expression. He was speaking, but I don't know what he said because someone was beating a drum in my ear. His head shrank and then ballooned up hugely, and I passed out again.

II

Water – clean, cold, pure water – is a marvellous substance. I've used it sometimes to make those packet soups; you get the dry, powdery stuff out of the packet which looks as unappetizing as the herbs from a witch doctor's pouch, add water and hey presto! – what were a few dry scrapings turn into luscious green peas and succulent vegetables.

I was very dehydrated after my week in the forest, and I'd lost a lot of weight, but within a few hours I felt remarkably chirpy. Not that I drank a lot of water because Fallon wouldn't let me and rationed it out in sips, but the sight of that water jug next to my bed with the cold condensation frosting the outside of the glass did me a world of good because I knew that all I had to do was to stretch my arm and there it was. A lovely feeling! So I was feeling better although, perhaps, like the packet soup I had lost a bit of flavour.

Fallon, of course, wanted to know what had happened in more detail than in the brief incoherent story I told when I stumbled into camp. He pulled up a chair and sat by the edge of the bed. 'I think you'd better tell me all of it,' he said.

'I killed a man,' I said slowly.

He raised his eyebrows. 'Rider? You mustn't think of it like that.'

'No, not Harry.' I told him what had happened.

As I spoke the expression on his face changed to startled bewilderment, and when I finally wound down he said, 'So we're under observation – and Gatt's out there.'

'With an army,' I said. 'That's what Pat Harris was trying to tell you – but you wouldn't listen. Gatt has brought his own men from the States and recruited chicleros to help him in the forest. And the fire in the radio shack wasn't an accident – nor was the crash of the chopper.'

'You're certain it was sabotage?'

'Harry was,' I said. 'And I believe him. I also think the other chopper – the big one at Camp One – was sabotaged. Your jet is stranded in Mexico City, too. We're isolated here.'

Fallon looked grim. 'How many men did you see with Gatt?'

'I didn't stop to count – but from first to last I must have seen twenty-five. Some of those I might have bumped into more than once, of course, but I'd say that's a fair reckoning.' I stretched my hand and laid it against the coolness of the water jug. 'I can make a fair guess at what they'll do next.'

'And what's your guess?'

'Isn't it obvious? They're going to hi-jack us. Gatt wants the stuff we've brought up from the cenote and any other trinkets we may have found. It's still here, isn't it?'

Fallon nodded. 'I should have sent it out before.' He stood up and looked out of the window. 'What puzzles me is how you – and Gatt – can be certain of this.'

I was too tired to yell at him but I made an effort. 'Damn it, I've been bringing the stuff out of the water, haven't I?'

He turned. 'But Gatt doesn't know that. How can he know, unless someone told him? We haven't broadcast it.'

I thought about that, then said softly, 'I was in the forest for nearly a week after the sabotage and Gatt still hasn't made a move. He's out there and he's ready, so what's holding him up?'

'Uncertainty, perhaps,' suggested Fallon. 'He can't really *know* that we've found anything valuable – valuable to him, that is.'

'True. But all he has to do is to walk in here and find a million and a half dollars that's here for the taking.'

'More than that,' said Fallon. 'Paul made a big find in the Temple of Yum Chac. He wasn't supposed to start excavating, but he did, and he stumbled across a cache of temple implements. They're priceless, Jemmy; nothing like this has been found before.'

'Nothing is priceless to Gatt,' I said. 'What would it be worth to him?'

'As a museum collection you couldn't put a price on it. But if Gatt split it up and sold the pieces separately, then maybe he could pick up another million and a half.'

I looked at Fallon sourly. 'And you had the nerve to tell me there wouldn't be any gold in Uaxuanoc. We know Gatt can recognize the value, and we know he can dispose of it through Gerryson. So what do we do! Just hand it to him when he comes calling with his goons?'

'In all fairness I think we'd better talk it over with the others,' said Fallon. 'Do you feel up to it?'

'I'm all right,' I said, and swung my legs out of bed.

It was a gloomy and depressing conference. I told my story and, after a few minutes of unbelieving incomprehension, I managed to ram it down their throats that we were in trouble. Fallon didn't need convincing, of course, but Paul Halstead was as contrary a bastard as ever. 'This whole thing sounds very unlikely,' he said in his damned superior way.

I bristled. 'Are you calling me a liar?'

Fallon put his hand on my arm warningly. Halstead said, 'No, but I think you're exaggerating – and using your imagination.'

I said, 'Take a walk out into the forest. If you run into a bullet it won't harm you if it's imaginary.'

'I certainly think you could have done more to help poor Rider,' he said.

I leaned over the table to grab him but he pulled back sharply. 'That's enough!' barked Fallon. 'Paul, if you haven't anything constructive to say, keep your mouth shut.'

Katherine Halstead unexpectedly attacked her husband for the first time. 'Yes – shut up, Paul,' she said curtly. 'You make me sick.' He looked at her in bewildered astonishment. 'You're not taking Wheale's side again?' he said in a hurt voice.

'There are no sides – there never have been,' she said in an icy voice. 'If anyone uses his imagination, it's not Jemmy.' She looked across at me. 'I'm sorry, Jemmy.'

'I won't have you apologizing for me,' he blazed.

'I'm not,' she said in a voice that would cut a diamond. 'I'm apologizing to Jemmy on my own behalf – for not listening to him earlier. Now just shut up as Professor Fallon says.'

Halstead was so surprised at this attack from an unexpected quarter that he remained silent and somewhat thoughtful. I looked across at Rudetsky. 'What do you think?'

'I believe you,' he said. 'We had some trouble with those goddamn chicleros back at Camp One. They're a murderous lot of bastards, and I'm not surprised they took a shot at you.' He squared his big shoulders and addressed himself to Fallon. 'But this guy, Gatt, is something else again. We didn't know about him.'

'It wasn't necessary for you to know,' said Fallon colourlessly.

Rudetsky's face took on a stubbornness. 'I reckon it was, Mr Fallon. If Gatt has organized the chicleros it means big trouble. Getting shot at wasn't in the contract. I don't like it – and neither do Smitty and Fowler here.' The other two men nodded seriously.

I said, 'What are you trying to do, Rudetsky? Start a trade union? It's a bit late for that. Whether or not Mr Fallon misled you is beside the point. In any case I don't think he did it deliberately. The point at issue now is what do we do about Gatt?'

Fallon said wearily, 'There's only one thing we *can* do. Let him have what he wants.'

Smith and Fowler nodded vigorously, and Rudetsky said, 'That's what I think too.' Katherine Halstead's lips tightened, while Halstead twisted his head and looked about the table with watchful eyes.

'Is that a fact?' I said. 'We just give Gatt three million dollars, pat him on the head and hope he'll go away. A fat chance of that happening.'

Rudetsky leaned forward. 'What do you mean by that?'

'I'm sure you're not as stupid as that, Joe. Gatt is committing a crime – he's stealing three million dollars of someone else's property. I don't know who this stuff legally belongs to, but I'm sure the Mexican Government has a big claim. Do you really think that Gatt will allow anyone to go back to Mexico City to put in an official complaint?'

'Oh, my God!' said Fallon as the reality of the situation hit him.

'You mean – hell knock us off – all of us?' said Rudetsky in a rising voice.

'What would you do in his position?' I asked cynically. 'Given, of course, that you don't have too much regard for the sanctity of human life.'

There was a sudden babble of voices, above which rose Rudetsky's bull-like tones cursing freely. Smith yelled, 'I'm getting out of here.'

I thumped the table and yelled, 'Belt up – the lot of you!' To my surprise they all stopped suddenly and looked towards me. I hadn't been used to asserting myself and maybe I over-did it – anyway, it worked. I stabbed my finger at Smith. 'And where the hell do you think you're going to go? Move ten yards into that forest and they've got you cold. You wouldn't stand a chance.'

Smith's face went very pale and he swallowed nervously. Fowler said, 'Jeez; he's right, Smitty! That's out.'

There was a sudden strength in Fallon's voice. 'This is impossible, Wheale; you're dragging up bogies. Do you realize what a stink there would be if Gatt went through with this . . . this mass murder? Do you think that a man can disappear with no questions asked? He'd never go through with it.'

'No? Who else but us knows that Gatt is here? He's experienced – he has an organization. I'll bet he can whistle up a hundred witnesses to prove he's in Mexico City right now. He'll make damned sure that there is no one to tie him up with this thing.'

Katherine's face was pale. 'But when they find us . . . find our bodies . . . they'll know that . . .'

'I'm sorry, Katherine,' I said. 'But they won't find us. You could bury an army in Quintana Roo and the bodies would never be found. We'll just disappear.'

Halstead said, 'You've put your finger on it, Wheale. Who else but us knows that Gatt is here? And the only reason we know is because of your say-so. *I* haven't seen him, and neither has anyone else – except you. I think you're trying to stampede us into something.'

I stared at him. 'And why the devil should I want to do that?'

He shrugged elaborately. 'You pushed your way into this expedition right from the start. Also, you've been very interested in the cash value of everything we've found. I don't think I have to say much more, do I?'

'No, you bloody well don't,' I snapped. 'And you'd better not or I'll ram your teeth down your throat.' All the others were looking at me in silence, letting me know that this was a charge that had to be answered. 'If I wanted to stampede you why would I prevent Smith going off? Why would I want to keep us together?'

Rudetsky blew out his breath explosively and looked at Halstead with dislike. 'Jesus! For a minute this guy had me going. I ought to have known better.' Halstead stirred uneasily under the implied contempt, and Rudetsky said to me, 'So what do we do, Mr Wheale?'

I was about to say, 'Why ask me?' but one look at Fallon made me change my mind. He was oddly shrunken and stared blindly in front of him, contemplating some interior vision. What he was thinking I don't know and I'd hate to guess, but it was evident that we couldn't rely on him for a lead. Halstead couldn't lead a blind man across a street, while Rudetsky was a good sergeant type, super-efficient when told what to do – but he had to be told. And Smith and Fowler would follow Rudetsky.

I have never been a leader of men because I never particularly wanted to lead anyone anywhere. I was always of the opinion that a man should make his own way and that if he used the brains God gave him, then he didn't have to follow in anyone's footsteps and, by the same token, neither should he expect anyone to follow him. I was a lone wolf, a rampant individualist, and it was because of that, perhaps, I was labelled grey and colourless. I didn't take the trouble to convert anyone to my point of view, an activity which seems to be a passionate preoccupation with others, and it was put down to lack of anything worthwhile to say – quite wrongly.

And now, in the quiet hut, everyone seemed to be waiting for me to take over – to do something positive. Everyone except Fallon, who had withdrawn, and Halstead, of course, who would be actively against me for whatever peculiar reasons occurred to his warped mind. Rudetsky said in a pleading voice, 'We gotta do something.'

'Gatt will be moving in very soon,' I said. 'What weapons have we?'

'There's a shotgun and a rifle,' said Rudetsky. 'Those are camp stores. And I have a handgun of my own packed in my kit.'

'I have a revolver,' said Fowler.

I looked around. 'Any more?'

Fallon shook his head slowly and Halstead just regarded me with an unwinking stare. Katherine said, 'Paul has a pistol.'

'A shotgun, a rifle and three pistols. That's a start, anyway. Joe, which hut do you think is most easily dependable?'

'Are you thinking of having a battle?' asked Halstead. 'If Gatt *is* out there – which I doubt – you won't stand a chance. I think you're nuts.'

'Would you prefer to let Gatt cut your throat? Offer your neck to the knife? Well, Joe?'

'Your hut might be best,' said Rudetsky. 'It's near to the cenote, which means they can't get close in back.'

I looked at the empty shelves. 'Where's all the loot?'

'I packed it all up,' said Fallon. 'Ready to go when the helicopter came in.'

'Then you'll have to unpack it again,' I said. 'We've got to get rid of it.'

Halstead jerked upright. 'Goddamn it, what are you going to do? That material is priceless.'

'No, it's not,' I said bluntly. 'It has a price on it – seven lives! Gatt may kill us for it, if he can get it. But if we can put it out of his reach he may not consider seven murders worth the candle.'

Fowler said, 'That figures. But what are you going to do with it?'

'Dump the lot back into the cenote,' I said brutally. 'He'll never get it out without a lengthy diving operation, and I don't think he'll stick around to try.'

Halstead went frantic. 'You can't do that,' he shouted. 'We may never be able to retrieve it.'

'Why not? Most of it came out of the cenote in the first place. It won't be lost forever. Come to that – I don't give a damn if it is; and neither do these men here. Not if it saves our lives.'

'Hell, no!' said Rudetsky. 'I say dump the stuff.'

Halstead appealed to Fallon. 'You can't let them do this.'

Fallon looked up. 'Jemmy appears to have taken charge. He'll do what he must.' His mouth twisted into a ghastly simulacrum of a smile. 'And I don't think you can stop him, Paul.'

'The cave,' said Katherine suddenly. 'We can put it in the cave.'

Halstead's head jerked round. 'What cave?' he demanded suspiciously.

There's an underwater cave about sixty-five feet down in the cenote,' I said. 'That's a good idea, Katherine. It'll be as safe and unavailable there as anywhere else.'

'I'll help you,' she said.

'You'll do no such thing,' snapped Halstead. 'You'll not lend a hand to this crazy scheme.'

She looked at him levelly. 'I'm not taking orders from you any more, Paul. I'm going my own way for a change. I'm going to do what *I* think is right. Uaxuanoc has destroyed you, Paul; it has warped you into something other than the man I married, and I'm not going to be used as a tool for your crazy obsessions. I think we're finished – you and I.'

He hit her – not a slap with an open palm, but with his clenched fist. It caught her under the jaw and lifted her clean across the hut to fall in a tumbled heap by the wall.

I wasted no time in thoughts of fair fights and Queensberry Rules, but grabbed a bottle from the table and crowned him hard. The bottle didn't break but it didn't do him any good. He gasped and his knees buckled under him, but he didn't go down, so I laid the bottle across his head again and he collapsed to the floor.

'All right,' I said, breathing hard and hefting the bottle, 'has anyone else any arguments?'

Rudetsky grunted deep in his chest. 'You did all right,' he said. 'I've been wanting to do that for weeks.' He helped Fowler to lift Katherine to her feet, and brought her to a chair by the table. Nobody worried about Halstead; they just let him lie where he fell.

Katherine was dizzy and shaken, and Fallon poured out a stiff drink for her. 'I pleaded with you not to have him along,' he said in a low voice.

'That's water under the bridge,' I said. 'I'm as much to blame as anyone.' Rudetsky was hovering solicitously behind Katherine. 'Joe, I want his gun. I don't trust the bastard with it.'

'It's in the box by the bed,' said Katherine weakly.

Rudetsky made a sign with his hand. 'Go get it, Smitty.' He looked down at Halstead and stirred him with his foot.

'You sure got him good. He's going to have one hell of a headache.'

Katherine choked over the whisky. 'Are you all right?' I asked.

She fingered the side of her jaw tenderly. 'He's insane,' she whispered. 'He's gone mad.'

I stood up and took Rudetsky on one side. 'Better get Halstead back into his hut. And if it can be locked, lock it. We have enough on our plate without having to handle that lunatic.'

His grin was pure enjoyment. 'I'd have done the same long ago but I thought Fallon would can me. Oh, boy, but you tapped him good!'

I said, 'You can have a crack at him any time you like, and you don't have to worry about being fired. It's open season on Halstead now; I've stopped being so bloody tolerant.'

Rudetsky and Fowler bent to pick up Halstead, who was showing signs of coming round. They got him to his feet and he looked at me blankly with glazed eyes, showing no sign of recognition, then Fowler pushed him out of the hut.

I turned to Katherine. 'How are you doing?'

She gave me a wry and lop-sided smile. 'As well as might be expected,' she said gently. 'After a public brawl with my husband.' She looked down at the table. 'He's changed so much.'

'He'll change a lot more if he causes trouble,' I said. 'And not in a way he likes. His credit's run out Katherine, and you can't do anything more for him. You can't be a barrier between him and the rest of the world any more.'

'I know,' she said sombrely.

There was a shout from outside the hut and I spun around to the doorway. A single shot sounded in the distance, to be followed by a fusillade of rifle fire, a ragged pattering of shots. I left the hut at a dead run and made for the outskirts of the camp, to be waved down by Rudetsky who was sheltering behind a hut.

I went forward at a crouch and joined him. 'What the hell's going on?'

'Halstead made a break for it,' he said, breathing heavily. 'He ran for the forest and we tried to follow him. Then they opened up on us.'

'What about Halstead? Did they fire on him?'

'I reckon he's dead,' said Rudetsky. 'I saw him go down as he reached the trees.'

There was a muffled sound from behind and I turned to see Katherine. 'Get back to the hut,' I said angrily. 'It's dangerous here.'

Two big tears squeezed from beneath her eyelids and rolled down her cheek as she turned away, and there was a dispirited droop to her shoulders.

I waited there at the edge of the camp for a long time but nothing happened; no more shots nor even the sound or sight of a living thing. Just the vivid green of the forest beyond the cleared ground of the city of Uaxuanoc.

III

Everything we did was under observation – that I knew. So I had a problem. We could take all the valuables down to the cenote quite openly and sink them, or we could be underhand about it and do it in secret. On balance, I thought that secrecy was the best bet because if we did it openly Gatt might get worried and jump us immediately with the job only begun. There was nothing to stop him.

That meant that all the packages Fallon had made up had to be broken open and the contents smuggled down piece by piece to my hut next to the cenote. Probably it would have been best to have just dumped the stuff as I had first suggested, but it seemed a pity to do that when the cave was available, so we used the cave. That meant going down there while Rudetsky lowered the loot, and that was something better left for after nightfall when prying eyes would be blinded.

For the rest of the daylight hours we contrived to give the camp an appearance of normality. There was a fair amount of coming and going between the huts and gradually all the precious objects were accumulated on the floor of my hut, where Rudetsky filled up the metal baskets we had used for bringing them from the bottom of the cenote in the first place.

Also on the agenda was the fortification of the hut, another task that would have to wait until after darkness fell, but Smith and Fowler wandered about the camp, unobtrusively selecting materials for the job and piling them in places where they could be got at easily at night. Those few hours seemed to stretch out indefinitely, but at last the sun set in a red haze that looked like dried blood.

We got busy. Smith and Fowler brought in their baulks of timber which were to be used to make the hut a bit more bullet-proof and began to hammer them in position. Rudetsky had organized some big air bottles and we hauled the raft into the side and loaded them aboard. It was tricky work because they were heavy and we were working in the dark. We also loaded all the treasure on board the raft, then Katherine and I went down.

The cave was just as we had left it and the air was good. I rose up inside, switched on the internal light I had installed and switched off my own light. There was a broad ledge above water-level on which the loot could be stored, and I sat on it and helped Katherine from the water. 'There's plenty of room to stash the stuff here,' I said.

She nodded without much interest, and said, 'I'm sorry Paul caused all this trouble, Jemmy. You warned me, but I was stupid about it.'

'What made you change your mind?'

She hesitated. 'I started to think – at last. I began to ask myself questions about Paul. It was something you said that started it. You asked me what it was I had for Paul – love or loyalty. You called it misplaced loyalty. It didn't take me long to find the answer. The trouble is that Paul hasn't – wasn't – always like this. Do you think he's dead?'

'I don't know; I wasn't there when it happened. Rudetsky thinks he is. But he may have survived. What will you do if he has?'

She laughed tremulously. 'What a question to ask at a time like this! Do you think that what we're doing here will do any good?' She waved her hand at the damp walls of the cave. 'Getting rid of what Gatt wants?'

'I don't know,' I said. 'It depends on whether we can talk to Gatt. If I can point out that he hasn't a hope in hell of getting the stuff, then he might be amenable to a deal. I can't see him killing six or seven people for nothing – not unless he's a crazy-mad killer, and I don't think he's that'

'Not getting what he wants might send him crazy-mad.'

'Yes,' I said thoughtfully. 'He'll be bloody annoyed. He'll need careful handling.'

'If we get out of this,' she said, 'I'm going to divorce Paul. I can't live with him now. I'll get a Mexican divorce – it will be valid anywhere because we were married in Mexico.'

I thought about that for a bit, then said, 'I'll look you up. Would you mind that?'

'No, Jemmy; I wouldn't mind.' She sighed. 'Perhaps we can begin again with a fresh start.'

'Fresh starts don't come so easily,' I said sombrely. 'We'll never forget any of this, Katherine – never!' I prepared to put on my mask. 'Come on; Joe will be wondering what has gone wrong.'

We swam out of the cave and began the long job of transferring the treasure from the basket which Rudetsky had lowered into the cave. Basket after basket of the damned stuff came down, and it took us a long time, but finally it was all put away. We had been under for two hours but had never gone below sixty-five feet so the decompression time was just under an hour. Joe lowered the hose which dangled alongside the shot line and we coupled the two valves at the end to the demand valves on our scuba gear. During the hour it took us to go up he fed us air from the big bottles on the raft instead of using the air compressor which would have made too much noise.

When we finally reached the surface, he asked, 'Everything okay?'

'Everything is fine,' I answered, and swore as I stubbed my toe on an air bottle. 'Look, Joe: tip all these bottles over the side. Gatt might start to get ideas – he might even be a diver himself. He won't be able to do a damned thing without air bottles.'

We rolled the bottles over the side and they splashed into the cenote and sank. When we got ashore I was very tired but there was still much to do. Smith and Fowler had done their best to armour the hut, but it was a poor best although no fault of theirs. We just hadn't the material.

'Where's Fallon?' I asked.

'I think he's in his own hut.'

I went to look for Fallon and found him sitting morosely at his desk. He turned as I closed the door. 'Jemmy!' he said despairingly. 'What a mess! What a godawful mess!'

'What you need is a drink,' I said, and took the bottle and a couple of glasses from the shelf. I poured out a couple of stiff tots and pushed a glass into his hand. 'You're not to blame.'

'Of course I am,' he said curtly. 'I didn't take Gatt seriously enough. But who would have thought this Spanish Main stuff could happen in the twentieth century?'

'As you said yourself, Quintana Roo isn't precisely the centre of the civilized world.' I sipped the whisky and felt the warmth in my throat. 'It's not out of the eighteenth century yet.'

'I sent a message out with the boys who left,' he said. 'Letters to the authorities in Mexico City about what we've found here.' He suddenly looked alarmed. 'You don't think Gatt will have done anything about them, do you?'

I considered that one, and said at last, 'No, I shouldn't think so. It would be difficult for him to interfere with them all and it might tip off the authorities that something is wrong.'

'I should have done it sooner,' said Fallon broodingly. 'The Department of Antiquities is goddamn keen on inspection; this place will be swarming with officials once the news gets out.' He offered me a twisted smile. 'That's why I didn't notify them earlier, I wanted the place to myself for a while. What a damned fool I was!'

I didn't spare him. 'You had plenty of warnings from Pat Harris. Why the hell didn't you act on them?'

'I was selfish,' he said. He looked me straight in the eye. 'Just plain selfish. I wanted to stay while I could – while I had time. There's so little time, Jemmy.'

I drank some whisky. 'You'll be back next season.'

He shook his head. 'No, I won't. I'll never be back here. Someone else will take over – some younger man. It could have been Paul if he hadn't been so reckless and impatient.'

I put down my glass. 'What are you getting at?'

He gave me a haggard grin. 'I'll be dead in three months, Jemmy. They told me not long before we left Mexico City – they gave me six months.' He leaned back in his chair. 'They didn't want me to come here – the doctors, you know. But I did, and I'm glad I did. But I'll go back to Mexico City now and go into a hospital to die.'

'What is it?'

'The old enemy,' said Fallon. 'Cancer!'

The word dropped as heavy as lead into the quiet hut and there was nothing I could say. This was the reason he had been so preoccupied, why he had driven so hard to get the job done, and why he had stuck to one purpose without deflection. He had wanted to do this last excavation before he died and he had achieved his purpose.

After a while I said softly, 'I'm sorry.'

He snorted. '*You're* sorry! Sorry for me! It seems as though I'm not going to live to die in hospital if you're right about Gatt – and neither is anyone else here. I'm sorry, Jemmy, that I got you into this. I'm sorry for the others, too. But being sorry isn't enough, is it? What's the use of saying "Sorry" to a dead man?'

'Take it easy,' I said.

He fell into a despondent silence. After a while, he said, 'When do you think Gatt will attack?'

'I don't know,' I said. 'But he must make his move soon.' I finished the whisky. 'You'd better get some sleep.' I could see Fallon didn't think much of that idea, but he said nothing and I went away.

Rudetsky had some ideas of his own, after all. I bumped into him in the darkness unreeling a coil of wire. He cursed briefly, and said, 'Sorry, but I guess I'm on edge.'

'What are you doing?'

'If those bastards attack, they'll be able to take cover behind those two huts, so I took all the gelignite I could find and planted it. Now I'm stringing the wire to the plunger in our hut. They won't have any cover if I can help it.'

'Don't blow up those huts just yet,' I said. 'It would come better as a surprise. Let's save it for when we need it.'

He clicked his tongue. 'You're turning out to be quite a surprising guy yourself. That's a real nasty idea.'

'I took a few lessons out in the forest.' I helped him unreel the wire and we disguised it as much as we could by kicking soil over it. Rudetsky attached the ends of one set of wires to the terminals of the plunger box and slapped the side of it gently with an air of satisfaction. I said, 'It'll be dawn fairly soon.'

He went to the window and looked up at the sky. 'There's quite a lot of cloud. Fallon said the rains break suddenly.'

It wasn't the weather I was worried about. I said, 'Put Smith and Fowler on watch out at the edge of the camp. We don't want to be surprised.'

Then I had an hour to myself and I sat outside the hut and almost nodded off to sleep, feeling suddenly very weary. Sleep was something that had been in short supply, and if I hadn't had that twenty-four hour rest in the forest tree I daresay I'd have gone right off as though drugged. As it was I drowsed until I was wakened by someone shaking my shoulder.

It was Fowler. 'Someone's coming,' he said urgently.

'Where?'

'From the forest.' He pointed. 'From over there – I'll show you.'

I followed behind him to the hut at the edge of the camp from which he had been watching. I took the field glasses he gave me and focused on the distant figure in white which was strolling across the cleared land.

The light was good enough and the glasses strong enough to show quite clearly that it was Gatt.

ELEVEN

There was an odd quality in the light that morning. In spite of the high cloud which moved fast in the sky everything was crystal clear, and the usual heat haze, which lay over the forest even at dawn, was gone. The sun was just rising and there was a lurid and unhealthy yellow tinge to the sky, and a slight breeze from the west bent the branches of the trees beyond the cleared ruins of Uaxuanoc.

As I focused the glasses on Gatt I found to my disgust that my hands were trembling, and I had to rest the glasses on the window-sill to prevent the image dancing uncontrollably. Gatt was taking his time. He strolled along as unconcernedly as though he were taking his morning constitutional in a city park, and stopped occasionally to look about at the uncovered mounds. He was dressed as nattily as he had been when he flew into Camp One, and I even saw the tiny point of whiteness that was a handkerchief in his breast pocket.

Momentarily I ignored him and swept the glasses around the perimeter of the ruins. No one else showed up and it looked as though Gatt was alone, a deceptive assumption it would be wise to ignore. I handed the glasses to Rudetsky, who had come into the hut. He raised them to his eyes, and said, 'Is that the guy?'

'That's Gatt, all right.'

He grunted. 'Taking his time. What the hell is he doing? Picking flowers?'

Gatt had bent down and was groping at something on the ground. I said, 'He'll be here in five minutes. I'm going out there to talk to him.'

'That's taking a risk.'

'It has to be done – and I'd rather do it out there than back here. Can anyone use that rifle we've got?'

'I'm not too bad,' said Fowler.

'Not too bad – hell!' rumbled Rudetsky. 'He was a marksman in Korea.'

'That's good enough for me,' I said with an attempt at a grin. 'Keep your sights on him, and if he looks like pulling a fast one on me, let him have it.'

Fowler picked up the rifle and examined the sights. 'Don't go too far away,' he said. 'And keep from between me and Gatt.'

I walked to the door of the hut 'Everyone else keep out of sight,' I said, and stepped outside, feeling like a condemned man on his way to the gallows. I walked towards Gatt across the cleared ground, feeling very vulnerable and uncomfortably aware that I was probably framed in someone's rifle sights. Obeying Fowler's instructions, I walked slowly so Gatt and I would meet a little more than two hundred yards from the hut, and I veered a little to give Fowler his open field of fire.

Gatt had lit a cigar and, as he approached, he raised his elegant Panama hat politely. 'Ah, Mr Wheale; lovely morning, isn't it?' I wasn't in the mood for cat-and-mouse chit-chat so I said nothing. He shrugged, and said, 'Is Professor Fallon available?'

'No,' I said shortly.

He nodded understandingly. 'Ah, well! You know what I've come for, of course.' It wasn't a question, but a flat statement.

'You won't get it,' I said equally flatly.

'Oh, I will,' he said with certainty. 'I will.' He examined the ash on the end of his cigar. 'I take it that you are doing the talking for Fallon. I'm surprised at that – I really am. I'd have thought he was man enough to do his own talking, but I guess he's soft inside like most people. But let's get down to it. You've pulled a lot of stuff out of that cenote. I want it. It's as simple as that. If you let me have it without trouble, there'll be no trouble from me.'

'You won't harm us in any way?' I queried.

'You just walk out of here,' he assured me.

'What guarantees do I have of that?'

He spread his hands and looked at me with honesty shining in his eyes. 'My word on it.'

I laughed out loud. 'Nothing doing, Gatt. I'm not that stupid.'

For the first time anger showed in him and there was a naked, feral gleam in his eyes. 'Now, get this straight, Wheale. I'm coming in to take that loot, and there's nothing you or anyone else can do to stop me. You do it peaceably or not – it's your choice.'

I caught a flicker of movement from the corner of my eye and turned my head. Some figures in white were emerging from the forest slowly; they were strung out in a straggling line and they carried rifles. I swung my head around to the other side and saw more armed men coming across from the forest.

Clearly the time had come to put some pressure on Gatt. I felt in my shirt pocket for cigarettes, lit one and casually tossed the matchbox up and down in my hand. 'There's a rifle sighted on you, Gatt,' I said. 'One wrong move and you're a dead man.'

He smiled thinly. 'You're under a gun, too. I'm not a fool.'

I tossed the matchbox up and down, and kept it going. 'I've arranged a signal,' I said: 'If I drop this matchbox, you get a bullet. Now, if those men out there move ten more yards, I drop this box.'

He looked at me with the faintest shadow of uncertainty. 'You're bluffing,' he said. 'You'd be a dead man, too.'

'Try me' I invited. 'There's a difference between you and me. I don't particularly care whether I live or die, and I'm betting that you do. The stakes are high in this game, Gatt – and those men have only five more yards to go. You had my brother killed, remember! I'm willing to pay a lot for his life.'

Gatt looked at the matchbox with fascination as it went up into the air, and winced involuntarily as I fumbled the next catch. I was running a colossal bluff and to make it stick I had to impress him with an appearance of ruthlessness. I tossed the box again. 'Three more yards and neither of us will have to worry any more about the treasure of Uaxuanoc.'

He broke! 'All right; it's a stand-off,' he said hoarsely, and lifted both arms in the air and waved them. The line of men drifted to a halt and then turned to go back into the forest. As I watched them go I tossed the matchbox again, and Gatt said irritably, 'For Christ's sake, stop doing that!'

I grinned at him and caught the box, but still held it in my fingers. There was a slight film of sweat on his forehead although the heat of the day had not yet started. 'I'd hate to play poker with you,' he said at last.

'That's a game I haven't tried.'

He gave a gusty sigh of exasperation. 'Listen, Wheale: you don't know the game you're in. I've had tabs on Fallon right from the beginning. Christ, I laughed back there at your airstrip when you all played the innocent. You really thought you were fooling me, didn't you? Hell, I knew everything you did and everything you thought – I didn't give a damn what action you took. And I've had that fool Harris chasing all over Mexico. You see, it's all come down to one thing, one sharp point – I'm here and I'm on top. Now, what about it?'

'You must have had some help,' I said.

'Didn't you know?' he said in surprise, and began to laugh. 'Jesus! I had that damned fool, Halstead. He came to me back in Mexico City and made a deal. A very eager guy, Halstead; he didn't want to share this city with Fallon – so we made the deal. He could have the city and I'd pick up the gold and get rid of Fallon for him.' The corners of his mouth downturned in savage contempt. 'The guy was too chicken to do his own killing.'

So it had been Halstead just as Pat Harris suspected and when we found Uaxuanoc he had tipped off Gatt. No wonder Pat had been running round in circles when Gatt knew our every move. It made me sick to realize how ambition could so corrupt a man that he would throw in his lot with a man like Gatt. The funny part about it was that Halstead had meant to cheat Gatt all along; he had never expected anything of value to turn up for Gatt to get his hands on.

I said in a hard voice, 'Where is Halstead now?'

'Oh, the guy's dead' said Gatt casually. 'When you chased him out my chicleros got a little trigger-happy and he caught one.' He grinned. 'Did I save you the trouble, Wheale?'

I ignored that. 'You're wasting your time here. You're welcome to come and take your loot but you'll get wet doing it.'

'Not me,' said Gatt. 'You! Oh, I know what you've done with it. Halstead didn't die right away and he told me where the stuff was – after a bit of persuasion. It took time or I'd have been here sooner before you put the stuff in the water. But it doesn't matter, not really.' His voice was calm and soft and infinitely menacing. 'You can get it back, Wheale; you're a diver, and so is that Halstead bitch. You'll swim down and get it back for me.'

'You don't know much about deep diving. It's not a five-minute job.'

He made a slashing motion with his hand. 'But you'll do it all the same.'

'I don't see how you can make me.'

'Don't you? You'll learn.' His smile was terrible. 'Let's say I get hold of Fallon and go to work on him, hey? You'll watch what I do to him and then you'll go down. I promise you.' He dropped the stub of his cigar and tapped me on the chest. 'You were right when you said there's a difference between you and me. I'm a hard man, Wheale; and you just think you're hard. You've been putting up a good imitation lately and you had me fooled, but you're like all the rest of the common punks in the world – soft in the middle, like Fallon. When I start taking Fallon apart slowly – or the girl, maybe – or that big ox, Rudetsky – then you'll dive. See what I mean?'

I saw. I saw that this man used cruelty as a tool. He had no human feeling himself but knew enough to manipulate the feelings of others. If I really had made an arrangement with Fowler I'd have dropped that matchbox there and then and taken my chance on being killed as long as he was eliminated. And I cursed my thoughtlessness in not bringing a pistol to shoot the bastard with.

I caught my breath and strove to speak evenly. 'In that case you must be careful not to kill me,' I said. 'You've heard of the goose and the golden eggs.'

His lips curled back from his teeth. 'You'll wish I had killed you,' he promised. 'You really will.' He turned and strode away and I went back to the hut – fast.

I tumbled in the door and yelled, 'Shoot the bastard!' I was in a blind rage.

'No good,' said Fowler from the window. 'He ducked for cover.'

'What gives?' asked Rudetsky.

'He's mad – staring stone mad! We've balked him and he's done his nut. He can't get his loot so he is going to take it out in blood.' I thought of that other madman who had shouted crazily, 'Weltmacht oder Niedergang!' Like Hitler, Gatt had blown his top completely and was ready to ruin us and himself out of angry spite. He had gone beyond reason and saw the world through the redness of blood.

Rudetsky and Fowler looked at me in silence, then Rudetsky took a deep breath. 'Makes no difference, I guess. We knew he'd have to kill us, anyway.'

'He'll be whipping up an attack any minute,' I said. 'Get everyone back in the hut by the cenote.'

Rudetsky thrust a revolver into my hand. 'All you gotta do is pull the trigger.'

I took the gun although I didn't know if I could use it effectively and we left the hut at a dead run. We had only got halfway to the cenote when there was a rattle of rifle fire and bits of soil fountained up from the ground. 'Spread out!' yelled Rudetsky, and turned sharply to cannon into me. He bounced off and we both dived for cover behind a hut.

A few more shots popped off, and I said, 'Where the hell are they?'

Rudetsky's chest heaved. 'Somewhere out front.'

Gatt's men must have gone on to the attack as soon as Gatt had gone into cover, probably by pre-arranged signal. Shots were popping off from all around like something in a Western movie and it was difficult to tell precisely where the attack was coming from. I saw Fowler, who was crouched behind an abandoned packing case on the other side of the clearing, suddenly run in the peculiar skittering movement of the experienced soldier. Bullets kicked up dust around him but he wasn't hit and he disappeared from sight behind a hut.

'We've gotta get outa here,' said Rudetsky rapidly. His face was showing strain. 'Back to the hut.'

He meant the hut by the cenote and I could see his point. There wasn't any use preparing a hut against attack and then being caught in the open. I hoped the others had had the sense to retreat there as soon as they heard the first shots. I looked back and cursed Rudetsky's neat and tidy mind – he had built the camp with a wide and open street which was now raked with bullets and offered no cover.

I said, 'We'd better split up, Joe; two targets are more difficult than one.'

'You go first' he said jerkily. 'I might be able to cover you.'

This was no time to argue so I ran for it, back to the hut behind us. I was about two yards from it when a chiclero skidded around the corner from an unexpected direction. He was as surprised as I was because he literally ran on to the gun which I held forward so that the muzzle was jammed into his stomach.

I pulled the trigger and my arm jolted convulsively. It was as though a great hand plucked the chiclero off his feet and he was flung away and fell with all limbs awry. I dithered a bit with my heart turning somersaults in my chest before I recovered enough from the shock to bolt through the doorway of the hut. I leaned against the wall for a moment gasping for breath and with the looseness of fear in my bowels, then I turned and looked cautiously through the window. Rudetsky was gone – he must have made his break immediately after I had moved.

I looked at the revolver; it had been fully loaded and there were now five shots left. Those damned thugs seemed to be coming from all directions. The man I had shot had come from *behind* – he had apparently come up from the cenote. I didn't like the implications of that.

I was wondering what to do when the decision was taken from me. The back door of the hut crashed open under the impact of a booted foot. I jerked up my head and saw,

framed in the doorway, a chiclero just in the act of squeezing off a shot at me with a rifle. Time seemed frozen and I
stood there paralysed before I made an attempt at lifting the
revolver, and even as my arm moved I knew I was too late.

The chiclero seemed to *flicker* – that movement you see
in an old film when a couple of frames have been cut from
the action producing a sudden displacement of an actor. The
side of his jaw disappeared and the lower half of his face
was replaced by a bloody mask. He uttered a bubbling
scream, clapped his hands to his face and staggered sideways, dropping his rifle on the threshold with a clatter. I
don't know who shot him; it could have been Fowler or
Rudetsky, or even one of his own side – the bullets were
flying thick enough.

But I wasted no time wondering about it. I dived forward
and went through that doorway at a running crouch and
snatched for the fallen rifle as I went. Nobody shot at me as
I scurried hell for leather, angling to the left towards the
edge of camp. I approached the hut by the cenote at a tangent, having arrived by a circuitous route, and I could not
tell if the door was open or even if there was anyone inside.
But I did see Fowler make a run for it from the front.

He nearly made it, too, but a man appeared from out of
nowhere – not a chiclero but one of Gatt's elegant thugs
who carried what at first I thought was a sub-machine-gun.
Fowler was no more than six paces from the hut when the
gangster fired and his gun erupted in a peculiar double
booom. Fowler was hit by both charges of the cut-down
shotgun and was thrown sideways to fall in a crumpled
heap.

I took a snap shot at his killer with no great hope of success and then made a rush for the door of the hut. A bullet
chipped splinters from the door frame just by my head, and
one of them drove into my cheek as I tumbled in. Then
someone slammed the door shut.

When I looked out again I saw it was useless to do anything for Fowler. His body was quivering from time to time as bullets hit it. They were using him for target practice.

II

The rifle fire clattered to a desultory stop and I looked around the hut. Fallon was clutching a shotgun and crouched under a window; Smith was by the door with a pistol in his hand – it was evidently he who had shut it. Katherine was lying on the floor sobbing convulsively. There was no one else.

When I spoke my voice sounded as strange as though it came from someone else. 'Rudetsky?'

Fallon turned his head to look at me, then shook it slowly. There was pain in his eyes.

'Then he won't be coming,' I said harshly.

'Jesus!' said Smith. His voice was trembling. 'They killed Fowler. They shot him.'

A voice – a big voice boomed from outside. It was Gatt, and he was evidently using some sort of portable loudhailer. 'Wheale! Can you hear me, Wheale?'

I opened my mouth, and then shut it firmly. To argue with Gatt – to try to reason with him – would be useless. It would be like arguing against an elemental force, like trying to deflect a lightning bolt by quoting a syllogism. Fallon and I looked at each other along the length of the hut in silence.

'I know you're there, Wheale,' came the big shout. 'I saw you go in the hut. Are you ready to make a deal?'

I compressed my lips. Fallon said creakily, 'A deal! Did he mention a deal?'

'Not the kind you'd appreciate,' I said grimly.

'I'm sorry that guy was killed,' shouted Gatt. 'But you're still alive, Wheale. I could have killed you right there by the door, but I didn't. You know why.'

Smith jerked his head and looked at me with narrowed eyes. There was a question in them which he didn't put into words. I closed my hand tighter round the butt of the revolver and stared him down until his glance slid away.

'I've got another guy here,' boomed Gatt. 'Big Joe Rudetsky. Are you prepared to deal?'

I knew very well what he meant. I moistened my lips and shouted, 'Produce him alive – and I might.'

There was a long pause. I didn't know what I'd do if he were still alive and Gatt carried out his threats. Whatever I did would be useless. It would mean putting the four of us into Gatt's hands and giving him all the aces. And he'd kill us all in the end, anyway. But if he produced Joe Rudetsky and began to torture him, could I withstand it? I didn't know.

Gatt laughed. 'You're smart, Wheale. You sure are smart. But not tough enough. Is Fallon still alive?'

I motioned to Fallon to keep quiet.

'Oh, I suppose he's there – with maybe one or two more. I'll leave *them* to argue with you, Wheale, and maybe you'll be ready to make a deal. I'll give you one hour – and no more. I don't think you'll be tough enough for that, Wheale.'

We stood there, quite still, for two full minutes and he said nothing more. I was thankful for that because he'd already said enough – I could see it in Smith's eyes. I looked at my watch and realized with a sense of shock that it was only seven o'clock in the morning. Less than fifteen minutes earlier I'd been talking to Gatt outside the camp. His attack had come with a ruthless suddenness.

Fallon eased himself down until he was sitting on the floor. He laid the shotgun aside carefully. 'What's the deal?' he asked, looking at his feet. The voice was that of an old man.

I paid far less attention to Fallon than I did to Smith. Smith held an automatic pistol; he held it loosely enough, but he could still be dangerous. 'Yeah, what's this deal?' he echoed.

'There's no deal,' I said shortly.

Smith jerked his head towards the window. 'That guy says there could be.'

'I don't think you'd like to hear it,' I said coldly.

I saw his gun hand tighten up and I lifted my revolver. He wasn't standing very far away but I don't even know if I could have hit him. They tell me that revolvers are very inaccurate in inexperienced hands. Still, Smith wasn't to know I wasn't a gunman. I said, 'Let's all kill each other and save Gatt the trouble.'

He looked at the gun in my hand which was pointed at his stomach. 'I just want to know about this deal,' he said steadily.

'All right; I'll tell you – but put the gun down first. It makes me uneasy.'

The thoughts that chased through Smith's mind were reflected on his face and were as clear as though he had spoken them, but at last he made his decision, stooped and laid the pistol at his feet. I relaxed and put my revolver on the table, and the tension eased. Smith said, 'I guess, we're all jumpy.' It was an apology of sorts.

Fallon was still regarding the tips of his bush boots as though they were the most important things in the world. He said quietly, 'Who does Gatt want?'

'He wants me,' I said. 'He wants me to go down and retrieve the loot.'

'I thought he might. What happened to Rudetsky?'

'He's dead. He's lucky.'

Smith hissed in a sudden intake of breath. 'What's that supposed to mean?'

'Gatt's way of persuading me to dive isn't pretty. He'll take any of us – you, Fallon or Mrs Halstead, it doesn't matter – and torture him to put pressure on me. He's quite

capable of doing it, and I think he'd relish using his imagination on a job like that' I found myself looking at it in a
detached manner. 'He might burn your feet off with a
blowlamp; he might chop you up joint by joint while you're
still alive; he might – well, there's no end to that kind of
thing.'

Smith had averted his face. He jerked nervously. 'And
you'd *let* him do it? Just for the sake of a few lousy trinkets?'

'I couldn't stop him,' I said. 'That's why I'm glad
Rudetsky and Fowler are dead. You see, we got rid of the air
bottles, and diving without them would be bloody difficult.
All we have are a few charged aqualung bottles – the big
bottles are at the bottom of the cenote. If you think I'm
going to dive in those conditions, with someone screaming
in my ears every time I come up, then you're even crazier
than Gatt.'

Smith whirled on Fallon. 'You got me into this, you crazy
old man. You had no right – do you hear me? You had no
right.' His face collapsed into grief. 'Jesus, how am I going
to get out of this? I don't wanna be tortured.' His voice
shook with a passion of self-pity and tears streamed from
his eyes. 'Good Christ, I don't want to die!' he wept.

It was pitiful to watch him. He was disintegrating as a
man. Gatt knew very well how to put pressure on a man's
innermost core, and the hour's grace he had given us was
not intended to be a relief. It was the most sadistic thing he
had done and he was winning. Katherine had collapsed;
Fallon was eaten up with cancer and self-recrimination, and
Smith had the pith taken out of him by the fear of death by
torture.

I was all knotted up inside, tormented by my sheer impo-
tence to do anything about it. I wanted to strike out and tear
and smash – I wanted to get at Gatt and tear his bloody
heart out. I couldn't and the sense of helplessness was
killing me.

Smith looked up craftily. 'I know what we'll do,' he whispered. 'We'll give him Fallon. Fallon got us into this, and he'd like to have Fallon, wouldn't he?' There was a mad gleam in his eyes. 'He could do things with Fallon – and he'd leave us alone. We'd be all right then, wouldn't we?'

'Shut up!' I yelled, and then caught hold of myself. This was what Gatt wanted – to break us down with a calculated cold cruelty. I pushed down the temptation to take out my frustrations on Smith with an awful violence, and spoke, trying to keep my voice firm and level. 'Now, you look here, Smith. We're all going to die, and we can die by torture or by a bullet. I know which I prefer, so I'm going to fight Gatt and I'm going to do my best to kill *him*.'

Smith looked at me with hatred. 'It's all right for you. He's not going to torture you. You're safe.'

The ridiculousness of what he'd just said suddenly struck me, and I began to laugh hysterically. All the pent-up emotions suddenly welled up in laughter, and I laughed uncontrollably. 'Safe!' I cried. 'My God, but that's funny!' I laughed until the tears came and there was a pain in my chest. 'Oh, safe!'

The madness in Smith's eyes was replaced by a look of astonishment and then he caught on and a giggle escaped him, to be followed by a more normal chuckle. Then we both dissolved in gales of laughter. It was hysterical and it hurt in the end, but it did us good, and when the emotional spasm was over I felt purged and Smith was no longer on the verge of madness.

Even Fallon had a grim smile on his face, remarkable in a man whose life and manner of death had just been debated by a semi-lunatic. He said, 'I'm sorry I got you into this, Smith; but I'm in it myself, too. Jemmy is right; the only thing to do is to fight'

'I'm sorry I kicked off like that Mr Fallon,' said Smith awkwardly, 'I guess I went nuts for a while.' He stooped and picked up the pistol, took out the magazine and flipped the action to eject the round in the breech. 'I just want to take as many of those bastards with me as I can.' He examined the magazine and inserted the loose cartridge. 'Five bullets – four for them and one for me. I reckon it's best that way.'

'You may be right,' I said and picked up the revolver. I wasn't at all certain whether I'd have the guts to put a bullet into my own head if it came to the push. 'Keep a check on what's happening outside. Gatt said he'd give us an hour but I don't trust him that far.'

I crossed over to Katherine and dropped to my knees beside her. Her eyes were now dry although there were traces of tears on her cheeks. 'How are you doing?' I asked.

'I'm sorry,' she whispered. 'I'm sorry I broke down – but I was afraid – so afraid.'

'Why shouldn't you be afraid?' I said. 'Everyone else is. Only a damn fool has no fear at a time like this.'

She swallowed nervously. 'Did they really kill Rudetsky and Fowler?'

I nodded, then hesitated. 'Katherine, Paul is dead, too. Gatt told me.'

She sighed and her eyes glistened with unshed tears. 'Oh, my God! Poor Paul! He wanted so much – so quickly.'

Poor Paul, indeed! I wasn't going to tell her everything I knew about Halstead, about the ways he went in getting what he wanted so quickly. It would do no good and only break her heart. Better she should remember him as he was when they married – young, eager and ambitious in his work. To tell her otherwise would be cruel.

I said, 'I'm sorry, too.'

She touched my arm. 'Do we have a chance – any chance at all, Jemmy?'

Privately I didn't think we had a snowball's chance in hell. I looked her in the eye. 'There's always a chance,' I said firmly.

Her gaze slipped past me. 'Fallon doesn't seem to think so,' she said in a low voice.

I turned my head and looked at him. He was still sitting on the floor with his legs outstretched before him and gazing sightlessly at the toe-caps of his boots. 'He has his own problems,' I said, and got up and crossed over to him.

At my approach he looked up. 'Smith was right,' he said wanly. 'It's my fault we're in this jam.'

'You had other things to think about.'

He nodded slowly. 'Selfishly – yes. I could have had Gatt deported from Mexico. I have that much pull. But I just let things slide.'

'I don't think that would have worried Gatt,' I said, trying to console him. 'He would have come back anyway – he has quite a bit of pull himself, if what Pat Harris says is correct. I don't think you could have stopped him.'

'I don't care for myself,' said Fallon remorsefully. 'I'll be dead in three months, anyway. But to drag down so many others is unforgivable.' He withdrew almost visibly and returned into his trance of self-accusation.

There wasn't much to be done with him so I arose and joined Smith at the window. 'Any sign of action?'

'Some of them are in those huts.'

'How many?'

He shook his head. 'Hard to say – maybe five or six in each.'

'We might give them a surprise,' I said softly. 'Any sign of Gatt?'

'I don't know,' said Smith. 'I wouldn't even know what he looks like. Goddamn funny, isn't it?' He stared across at the huts. If they open fire from so close, the bullets will rip through here like going through a cardboard box.'

I turned my head and looked at the plunger box and at the wires which led to it wondering how much explosive Rudetsky had planted in the huts and whether it had been found. As a kid I'd always been overly disappointed by damp squibs on Guy Fawkes Night.

The hour ticked away and we said very little. Everything that had to be said had been torn out of us in that explosive first five minutes and we all knew there was little point in piling on the agony in futile discussion. I sat down and, for want of something better to do, checked the scuba gear, and Katherine helped me. I think I had an idea at the back of my mind that perhaps we would give in to Gatt in the end, and I would have to go down into the cenote again. If I did, then I wanted everything to work smoothly for the sake of the survivors in Gatt's hands.

Abruptly, the silence was torn open by the harsh voice of Gatt magnified by the loudhailer. He seemed to be having trouble with it because it droned as though the speaker was overloaded. 'Wheale! Are you ready to talk?'

I ran at a crouch towards the plunger box and knelt over it, hoping that our answer to Gatt would be decisive. He shouted again. 'Your hour is up, Wheale.' He laughed boomingly. 'Fish, or I'll cut you into bait.'

'Listen!' said Smith urgently. 'That's a plane.'

The droning noise was much louder and suddenly swelled to a roar as the aircraft went overhead. Desperately I gave the plunger handle a ninety-degree twist and rammed it down and the hut shook under the violence of the explosion. Smith yelled in exultation, and I ran to the window to see what had happened.

One of the huts had almost literally disappeared. As the smoke blew away I saw that all that was left of it was the concrete foundation. White figures tumbled from the other hut and ran away, and Smith was shooting fast. I grabbed his shoulder. 'Stop that! You're wasting bullets.'

The plane went overhead again, although I couldn't see it. 'I wonder whose it is,' I said. 'It could belong to Gatt.'

Smith laughed excitedly. 'It might not – and, Jeez, what a signal we gave it!'

There was no reaction from Gatt; the loud voice had stopped with the explosion and I desperately hoped I'd blown him to hell.

III

It was too much to hope for. Everything was quiet for another hour and then there came a slow and steady hail of rifle fire. Bullets ripped through the thin walls of the hut, tearing away the interior insulation, and it was very dangerous to move away from the cover of the thick baulks of timber Rudetsky had installed. The chief danger was not from a direct hit but from a ricochet. From the pace of the firing I thought that not more than three or four men were involved, and I wondered uneasily what the others were doing.

It was also evident that Gatt was still alive. I doubted if the chicleros would still keep up the attack without him and his bully boys behind them. They wouldn't have the motive that drove Gatt, and, besides, an unknown number had been killed in the hut. I was reasonably sure that none of the men in that hut could have survived the explosion, and it must have given the rest a hell of a shock.

The fact that the attack had been resumed after an hour also demonstrated that Gatt, no matter what else he was, could lead – or drive – men. I knew personally of three chicleros that had died; say another four, at a low estimate, had been killed in the hut, and add to that any that Fowler or Rudetsky had killed before being slaughtered themselves. Gatt must be a hell of a man if he could whip the chicleros into another attack after suffering losses like that.

The aircraft had circled a couple of times after the hut blew up and then had flown off, heading north-west. If it belonged to Gatt then it wouldn't make any difference; if it belonged to a stranger then the pilot might be wondering what the hell was going on – he'd certainly been interested enough to overfly the camp a couple of times – and he might report it to the authorities when he got to wherever he was going. By the time anything got done about it we'd all be dead.

But I didn't think it was a stranger. We'd been in Quintana Roo for quite some time and the only aircraft I'd seen were those belonging to Fallon and Gatt's little twin-engined job that had landed at Camp One. There's not much call for an air service in Quintana Roo, so if it wasn't Gatt's plane then it might be someone like Pat Harris, come down to see why Fallon had lost communication with the outer world. And I couldn't see that making any difference to our position either.

I winced as a bullet slammed through the hut and a few flakes of plastic insulation drifted down to settle on the back of my hand. There were two things we could do – stay there and wait for it, or make a break and get killed in the open. Not much of a choice.

Smith said, 'I wonder where all the other guys are? There can't be more than four of them out front.'

I grinned tightly. 'Want to go outside and find out?'

He shook his head emphatically. 'Uh-uh! I want them to come and get *me*. That way *they're* in the open.'

Katherine was crouched behind a thick timber, clutching the revolver I had given her. If she had not lost her fear at least she was disguising it resolutely. Fallon worried me more; he just stood there quietly, grasping the shotgun and waiting for the inevitable. I think he had given up and would have welcomed the smashing blow of a bullet in the head which would make an end to everything.

Time passed, punctuated by the regular crack of a rifle and the thump of a bullet as it hit thick timber. I bent down and applied my eye to a ragged bullet hole in the wall, working on the rather dubious principle that lightning never strikes twice in the same place. The marksmen were hidden and there was no way of finding their positions; not that it would have done us any good if we knew because we had but one rifle, and that had only two rounds in the magazine.

Fowler's body was lying about thirty feet from the hut. The wind plucked at his shirt and rippled the cloth, and tendrils of his hair danced in the breeze. He lay quite peacefully with one arm outflung, the fingers of the hand half-curled in a natural position as though he were asleep; but his shirt was stained with ugly blotches to mark the bullet wounds.

I swallowed painfully and lifted my eyes higher to the ruined hut and the litter about it, and then beyond to the ruins of Uaxuanoc and the distant forest. There was something about the scene which looked odd and unnatural, and it wasn't the ugly evidence of violence and death. It was something that had changed and it took me a long time to figure what it was.

I said, 'Smith!'

'Yeah?'

'The wind's rising.'

There was a pause while he looked for himself, then he said tiredly, 'So what?'

I looked again at the forest. It was in motion and the tree-tops danced, the branches pushed by moving air. All the time I had been in Quintana Roo the air had been quiet and hot, and there had been times when I would have welcomed a cool breeze. I turned carefully and strained my head to look out of the window without exposing my head to a snap shot. The sky to the east was dark with thick cloud and there was a faint and faraway flicker of lightning.

'Fallon!' I said. 'When does the rainy season start?'

He stirred briefly. 'Any time, Jemmy.'

He didn't seem very interested in why I had asked.

I said, 'If you saw clouds and lightning now – what would you think?'

'That the season had started,' he said.

'Is that all?' I said, disappointed.

'That's all.'

Another bullet hit the hut and I swore as a wood splinter drove into my calf. 'Hey!' shouted Smith in alarm. 'Where the hell did that one come from?' He pointed to the ragged hole in the wooden floor.

I saw what he meant. That bullet had hit at an impossible angle, and it hadn't done it by a ricochet. Another bullet slammed in and a chair jerked and fell over. I saw a hole in the *seat* of the chair, and knew what had happened. I listened for the next bullet to hit and distinctly heard it come through the roof. The chicleros had got up on the hillside behind the cenote and were directing a plunging fire down at the hut.

The situation was now totally impossible. All our added protection was in the walls and it had served, us well, but we had no protection from above. Already I could see daylight showing through a crack in the asbestos board roofing where a bullet had split the brittle panel. Given enough well-aimed bullets and the chicleros could damn near strip the roof from the top of us, but we'd most likely be dead by then.

We could find a minimum shelter by huddling in the angle of the floor and the wall on the side of the hut nearest the hill, but from there we could not see what was happening at the front of the hut. If we did that, then all that Gatt would have to do was to walk up and open the door – no one would be in a position to shoot him.

Another bullet hit from above. I said, 'Smith – want to break for it? I'll be with you if you go.'

'Not me,' he said stubbornly. 'I'll die right here.'

He died within ten seconds of uttering those words by taking a bullet in the middle of his forehead which knocked him back against the wall and on to the floor. He died without seeing the man who killed him and without ever having seen Gatt, who had ordered his death.

I stooped to him, and a bullet smacked into the wall just where I had been standing. Fallon shouted, 'Jemmy! The window!' and I heard the duller report of the shotgun blasting off.

A man screamed and I twisted on the ground with the revolver in my hand just in time to see a chiclero reel away from the already long-shattered window and Fallon with the smoking gun in his hand. He moved right to the window and fired another shot and there was a shout from outside.

He dropped back and broke open the gun to reload, and I leaped forward to the window. A chiclero was jumping for cover while another was staggering around drunkenly, his hands to his face and crying in a loud keening wail. I ignored him and took a shot at a third who was by the door not four feet away. Even a tyro with a gun couldn't miss him and he grunted and folded suddenly in the middle.

I dropped back as a bullet broke one of the shards of glass remaining in the window, and shuddered violently as two more bullets came in through the roof. Any moment I expected to feel the impact as one of them hit me.

Fallon had suddenly come alive again. He nudged me with his foot and I looked up to find him regarding me with bright eyes. 'You can get out,' he said quickly. 'Move fast!'

I gaped, and he swung his arm and pointed to the scuba gear. 'Into the cenote, damn it!' he yelled. 'They can't get at you there.' He crawled to the wall and applied his eye to a bullet hole. 'It's quiet out front. I can hold them for long enough.'

'What about you?'

He turned. 'What about me? I'm dead anyway. Don't worry, Gatt won't get me alive.'

There wasn't much time to think. Katherine and I could go into the cenote and survive for a little longer, safe from

Gatt's bullets, but then what? Once we came out we'd be sitting targets – and we couldn't stay down forever. Still, a short extension of life meant a little more hope, and if we stayed where we were we would certainly be killed within the next few minutes.

I grabbed Katherine's wrist. 'Get into your gear,' I yelled. 'Get a bloody move on.'

She looked at me with startled eyes, but moved fast. She ripped off her clothes and got into the wet-suit and I helped her put on the harness. 'What about Fallon?' she said breathlessly.

'Never mind him,' I snapped. 'Concentrate on what you're doing.'

There was a diminution in the rate of rifle fire which I couldn't understand. If I'd have been in Gatt's place now was the time when I'd be pouring it on thick and heavy, but only one bullet came through the roof while Katherine and I were struggling with the harnesses and coupling up the bottles.

I turned to Fallon. 'How is it outside?'

He was looking through the window at the sky in the east and a sudden gust of wind lifted his sparse hair. 'I was wrong, Jemmy,' he said suddenly. 'There's a storm coming. The wind is already very strong.'

'I doubt if it will do us any good,' I said. The two-bottle pack was heavy on my shoulders and I knew I couldn't run very fast, and Katherine would be even more hampered. There was a distinct likelihood that we'd be picked off running for the cenote.

'Time to go,' said Fallon, and picked up the rifle. He had assembled all the weapons in a line near the window. He shrugged irritably. 'No time for protracted farewells, Jemmy. Get the hell out of here.' He turned his back on us and stood by the window with the rifle upraised.

I heaved away the table which barricaded the door, then said to Katherine, 'When I open the door start running.

Don't think of anything else but getting to the cenote. Once you are in it dive for the cave. Understand?'

She nodded, but looked helplessly at Fallon. 'What about . . .?'

'Never mind,' I said. 'Move . . . now!'

I opened the door and she went out, and I followed her low and fast, twisting to change direction as soon as my feet hit the soil outside. I heard a crack as a rifle went off but I didn't know if that was the enemy or Fallon giving covering fire. Ahead, I saw Katherine zip round the corner of the hut and as I followed her I ran into a gust of wind that was like a brick wall, and I gasped as it got into my mouth, knocking the breath out of me. There was remarkably little rifle fire – just a few desultory shots – and no bullets came anywhere near that I knew of.

I took my eyes off Katherine and risked a glance upwards and saw the possible reason. The whole of the hillside above the cenote was in violent motion as the wind lashed the trees, and waves drove across as they drive over a wheat-field under an English breeze. But these were hundred-foot trees bending under the blast – not stalks of wheat – and this was something stronger than an English zephyr. It suddenly struck me that anyone on the hillside would be in danger of losing his skin.

But there was no time to think of that. I saw Katherine hesitate on the brink of the cenote. This was no time to think of the niceties of correct diving procedure, so I yelled to her, 'Jump! Jump, damn it!' But she still hesitated over the thirty-foot drop, so I rammed my hand in the small of her back and she toppled over the edge. I followed her a split-second later and hit feet first. The harness pulled hard on me under the strain and then the water closed over my head.

TWELVE

As I went under I jack-knifed to dive deeper, keeping a lookout for Katherine. I saw her, but to my horrified astonishment she was going up again – right to the surface. I twisted in the water and went after her, wondering what the hell she thought she was doing, and grabbed her just before she broke into the air.

Then I saw what was wrong. The mask had been ripped from her head, probably by impact with the water, and the airline was inextricably tangled and wound among the bottles on her back in such a position that it was impossible for her to even touch it. She was fast running out of air, but she kept her head, and let it dribble evenly and slowly from her mouth just as she had done when I surprised her in Fallon's swimming pool back in Mexico City. She didn't even panic when I grabbed her, but let me pull her under water to the side of the cenote.

We broke into air and she gasped. I spat out my mouthpiece and disentangled her airline, and she paused before putting the mask on. 'Thanks!' she said. 'But isn't it dangerous here?'

We were right at the side of the cenote nearest the hill and protected from plunging fire by the sheer wall of the cenote, but if anyone got past Fallon we'd be sitting ducks. I said, 'Swim under water for the shot line, then wait for

me. Don't worry about the shooting – water is hard stuff –
it stops a bullet dead within six inches. You'll be all right if
you're a couple of feet under; as safe as behind armour
plate.'

She ducked under the water and vanished. I couldn't see
her because of the dancing reflections and the popple on the
water caused by the driving wind, but the boys on the hillside evidently could because of the spurts of water that
suddenly flicked in a line. I hoped I was right about that bit
of folklore about bullets hitting water, and I breathed with
relief as there was a surge of water at the raft as she went
beneath it and was safe.

It was time for me to go. I went down and swam for the
raft, going down about four feet. I'll be damned if I didn't
see a bullet dropping vertically through the water, its tip
flattened by the impact. The folklore was right, after all.

I found her clinging to the shot line beneath the raft, and
pointed downwards with my thumb. Obediently she dived,
keeping one hand in contact with the rope, and I followed
her. We went down to the sixty-five-foot level where a
marker on the rope indicated that we were as deep as the
cave, and we swam for it and surfaced inside with a deep
sense of relief. Katherine bobbed up beside me and I helped
her climb on to the ledge, then I switched on the light.

'We made it,' I said.

She took off her mask wearily. 'For how long?' she
asked, and looked at me accusingly. 'You left Fallon to die;
you abandoned him.'

'It was his own decision,' I said shortly. 'Switch off your
valve; you're wasting air.'

She reached for it mechanically, and I turned my attention to the cave. It was fairly big and I judged the volume to
be in excess of three thousand cubic feet – we'd had to
pump a hell of a lot of air into it from the surface to expel
the water. At that depth the air was compressed to three

atmospheres, therefore it contained three times as much oxygen as an equal volume at the surface, which was a help. But with every breath we were exhaling carbon dioxide and as the level of CO_2 built up so we would get into trouble.

I rested for a while and watched the light reflect yellowly from the pile of gold plate at the further end of the ledge. The problem was simple; the solution less so. The longer we stayed down, the longer we would have to decompress on the way up – but the bottles in the back-packs didn't hold enough air for lengthy decompression. At last I bent down and swished my mask in the water before putting it on.

Katherine sat up. 'Where are you going?'

'I won't be long,' I said. 'Just to the bottom of the cenote to find a way of stretching our stay here. You'll be all right – just relax and take things easy.'

'Can I help?'

I debated that one, then said, 'No. You'll just use up air. There's enough in the cave to keep us going, and I might need what you have in that bottle.'

She looked up at the light and shivered. 'I hope that doesn't go out. It's strange that it still works.'

'The batteries topside are still full of juice,' I said. 'That's not so strange. Keep cheerful – I won't be long.'

I donned my mask, slipped into the water and swam out of the cave, and then made for the bottom. I found one of our working lights and debated whether or not to switch it on because it could be seen from the surface. In the end I risked it – there wasn't anything Gatt could do to get at me short of inventing a depth charge to blow me up, and I didn't think he could do that at short notice.

I was looking for the air cylinders Rudetsky and I had pushed off the raft and I found them spread out to hell and gone. Finding the manifold that had followed the cylinders was a bit more tricky but I discovered it under the coils of air hose that spread like a huge snake, and I smiled with satisfaction as I saw the spanner still tied to it by a loop of rope. Without that spanner I'd have been totally sunk.

Heaving the cylinders into one place was a labour fit for Hercules but I managed it at last and set about coupling up the manifold. Divers have very much the same problem of weightlessness as astronauts, and every time I tried to tighten a nut my body rotated around the cylinder in the other direction. I was down there nearly an hour but finally I got the cylinders attached to the manifold with all cocks open, and the hose on to the manifold outlet with the end valve closed. Now all the air in the cylinders was available on demand at the end of the hose.

I swam up to the cave, pulling the hose behind the, and popped up beside the ledge holding it triumphantly aloft. Katherine was sitting at the further end of the ledge, and when I said, 'Grab this!' she didn't do a damn thing but merely turned and looked at me.

I hoisted myself out of the water, holding the end of the hose with difficulty, and then hauled in a good length of it and anchored it by sitting on it. 'What's the matter with you?' I demanded.

She made no answer for some time, then said cheerlessly, 'I've been thinking about Fallon.'

'Oh!'

'Is that all you can say?' she asked with passion in her voice, but the sudden violence left her as soon as it had come. 'Do you think he's dead?' she asked more calmly.

I considered it. 'Probably,' I said at last.

'My God, I've misjudged you,' she said in a flat voice. 'You're a cold man, really. You've just left a man to die and you don't care a damn.'

'What I feel is my business. It was Fallon's decision – he made it himself.'

'But you took advantage of it.'

'So did you,' I pointed out.

'I know,' she said desolately. 'I know. But I'm not a man; I can't kill and fight.'

'I wasn't brought up to it myself,' I said acidly. 'Not like Gatt. But you'd kill if you had to, Katherine. Just like the rest of us. You're a human being – a killer by definition. We can all kill but some of us have to be forced to it.'

'And you didn't feel you had to defend Fallon,' she said quietly.

'No, I didn't,' I said equally quietly. 'Because I'd be defending a dead man. Fallon knew that, Katie; he's dying of cancer. He's known it ever since Mexico City, which is why he's been so bloody irresponsible. And now it's on his conscience. He wanted to make his peace, Katie; he wanted to purge his conscience. Do you think I should have denied him that – even though we're all going to die anyway?'

I could hardly hear her. 'Oh, God!' she breathed. 'I didn't know – I didn't know.'

I felt ashamed. 'I'm sorry,' I said. 'I'm a bit mixed up. I'd forgotten you didn't know. He told me just before Gatt's attack. He was going back to Mexico City to die in three months. Not much to look forward to, is it?'

'So that's why he could hardly bear to leave here.' Her voice broke in a sob. 'I watched him looking over the city as though he were in love with it. He'd *stroke* the things we brought up from here.'

'He was a man taking farewell of everything he loved,' I said.

She was quiet for a time, then she said, 'I'm sorry. Jemmy, I'm sorry for the things I said. I'd give a lot not to have said them.'

'Forget it.' I busied myself with securing the hose, then began to contemplate what I'd do with it. The average diver doesn't memorize the Admiralty diving tables, and I was no exception. However, I'd been consulting them freely of late, especially in relation to the depths in the cenote, and I had a fairly good idea of the figures involved. Sooner or later we'd have to go to the surface and that meant decompressing on the way up, the amount of decompression time depending on the depth attained and the length of time spent there.

I had just spent an hour at nearly a hundred feet and came back to sixty-five and I reckoned if I spent another hour, at least, in the cave, then I could write off the descent to the bottom of the cenote as far as decompression went. The nitrogen would already be easing itself quietly from my tissues without bubbling.

That left the ascent to the surface. The longer we spent in the cave the more decompression time we'd need, and the decompression time was strictly controlled by the amount of air available in the big cylinders at the bottom of the cenote. It would be unfortunate, to say the least, to run out of air while, say, at the twenty-foot decompression stop. A choice between staying in the water and asphyxiation, and going up and getting the bends. The trouble was that I didn't know how much air was left in the cylinders – Rudetsky had been doing the surface work on the raft and he wasn't available to tell me.

So I took a chance and assumed they were half full and carried on from there. My small back-pack bottles were nearly empty, but the ones on Katherine's harness were nearly full, so that was a small reserve. I finally figured out that if we spent a total of just over three hours in the cave I would need an hour and three-quarters, decompression – a total of five hours since we had dived under the bullets. There could possibly have been a change up on top in five hours. I grinned tightly. There wasn't any harm in being optimistic – Gatt might even have shot himself in frustration.

I consulted my watch and considered it lucky that I'd made a habit of wearing the waterproof and pressureproof diver's watch all the time. We'd been down an hour and a half, so that left about the same time to go before vacating the cave. I stretched out on the hard rock, still weighing down the hose, and prepared to wait it out.

'Jemmy!'

'Yes.'

'Nobody ever called me Katie before – except my father.'

'Don't look upon me as a father-figure,' I said gruffly.

'I won't,' she promised solemnly.

The light went out – not with a last despairing glimmer as the batteries packed in, but suddenly, as though a switch had been turned off. Katherine gave a startled cry, and I called out. Take it easy, Katie girl! Nothing to worry about.'

'Is it the batteries?'

'Probably,' I said, but I knew it wasn't. Someone had turned the light off deliberately or the circuit had been damaged. We were left in a darkness that could be felt physically – a clammy black cloak wrapped around us. Darkness, as such, had never worried me, but I knew it could have peculiar effects on others, so I stretched out my hand. 'Katie, come here!' I said. 'Let's not get too far away from each other.'

I felt her hand in mine. 'I hope we'll never be that.'

So we talked and talked in the blackness of that cave – talked about every damned thing there was to talk about – about her father and his work at the college, about my sports of fencing and swimming, about Hay Tree Farm, about the Bahamas, about my future, about her future – about our future. We were forgetful enough in that darkness to believe we had a future.

Once she said, 'Where did the wind come from so suddenly?'

'What wind?'

'Just before we ran for the cenote.'

I came back to the real and bloody world with a jerk. 'I don't know. Rider was telling me there was a hurricane off-coast. Maybe it swung inland. He was keeping an ear open for the weather forecasts, I do know that.' The crash of the chopper and the chase in the forest seemed to have happened an aeon before.

I looked at my watch and the luminous dial swam ghost-like in the darkness. It was just about time to go and I said so. Katherine was practical about it. 'I'll get ready,' she said.

My mouth was dry and I could hardly get the words out. 'You're not coming,' I said.

There was a brief gasp in the darkness. 'Why not?'

'There's only enough air to take one of us to the top. If we both go we'll both die. You can't go because God knows what you'd find up there. Even if Gatt has given up you'd still have to find the compressor parts which Rudetsky hid away and get the compressor going again. Could you do that?'

'I don't think so,' she said. 'No, I couldn't.'

'Then I must do it. God knows I don't like leaving you here, but it's the best way.'

'How long will you be?'

'Nearly two hours going up and maybe another hour to get the compressor going. You won't run out of air here, Katie; you should have enough for another seven or eight hours.'

'Seven hours will be too late, won't it? If it's as much as seven hours you won't be coming back at all. Isn't that right, Jemmy?'

It was – and I knew it. 'I'll be back long before then,' I said, but both of us knew the chances against it.

Her voice was pensive. 'I'd rather drown than just run out of air slowly.'

'For God's sake!' I burst out. 'You'll stay in this bloody cave until I get back, do you hear me? You'll stay here – promise me!'

'I'll stay,' she said softly, and then she was suddenly in my arms. 'Kiss me, darling.' Her lips were on mine and I

held her tight, despite those damned clammy and unro-
mantic rubber wet-suits we wore.

At last I pushed her away. 'We can't waste time,' I said,
and bent down, groping for the hose. My fingers encountered something metallic which clattered on the rock, and
I grasped it, then found the hose with my other hand. I
pulled down the mask and whatever I was holding was in
my way so I thrust it impatiently under the harness straps.
'I'll be back,' I promised, and slipped into the water, dragging the hose.

The last thing I heard before going under the water was
Katie's voice echoing desolately round the cave. 'I love
you – love you.'

II

I was holding the weight of about seventy feet of hose
which tended to drag me down and I lost some height
before I reached the shot line, but once there I was able to
hold on to it while I hauled up more hose. When I felt
resistance I stopped, and fastened the hose to the line with
one of my finfasteners. I wouldn't need the fins from now
on and the hose needed to be fastened so as to take the
weight off me. That done, I went up slowly to the thirty foot
mark, letting the air bubble from my mouth as it expanded
in my lungs due to the lessening pressure and holding down
my speed to less than that of the rising bubbles.

At thirty feet I climbed into the slings on the shot line
and plugged the air hose into the demand valve on the harness, thus taking air from the big bottles at the bottom of the
cenote and leaving the smaller harness bottles as a reserve.
Then I looked at my watch. I would have to wait fifteen
minutes at thirty feet, thirty-five minutes at twenty feet,
and fifty minutes at ten feet.

Decompression is a slow and wearisome business at the best of times but this time the uncertainty of what I was about to meet when out of the water made it much worse. At the ten-foot level the suspense was awful because I knew I would be perfectly visible to anyone standing on the edge of the cenote. To make matters more nerve-racking the air gave out after only ten minutes at ten feet and I had to switch on to reserve; there had not been as much in the big cylinders as I thought and I was cutting things damned fine. And Katherine had been a little wasteful with the air from her bottles because it ran out fifteen minutes before my time was up, and I was forced to the surface.

I came up under the raft and hoped it wouldn't matter, pleased to be able to gulp in mouthfuls of sun-warmed air. I clung on to the underside of the raft with my head in the air space and listened intently. There was nothing to be heard apart from the soughing of the wind, which seemed to have dropped considerably in strength while we had been under water. I certainly heard no voices or anything human.

After a while I swam from under the raft and wearily climbed on board and shook off the scuba harness. Something clattered to the deck of the raft and I looked around in alarm for fear that it might have been heard before I bent to pick it up. It was a gold piece from the cave – the little statue of the Mayan maiden that Vivero had cast. I thrust it into my belt and then listened again and heard nothing of consequence.

I swam ashore to the rough dock that Rudetsky had made and trudged up the steps that had been hewn in the clifflike side of the cenote. At the top I stood in shaken amazement. The camp was a total wreck – most of the huts had disappeared completely, leaving only the foundations, and the whole area was a tangle of broken branches and even whole tree trunks from God knows where. And there was not a man in sight.

I looked towards the hut where we had made our stand and saw it was crushed and smashed under the weight of a big tree whose roots pointed skywards incongruously. Twigs cracked underfoot as I picked my way towards it and, as I got near, a brightly coloured bird flew out of the wreckage with a flutter of wings that momentarily alarmed me.

I prowled around, then stepped inside, climbing with difficulty over branches as thick as my own body. Somewhere among this lot were the spare scuba bottles I needed to bring Katherine to surface.

And somewhere among this lot was Fallon!

I found two machetes lying crossed as though someone had laid them down for sword dancing and took one to cut away at the smaller branches near where I would expect to find Fallon. After ten minutes of chopping I disclosed a hand and an arm outflung in death, but a few more cuts revealed the blood-smeared face of Smith. I tried again a little further along the line of the wall and this time I found him.

He was pinned to the ground by the branch that had struck him down, and when I put my hand on his arm I found, to my astonishment, that he was still warm. Quickly, I felt the pulse at his wrist and detected the faintest pulsation. Fallon was still alive! He had died neither by the hand of Gatt nor of the ancient enemy, but, incredibly, was still alive in spite of the violence of nature that had crashed a whole tree on to the hut.

I swung the machete and began to chop him free, which was not too difficult because he lay in the angle between floor and wall which had protected him from the tree in the first place, and I was soon able to drag him free and to put him in better comfort out of the sun. When I had done that he was still unconscious but his colour had improved and there didn't seem much wrong with him apart from the dark bruise on the side of his head. I thought he would presently regain consciousness naturally, so I left him for more important work.

The compressor parts had been hidden in a hole near the hut and covered with earth, but the whole area was covered with torn tree branches and other debris, including whole tree trunks. I wondered momentarily where they had come from and looked across the cenote to the hillside behind, and the sight of it took my breath in sharply. The ridge had been wiped clean of vegetation as if Rudetsky's gang had worked on it with power saw and flame-thrower.

There had been a wind – a big wind – that had assaulted the shallow-rooted forest trees and torn them clean out. I turned to look again at the hut and saw that the tree whose roots stuck up so ridiculously into the air must have been hurled from high on the hillside to strike downwards like some strange spear. And that was why the whole camp area, as far as I could see, was a wreck of timber and leafage.

The hillside was scraped clean to reveal the bare rock that had been hidden beneath the thin soil and, on top of the ridge, the temple of Yum Chac stood proudly against the sky very much as it must have looked when Vivero first saw it. I stepped back to get a better view of the whole ridge and looked past the ruined hut, and a great feeling of awe came upon me.

Because I saw Vivero's sign written in burning gold in the side of the ridge. I am not, in any sense, a religious man, but my legs turned to water and I sank down upon my knees and tears came to my eyes. The sceptic, of course, would write it off as a mere trick of the sun, of light and shade, and would point to parallels in other parts of the world where some natural rock formations are famous and well known. But that sceptic would not have gone through what I had gone through that day.

It may have been a trick of light and shade, but it was undeniably real – as real as if carved by a master sculptor. The setting sun, shining fitfully through scudding clouds, shed a lurid yellow light along the ridge and illuminated a great figure of Christ Crucified. The arms, spread along the ridge, showed every tortured muscle, and the nail heads in the palms of the hands cast deep shadows. The broad-chested torso shrank to a hollow stomach at the foot of the ridge, and there was a gaping hole in the side, just under the rib cage, which a sceptic would have dismissed as a mere cave. All the rib structure showed as clearly as in an anatomical drawing, as though that mighty chest was gasping for breath.

But it was the face that drew the attention. The great head lolled on one side against a shoulder and an outcrop of spiky rocks formed the crown of thorns against the darkening sky. Deep shadows drew harsh lines of pain from the nose to the corners of the mouth; the hooded eyes, crow-footed at the corners, stared across Quintana Roo; and the lips seemed about to part as though to bellow in a great voice of stone, 'Eloi! Eloi, Lama Sabacthani!'

I found my hands trembling and I could imagine what impression this miracle would have made on Vivero, a child of a simpler, yet deeper, faith than ours. No wonder he wanted his sons to take the city of Uaxuanoc; no wonder he had kept it secret and had baited his letter with gold. If this had been discovered in Vivero's time, it would have been one of the wonders of the Christian world, and the discoverer might even have been revered as a saint.

Probably this effect was not a daily occurrence and might depend on certain angles of the sun and, perhaps, times of year even. The Mayas, brought up in a different pictorial tradition and with no knowledge of Christianity, might not even have recognized it for what it was. But Vivero certainly had.

I knelt entranced in the middle of that devastated camp and looked up at this great wonder which had been hidden for so many centuries under a curtain of trees. The light changed as a cloud passed over the sun, and the expression of that huge and distant face changed from a gentle sorrow to inexpressible agony. I suddenly felt very afraid, and closed my eyes.

There was a crackle of twigs. 'That's right; say your prayers, Wheale,' said a grating voice.

I opened my eyes and turned my head. Gatt was standing just to one side with a revolver in his hand. He looked as though the whole forest had fallen on top of him. Gone was the neat elegance of the morning; he had lost his jacket, and his shirt was torn and ragged, revealing a hairy chest streaked with bloody scratches. His trousers were ripped at the knees and, as he walked around me, I saw that he had lost one shoe and was limping a little. But even so he was in better shape than I was – he had a gun!

He rubbed his hand over one sweaty cheek, streaking it with dirt, and lifted the other which held the revolver. 'Just you stay right there – on your knees.' He walked on a little further until he was directly in front of me.

'Have you seen what's behind you?' I asked quietly.

'Yeah, I've seen it,' he said tonelessly. 'Some effect, hey? Better than Mount Rushmore.' He grinned. 'Expecting it to do you some good, Wheale?'

I said nothing, but just looked at him. The machete was at my side and within reach of my fingers if I stooped a little. I didn't think Gatt would let me get that far.

'So you been praying, boy? Well, you gotta right.' The cultivated accent had vanished along with the elegance of his clothes; he had gone back to his primitive beginnings. 'You got every right because I'm gonna kill you. You wanna pray some more? Go right ahead – be my guest'

I still kept my mouth shut, and he laughed. 'Cat got your tongue? Got nothing to say to Jack Gatt? You were pretty gabby this morning, Wheale. Now, I'll tell you something – confidential between you and me. You got plenty time to pray because you're not going to die quick or easy. I'm going to put a hot slug right in your guts and you'll take a long, long time to join our pal over there.' He jerked his thumb over his shoulder. 'You know who I mean – Holy Jesus up in the sky.'

There was a maniac gleam in his eyes and a tic convulsed his right cheek. He was now right round the bend and beyond the reach of reason. Gone was any idea he might have had of making me dive for the treasure – all he wanted was the violence of revenge, a booby prize for being cheated.

I looked at the gun he was holding and couldn't see any bullets in it. What I don't know about firearms would fill a library of books, but the revolver I'd used had rotated the cylinder when the trigger was pressed to bring a cartridge under the hammer, and before the gun was fired that cartridge would be visible from the front. I couldn't see any such cartridge in Gatt's gun.

'You've caused me a lot of trouble,' said Gatt. 'More trouble than any man I knew.' He laughed raucously, 'Get it? I put that in the past tense because guys who cause me *any* kind of trouble don't stay alive. And neither will you.' He was relaxed and enjoying his cat-and-mouse game.

I was anything but relaxed. I was about to stake my life on there not being two kinds of revolver. Slowly I stooped and curled my fingers around the handle of the machete. Gatt tensed and jerked the gun. 'Oh, no,' he said. 'Drop it!'

I didn't. Instead, I started to get to my feet. 'All right buster,' shouted Gatt. 'Here it comes!' He squeezed the trigger and the hammer fell on an empty chamber with a dry click. He looked at it with startled eyes, and then backed away fast as he saw me coming at him with the upraised machete, turned tail and ran with me after him.

He scrambled over a tree trunk and became entangled in branches. I took a swing at him and a spray of leaves and twigs flew up into the air. Gatt yelped in fear and broke free, trying to make for the open ground and the forest beyond, but I ran around the tree, cutting him off, and he backed away towards the cenote.

He was still holding the useless gun which he raised and tried to fire again, giving me another bad moment, but it clicked harmlessly. I stepped forward again, manoeuvring him backwards, and he stepped back cautiously, not daring to take his eyes off me until he stumbled over the concrete foundations of the hut.

I will say he was quick. He threw the gun at me with an unexpected movement and I ducked involuntarily, and when I recovered he also was armed with a machete, which he had picked up from the floor of the hut. He squared his shoulders and a new confidence seemed to come over him as he hefted the broad-bladed weapon. His lips parted and his mouth broke into a grin, but there was no humour in his watchful eyes.

I automatically fell into the sabre stance – the classic 'on guard' position. As from a great distance seemed to come the ghostly voice of the maître d'armes crying. *'Use your fingers on the cut, Wheale!'* I hefted the machete. This was no light sporting sabre to be twitched about by finger action as the Hungarian masters have taught; it could be more appropriately compared with a naval cutlass.

Gatt jumped and took a swipe at me and I instinctively parried with a clash of steel, then jumped back six feet and felt the sweat start out on my chest beneath the rubber suit. I had used the wrong parry, forgetting the machete had no guard for the hand. Gatt had used a sideways slash and I had parried in seconde, catching his blade on mine. If I hadn't jumped back his blade would have slid along mine and chopped my hand off – something that couldn't happen with a sabre.

I feinted at him to gain time to think and to watch his reaction to an attack. He tried to parry clumsily, missed my blade, jumped back and nearly fell. But he was agile for his age, and recovered quickly, successfully parrying again. I gave ground, well satisfied with what I had learned. Gatt was definitely no fencer. As a young mafioso he may have been an adept with a knife, but a machete is more like a sword than an overgrown knife, and I had the advantage.

So here we were, fulfilling the hypothetical prophecy of Pat Harris – Gatt and I alone in Quintano Roo with Gatt separated from his bodyguards. I was determined to make it as quick and as short as possible; I was going to kill Gatt as soon as I could. I didn't forget, however, that he was still highly dangerous, and advanced on him with due caution.

He had the sense to manoeuvre sideways so he would not have the wreckage of the hut behind him. That suited me because he could not retreat very far without coming to the edge of the cenote. He was sweating and breathing heavily, standing square on with his feet apart. He moved again, fast, and chopped down in a swing that would have cleaved my skull had it connected. I parried in quinte and stood my ground, which he didn't expect. For a split second he was very close and his eyes widened in fear as I released his blade and cut at his flank. It was only by a monstrous leap backwards that he avoided it, and the point of my machete ripped his shirt away.

I took advantage and pressed home the attack and he gave way slowly, his eyes looking apprehensively at my blade which is the wrong thing to watch – he ought to have been looking at my sword hand. In desperation he attacked again and I parried, but my foot slipped on a branch which rolled under the instep and I staggered sideways. I lost contact with his blade and it sliced downwards into my side in a shallow cut.

But I recovered and engaged his blade again and drove him back with a series of feints. He parried frantically, waving the machete from side to side. I gave ground then and put my hand to my side as though tiring and he momentarily dropped his guard in relief. Then I went in for the kill – a flèche and a lunge in the high line; he parried and I deceived his parry and chopped at his head.

The edge of the machete hit the side of his head just below the ear and I instinctively drew it back into a cut as I had been taught, and the blade sliced deep into his neck. He was dead before he knew it because I had damn near cut his head off. He twisted as he fell and rolled to the edge of the cenote, then slowly toppled over to fall with a thump on the wooden dock.

I didn't bother to look at him. I just staggered to the nearest support, which was a fallen tree, and leaned on the trunk. Then I vomited and nearly brought my heart up.

III

I must have passed out for a while because the next thing I knew was that I was lying on the ground, staring sideways at a column of industrious ants that looked as big as elephants from that angle. I picked myself up wearily and sat on the trunk of the tree. There was something nagging at the back of my head – something I had to do. My head ached abominably and little pointless thoughts chattered about like bats in an attic.

Oh, yes; that's what I had to do. I had to make sure that Jack Edgecombe didn't make a balls-up of the farm; he wasn't too enthusiastic in the first place and a man like that could make an awful mess of all the Mayan rains. There was that pillar I'd found right next to the oak tree great-grandfather had planted – Old Cross-eyes I'd called him, and Fallon had been very pleased, but I mustn't let Jack Edgecombe near him. Never mind, old Mr Mount would see to everything – he'd get a farm agent in to see to the excavation of the Temple of Yum Chac.

I put my hands to my eyes and wiped away the tears. Why the devil was I crying? There was nothing to cry about. I would go home now and Madge Edgecombe would make me tea, with scones spread thick with Devonshire cream and homemade strawberry jam. She'd use the Georgian silver set my mother had liked so much, and it would all be served on that big tray.

That big tray!

That brought it all back with a rush and my head nearly burst with the terror of it. I looked at my hand which was covered with drying blood and I wondered whose blood it was. I had killed a lot of men – I didn't know how many – so whose blood was this?

There and then I made a vow. That I would go back to England, to the sheltered combes of Devon, and I would never leave Hay Tree Farm again. I would stick close to the land of my people, the land that Wheales had toiled over for generations, and never again would I be such a damned fool as to look for adventure. There would be adventure enough for me in raising fat cattle and sinking a pint in the Kingsbridge Inn, and if ever again anyone called me a grey little man I would laugh, agree that it was so, and say I wouldn't have it otherwise.

My side hurt and I put my hand to it and it came away sticky with blood. When I looked down I saw that Gatt had cut a slice from my hide, chopping through the wet-suit as cleanly as a butcher with a cleaver. Bone showed – the bones of my ribs – and the pain was just beginning.

I suddenly thought of Katherine in the cave. Oh, God, I didn't want to go into the cenote again! But a man can do anything he has to, particularly a grey little man. Gatt wasn't a grey man – more like red in tooth and claw – but the grey men of the world are more than a match for the Gatts of this world – for one thing, there are more of them – and the grey men don't like being pushed around.

I pulled my weary bones together, ready to go looking again for those compressor parts and brushed the back of my hand across my eyes to rid them of the trace of those tears of weakness. When I looked across the city of Uaxuanoc there were ghosts there, drifting about in the ruins and coming closer – indistinct white figures with rifles.

They came soft-footed and looked at me with hard eyes, attracting each other with faint shouts of triumph, until there were a dozen of them in a big semi-circle surrounding me – the chicleros of Quintana Roo.

Oh, God! I thought desperately. Is the killing never going to end? I bent down and groped for the machete, nestled the hilt in the palm of my hands, then rose creakingly to my feet. 'Come on, you bastards!' I whispered. 'Come on! Let's get it over with!'

They closed in slowly, with caution and an odd respect in their eyes. I lifted the machete and one man unslung his rifle and I heard the metallic noise as he slammed home a round into the breech. There was a great throbbing sound in my ears, my vision darkened, and I felt myself swaying. Through a dark mist I saw the circle of men waver, and some began to run, and they shouted loudly.

I looked up to see a cloud of locusts descending from the sky, and then I pitched forward and saw the ground coming up at me.

IV

'Wake up!' said the voice distantly. 'Wake up, Jemmy!'

I moved and felt pain. Someone, somewhere, was speaking crisp and fluent Spanish, then the voice said close to my ear, 'Jemmy, are you okay?' More distantly it said, 'Someone bring a stretcher.'

I opened my eyes and looked at the darkening sky. 'Who is the stretcher for?'

A head swam into view and I screwed up my eyes and saw it was Pat Harris. 'Jemmy, are you okay? Who beat you up? Those goddamn chicleros?'

I eased myself up on one elbow and he supported my back with his arm. 'Where did you come from?'

'We came in the choppers. The army's moved in.' He moved a little. 'Look, there they are.'

I stared at the five helicopters standing outside the camp, and at the busy men in uniform moving about briskly. Two of them were trotting my way with a stretcher. The locusts coming from heaven, I thought; they were helicopters.

'I'm sorry we couldn't get here sooner,' said Pat. 'It was that goddamn storm. We got a flick from the tail of a hurricane and had to put down half way.'

'Where have you come from?'

'Campeche – the other side of Yucatan. I flew over this morning and saw all hell breaking loose here – so I whistled up the Mexican army. If it hadn't been for the storm we'd have been here six hours ago. Say, where is everybody?'

That was a good question. I said creakily, 'Most of us are dead.'

He stared at me as I sat up. 'Dead!'

I nodded wearily. 'Fallon's still alive – I think. He's over there.' I grabbed his arm. 'Jesus! Katherine's down in the cenote – in a cave. I've got to get her out.'

He looked at me as though I had gone mad. 'In a cave! In the cenote!' he echoed stupidly.

I shook his arm. 'Yes, you damn fool! She'll die if I don't get her out. We were hiding from Gatt.'

Pat saw I was serious and was galvanized as though someone had given him an electric shock. 'You can't go down there – not in your condition,' he said. 'Some of these boys are trained swimmers – I'll go see the teniente.'

I watched him walk across to a group of the soldiers, then I got to my feet, feeling every pain of it, and limped to the cenote and stood on the edge, looking down at the dark water. Pat came back at a run. 'The teniente has four scuba-trained swimmers and some oxygen bottles. If you'll tell them where the girl is, they can take oxygen down to her.' He looked down at the cenote. 'Good Christ!' he said involuntarily. 'Who's that?'

He was looking down at the body of Gatt which lay sprawled on the wooden dock. His mouth was open in a ghastly grin – but it wasn't really his mouth. 'It's Gatt,' I said unemotionally. 'I told you I'd kill him.'

I was drained of all emotion; there was no power in me to laugh or to cry, to feel sorrow or joy. I looked down at the body without feeling anything at all, but Harris looked sick. I turned away and looked towards the helicopters. 'Where are those bloody divers?'

They came at last and I explained haltingly what they were to do, and Pat interpreted. One of the men put on my harness and they jury-rigged an oxygen bottle and he went down. I hoped he wouldn't frighten Katie when he popped up in the cave. But her Spanish was good and I thought it would be all right.

I watched them carry Fallon away on a stretcher towards one of the choppers while a medico bandaged me up. Harris said in wonder, 'They're still finding bodies – there must have been a massacre.'

'Something like that,' I said indifferently.

I wouldn't move from that spot at the edge of the cenote until Katie was brought up, and I had to wait quite a while until they flew in proper diving gear from Campeche. After that it was easy and she came up from the cave under her own steam and I was proud of her.

We walked to the helicopter together with me leaning on her because suddenly all the strength had left me. I didn't know what was going to happen to us in the future – I didn't know if such an experience as we had undergone was such a perfect beginning to a marriage, but I was willing to try if she was.

I don't remember much about anything after that, not until I woke up in a hospital in Mexico City with Katie sitting by the bedside. That was many days afterwards. But I vaguely remember that the sun was just coming up as the chopper took off and I was clutching that little gold lady which Vivero had made. Christ was not to be seen, but I remember the dark shape of the Temple of Yum Chac looming above the water and drifting away forever beneath the heavily beating rotors.

POSTSCRIPT

To write about one's own novels is risky, indeed. On those few occasions when my editor has asked me to write a blurb my mind has gone blank and I have become tongue- or, rather, typewriter-tied. Of course, then I was to write about a current book which was much too close for objectivity; here I feel detached and distanced enough in time for it to work – perhaps.

The first novel here, THE GOLDEN KEEL, was the first to be written and, as is often usual with the first effort of the apprentice hand, contains many autobiographical elements. In the early 1950s I worked in an office in Durban, South Africa, and a colleague told me a curious yarn. During the war he had been captured at Tobruk and transferred to a prison camp in Italy from which he had escaped to join the partisans fighting behind the German lines. During that period he, another South African, and some Italians had ambushed a convoy of German trucks and found it to contain a quantity of gold and other goodies which they had promptly buried.

Now came the question: would I go with him to Italy and help him recover the loot? Not averse to a bit of adventure I agreed, but nothing came of it because there was a report in the *Natal Mercury* to the effect that 16 Italians had just been jailed for alleged complicity in the disappearance of Mussolini's treasure. My friend called off the project.

But the incident remained in my mind and ten years later I used the incident to write THE GOLDEN KEEL which turned into a sea story and was written in Johannesburg, about as far from the sea as one can get in Southern Africa. One character, Metcalfe, more of an anti-hero than a villain, was a composite of two of the biggest con men and scallywags ever to hit South Africa. I had some strange friends in those days.

Drunk with the success of my first book, I was resting on my laurels when it was gently brought to my attention that my publisher expected another book, and I had not an idea in my head. KEEL had been written in the first person but I wanted to tackle a novel in the third person, something I had never tried. So, one morning I slipped a sheet of paper into the typewriter and began to write in the third person, very much as a pianist might practise five-finger exercises. At the end of the day I was interested enough to continue and by the end of the third day I realized I had a novel on my hands. I stopped for necessary research and completed the book with my study being taken apart around me in preparation for a journey to England. I carried that one-and-only copy of the first draft to Britain, doing revisions on the way, and it became HIGH CITADEL.

THE VIVERO LETTER was my fifth book and I was now much more professional and confident though still not well-breeched enough to actually go to the places I was writing about. However, I did start off the book in Totnes, Devon, where I then lived. When I wanted to enquire about police procedure I walked into the friendly neighbourhood police station, approached the desk sergeant, and said baldly, 'I want to talk about a murder.'

He went very still, then leaned forward and said gently, 'Yes, sir; what have you to tell me?' It was the beginning of a beautiful friendship. It turned out that there had not been a murder in Totnes within living memory and he would have to look up the details in the books.

In writing this novel I studied the geography of Yucatan, Mayan architecture, deep diving techniques, the Spanish Armada and a few other things. Two years after the book was written I was pleased to see photographs which showed that the archeological techniques I had devised in my own head were in actual use. I was even more pleased the other day when I gave a copy of VIVERO to one of the experienced divers from HMS *Inslow*, the naval diving tender, and asked him to point out any flaws in the diving techniques described. He could not find any, so I must have done something right.

Later, RUNNING BLIND was the first book I researched on the ground and the improvement in authenticity of background was immediately apparent. All subsequent books have been so researched leaving my seat in the library to others. It was my first espionage book and was written just after the death of Ian Fleming whose James Bondery had hitherto made the writing of a serious spy story impossible. Set in Iceland it was my attempt to illustrate the utter absurdity of the international espionage scene and I think that, in part, I succeeded, although it is most difficult to satirize the antics of the CIA – one cannot satirize the already ludicrous. Again I had apparently done something right – the novel was adapted as a three-part serial by the BBC.

While the task of writing novels is as lonely a job as being a lighthouse keeper there are associated compensations, the biggest of which is the opportunity to travel once one is away from the typewriter keyboard. This is a real bonus. When I wrote RUNNING BLIND I was bitten by the travel bug; I have visited Greenland, crossed the Sahara, been to the South Pole by courtesy of the US State Department and the US Navy, and travelled in every continent except Asia.

In these countries there is the opportunity to find interesting places and to meet interesting people. On a recent visit to North America I did a night patrol in a police car in Pasadena, drifted over Los Angeles at an incredibly low altitude in one of the Sheriff's helicopters, rode an airboat through the Florida Everglades, went over the Jet Propulsion Laboratory in California from which the Voyager/Jupiter and Viking/Mars unmanned space shots are controlled, visited the Massachusetts Institute of Technology, and played with computers in Toronto. It is from these experiences that I weave my tales.

Referring to computers I suppose I must mention my own which has attracted a certain amount of journalistic attention. These days one can hardly pick up a newspaper without finding an article about word processing and text editing controlled by machines using the ubiquitous silicon chip. Some years ago, when I installed my computer, I suppose I was ahead of my time, although not ahead of Len Deighton.

The computer is a data manipulating machine. I can write the first draft of a novel into the computer and then make changes selectively without having to type out the whole thing again. I can alter or switch about words, sentences, paragraphs or whole chapters. I can even change the names of characters if the names I have chosen are unsatisfactory and the machine will run through the whole book and make the alterations automatically. Then, when everything is to my satisfaction, I instruct the computer to print the whole book which it does largely unsupervised.

The computer also looks after the business side of my career, so much so that my publisher now complains that I know more about his business than he does. And on a rainy Saturday afternoon I can play an eighteen hole round of golf on the computer or land a spaceship on Venus.

But when all is said and done the computer remains merely an electronic quill pen, taking the donkey work out of writing and leaving more time for creativity. It is hard to convince journalists that this is so and that the machine does not actually plot and write my books for me.

I hope you have as much fun reading my books as I had in the writing.

DESMOND BAGLEY
1979

DESMOND BAGLEY

'Unbeatable for sheer gripping excitement.'

Daily Telegraph

RUNNING BLIND

The assignment begins with a simple errand – a parcel to deliver. But to Alan Stewart, standing on a deserted road in Iceland with a murdered man at his feet, it looks anything but simple. The desolate terrain is obstacle enough. But when Stewart realises he has been double-crossed and that the opposition is gaining ground, his simple mission seems impossible . . .

THE FREEDOM TRAP

The Scarperers, a brilliantly organised gang which gets long-term inmates out of prison, spring a notorious Russian double agent. The trail leads Owen Stannard to Malta, and to the suave killer masterminding the gang. Face to face at last with his opponents, Stannard must try to outwit both men – who have nothing to lose and everything to gain by his death . . .

'Literate, exciting, knowledgeable adventure stories – Desmond Bagley is incomparable.' *Sunday Mirror*

978-0-00-730474-5

DESMOND BAGLEY

'Sizzling adventure.'   *Evening Standard*

THE TIGHTROPE MEN

When Giles Denison of Hampstead wakes up in an Oslo hotel room and finds the face looking back at him in the mirror is not his own, things could surely get no more bizarre. But it is only the beginning of a hair-raising adventure in which Denison finds himself trapped with no way to escape. One false move and the whole delicately balanced power structure between East and West will come toppling down . . .

THE ENEMY

Wealthy, respectable George Ashton flees for his life after an acid attack on his daughter. Who is his enemy? Only Malcolm Jaggard, his future son-in-law, can guess, after seeing Ashton's top secret government file. In a desperate manhunt, Jaggard pits himself against the KGB and stalks Ashton to the silent, wintry forests of Sweden. But his search for the enemy has barely begun . . .

'Bagley has become a master of the genre – a thriller writer of intelligence and originality.'   *Sunday Times*

978-0-00-730475-2

DESMOND BAGLEY

'Compulsively readable.'   *Guardian*

FLYAWAY

Why is Max Stafford, security consultant, beaten up in his own office? What is the secret of the famous 1930s aircraft, the Lockheed Lodestar? And why has accountant Paul Bilson disappeared in North Africa? The journey to the Sahara desert becomes a race to save Paul Bilson, a race to find the buried aircraft, and – above all – a race to return alive . . .

WINDFALL

When a legacy of £40 million is left to a small college in Kenya, investigations begin about the true identities of the heirs – the South African, Dirk Hendriks, and his namesake, Henry Hendrix from California. Suspicion that Hendrix is an impostor leads Max Stafford to the Rift Valley, where a violent reaction to his arrival points to a sinister and far-reaching conspiracy far beyond mere greed . . .

'From word one, you're off. Bagley's one of the best.'
The Times

978-0-00-730476-9